The Sendaxa Chronicles:

The Complete Series

By

REBECCA HEFNER

Cover Design: The Book Brander
Editor: Megan McKeever
Proofreader: Nay's Notations – Editing and Proofreading Services

Contents

Repressed Echoes
Copyright
Dedication
Chapter 1
Chapter 2
Chapter 3
Chapter 4
Chapter 5
Chapter 6
Chapter 7
Chapter 8
Chapter 9
Chapter 10
Chapter 11
Chapter 12
Chapter 13
Chapter 14
Chapter 15
Chapter 16
Chapter 17
Chapter 18
Chapter 19
Chapter 20
Chapter 21
Chapter 22
Chapter 23
Chapter 24
Chapter 25
Chapter 26
Chapter 27
Chapter 28
Chapter 29
Chapter 30
Chapter 31
Chapter 32
Before You Go

Scorched Redemption
Copyright
Dedication
Chapter 1
Chapter 2
Chapter 3
Chapter 4
Chapter 5
Chapter 6
Chapter 7
Chapter 8
Chapter 9
Chapter 10
Chapter 11
Chapter 12
Chapter 13
Chapter 14
Chapter 15
Chapter 16
Chapter 17
Chapter 18
Chapter 19
Chapter 20
Chapter 21
Chapter 22
Chapter 23
Chapter 24
Chapter 25
Chapter 26
Chapter 27
Chapter 28
Chapter 29
Chapter 30
Chapter 31
Chapter 32
Chapter 33
Chapter 34
Epilogue
Before You Go

Fated Salvation
Copyright
Dedication
Part 1 - The Past
Chapter 1
Chapter 2
Chapter 3
Chapter 4
Chapter 5
Chapter 6
Part 2 - The Present
Chapter 7
Chapter 8
Chapter 9
Chapter 10
Chapter 11
Chapter 12
Chapter 13
Chapter 14
Chapter 15
Chapter 16
Chapter 17
Chapter 18
Chapter 19
Chapter 20
Chapter 21
Chapter 22
Chapter 23
Chapter 24
Chapter 25
Chapter 26
Chapter 27
Chapter 28
Chapter 29
Chapter 30
Chapter 31
Chapter 32
Part 3 - The Future
Chapter 33
Before You Go
About the Author

Repressed Echoes

The Sendaxa Chronicles, Book 1

By

REBECCA HEFNER

For everyone else who needed a book that was a mash-up of The Last of Us and Fifty First Dates. I can't be the only one who loves steamy post-apocalyptic romances with a little amnesia thrown in...right??

Chapter 1

Sometime in the not-so-distant future...

D r. Danica Lawson's eyes flew open, darting to each corner of the dim room. The only sounds that marred the silence were her soft, labored pants and the pounding heartbeat that infiltrated her inner eardrums. Touching her tongue to the dry roof of her mouth, she tried to swallow, but her throat failed to bob. A soft whimper escaped her lips, and she placed her palm flat on the bed, attempting to push into a sitting position.

Pain seared her side and she gasped, collapsing on the mattress as her fingers found the wound. A thick bandage covered the tender skin, and she wondered how she'd sustained the injury.

Closing her eyes, she took a moment to center herself.

You can do this, Dani. Try to remember.

Cobwebs clouded her brain, obstructing any semblance of rational thought. Her pupils roved under closed lids, searching the darkness for a trace of where she was...how she'd been injured...and how she'd ended up in a strange bed in a dark room.

Obscure shadows were her only answer, and she struggled with the realization she needed to *run.* Lifting her lids, she hastily scanned the room. Whoever had placed her here wasn't present, but they could return any moment.

Now was the time to break free.

Sucking in a breath, she palmed her side, holding the bandage tight, and maneuvered into a sitting position. Glancing down, she noticed the thin shorts and tank top that covered her frame. Black sneakers sat at the foot of the nearby nightstand, and she grabbed them, tugging them on under the small shaft of light that filtered through the curtains of the lone window in the room. Once the shoes were tied, she gradually rose to her feet, placing a hand on her head as the room began to spin.

"Come on, Dani," she whispered, lowering her hand and straightening her spine. "Let's go."

Gritting her teeth, she began to push forward—one foot, then the other—inching toward the door. Her shaking fingers gripped the knob and turned. Ever so gently, she eased the door open, relieved to find an empty hallway. Gathering her courage, she stepped across the threshold.

A muscled arm snaked across her line of view, causing her to flinch as she drew back. The hand attached to the sinewy arm landed flat on the nearby wall as a warm body pressed into her uninjured side. Closing her eyes, she balled her fist, ready to strike.

"Not so fast there, slugger," a rugged baritone chimed in her ear, causing her to shiver. "You need rest before you charge back into the world—"

Swinging with all her might, Dani brought her fist high, aiming for the man's face. Although she didn't have time to align her blow, she aimed to strike his nose above the lips that had brushed her ear as he spoke.

The man's hand caught her fist, crushing it as he lowered her arm, causing her to cry out.

"You son of a bitch!"

"I don't want to hurt you, Dani," he said, his tone soothing even though her body was fraught with nerves and fear. "Take a deep breath and relax."

Lifting her gaze to his, she noted the silver flecks that glinted in his gunmetal gray eyes. His features were angular as he loomed over her although she was five feet, eight inches tall. She might not remember much, but for some reason, she remembered that.

"What do you want?" she asked, struggling to keep the fear from her voice. "Whatever it is, I'm sure we can negotiate."

His firm lips curved into a roguish smile, causing her knees to shake. Dark hair fell over his forehead, tinged with a bit of gray at the temples, and she had the insane thought he might be the most attractive man she'd ever seen. Dangerous. Mysterious. *Hot.*

"You try to negotiate every time," he murmured, lowering so his warm breath floated across her cheek. "It's so cute, babe."

Attempting to wrench her fist from his grasp, she glared at him until he released her. Drawing back, she let another blow fly, but he quickly caught her fist again, smirking as she writhed to break free.

"I know your tells by now, Dani. Believe me, you got me pretty good the first few times we did this, but now I can read your punches from a mile away. Don't get me wrong, it's sexy as hell when you try to slug me, but it's not conducive to moving the mission along."

"What mission?" she asked, infuriated by his tender endearments along with the fact he was all but *laughing* at her. "I have no idea who you are! If you want to kill me or...*worse*...then do it. But I'm certainly not involved in any sort of mission with you."

Something flashed in his eyes—tender and almost sad—before his grip relaxed on her fist. "I know this is scary. I'm sorry. It's my fault—"

"Why can't I remember anything? Did you drug me?"

Remorse crossed his features as he slowly shook his head. "It's your brain injury. You sustained it over three months ago, and your memory hasn't recovered."

"Three months? I've lost my memory for three months?"

"Yes," he softly confirmed. "You sustained it at your lab while you were working for Sendaxa."

Furrowing her brow, she tried to recall her last memory. "I don't work for Sendaxa. I work at Columbia University as a professor and head of their genetics lab." Pausing, she indexed her thoughts for any memory of working for the largest pharmaceutical company in the United States. "I vaguely remember receiving an email from an executive at Sendaxa expressing interest in working with me. That's all I remember about them."

Gray eyes assessed her as he nodded. "They recruited you to work on EverLife."

Blowing out a breath, she racked her brain, frustrated at the murky images that didn't quite form. "But I was so close to a cancer vaccine."

"Yes. Sendaxa offered you a deal: work for them to develop EverLife, and once it was approved for use, they would fund your cancer research."

Latching onto his gaze, she swallowed. "I'm assuming things didn't exactly go as planned."

Huffing a laugh, he shook his head. "You were successful in creating the EverLife formula but didn't realize it would be highly addictive. Once the side effects became known, you dedicated yourself to developing an addiction antidote. Cancer took a backseat to reversing the damage."

"Damage?" Dread filled her heart as her throat bobbed. "How much damage?"

Lifting his hand, he slowly extended it toward her cheek. Dani's brain screamed to recoil, but her body subconsciously leaned toward his.

Once he'd placed his rough palm over her cheek, his lips curved into a sad smile. "I'm happy to tell you everything, but you're hurt and I don't want to reopen your wound." Craning his neck, he eyed the side of her body with the laceration. "We have a protocol for when you wake up. I messed that up today and I'm sorry. I thought you'd sleep longer since you're recovering. I should know by now not to underestimate you."

Butterflies of anxiety flitted in her belly as she studied him. A strange desire to arch toward him and seek comfort in his muscular arms overwhelmed her. Squinting up at him, she asked, "Who are you to me?"

His broad lips twitched, causing her heart to slam between her ribs.

"One of these days, you're going to remember, and it will be the happiest day of my life, babe."

"Don't call me that," she said, feeling her nostrils flare. "I hate that endearment."

A deep chuckle rumbled in his chest. "I know. You seem to prefer 'slugger.' But I like 'babe.' Call me old-fashioned." Lifting his hand from her cheek, he tucked a strand of silky brown hair behind her ear.

"Please stop mocking me. I don't recognize you, but you seem so familiar..." Lifting her palms to her temples, she squeezed. "Fuck, my brain hurts."

"Hey," he murmured, gently encircling her wrists and dragging her hands away. Drawing her hands to his chest, he splayed one of her palms over each of his pecs. His heartbeat thrummed beneath her skin as he covered the backs of her hands with his. "It's okay, Dani. Look at me. *Feel* me."

Shallow breaths exited her lungs as his pulse ticked beneath her fingers. Staring deep into his stunning irises, she waited.

"Good," he soothed, lifting one hand to cup her jaw, stroking the skin with his thumb. "Who do you think I am?"

Her mouth opened and closed as she struggled to form words. "I have no idea. I have so many questions—"

"Do you remember my name?"

Tears stung her eyes as she shook her head. "I don't know you..."

Sighing, he removed his hand from her jaw before harshly rubbing his forehead. Lifting his gaze to hers, he said softly, "I'm Maverick."

Her features contorted. "Like *Top Gun*?"

Rolling his eyes, he scoffed. "Yes, like *Top Gun*. You ask me that every time I tell you my damn name. From the first time we met until right now. One day, you'll just accept that my parents were weird and gave their kid a strange name."

A laugh escaped her throat, surprising her as she stared up at the man who was both reassuring and mysterious. "When did we first meet?"

"Five years ago."

Dani gazed down, trying to remember.

"Since your brain injury, you only seem to remember as far back as your last days at Columbia and Sendaxa contacting you. But you don't ever remember moving to Bethesda to start the job."

Rapidly blinking, she worked to amalgamate the thoughts racing through her mind. Concern jolted down her spine as visions of her sisters' faces appeared. "Where are Raquel and Arianna?"

"Your sisters are safe," he assured, his tone calm. "They're here with us and you can see them, but first you need to rest. You're pretty banged up there, slugger."

Filled with trepidation—and a hefty surge of curiosity—she cemented her eyes to his. "Are we...lovers?"

White teeth flashed as he smiled, transforming his features into something so sexy her knees almost buckled.

"I guess you could say that..."

Narrowing her eyes, she regarded him.

"But I'm a lot more than your lover."

Swallowing thickly, she whispered, "You are?"

Nodding, he leaned closer, those swirling eyes searching hers.

"Danica Lawson, it's nice to meet you all over again. We do this dance every day, and it never gets old." Drawing back, he extended his hand. "Maverick Ward."

Tentatively shaking his hand, she tilted her head. "Maverick Ward...my lover...and..."

"Husband," he said, lips twitching at her rapid inhale. "I'm your husband, Dani. Pleasure to meet you, as always."

Suddenly, the floor seemed to melt away as the wound at her side throbbed. Unable to stand, she collapsed into her husband's arms, wondering if she would remember him the next time she regained consciousness.

Chapter 2

Maverick caught his wife in his arms, careful of her wound, and lifted her as her head lolled.

"She fainted again?" a deep voice asked, attached to the man striding down the hallway.

"Yeah. I don't want to restrain her, but I might have to if she keeps waking up and trying to bolt."

Striding toward the bedroom, he placed Dani on the bed before tugging off her sneakers. Tossing them to the floor, he checked her wound before covering her with the comforter.

"Why didn't you leave the phone by her bed?" Dominic asked.

"I didn't think she'd wake this early. Her wound is healing, but the phone was almost dead last night so I decided to charge it. Rookie mistake," Maverick said. "If there's one thing we know about my wife, she's determined to escape every time she wakes up if the phone with the video she recorded isn't accessible." Grinning, he softly stroked her cheek. "For a geeky scientist, she's pretty badass."

"That's why we all love her," Dominic said quietly.

Maverick glanced at the man, six feet, six inches of thick, sinewed muscle under a buzz cut and austere features. A jagged scar ran from the corner of one eye, over his nose and ended at the opposite corner of his broad lips. Tattoos covered the arms crossed over his chest, and his dark eyes were filled with concern. It made sense considering one thing they both knew to be true: they both were in love with Maverick's wife.

An unspoken agreement lingered between Maverick and the stoic man with whom he'd forged a solid friendship over the years. They would never discuss Dominic's feelings as long as he never acted on them. It would be futile anyway considering Danica loved Maverick as fiercely as he loved her. Gazing at her, he stroked her chestnut-colored locks atop the pillow as she slept, thanking the universe she'd chosen him. Dominic was a good man, but for some reason, Dani had chosen Maverick.

Perhaps miracles were still possible.

Dominic and Maverick were aligned in the cause, and his friend was a damn good soldier, so Maverick was content to overlook the fact he was in love with his wife. He hoped that one day, once they set things straight and returned to some sense of normalcy, Dominic would find a woman who would capture his heart too. Only time would tell.

"Has Arianna returned from the scouting mission?" Maverick asked, tucking the covers around Dani's shoulders before rising.

"No, and she didn't take a comm device with her either," Dominic muttered, rubbing his forehead. "Stubborn woman. She looked me straight in the eye and told me she'd have one in her ear at all times, but I found it lying on the table by the front door. It's like she left it there to tell me to go fuck myself."

Breathing a laugh, Maverick cupped his chin. "I've never seen two people who detest each other work so brilliantly together. It defies logic. Half the time, I'm convinced she'd rather kill *you* than the Sen Force soldiers."

Dominic scoffed. "Or I'd rather kill her. I swear, most days I'm this close." He formed a circle with his hands, mimicking choking someone. "But then she usually ends up doing something cool, like protecting Raquel when she goes on her berry-picking excursions or kicking my ass when we spar, and I don't have the heart to go through with it."

Grinning, Maverick strode by his friend, gesturing with his head for the man to follow him so they could leave Dani to sleep and heal. As they trekked down the hallway, he patted Dominic's shoulder. "Are you admitting Arianna is a better fighter than you?"

Dominic's eyebrow arched. "I'll admit she's one of the best soldiers I've ever met. Better than me? No fucking way. But she's pretty damn awesome."

"That's a pretty big declaration from the best fighter *I've* ever met," Maverick said, entering the large back room of the abandoned home where they'd set up their temporary headquarters. "I have a feeling she'd say she was better than you, but who's keeping score?"

Dominic grunted in annoyance as they entered the makeshift lab Dani and Raquel had built in the den of the home they'd been residing in since Dani's brain injury.

"Where's Raquel?" Dominic asked, craning his neck to look outside. "I told her to stay inside until I was ready."

"She's obsessed with the mushrooms growing by the old shed," Maverick said, gesturing toward the window. "Maybe she's picking them."

"She's determined to recreate the antidote," Dominic said, craning his neck to look out the window.

"She was a preeminent biologist before the world went to shit, and I appreciate her trying to formulate an antidote," Maverick said, shaking his head. "But Dani is still our best hope...if her memory ever comes back."

"It will, Mav," Dominic said, cupping his shoulder. "And then we'll break into the Sendaxa lab to steal the secret antidote stash, and the world can begin to wake up from this nightmare."

"Raquel insists she can get Dani's memory back with some perseverance. The teas she concocts seem to help, and Dani logs everything," Maverick said, pointing to the notebook that sat beside the vials on the lab table. "Sometimes, when she looks at me, I see flashes of...*something* in her eyes. A small tendril of recognition, and that gives me hope."

"Never doubt the Lawson sisters," Dominic muttered. "If Raquel says Dani can get her memory back, I'm apt to believe it. Those three are stubborn as hell when they set their mind to something."

"No doubt, but I kind of dig that about Dani," Maverick said with a sly grin. "I love it when she tries to beat the crap out of me when she wakes up. It's hot."

"You're weird, man," Dominic said, shaking his head. "I'm going to head out and keep an eye on Raquel. Arianna and I haven't observed any Sen Force soldiers or deserters on any recent scouting missions, but I want to stay alert."

Before he could pivot and exit the room, a door slammed in the distance and heavy bootsteps echoed down the hallway. Arianna breezed in, silky dark hair hanging over one eye from the half of her head that wasn't shaved.

"Hey," she grunted, giving them both a quick salute. "Did Dani wake up?"

"The phone was charging so I blew it," Maverick said.

"Oh shit. Did she *Top Gun* you?" Amusement clouded her expression under her piercing hazel eyes.

"Yeah. She's a broken record with that one."

Nodding, Arianna crossed her arms and glowered at Dominic. "What the fuck is wrong with your face?"

With a sardonic eye roll, Dominic placed his hands on his hips. "You left your comm device behind again. You promised, Ari."

"Don't call me that," she snapped. "Only Dani calls me that. And why do you care?"

Thick nostrils flared as he studied her. "You know what? I don't. Go scout alone and get yourself killed for all I care."

She tilted her head, cheeks reddening with anger. "I would but I do need your back up *sometimes*," she snorted. "And Magic Mike over there can't do it because he needs to keep an eye on Dani."

"Am I Magic Mike in this scenario?" Maverick asked, pointing to his chest.

"Yep," Arianna said with a nod. "You and that pretty face. It's annoying. Try to be uglier, like this one." She pointed to Dominic. "Okay, I'm starving. The fields are clear, by the way. No Sen Force spies within a two-mile perimeter. The farmhouse has been our longest-lasting base, and I don't want to search for another one. For now, it's secure and they don't know we're here."

"Let's hope it lasts," Maverick said. "I'm going to make sure the phone is ready for the next time Dani wakes."

Arianna nodded before stomping out of the room toward the kitchen where they kept their meager food supplies.

Dominic grunted before pivoting and exiting as well.

"Lots of tension between those two," Maverick mumbled to himself, striding toward the table where vials, concoctions, and other supplies Raquel used to create her potential antidotes and teas resided. As he inspected the items, he reflected on the obvious distaste between his best friend and his wife's sister.

Narrowing his eyes, he drew a finger over one of the tea leaves as he pondered. Was it a love-hate thing? Maybe they just needed to have sex and see if that changed the dynamic. Chuckling, Maverick admitted that would certainly make things interesting, although it wasn't likely to happen.

Dominic fixated on Danica because she was safe. Easy. Unavailable. Exploring feelings for Arianna would open a Pandora's box he wasn't sure his friend would even consider. Dominic could be pretty oblivious and had one goal: to destroy the shell government that had taken over Washington, DC and restore the world to some semblance of normal. Dominic's sister had died of cancer, and he wanted to start a new chapter so Dani could finally develop her cancer vaccine.

But a man needed a release every once in a while, and Maverick wondered if his friend would eventually get tired of his own hand. The raw energy that vibrated between Dominic and Arianna was damn near combustible. They might kill each other if they had sex—but there were worse ways to go, Maverick mused, flattening his lips to contain his grin.

On that note, he needed to check on his wife and make sure he didn't fuck up again the next time she awoke. Turning, he approached her room, intent on making sure she didn't try to punch him when she regained consciousness.

Chapter 3

The next time Dani's eyes flew open, she shot up in bed, her hand darting to her laceration. It still marred her side, covered by the thick bandage, but she *remembered*. Maverick. Their conversation. The insane assertion he was her husband.

Baffling since she couldn't recall ever having met the man, and yet he seemed so familiar...

"Hey, sleeping beauty," the object of her musings said, striding into the room and pointing to the bed. "Mind if I sit?"

Dani blinked, wondering when she was going to wake up from the strangest dream she'd ever had. Clearing her throat, she nodded, unconsciously clenching the covers and drawing them higher.

Tilting his head, he studied her with those deep eyes. "You remember waking up before?"

"Yes," she rasped, her throat dry as the wound at her side throbbed. "How?"

Reaching into his pocket, he pulled out a cell phone and shook it. "I have the answer here."

"You're going to call someone?"

Huffing a laugh, he shook his head. "Most cell phone towers in America haven't worked in over a year, although some are still known to function, especially ones near the Sendaxa cities. The phone has some important videos, and Arianna was smart enough to toss some chargers in her bag before we all went into hiding."

Dani glanced at the bedside lamp before reaching over and turning it on. "We still have electricity?"

"This place has a generator. Pretty fortuitous find. We've been staying here for months. Arianna and Dominic regularly patrol to ensure we're not on Sen Force's radar."

"Sen Force...?"

"Soldiers employed by Sendaxa to ensure the new world order they've created stays in place. Most are remnants of the old U.S. Army, which disbanded once the government collapsed."

Dani blinked once...twice...and once more for good measure before expelling a breath. "This is seriously the weirdest dream I've *ever* had."

His warm chuckle surrounded her, caressing her skin as tiny bumps rose along her arms. Somewhere in the far reaches of her mind, she remembered that laugh...rumbled in her ear as he covered her with his muscled body and kissed her until she breathed his name...

"Babe?"

Shaking her head to rid it of the madness, she scowled. "I really wish you wouldn't call me that."

A challenge flared in his eyes as he scooted closer. "Okay." Lifting the phone, he brought up a video before placing it in her hand. Leaning forward, he whispered, "But just so you know, there have been several times in the past when you *liked* when I called you that."

Bristling, she opened her mouth to give him a piece of her mind before he showed her his palms and stood. "Don't want to fight with you. Go on," he said, gesturing with his head. "Watch the video and we'll discuss after."

Shooting him one last glare, she pressed play on the video and gasped when she saw her own face.

"Hello, Dani. I know this is probably very shocking to you, but Maverick and I thought it was the best way to help you acclimate and navigate each day with your condition. Maverick is usually by your side when you watch this video, but if he's not, you'll meet him soon. I know it's hard to believe, but he is your husband and you can trust him. Take it from...well, yourself."

Dani's eyes darted to Maverick's before they lowered again. Heart racing, she concentrated on the sound of her own voice.

"I'm going to be succinct but try to hit all the important points. Maverick can fill in the time stamps and answer your questions afterward."

Pausing the video with shaking fingers, she asked, "How many days ago did I make this?"

"You made this video almost three months ago," Maverick said softly.

Lowering her gaze, she struggled to control her errant heartbeat and shallow breathing. "After my brain damage where I lost my memory."

"Yes." Rubbing his chin, he gestured with his head. "Keep going."

Pushing through the sticky fear that laced her veins, she pressed play.

"You most likely just asked Mav how long it's been since you made this video. I pray there aren't many days left you'll have to watch it."

Dani squirmed in the bed, straightening in an attempt to brace herself for what was to come.

"Several years ago, you were hired by a company called Sendaxa to spearhead a campaign to create a drug that could double human life expectancy. This drug was called EverLife. I'm going to assume Mav has explained this to you, but if not, pause here and he can."

Pausing the video, she scrunched her features as she contemplated. "I think I have the basics. Sendaxa recruited me to create EverLife, and I agreed on the contingency they would fund my cancer vaccine development afterward. It went terribly wrong and I created a highly addictive drug that was consumed by the masses."

Maverick crossed his arms over his thick chest and gave an affirmative nod.

Pursing her lips, she resumed the video.

"You were determined to eventually save humanity, and now—although it wasn't how you envisioned it—you have your chance."

Glancing at Maverick, she asked, "I assume this is the mission you were referring to?"

"Yep. Your sisters and my friend Dominic are all on our team, and we've been living in this abandoned farmhouse while we figure out next steps. I'll explain more after you finish."

Clicking the screen, she continued watching. *"EverLife's addictive side effects were worse than any drug ever created. The need for the drug began to overtake people from all walks of society. They left their jobs and families, consumed with finding the drug on the black market as it became sold out in pharmacies. Sendaxa tasked you to create an antidote to counteract the side effects, which you did."*

"Wait," Dani said, sitting up straighter in the bed. "If we have an antidote, what the hell are we doing here? Let's cure everyone and get back to normal."

"It's not that easy, sweetheart," he said, resignation in his voice.

Frustration swamped her as she resumed the video.

"As the addiction spread, society began to break down. Homeless addicts roamed the streets, and the worldwide economy could no longer function. Sendaxa's CEO, Luthor

Cromwell, gained immense power while the government was simultaneously indicting him on charges of duping the public about EverLife's addictive tendencies. He saw an opportunity to escape persecution by destroying the government."

"Holy shit," Dani whispered, overwhelmed by the unbelievable story.

"Using the vast wealth he'd made from EverLife, Luthor closed off the major cities, fortifying them and ensuring only people inside the walls had the antidote. The ones who remained outside were left to die. The people inside the cities were given a watered-down antidote that offers small relief but doesn't cure the addiction. Your only hope is to retrieve the full-strength antidote you created, replicate it, and begin distributing it. You try every day to recreate it in the makeshift lab you and Raquel created, but you've been unsuccessful so far. You need the original antidote to duplicate it effectively."

Tears stung her eyes as her chin began to warble. "So many people are suffering...because of me. Why haven't I retrieved the antidote yet?"

Maverick stepped closer and tapped the phone to pause the video. "The world is in shambles, Dani. The wealthy retreated inside their fortified walls, able to continue their use of the drug and survive with the modified antidote, although I'd barely call that survival. Those left outside the walls with no antidote suffered most of all. Societies across the globe fell, and the world is now composed of those who live in the fortified cities and those who fend for themselves on the outside. Villages and towns have formed outside the cities, mostly run by connected dealers who can supply addicts with black-market substitutes for EverLife."

"Then we have to go now," she said, tossing the phone on the bed and throwing off the covers, attempting to stand. "I have to retrieve the antidote—"

"Whoa," he said, gently gripping her shoulders and urging her back against the headboard. "That's what we're trying to do, Dani. Three months ago, you attempted to steal a secret stockpile of the antidote from the Sendaxa lab so you could replicate it. Unfortunately, someone banged you on the head before you could retrieve the stash, and we went on the run until we figure out a solution."

"Well, let's go back and break in again," she said, exasperated. "I'm ready."

Breathing a laugh, he shook his head. "There are reasons why we haven't done that yet, sweetheart."

"Being?"

"The lab where you created the antidote is under Sen Force security. You set up some extra security measures to ensure no one but you could access the hidden antidote."

"Shit." Harshly rubbing her forehead with her fingers, she said, "I would've set up a secure keypad with a numerical security code only I knew."

"Along with a separate keypad that only opens if touched by your index finger. It reads temperature and pulse to prevent someone from chopping off your finger and using it while...not attached to you," he finished, arching a brow.

"Wow," she said, lips flapping as she expelled a breath. "I was resourceful."

Admiration entered his gaze as he grinned. "Yep. As head of security at the lab, I was able to approve the extra security measures without Luthor Cromwell's knowledge. That kept it under the radar."

Her shoulders crumpled as she sank into the bed. "Don't tell me I didn't write down the security code once you installed the keypad. I must've emailed it to myself...or made a jump drive with the information?"

Gently tapping her forehead, he gave a soft grin. "Everything only exists here. You were too paranoid to write things down and prided yourself on your photographic memory. When society began to crumble, you were afraid to email anything to yourself or write notes in your phone. Sendaxa essentially took over the government, and you didn't want the secret antidote stash to be discovered."

Harshly rubbing a hand over her face, she groaned. "I can't believe they talked me into working for them. They must've really played on my desire to cure cancer."

"They knew about your mom," he said, lowering to sit beside her before sliding his hand over her leg and squeezing through the covers. "They're a company with limitless means and investigated you thoroughly before they recruited you. They knew you were the best geneticist in your field and understood how devastating your mom's death was. They preyed on your nobility, and it worked."

"Son of a bitch. And now I have amnesia."

"And now you have amnesia," he affirmed with a slow nod. "You were hit in the head the night you tried to steal the antidote. We still don't know who injured you. Dominic found you unconscious on the floor before we carried you out and went on the run."

She stared blankly at the phone as she tried to digest the overwhelming information. "I need to remember the code so we can break in again and steal the antidote."

"Bingo," he said with a nod. "We don't have the tools or compounds out here to replicate the antidote—although Raquel might die trying—but if you got your hands on a vial, you'll duplicate it in a heartbeat."

"I will," she said confidently, "with Raquel's help. But I definitely need the sample. Damn it."

Taking her hand, he slid his palm over hers, the skin coarse and warm. "Which is why we're trying like hell to restore your memory."

Shaking the phone, she narrowed her eyes. "How did you convince me to make this video?"

"Every once in a while, we have a good day where you're able to let your guard down by the end of the night and trust me. They're rare but they happen."

"And we had one of those days and you had the idea to make the video?"

"*You* had the idea," he said, cocking a brow, "and it was brilliant. Watching the video seems to help you trust me."

Dani allowed her eyes to rove over his face, wishing she recognized this man who claimed to be her husband. He was sinfully handsome and stared back at her with deep emotion. Although the situation was disconcerting, he truly seemed to care for her. Deciding to lighten the moment, she lifted her brows. "If this is some elaborate ruse to get laid, you get an A-plus for effort."

Tossing back his head, laughter bellowed from his throat. His neck was thick with a prominent Adam's apple, and a vision of trailing wet kisses along the skin there flashed through her brain. It was...*familiar*...as if her lips had already traveled the path a thousand times before...

"Babe, you've been through the ringer, but you never lose your sense of humor." Taking the phone, he set it on the nightstand before clutching both her hands and squeezing. "God, I miss you so much. I think it's only a matter of time before your memory returns."

Licking her parched lips, she asked, "Are Raquel and Ari okay?"

"They're both fine and valuable members of our team. Arianna and Dominic perform scouting missions to make sure we're safe, and Raquel is continuing your work when you're not able to help."

"She's an exceptional biologist and botanist."

Nodding, he scooted closer and craned his neck to look at her side. "How's your side feeling?"

"It hurts but I'll survive." Glancing down, she asked, "How was I injured anyway?"

"You and Raquel went out to pick some berries on the outskirts of the farm. Dominic was keeping watch and heard a sound in the distance that alarmed him. It ended up being nothing, but he sent you and Raquel back to the house so he could check it out. You tripped on a log and fell straight into an old pitchfork lying on the ground." Shaking his head, he sighed. "You have some terrible luck, Dani. I wouldn't suggest *ever* playing the lottery."

Laughing, she leaned farther back on the bed, snuggling into the soft mattress. "Seriously. So, do I lose my memory nightly? Is that why I remember our encounter earlier?"

"Yes." Resignation laced his features as his thumb tenderly skated over her skin. "You can take short naps and retain memories during a one-day span, but after a longer sleep, you always wake up unable to remember." Lifting his hand, he tucked a strand of hair behind her ear. "I'm so sorry. I hate it for you."

Curiosity squeezed her throat as a multitude of questions swirled in her mind. Gathering her courage, she asked, "Do we...sleep together?"

That sexy smile overtook his lips as he slowly dragged the pad of his thumb over the back of her hand.

"Sometimes. We did the night you made that video. Sometimes we sleep together..." leaning forward, he whispered, *"and sometimes we even have sex..."*

Air rushed from her lungs as she assessed him. "How in the hell did we end up together?"

Laughing, he dragged a hand over his face. "Wow. Are you trying to decimate my ego?"

"The opposite," she rushed to assure him. "I'm a workaholic scientist and you're"—waving her hand over his body, she struggled to speak—"the hottest guy I've ever seen. I can't imagine a scenario where we would've ever crossed paths."

His low-toned chuckle caused sparks of arousal to ignite deep within, and she squeezed her thighs together. "I was head of security for the Sendaxa lab. We met when you took the job." Lifting her hand, he grazed a kiss over her knuckles. "I guarded you when you worked, and since you're a workaholic, that meant I spent a lot of time with you. As we got to know each other, we fell in love."

Tilting her head, her eyebrows drew together as she allowed her eyes to assess his muscular frame. "It's a nice story. I'd love to hear the details sometime."

"Anytime. I never get tired of telling you that story."

Swallowing thickly, she gazed into his eyes, unable to look away. "You must know I love tulips," she said with a cheeky grin. "Just trying to think of ways I can help you get on my good side."

"I do," he said, winking and sending a rush of elation through her veins. "And chocolate. And being touched right here..." Eyes cemented to hers, he gently placed the pads of his fingers on her collarbone before lightly tracing the skin there.

Licking her suddenly dry lips, Dani sat frozen as the most gorgeous man she'd ever seen caressed her rapidly heating skin.

"You like me to go lower too," he murmured, running his finger along the neckline of her black tank top. "Eventually, you always ask me to kiss you...here." Never breaking their gaze, he ran his finger over the mound of her breast above the fabric. "You're *very* sensitive here, Dani."

Clearing her throat, she lowered her gaze to his hand. He let it rest for another moment before withdrawing it. "But I think that's enough for today."

Overcome with the need to fan herself, Dani sank into the bed, determined not to showcase her arousal. It was just too...confusing...and hot...and weird...

"Today's pretty much shot, so I'd suggest you continue to rest before dinner." Rising, he urged her to lie back and covered her with the blankets. "After that, we'll do it all again tomorrow, but I'm not going to mess up the routine." Lifting the phone, he shook it.

"Okay," she whispered, wondering why she could still feel the heat of his touch on her skin. Rapid heartbeats pounded as he smiled down at her. Reaching over, he clicked off the bedside lamp. "I'll wake you before dinner. Sweet dreams." Turning to leave, he paused when she called his name.

"Hmm?" he asked, facing her.

"I'm sensitive behind the knees too, especially my left one where the birthmark is."

His lips quirked as he studied her in the dim light shining through the curtains. "Your birthmark is behind your *right* knee, sweetheart, but good try. And believe me, I know you're sensitive behind both of them. Good night."

His broad shoulders exited the room, leaving the door cracked behind him, and Dani pulled the covers to her chest, unable to control her grin. The birthmark had been a test, which Maverick had passed.

"Holy shit, Dani," she whispered, closing her eyes to steady herself. "You have a husband and he's...probably the sexiest man on Earth. How did you manage that?"

Overwhelmed with questions, she allowed them to flit through her head as she attempted to catalog them all. Of course, the effort was futile since she wouldn't remember a damn one of them when she awoke the next morning.

Chapter 4

Arianna Lawson waited for the house to get dark and quiet. She rarely slept, so she figured instead of wasting hours lying in bed staring at the ceiling, she'd let everyone else fall asleep before heading out. She'd noticed something during her scouting session earlier and wanted to check it out. Since she didn't deem it a threat, she hadn't told anyone else, but it still lingered in her mind hours later, which meant it required attention.

Once midnight hit, she rose, tossing on some of the black clothing she'd managed to stuff into her bag before they all went into hiding the night Dani lost her memory. Arianna preferred black, perhaps because it was the color of her thick, straight hair—well, the half she kept, at least.

She'd shaved the other half of her head bald on a whim once she left the army. Something about choosing her own damn hairstyle was freeing. The remaining half had grown long and often fell over her eye unless she twisted it in a braid. Striding to the hazy mirror in the room she'd claimed in the farmhouse, she began twining the strands, wanting it off her face for tonight's excursion. Once the tip was secured in a rubber band, she gazed at her greenish-brown eyes in the mirror.

"Well, you're not winning any beauty contests, Ari," she muttered, "but you could probably kick the shit out of the judges." Snickering, she secured her gun and knife to her belt and headed downstairs to the foyer by the front door, careful that her boots remained silent on the wooden steps.

Stopping by the front table, she picked up the tiny comm device, examining it between her fingers as she debated wearing it. No one would be listening on the other end anyway. Dominic was usually her comm partner, but he was sleeping. The tiny devices communicated like walkie-talkies and didn't require any telecommunication equipment. Good thing since most telecom equipment no longer worked.

"Fuck it," she murmured, setting it back on the table. "You'll be back in an hour, and they'll never even know you were gone." Grabbing her backpack, she headed to the kitchen and stuffed the bag full of apples, strawberries and some of the chicken Raquel had cooked for dinner. Finding an abandoned house with a generator had been a godsend, and Arianna only took the appropriate amount of food she knew the others wouldn't notice.

Trailing back to the front door, she reached for the knob and froze when someone cleared their throat behind her. Annoyed, she glanced toward the ceiling in frustration before turning to face Dominic.

His face was a jagged piece of beauty, anger marring the smooth skin that surrounded the ragged scar that ran from his eye, across his angular nose, to the other side of his perfectly full lips. He should've been ugly. God, she wished he were. But her heart leapt in her chest like the traitorous organ did every time he approached her.

Of course it did.

Because Arianna was deeply, inexplicably, unavoidably in love with Dominic Cavalleri.

And he was in love with her sister.

Furious at the feelings she couldn't contain, Arianna bristled and lifted her chin. "Can I help you?"

Scoffing, he strode closer and jabbed his finger toward her face. "Are you fucking serious?" he hissed. "You're going out alone after midnight? Do you have a death wish?"

"Don't point your finger in my face!" she whispered, swatting it away before gesturing upstairs. "I don't want to wake anyone up. I'll be back hours before sunrise."

Crossing his arms over his chest, he glowered at her as he tapped his bare foot. Arianna stared back, determined to maintain his unwavering gaze. He thought he was tough? She'd stare him down all fucking night long. She was stubborn as hell and certainly not intimidated by a man whose ass she could kick any day and twice on Sunday.

Probably. Of course, he was bigger than her, which was a feat since she was almost six feet tall and a hundred and sixty pounds of pure muscle. No one would ever accuse Arianna of being a shrinking violet, that was for damn sure.

Even though Dominic was several inches taller and built like a freight train, she'd sparred with him enough to know his tells. He was a good fighter and incredibly strong—but she was faster. Better at adapting and shifting tactics in the heat of a battle. He wasn't a bad soldier—hell, he was probably the best she'd seen, besides herself—but he wasn't invincible. And if she had to physically take him on in order to accomplish what she meant to do, she would without hesitation.

Sighing, he swiped a hand over his chin and shook his head. "Stay here." Pivoting, he began to walk away.

"Um, I'm not sure who you think you're talking to, but I don't take orders from you—"

"Shut up," he rasped, turning and slicing a hand through the air. "Do you want to wake the whole house up? I'm going with you. I just need to get dressed. Don't fucking move."

Crossing her arms, she huffed as her features contorted into a mask of annoyance. Although she didn't take orders from anyone, she'd also learned Dominic was as stubborn as she was and didn't want to waste time arguing. "Fine. Hurry the fuck up."

Shooting her one last glare, he pivoted and strode toward the small bedroom on the opposite side of the kitchen. He'd claimed it when they moved in, probably because it was on the ground floor near Dani's. She had some valuable info inside her head, and Dominic was in love with her, so it made sense. Arianna was fine sleeping upstairs, as did Raquel and Maverick on the nights Dani didn't trust him enough to bang him. Poor Mav. He did his best to win her over every day. Arianna had respect for him. He hadn't wavered in his dedication to Dani once. Maybe true love existed after all—for women like Dani, of course.

Craning her neck to look in the mirror that hung in the foyer, Arianna reminded herself it was okay men didn't think about her that way. Women like her didn't get roses and poems. They got scowls from men who were intimidated pussies because she was a better soldier. Fine with her. She'd use her skills to protect their team until Dani regained her memory and they'd retrieved the antidote from the lab.

Then Arianna would let Dani and Raquel heal the world while she retreated somewhere quiet and serene. She'd conceive through artificial insemination and have the child she craved without ever needing a man. It was a solid plan and one she planned to see to fruition once the mission was accomplished. For someone like her who had no blood relatives, it had become extremely important somewhere along the way to have a child. Someone who shared an unbreakable connection to her.

A twinge of guilt flared in her chest as Cynthia Lawson's beautiful face appeared in her mind. Her adoptive mother had always treated Arianna as her own and never made her feel different. She'd taken Arianna in when her birth parents had died in a car accident when she was only four years old. Their will had designated custody to Arianna's maternal grandmother, her only living relative at the time it was written. Unfortunately, Arianna's grandmother had passed of natural causes six months before her parents' accident, and they hadn't rewritten the will at the time of her death.

With no other relatives to take her in, Arianna was set to be shuffled into the foster system. Cynthia had been friends with her parents and lived next door. The kind woman had petitioned the court for custody of Arianna and given her a home. It had been one of the best turns of fortune in Arianna's life, and she was extremely thankful.

But still, in the hidden corners of her heart, she wanted someone who was...*hers*. True family, related by blood. Since she was a few months shy of forty, she really needed to get on that because the window to pop out a kid closed a fraction every day. But first, she needed to complete the mission and ensure they retrieved the antidote.

Mission, then baby. Lifting her brows in the reflection, she nodded. "Good plan, Ari."

"Sounds like a titillating conversation you're having with yourself out here," Dominic muttered, stalking down the dim hallway.

Shooting him the bird, she resisted the urge to tell him to go to hell. Those broad lips just smirked, driving her insane, so she turned and opened the door. Dominic followed behind, quietly securing the multitude of locks he and Maverick had installed. Hesitating, he lifted his gaze to her, his deep brown orbs swimming with concern. "Maybe we should tell Mav before we go."

"He's a trained soldier just like we are," she said, walking down the wooden porch stairs. "And you don't have to come. You're not invited anyway." Approaching the mist-covered grass, she began walking toward the gravel road that led to the woods, which were her destination.

When she approached the protective fence she, Dominic and Maverick had built, she carefully opened the barbed-wired gate. The circular perimeter wasn't perfect, but it added an extra layer of protection around their temporary home. Closing the gate behind them, she resecured the rope that held it closed and headed into the darkness.

Dominic fell into step beside her, his presence comforting, which annoyed her. If she were honest, she'd admit that having him near her sent a smooth wave of warmth throughout her entire body. His scent always seemed to invade her nostrils—crisp like the evergreen trees that grew in her back yard as a kid. It was...calming...refreshing...*sexy*...

Tamping down her unwanted attraction, she remained silent as she traipsed over the gravel and into the forest. Dominic followed her without a word, and something coiled deep in her belly at his silent faith in her even though he didn't have a clue where they were headed.

"I spotted a clearing with some sleeping bags, blankets and a banked fire," she said softly, feeling the need to explain. "There was a soccer ball nearby. I think there are some addicts living out here, and they have a kid...or kids. If so, I want to leave them some food."

Dominic glanced at her from the corner of his eye before nodding. "Okay."

Rolling her eyes, she continued walking under the dense canopy of leaves from the surrounding trees. "I don't need protection. You should've stayed home and kept an eye on Dani. She's the one who's integral to our mission."

Dominic remained silent, which drove her a thousand shades of crazy. Thinning her lips, she told herself she didn't owe him any explanations.

"You're important too, Ari," he finally said, the words sending shivers of pleasure through every cell of her skin. "I need you. Maverick and I couldn't do this on our own. Even with the three of us, we're outnumbered, but I like our chances better with you on our side." Reaching over, he squeezed her upper arm. "So stop doing stupid shit like scouting alone and going on secret missions without me. We're a team."

It was a warm summer night, so Arianna had only donned a black tank top, leaving her arms bare against the night air. As Dominic's palm covered her exposed skin, she felt herself flush and desperately wanted to pull away. God, she wished he wouldn't touch her. It swirled too many murky feelings deep in her core she'd never be able to extinguish.

"Thanks for your help," she mumbled, drawing her arm away and slightly shaking it, as if to shake off the remnants of his touch. "I know how much you want to protect Dani, and I'll keep doing my part."

A slow breath exited his lips as leaves and twigs crunched underneath their boots. Arianna sensed frustration in the soft breath, as well as longing and something else she couldn't quite identify. Finally, he said, "You don't have to throw it in my face all the time, you know? I understand she's Mav's. I know you don't give a shit about emotion, but some of us feel it even if we don't want to."

If he only knew. Squeezing her eyes closed for a brief moment, she wondered what he would do if she turned to face him and professed her love for the entire forest to hear. Considering he thought she hated him and was in love with her sister, he'd probably toss his head back and laugh in her face until his fucking lungs collapsed. Because if there was one thing Arianna had learned a long time ago, it was that men would never want a declaration of love from her.

She'd learned it from her high school boyfriend, who'd thoughtlessly taken her virginity and then laughed in her face when she exclaimed her love for him afterward.

From her college boyfriend, whom she discovered had a fantastic ass from behind...when she came home to find him fucking her roommate.

And from the man who'd proposed to her with such zeal over a decade ago. The soldier in her squadron who'd convinced her he loved her...until she'd realized he saw sleeping with her as the fastest way to move up the ranks.

Three attempts at love, which Arianna considered a full execution of the "three strikes and you're out" rule. She'd tried. She'd failed. She'd learned to never put her feelings on display for a man *ever* again. End of story. Thank you, drive through, please.

"Emotion isn't something I have time for," she said, swiping a branch out of their path as they walked down a haphazard trail. "But I'll try to leave you alone about Dani. Sucks to want something you can't have, but that's life, I guess."

He surprised her by snickering, and she craned her head to look at him, unable to control her corresponding smile. "What?"

"I just think it's funny to hear you say you'll let up on me. It's never going to happen." Grasping a low branch, he lifted it high and urged her to walk underneath it before he followed her. "I think you live to razz me, Ari."

"Don't call me Ari," she said, shooting him a glare over her shoulder, although her tone was light. "It's a nickname meant for people who care about me. Only my sisters call me that."

His broad fingers encircled her arm, drawing her to a stop and tugging her slightly closer. Those gorgeous eyes stared into her own, the hurt simmering there illuminated by the soft moonlight above. "I care about you, Arianna. Even though I want to strangle you most of the time, I care about you."

Huffing a laugh, she drew his arm away, her own palm on fire from the contact with the prickly hairs. "Wow, you're really in the feels tonight. It's weird." Glancing toward the nearby clearing, she gestured with her head. "Come on. The camp I spotted is in that clearing. Let's go."

She lurched ahead, needing to create space between them so she didn't drown in the warm heat of his body or the heady evergreen scent that shot straight to the place between her thighs. Determined to remain indifferent, she approached the campsite, noticing the pale glow of the fire. A woman and girl were nestled in two sleeping bags on the far side, and a boy, who Arianna guessed to be eight or nine, sat beside the fire, cradling bent legs as he stared into the flames. His chin rested on his knees as he slowly rocked back and forth, and sympathy swelled as she noticed how skinny he was.

"Hey," she whispered, holding up a hand when he gasped. Wide eyes latched onto hers, laced with fear and surprise.

"Don't be scared," she said, her soft tone reassuring. Slowly approaching, she crouched before him. "I'm Arianna and that's Dominic." She pointed over her shoulder. "He's really ugly, but he's harmless."

Dominic scoffed behind her, and the boy's shoulders seemed to relax slightly. Gripping the straps, she slowly eased the backpack off her shoulder. "Is that your mom and sister?"

He nodded, looking toward their sleeping forms before resuming eye contact with Arianna. "She's sick from the medicine she took. We live out here since we lost our house."

Nodding, Arianna slid the backpack over the ground as the boy warily watched her. "We brought you some food. Figured you might be hungry." The boy's eyes gleamed with hope, and she grinned. "It's okay. I'll leave the bag here but only if you'll share with your mom and sister when they wake up."

The boy nodded his head with vigor as he reached over, grabbing the bag and tugging it toward him. Unzipping it, he sucked in a breath as he observed the contents inside. Pulling out the container with the strawberries, he took a huge bite, his lips curving as he began to chew.

"How long have you been staying here?"

Squinting one eye, he stared up at the sky. "A few days. Mom says that once she feels better, we're going to walk to the compound where her brother lives. They take in people who need the medicine like she does."

Anger flared in Arianna's chest as she took a moment to rail at the state of the world. The entire fabric of society collapsed because people wanted to take a drug to stay young forever. Now, most of them were battered and broken by addiction and would die meaningless deaths. So much destruction because people wanted to play God with their own bodies. It was a terrible tragedy she hoped to end before humanity reached the point of no return.

Only time would tell if she would succeed.

"It's time to go," Dominic said, cupping Arianna's shoulder and urging her to rise. "Safe travels to the compound, son. I hope your mom feels better."

"Thank you for the food," he said, lifting the strawberry and waving. "I promise I'll share."

A twig snapped to Arianna's right, causing her to surge to her feet. Dominic rose beside her, heat emanating from his large frame as they gazed into the dark woods.

"Sen Force?" Dominic asked softly.

"I didn't see any evidence when I scouted, but I could've missed it—"

A loud bang sounded a millisecond before a bullet whizzed by her ear. Grasping the gun at her waist, she drew, aiming at the dense forest. Dominic drew his gun and tried to step in front of her as the woman and girl beside the fire jolted awake and screamed.

"Protect the camp," she said, pushing in front of Dominic and stepping toward the brush where the shot commenced. "I'll check it out."

"Ari..." Dominic warned.

"Come out and face us!" she yelled, squinting at the man she could barely see hiding behind a tree set a few feet into the clearing. "Coward!"

The man slowly edged away from the tree, gun held high as he aimed at Arianna. They faced off, hands gripping their weapons, as he entered the campsite.

"I'm not Sen Force," the man said in a gravelly voice. Judging by the deep wrinkles around his eyes and parched lips, Arianna surmised he hadn't had proper shelter or water in some time.

"Well, you have a gun and I'm not feeling real friendly right now," she said through clenched teeth.

"I'm a deserter," he said, moving forward as Arianna lifted the gun to aim between his eyes. "And I need some EverLife. I know the woman has some stashed in her bag. I've been following them for two days."

"I only have enough left to get to my brother's compound," the woman pleaded, holding her daughter as they rocked on the ground. "I need a fix every few hours or I'll die."

"Lady," the man said, lifting his gun and aiming it directly at her. "I hate to tell you this, but you're already dead."

A loud growl shot through the forest before Dominic barreled into the man's side, knocking him to the ground. Arianna had observed him creeping up on the deserter as the situation unfolded. Another shot was fired, and Arianna urged the family to scurry behind her as she trained the gun on the men.

They rolled and scuffled, each grunting as they punched and kicked. Arianna's heart pounded as she tried to find a clean shot that wouldn't hit Dominic.

Suddenly, Dominic seized control of the man's gun, pressing the barrel to his temple and firing a fatal blow. The deserter crumpled beneath him, muscles turning lax as Dominic expelled a deep breath.

"Damn it," he breathed, rising and planting a fist on his hip. "I didn't want to kill him."

Arianna rushed over, lowering to place two fingers on his neck. "Well, you did, and I'm glad. He sealed his fate when he deserted Sen Force." She tapped her fingers on the brand that had been burned into his neck. The one all deserters were forced to bear before being exiled from the District.

"Mama," a high-pitched voice cried.

"I'm here, baby," the woman soothed, pulling both children into her sides as they sat on the ground.

"You should have enough food in the bag I gave your son to get to your brother's compound," Arianna said, facing them. "I'd go now. You'll be less detectable in the dark."

The woman rose, extending shaking hands to her children. "Come on. Let's go."

The boy grabbed the food sack and the small pack that must've held their meager belongings. After grasping his mother's hand, the boy turned to look over his shoulder as she led them away. His eyes shone with fear and gratitude as they locked onto Arianna's. His soundless *thank you* almost broke the heart that had hardened into a lifeless rock years ago.

Once they disappeared, she sighed and rubbed her forehead. "Fuck. We probably made too much noise. Do you think we're blown?"

"I don't know, but we need to bury the body," Dominic said, approaching her. "This is why—"

"I swear to god," she interjected, holding up a hand. "If you lecture me right now on why this was a bad idea, I'll shoot you. Those kids needed food."

Deep brown eyes darted between hers before he nodded. "Okay. Let's head back, get a shovel, and finish this while the moon's still high."

Nodding, she fell into step beside him, shoulders drooping at the disastrous turn of events. Closing her eyes, she sent out a soft prayer for the family's safety. Arianna wasn't religious, but she figured it sure as hell wouldn't hurt.

They each grabbed a shovel from the shed behind the farmhouse and returned to the site. The fire burned low, the remaining shards of wood glowing a deep orange. Glancing toward the spot where they'd left the body, Arianna's eyes grew wide as her spine straightened with alarm.

The body they'd left dead and cold upon the grass was gone.

An hour later, after thoroughly searching the site and surrounding woods, Arianna and Dominic stood beside the now-banked fire. Hands upon their hips, they both absently stared at the charred wood, Arianna gnawing her lip as she debated.

"There are no footprints and no evidence of the body being dragged," she said. "He literally disappeared."

"The only explanation is that someone—or a group of people—lifted him and carried him away."

"Who would rescue a deserter's body?" she asked, lifting her gaze to his. "Certainly not Sen Force."

"It makes no sense," Dominic said, shaking his head. "But it's got to be close to three a.m., and we're both beat. Let's come back tomorrow and examine the site in the daylight. We're not going to accomplish anything tonight."

Defeated, Arianna nodded and began the trek home. Regret coiled in her stomach, mostly because her intended good deed had turned horribly wrong. Two kids were now traveling in the dark, scared and vulnerable.

"They weren't safe in the open either, Ari," Dominic said, reaching over and squeezing her hand. "They won't be safe until they get to the compound. It's probably better that you spurred them along."

Taking comfort for one small moment, she squeezed his hand. "I'll choose to believe that. Thank you."

They reached the porch steps, the wood creaking under their boots as they climbed. After resting the shovels against the porch wall, they entered the darkened house. Arianna kicked off her boots as Dominic clicked the locks behind her. Straightening, she almost banged into the thick wall of his chest. His broad hands gripped her upper arms, steadying her as she cursed herself for taking off the boots here instead of in her room. Without them, she was an inch shorter, causing her to feel vulnerable next to his thick frame.

"Let's return to the site at seven a.m. sharp. Good night." She turned to bolt up the stairs as his hand snaked around her arm. Whirling back, she opened her mouth to tell him that if he ever grabbed her again, she was going to punch his nose clean off his face.

But his expression froze her, turning every muscle in her body to stone. He was gazing at her with an intensity and...*respect*. It unnerved her to her very core.

"It was noble to take food to the kids, Ari," he said softly. "We'll figure out who moved the deserter's body. We knew we wouldn't be able to hide here forever."

"We need to tell Mav."

He gave a curt nod. "We'll tell everyone tomorrow. You and I will go back to examine the site and leave Dani and Raquel to work on science-y stuff. We'll stay on high alert."

Arianna's lips twitched. "Science-y stuff? Is that a technical term?"

A dark eyebrow arched, causing her heart to lurch. Why did she find him so fucking sexy?

"It's all I've got." Lifting his hands, he took a step back. "Don't beat yourself up about tonight. You're too hard on yourself. You're a good one, Ari."

She wanted to be angry at his continued use of her nickname, but her throat was suddenly tight with a thousand emotions she couldn't name and desperately wanted to eliminate. Unable to stop herself, she asked, "A good what?"

His eyes roved over her face, lowering to her neck and the rapidly reddening skin above her collarbone before lifting back to hers. Leaning closer, he whispered, "A good soul, no matter how mean you are. You might fool everyone else, but you can't fool me."

Straightening her spine, she swallowed the lump in her throat and forced herself to speak. "You don't know me. Don't pretend you do." Turning, she began to head up the stairs before turning back and lifting a finger. "And if you ever grab my arm again, I'll chop off your fucking hand. Got it?"

Those broad lips twitched before slowly curving into the sexiest smile Arianna had ever seen. Convinced her knees were going to collapse, she pivoted and resumed walking up the stairs.

"With a knife or a saw?" he taunted, his gruff voice washing over her as she tackled the stairs. "Just so I'm prepared..."

Extending her middle finger, she shot him one last silent "Fuck you" before cresting the second floor. She quickly washed her hands and face in the upstairs bathroom, thankful for the running water. Striding into her bedroom, she tugged off her pants and shirt and climbed between the sheets clad in her underwear and bra. As she relaxed, she stared at the ceiling, hoping like hell she hadn't blown their cover.

Minutes later, she turned on her side and forced her eyes closed, determined to sleep. As she drifted, she imagined Dominic's warm body cradling her as that deep voice whispered in her ear...

You're a good one, Ari...such a good girl for me...

Groaning, she punched the pillow before eventually falling into a restless slumber.

Chapter 5

Maverick rose with the sun the next morning and entered Dani's room, careful to remain quiet. There was a note he liked to leave by the phone so she'd see it when she awoke, and he placed it on the nightstand before exiting.

Open the camera app and watch the first video, then come and find me.

Love, Maverick.

Heading to the kitchen, he brewed some of the tea the previous owners had stashed in the pantry. They'd been stocked full, and Maverick was grateful for that. Sadly, they'd run out of coffee after their first month in the farmhouse, which had led to an overall rise in morning crankiness for everyone. Now, after several months, he'd gotten used to the tea and was thankful they'd found a place with a generator and working well in the back yard.

The kettle began to boil, and he turned off the stove before pouring the tea and dunking the bag into the scalding liquid. Returning to the sink, he stared out the window at the shed and the meadow beyond. They'd been lucky, remaining off the grid in the abandoned home, but Maverick knew that luck always ran out.

The time to break into Sendaxa's lab and retrieve Dani's secret antidote was near. If she didn't regain her memory, they'd have to forge ahead and try like hell to succeed.

"Good morning," Raquel's sweet voice chimed, and Maverick turned to smile at his wife's youngest sister. Arianna looked nothing like Dani or Raquel since she was adopted, but the two younger sisters bore a resemblance to each other. They shared the same light green eyes, although Dani's had gorgeous honey-colored flecks that were absent in Raquel's, and both had a smattering of freckles across their nose and cheeks. Dani was stunning in an almost ethereal way, with her pert nose, bright smile and thick brown hair...but of course, he was biased because he was her husband.

Raquel was pretty in a more muted way, and Maverick had heard her say on many occasions that Arianna got the brawn, Dani got the looks and the brains, and she'd gotten the baby fat along with a hefty side of awkwardness. It was a self-deprecating statement she made with a teasing grin, but it always stirred compassion inside Maverick's heart. Raquel was a sweet, loving person who was a fantastic scientist in her own right, and he hated it when she disparaged herself.

"Good morning to you," he said, noticing she was wearing sneakers. "You must be planning an early-morning walk."

"Yeah," she said, trailing over to pour some water before stuffing a tea bag inside. Blowing on the hot liquid, she took a sip and leaned her hip against the counter. "I spotted a bush that's growing some sort of new berries I've never seen at the far end of the meadow." She gestured toward the window above the sink. "Figured I'd pick them and test them to see if they're poisonous or if they could possibly help with the antidote formula I've been working on."

"I snooped around your lab yesterday," he said, flashing a grin. "You've done a great job rigging up a full-fledged science lab in the den of an abandoned farmhouse." He lifted his mug in a salute.

"We were lucky to find a house with so much vegetation nearby. I like trying different combinations and hope one of the teas I make will help Dani. Blueberries are known to strengthen memory, as well as kale and rosemary, which the previous owners planted in their garden. The teas don't taste that great, but hopefully, they're helping."

"She had a good day yesterday after I messed up," he said, swiping a hand over his face. "Even told me where to find her birthmark. Hopefully, today will be even better. You never know."

A throat cleared in the doorway, and their heads snapped toward Dani, who stood in the frame, knuckles white as she clutched a long metal candlestick in one hand. "I wouldn't be so sure, buddy," she muttered. "I'm assuming you're Maverick?" Lifting the phone, she shook it.

He gave a deep bow fit for the finest queen. "At your service, my lady."

"Hey, Dani," Raquel said with a soft smile.

"Hey," she said, gingerly approaching before setting the phone on the round dining table, although she held the candlestick firm. "Does the principal need to see you in the office?"

Maverick's lips curved at the inside phrase used between the sisters to signal something might be wrong. Dani used to save Raquel from having to participate in physical education class by showing up and telling the teacher the principal needed to see Raquel.

"Nope," Raquel said, shaking her head. "Everything's fine and we're not in danger. Promise."

Exhaling, Dani gingerly lowered the candlestick to the counter. "Holy shit. What the fuck is going on?"

Raquel approached her, and they shared a tight hug before Dani drew back and patted her side. "It seems like I destroyed the world, which I can't even begin to wrap my head around, and I have a huge fucking laceration on my side. What the hell?"

"Pitchfork accident about a week ago," Maverick interjected. "Raquel was with you when you fell."

"The sun was setting and you tripped and..." biting her lip, Raquel shrugged. "I mean, it wasn't funny, but it kind of was...until you got hurt and then I felt really bad. I lugged you back here, and Mav cleaned your wound."

Glancing at Maverick, Dani asked, "So, were your parents huge Tom Cruise fans? I'm not getting the name."

"Every fucking time," he muttered, rubbing his forehead as Raquel giggled. "I need you to get your memory back so we don't go through this every morning."

"Did I miss Mav getting '*Top Gunned*'?" Arianna asked, striding into the kitchen.

"Barely," Raquel chimed.

"Shut it, you two," Maverick warned the sisters. "I'm going to make some breakfast and then I'll bring you up to speed, Dani. After that, Dominic and I need to head out and get more gas from that farm we scouted with all the tractors."

Their makeshift home had an abandoned pickup truck they were planning to drive to the Sendaxa lab in what was formerly Bethesda, Maryland, when they were ready to retrieve the antidote. Although Bethesda was now a ghost town since the wealthy had moved inside the fortified walls of Washington, DC, and the addicted had perished or relocated to one of the black-market compounds, the lab was still guarded by Sen Force soldiers. It was ground zero for the beginning of the world's downfall, and Sendaxa hadn't destroyed it...yet. But the knowledge the lab could be demolished—and any hope of retrieving Dani's secret antidote along with it—kept an urgency to their mission that couldn't be ignored.

"Will you go on foot?" Dani asked, lowering to one of the chairs at the dining table. "How far is it? Where the hell are we?"

"We're in an abandoned farmhouse in Waterford, Virginia, with a generator and a well, thank god. Dominic and I have been syphoning gas from nearby farms to make sure we have enough to drive to the lab once we're ready," Maverick said, striding over to her and lifting a tentative hand. Ever so gently, he placed it on her soft curls, thrilled when she didn't pull away. "Good morning, sweetheart," he said reverently.

Dani swallowed thickly, her eyes growing wide as she studied him, and Maverick dropped his hand, not wanting to push her or make her uncomfortable. Still, he missed touching her...missed the soft moans she expelled when he trailed kisses over the valley between her breasts...and the sexy purrs that escaped her pretty lips when he went lower...

Not wanting to be a creep, he strode back to the stove and pulled two pans from the cabinet. "Eggs as usual?" he asked, lifting his brows.

"Works for me," Arianna said, trailing to sit beside Dani before giving her a firm hug. Maverick heard her say softly, "He's a good one, sis. I wouldn't steer you wrong," to which Dani whispered, "Thank you," before releasing the embrace.

"No eggs for me," Raquel said, inching toward the back door. "Even in a world with limited food options, I can't seem to lose the baby weight." Her lips curved into a smile that didn't quite reach her eyes. "I'm going to go pick some of the wild raspberries."

"I'll go with you," Ari said, standing.

"No, it's fine," she said, turning the knob and opening the door. "They're on the far end of the yard by the tall evergreens, and still inside the perimeter you all built." Pointing toward the window above the sink, she added, "Mav can see me as he cooks."

Looking up from scrambling the eggs, which had been supplied by the chickens in the coop out back, Maverick squinted out the window. "I can barely see it, but yeah, I'll keep an eye out. Arianna scouted yesterday and everything was fine."

"About that," Arianna said as guilt clouded her features. "Something happened last night that I need to update you on."

"Is it a soldier thing?" Raquel asked. "If so, you can update me after my walk."

"That's fine," Arianna said. "I'll come find you after breakfast. I can tell you're itching to get outside. Go on."

"See you in a bit." With a wave, Raquel headed outside, closing the door behind her.

Maverick turned off the stove and scraped the eggs onto four plates in equal portions. He carried two to the table for Dani and Arianna before walking back and grabbing the two other plates. Dominic exited his bedroom that adjoined the kitchen, inhaling a deep breath.

"I smell eggs," he said in his deep baritone.

"Eat them while they're hot," Maverick said, gesturing to the seat next to him as he lowered into his own. "Arianna was about to give us an update."

A look passed between Arianna and Dominic.

"Before she starts, I'd like to say good morning, Dani," Dominic said. "I'm Dom and I'm part of the team. Hope the scar doesn't scare you. Arianna thinks it's hideous."

Arianna rolled her eyes as Dani glanced between Dominic and Maverick. "I have so many questions. Did I meet you at Sendaxa? I don't understand—"

"I'm going to answer them all for you," Maverick said, reaching over and squeezing her wrist. "But for now, let's just eat breakfast and pretend the world is normal for five minutes."

"Might as well update you while we eat," Arianna said gruffly. "I'll preface this by saying that my goal was to help some hungry kids. Unfortunately, things devolved..."

Arianna updated them while Dominic filled in some pieces along the way. Once she'd finished recounting the events of the previous night, she sat back and laced her fingers behind her head.

"So, that's it. Feel free to tell me how dumb it was to go out at night and possibly attract attention to our location."

"You wanted to bring some kids some food," Dani said, reaching over to squeeze her wrist. "I'd be pissed if you didn't help them, Ari. You couldn't have known a deserter would show up." She pursed her lips. "I'm going to need a briefing on what army he deserted from, but I assume one of you will catch me up."

"I will," Maverick said with a nod. "We'll take a walk after breakfast and I'll explain everything."

"Arianna and I will head out to examine the site," Dominic said. "The disappearance of the body is alarming, and we want to figure out who took it. But it's also pointless to worry about something we can't change."

Dani ate a forkful of eggs before asking, "Whose idea was it to make the video? That definitely helped when I woke up in a strange room with no memory."

"Yours," Maverick said, grinning. "We'd had a good day, and you wanted to ensure we had more of them."

"What does a good day entail?" she asked, her green eyes lit with curiosity.

"It means Mav gets laid," Arianna muttered.

"Jesus, Ari," Dominic interjected.

"Well, it's true." Wooden legs scraped the floor as she abruptly stood and carried her empty plate to the sink. "I'm going to go make sure the area around Raquel is safe and then we can head back to the site. Dani, do you want me to examine your side first or are you okay if Mav does it?" She pointed between Maverick and Dani.

"I..." Dani said hesitantly. "I guess it's okay if Maverick looks at it."

Arianna nodded before heading through the back door and closing it firmly behind her.

"Still the same Ari," Dani said, her gaze filled with wonder. "I'd be more weirded out if she and Raquel weren't here. For now, I'm just...overwhelmed."

Maverick smiled as admiration covered his features. "You're getting better each day at accepting the situation. I think you're building some muscle memory, even if you don't physically remember." He tapped his temple.

Dani remained silent, studying him as she often did each morning.

Maverick rose, collecting the dishes and washing them as he prepared himself for his daily briefing to his wife.

Chapter 6

After breakfast, Dani followed the incredibly handsome man who looked like the result of a baby between Timothy Olyphant and Patrick Dempsey into the living room. Forget Dr. McDreamy. Somehow, she'd woken up and the hottest silver fox in the world claimed to be her husband.

It would be cool if she hadn't destroyed humanity.

Which she was pretty sure she'd done, even though that certainly hadn't been her intention.

Man, life was a bitch sometimes.

"You okay?" Maverick asked, gesturing toward the weathered red plaid couch. "It was here when we found the house and it's ugly but comfortable."

Nodding, Dani sat, stiffening a bit when he lowered beside her.

"Don't worry," he said, the curving of his lips causing slight dimples to form under cheeks covered with a light smattering of black and gray stubble. "I'm not going to bite."

That's a shame...

The words flashed through her head before she cleared her throat and reminded herself she'd never seen this man in her life...but he and her sisters claimed he was her *husband*. Since it was too surreal to process, she glanced at her side.

"Soooo...do you want to treat my...pitchfork accident?" Scrunching her features, she said, "Wow. Those are two words I never thought I'd say together."

Chuckling, he rose and lifted a finger. "Be right back. Need to grab a wet cloth, fresh bandage and some of the antibiotic ointment the previous residents stocked in the upstairs bathroom cabinet. It's expired, but you and Raquel say it's better than nothing."

"Antibacterial cream is usually good years after expiration," she affirmed. "Should I...uh...take off my shirt?"

He cocked a brow. "Honestly, yeah, that will make it easier. Wait until I get back since you're not wearing a bra. I'll grab you one from your bedroom on the way."

"How do you know I'm not wearing a bra?"

"You never sleep in a bra, babe. Be right back."

Glancing down, she admitted he was right while simultaneously wondering who'd dressed her in the black tank top and boxer shorts. Had she dressed herself or had he done it? Shivering at the thought, she gnawed her lip while she awaited his return.

He returned, extending a hand with a functional beige bra hanging from one finger. Frowning, Dani grabbed it and stood. "Turn around," she said.

He breathed a laugh before turning and setting the supplies on the side table while she chucked her shirt and put on the bra. Once it was secure, she said, "Okay, ready."

"It's best if you lie on your back with your injured side facing me."

Dani's eyes darted between his as breath lodged in her throat.

"I won't try anything, Dani. Not really my style. If you want me to touch you, you'll ask. Come on. Let's get it done so we can head outside and I can brief you."

Feeling her heart thunk in her chest, she lay down on the couch.

"Lift your arm above your head," Maverick gently commanded, sending a jolt of pure arousal through her veins. Cognizant of the rising and falling of her chest, she lifted her arm, resting it beside her head.

Lowering, he sat beside her, his face a mask of concentration as he touched his fingers to the area where her skin met the adhesive tape. Dani sucked in a breath, and his striking eyes lifted to hers. "Are my fingers cold?"

Unable to speak, she shook her head, and he blinked before lowering his gaze to the bandage. His fingers scraped at the white gauze, gently tugging until he drew the bandage from her body. Studying the wound, he gently pushed the red skin surrounding the three circular punctures.

"Does that hurt?"

"It's tender, but it's not too bad," she rasped, wondering when someone had dropped a bag of gravel down her throat.

"Okay. I'll clean it, apply the ointment and put on a new bandage. I think we'll only need to do this two or three more times and it will be healed enough you won't need me to clean it for you."

Bummer. She'd have to give up having Silver Fox Hottie touch her while she lay sprawled on the couch? Was there another pitchfork she could walk into? Where was a random pitchfork when a girl needed one?

Maverick's lips pursed as mirth entered his eyes. "Were you just wondering if there's another pitchfork lying around you could fall into?"

Laughter bounded from her throat. "Yep. Busted."

His warm chuckle washed over her as he lifted the wet cloth and began to clean her wound. "Your sense of humor is what I noticed first, and it's killer. I couldn't believe a world-renowned geneticist could be so damn funny."

"How did we meet?"

"Sendaxa recruited you to develop EverLife and I was head of security at your lab. You worked a lot, which meant we spent a lot of time together."

"And you couldn't resist my dazzling knowledge of mitochondrial DNA?"

White teeth flashed as he grinned. "That and...other things." He slid the cloth over her skin one more time before setting it on the table and picking up the ointment. As he spoke, he spread the smooth gel over her wound. "You were so damn funny, and so determined to succeed. Every time you created a formula that failed, you'd pour yourself a glass of champagne and toast to another fantastic failure."

"I'm a huge fan of failure," she said, watching his fingers as they worked. "It's the only path to success."

"One of your favorite sayings," he confirmed with a nod. "Eventually, you roped me into having a sip of champagne with you here and there. It was so refreshing to meet someone who embraced failure. I'd never really contemplated having a positive attitude toward failing, and you were always so cute as we drank together."

"I'm sure Sendaxa wasn't happy their star scientist and head of security were drinking on the job."

"They never knew," he said, arching a mischievous eyebrow. "What use would I have been if I hadn't known how to hide from their cameras?"

"Indeed," she said, biting her lip. "But sharing stolen champagne is a long way from marriage. I'm exceedingly curious how that happened."

Remaining silent, he wiped his fingers on the wet cloth before picking up the large bandage. Removing the adhesive covering, he pressed the white gauze to her skin before patting the sides to ensure the adhesive stuck to her skin. After several firm presses, he straightened and ran his fingers over the bandage, causing her to shiver. "I think it's set," he said softly.

"Did I say something wrong?"

Those deep eyes lifted to hers. "No," he murmured, running a hand over his face. "It just makes me sad that you don't remember."

Dani's eyes widened as she studied him, something welling in her chest that felt a lot like...*remorse?*

"I'm sorry—"

"It's okay," he interjected, shaking his head. "One day you're going to remember, and it's going to be the happiest day of my damn life."

Slowly rising, she sat on the edge of the couch, wondering why she didn't feel more vulnerable in front of this man who was essentially a stranger. Here she was, clad in only a bra and boxer shorts, completely exposed. She should've felt trapped. Wary. Afraid. Instead, she felt drawn to the man whose face was now a mask of sadness and longing.

"Then tell me," she whispered, lifting her hand to gently rest her palm on his stubbled cheek. "Tell me how we fell in love. I'd really like to hear the story."

Emotion flared in his eyes as he smiled. "I promise, I'll tell you the story later. For now, I want to brief you. There's an urgency to our mission, and I have a feeling last night's events will only add to it. I've got work to do, but I don't want to leave you hanging." Rising, he extended his hand. "Come on, slugger. Let's get to it."

CHAPTER 7

After throwing on a t-shirt and sneakers, Dani headed outside with Maverick, taking in the expansive meadows and forests that surrounded the farmhouse. "Who lived here before?"

"We don't know," he said, shaking his head as he walked beside her. "Once they locked down the cities and medical care became scarce outside the city walls, people began to migrate toward the black-market compounds. Many left their lives and belongings behind, only concerned with finding more EverLife. Whoever owned this farm was long gone before we arrived."

"How do you know?"

"The food in the fridge and on the counter was rotted, and there was a severe ant problem, which Raquel insisted on eradicating." He flashed a grin. "Waterford is far enough off the grid, and this place is remote enough that Dom, Arianna and I decided to set a temporary base here."

"How long ago?"

"We've been here for three months."

A heavy rush of air escaped her lungs. "I lost my memory three months ago," she said flatly. "After I created a drug that hurt so many." Halting, she turned to face him, the sun burning her eyes as they welled. "How many people have died?"

"Don't do this to yourself, sweetheart," he said, gently rubbing her upper arm. "No one could've foreseen this—"

"*I* should've foreseen it," she said, angrily swiping the tear that escaped and trailed down her cheek. "I should be arrested and tried for murder. It's no less than I deserve."

His nostrils flared as he inhaled a deep breath, the smooth strokes of his palm against the skin of her upper arm soothing. "We can't turn you in. We need you, Dani. You're going to remember the code, and we're going to break into the lab so we can fix this."

"I just want to help people," she whispered, her throat bobbing as it burned with clogged emotion. "To cure cancer so people won't suffer like we did with Mom. That's what I was working on at Columbia. How did I fuck everything up so badly?"

"Your intentions were good, sweetheart." Stepping forward, he drew her close, aligning their bodies, the firm ridges of his chest and thighs pressing into hers. "Sendaxa promised they'd fund your cancer vaccine research once you finished EverLife. Sometimes shit happens even when we try our best and have good intentions."

Her throat bobbed as she stared deep into his eyes, smoldering with love and compassion. "I have to fix it," she said softly.

"We will. That's what we're doing here. We're working our way up to breaking into the lab to steal the secret stash of antidote you hid before you lost your memory. Once we have that, you and Raquel can replicate it, mass produce it, and we can begin to distribute it to the black-market compounds."

Dani mulled the plan over in her head, both overwhelmingly complex and simple at once. "It's a lot for a five-person team to take on, especially when you have to spend hours explaining the situation to me every day."

Huffing a laugh, he nodded. "It would be easier if we could cut the daily recaps. I haven't figured out how yet. The video helps, but you're still wary until we have a chance to talk like we are now."

Dani's eyes lowered, roving over the neckline of his t-shirt and the tiny black and gray hairs that sprung around the collar. How many times had she trailed her fingers through them? How many times had she made love with this stranger who spoke to her with such familiar reverence? Lifting her hand, she placed it over his heart, strangely comforted by the firm beats beneath her palm.

Maverick's eyes closed as he seemed to melt underneath her touch. A muscle ticked in his jaw, the strong muscles of his neck chording as he allowed her to explore. Sliding her hand to his collar, she delved her fingers inside, brushing the backs against the prickly hairs. A low groan escaped his throat, causing her body to inflame.

"Babe," he rasped, his breath choppy as he squeezed his eyelids together. "I want you to touch me...*everywhere*...believe me." Lifting his lids, his gaze drilled into hers. "But Dom and I have to go retrieve some gas today, so I need to finish our briefing and get on the road."

"Okay," she whispered, aware of the swirling emotions deep in her gut. Guilt she'd hurt so many people. Remorse she couldn't bring back the ones that were already lost. Determination to save those who still had a chance. Desire for the man who seemed intent on helping her accomplish that task. "Have I tried keeping a journal? What methods have I tried to condense this daily process?"

"You do have a notebook where you write things down, but in the end, it's always easier for us to talk." Grasping her hand, he brought it to his lips, gently kissing her palm. "You don't remember me here when you wake up," he tapped her forehead, "but your body remembers me. Your hands remember me." He placed another reverent kiss before lowering her hand and releasing it. Dani flexed her fingers, already missing his touch. "So, it was just easier to do this every morning"—he circled his hand between them—"than for you to spend an hour reading a journal."

Lowering her gaze, she stared at the spongy grass as she gnawed her lip, pondering how to jog her memory so they could escape this nightmare and enter the next phase of their plan. Cementing her gaze to his, she said, "We have to find a solution. Three months is too long. We can't remain inactive, especially if bodies are mysteriously disappearing."

"I agree," he confirmed, gently brushing away the hair that blew across her cheek. "If you don't recover your memory soon, we're going to just break into the lab and try to blow the locks to bits so we can retrieve the antidote. You armed the door to the secret storage unit with a ten-digit security code, which we hope you'll remember. If not, you'll still need to scan your fingerprint. Without the code, the chances of us breaching the lab, retrieving the antidote and escaping intact are slim, but we're going to try."

"You know the layout since you were head of security?"

"Yes, and Dom worked there too. We know it intimately."

Chewing the inside of her lip, Dani digested the information. "Okay. The lab is heavily guarded, I assume?"

"It is, but it's outside the city walls, which gives it a vulnerability it wouldn't have otherwise. Between Dom, Arianna and I, we think we can take the soldiers. Raquel isn't a soldier, so we'll retrieve her after the mission. Or she'll continue the mission if we fail."

"I don't want her left alone," Dani said, concern for her sister flaring in her chest.

"Then we'll have to succeed," he said firmly. "You're determined to save the world, and I've never met a more tenacious woman than you, sweetheart. Along with Arianna and Raquel. The Lawson sisters are fierce."

Sighing, she ran a hand through her hair. "I failed at helping people and created a huge disaster instead. I feel anything but fierce. It's unforgiveable."

"There's no point in dwelling on things we can't change, Dani," he said, sliding his fingers under her chin to stare deep into her eyes. "All we can do now is fix it."

"I'm ready," she whispered, straightening her spine. "Let's get fucking started."

Chuckling, he leaned down and brushed a kiss across her lips, his lips soft yet firm as they caressed hers.

"Sorry," he whispered, shaking his head. "You're just so cute when you get that determined glint in your eye. I couldn't resist."

"Will you tell me about our first kiss one day? I'd really like to know."

"Yeah." Dropping his hand, Dani shivered at the loss of his warm fingers against her chin. "How about when Dom and I get back tonight?"

"It's a date," she breathed, her voice raspy as they stood in the warm breeze, their bodies humming in tune even though they were no longer touching.

"Come on. Let's get you set up in Raquel's lab. You like to work with her on the various vegetation and tea combos. I think you're healed enough to work today."

Stepping back, he extended his hand and she took it, interlacing their fingers before he led her back to the house. He gave her a quick tour of the lab, which was impressive considering the lack of scientific equipment at the farmhouse, and kissed her once more on the forehead before he headed outside to wait for Dominic and Arianna to return.

Staring at the various concoctions and the vegetation spread across the large table, Dani grabbed the nearby notebook that had her scrawled notes and got to work.

Chapter 8

Dominic returned from scouting the campsite, annoyed he and Arianna found no clues of who moved the deserter's body. After heading to his room and fishing a pesky rock from his boot, he slipped it back on and stood from the rickety bed. It was better than sleeping on the floor, so he wouldn't complain, but a part of him detested the fact the Sendaxa executives and their supporters slept in luxury every night. Safe in their walled-off cities, they'd left the destruction of society behind, carelessly hoarding all available EverLife and the antidote supplies and shutting out the rest of the world.

They were a bunch of bastards, and Dominic couldn't wait to bring them down.

The odds against him and the rest of their scrappy team were vast, but Dominic knew they'd do their best to accomplish their goal or die trying. There was honor in that, and it was extremely important to Dominic to live with honor since so many others had lost their chance.

The image of his parents and sister flashed through his mind, causing him to smile as he rested his palms flat on the dresser. He stared into his withered face and dark brown eyes, remembering how his sister, Pam, used to tease him after he'd sustained the scar that now marred his features.

He'd been deployed on a special ops mission back when he was still a Navy Seal. A young man who'd believed in optimistic ideals like democracy and freedom. His team was tasked with taking out a high-level operative in a terrorist regime in Pakistan. It wasn't his first mission designed to target and assassinate a threat, but it would end up being the deadliest.

Somehow, the terrorist cell and their leader had known about the impending attack. Dominic's team of twelve men charged into an ambush and only three survived. A rebel soldier had pulled a machete from his belt, slashing it across Dominic's face before he regained his wits enough to shoot a spray of bullets from his rifle into the man's chest. Dominic could still remember the blood dripping from his nose and cheeks as his commander gripped his arm and tugged him out of the cave into the dark night. Dominic returned home with his commander and one fellow comrade, their bodies bludgeoned and their spirits broken.

Dominic's parents and sister had taken him in, nursing him back to health after he was honorably discharged from duty. In those days after his release from the hospital, Pam would tiptoe into the room and leave snacks for him on the bedside table. Sometimes, she brought him ice cream, and they ate together as she teased him about his scar. She'd tell him he needed to create an online dating profile specifically looking for girls who dug scars and wounded men.

His nineteen-year-old sister had been wise, even though she was five years his junior. She would always gently remind him that he'd lived when others hadn't, and he had a duty to attempt to thrive. So, Dominic had reentered the world, picking up various short-term security jobs as he struggled with PTSD. Pam urged him to see a therapist, and the bi-monthly visits with Dr. Langone helped as he slowly began to rebuild his life.

And then, he came home one evening to find his parents dead in their Washington, DC townhome. Although their Adams Morgan neighborhood was relatively safe, Dominic had later learned the burglars had followed his parents home. The attack had been calculated, and when the criminals forced themselves inside, his parents hadn't stood a chance. The two men shot them dead before absconding with his mother's jewelry and his dad's wallet, taken from his lifeless body.

Dominic had been at a PTSD recovery meeting, and Pam had been at study group at George Washington University, where she was a sophomore. She'd returned home to find their living room swarming with cops and EMTs. They'd held each other as members of the coroner's office wheeled away their parents' bodies, unable to comprehend the loss. Three weeks later, the two burglars were apprehended and eventually put on trial, where they were both sentenced to life in prison.

It all seemed so senseless to Dominic, who'd lost most of his team in Pakistan only to return and lose his parents a year later.

And then, as Dominic and Pam began to settle their parents' estate, she began to feel sick. He urged her to go to the doctor, but she brushed him off, saying it was something she ate or allergies. "I'm twenty, bro," she'd say with a cheeky grin. "Healthy as a horse. I don't want you worrying about me."

As her sophomore year wound down and she began to lose weight, Dominic threatened to carry her to the doctor's office if she didn't make time for a checkup. She'd stared at him with eyes the color of his own, with dark circles underneath that had only recently appeared, and finally agreed to a physical.

The cancer diagnosis came several weeks later. Lung cancer, although she'd never smoked a day in her life and was a few months shy of twenty-one years old. A crushing diagnosis that was already in Stage 4 when discovered. She withdrew from school to focus on her health—and the various chemo, radiation and drug therapies—before her body began to truly break down several months later.

Living in the home where his parents were murdered, Dominic nursed his dying sister until he accepted the inevitable. Hospice was brought in, and he sat by her bedside every night, holding her hand as he tried to memorize everything about his last living blood relative.

"You've had so much pain," Pam rasped one night, coughing as she lay on the cool sheets. Bones jutted from her thin, cancer-ridden body and the smell of death pervaded the room even though she continued to smile through the agony. "And now I'm going to leave you too, and I'm afraid you're never going to allow yourself to love again."

Dominic studied her, wishing he could promise her he would but unable to utter the words. What was the point of connecting with people—of having a family—only to live with the knowledge they could be ripped away at any time? The thought of caring for someone else and reliving the intense pain he felt as he gazed into his sister's eyes, dull from pain medication, made him cringe. It was something he couldn't possibly fathom in the moment. Perhaps never again. Time was a powerful healer but only for those who wished to be healed.

Dominic was quite sure he'd lost that desire. He wasn't sure where that left him, but it most likely led to a lonely life working dead-end security jobs until he met his maker. Still, being lonely was better than the terrible suffering he'd experienced in his two and a half decades on the planet, so he accepted that fate as the preferable alternative.

Until he'd met Dr. Danica Lawson.

Over a decade later, Dominic was in between security jobs when a buddy told him about an opening at Sendaxa. The pharmaceutical-biotech company was working on a new drug in their fancy lab at the facility in Bethesda. They wanted experienced security specialists who could work long shifts for abnormal hours since the scientists were on a deadline to create a new drug to satisfy investors.

After his first interview with Maverick Ward, Dominic knew it was a job at which he would excel. He liked Maverick, who was also former military, and he was offered the job after two more rounds of interviews and various background checks. Dominic had sold his parents' townhome years before, so he ended his lease on his apartment in Washington, DC and relocated to a one-bedroom unit in Bethesda.

"Before the world went to shit," Dominic murmured to his reflection. Pushing away the morbid thoughts, he secured the holster on his belt before exiting his room and heading toward the makeshift lab where Raquel and Dani often worked.

Striding up to the open doorframe, Dominic leaned against it, grinning as he observed Dani sitting at the lab table scrawling in a notebook. Her tongue was situated between her teeth as she wrote out some equation he'd never understand, tossing him back into his memories.

He'd first seen her like this—in her element clad in a white lab coat—at the sterile lab at Sendaxa. The lab was a marvel of technology, complete with every modern upgrade Dani would need to create EverLife and make the company billions. As she'd worked, lifting a dropper to dispense something onto a Petri dish, she must've sensed his presence. Her green eyes latched onto his and widened as she gasped.

"Holy shit," she whispered, lowering the dropper and dish and placing her hand over her heart. "You scared me. You must be the new security guard. Maverick told me you'd be starting today."

"I am." Stepping into the lab, he walked forward until a few feet separated them. "I'm very sorry to scare you, ma'am. I'm Dominic Cavalleri, and I asked Mr. Ward to tell you about the scar." He pointed at his face, understanding that seeing the ugly wound was usually a shock for people.

"Oh, he did," she said, waving her hand, "and it's not that bad. We all have scars, right? Some are just on the inside where people can't see."

"True," he said, feeling his lips curve at her kindness. "Well, it's nice to meet you, Dr. Lawson." He extended his hand.

"Oh, please call me Dani. Everyone does." They shook as Dominic felt an undeniable spark in his chest. He would later realize the flare was emotion—something he hadn't allowed himself to feel in so long. But he'd felt it for the lovely woman who accepted him, scars and all, from the first day they met.

Returning to the moment, Dominic cleared his throat so he wouldn't startle her as she worked at the makeshift farmhouse lab.

"Oh...hello, Dominic," Dani said, lifting her head from the notebook, curiosity in her eyes. "I think Maverick was looking for you."

"He's getting ready and then we're heading out." Tentatively striding forward, he pointed at the notebook. "Any science miracles happening here today?"

"Well, I just got started," she said, chewing on the pen cap as she flipped through the notebook, "but Raquel has some great notes here, and I've left some too. I can tell since my handwriting is ten times worse than hers." Smiling, she tilted her head. "Guess I'm not in the twilight zone after all. I'm just an amnesia survivor who needs to get her memory back."

"I'd say our reality is way stranger than the twilight zone, but that's just my take" was his sardonic reply as he cocked a brow. "But it's still exciting, I guess."

She studied him as she often did each day after she woke up and met him for the "first" time. After a few moments, she asked, "Were we good friends? Before the world fell apart?"

Nodding, he closed the distance between them, leaning his hip on the table as he crossed his arms over his chest. "We were. You worked all the time and liked to chat while you worked. Since Mav and I were the only ones there with you most of the time, depending on what shifts we were working, you talked to us a lot."

Her eyebrows lifted as she flashed a cheeky grin. "Maverick says I forced him to drink champagne with me and that's how we fell in love. What did you and I bond over? I didn't make you smoke a joint with me, did I?"

Laughter sprung from his throat as he shook his head. "No, but that would've been fun." Tracing the wooden lab table with his finger, he cleared his throat. "You told me about your mom...and my sister also died of cancer. We eventually bonded over the shared experiences and...comforted each other, I guess you could say."

"Oh, Dominic," she said, rising and placing her hand on his bicep. Squeezing, she gazed up at him, empathy shining in her eyes. "I'm so sorry. She must've been young."

"Twenty-one years old," he said, his voice raspy. "My parents died the year before and then she passed. It was quite overwhelming. Years later, I met you." Lifting his hand, he cupped her shoulder, returning her comforting gesture. "Talking about it with someone else who had been through it was cathartic."

"I'm sure it was for me too. Watching my mom die from cancer is the entire reason I wanted to create a cure. I knew if I worked hard enough and secured funding, I could create a vaccine so no one else would have to suffer like that."

"You still can, Dani." His fingers dug into her shoulder, gentle but sure. "We've just got to help those affected by EverLife first. And then, I promise you, we're going to ensure you create your cancer vaccine."

"Thank you," she whispered, tears welling along her lashes.

"Okay, buddy, hands where I can see them," Maverick teased, striding into the room. "Ready to syphon some gas?"

"Ready," Dominic said, dropping his hand. Maverick was his best friend and cool as fuck regarding the fact that Dominic was in love with his wife, but he didn't want to push it. After all, his feelings for Dani could never go anywhere, and Dominic was perfectly fine with that.

Loving Dani wasn't about reality. He'd given up on experiencing any form of real emotion after his parents and sister died. No, loving her was an...*idea* more than anything. A way for him to connect with someone who'd had a similar experience without any possibility of actually having to put himself out there.

Dani would always belong to Maverick, which meant she was safe. Loving her would never hurt. It would offer comfort but allow him to keep the wall he'd built around his heart intact. After the crushing agony he'd experienced from his family's death, it was the only way he knew how to process emotion.

So, he loved her from afar, thankful to every god in the universe she loved someone else.

It might have seemed a sad tale to someone else, but Dominic rarely gave a shit what others thought. Loving Dani these past few years had led to a healing, of sorts, if not all the way, and that in itself was a small miracle he would allow himself to enjoy.

"Dom?" Maverick called, gesturing him toward the kitchen. "Let's go."

Sending an affable salute to Dani, he followed her husband so they could complete the day's mission.

Chapter 9

M averick and Dominic began the trek across the fields, careful to walk through wooded areas when possible. Although they were in a remote area, they both understood the importance of remaining inconspicuous.

As his boots crunched the grass, Maverick observed the evidence of destruction. Power lines that had once traversed the countryside were now strewn across the fields. Some of the utility poles were charred, perhaps from addicts who'd camped out and used them to build fires. Others were chopped into parts, some of the wood carried off by people who could use it to build makeshift encampments or bonfires.

Entering an area with a dirt path, they hiked as Maverick noticed the discarded syringes scattered along the trail. The surrounding trees would've created a hideout for addicts when the world began to fell apart. Now, it was empty. Anyone who'd camped here had long since moved on. Either to a black-market compound...or to meet their maker. Maverick's lips thinned at the somber thought.

When they exited the thicket, a tall metal tower greeted them. It was now a fossil in a world once dominated by cell phones and technology. It sat eerily under the glowing sun, rusting as the world adjusted to the new normal.

Maverick glanced at Dominic as they passed the tower. "You're quiet today, man," he said as they navigated through the uncut grass.

"I'm always quiet."

Huffing a laugh, he nodded. "True. But something's off today."

Dominic scowled as he harshly rubbed his forehead. "Bodies are disappearing, man. I'm afraid our cover's blown. I wanted to wait for Dani's memory to come back, but..."

"I know," Maverick softly replied. "We're going to have to initiate Phase II, whether we're ready or not. Since Dani can't remember the code, we're going to have to make a damn good plan."

"Agreed."

They strode in silence as they pondered the huge task before them. Finally, Dominic said, "We'll never succeed if Sendaxa decides to use military force outside the cities. Luthor Cromwell isn't going to accept us distributing the antidote to those who need it. If Sen Force begins attacking the compounds, people will die before we can save them."

"Do you really think they want a war?" Maverick asked, eyes narrowing as he considered the prospect. "Luthor has everything he wants. He controls all the remaining technology in the world and is the leader of the Sendaxa cities. Every former general and commander of the US military reports to him since he stepped in and took over the government when President Johnson overdosed on EverLife." He shook his head at the sadness and senselessness of the president's demise.

"Such a waste," Dominic murmured. "Wanting to stay alive forever, so you shove shit in your body that kills it. I'll just never understand it."

"I think it's just human nature," Maverick said, patting him on the shoulder.

"I guess." They approached the clearing where three tractors sat. Each were nearly full with gas, and both men would fill the empty containers attached to their packs, strap them back on and lug the gas back to the farmhouse. They'd decided not to chance driving during the day since a moving truck would draw attention and they needed to remain hidden.

Removing his pack, Dominic sat it on the ground and rubbed the back of his neck, massaging the tight muscles there. "I think I worry because men like Cromwell are never satisfied with getting everything they want. They always want more power until it eventually destroys them and everyone around them. Look at what happened when he decided to play God and create a drug that would double humans' lifespans." He snapped his fingers. "Up in flames, Mav. A guy with that ego isn't done yet, and he has limitless resources. I think it's only a matter of time before he begins to attack the black-market compounds."

"To what end?" Maverick asked, pulling the rubber hose with the pump he'd fashioned on the end out of his bag.

"To create a world in his image," Dominic said, shrugging. "A world where only the Sendaxa cities exist and everyone else is exterminated."

"Wow," Maverick said, shaking his head as he unscrewed the gas cap on the nearest tractor. "Did you read a lot of George Orwell and Stephen King as a kid? That's dark, man."

"I'm kind of a pessimist, in case you haven't noticed," he muttered, cocking a brow.

"Uh, yeah, I got the memo. Come on. Help me with this."

They began to syphon the gas, extending the tube into the tank and the other end into one of the eight containers they'd brought. Maverick had fashioned the tube with a bicycle pump he found in the garage, allowing them to pump the liquid. Once full, they would lace a rope through the handles of the containers, strap them on their backs, and carry them home.

As they worked, Maverick thought about the best possible outcome, if their plan actually succeeded.

First, Dani would have to replicate the antidote, and while they aligned with trustworthy people at the compounds, people who wouldn't be seduced by the lure of riches and technology that still existed in the walled-off Sendaxa cities.

Second, they'd need to find an abandoned warehouse or factory to produce enough quantities to distribute to all the people who so desperately needed it.

Third, they would need protection as they extended their reach across the country and eventually the globe. Sendaxa employed the Sen Force, which was essentially the former US military, and it made them formidable. The more Maverick thought about it, the more he realized they needed to begin recruiting soldiers. But where? Strung-out addicts from black-market compounds certainly wouldn't be ready for combat. They'd somehow need to recruit soldiers who weren't addicted to EverLife nor loyal to Sendaxa. No small feat in their current situation.

"We need to start building a militia," Dominic murmured, echoing his thoughts. "It's the only way we're going to have half a chance, Mav."

"I know," he said, working the pump. "We were so focused on regaining Dani's memory." He drifted off, tapping the hose against the full container before sliding it into the nearby empty one. "And, selfishly, I don't want her to get hurt. But she wants to save the world, and I've got to help her try."

"Even if our chances are close to zero."

Maverick's lips pursed. "You know, I think I liked you better when you weren't talking."

Laughing, he nodded. "You and Ari both. I think she tells me to shut up as much as I tell her."

Keeping his gaze averted in the hopes Dominic wouldn't feel interrogated, Maverick asked, "You ever think about her? In that way? Might take your mind off other things."

Dominic's hand froze as he was moving an empty container toward the one Maverick was rapidly filling. "Arianna?" he asked, stunned. "She hates me."

Maverick lifted a shoulder. "For someone who hates you, she exudes some palpable energy toward you, and you shoot it right back. It's impossible not to notice, man."

"Because she's a loner who hates that I want to help her. She's a skilled soldier and we need her, but I hate that she puts herself at risk when she tries to do everything alone."

Pausing, Maverick stared into his friend's eyes. "Sounds like you care about her and don't want her to get hurt."

With a *pfft*, Dominic sliced his hand through the air. "I'm just smart enough to realize we need her. And she's been very clear she thinks I'm an ugly jerk and she'd rather wrap herself around a frayed electrical wire before being anywhere near me."

"Maybe she just doesn't want to try with a man who's decided he wants someone else. She's got a lot of pride. It's a Lawson family trait."

Dominic remained silent, digesting Maverick's words as he finished filling the gas. Once all the containers were full, they carefully tied them to their packs and strapped them on their shoulders, ready to head back.

Something snapped in the distance, and their heads swung toward the nearby forest before they locked gazes.

"Gun cocking," Maverick said softly.

"Confirmed," Dominic replied.

With confident nods, they each dropped their heavy, gas-laden packs to the ground and drew their guns, aiming them at the forest. Another click sounded and Maverick commanded, "Take cover."

Maneuvering behind the tractors, they crouched, each lifting their arms to rest on the green metal of the tractors and aimed into the woods.

"Show yourself!" Maverick shouted. "We're armed and ready to fight!"

A man stepped from the forest, tall and toned, the bronzed skin of his arms glistening in the afternoon sunlight. Five men followed behind him, and he held up a fist, commanding them to halt.

"Well, boys, looks like it's six against two," the man said, his tone slightly ominous. "I like those odds, but we're not here to harm you."

Glancing at Dominic, Maverick felt his chest swell at his friend's affirmative nod, indicating he was willing to fight the six men, just the two of them. Straightening, Maverick cocked his gun and tilted his head. "The rifles slung over your shoulders would suggest otherwise. Bring it on, motherfucker. We'll fight you all day long."

The leader still held his fist high, but the men behind him disobeyed the order, lifting their guns. Maverick and Dominic spared each other one last glance before opening fire.

In an instant, the soft chirp of birds gave way to the sounds of bullets being sprayed across the dry, uneven grass as all hell broke loose.

Chapter 10

D ominic heard the bullet whiz past his ear as he crouched behind the tractor. Rising, he fired a few precise shots, elation coursing through him when one of the men fell. One down, five to go. Glancing over at Maverick, he jerked his head toward the men, indicating they should begin to advance. Maverick gave a curt nod, and they slowly edged toward the side of their respective tractors.

Maverick straightened and shot one of the attackers directly between his dark eyebrows. The soldier's eyes widened before he expelled his last breath and crumbled to the ground. Dominic's boots crunched the grass as he continued the advance, thankful to get a clean shot in one of the men's necks. Groaning in pain, the soldier fell as the leader glared at him in frustration. Lifting his hand, the leader halted the fighting.

"Enough," he said, slowly lifting his rifle before slinging it behind his shoulder. "I meant it when I said I didn't want to shoot you." Glancing at the fallen men, he shook his head. "Such a waste. They shouldn't have raised their weapons."

Dominic's eyes narrowed as he clutched his gun, still holding it high as he aimed it between the leader's eyes. The injured soldier lay on the ground, writhing in pain as he cupped his bleeding neck. Glancing toward him, the leader sighed and lifted a handgun from his belt. Aiming it at his comrade as he wiggled on the ground, he shot him directly in the temple. The soldier gasped, his body stiffening, before his muscles lost their rigidity and he melted against the ground.

"Jesus, man," Maverick said, still holding his gun high. "You killed your own soldier."

"He was suffering and never going to make it," the leader said, his tone unwavering. "I did him a favor. And it's Tristan. Tristan Holder."

"Sir, we should retreat," the remaining soldier said, his expression wary as he contemplated Maverick and Dominic.

"Go back to the jeep and wait for me," Tristan said, gesturing with his head toward the woods. "I want to talk to these two alone. I'll be there in five minutes, and we'll head back to the Sendaxa District."

The soldier spared Maverick and Dominic one last cautious glare before pivoting and striding into the woods.

"You can put away the guns," Tristan said, holstering his handgun and resting his hands on his hips above camouflage pants. "I have no desire to kill you."

"Hard to believe since you just opened fire on us," Dominic muttered.

"Do you work for Sendaxa?" Maverick asked. "Are you on the Sen Force?"

Tristan squinted one eye. "I'm more of a...mercenary you could say. I do the dirty stuff Luthor Cromwell doesn't want to claim."

"He's already pretty dirty," Dominic said acerbically. "His drug eliminated over half the world's population and destroyed society as we know it."

"True, but he still longs to maintain a cultured appearance. Most men with overgrown egos do. It's important his wealthy friends see him as a savior instead of a savage. Sometimes the line between them is very thin." He held his thumb and forefinger an inch apart.

"Did you remove the body from the campsite last night?" Dominic asked.

"Yes. Bodies are valuable in today's world, especially ones that are barely cold." Tristan's lips thinned. "I sold it to a group of dealers on their way to a black-market site in West Virginia. They paid well."

Disgust coiled in Dominic's stomach. Food was scarce in some of the more derelict compounds, and he'd heard rumors that some had resorted to extremes in order to survive. Still, he didn't want to believe people had sunk so low they would turn cannibalistic.

"Are you telling me they...?" Maverick's voice drifted off.

"I don't give a shit what they did with the body," Tristan said, showing his palms. "I just wanted the money."

"Why?" Dominic asked. "You just told us you work for Luthor Cromwell."

"He *thinks* I work for him. But things aren't always as they appear. I need money because I have my own plans."

Gazing over his shoulder, Tristan pointed in the direction of the farmhouse. "Cromwell knows you're here. His soldiers discovered your location last week, but he hasn't given the order to kill Dr. Lawson...yet"—he arched an ominous brow—"because he has other plans for her."

Stiffening, Maverick's jaw clenched so tight Dominic thought it might snap off his face. "No one is laying a finger on my wife, asshole. Got it?"

"I have no desire to harm her," he said, showing his palms. "But Cromwell is drunk with power and sees her as the key to gaining more."

"How? She'll never work for him again. She wants to heal people, not harm them."

Tristan cocked a brow. "Let's just say Cromwell thinks he's smarter than everyone, but I'm betting your scrappy little team might just best him."

Maverick and Dominic shared a glance as the tension thickened.

"Even though I've been given refuge inside the District, it's not a safe place for vagrants like me," Tristan continued. "There's an underlying current of realization that's rapidly dawning: the rich are safe and the rest are expendable."

"How so?" Dominic asked.

"The wealthy cronies who made it into the District don't know how to exist without their servants, yachts and opulence. They've begun to call for the middle-class residents to take up laborers' jobs. House cleaning, cooking, child care. All the shit the uber-wealthy don't want to do. Regular people thought they'd be accepted by the elite, but they're starting to realize it was a pipe dream."

"So the addicted and homeless suffer outside the walls, and half the people inside the walls realize life was better before society fell." Maverick shifted his weight, placing a fist on his hip as he contemplated. Finally, he said, "There's going to be a rebellion."

"Maybe," Tristan said, lifting a shoulder. "Most people I've met in the District aren't *that* impressive...but there's hope."

Maverick studied him. "So, what's your objective? You don't seem like Cromwell's biggest fan."

A muscle ticked in Tristan's jaw. "I'm not, but staying close to him gives me access I need to put my own plans in motion. And before you ask me what they are, I'll kindly tell you they're none of your business."

Maverick and Dominic remained silent, understanding they weren't getting more information from the mysterious man.

"I have a map saved in here of all the black-market compounds," Tristan said, lifting a smart phone from his belt and shaking the device. "I'll share it with you once you break into the lab and retrieve the antidote. Some compounds have smart, capable leaders who've controlled the rampant addition within their walls. I'd start with those if you want any chance of success."

"Are you always this bossy?" Dominic muttered.

Ignoring him, Tristan continued. "If you're lucky, I might even leave some weapons for you in the shed to increase your chance of success."

Exasperated, Maverick extended his hands at his sides. "What's in this for you? I don't understand your motives."

Tristan's eyes shone under the late afternoon sunlight as he studied them. "There are many things in play here you don't understand." He held up a finger when Maverick opened his mouth to argue. "But it's time to break into the lab. The clock is ticking and Cromwell isn't stable." He began slowly easing back into the woods.

"Wait!" Maverick called, stalking forward before Tristan slung his rifle around and aimed it at him.

"That's far enough," Tristan warned, continuing his retreat. "Get the gas back home and make a plan with your team so my comrade and I can bury these soldiers." He gestured with his head toward the slain bodies. "Each day you wait, the odds stack more against you. Stop wasting time." With a salute, he turned and stalked into the forest.

"What the fuck?" Dominic breathed.

"Tristan Holder," Maverick said, tapping his forehead. "We need to ask Arianna if she ever heard the name during her time in the military. Maybe she can shed some light on him."

Glancing back at the gas containers, Dominic nodded. "Let's get the fuck out of here. I don't like being exposed, or the fact that bastard snuck up on us."

"Heard," Maverick said, patting him on the shoulder.

They strapped the containers on their backs once again and marched across the field under the late afternoon sun.

Chapter 11

D ani sat on the uncomfortable stool, absently shifting her weight as she leaned over the notebook. She'd written pages of meticulous notes, mostly with chemical equations that could possibly lead to an antidote for EverLife. There were other notes too, about different herbs and teas Raquel had mixed to try and regenerate her memory, as well as random notes that didn't make much sense at all.

In several places, Dani had written various Latin phrases. She'd always loved Latin, and very few people understood it, so she sometimes thought of it as a secret language all for herself. Silly since entire civilizations had spoken it in the past, but they were long gone and it always gave her a tiny thrill whenever she observed the language being used in modern society.

Running her finger over the Latin scrawling, she read aloud—quietly since Arianna and Raquel were preparing dinner in the kitchen. Arianna had stayed back to keep watch while Maverick and Dominic traveled to syphon the gas, and having her sisters nearby comforted Dani.

Many of the Latin phrases she'd written were well known and quite inspirational.

- *Acta non verba* (deeds, not words)

- *Audentes fortuna iuvat* (fortune favors the bold)

- *Aut viam inveniam aut faciam* (I will find a way or make one)

But there were others as she read further, each becoming more ominous as she scrolled down with her finger.

- *Fere libenter homines id quod volunt credunt* (Men generally believe what they want to)

- *Nemo mortalium omnibus horis sapit* (Of mortal men, none is wise at all times)

- *De omnibus dubitandum* (Be suspicious of everything)

And finally, at the very end, *et tu, Brute?*, which was one of the most commonly known Latin phrases, even by those who didn't speak it. A phrase that expressed Julius Caesar's shock at the discovery his friend Brutus conspired to murder him. Narrowing her eyes, she focused on the missives.

"What were you trying to say here, Dani?" she asked, frustrated her memory was a pit of blackness. Closing her eyes, she squeezed her lids tight, trying to remember something...*anything* after her last memory all those years ago when she lived in New York and worked as a professor at the genetics department at Columbia University.

Settling into the darkness, she allowed the puffs of light to creep into the corners of her vision, almost like smoke billowing from the recesses of her subconscious. Resting her forehead on her hands, her elbows dug into the table as she concentrated.

Echoes of metal clicking ticked in the background, and Dani saw her own hands, unlatching a steel door with biomedical warning symbols. Pulling it open, she reached inside, ready to grasp the contents before she felt the presence behind her. Gasping, she turned, unprepared for the explosion of pain in her skull as someone struck her...

"Dani?" Raquel asked, causing her to flinch and place her hand over her rapidly beating heart. "Are you okay?"

"Shit," Dani whispered, shaking her head. "I think I just had a flashback...possibly to the few moments before encountering the person who did this to me." Reaching toward the base of her head, she rubbed the area that covered her hippocampus. As a scientist, she knew that was the region that had been injured when she'd been struck. It was responsible for episodic and connected memories.

"That's amazing, Dani," Raquel said, squeezing her shoulder. "Every once and a while you have a flashback, but it only lasts a few seconds and you don't remember it when you wake up the next day."

"Which is something I have to change." Straightening, she pointed at the notebook. "I've been writing random notes in here, but we both know nothing I do is random."

"Truth," her sister said, grinning. "Your brain is always leaving clues behind. It gives me hope you're going to see something you scribbled down and it will jog your memory. I think once you cross the threshold of having full-on memories instead of flashbacks, you'll regain everything that was lost."

"Let's hope so." Pointing across the table to the counter where Raquel kept her tea leaves and other herbs, Dani asked, "What tea concoctions have worked best? Which ones led to days with flashbacks?"

"Well, the one I made you earlier had rosemary and sage. Those seem to work well. And the mushrooms help too."

"Must be why it tasted awful," she said, wrinkling her nose, "but if it works, I'll drink it all day long."

Arianna strode into the room, wiping her hands on a dishcloth. "Dinner's almost ready. And if either of you tell the men I cooked, you're toast." She pointed between her sisters. "I was in the mood for quiche, and the chickens have been giving us eggs in droves, so I made two of them. Raquel's taking credit for cooking though."

"I don't think anyone's going to accuse you of being the 'little woman,' Arianna," Raquel said, making quotation marks with her fingers. "But I love quiche, so your secret is safe with me." She made an X over her heart as her green eyes sparkled under her shoulder-length brown hair.

"Good. Last thing I need is Dominic making fun of me."

"He wouldn't do that," Raquel said, her features contorting with incredulity. "Why are you so hard on him?"

"He's tough and can take it," Arianna said, shrugging. "What's the big deal?"

"Tell me more about Dominic," Dani said, curious about the man who'd lost his sister to the terrible disease that had claimed their mother. "He seems really nice."

"He is to *you*," Arianna mumbled.

"Ari…" Raquel scolded.

"What? It's true."

"He's nice to *all* of us," Raquel said. Reaching over, she covered Dani's hand. "There's a bit of common knowledge you're missing. Dominic is…well, he's kind of in love with you, Dani. It's just something we all accept and don't really acknowledge out loud."

"Ohhhh," Dani said, softly expelling the word as she digested the information. "And he and Maverick are best friends?"

"Yes," Raquel said, squeezing her hand. "Maverick understands you two bonded over Mom and his sister, and he's hella cool about it."

"Wow, that's…weird." Extending her bottom lip, she blew out a breath, fanning the hair at her forehead as she contemplated. "How did two men fall in love with me? What the hell was I doing at the Sendaxa lab?"

"You've always been amazing, Dani," Raquel said, admiration and a hint of longing in her tone. "The prettiest and the smartest of all of us." She gestured between them.

"Speak for yourself," Arianna said, crossing her arms and tapping her boot as her eyes narrowed. "I'm hot in my own fucking way, and most men are pussies who can't handle it."

Laughing, Raquel nodded. "You've always been the most confident and kick-ass, Ari. That leaves me." Her eyes lowered over her body, clad in faded pants and an oversized, baggy shirt. "Chunky and plain. I'm a competent botanist, but I was never chosen by an Ivy League school to run my own lab. Dani's the genius."

"Hey," Dani said, standing and resting her hands on Raquel's shoulders. "I don't want to hear you talk like that, okay? You're my little sister, and you're the most special person on the fucking planet. I'll beat the hell out of anyone who disagrees."

"Thanks," Raquel said softly before pulling out of Dani's grasp. "You've always been my champion. You both have. I was so happy to get recruited by Sendaxa right after they reached out to you. It was the highlight of my career." Her lips formed a sad smile. "Then, the Medical Director told me they'd reached out because you asked them to, Dani. That you wouldn't come on board unless they hired me too. It was above and beyond and I was really thankful."

"I wish I could remember," Dani said, lowering back to the stool and rubbing her head. "But of course I would've wanted you on my team, Raquel. I need your brain. You're smart as hell."

"Thanks." Glancing down, Raquel twined her hands at her waist, and Dani thought she saw her chin quiver ever so slightly. "Well, anyway," she said, lifting her chin. "Enough Debbie Downer for today. I'm going to go feed the chickens before the guys get home."

"I'll help you," Arianna offered.

"It's fine," she said, edging toward the doorway. "I think I just need a few minutes alone. Can't wait for the quiche." Quick as a scuttling mouse, she pivoted and left the room.

"Still the same Raquel," Dani said, sighing as she rubbed the back of her neck. "She just never grew into herself or gained the self-confidence someone as amazing as she should have."

"There's still time," Arianna said, lifting a shoulder. "She's thirty-two, and I grew into myself a lot in my thirties."

"I guess so." Gnawing her lip, Dani asked, "How long did EverLife increase lifespan again?"

"The promise was it would help someone to live to be two hundred years old on average." Arianna grimaced. "Too fucking old if you ask me. Who wants to live that long? Kind of defeats the purpose of having goals, accomplishing them and then using your remaining years to enjoy them."

Dani smiled and leaned her chin on her fist. "What goals do you want to accomplish? All I remember is that you wanted to open your own security firm after you left the military."

"I did, before the world ended," she said with a nod. "Now, I just want to save the world, have a baby or two, and relax somewhere where no one can find me."

Dani's eyes widened with excitement. "You want to have a baby? Aw, Ari, that's so sweet. Aunt Dani is ready to spoil her rotten."

"Okay, calm down," she said, rolling her eyes and holding up her hands. "We've got a lot of shit to do first."

"But once we're done, you'll find a super-hot guy, make him fall madly in love with you and have lots of nieces and nephews for Aunt Dani," she said, holding up a finger.

"A man isn't required in this scenario," Arianna muttered. "Just me, a turkey baster and a nice cabin somewhere in some very dense woods."

The sentiment was quite sad to Dani, who'd always been a sucker for romance and true love. "But you deserve someone who loves you—"

"I've got you and Raquel, and that's enough, believe me." She flashed a grin to soften the harshly spoken words. "On that note, you and Maverick seem good today. I feel for the poor guy. Some days you won't let him near you. Since you're vibing with him today, maybe let him kiss you after dinner."

"He's so fucking hot, Ari," she almost whispered, running her hand through her hair. "It's so bizarre."

"Like Raquel said, you're the catch here. He fell for you as hard as you fell for him. It's kind of sweet. I actually enjoyed your wedding, and I hate weddings." Frowning, she shrugged. "Until Dominic asked me to dance. Motherfucker stepped on my toes a hundred times. That was the first weekend I met him, and I've hated him ever since."

"You're joking, right? Because if you don't want him here, he has to go."

Something flashed across Arianna's face before she scrubbed it with her hand. "He's fine. I'm just being my usual acerbic self. He's actually not a bad fighter. He *might* come in handy one day."

Chuckling, Dani nodded. "Okay, but let me know if you want me to boot him. My loyalty is to my sisters. I'm so glad we stuck together after the world ended."

"No doubt."

"How did that happen anyway?"

Arianna gazed at the ceiling as she recalled the night Dani was injured. "Maverick called me and said they were going on the run with you. Raquel was with them and they wanted me to come. I didn't even think twice."

Grateful for her, Dani felt her features soften. "Thank you, Ari. I'm sure they were thrilled to have someone with your military experience on board."

"Yep," she confirmed with a nod. "I'd been working odd jobs after resigning from the army. But once the world began collapsing, I wasn't working at all. I spent a few weeks wondering if I should go on the run or try to get accepted into a fortified city to perform private security and then Mav called." Lifting a shoulder, she said, "No contest. I was going to protect my sisters. I threw everything I thought I needed into a backpack and met up with you all outside Bethesda. We traveled around a while until we found the farmhouse."

"And here we are," Dani said with awe. "Ready to try and fix everything."

"We'll try our best." Perking her ears, she turned her head toward the doorway. "Mav and Dominic are back. I'm going to go see if they need help. If I'm not back in ten minutes, take the quiches out of the oven."

"Yes, boss," Dani said, saluting.

Once she was alone again, Dani studied the Latin phrases once more before turning to the next page in the notebook. It was labeled "Flashbacks" at the top and had a small list underneath:

Walking inside the lab and hearing a door creak behind me

Dominic shaking me as I lay on the floor, screaming my name as I floated in darkness and my head throbbed

Maverick clinking his champagne glass to mine

Maverick's warmth behind me as his body bracketed mine and his lips brushed my ear

The soles of my sneakers squishing the hallway floor as I retreated from a conversation with someone whose name and face I can't remember. All I could feel in the flashback was anger...uncontrolled rage directed at the person I'd had the conversation with...

Had that conversation been with Luthor Cromwell? Had she tried to tell him they had to stop production of EverLife but he insisted on selling it anyway? Studying the words, she tried to recall the recorded flashbacks in the present moment. Minutes later, she gave up the futile effort. Grabbing the nearby pen, she added a new entry:

Unlatching the door to a biomedical unit and realizing someone was behind me before pain exploded in every part of my skull

"Yikes," Dani murmured, wishing she could recall who'd hit her. The person who'd erased her memory must have worked in the lab. If it was a secure lab owned by a huge biotech company, it was the only logical explanation as to why they would be allowed inside.

Someone who worked with me at the lab had tried to kill me. The thought was extremely unsettling and a vivid example there were very few people she could trust. Whoever they were, they must've been very loyal to Sendaxa if they were willing to kill for them.

It was a mystery that needed solving, and she added it to the mental checklist of things she needed to accomplish.

"Regain memory, steal antidote, reproduce antidote, heal everyone addicted," she said, lifting a finger as she named each task, "*and* figure out who tried to kill you, thus generating your amnesia." Pursing her lips, she almost laughed at the absurdity of the situation. "How in the hell did you get here, Dani? Good grief."

Since the quiet room held no answers, she closed the notebook and headed to the kitchen to focus on the menial task of ensuring their dinner didn't burn. That, at least, was something she could control.

Chapter 12

During dinner, the mood was somber as Maverick and Dominic relayed their encounter with Tristan Holder to the Lawson sisters. Arianna was furious, pounding her fist on the table and exhibiting frustration she hadn't been there to help them. The men reassured her that someone had to stay and protect Dani and Raquel, which was of utmost importance.

"Well, I've never heard of Tristan Holder," Arianna said, squinting at the ceiling as she tried to recall the information. "But he seems like a slimy bastard."

"He didn't kill us, so I'll take that as a good sign," Dominic said. "He certainly is no fan of Cromwell even though he works for him."

"A man who plays both sides of the fence," Raquel said. "Sneaky."

"I can't discern his motives, but he knows ours," Maverick said, sitting back in the chair and running his hand through his hair. "We've got to speed up the timeline, especially since Cromwell knows we're here." Reaching over, he slid his hand over Dani's. "Today's been a long day, so let's have a group meeting in the morning when we're fresh. I'll bring you up to speed early so we can get to work."

Nodding, Dani did her best to process the information, added to the pile of unbelievable facts she'd learned throughout the day. After dinner, Raquel excused herself and headed upstairs to her room. Arianna and Dominic retired to their rooms shortly thereafter.

Once the dishes were washed and the house was quiet, Maverick asked Dani to sit with him in the living room. She slid beside him on the couch, curiosity coursing through her veins.

"Can I...?" She cleared her throat. "How did you fall in love with me? I'm dying to know."

White teeth flashed as he scooted closer and brushed her hair off her shoulder. "I'm not sure I can pinpoint a specific time, but it was probably when I caught you talking to the mice."

She bit her lip to contain her smile. "Occupational hazard. I always got attached to those little critters."

Chuckling, he nodded. "When you first started, I would stand in the hallway outside the lab. But your voice would always carry, and you'd soothe the mice before you injected them with whatever concoction you were testing."

Dani smiled, silently urging him to continue.

"Eventually, I moved inside the lab, content to guard you from inside so I could hear your conversations. You were cute and formidable at the same time. I'd never met anyone as smart as you. You would scribble formulas and run all these equations on your laptop. I was entranced. A genius who cared about mice. It was refreshing."

"Surely you dated."

"I dated," he said with a grin. "And I told myself I'd eventually settle down. My parents had a happy marriage, and I wanted that too. But I wasn't in a rush."

"And you took one look at this and it was over?" she teased, pointing at her face.

His lips twitched, and Dani realized she was thoroughly enjoying the conversation.

"It was a combination of talking to the mice, your intelligence and those pretty eyes. They all hooked me. But I also noticed your determination. You were an unstoppable force, determined to create EverLife so you could move on to your cancer vaccine. You had unwavering purpose."

Dani noted the admiration in his eyes as her body thrummed. They studied each other, smiles curving their lips as she settled into being in his presence.

Maverick yawned before lifting his hand to rub his neck, and she felt the pressing urge to comfort him. It should've been strange, wanting to comfort this man she didn't know. And perhaps there was a slight discomfort in her gut, but it was drowned out by the suddenly voracious need to soothe him after the long day.

"Can we, uh...go to my room?" she asked, her voice raspy. "You look exhausted, and it seems like you've got knots in your shoulders. I can..." Lowering her gaze, she swallowed thickly. "I can try and get them out if you want?"

His lips curved into a slow, sexy grin. "You offering to give me a massage, slugger?"

"Yeah," she whispered, pressing her teeth into her lower lip. "Is it weird? God, this whole thing is so weird. I'm just really grateful for you...and the rest of the team. You've all protected me for months without asking anything in return...*after* I destroyed the world." Tears welled as she struggled to tamp down the emotion burning in her chest. "I just wanted to try and help you for once."

"Okay," he murmured, extending his hand. "Come on."

Sliding her palm over his calloused one, she smiled shyly when he interlaced their fingers and tugged her toward the large downstairs bedroom. They entered, and Dani let go of his hand, crossing the room to switch on the bedside lamp. The door latch clicked, and she realized he'd locked it.

"I'm protecting us from sleepwalkers," he teased when she turned to gaze into his eyes. "I can unlock it if you want—"

"No, it's fine." Glancing at the bed, she crossed her arms over her chest, palming her throat as she wondered what the hell she was doing. Had she really offered to massage him? Now that she was alone with him in a room with a rather large bed, it seemed daunting.

"Dani," he said, the low tone of his voice sending shivers over her skin as he approached. Cupping her upper arms, he soothed her as his hands slid over her suddenly heated skin. "We don't have to do anything. If you want to go to sleep, that's fine. I can give you some solitude. You've had a long day."

Feeling her throat bob, she shook her head. "You deserve a moment to relax too. I guess you should...uh, take off your shirt. Then you can lie down on your stomach and I'll massage your back and shoulders."

Anticipation flared in those gorgeous eyes as he smiled down at her. His height was sexy, and she was suddenly aware of how much bigger he was. Although she was pretty tall, she was lanky and didn't have a ton of muscle definition since she'd worked in a lab most of her life.

Her husband, on the other hand, was chiseled. Bands of muscle ran down his biceps to his forearms, and his torso was thick and firm. Licking her lips, she wondered if the hair on his chest was sprinkled with silver all the way down to his navel. Suddenly dying to find out, she banked the urge to snake her hand under his shirt and trace her fingers over his abdomen.

"Are you sure, Dani?"

"Yes."

He gripped the base of his shirt, dragging it off in one fell swoop before dropping it to the floor. Black and gray hairs swirled over his copper nipples and toned pecs before forming a V that led over his stomach to the waistband of his pants. Touching the tip of her tongue to the dry roof of her mouth, she pointed to his boots. "Take those off too."

He complied, sitting on the bed before removing his shoes and socks. He'd removed his weapons when he returned home, but the belt remained, so he touched the buckle and gazed up at her. "This will be uncomfortable to lie on."

Nodding, she said, "Take it off too."

Thick fingers unclasped the buckle, the movements deft and measured. After sliding it out of the loops of his black pants, he dropped it on the floor and pointed. "Should I lie down?"

Dani nodded, unwilling to speak since she was pretty sure she'd lost the ability to perform basic functions once she'd seen his chiseled chest. He lowered to the bed, sprawling on his stomach and lifting his hands to fluff the pillow a few times. Once it was full, he rested his cheek on the pillow, facing her as he rested his arms at his side. "Do your worst, Dr. Ward."

Dr. Ward. That would be her name if she were married to him, wouldn't it? Wrinkling her nose, she said, "I'm pretty sure I kept Lawson. Mom was a feminist, but she loved my dad and loved that name."

Chuckling, he nodded against the pillow. "Dr. Lawson-Ward. That's what you decided on. It has a nice ring to it."

Grinning, she tilted her head. "It does."

Willing her frozen muscles to move, she rested one knee on the bed, extending her hand to lightly press her fingertips against his back. Maverick sucked in a breath, and she stilled. "You okay?"

He squeezed his eyelids so tight, she thought they might fuse together. Slowly exhaling, his fingers gripped the comforter at each side. "It just feels good to have you touch me, babe."

Unable to control her grin, she willed herself to relax—tough since her heart was two seconds away from violently pounding out of her chest. Situating her other knee on the bed, she slid over him, straddling his thighs as she settled against his body.

"I'm really going to need the story of how you talked me into letting you call me 'babe,'" she said, pressing her palms to his back before digging the heels of her hands into the tight muscle. A deep, guttural groan escaped his throat as she began kneading the firm skin, sending a rush of heat to her core. Could he feel it through their clothes? Turned on by the thought, she continued as he slowly relaxed beneath her.

"We'd been dating a few weeks," he mumbled, eyes closed as his face pressed into the pillow. "You were so cute when you stayed late working at the lab. It was pretty much every night since you were a workaholic, and I remember you waving at me through the glass as I returned from getting a soda in the cafeteria. You had a cheeky grin, and I knew you were going to tell me we needed to cancel dinner so you could work for several more hours."

Breathing a laugh, she said, "Yep. That sounds like me."

"Mmm hmm," was his smooth reply as he emitted another soft moan. The fact he found her strokes pleasurable awoke something inside her. Something that felt a lot like desire and unsated lust. Holy shit, she wanted him. Dani was suddenly very aware she was yearning for her husband as vehemently as a Henry Cavill superfan watching *The Witcher* bathtub scene. Wiping her slightly damp brow with her wrist, she remained silent so he would continue.

"I entered the lab—which you told me not to do because it distracted you. But I entered anyway and came up behind you to tease you for cancelling our date. You swatted me away, but I took the opportunity to sneak in a kiss since you were going to diss me in favor of genetic engineering. I mean, that can really shake a man's ego."

Dani recalled the flashback she'd found in the journal. Was this the moment she'd remembered when Maverick had bracketed her body?

"I leaned down and kissed your neck before whispering in your ear, 'You're going to give me a complex, babe. I finally got you to agree to date me, even though you swore your work was too important and you didn't have time.' You leaned back against me and gazed up at me with those pretty eyes and said, 'Don't call me babe.'"

Chuckling, she said, "I'm with you so far."

"And I pulled you closer and said, 'What if I make you beg for it? Hmmm? Will you let me then?'"

Shivering, Dani attempted to breathe as her throat threatened to close.

"I do love a challenge."

His warm chuckle vibrated through his chest, surrounding her in its warmth as he nodded. "You sure do. Much later that night, I drove you home and you invited me in. You taunted me that I couldn't make you beg." Opening one eye, his lips curved as he stared at her with a lazy gaze. "Let's just say you lost."

Desire hummed as her body threatened to overheat atop his strong thighs. "I...uh...wow. I guess I shouldn't have underestimated your...*abilities.*"

Sliding his hand up her thigh, he gently squeezed. "My ability to love you is my greatest accomplishment."

Tears stung her eyes as emotion overwhelmed her. Frustration she couldn't share in the memories he so obviously cherished. Anger that years had been ripped away from her with one striking blow. Fear at the feelings welling in her chest for a man she couldn't remember but somehow knew.

"Sweetheart," he whispered, his face a mask of concern as he slowly rolled beneath her to lie on his back. "Come here. Lie on your side that isn't hurt. Come on." She settled into his side, allowing him to slide her leg over his thighs. Once they were twined together, he lifted his fingers to her temple and brushed away a curl. "It's okay. Just feel me, honey."

His angular features began to blur as wetness clouded her eyes.

"Shhh..." he soothed, kissing her forehead. "I know it's scary—"

"It's infuriating!" she gritted, angrily swiping away a tear. "How dare the universe allow me to marry someone as caring and sexy as you and not even remember it? I guess that's what I get for hurting so many people." A sob escaped her throat. "I've killed so many...and I don't remember anything." Closing her eyes, the magnitude of it all washed over her. "Oh god..."

He whispered her name, cupping her head as she pressed her face into his neck. Huge sobs racked her body as she released all the emotion and anger that had built over the day. She'd awoken to a video of herself explaining the state of the world and her tragic role in it, met her husband she didn't remember, and discovered cryptic notes she'd left for herself along the way. For an instant, she wondered if they'd all be better off if they left her behind and continued the mission alone. Arianna was a formidable, cunning soldier, and Raquel was a brilliant scientist. Perhaps their chances were better without her?

"Don't do this, sweetheart," Maverick said, almost crushing her as he held her, attempting to comfort her as she threatened to drown under the weight of her actions. "It sucks, but we can't change the past. We need you to change the future though." Bringing both hands to cup her cheeks, he lifted her face to his as their heads shared the same pillow. "We need you, Dani. Don't give up."

Sniffling, she shook her head. "I have to save everyone who's left. It's the only way I can go on."

"You will, sweetheart. *We* will. Or we'll die trying."

Her eyes darted between his as she contemplated. "Have I ever mentioned having flashbacks?"

Nodding, he wiped her cheek with his thumb. "You write them in your notebook along with all the weird Latin phrases no one understands."

Uttering a laugh, she bit her lip. "Yeah, I think they're some sort of breadcrumbs I'm leaving myself, but they don't really make sense."

"Did you have a flashback today?" His tone was soothing as his fingers continued to caress her cheek.

"Yes. I think it was of the instant before I was knocked unconscious and lost my memory."

His eyes widened as he digested the information. "Did you recognize anyone? Any familiar smells or senses that could help us identify the person who attacked you?"

Shaking her head on the pillow, she sighed. "It was like my brain shifted into rewind for a few seconds and then it was gone." She snapped her fingers.

Maverick chewed his inner lip as he pondered. "You've been getting the flashbacks more frequently," he finally said. "I think it's a good sign your memory is slowly coming back."

Dani contemplated for a while before she lifted her head to look at the nightstand. "I want to make another video."

"Okay." Turning, he picked up the phone and unlocked the screen before handing it to her. "Go for it."

She settled back against him, noticing how well her body fit with his as she held the phone high with one arm. Ensuring both their faces were on the screen, she hit record.

"Hi, Dani. I know you're probably still in shock, but it's been a long day, as I imagine all of them are." Glancing at Maverick, she smiled before looking back at the phone. "You're smart enough to understand you have to cut the explanation time each day. The first video is good because it contains a lot of information. But I'm making this second video to tell you to stop having everyone explain things to you for hours after you wake up."

"Dani—"

"No, I need to say this," she said, shushing him. "Dani, the fate of the world is quite literally in your hands, and you've got to put on your big girl pants and go out and fix what you fucked up. You can't do that if Maverick has to spend hours bringing you up to speed and making you feel comfortable each day."

"I don't mind, even if you're a pain in the ass," he teased, chucking her on the nose.

"As you can see, he thinks he's funny, and he's going to call you 'babe,' which he swears you approved somewhere along the way. You're not going to like that, but secretly, deep down, your insides kind of melt when he says it."

"Damn straight," Maverick muttered.

"Shhh!" she scolded before staring back at the screen. "Get to work, Dani. Trust Maverick, Dominic and your sisters. Time is running out and you're practical. You know you can't waste it. Also, there's a hidden message in the Latin phrases in your notebook. Figure it out. Good luck."

Clicking stop, she turned her head on the pillow and grinned at Maverick. "Well, what do you think? Can you make sure I watch that one each morning after watching the first one?"

His eyes roved over her face, filled with admiration and desire, before he took the phone and set it on the nightstand. Rolling over, he slid his hand over her lower back, drawing her into his body as their legs twined below.

"Babe, all I can think right now is that I want to kiss you."

Swallowing the huge lump in her throat, she placed her hand on his jaw. "Tell me about the first time we kissed."

His fingers drew lazy circles on her lower back above her shirt as he spoke. "You were celebrating another failure and roped me into having a sip of champagne with you. It was against protocol for me to drink while on duty, but I'd done it with you a few times before and I couldn't resist..."

Dani was mesmerized by his smooth voice as he recounted the memory...

Maverick clinked his glass with Dani's, overcome by her bright smile and the scent of her hair, even though it was cinched atop her head in a messy bun. He liked her curls down, but there was something adorable when she gathered all that hair and tied it together, baring the line of her neck and the silken skin there. Taken by the sight, he didn't realize he was staring until she called his name.

"Huh?" he asked, lifting his eyes to hers. Setting down the glass, he told himself to back away. "Sorry, I have to get back to work."

"Oh, you're no fun," she said, wrinkling her nose. "And honestly, my workaholic ass isn't much fun either, so I guess we're both a bunch of losers."

Maverick knew he should walk away, but for some reason, he wanted to reassure her. That she was definitely fun. And gorgeous. And brilliant. And somehow, he'd begun thinking of her all the damn time. He'd been head of security at the lab for a few years, but during Dani's tenure, he'd picked up every extra shift available in order to be near her. To see her smile when she arrived each morning and experience her tired wave when she exited after midnight each evening.

To see the way she treated Dominic, whose gruff exterior was no match for her open heart and desire to comfort him due to the loss of his family. Or the way she was with Raquel, who she'd bent over backward for to secure a job at Sendaxa. Maverick understood this because he'd done the background checks on all the applicants, and several scientists were more qualified. But Dani wanted Raquel, so she ultimately got Raquel.

To see how relentless she was in pursuit of the perfect formula for EverLife. It was only a stepping stone on her path to creating a cancer vaccine, and she was determined to finish the project and move on so she could tackle what she considered her life's purpose.

Unable to stop himself, he reached for her, observing his hand as it slid through the air in slow motion. Cupping her chin, he tilted her face to his. "You're not a loser. You're a force of nature, Dani. It's so beautiful. You're beautiful."

Those plump pink lips parted as her eyes widened, the honeyed flecks so pretty under the staid fluorescent lighting of the lab. The vein at her neck fluttered, and Maverick felt himself falling. Never had he been so consumed by a woman. He was a confident man who dated sporadically and never had to search far to find a willing participant to sate any sexual desires. But looking at her...touching her...was different, and he slowly understood why people referred to it as "falling..."

"What the hell is happening?" she whispered, her knuckles white as her fingers tightened on the glass. "Maverick?"

"Set down the glass, Dani," he commanded softly.

Her tongue darted out to bathe her lips, leaving them shiny as his muscles hardened with desire.

"Why?"

"Because I want you to put your arms around my neck when I kiss you."

"I...oh...uh, well, this isn't really...I mean...we can't do that here—"

Grasping the glass, he all but ripped it from her hands and set it on the metal table. Gliding his arm around her waist, he drew her into his warm body. "Slide your arms around my neck."

"I'm a dorky scientist," she rasped, her arms lifting even as she tried to talk herself out of kissing him. "I'm sure there are many other women who'd...fit you better."

"I'm sure there are," he murmured, lowering his head and nudging her nose with his. "But right now, all I can think about is you." He brushed his lips over hers, gentle and slow, and his knees turned to jelly as she trembled in his arms. "Scratch that. No one has ever fit like you, Dani." Resting his forehead against hers, he whispered, "Ever."

"Maverick—"

Inhaling his own name from her lips, he devoured her with one relentless stroke of his tongue.

"Wow," Dani breathed, her chest visibly rising and falling as he recounted the story. "That's pretty romantic."

"Sure is." The backs of his fingers skated over her cheek as they stared into each other's eyes. "From that night forward, it was only you, Dani. Forget falling. I dove over the cliff and never wanted to look back."

She ran her tongue over her bottom lip, wishing it was *his* tongue as she shimmied further into his body. A soft growl exited his throat as he pressed his hips against hers, and her heart slammed when she felt his erection against her thigh.

"Fuck," he rasped, closing his eyes as he pulled her close. "I want you so much."

"I want you too," she admitted, acknowledging the pulsing arousal skating through every inch of her body. Her nipples had pebbled into hard, aching peaks, and wet arousal pulsed between her thighs. Heat flushed every cell in her skin, setting it on fire as she slid her fingers through his thick hair and squeezed. "Kiss me, Maverick."

Groaning, he dove for her, clenching her hair and tilting her face to his. His lips pressed against hers, consuming them before plunging his tongue in her mouth and sweeping to taste every crevice. Dani wriggled into his body, desperate to sate the lust that threatened to burn her alive. She tentatively touched her tongue to his, and he rewarded her with a desire-laden groan before urging her to her back and sliding atop her quivering body. He was careful to rest his weight on her uninjured side, and pushed her legs open to press his hard shaft between them.

Dani moaned, overwhelmed with the weight of his strong body against hers. Clenching her hair, he broke the kiss, panting wildly as he undulated his hips into hers.

"Do you feel that, baby?" he asked, grinding his cock into her as her body jutted up to meet his ragged thrusts. "Feel how much I want you?"

"Yes," she groaned, her head lolling on the pillow as her hair skated across the pillowcase. "Oh god, this is insane. I want you too. *Maverick...*"

Pressing his lips to hers, he drew her into another molten kiss, the movements of his hips steady and strong between her legs. Dani's nails dug into his back, causing him to buck against her, and she felt her inhibitions melt away. Twelve hours ago, she didn't even know this man. Now, she was seconds away from ripping away their clothes and begging him to fuck her.

Reaching for her shirt, she began to bunch the fabric to slide it off and gasped. She'd also inadvertently grabbed the bandage, and the resulting twinge of pain shot through her side.

Tensing, Maverick froze and broke the kiss. "Is it your side?" Lowering his hand, he gently grasped her wrist. "Let me look at it."

Sliding off her trembling body, he sat beside her and lifted her shirt. Frowning, he shook his head. "The bandage came off. Let me get another one, and I'll clean the wound."

"I cleaned it when I showered earlier," she said, feeling like someone had thrown a bucket of ice water over her head. Sexual frustration buzzed in her frayed nerve endings as he warily studied her. "I think I should actually leave the bandage off and let it get some air tonight."

Exhaling, he nodded as his warm breath trailed across her skin. "Okay." Gazing at her, he placed his fingers over her collarbone and began to rub the soft skin, soothing her as she relaxed on the bed. "Well, that was fun...for a while at least. Right?" He gave her a goofy grin as a question simmered in his eyes. "It wasn't too much, was it? I never want to cross a line with you, Dani."

"It wasn't too much," she said, disappointed the sexy encounter was over. "Do we...um, how often do we...go all the way?"

Breathing a laugh, he continued to caress her. "Every so often. It's just hard because I don't want to take advantage of you. Earning your trust every day is very important to me, and if I don't have it, I won't touch you."

She slowly shook her head on the pillow. "Thank you."

Smiling, he caressed her cheek one last time before rising. Leaning over, he kissed her forehead and brushed the tiny tendrils of hair away. "I'm going to let you get some rest.

We've got a big day tomorrow with a new video. I'm interested to see if we can cut the time it takes for you to settle in and accept your new reality each day."

Placing one last reverent peck on her lips, he rose. "Sweet dreams." Striding to the door, he opened it and turned to face her. "I love you so much, Dani. I have to say it right before I leave because I don't want you to feel pressure to say it back. But it's true, and I hope you'll lock that somewhere in your memory so you can cherish it in your dreams." He gently rapped his fist on his forehead, imitating stimulating the brain to remember. "Night."

The door clicked behind him, the sound almost tangible in the quiet room. As her body attempted to cool from unrealized sexual desire, she rose to inspect her wound one last time. Then, she prepped for bed in the adjoining bathroom, noting her flushed skin in the reflection.

Lowering between the sheets, she glanced at the phone and spoke softly. "Don't let them down, Dani. Listen to yourself on the videos. Time to kick it into high gear."

Clicking off the lamp, she stared at the ceiling, willing herself to be strong enough to quickly accept her new reality so she could fix what she'd so badly broken.

Chapter 13

Tristan strode into the opulent penthouse offices, frustration oozing out of every pore at the senseless loss of life in the earlier confrontation with Maverick and Dominic. His men should've heeded his order not to fire, and it cost them their lives. Now, he'd have to ask Luthor for more men, and he hated asking Luthor for *anything*.

Luthor still kept his offices at the Sendaxa corporate headquarters in DC. Moving into the White House would've afforded too much nostalgia and symbolism to a government that was long gone and would never exist again. He understood he had to build a new society from the headquarters of the company that now controlled the world.

And Luthor Cromwell was the dictator.

After walking through the empty sitting room, Tristan placed his palms on the large wooden doors and pushed them open. Freezing, he observed the display before him as fury ignited in his gut. It swirled and twisted, making him queasy, and he cleared his throat to indicate his presence.

"Oh, Tristan, hello," Luthor said, his gravel-laden, weathered voice making Tristan's skin crawl. His face had aged better than his voice, making him appear middle-aged although he was almost seventy. Running a hand over the woman's hair who was kneeling before him, he chucked her chin. "Thank you, Jessica. You can button your blouse now."

Jessica stood, buttoning her blouse as Luthor stuffed his flaccid cock back in his pants before sliding up the zipper. Tucking in his shirt, he gestured toward the counter on the far side of the room. "There's a vial of EverLife and an antidote vial to manage the aftermath. Goodbye, dear." Leaning down, he kissed her forehead, and Tristan resisted the urge to march over and kill him on the spot.

It was the least the bastard deserved for the way he treated his sister. She was hooked on EverLife, as most of society now was, and Luthor held that addiction over her head like a fucking twisted pied piper. He had several women in his rotation, and the dance was the same with all of them: they traded sexual favors for EverLife with no end in sight.

The cycle made Tristan want to retch.

He would certainly find the situation terrible if his sister wasn't one of those women, but the fact she'd literally just finished sucking the bastard's dick to fuel her addiction ripped him in half.

And that was why Tristan Holder was determined to murder Luthor Cromwell.

Of course, it couldn't be *now*, since there were two armed guards in each corner of the room. Two men who'd watched his sister suck off a crazed old man who held limitless power. Running a hand over his face, Tristan shifted his weight before placing his fists on his hips. "Go on, Jess," he said, giving her the permission he felt she was waiting for. "I need to speak to Luthor alone."

She nodded, scuttling over to grab both vials before heading toward him. Staring up at him with dull, addiction-ridden eyes the color of his own, she stood on her toes and kissed his cheek. "Thank you."

With a curt not, he dismissed her, furious she hadn't been strong enough not to take the drug in the first damn place. She'd had a messy divorce two years before EverLife hit the market, and the promise of looking young forever was too tempting to resist. She'd been addicted from the first pill, and now she was shooting the shit straight into her veins. It was appalling to Tristan, who'd never touched a drug in his life and never would.

"Did you give her the pure antidote?" Tristan asked, already knowing the answer.

"You know I only offer the pure antidote to people in my inner circle, Tristan," Luthor said, striding over to look over the city he now controlled. The sun was setting in the distance, and he latched his hands behind his back as he stood firm, without remorse, as most monsters did. "The common antidote will ease your sister's symptoms and cravings for a while, which should bring you solace. When they return, she knows where to find me."

The "common antidote" was the name given to the watered-down version of the antidote Dani had created. It was now manufactured in one of the biotech facilities Luthor had seized when he overtook the District. He'd relocated all remaining scientists and manufacturers to the facilities, which now only produced EverLife and the common antidote. Tristan had a feeling Luthor knew about the employees who sold portions to the black-market drug dealers for them to dispense outside the walls. The more people addicted to EverLife, the better in Luther Cromwell's view. It made him indispensable and allowed him to remain the most powerful man on the planet.

"I only agreed to work for you if she's protected—"

"And she is," Luthor interrupted, holding up a hand. "I'm very busy, Tristan. Are you here to update me on Danica Lawson?"

"Yes." Stepping forward, he addressed Luthor as he slid into the leather chair behind his mahogany desk. "I made contact with Maverick and Dominic and confirmed they plan on breaking into the lab even if Dani doesn't regain her memory."

"Good," he said, steepling his fingers and touching them to his lips. "Capturing her crimes on video and televising her trial—and subsequent execution—will cement my place as leader. The people are starting to yearn for a scapegoat, and we can't have them blaming me." He cocked an arrogant brow.

"Wouldn't it be easier to just kill her?"

"No." Lowering his gaze, he touched his palm to the desk and stroked the wood as he recounted his master plan. "The people want a villain, and Dani created EverLife. Her death will be meaningless unless I exploit it for all to see."

"And she'll play right into your hands," Tristan said, flattening his lips.

"Of course. She'll break into the lab to steal the antidote, and my cameras will capture everything. We'll portray her as a thief who wanted to steal EverLife and sell it to black-market dealers."

"And you'll get your scapegoat," Tristan said, crossing his arms over his thick chest.

"I'll disseminate the footage of her break-in and capture to every remaining news outlet. Then I'll put her on trial for the world to see." He flashed a malevolent grin. "With a judge of my choosing, of course."

Tristan had to refrain himself from rolling his eyes at the man's arrogance and haughtiness.

"Once she's found guilty, we'll inject her with EverLife on live TV over several weeks. Get her hooked, throw her into a cell, and let the world watch her die from the addiction."

Rubbing his chin, he asked, "Do you think you could be underestimating the desire people have to watch an innocent woman die?"

"*Pfft,*" he scoffed, slicing a hand through the air. "She's no more innocent than I. She created the drug that destroyed the world."

"She formulated the drug, but *you* funded EverLife and allowed it to be dispensed after you learned of the side effects. You are the villain, Luthor."

The evil man's lips twitched in a humorless laugh. "I've been called the villain for so long it's lost its luster. The fucking government pushed me into this position, with their constant investigations and indictments against me."

"Your company was a monopoly they wanted disbanded. No company should have that much control over a nation's pharmaceutical supply."

"And what did it gain them?" Luthor asked, lifting his hands. "Their persecution of me only made me detest the government more. I began to understand that I was the one who needed to seize control. That people like me would never be safe from their constant oppression."

"Billionaires are rarely oppressed," Tristan muttered. "You had everything you could possibly desire."

"No," Luthor said, frowning. "I had money, but I didn't have power. EverLife was the key I needed to seize control. The system is fair again. Balanced. Those who live in the walls are grateful and play their roles. This is how society should function. The old government was obsessed with tearing down the rich, when all we wanted was the ability to enjoy the spoils of our hard work." Fixing his gaze on Tristan, his eyes narrowed. "We just wanted to be left the hell alone."

"Criminals are often prosecuted by government. That's the way it works, Luthor."

Rising, he jabbed an angry finger as he spoke. "I'd watch your tone, young man. I agreed to let you work for me because you have military skills and I like your sister. I *really* liked having her mouth around my cock a few minutes ago."

Tristan clenched his fists so hard he thought they might crumble and turn to dust.

"But she's expendable and so are you, so I'd suggest showing me the respect I deserve. Now, I'll say thank you for completing your task today and ask you to leave me the fuck alone so I can get back to running the world." He dismissively waved his hand, shooing Tristan from the room.

Pivoting, Tristan stomped toward the door, rage surging at the old man's arrogance. Before he could pull the handle, the door flew open and he closed his eyes. The scent of spring and heartache surrounded him, and Tristan cursed the organ that pounded in his chest.

Lifting his lids, he forced himself not to sneer at the woman who breezed into the room. His expression remained void of emotion as he spoke. "Grace," he said with a slight tilt of his head.

Those ice-blue eyes he saw in every fucking dream widened slightly before her face dropped into an expressionless mask as well. God, they were both experts at hiding the intense emotion that roared within.

Roared within *his* gut, at least. Grace Cromwell hadn't shown emotion in years. Especially not toward him.

"Tristan," she said, that honey-gravel voice almost causing his knees to buckle.

"Ah, my darling wife," Luthor said, striding over and placing a peck on her cheek.

Tristan saw the minuscule flash of distain before she pasted on a smile and greeted her husband. Or perhaps he imagined it. Deep in his mind, a small part of him still hoped his wife hated her husband.

Rather his *ex*-wife. After all these years, he could barely bring himself to say it. His wife now belonged to the man he detested. Dark and sticky anger surged in his veins, and he clenched his fists to ground himself.

"To what do I owe the honor?"

Grace's eyelids fluttered as her fake smile deepened. "I invited the Luddingtons to dinner tonight. George feels left out since you didn't invite him on your lake excursion last week. We need to keep him happy."

Luthor rubbed a hand over his face. "I hate that fat bastard, but he has connections to many of the wealthy in the District who support me. Well done. I'll be on my best behavior."

With a nod, she turned and glanced at Tristan. Her eyes skated over his neck, and flashes of having her soft lips trail over the skin blazed through his brain.

"Tristan," she said, the word husky as she reclaimed his gaze. And then, she was gone. Lost to him as she'd always been.

"How uncomfortable it must be for you," Luthor murmured, "knowing I'm married to your ex-wife and fuck your sister. You have an unbearable tolerance for pain, my friend."

Tristan recoiled and backed toward the door before he gave into his base instincts and strangled the bastard. He needed to protect Jessica at all costs, and attacking the man who kept her alive—for now—wouldn't help his cause. Once Danica retrieved the antidote, he wouldn't need the bastard anymore. But for now, he needed to retain close proximity to the man he planned to kill one day.

Clenching his jaw, he turned and stalked from the office, anticipating the day Luthor Cromwell expelled his last breath.

Chapter 14

Maverick stood at the stove the next morning, cooking as he anxiously awaited Dani's arrival in the kitchen. He relished the idea of her accepting her current reality without a ton of explanation each day because it would afford more time for them to plan. She usually entered the kitchen wary, and sometimes holding a makeshift weapon like a candlestick or even a shoe, but perhaps the second video would make her feel more comfortable.

Something rustled behind him, and Maverick turned to see his wife standing in the doorway. Inquisitive green irises roved over his frame as he let her look her fill. Finally, she opened her mouth to speak.

"So, um, apparently we have some work to do." She traced the floor with her bare toe as she gazed down. "I'm terrified and have a million questions, but my brain also accepts you're not going to hurt me." Lifting her gaze, she said resolutely, "Bring me up to speed and let's get to it."

Love for her swelled in his chest as he admired her grit and strength. It was one of the many reasons he'd fallen so hard for her, and he couldn't control the desire to touch her. Setting down the spatula, he slowly trailed toward her, opening his arms when he was close. She pursed her lips, contemplating, before she stepped forward into his embrace.

"Good morning, sweetheart," he whispered, kissing her hair.

Drawing back, her fingers clenched his shoulder. "Hi." She gently ran her fingertips over his chest, covered by his black t-shirt. Maverick let her explore, determined to make her feel comfortable.

"Sit at the table and I'll answer anything you like," he said, gesturing toward it before he resumed cooking.

Dani asked him questions as he maneuvered around the kitchen. Eventually, her sisters and Dominic arrived, all sitting at the table and "meeting" Dani as they did each morning. Her resolve seemed firm, and Maverick felt they were crossing a new threshold. It was time to make a solid plan to break into the lab and retrieve the antidote.

After breakfast, they moved to the living room, where they spent hours going over the map of the lab Maverick and Dominic had drawn on a piece of cardboard they'd found in the basement. Eventually, they formulated a plan—one that didn't involve Dani regaining her memory.

"So, we'll just assume Dani will still have amnesia when we attack," Maverick said, pointing at the spot on the map that signified the entrance to the biomedical storage room where she'd hidden the antidote. "You'll still need to scan your fingerprint, Dani, and Dom and I will search the farmhouse basement to find materials we can use to make explosives to hopefully blow open the locks."

"I'm still going to try like hell to remember the code," Dani said.

"I know you will," Maverick said, reaching over and squeezing her knee.

"I have a new tea I created yesterday. It's got some herbs and mushrooms that should help with memory."

"Thanks," Dani said, grinning. "You're my botany whiz, so I look forward to trying it."

"You're both geniuses," Arianna confirmed. "But the rest of us can still kick some ass. Dom, remember that fertilizer we saw in the shed? We could probably use that to make explosives."

"We can combine it with the fuel we collected yesterday and make some heavy-duty IEDs," he said with a nod.

"Great," Maverick said, tapping the cardboard. "Why don't you two work on making those? You can use the empty milk crates and jars in the basement. I'd like to take a quick walk with Dani to make sure I answer any lingering questions. Although the explanation time seems to have been cut shorter by the making of the second video. Great idea, babe."

"Ew," she said, wrinkling her nose.

Emitting a hearty laugh, he lifted a shoulder. "Sorry. Old habits die hard. After we walk, I'll come help you all while Dani works in the lab with Raquel."

"Where do I keep the notes I mentioned in the video?"

"In a notebook we found in the small office off the kitchen." Raquel pointed toward the doorway. "Your notes don't make a ton of sense, but you've always loved being cryptic."

"At least that hasn't changed," Dani said, chuckling as she ran a hand through her hair.

"Okay, I think we've got it," Arianna said, rising. "And I want to spar and do some target practice with you two so I'm prepared when we infiltrate the lab." She pointed between Maverick and Dominic. "Are we set on the timeline?"

"A week is enough time to prepare, I think," Maverick said. "If we're assuming Dani's not going to recover her memory, I don't see any point in waiting longer than that. We've been here for three months, and we need to take action. Our encounter with Tristan proved that."

"Tristian said he didn't wish to harm us, but we don't know if he can be trusted," Maverick continued. "As we prepare, we'll also get supplies ready so we can camp along the way to the first black-market compound after we retrieve the antidote. We'll need to travel on foot once the gas runs out in the truck, and it will be too dangerous to return here."

"Let's hope we get a friendly reception at the compounds," Arianna said. "It's possible they'll be skeptical of our intentions. There's not a lot of trust floating around these days."

"We don't have a lot of options, so we'll do our best," Maverick said. "Having a compound of addicts isn't a fulfilling goal as a leader. Hopefully, the compound leaders want to return to some semblance of normal. If so, we'll begin to recruit militia at the compounds as we cure people. Once we're formidable enough, we'll formulate a plan to take down Cromwell."

"And the Ten Cities will fall too," Arianna said.

"Yes," Maverick nodded. "DC, New York, Miami, LA and all the others that were walled off. I think if we capture Cromwell and liberate DC, the rest will follow."

"And who will lead then?" Arianna asked. "In this new society? You?"

"Uh, no thanks," Maverick said, rubbing the back of his neck. "My only desire is to help Dani save the world and regain her memory." Glancing at his wife, he grinned. "And maybe have a few kids while we're still young enough, but that's a discussion for another time."

"I always wanted kids," Dani said wistfully, leaning back against the couch. "Once I created my cancer vaccine, I was going to have a gaggle of babies."

"Well, let's start with one and see where that takes us," Maverick teased.

Dani contemplated him before her lips curved ever so slightly. "We'll see. I'm still not sure we're actually married. I'm going to need some details."

"Come on, then. Let me debrief you so we can get to work."

Dani stood, ending the meeting as she followed her husband outside under the blue sky.

Chapter 15

D ani's sneakers crunched the gravel as she walked beside Maverick. Biting her lip, she stared up at him. "I need details. How the hell did this happen? How bad is the damage—"

"I try not to focus on the damage with you. It detracts from our purpose."

Stopping short, she faced him, lifting her chin in defiance. "I need to know, Maverick."

Gray eyes roved over her face. "Mav is fine. And I think we should sit for this."

He led her to a large stump, left behind from a nearby tree that had snapped in half. They lowered onto the withered wood as Maverick inhaled a deep breath.

"Sendaxa recruited you five years ago. The CEO, Luthor Cromwell, wanted you, and was prepared to offer anything to get you."

"He offered to fund my cancer vaccine," she said, tracing her fingers over the stump. "Smart play."

"It helped to overcome your objections, and you began working for him. This was a few months before the US government appointed a special council to look into his business dealings." His lips drew into a thin line. "He wasn't a good man. Not only did he falsify clinical trial data of drugs created before EverLife, but he eventually falsified the data from EverLife trials too."

"I must've been livid when I found out," Dani said, exasperated. "There's no way I would've continued working for him."

"You were in a bind. You knew the drug was more addictive than the clinical trials reported—thanks to Luthor's meddling—but you also knew you had the best chance of creating an antidote in the Sendaxa lab. It was state of the art. Nothing else came close."

Her lips fluttered as she expelled a breath. "So, I created a ruse and continued to work there so I could fix what I'd broken."

Maverick nodded. "The FDA fast-tracked the drug, and it began selling over the counter while you worked on the antidote. You were tireless. Dom and I made sure one of us was always there to protect you."

"Luthor believed I was still on board?"

"He had suspicions, but you were convincing. There were times when he visited you in the lab and your discussions became...heated. You eventually cooled off enough to remember your goal. Luthor was rapidly gaining power as more people consumed EverLife, and you had to keep him on your good side to maintain access to the lab."

"Why would he let me create an antidote? If what he wanted was ultimate power?"

"You can't have power if everyone is dead," Maverick said, lifting a sardonic brow. "He needed the antidote so he could water it down and keep people alive but addicted. Addicts are controllable."

Steeling herself, she asked, "How deadly is EverLife? And why the hell did everyone start taking it?"

"Social media is a powerful force. People have been swayed to take drugs for years. You remember the craze surrounding the diabetic drug that also fostered weight loss. Tons of non-diabetics began taking it solely to lose weight."

"But it wasn't addictive," she said solemnly, running her toe over the grass.

"No. For EverLife, you realized you needed to include minute amounts of narcotics in the formula to dilute the pain from the increased cellular manipulation." He flashed a grin. "Making people stay young forever is hard on the body."

"Did I use poppy plant extract? Why in the hell didn't I use Psilocybin or THC?"

"You tried, but they weren't strong enough. The poppy plants were the only pain suppressant that worked effectively...as long as the drug was taken properly."

"The amount a person would have to take in order to become addicted would be extreme. Taking that many pills would rip open someone's stomach."

"You compensated for this in the clinical trials. You had two groups of people take double and triple doses and documented the side effects. One was the destruction of stomach lining, and the other was addiction. People who took the triple doses experienced addiction and needed to go through withdrawal."

"I would've recommended it be categorized as a Schedule II drug so it could be regulated and only available by prescription after consulting with a physician."

"And having a Schedule II drug wouldn't make nearly enough money for Luthor," Maverick confirmed. "He falsified your data, and it was approved by the FDA as a Schedule IV drug, similar to several over-the-counter sleep medicines. Anyone could get it."

"Bastard," Dani breathed, punching the log. "And I was stuck because I needed to stay on his good side to create the antidote in my fancy lab. Geezus. I really dug a fucking hole."

"It got worse when social media got a hold of it. Several reality stars with big followings touted EverLife as the 'miracle drug.' Luthor paid them to promote the drug on their platforms. People began stockpiling the drug and selling it on the black market."

"Which means they didn't stick to the recommended doses."

Shaking his head, Maverick sighed. "Addiction grew in every portion of the country. No race, class or town was immune. People began crushing the pills and injecting them intravenously to experience the high. It was a vicious cycle."

"So many lives destroyed," she said, swiping away a tear. "All because I didn't foresee the inevitable."

"You couldn't have foreseen this, sweetheart," he said, gently rubbing her arm. "You have an optimistic heart when it comes to science. Honestly, I don't think anyone could've foreseen this."

Dani remained quiet, allowing the shocking details of her destruction to settle deep in her bones.

"Luthor became the most powerful man in the world. The president of Sendaxa's board overdosed on EverLife, leaving Luthor in power of the company's massive funds when he dissolved the board shortly thereafter. Without any votes needed to make decisions, he began closing off large cities, urging the wealthy to remain inside where they could obtain EverLife and the watered-down antidote he created from your formula."

"The army didn't stop him?"

"President Johnson overdosed, and Luthor took control of the army, Dani. He ultimately achieved his goal of taking down the government."

"Jesus," she breathed, raking a hand through her hair. "And once he had the antidote, he didn't need me."

"We knew the writing was on the wall," Maverick said, covering her thigh and squeezing. "Dom and I thought he might kill you once he had everything he needed. You hid a secret stash of antidote, and we bided our time so that you could resign and bring the antidote with you."

"And then some fucker hit me in the head," she exclaimed, rubbing the base of her scalp. "I guess we didn't anticipate everything."

"Unfortunately not. We went on the run and scouted safe places to stay. By the time you got amnesia, the world was in chaos. Many houses were abandoned because people had moved inside the Ten Cities or to a black-market compound. We finally found this place, and now it's time to enact our plan. I'd hoped you would regain your memory, but we can't wait anymore. I'm sorry, slugger."

"I get it," Dani said, straightening her spine. "And I can't live with myself until I try to fix this mess." Rising, she faced him and formed a lopsided grin. "You know we're probably going to fail, right?"

Standing, he cupped her shoulders. "Where's my optimistic scientist?" he teased. "I never would've imagined you could destroy the world, but you did."

Dani shot him a droll look.

"So, who's to say you can't save it as well?"

Straightening her shoulders, Dani inhaled a breath. "Good point. Maybe we have a tiny shot." She squinted and held her thumb and forefinger an inch apart.

Laughing, Maverick rested his forehead against hers. "With you at the helm, I like our chances. Come on. We've got work to do."

Dani leaned into her husband's side when he slid his arm around her waist. She sure as hell hadn't meant to decimate the world but knew it was damn well time to save it.

Chapter 16

After her walk with Maverick, Dani entered Raquel's makeshift lab and got to work. As Raquel toiled with combining the various herbs she'd collected over the past few days, Dani read over the notes she'd left in the notebook. She'd warned herself in the video that she was leaving breadcrumbs, and she was determined to decipher the cryptic phrases.

Raquel returned from the kitchen, carrying a mug with steam rising from the center. Handing it to Dani, she said, "This is a brand new concoction. I'm hoping it will help your memory. Drink up."

Dani took the mug, blowing on the hot liquid before she drank. Touching the rim to her lips, she took a sip before breaking into a coughing fit.

"Dani?" Raquel asked, rubbing her back.

"I don't care if that gives me the memory of a fucking elephant," she sputtered, wiping her mouth. "It tastes awful. I'm not drinking it."

Raquel's face fell. "Okay. I was just trying to help."

"I know," Dani said, cupping her shoulder, "and I appreciate it, but I just can't. I'd rather forget my name than drink that."

Something flashed in her sister's eyes—so quick Dani couldn't read it—before it disappeared. Sighing, Raquel nodded. "Okay. Maybe I can try putting some mint in the next one. Sorry."

"It's fine. Thanks for trying."

Raquel circled the table, returning to the other side as she began to fiddle with the various plants and herbs on the table. Dani picked up the pen and wrote in the notebook. *Raquel's teas taste terrible. Stopped drinking them on...* Glancing up, she asked, "What's today's date?"

Raquel informed her it was July 28, and the year was several past the one Dani last remembered, but she jotted down the date anyway, vowing to have a written reminder she hated the teas. It might hurt Raquel's feelings, but there was no use in ingesting something she was pretty sure would make her puke.

Eventually, the sun began its descent behind the rolling hills that met the horizon outside the farmhouse window. Dominic entered, asking them both how they were faring and informing them Maverick and Arianna were still doing target practice. Dominic approached and sat in the open seat beside Dani as Raquel excused herself to get some fresh air before the sun set.

"So, tell me about you," Dani said, observing his scar, which he'd explained at breakfast he'd received during his tour in Pakistan. "Maverick told me on our walk we're good friends."

"We were," he said with a nod, circling his thumbs as they sat atop his thighs. "And maybe we'll be again one day, if you ever get that noggin' to remember." He tapped his temple.

Chuckling softly, she shrugged. "I want that more than you, believe me."

His resulting smile caused tiny wrinkles to form under his eyes, making Dani guess he was somewhere around forty. Weathered enough to have seen combat so fierce he sustained scars but still young enough the wrinkles softened when his lips flattened again. "You were the last person to see your mom alive, and I was the last person to see my sister alive. We both held their hands as they passed from cancer. It's a terrible experience."

"So true," Dani said, blowing out a breath as she shook her head. "Mom asked to see Arianna first, and they said their goodbyes, then I went in next. I probably took too long with her, but I just didn't want to say goodbye." Tears clouded her eyes as she struggled with the emotion blocking her windpipe. "Suddenly, her face fell and she let out this long breath. I called for Raquel, and she ran inside but it was too late. She didn't even get to say goodbye. Mom just slipped away...and I felt so helpless."

"There was nothing you could do," he said, gently rubbing her upper arm.

"I know, but it burns." Rubbing her chest, she felt the fire of failure simmer deep within. "I want so badly to save other people from that experience. Now my cancer vaccine seems so far away. All because I made terrible choices."

"I would argue you made the choices you thought would bring you to a vaccine faster. You couldn't have known what would unfold with EverLife. You're pretty brilliant, Dani, but you're not psychic."

"I guess." Sighing, her teeth toyed with her lip as she pondered. "But one day, I'm going to do it, Dominic. Save people like us from having to suffer."

"I have no doubt."

Gazing tenderly at the kind man who had such a gruff exterior, Dani asked softly, "Tell me about your sister. I'd love to know her story."

Feeling the tension ease slightly from her muscles, she settled in and listened to her friend tell the sweet story of how much he loved his little sister.

Arianna stepped through the back door, loving the slight pain in her muscles after her sparring session and target practice with Maverick and Dominic. She'd been an officer in the army before she resigned, and missed the thrill of always being alert and combat ready. She'd been deployed to Afghanistan twice before receiving another promotion—and realizing that being a female officer in the army was never going to make her truly happy.

The ranks were rife with sexism and misogyny, and although strides had been made, Arianna understood she could only advance so far in a structure designed for men, by men. Her stoic exterior certainly didn't help, but she'd refused to paste on a smile and fake it. Men had told women to "smile more" since the dawn of civilized society, and Arianna wasn't interested in playing that game. Take her or leave her, she was true to herself and there was honor in that.

So, she'd resigned from the army around the time Sendaxa released EverLife to the masses. Dani had been thrilled the FDA fast-tracked the drug's approval since it brought her closer to working on a cancer vaccine. Arianna had been extremely proud of her little sister, who they'd all believed was going to save the world.

Frowning, Arianna smoothed her hand over her half-bald head, wishing they hadn't been so horribly wrong. In the months that followed EverLife's release, addiction spread across the globe, signaling the beginning of society's downfall. And then she'd received the voicemail from Maverick.

"Arianna, it's Mav. Dani's sustained a terrible head injury, and we've been banned from the lab. We've also been placed on the black list for entry into the District. We're going on the run and we need you. Call me when you get this. Everything is going up in flames, and I don't know how long the cell phone towers will be functional."

Arianna had eventually connected with Maverick and joined them as they searched for a place to hide. Thankfully, they'd found the farmhouse, and it had given them a few months of refuge. Now, the time had come to attempt to right Dani's wrongs. Although not intentional, her sister had fucked up royally, and Arianna was determined to help her set things right.

Cynthia Lawson would expect nothing less from her daughters than to help each other through crisis.

Arianna had loved Cynthia with a ferocity she couldn't quantify. She'd been young and most likely unprepared for a child when she adopted Arianna. But they'd learned together—grown together—and Cynthia met Bill Lawson several months after her adoption. He was kind, and Arianna observed him fall like a rock for her adoptive mother. Even though she'd been a child, she understood their connection and thought it beautiful.

They married shortly after Arianna turned five, Cynthia's belly already swollen from the baby growing inside. Cynthia would sing to Arianna, taking her hand and placing it over her stomach as Dani kicked beneath. Arianna had formed a connection with Dani before she was born and relished being the oldest sister. Protecting Dani and Raquel was an honor, and she'd felt a calling to protect them all her life.

Now, she could use the skills she'd learned in the military to help Dani and hopefully save countless others. It was a worthy cause, and Arianna would do her best to achieve it.

After removing her boots and tossing them by the back door, she silently strode toward the den, her ears perking as she overheard Dani and Dominic's conversation. Glancing around the doorframe, she watched them. They shared a comfortable comradery as Dominic spoke about Pam, even though Dani didn't remember their past. Feeling her heart squeeze in her chest, Arianna observed their interaction.

Every so often, Dani would reach over and soothe him, rubbing his corded arm as he recounted stories about his sister. Being nurturing came easily to Dani, and it was one of the reasons Dominic had been drawn to her. Arianna understood this and tamped down the swell of jealousy that threatened to choke her as she listened.

Arianna had always been quiet. Stoic. Thoughtful. And yes, perhaps she was a bit harsh. She was no psychoanalyst but figured it stemmed from the fact she'd always felt the need to prove her worth to her family. Although Cynthia and Bill had adopted her and loved her intensely, the nagging feeling she didn't belong always lingered in the corner of her mind.

She was the adopted sister while Dani and Raquel were blood sisters.

When Arianna was seventeen, Bill was struck by a drunk driver and passed away. It was devastating, and the Lawson family did their best to grieve and move on. During that time, Arianna took on the nagging fear that Cynthia would gain more comfort from Dani and Raquel since they were Bill's biological daughters. That fear caused her to retreat...to sink further into silence so Bill's "real" daughters could grieve with Cynthia.

Cynthia had drawn Arianna back in, pulling her from the abyss of her fears and assuring her she was as much her daughter as Dani and Raquel. But the fear and self-doubt always lingered, even for someone as outwardly confident as Arianna.

Years later, when Cynthia lay in her bed, minutes from death from the cancer that was ravaging her body, she'd called for Arianna. She'd stepped into the dim room, unable to control the tears she rarely shed. Sitting by her mother's bedside, she'd gripped her clammy hand, stroking it as Cynthia struggled to speak.

"You've always been so strong, Ari," she rasped, her green eyes devoid of the sparkle that had lived there for so long. "I need you to watch over the girls. You're the strongest of all of us, and I love you with all my heart."

"I love you too, Mom," she'd whispered, unashamed when a tear fell on her mother's cotton nightgown. "I'll take care of them. I promise."

"Good girl," she said, patting her hand. "You were my first baby and taught me how to love. Don't ever forget that. My beautiful baby..."

She'd drifted off, her eyes drooping, and Arianna had placed a tender kiss on her forehead before rising and allowing Dani to take her place. Cynthia had passed away moments later, before Raquel had a chance to say goodbye. Arianna held her youngest sister, soothing her as she railed at the unfairness of the world and the misery of being denied one last goodbye.

Shortly thereafter, they'd buried their mother and further cemented their bond. The Lawson sisters would always remain loyal and steadfast to each other, no matter the circumstances. It was a promise to their mother they intended to keep, and Arianna was grateful to have Dani and Raquel in a world she found quite lonely.

Gazing at Dani and Dominic, Arianna wondered if things would've been different if Bill and Cynthia had survived. Would she be as harsh and unyielding? When she'd first met Dominic, could she have been the one to offer him a safe place to tell his stories instead of Dani? Could he possibly have chosen to love her instead?

Scoffing, Arianna shook her head, ridding it of the pointless, meandrous thoughts. Long ago, she'd accepted she wasn't meant to have a great love. Some were—Dani and

Maverick proved that. But many were also like her. Impenetrable. Different. Outliers. She'd just never understood how to reach out and connect with someone. In the deep corners of her heart, she yearned to offer Dominic comfort. To ease his head against her chest and stroke his short dark hair as he told her about Pam.

In reality, the idea scared her to death. Dominic didn't want someone cold and unyielding to soothe him. Dani was exceedingly better at emotion, and Arianna understood that. Maybe one day, when she had her own child, she could allow herself the space to be vulnerable. To trust she had the emotional bandwidth to truly love and nurture someone...and to be loved in return.

For now, she'd accept the man she loved was better off taking comfort from someone who understood how to offer it completely. Annoyed with herself at the unusually sappy thoughts, Arianna pushed off the door frame and headed upstairs to seek solace in her room before dinner.

Chapter 17

D ani spent the next few days acclimating to her new normal. The wound at her
side—which she'd sustained by falling into a pitchfork according to her notes and
her sisters—was healing nicely and only stung occasionally. She continued to write more
notes for herself, making sure to record instances of small flashbacks and any patterns she
could find.

She also began writing notes about Maverick on a fresh page titled "My Husband" at
the top. There, she would jot down things she wanted to remember. Every morning, as she
watched the video where she intimately cuddled with the handsome stranger and spoke
to herself, her heartbeat accelerated furiously in her chest. Armed with the knowledge he
wouldn't hurt her, she always rose and headed to find him and her sisters.

The idea she'd fallen in love was so intriguing to Dani, she decided she wanted to
write down the little quirks and gestures Maverick exhibited each day. After all, she was a
scientist, and the best way to study a subject was to keep copious notes. She hoped to ease
herself down a new path where she finally remembered him.

Several days before the planned break-in, she sat at the lab table, reading her list as
Raquel toyed with some concoctions across the room. Maverick, Arianna and Dominic
were outside training, and they'd fallen into a nice daily rhythm. Dani would wake up,
watch the videos and they would all have breakfast. Then, they would sit and study the
map as they discussed their plan and theorized ways they could succeed and fail. Maverick
would walk with Dani while Arianna and Dominic worked on the IEDs and Raquel
toiled in the lab. They would all reconvene for dinner before her sisters and Dominic
retired to their rooms and Dani spent some time with Maverick.

Narrowing her eyes, she read the notes she'd left over the past few days.

Maverick and I had a nice evening. He's funny and has a chip on his shoulder about his parents' love of Top Gun and all things 80s. He's also a great kisser. You tiptoed back into the den to make this note so you wouldn't forget. Make sure you do it again. Soon.

Snickering, Dani closed her eyes for a moment, trying to imagine the kiss. Had his lips been firm against her softer ones? Lifting her lids, she read some of her other missives.

Maverick knows where your birthmarks are. The one behind your knee, the one on your elbow...and others. It's so weird but also kind of hot. Like he's touched you in places that only belong to him...

Maverick was so sweet as he tucked you in tonight. He kissed you and then walked to the door and turned around before telling you he loved you. It wasn't timid or shy, like several of the duds you dated in the past. He said it so firmly, with that deep voice that makes your insides vibrate. "I love you so much, Dani." God, it makes my knees shake as I'm writing this. I think you need to trust him enough to go all the way...

And then, there was the note from last night:

Okay, Dani, enough is enough. You're writing this in the dark as parts you don't think about in polite society are quite literally throbbing. Maverick just kissed you like your lives depended on it and left you sweaty and needy in a lonely bed. You have a dangerous mission ahead of you and might not survive. For god's sake, let him hold you. Let him love you. He's safe. You know that deep within even if your brain can't recall the memories...

Sucking in a breath, Dani lifted her gaze to the ceiling, contemplating. Could she really make love to a man she only remembered meeting that morning? Chewing the top of her pen, she didn't notice Raquel approach until she was right beside her.

"Okay, this one should taste better," she said, her gaze slightly wary as she extended a mug. "If it's too cold, let me know."

Flipping through the notebook, Dani pointed at one of her entries. "Sorry, sis, but I have a written directive not to drink any teas you make. I also made a note to tell you that you're amazing, remind you I love you and not to take it personally."

"Okay," Raquel said, her eyes drifting to the notebook. "Can't mess with the notes," she teased. "It also seems like you're having more flashbacks, which is a good sign."

"Yes." Turning to the page where her flashbacks were recorded, she tapped it. "I'm having at least one flashback every day, sometimes two." Excitement bloomed as Dani felt herself inching closer to regaining her memory. "I feel like we're close, Raquel."

Her sister stayed silent a moment before she smiled. "I hope so. In the meantime, I'm going to take a walk and drink the tea since you don't want it." She took a sip as her eyebrows rose in delight. "This one actually tastes good. See you in a bit."

After Raquel stepped outside, Dani flipped to the page with the Latin phrases. Zeroing in, she felt drawn to them for some reason. Reading in a hushed voice, she recited the words.

- *Fere libenter homines id quod volunt credunt (*Men generally believe what they want to)

- *Nemo mortalium omnibus horis sapit (*Of mortal men, none is wise at all times)

- *De omnibus dubitandum (*Be suspicious of everything)

- *et tu, Brute?*

Frustration consumed her as she tried to decipher any hidden meaning. Sadly, it was no use. Annoyed, she flipped the notebook closed and rubbed her tired eyes.

Pushing away from the table, she decided she needed some fresh air before the group gathered for dinner.

Chapter 18

During dinner, Maverick observed Dani, grateful for her progress over the past few days. Although her memory hadn't returned, she'd had several murky flashbacks, making sure to record them all in her notebook. Her disposition seemed more resolved and also...*lighter* in a way. It reminded him of when they'd met. The focused head of security and the meticulous, steadfast scientist. Each drawn to each other in ways they couldn't explain but somehow made sense.

After dinner, Dani and Maverick headed to the living room, leaving Dominic, Arianna and Raquel to a raucous game of poker at the kitchen table. As their shouts of disbelief at their misfortune and bursts of laughter echoed through the house, Dani snuggled into Maverick's side on the comfortable couch as he gently rubbed her arm.

"Did you have a flashback today?" he asked, loving her resulting shiver as his voice washed over her. She'd told him often how sexy his voice was, and he reveled in how her body still responded to it, even if her mind didn't remember.

Picking at a stray thread on her pants, she nodded. "It wasn't anything tangible though. I keep seeing the lab and the biohazard symbols...but that's all I can remember."

"Hey, it takes time, sweetheart."

She hesitated, biting her lip as she contemplated. Finally, she said softly, "I do have several notes where I tell myself to..." Her cheeks flushed as her gaze tentatively lifted.

Sliding his fingers under her chin, he grinned as he stared into her eyes. "Yes?"

"I told myself to...let you kiss me...and touch me." Her eyelids squeezed together. "Oh god, this is embarrassing."

"I love touching you," he murmured, reveling in the swirls of emotion that clouded her eyes when they popped open. "But I won't push you. We can just sit here and relax if you want. We've only got a few days until the shit hits the fan, and I'm happy to just hold you."

She studied his face and throat, from his angular nose to the muscles that were corded in his neck from her tender caresses. Curiosity entered her expression and she cleared her throat. "How long has it been since we had sex?"

Maverick couldn't resist teasing her, considering she looked so serious, and he relished making fun of her when she fell into a serious mood. "Did you have a flashback about us having sex? That's hot."

Wrinkling her nose, she laughed and swatted his chest. "No. I just...I was just wondering. Forget it."

His deep chuckle blanketed them as he leaned closer, brushing his lips across her ear. "It's been a while, babe. I miss you."

A dull ringing sounded in his ears as breath rushed from her throat. Her chest lifted in a chaotic rhythm as his body hardened. Consumed by her, he waited, determined to let her take control.

"How long?" she whispered, her voice raspy.

His tongue darted out to bathe his parched lips as he slowly drowned in her scent. Letting his eyes rove over her pert nose, dash of freckles and plump pink lips, he stopped trying to control his jagged heartbeat. How could he when she looked at him like this, inquisitive and stunning, with her lithe body pressed against his? Placing his fingers at her temple, he tenderly tucked a curl behind her ear.

"Honestly, it happened more in the beginning...before we ran out of wine and beer." Cocking a brow, he gestured with his head to the kitchen. "Every once in a while, when we first moved here, you would get tipsy at dinner and after that..." He drifted off, shaking his head as he grinned. "I don't want to sound like a creep. I never seduced you when you were drunk or anything. I just—" He rubbed a hand over his face. "You're always more...*open*...when you're tipsy, and if we had a good day, you'd drag me into your room. I made sure to ask several times for your consent. Promise." He made an X over his heart.

Dani expelled a breath, her cheeks puffed as she digested his words. "It's true. I like to get down when I'm tipsy."

Laughing, he tugged a strand of her hair. "One of the many things I love about you. Two glasses and you're a sure thing."

Enchantment at his teasing marred her features, and she bit her lip, almost sending him over the edge as her teeth toyed with the flesh. "But then we ran out of booze?"

"Yeah." His fingers trailed through her tresses, the soft strands silky against his skin as they spoke. "There wasn't a huge stash anyway, and we fell into our roles. We began formulating a plan for when you recovered your memory and hoped like hell it would happen."

"Until dead bodies started disappearing and a stranger appeared to tell you to get on with it."

"Yep," he said, chuckling as he nodded.

She remained silent as he traced his finger over the smooth skin of her jaw. He continued the caress, moving lower, causing her to shiver as he drew tiny circles on the sensitive skin of her neck. Sensing her acquiescence, he tilted her face to his and waited for her to speak.

"Maverick?"

"Hmm?"

"I want..." Inhaling a deep breath, she straightened slightly. "I want to make love to you."

A ragged breath escaped his lungs, washing over her as his eyes narrowed and grew heavy with desire. Continuing to trace her neck, he remained silent.

"I mean...if you want to. I—"

"I want to," he interjected, gently squeezing her neck, the possessive gesture causing her to close her eyes as her body swayed toward his. Maverick knew she loved it when he took control, and her body always arched into his, which drove him wild. "I just want you to be sure, babe."

Lifting her lids, she cemented her gaze to his. "I'm sure. Although, I have no idea how I ever let you call me that—"

His fingers snaked up from her neck, covering her lips as she gasped. Sliding his free hand to her ass, he palmed the flesh and dragged her against him. "Give me ten minutes and I'll show you," he rasped, pressing his forehead to hers.

A small eternity passed for Maverick before she nodded. "Deal."

A growl ripped from his throat before he pulled her into his lap. Sliding an arm under her knees and one under her back, he rose, lifting her in his arms. Exiting the living room, he called to the kitchen, "We're going to bed. The door will be locked. See you all in the morning."

"Woo hoo!" Arianna called from the kitchen. "Mav's getting laid. Nice job!"

"Fucking peanut gallery," Maverick muttered, striding into Dani's room and kicking the door closed.

Her melodious laughter filtered through the room as he placed her on the bed. "Arianna's still so fucking acerbic. I love her."

"I love her too, but she's a ball buster," he said, slowly covering her body with his as he sunk his fingers into the thick tresses that fanned across the comforter. "If I didn't love you so much, I'd tell her to fuck off."

Tossing back her head, she laughed, baring the delectable skin of her throat. Unable to resist, Maverick touched his lips to the soft skin, grateful to taste her once more. Sucking in a breath, she plunged her fingers into his hair, tugging as she pulled him closer.

"Show me," she pleaded, her hips undulating to meet his. "I need to see these 'babe-inducing' skills in action."

Chuckling, he placed tender kisses along her neck, gently running his tongue over the smooth skin before nipping her with his teeth. Her body quaked, and he surged the hard ridge of his erection against her mound, frustrated at the barrier of clothes between them. "I'm going to make you scream, Dani." Lifting his head, he clenched his hands in her hair. "But be honest with me, okay? I can get...carried away." He waggled his eyebrows.

The little vixen just smiled and slowly lifted her arms above her head on the mattress. "I'm all yours and I won't break. Just be careful with my side. It's healing nicely, but let's not take any chances."

Lust racked his frame as he gazed at her beauty, sprawled before him like a feast he was ready to devour. Rising, he gripped the hem of her shirt, heart pounding in anticipation of seeing his wife's pretty little breasts for the first time in so damn long...

Chapter 19

Dani observed her husband as he loomed over her, his broad shoulders blocking the light from the bedside lamp as he fisted her shirt in his broad hands. Bands of muscle flexed in his arms as he tore the shirt from her body, and his expression turned reverent as he placed his fingers atop her collarbone. Slowly dragging them across her flushed skin, his breath was heavy as he toyed with the top of her functional bra.

"I'd tell you to rip it off, but I'm guessing we don't have a ton of extra clothes lying around."

A sultry smile crested his lips as he shook his head. "No. We need to keep this one intact." Sliding his hands beneath her, Dani arched her back so he could unfasten the clasp. Tossing the garment to the floor, Maverick rested on his elbow, gazing at her breasts as he cupped one in his palm.

"I think about these pretty little breasts all the time," he murmured, lowering his head to nudge the underside of her breast with his nose. "And your scent..." Inhaling deeply, he breathed her in. "God, Dani, you smell so good. Once I drank you in, I never wanted to let go."

"I wish I could remember," she warbled as tears stung her eyes.

"We'll remember together, sweetheart," he said, repositioning so he could press his lips to hers. He kissed her softly, massaging her lips with his as he breathed her name. "Kiss me back."

Gliding her arms around his neck, Dani tugged him close, opening her mouth to draw him inside. He groaned, surging his hardness between her thighs. His tongue tasted and explored, and Dani almost giggled at his zeal. It was as if he'd been on the verge of starvation and she was his only source of sustenance.

"And what are you laughing at?" he teased, nipping her nose.

"You're so into it. And I'm *really* into it. Holy shit, we have awesome sex, don't we?"

Laughter bounded from his throat as he tossed back his head. Joy emanated from his strong frame, and Dani's heart splintered at his laughter. It brought her almost as much pleasure as his lips against hers, and his hand against her breast. *Almost.*

"We do," he said, grinning as he placed soft kisses along her wet lips. "Since you're thirty-five now and I'm seven years older than you, we always joked we didn't have time to waste having bad sex. We know what we want and are forthright enough with each other to ask."

"I'm on board with constructive feedback, although I don't remember turning thirty." Furrowing her brow, she touched the corner of her eye. "Do I have wrinkles?"

"I wouldn't care if you had a thousand wrinkles" was his sweet reply as he kissed the place she'd touched. "You'll always be gorgeous to me. You're my wife, hon. I'm kind of stuck with you." He winked as she emitted a soft laugh.

Palming his cheeks, she shook her head against the comforter. "You've been so patient. So loyal. Arianna and Raquel both told me today, and I wrote it in my notebook several times." Running her thumb over his bottom lip, she asked, "Do I deserve this? I mean, I destroyed the world. I should probably be in prison."

"We're going to fix it, slugger. For now, just feel, okay? Can you do that for me?"

She nodded, cupping his cheek as she whispered, "Don't let me kill the vibe. Sex first, then save the world. Got it."

Low-toned laughter vibrated in his chest as his hand caressed her breast. His shaft pushed against her thigh, hard and ready to claim her as she shivered. Widening her legs, a sense of female satisfaction coursed through her when he groaned. Pressing his forehead to hers, he gazed at her with a question in his eyes.

"Keep going," she said, her tone shy as anticipation bloomed deep within.

He pecked the tip of her nose before sliding down her body, his hand reaching to cup her breast once more. Touching his lips to the small mound, he began to trail kisses over the quivering skin. Bringing his other hand to the other breast, his fingers surrounded both nipples as he kissed the valley between them.

"*Ohhhhh*...that feels so good..." she moaned, writhing beneath him.

"You like it when I pinch these tight little nipples and kiss you here," he rasped against her skin. Extending his tongue, he licked her, wetting the flesh between her breasts as his fingers tugged and toyed with the sensitive buds.

Tossing her head back, she closed her eyes and mewled beneath him.

Strong fingers twirled and pulled the tight points, shooting a rush of moisture to her core. Squeezing her eyelids together, she felt the warm honey flow between her thighs, aching to relieve the intense pressure.

"Do we use protection?"

"You have a contraceptive implant." He tapped her arm, indicating the location. "We were going to wait to have kids until you cured cancer."

"Got it. So you're safe and I'm safe, right?"

Resting his chin between her breasts, he gently squeezed one of the soft mounds. "Look at me, sweetheart."

Dani lifted her head, overwhelmed with the emotion...with the *love* shining in his eyes. "You're *always* safe with me. Do you hear me?"

Nodding, she licked her lips, rapt with anticipation as his lips curved. "Good girl." Lowering his head, he blew a warm breath on her nipple, causing her to moan. "Now let me taste you, honey."

Lost in the most erotic moment of her life, Dani watched him open those firm lips before closing them over her nipple. Threading her fingers in his thick hair, she clenched the tresses as he sucked her deep, each corresponding pull of the nub throbbing in her deepest place. Soft moans leapt from her throat as he worked his mouth, wetting the flesh as he lavished her with his tongue.

After thoroughly devouring her nipple, he kissed a wet pathway to her other breast. Touching his tongue to the tip, he flicked it several times, chuckling when she groaned in frustration.

"You're teasing me," she rasped, her lips forming a pout. "Please, Maverick."

Forming a sexy smile, he tilted his head. "Beg me again, babe. Fuck, I like it so much when you beg. That's how I originally gained nickname approval." Waggling his brows, he nipped her sensitive bud.

"*Please*," she cried, unable to deny him since her body was slowly combusting beneath him. "Call me whatever you want. Please just don't stop."

"Never." Cupping her other breast, he gently massaged it as he lowered his mouth over her nipple. Dani squirmed against the maddening ministrations, realizing her husband had already learned how to play her body like a musician performing a beautiful symphony. Giving in to the pleasure, she closed her eyes and let him work her nipple on his tongue. He moaned against the quivering flesh, indicating his mutual desire, and she allowed herself to feel a moment of happiness.

Yes, tomorrow would come and then the day after, and eventually they would try to save humanity. But for now, Dani was content to lie in her husband's arms and experience pleasure instead of sorrow for a small window of time.

Once her nipples were wet, turgid peaks, Maverick moved lower, kissing her stomach and abdomen before dipping his tongue in her navel. Dani shivered and pushed her waistband, longing to be naked so he could go lower. Rising to his knees, he shucked her pants, tossing them to the floor before removing his shirt.

"Take off the rest," she commanded softly, loving the arousal that flared in his eyes.

Standing, he removed his pants and hooked his fingers around the hem of his boxer briefs. "You sure?"

Biting her finger, she nodded from the bed. Giving her another sultry wink, he pulled off his underwear before facing her on the bed. His erection stood firm and full, jutting from the springy hairs between his thighs, and her mouth began to water. Firm, ridged muscles skated across his abdomen before leading down to his pulsing cock and thick thighs. God, he was gorgeous. Thanking the universe for the fortune of finding him, she grinned and hooked her finger.

"Come back here and play with me."

Lowering to his knees, he gripped the back of her thighs, drawing her across the comforter as she squealed. Placing one leg over each of his shoulders, his gaze burned as he stared into her eyes. "I give the orders here, sweetheart."

Gasping, her body arched as he pressed his fingers to her folds, spreading her apart and burying his face in her wet warmth. Speaking became a lost cause, along with thinking and most likely breathing as he swiped his tongue over her silken slit.

"You laughing at me?" he teased, the words murmured into her deepest place.

"I'm laughing because I...*oh god*...I might lose the ability to breathe." Pushing against him, she silently begged for more. "And honestly, I don't care."

Knowing laughter reverberated against her wet folds. Sliding his fingers through her slickness, he dragged them to the tiny nerve-filled nub. Warm breath skated across her tender skin as he began to slowly circle her engorged clit.

Clenching the covers, she shook her head in frustration, needing more pressure. Gripping his hair, she undulated into his fingers, her body on fire as her core brushed his lips. "*More...*"

Her husband took pity on her, increasing the pace of his firm strokes as he touched his tongue to her opening. Whispering words of praise and desire, he sipped her honey, sucking her wet skin into his mouth before pressing his tongue to her dripping core. As his fingers circled and stroked, he impaled her with his tongue, darting it inside before retreating and surging back for more.

The act was so intimate...so *raw*...that tiny flames of arousal consumed her. They blossomed into blazes, threatening to burn her alive as her skin flushed a thousand shades of red. Moaning her husband's name, Dani let him take her to heaven with his skillful tongue and incessant strokes. Stars formed behind her closed eyelids, bursting in the dark, until she opened her mouth in a silent scream. Unable to hold back, she dove over the cliff into a blinding orgasm, her husband purring moans of approval against her swollen flesh as she crashed into the abyss.

Shudders racked her frame, engulfing her as wave after pleasurable wave enveloped every cell of her skin. Feeling her muscles liquify, she collapsed on the bed as Maverick rested his cheek against her inner thigh. Sighing, she lifted her head, biting her lip to hide her smile at his smug, satisfied expression.

"Oh man," she sighed, collapsing back on the bed. "I see how you got me to agree to the endearment. I didn't stand a chance."

Rising, he slinked over her body, firmly planting one knee and then the other on the mattress. Slithering over her, sexy and lithe as a snake stalking his prey, he slowly aligned his body with hers. The spiky hairs that covered his body pressed into her sweaty skin, and Dani ran her calf over his, delighting in his growl of approval.

Resting his elbows at her side, he slid his fingers into her hair, massaging her scalp as his cock searched for her. Gray eyes locked with hers as he began to push inside.

"Dani," he whispered, cementing his lips to hers in a torrid kiss as he pressed inside, inch by slow inch. "I've missed this so much."

"I'm sorry," she whispered, aching to comfort him...hating she'd ever denied him anything.

"No, sweetheart," he whispered against her lips. "No apologies. I just need to feel you." Pushing deep inside her tight heat, his length pulsed against her inner walls. "That's it. Open up for me."

Dani widened her legs, allowing him to press farther, his sensitive tip pressing against the inner spot he seemed to intimately know. His fingers continued their pleasurable assault against her scalp, maneuvering the skin around her damaged brain, almost as if he were trying to heal her.

"I don't need to remember to know this is real," she whispered, digging her nails into his neck. His resulting hiss resonated in her bones as she undulated against him. "Show me, Mav. I just need you to show me."

His strong hips began to move, dragging his steel through her softness. Her body mourned the loss every time he retreated and shuddered each time he filled her once more. Gazing into her with hooded eyes, he whispered unintelligible words she somehow understood. Never had she experienced a connection so intense. Needing him to know, she opened her mouth, frustrated when she could only emit a soft mewl.

"I know," he breathed, the pace of his hips increasing as he hammered into her. "It's always like this..." Brushing his lips against hers, his words ripped her heart open. "I love you so much, Dani."

The intensity of the words choked her, breath halting in her lungs as she struggled to amalgamate her feelings with the lingering notion she'd lost every memory they'd ever made together.

"No thinking," he commanded, sliding one hand down to cup her ass as he continued to increase the pace. "Just concentrate on taking me deep...right there." Circling his hips, his cock stroked her clit before jutting inside and reaching the spot deep within.

"Ohhh...*fuck!*" she cried, closing her eyes as his pounding became swift and furious. Clenching her hair, he anchored her, slamming inside her as another orgasm threatened to take hold.

Searching for a stronghold, she gripped his shoulders, finding the muscles strained and rigid beneath her fingers. A ragged groan leapt from his throat as he closed his eyes. His cock filled her, sliding through her honey as his jaw clenched. Jabbing her nails in his flesh, Dani succumbed to another climax. It burst through her, dragging her into its depths as Maverick stiffened above her.

With one last thrust, he cried her name before burying his face in her neck. Jerks and spasms overtook his frame as he emptied himself into her. Dani squeezed him tight, feeling him pulse against her inner walls as his release jetted into her body. Eventually, his jerks turned to slight tremors as he settled against her. Wrapping himself around her, he pulled her into every crevice of his body.

Dani settled against him, craving his warmth as her body cooled. His fingers toyed with her hair as his lips nuzzled her neck, and he shivered as she slid her nails up and down his back. They lay there for a small eternity before she felt him begin to slip from her body.

"Damn it," he whispered, sighing against her neck. "I don't want to move."

"Let's get under the covers so you can hold me."

Lifting his head, he gazed at her with wary eyes. A dull throb pounded deep within as she realized he wasn't going to stay. Pecking her lips, he lifted on straight arms and said, "Be right back."

Dani's eyebrows drew together as he rose and walked to the dresser. Opening the drawer, he pulled out a cloth before returning to the side of the bed. Silently, he pushed her legs open and wiped away the evidence of their loving. His eyes bore into hers, resolute, silently informing her he couldn't stay. After cleaning himself, he reached for his underwear and slid them on.

"Maverick?" she asked, feeling her heart crumble into tiny pieces as he frowned.

"It never works if I stay, sweetheart," he said, sitting on the side of the bed and caressing her leg. "You wake up and have no idea who I am and usually want to slug the shit out of me." The corner of his lips twitched. "I mean, it's kind of hot, but it's not conducive to us having a productive day."

Feeling exposed, she tried to cover her body before he lifted her from the bed. Holding her against his warm chest, he pulled back the covers and placed her inside before drawing them up to her chin. Kissing her forehead, he cupped her jaw as she stared up at him.

"You won't even cuddle with me? After all that?"

Sitting beside her, he shook his head as he tried to explain. "The problem with cuddling is that I fall asleep in about three seconds. Your body's just too warm, and I'm used to sleeping against you."

Tugging her lip between her teeth, she processed his words. They made sense logically, but her heart wasn't getting the message. "Can't we try? I can make a video."

A brow arched over those gunmetal gray eyes. "That's a lot of videos to watch when you wake up, sweetheart."

"I'll make one to watch first. Come on." Shooing him off the bed, she lifted the covers, urging him to crawl under. "Leave the underwear on. That's definitely less creepy."

A laugh escaped his lips. "Dani, it's not going to work—"

"In. Bed." She pointed under the covers. "Now. You just banged me senseless, and I want to cuddle, mister."

His features contorted with love and affection as he contemplated. Inhaling a deep breath, he nodded and slid in beside her, taking the side closest to the wall so she could reach the nightstand.

"Okay," she said, picking up the note that said *Watch Me, Dani* and making sure it was visible on the nightstand surface. Shimmying underneath the covers, she threw her leg over Maverick's thighs, pressing against him as she lifted the phone high and pressed record.

"Dani, you're going to be scared shitless and that's okay, but take a look at this man." Glancing at Maverick, she planted a kiss on the tip of his nose before turning back to the phone. "He just gave you two amazing orgasms, and you refused to let him leave. *You* asked *him* to stay. He's very special to you, and I need you to not freak out."

Turning her head on the pillow, she grinned. "Now, tell future Dani you won't hurt her."

"I won't hurt you." The words surrounded her as he stroked her hair, gazing into her eyes instead of looking at the camera. "I love you, Dani."

Glancing back at the screen, she gave a cheeky grin. "Dani, if you mess this up, I'm disowning you. You're safe with Maverick, and you still need to ask him why his parents gave him that ridiculous name."

He rolled his eyes at her teasing.

"Now, go watch the next two videos and they'll explain everything. Be cool, okay? You scored a super-hot dude, and you have *way* more important shit you need to focus on. Capisce? Bye for now." She waved at the screen before saving the video and placing the phone on the nightstand and clicking off the lamp.

Turning into his body, she nuzzled against him, releasing a satisfied sigh when his strong arms surrounded her. Sated and content, she inhaled his musky sandalwood scent until her eyes drifted closed.

Chapter 20

Dani clawed toward consciousness, trying to escape the darkness as her eyelids fluttered. Opening them wide, she gasped, turning her head on the pillow to survey her surroundings. A man lay next to her, his broad back facing her. He appeared to be naked, and her eyes drifted to where the sheet rested against his waist. Why was she in bed with a naked man? Had she gotten drunk and had a one-night stand? It was certainly against her nature, but her sleepy brain couldn't devise any other plausible scenarios.

Looking toward the other side of the room, she noticed a note on the nightstand beside a cell phone. *Watch me, Dani.* Although she desperately wanted to run, her arm reached for the phone, almost as if in slow motion, and lifted it. Tapping the screen, she pulled up the videos. With a nervous glance toward the man softly snoring beside her, she pressed play.

Confusion clouded her brain as she watched herself on the screen. In bed. With flushed cheeks and a bright smile, stating everything would be okay. That she was safe.

The man next to her stirred, slowly rolling over until he pierced her with his deep gaze. Sliding his hands underneath his cheek, he relaxed into the pillow, watching her as she debated starting the next video.

He remained quiet, and she didn't sense any danger. Looking back at the phone, she played the next video.

In all, there were three videos, all of them explaining the events of the past few years, her memory loss and who the man next to her was. Her husband. The man next to her was her *husband*.

Setting the phone on the nightstand, she turned to her side, facing him as blood pounded through her veins. Resting her cheek on the pillow, she stared into his eyes, feeling a palpable connection although she'd never laid eyes on him.

Sliding her legs over the cool sheets, she grimaced. Sympathy marred his expression, and he lifted a shoulder. "Last night was the first time in a while. You're probably sore...down there and on your side. You had an unfortunate incident with a pitchfork."

"Yikes."

His lips twitched. "It's healing nicely and shouldn't hurt too badly anymore."

The deep timbre of his voice soothed her as she studied him. As her mind processed the wealth of information she'd just absorbed, her nostrils flared. Shaking her head on the pillow, she asked softly, "How many people did I hurt?"

"Sweetheart," he said, gingerly moving closer, asking permission with his eyes and open expression.

Dani nodded, and he drew her into his arms. Clutching on for dear life, she buried her face in his neck and let the tears fall.

Minutes later, she told herself to get it together and lifted her head to look at her...husband. Resting her face in her hand as her elbow dug into the mattress, she tenderly touched his nose. Tracing the angular feature, she continued tracing his eyebrows before reaching the skin beneath his eyes, marred with slight wrinkles that were way too sexy. Moving toward his chin, she caressed the stubble there.

"Maverick," she whispered, the name slow on her tongue as she felt it out. "At least your parents didn't name you Goose."

"Every fucking time," he droned, playfully rolling his eyes.

Although she was an emotional wreck, his sentiment was funny and she breathed a laugh. "Is it your real name?"

Full lips curved as he nodded. "It was the movie my parents watched on their first date when they were seventeen. Dad fell for Mom on the spot, and when they left the theater, he took her hand and told her he was smitten."

"Aw. Cute." Dani bit her lip.

"Yeah. Well, Mom wasn't as into him and told him she wasn't feeling it. Dad bet her he could make her fall in love with him. She thought him so ridiculous she almost laughed him off the sidewalk and told him if he accomplished the task of making her fall in love with him, she'd name their first kid Maverick."

"Yikes. Talk about a hell of a bet."

Chuckling, he nodded. "Well, she lost, but in the end, they both won. They had a very happy marriage and had me. I was their only kid or maybe they would've had a 'Goose.' We'll never know."

"Where are they now?" Dani asked, hoping they hadn't been a casualty of the drug she'd created.

"They'd already retired to Florida when shit hit the fan with EverLife. There was a cruise ship senior citizens could buy a lifetime ticket for if they had enough money. Mom and Dad had just enough. I urged them to go, and I imagine they're somewhere safe in the Atlantic Ocean enjoying the last years of their life. I want them as far away from what's left of society as possible."

"And if we save everyone?" she asked, resting her hand at the juncture of his neck and shoulder. "Can I meet them?"

"They love you," he said, chucking her nose. "And yes, if it's ever safe for them to return to land, I'd love for them to meet you again if you haven't regained your memory. Especially if we can set things right *and* have a baby. They'd be amazing grandparents."

"A baby," she whispered, fear squeezing her throat as she tried to accept the fact she'd fallen asleep a single scientist in New York City and woken up a married amnesiac. "How old am I now? Thirty?"

"Plus five years, slugger." His lips formed a tender smile. "But still as beautiful as the day I met you."

Swallowing the lump of emotion, her brain scrambled to accept she'd lost so many years. Anger and frustration swelled before it was overtaken by the rumbling of her stomach.

"I know it's overwhelming, but you need to eat." Smoothing her hair, he smiled, and her insides quivered from the flash of his straight, white teeth. "Arianna and Raquel are here, and you can meet Dominic...again."

"You said we haven't..." Gazing down, she pressed her thighs together. "Do we...uh...do that often?"

"No," he said, shaking his head. "But apparently, you've been making some naughty notes in your journal, Dr. Lawson-Ward. I might have to punish you." Mirth sparkled in his eyes, along with a hefty dose of desire. "I will say, this is the first morning I've woken up beside you and you haven't tried to slug me, so we're definitely making progress."

A tiny laugh escaped her lungs. "You're funny."

"One of the reasons you fell for me," he said, his tone cocky as he arched a brow. "You never had a chance, babe. This face with my sense of humor?" He pointed at himself. "I had you from Day One."

"I'm not sure about that, but I'm open to hearing the story." Pushing up from the mattress, she grinned. "On that note, I'm guessing we have a lot of shit to accomplish."

Rising, he pecked her lips before climbing out of bed. "We definitely do. We're going to break into a highly secure lab and steal a secret antidote in a few days." Extending his hand, he waited. "Can't wait to tell you how we plan to do it."

Placing her hand in his, she rose to start another day and learn everything again for the very first time.

Chapter 21

The next few days were serious and solemn as the crew prepared for the break-in at the Sendaxa lab. They all knew the plan presented serious challenges, but the time for action had arrived.

The plan was simple. Dominic and Arianna would approach the building first, attacking the Sen Force soldiers who guarded the outside. Then, they would blow open the front doors with the homemade IEDs and continue down the long hallways, taking out guards along the way until they made it to the lab. Maverick and Dani would follow behind, Maverick armed to protect his wife the entire way.

Dani would scan her finger to open the hidden secure biolab compartment, which would lead them to the second door with the unknown ten-digit code. Arianna would keep watch outside as Dominic and Maverick blew open the door and Dani retrieved the antidote. Then, they would high-tail it out of Bethesda and reconvene with Raquel, who would be waiting ten miles away in a hidden wooded area.

After that, they would head to the first black-market compound and make contact with the leader in the hopes he or she was receptive. If so, they would find lodging with a generator, set up a makeshift lab and Dani would replicate the retrieved antidote.

As the team sat in the living room one morning, two days before the break-in, Arianna rubbed her hand over her head as she sighed. "We've gone over it a thousand times now, guys." Standing, she began to pace, flexing her fingers as she paced back and forth. "I can't do it anymore. We've got it. Even Dani's got it," she said, pointing at her sister, "and she can't remember shit."

"Thanks," Dani mumbled, rolling her eyes.

"Well, it's true," Arianna said, slicing her hand through the air. "Dom, let's spar before it rains. I need to kick someone's ass before the sky opens up. See you outside."

Stalking from the room, she disappeared down the hallway before the front door slammed, causing Dani to flinch.

"She's just tense," Dominic said, standing and rubbing the back of his neck. "We all are. Tristan said he might leave weapons in the shed but, so far, nothing. Of course, we have no reason to trust him, but extra weapons would be nice. See you all in a bit."

Once his broad shoulders retreated, Raquel stood, wiping her palms on her pants. "I need some fresh air too. I'll be back in a few."

She flitted from the room, leaving Dani and Maverick alone.

"Everyone is tense as hell," Maverick said, harshly rubbing his forehead. "We need to be aligned if we're going to succeed."

"We're only human," Dani reassured him, rubbing his shoulder as they sat on the couch. "It's normal to feel anxious."

"Yeah." Blowing out a breath, he stood. "Come on. Let's take a break and clear our heads before it rains."

They headed outside, strolling around the house before stopping at the shed behind the kitchen. "This is where Tristan is supposed to leave weapons for us?"

"Yes," Maverick said, lifting the latch. "But so far, we haven't seen—" Breaking off, his eyes widened as he opened the door.

"Maverick?"

"Holy shit," he said, drawing the door back so they could both look inside.

"Whoa," Dani said, taking in the menagerie of rifles and handguns that sat strewn on the dirty wooden floor. "Guess ol' Tristan came through after all."

Eyes filled with disbelief and relief cemented to hers. "Well, I'll be damned. I guess he did."

Straightening her spine, Dani steeled herself. "Do I know how to shoot these?"

"I've done some target practice with you and Raquel, but neither of you are fans of semi-automatic rifles. You're both better with a handgun. Raquel carries one sometimes when she heads out on her own and wants space from Arianna and Dominic."

"Fine. Select a handgun for me and let's go practice. You, Arianna and Dominic are fierce, but I should be armed too."

Hesitating, he lifted his brows. "You sure, slugger? We're trained soldiers and I'm confident we can protect you."

"I'm sure." Extending her hand, she turned her palm up. "Give me a gun and let's practice."

Cocking his head, he said, "All right, then. Fair warning: I get really turned on when you hold a gun."

Tossing back her head, she broke into joyful laughter. "Then we *really* need to practice. Let's do it."

Chapter 22

Tristan stood in the shadows, the forest dim from the tall oaks that offered shelter. He'd come to drop off the weapons and had parked at the other end of the forest so his jeep wasn't spotted. At the edge of the trees, a row of mushrooms grew in the grass where the meadow began. A woman bent down, tugging several of the mushrooms from the ground. Every so often, she would grunt if one was stuck, but eventually, she would remove it and continue on.

Careful to remain silent, he watched her work. Eyeing the mushrooms, he wondered why she was picking that particular variety. Curious, he deliberately stepped on a twig, crunching it with his boot to alert her of his presence.

Whirling around, she dropped the basket and placed her hand over her heart. Wide, light green eyes roved over him as he approached. Reaching into her pocket, she pulled out a gun. Lifting it, her hands violently shook as she aimed it straight at him.

"Don't move a muscle, buddy, or I'll blast a bullet into your heart."

Chuckling, he stepped forward, silently admiring her fortitude. From what he'd heard, Raquel Lawson was the quiet younger sister who lived in Danica's shadow. He hadn't expected her to have grit.

"You've got the safety on," he said, arching a brow. "Can't really blow my brains out unless you fix that."

She emitted a frustrated huff before sticking her tongue between her teeth and fiddling with the safety. Closing the distance between them, he yanked the weapon from her hand and tossed it aside.

"Hey!"

"Calm down, little mouse," he said. "I'm not going to hurt you."

"Well, I might hurt *you*," she said, her eyes darting to the gun. "I can dive for that thing, and I'm closer."

"Let's save the drama," he muttered. "Now, why don't you do me a favor"—he gestured toward the basket—"and tell me why you're picking poisonous mushrooms."

"I don't have to tell you anything." Lowering to pick up the basket, she turned and attempted to walk away. Tristan grabbed her arm, tugging her back and stilling her. Fury flashed in her eyes as she glanced down at the basket.

"Don't try and hit me with it," he said, surprised at the mirth in his tone. "My cause of death can't be 'death by basket.' That's really lame."

"Who are you and why are you following me?" she asked through clenched teeth.

"You answer mine and I'll answer yours. Why are you picking false morels? They're toxic."

"None of your fucking business."

Tristan smirked, unable to believe the frumpy-clothed woman was holding her ground. She was young with an air of innocence that reminded him of Jessica before things turned so horribly wrong. Noting the protective swell, he studied her.

"You can't use those in any foods or formulas..." he murmured, rubbing his chin before recognition dawned. "Unless you want to harm someone."

"Small doses of toxic fungi help with efficacy of formulas and teas," she said, jutting out her chin. "Not that I would expect *you* to know that. It's something only a botanist with years of training could comprehend."

Tristan grunted, doubtful but willing to admit he was no scientist.

"My sister is sparring just over that hill." Her finger jutted toward the horizon, which was rapidly filling with dark clouds. "If I scream, she'll be here in a heartbeat. If she sees you harassing me, she'll kill you."

Nonplussed by her threat, Tristan rocked back on his heels, taking in her appearance as he pondered. She was different than the rich, snooty women he was used to inside the walls of the District. Her innocence hadn't been shattered by their dark world, and he found himself hoping it never would be. He hadn't been able to save Jessica from traversing her torrid path, but he hoped this woman never felt the ravages of addiction or pain.

"*Excuse you*," she droned, waving her hand in front of his face. "I'm going to tell you one more time. Leave me alone—"

"I just dropped a shit-ton of weapons in your shed," he interjected, pointing toward the farmhouse. "So I don't appreciate the tone."

Her expression fell as she studied him. "Thank you. That will help the others with the raid."

Tristan's eyes darted between hers. "You aren't joining them?"

"I'm not a soldier" was her soft reply as she shook her head. "They're going to reconvene with me when they're finished."

"Hmm..." Narrowing his eyes, he asked. "And what will you do if they fail?"

"Failure isn't an option."

Admiration surged at her confidence, even though it was unwarranted. Although he hoped Dani and her team succeeded, the chances were small.

Stepping back, he placed his hands on his hips and regarded her. "If they fail, you're welcome to search me out in the District. You'll need protection if they don't return to claim you."

She scoffed. "Thanks, but I'm all set."

Before he could respond, a gun discharged from the far-off hill, and Tristan could see Arianna Lawson's tall figure as she sprinted toward them.

"Gotta go," he mumbled, turning to jog back into the forest. Looking back over his shoulder, he warned, "Don't die because you're stubborn. Search me out if you need me."

Her muttered *"Like hell"* followed him into the woods as he ran back to his jeep and started the engine. Hightailing it back to the District, his thoughts drifted to Raquel Lawson. She had a conflicting purity and defiance that didn't make sense to his logical brain.

Tristan lived in absolutes. A person was generally good or evil in his world. There was no in between. But for some reason, as he drove on the withered gravel, he couldn't shake the feeling there was more to Raquel Lawson than met the eye.

Chapter 23

Dani rushed to meet Raquel and Arianna as they hurried to the back door. Rain fell in large drops, intensifying as her sisters stepped inside. Worried, Dani gripped their shoulders.

"Are you okay? We heard a gunshot."

"Thank you for checking on me," Raquel said, pulling Arianna into a hug. "He snuck up on me and I was terrified." Drawing back, she looked at Dani. "I was picking mushrooms, but I dropped them all when he confronted me. I was going to try putting false morels in a tea tomorrow. They have a slight toxin known to increase memory output. If you'd agree to drink it, which I know you probably won't." She gave a resigned shrug.

"A slight toxin, huh? Should I be worried?" Dani teased.

"I would've tried it first," Raquel said, grinning. "And you know as well as I do that a small amount of toxicity can jumpstart neuron function."

"That's true," Dani said with a nod. "Enough about mushrooms. I'm just glad you're okay." Slipping her arm over Raquel's shoulders, she led her into the living room.

Arianna followed, and they sat on the couch as Dominic and Maverick entered.

"Do we know who the perp was?" Dominic asked.

"I'm assuming it was Tristan Holder," Arianna said. "Six two, black hair, lean but muscular?"

"That's him," Maverick said with a nod. "He must've been returning to his vehicle after dropping off the weapons."

"Well, he scared the crap out of me," Raquel said, expelling a breath as she held her hand over her heart and sank into the couch. "Geez."

"I didn't deem him a threat, especially since he left us the weapons," Maverick said, his brow furrowing. "Did he threaten you?"

"No. He was just an arrogant jerk. If I see him again, I'm going to kick him in the balls."

"Atta girl," Arianna said, rising and patting her sister on the shoulder. "I always knew you had it in you. Come on, guys." She gestured toward Dominic and Maverick. "We need to check on the IEDs in the barn. The rain is harder than I expected, and we're probably going to need to plug some leaks so we don't ruin the explosives before we have a chance to use them."

Maverick stood, cupping Raquel's shoulder and squeezing. "Do you need anything from me?"

Dani's heart quivered at the reverent show of affection from her husband toward her sister.

"I'm fine. Thank you, Mav."

"Sure thing." After placing a tender kiss on Raquel's forehead, he followed Dominic and Arianna through the doorway.

"Whew," Dani said, scooting closer to Raquel and rubbing her arm in soothing strokes. "Close call."

"Yeah. I'm fine now. Sorry I freaked."

"It's okay. That must've been scary as hell. Where were you picking mushrooms?"

"Over by the edge of the forest."

Gnawing her lip, Dani saw the logic of trying something different. "I see why you wanted to try, but I'm done with the teas, Raquel. I've had more flashbacks without them anyway."

"Thank god."

Wetness clouded Dani's eyes as she studied her little sister. "I'm scared to leave you while we raid the lab," she said, the words thick with emotion. "What if something happens to you?"

"I'll be fine," Raquel said, drawing her into a hug. "You're going to steal back the antidote, and I'm going to help you create a kick-ass remedy that will cure everyone. As I told Tristan, failure isn't an option."

"I love you," Dani said, drawing back and chucking her chin. "Mom made me promise to take care of you, and I take that vow very seriously."

"I can take care of myself," Raquel said, smoothing a hand over Dani's hair. "You're the important one in this scenario."

"Don't say that." Dani squeezed her hand. "You're important too, Raquel."

Something flashed across her face—so quickly Dani almost missed it—and then the reverent expression returned before she stood. Wiping her palms on her thighs, she uttered a soft "Thanks. I'm going to take a shower. I just need some time to process the encounter. It was intense."

"Of course. Let me know if you need anything."

Raquel nodded before scampering away. Resting back on the couch, Dani crossed her legs, her foot shaking back and forth as she contemplated. Tensions were high and they all were on edge. Hopefully, they would regain some composure before the raid.

If they didn't, Dani worried they would make mistakes, and mistakes were unacceptable. Fear crept in as the importance of their mission preyed on her weary soul.

Chapter 24

The next afternoon, Arianna clenched her jaw as she fired several rounds into the target. She didn't want to waste them, but it was important her aim was sure for the raid. And, if she was being honest, she was pissed as hell that Tristan Holder had approached her sister without Arianna knowing. It was her duty to protect her sisters, and her failure to uphold that vow churned in her gut as her finger pulled the trigger.

Lowering her gun, she cursed as she realized she was out of bullets. She didn't want to use any more since they needed them for the raid, so she clicked the safety in place before throwing the gun on the ground in a completely pointless, annoyed gesture that alleviated a twinge of her frustration.

"You're supposed to shoot it," Dominic's voice called behind her. "Not throw it."

Whirling around, she almost took pity on him. He'd picked the wrong time to meddle with her, and she was good and ready to attack. Sucking in a breath, she pointed her finger in his face and opened verbal fire.

"You son of a bitch! If you ever sneak up on me again, especially when I have a gun in my hand, I'll stick it in your neck and fire a bullet right into your jugular."

The sun was beginning to set over the horizon, leaving gorgeous streaks of orange and yellow in the cloud-filled sky. His scar seemed to glow in the warm colors as he scowled, and Arianna wondered if he was going to yell back. Usually, when she ripped into him, he responded with acerbic comebacks that shot tiny little thrills down her spine. She loved verbally sparring with him more than physically sparring, and that was saying a *lot* since she wasn't a big fan of talking in general.

"Well?" she asked, extending her hands at her sides as exasperation consumed her. "Are you just going to stand there? No quippy comebacks today?"

Approaching her slowly, as if she were a snake about to strike, he drew close enough she could smell his evergreen scent. His proximity shot all sorts of unwanted rushes to her nether regions, filling her with rage. Flaring her nostrils, she wavered between the urge to scream and the yearning to close her eyes and inhale his musky scent until it invaded every corner of her lungs.

He opened his mouth to speak, hesitating as he worked his jaw. Finally, he said softly, "What happened to Raquel isn't your fault."

"Yeah? Tell that to my dead mother. I promised to protect them. *Both* of them."

"And you do. Brilliantly. But even you aren't perfect, Arianna."

Scoffing, she kicked the ground with her toe. "I never claimed to be perfect."

He blinked several times, as if processing what to say next. His indecision drove her insane considering it went against his nature. One of the things she loved about Dom was his assurance and confidence. Clenching her fists so she didn't do something awful like punch him, she began to stomp off. "I don't have time for this—"

"Ari," he said, encircling her arm. "Wait."

Yanking her arm from his grasp, she picked up the gun lying in the nearby grass and aimed it directly at his face. "I told you never to grab my arm again," she uttered through clenched teeth.

Sighing, he rubbed his hand over his short hair, frustration emanating from his large frame. "You're out of bullets, but you can point it at me all day if it makes you feel better."

"What will make me *feel* better is if we accomplish our mission so I can get on with my damn life. I can reclaim my independence, and Raquel can live with you three weirdos who don't seem to give a shit you're both in love with the same woman."

Anger flashed in his eyes as he studied her. "You know, I always wondered why it bothered you so much. My feelings for Dani." Stepping closer, he balked when she cocked the gun, the gesture symbolic even though it held no bullets. "Jesus, Ari. Why the fuck do you even care? You obviously hate me."

A sob escaped her throat, sending shockwaves of embarrassment through her frame at the small outburst of emotion. Arianna never exhibited uncontrolled emotion, especially near Dominic, who was smart enough to sense her feelings if she slipped and bared herself to him. Craving solace, she tossed the gun to the ground and began to stalk away.

"Ari—"

"Leave me alone!" she yelled, angrily swiping a tear that never should've fallen. God-damnit. Tears had no place in their world. What the fuck was wrong with her?

Clutching onto the silver lining that tomorrow they would attack the lab and begin the next phase of their lives, she took several calming breaths as she stalked across the nearby field. Stepping into the adjacent woods, she collapsed to the ground and rested her back against one of the thick oak trees as she drew her knees to her chest and began to rock.

Placing her hand over her pounding heart, she cursed her feelings for the millionth time.

"Get it together, Ari," she chided, gently rapping the back of her head against the tree. "You aren't the first person to fall for someone in love with someone else, and you won't be the last. This emotional baggage has got to go. Tomorrow's a big fucking day."

Willing her heartbeat to return to normal, she reminded herself there were more important things at stake than her stupid heart. After the break-in, she could sulk and rail at the world all she wanted. *Alone.* As she damn well preferred.

Rising, she wiped the dirt off her butt, inhaled a deep breath and strode back to the house, determined to keep her feelings buried so deep inside they no longer existed.

After dinner, the mood was heavy as everyone packed and prepared to leave the following morning. Once his meager belongings were stuffed into his backpack, Dominic walked outside to place it in the truck, craving fresh air.

The bed of the truck was filled with the weapons Tristan had supplied and the IEDs he and Arianna had made together. Smirking, Dominic found it fitting he and the stubborn woman had found one thing they could make together without killing each other: bombs. Yep, that sounded about right, considering the way she'd blown up on him earlier.

Dominic had no idea why she detested him so vehemently. He figured it sprang from the protective streak she carried for Dani, but she had to realize by now he would never harm Dani or act on his feelings. They were a shield more than anything and helped him cope in a life where he'd lost every person he loved.

Halting on his trek back to the house, he spotted Arianna in the moonlight. Tall and regal, she stood facing the far-off hills, her eyes closed as she inhaled the warm air. Her half hair was in a braid, cascading over her shoulder to rest against the curve of her breast under her tight black tank top.

Dominic had never seen Arianna in any state of vulnerability. She always carried an air of impenetrable toughness. But now, watching her in the shadows, he stood frozen, mesmerized at finally seeing the woman inside. As the silver light washed over her skin, she appeared...sad. Something cracked in his chest at her forlorn expression, and he realized it was his heart. Placing his palm over the organ, he rubbed, barely able to breathe as he gazed at her.

She slid her fingers to the back of her neck, massaging the tense muscles as she sighed. Blood pounded in his veins as the image of replacing her fingers with his own took shape. What would she do if he trailed toward her, gently pushing her hand away so *he* could comfort her instead?

Had anyone ever comforted Arianna? Frowning, Dominic realized it was doubtful. Arianna was a protector. A warrior who felt it her duty to show strength so others could achieve their dreams and goals. When Maverick had asked her to join their cause, she didn't hesitate.

It was noble and selfless to put others' goals and dreams before her own, but what did that mean for *her?* Didn't she have dreams she wished to fulfill? Strangely, the need to find out roared inside, and Dominic promised himself he would be gentler with her. He'd always been harsh to mirror her tone, which was as far away from puppies and butterflies as humanly possible. But now, observing the slight hunch of her shoulders and the heartbreaking aura of loneliness surrounding her, he realized it was a defense mechanism.

If there was one thing Dominic excelled at, it was defense mechanisms. He'd had his own iron-clad defenses for years.

Inwardly chiding himself for lingering longer than he should have during her moment of solace, Dominic forced his legs to move. Entering the kitchen, he headed to his room, content to enjoy the soft bed. It might be the last time he slept in one for the foreseeable future, and he would relish a good night's sleep.

Usually, as he drifted off, his mind would remain blank, pushing away the day's events so he could reset during slumber and wake up fresh. But tonight, for some inexplicable reason, he fell asleep to the image of Arianna's neck glistening in the moonlight as her fingers massaged the soft flesh.

Chapter 25

Maverick rose with Dani as the sun was peeking over the horizon. After watching the videos, she understood that today held great importance. As light streamed through the window, she felt grateful they would have a sunny day for the raid. Although she wasn't superstitious, she decided to take it as a good omen. Perhaps they would prevail and begin to set things right.

After breakfast, they huddled in the living room to go over the plan one last time. Around noon, they placed their bags in the bed of the pickup truck and tidied up the home. Perhaps someone else would find it in their travels and it could offer them safe haven as well. Closing the doors behind them, Maverick slid behind the wheel of the truck as Dani and Raquel sat beside him. Dominic and Arianna sat in the bed of the truck, tasked with keeping an eye on the explosives. They weren't set to ignite without being lit with the lighter Dominic had found in one of the kitchen drawers, but one could never be too safe.

They drove over unkept roads, some gravel and some paved, and Dani noted the eeriness of her surroundings. There were no other cars on the road, no people to pass, and the vastness of the consequences of her actions overwhelmed her. Because of her, people had been pushed into black-market compounds or walled-off cities to seek shelter. Society had been irrevocably altered, and the journey back seemed daunting.

"You okay?" Maverick asked, reaching over and squeezing her hand as they puttered along in the truck.

She nodded and willed the emotion away, understanding it wouldn't solve anything. Only their actions could set things right.

The stumps of downed utility poles dotted the horizon, confirming she'd relegated the world to darkness. They passed a row of houses that had been badly burned. Only a few shards of glass remained in the shattered windows. The front doors were marked with red or black *X*s, and she wondered what they meant. Most likely red for houses where bodies remained and black for homes that were merely abandoned.

Who was left to bury the dead? How many had died, addicted and alone?

When they passed a large field, Dani craned her neck, attempting to identify the mass of crumpled metal in the tall grass.

"It's a helicopter," Maverick said. "Or, it was. Probably ran out of gas and crashed. Hopefully the pilot and passengers survived."

"I hope so," Dani said softly, overcome with the devastation. Tears burned her eyes, but she knew they were pointless. Crying wouldn't resolve the situation. Action was her only course.

Twenty miles from Bethesda, they spotted two forms in the distance, lying on the side of the road. Maverick slowed, parking several yards away before exiting and drawing his handgun.

"You two stay here," he said to Dani and Raquel. "Dominic, come with me. Arianna, keep them safe."

Arianna gave a salute from the bed of the truck as Dominic hopped out and pulled his gun. Their broad shoulders grew smaller as they approached the bodies, and Dani lifted her fingers to her lips as she observed Maverick kneel and shake his head. The scientist in her yearned to examine the situation, needing to understand what happened. Disregarding Maverick's orders, she exited the truck and approached.

"Sweetheart," he said, rising and showing her his palms. "You don't want to see this."

"What did they die of?" she asked, inching closer. "Were they addicts?"

"It appears so," Dominic said, his tone sad. "They exhibit the traits of EverLife addiction."

Swallowing thickly, she lifted her chin and urged Maverick to step aside. "I need to see the damage, Maverick. It will only make my resolve stronger."

Deep eyes contemplated before he nodded and backed away. Stepping toward the two bodies, Dani gasped as she took in their disheveled corpses. Dark bags stretched under their eyes, which barely seemed attached to the sockets. The female's mouth was open, showing only one tooth and gums that were rotted and scabbed. The man's lips were chapped and caked with dried blood, and there were infected puncture wounds in the crook of both his elbows.

"They were shooting it intravenously," she murmured, crouching to get closer. "It was destroying them from the inside out."

"The bodies aren't decomposed, so they must've died recently," Dominic said.

"Two lives ended with such senselessness," Dani said, pressing her fist to her mouth so she wouldn't scream.

"Hey," Maverick said, encircling her arm and pulling her to stand. "That's not going to help us here, Dani. Your sadness and guilt are justified, but focusing on it just makes things worse."

Glancing back at the bodies, she expelled a long, slow breath. "You're right. We need to bury them though. It's the least I owe them. To give them a proper resting place."

"We'll bury them," Dominic said, cupping her shoulder. "There's a shovel in the truck bed I decided to bring with us. I wasn't sure we'd need it, but you can never have too many blunt objects." Training his gaze on Maverick, he said, "Let's bury them and then get back on the road. We need to drop Raquel off and get to the lab before sundown."

"I can help," Dani offered.

"Let us do it," Maverick said, rubbing her arm. "Go sit with Arianna. Have her tell you about our wedding. She wasn't a fan of Dom's dancing." Dominic scoffed.

They headed back to the truck, Dani crawling in the truck bed with Arianna as Raquel joined them. Dominic and Maverick buried the bodies as the sisters spoke. As they recounted stories about the weekend wedding that happened years before the world fell apart, Dani studied her sisters. Reaching over, she squeezed both of their hands.

"I love you both so much. Thank you for sticking with me after what happened. I understand if part of you wants to hate me for the destruction I caused."

"We could never hate you," Raquel said. "We're family, and Mom would want us to support each other."

"What she said," Arianna uttered, grinning to soften the harsh tone. "You're stuck with us, Dani."

Maverick and Dominic returned, and after washing their hands with some of the soap and water from their supply stash, the trip resumed. Eventually, they made it to the location ten miles from the lab where Raquel would camp until they returned to retrieve her.

Once she was settled in the clearing in the dense woods, she hugged everyone before nervously twisting her fingers as she spoke. "I'll be sending you all the good vibes, guys.

Just think, eight hours from now, you'll be back here with the antidote, and we'll be on our way to making things better. You've got this."

"You remember how to use the gun?" Arianna asked.

"Well enough," Raquel said with a shrug. "It's only a few hours. I'm going to rest in the sleeping bag and try to relax. Don't worry about me. Go kick some ass."

After one last round of hugs, they left their sister behind, ready to enact their plan.

Chapter 26

As the last rays of light glimmered over the horizon, the team arrived at an abandoned parking lot two hundred yards from the Sendaxa lab. Exiting the truck, they began preparing, buckling duty belts and arming themselves with guns, knives and the IEDs. Dani was given a handgun, which Maverick assured her he'd trained her to use, while the three soldiers were much more heavily armed.

They snuck through the woods surrounding the lab, Maverick leading as he observed the entrance. "Two soldiers flanking the door and four additional soldiers visible surrounding the building," he whispered.

"Confirmed," Dominic and Arianna said in unison.

"Dominic, you'll take out the soldiers on the right flank, Arianna will target the ones on the left. Shoot to wound first, but if you need to make a kill shot, do it."

They both nodded.

"Remember the plan?" Maverick asked Dani.

"Once they take out the guards, you and I will head inside. I'm to stay directly behind you in case we encounter guards along the way. You'll lead us to the storage area in the lab where I hid the antidote. I'll scan my finger to unlock the first door, and you'll use the IEDs to blow open the second door. Ari and Dom will keep an eye on the outer hallways to protect us."

"Pretty good for a woman whose memory is broken," he said, pecking her lips. "Remember, stay near me at all times. I can't lose you, Dani."

Dani's heart leapt in her throat as she nodded, the magnitude of the mission truly washing over her. They were going to break in to a heavily guarded lab to steal something that was sealed behind nearly impenetrable locks. The chances of success were slim, at best.

"It's this or let the world continue to crumble, Dani," Maverick said, squeezing her wrist. "We have to try. You won't forgive yourself if we don't."

Exhaling a shaky breath, she straightened her shoulders. "I'm ready."

Her husband flashed a grin filled with admiration and resolve before turning and beginning to advance toward the edge of the woods. Lifting his fist, he extended his fingers and began lowering them in a silent countdown. Three. Two. One. Slicing his hand through the air, he gave the soundless order for Arianna and Dominic to advance.

They crept toward the edge of the trees, Arianna aiming her rifle at the guard on the left side of the door, Dominic aiming at the guard opposite him. They glanced toward each other, and Arianna muttered, "Bet I get a cleaner shot than you."

"You're on, Lawson," he murmured. "Stay close."

Shots fired from each rifle, the sound echoing through the air before each guard clasped a knee cap, screaming before falling to the ground. They writhed in pain as they each gripped their bleeding legs.

"That will keep them down for a bit," Arianna yelled, jogging toward the left side of the lab entrance. "Come on."

Dominic ran to the right flank, both of them taking out the two remaining guards on each side before approaching the front door. After yanking the badge from the writhing guard's neck, she swiped it through the reader that would unlock the door.

"You fucking bitch!" the guard screamed, lifting his handgun as he still clung to his knee with his other hand. Grunting, Arianna kicked him in the face with her boot. His body went lax as he fell unconscious, and Dominic raised his eyebrows. "Nice kick. Does the badge work?"

Arianna swiped it again, her eyes widening with excitement when the little red dot turned from red to green. Pulling open the door, she turned and waved to Dani and Maverick.

Maverick shot Dani a quick nod, and she followed him as he jogged toward the lab. After ushering her inside, he began leading them down the darkened hallway.

"Stay alert," he commanded as Arianna and Dominic flanked them. "Although the lab is no longer functional, Cromwell knows we're coming, according to Tristan. There are cameras everywhere, and who knows who's watching on the other end?"

They rounded a corner, startling a guard who sat in a metal folding chair, head hung as he dozed. Lifting his head, he scrambled for his gun as Arianna held up her rifle. "Don't do it. I've got a clean shot between your eyes. Lower your gun and let us restrain you. Your choice."

The guard's eyes widened as his hand froze on the gun. Nostrils flared as he debated pulling the gun or following Arianna's command.

"You've got two seconds, buddy—"

"Okay," he said, lifting his hands. "Restrain me."

Dominic moved forward, jerking the guard's hands behind his back and tying them with the rope he'd secured on his belt. Instructing the guard to lie down on the concrete floor, he tied his ankles together, removed the man's duty belt and tossed it to the other side of the hallway.

"Come on," he said, jerking his head. "We're almost there."

They continued down the hallway, turning another corner. Dani gasped as she observed the lab before her, enclosed behind glass windows. It was expansive with rows of metal tables lined with all the equipment she would ever need to create plentiful stockpiles of antidote as well as her cancer vaccine. No wonder she'd been lured by the promise of working in the lab. So much opportunity, wasted because evil men wanted to profit on the pain of so many.

Shouts echoed in the distance, and Maverick faced Dominic and Arianna. "I've got four IEDs in my bag and one of the lighters." He patted his backpack. "You two hold off whoever that is so we can grab the antidote."

Arianna began to follow Dominic but turned to squeeze Dani's arm. "See you on the other side, sis. You've got this."

Dani smiled at the display of affection, which was rare from her stoic sister, and whispered, "I love you."

Arianna's lips formed a smile before she pivoted and followed Dominic down the hallway.

Facing her husband, Dani said, "I'm ready."

Covering his fist with a cloth, he punched through the glass door, spraying glass over the floor as he reached inside to grab the handle. Opening it, he ushered her inside. As she trailed through the rows of tables and equipment, something tingled in the far reaches of Dani's mind. The room felt so familiar, and as she glanced at the microscope across the room, she gasped.

"Dani?" Maverick asked, halting and grabbing her hand. "What is it?"

"I remember," she whispered, blood thrumming in her veins as she surveyed the room before staring into her husband's eyes. "I remember...champagne. Did we drink champagne in the lab?"

"Holy shit," he whispered, excitement flashing in his eyes. "We did, but I don't have time to tell you the story now." He tugged her hand, leading her to the secure area in the back of the room.

Once they arrived, he pointed to the pad on the side of the door. "This one needs your index fingerprint."

Lifting her finger, Dani touched the pad. A blue light scanned her finger before several beeps sounded. After a moment, the door clicked open.

"Fuck yes!" Maverick hissed, pushing open the door. Approaching the next door, he pointed at the keypad. "Any chance you remember the ten-digit code since you remember the champagne?"

Massaging her temples, Dani willed herself to remember, but her brain was fogged. "I can't. I'm sorry."

"It's okay. Stand back." Slinging his pack off his back, he pulled out the four IEDs, placing the small containers at the bottom of the door. "This will be loud and alert everyone to our presence. Plug your ears and crouch outside the first door. I'm going to light it, let it blow and then we'll head inside and grab the antidote."

Nodding furiously, Dani followed his orders, stepping back outside and crouching down to hold her ears. The silence was deafening as she waited with bated breath, anticipating the blow. Maverick appeared at her side, lowering beside her before the ground shook. Rising on shaky feet, she followed him back to the door, waving away the smoke as it cleared.

"Okay, you always said the antidote was stashed in a biomedical storage container in this room," he said, pushing open the crumbled door and leading her inside the dark room. "I know nothing about biomedical storage, so this is all you, Dani."

Allowing her eyes to adjust to the dim light, she observed the rows of cylindrical containers. Walking toward the first row, she unlatched the lid and lifted it as a cloud of cold air puffed from inside.

"They're refrigerated," she said, lowering the container when she found it empty. "There must be a different stash. I don't think I would've created an antidote that required refrigeration. It would make it less accessible. We need to find the room temperature storage area."

"How about there?" he asked, pointing to a metal door with a biohazard sign.

"Yes," she said, inching forward. "I wonder if there's a lock..." Feeling the cool metal, she inserted her fingers in the metal ring, drawing it back and tugging. "I think it's stuck." Grunting, she gripped harder and pulled.

"Let me try." Maverick clenched the ring attached to the door, muscles flexing as he yanked. It flew open, revealing a square cabinet built into the wall. Approaching it, Dani grasped the handle and opened the cabinet drawer.

Peering inside, she spotted a white box with a biohazard symbol on top. Reaching inside, she peeled open the lid to find ten vials full of milky liquid. "This is it," she said. "It has to be."

Reaching with both hands, she palmed the box, halting when she heard a *thunk* behind her. Rotating, she saw Maverick fall to the ground, unconscious. Sinking into a surreal dream that was rapidly becoming a nightmare, Dani slowly turned to face the woman holding a crowbar high, ready to strike.

Chapter 27

Dominic heard the sound of boots smacking the hard floor and knew the Sen Force reinforcements were on the way. Arianna jogged beside him, back toward the entrance, and he was thankful she was with him. If they had to fight to the death, he'd relish having her by his side.

They crested the corner, meeting a flurry of bullets before Dominic grabbed her arm and tugged her back into an adjoining hallway. Panting from exertion, he said, "I spotted at least five."

"That's how many I saw," she said, drawing the rifle from behind her shoulder so it hung above her abdomen, ready to be fired. Retrieving her handgun, she cocked it, the movement firm and sure. "I'll attack from left to right and you'll do the opposite."

He nodded, acknowledging their agreed tactical method. Since she was left handed, the strategy gave them the best odds. "I think we need to shoot to kill on this one."

"Fuckers. I know. The vests the guards outside wore left a small opening in the neck. Go for that or the head."

"I'd chide you for bossing me around, but we don't have time."

Her eyes lifted to his, green flecks sparkling in her hazel irises, and she grabbed his sleeve before twisting the fabric. "Don't die. You hear me?"

A small hum ignited in every cell as he stared down at her, wishing he could stop time. Why was her gaze so intense? It was as if he felt her energy wrapping around him, and it was shifting something profound and deep each millisecond.

"Ari—"

"Let's go."

Releasing the fabric, she inhaled a deep breath before charging forward. Dominic followed her, determined to protect Dani and Maverick in the lab, but also to protect

Arianna. There had been something in those limitless eyes he needed to explore, and he'd damn well do it once they were safe.

They surged into the oncoming onslaught, Dominic thankful for the bulletproof vests he'd packed when he originally went on the run. They wouldn't protect every part of their bodies, but they were better than nothing.

Lifting his gun, he squinted one eye, aiming at the guard on the far right and shooting him in the forehead. He fell, causing the guard beside him to trip over his body, and Dominic lodged a bullet in that man's throat. Arianna took out two guards on the left, leaving only one rushing toward them.

Holstering her handgun, Arianna lifted the rifle, unloading a spray of bullets into the man's chest. Before he fell, he discharged one final round and fell to the floor.

Air jetted from Dominic's lungs, and he lifted his hand to his neck, palming the area of his skin that had somehow exploded. Sucking in deep breaths, he realized he was inhaling his own blood. Feeling his eyelids droop, his legs collapsed beneath him and he fell to the ground.

"No!" Arianna screamed, slinging the rifle behind her back and crouching beside him. Resting on her knees, her hands patted his chest before she drew his hand from his bleeding neck. "Fuck!" she cried, pressing her palm to the gushing wound as Dominic choked on his blood. "You're hit."

His lips moved, unable to form words as her arms moved furiously above him. Removing the rifle, she set it on the floor and yanked off her shirt, the expanse of her smooth skin glowing around her black sports bra. Balling her shirt, she pressed it to his wound, the pressure causing Dom to howl in pain.

"I know it hurts. We have to stop the bleeding. Can you breathe? Damn it, Dom. I need you to breathe." Pulling him to a sitting position, she pushed his back against the cinderblock wall, opening his airway a bit as she held compression. "That should help."

Dominic saw something over her shoulder. Just a tiny blip as someone passed between the hallways in the distance. Was it Raquel? No, it couldn't be. They'd left her in the woods, right? Overcome with pain, Dominic's mind was muddled as he tried to retain consciousness.

"Someone's...here..." he sputtered, attempting to point toward where he'd seen the flash. "Have to go to Dani and Mav. Trouble..."

"I can't leave you here," she said, her voice more erratic than he'd ever heard. Arianna was always so composed. So infallible. But now, as he felt the life dripping from his bones, he saw the emotion she kept buried deep inside.

"Ari," he whispered, lifting his bloody hand to cup her cheek. "Can't...save...me. Go..."

A sob tore from her throat as she shook her head. Her chin trembled as she maneuvered the shirt, pressing it tighter against his skin.

"It's okay..."

"Dominic..." Emotion swirled in her eyes, laced with such agony he longed to draw it from her. Squeezing her jaw, he silently urged her to leave him.

Staring deep into his eyes, she shook her head, her gaze unblinking as she let him finally see her. Past all the walls and the suppressed emotion, Dominic finally understood why she hated him so vehemently.

Because it wasn't hate after all. Arianna Lawson's brilliant orbs gazed at him, filled with all the unrequited love she felt for him and he'd never even thought to give her. What a waste. All this time, he'd hidden behind a false love for Dani to protect himself when Arianna had been beside him the entire time. And now, he was going to die before he could do a damn thing about it.

"You can't die," she rasped through clenched teeth, shaking her head as she pressed the shirt to his neck. "You son of a bitch, if you die, I'm going to murder you myself. Do you fucking hear me?"

Dominic tried to laugh at the nonsensical words, although the sound was garbled by the blood mixed with the air in his throat. Moving his hand to hers atop the compress, he tried to tug it away. "I'll hold...you go... Dani needs you..."

Pain flashed in her eyes, and he wanted to kick himself, knowing she interpreted his statement as yet another avowal of love for her sister. If he only had more time, he'd tell her he hadn't known. Hadn't even fathomed she cared for him. That his love for Dani had been a shield because he was too scared to love again.

That, for her, if they had just a bit more time, he might be willing to try.

Cursing the fates that led them here, he slumped to the floor, unable to support the weight of his body any longer.

"Hold this tight," she said, leaning over him as he rested on his back. "I'll be back soon." Leaning forward until their noses grazed, she gritted one last time, "Don't. Fucking. Die. I mean it, you son of a bitch." Closing her eyes, she rested her forehead against his for a moment that lasted an eternity. Then, she rose, slung her rifle back over her shoulder and ran to help her sister.

CHAPTER 28

D ani's mouth fell open as she observed her husband unconscious on the ground. Furious heartbeats clamored in her chest as she slowly lifted her gaze. Focusing on eyes similar to her own, a sob escaped her lips as her legs threatened to collapse. Betrayal, thick and suffocating, circulated through her veins as she worked her jaw, unable to speak due to the pervasive shock.

"You really should've trusted your little notes, Dani," Raquel said, her tone menacing as she held the crowbar high. "Now Maverick's down for the count, and I'm sorry to say, you're next."

"How did you get here?" Dani asked, shock pervading her veins.

"I'm not an idiot, contrary to what you all think," she spat. "I found a car nearby and hotwired it as soon as you left. Pretty resilient for your boring little sister, huh?" she taunted, rapidly blinking as she smirked.

Pain speared through Dani's brain, and she pressed her palms to her temples as a memory surged deep within. *The sound of sirens blaring as Sendaxa ordered everyone out of the lab. Rushing to this very room to retrieve the antidote. Hearing someone behind her and whirling to see who it was...*

She'd assumed it was a guard, even though she heard Raquel's voice in the background too...and she'd turned to find her sister, standing in the same position she was now...holding a crowbar high before slamming it down on her head.

"You were the one who hit me!" Dani exclaimed, outraged and heartbroken at her sister's betrayal. "Why would you do that?"

Scoffing, Raquel's eyes filled toxic rage, causing anguish to churn in Dani's gut. "Because you're so fucking *perfect,* right, Dani? Why would anyone hurt you?"

"I don't understand," she said, extending her hands. "I love you, Raquel—"

"Shut up!" Advancing forward, Raquel lifted the crowbar higher. "Just shut the fuck up. You've taken from me my entire life and relished having me in your shadow. That ends today. I'm going to be the one who leaves here with the antidote, and I'm going to *finally* earn something on my own for once."

"What the hell are you talking about?"

"You just couldn't let me have *anything*, could you?" Her chin warbled, showing a brief moment of indecision. "I didn't want to hurt you, Dani, but you just can't get out of my way."

"I don't understand—"

"The job here?" She gestured with her hand. "I applied and was more than qualified, but no, you had to swoop in and meddle to make sure I got it. It was the same thing when I applied at Columbia. You just can't help yourself."

"I was trying to help you!" Dani said, exasperated. "I want the best for you, Raquel. I always have."

"Have you?" Arching a brow, she inched closer. "Because you took the final moments I'd ever have with her, and you didn't even care. Why would you? You always thought yourself so fucking important. So much better than me."

Dani struggled to understand her cryptic words. "With Mom?"

"Yes, with Mom," she hissed. "Arianna got to say goodbye, and then you went in after her. You were only supposed to stay a few minutes, but you lingered because you thought your goodbye was more important than mine. Who needed to say goodbye to the ugly, imperfect daughter? The afterthought? You created that role for me and I hate it! You've kept me in a gilded cage, and I won't live in your shadow anymore."

Tears burned Dani's eyes as she regarded the person she loved more than anyone in the world, along with Arianna. Her sisters were her rocks, and her mind was struggling to process the intense hatred in Raquel's green eyes. Swiping away a tear, she emitted a soft sob. "All along, it was you who gave me amnesia."

"Yes. My plan was to steal the antidote and take it to the District to make a deal with Luthor Cromwell. They had just started to wall off the cities, and I knew he would need scientists. This time, I could secure my *own* future."

"But he's evil, Raquel—"

"I don't think you have any room to point fingers," she said, arching a brow. "After all, you're the one who created this disaster. I tried to tell you the EverLife formula would be too addictive. You were so sure the poppy extracts wouldn't be a problem. So sure that people would stick to the recommended dose. Your optimism has always been your downfall."

"Did you know that Sendaxa falsified the clinical trial data?"

Malicious laughter exited her throat. "For god's sake, Dani, wake up! Sendaxa is the most powerful company in the world, and EverLife was a goldmine. Of course I knew. They paid off the FDA regulators and sent it into full production. The consumers never stood a chance."

Shaking the crowbar, Raquel's lips formed a nefarious smile. "Look at me. You never once believed your frumpy little sister could harm you. I knew eventually we'd end up here again, but this time, I'm not going to fail."

"You pushed me into the pitchfork," Dani accused softly.

"You'd had a flashback that day of seeing me in the lab with something in my hands." Shaking the crowbar, she smirked. "We got in an argument and I pushed you. I didn't mean to ram you into a pitchfork, but it certainly came in handy."

A warbled cry leapt from her throat. "Are you going to kill me? God, Raquel, do you hate me that much?"

"I have no wish to kill you," she murmured, a small flare of emotion contorting her features. "I just want to be free of you and all the painful memories I have because of you. It's time for me to have my turn as the one everyone reveres. The one who inspires greatness."

"Please, Raquel," Dani pleaded, holding up her hands. "I never meant to hurt you. I didn't realize your feelings about Mom's goodbye, but I should have. I'm so sorry."

"I never wanted to hurt you either," she said, stepping forward. "Unfortunately, I've learned the hard way we never get what we want in life unless we take it." Lifting the weapon, Raquel snarled as her arms began to swing.

Dani crossed her arms in front of her face, turning to try and escape the blow. And then, everything went black as she fell to the ground.

Chapter 29

Arianna ran to the main hub of the lab, more concerned with finding Dani, grabbing the antidote and returning to Dominic than anything else. Their interaction last night played in a constant loop in her brain, and she hoped to hell it wasn't the last cognizant conversation they would ever have. She'd stormed off like a petulant child. Now, she vowed to treat him differently if he survived. Hell, he couldn't control his feelings for Dani. Moreover, she'd never given him a reason to try. Frustrated with her emotional ineptitude, she charged over the broken glass, entering the lab as it crunched beneath her boots.

Approaching the thick metal doors, she stepped through the first one and noticed the second one blown apart by the IEDs. Drawing her handgun, she stepped over the threshold. Confusion marred her features as she tilted her head.

"Raquel?"

"Don't come any closer!" her sister yelled, whirling as she held a crowbar high. "They're both unconscious and I don't want to hurt them. But if you force me to, I'll slam this so hard on Dani's temple, it will crack in half before you shoot me." She shook the weapon, and Arianna noticed her hands were trembling quite fiercely. Arianna judged her words an empty threat, but she had no desire to shoot Raquel, despite her treachery. Something awful must've prompted her actions, and Arianna would always give her sisters the benefit of the doubt.

But just because she didn't want to hurt her didn't mean she wasn't pissed as hell. "What the fuck, Raquel? You don't have to do this."

"No, I don't," she said, lifting her chin. "I could choose to remain someone no one sees and live an uneventful life. But I'm choosing another path."

"You're not going to best me when I'm holding this and you've got a crowbar," Arianna said, shaking the gun. "You know this, Raquel."

"That's where you're wrong, I'm afraid," a deep baritone said behind her. The sound of a gun cocking beside her ear caused Arianna to freeze. Ice coursed through her veins as she debated turning to see who was behind her.

"Well, little mouse," the man droned, "you've certainly surprised me. Luthor Cromwell has plans for what needs to happen in this lab, and you're fucking it up. But I admire your spunk, so I'm going to help you."

"I'm not working with you!" Raquel cried. "I'm stealing the antidote and heading to the District, where I'm going to approach Cromwell. I'll be able to replicate it when I have access to technology inside the wall and I can create a better lite version than he's using now."

The man hesitated, and Arianna took the moment to spin and point her gun in his face. Tossing back his head, he laughed before shrugging. "Go ahead. Shoot me. But I'll shoot her first." He pointed the gun at Raquel. Arianna stood firm, calculating in her mind how long it would take to shoot him and then shoot to wound Raquel.

"I assume you're Tristan Holder. Thanks for the weapons, by the way." Arianna arched a sardonic eyebrow. "*Really* helpful."

"You're welcome," he said with an arrogant nod. "I needed you to end up here. I didn't count on *her* though," he said, gesturing to Raquel with his gun. "And if you don't drop your weapon, I'll shoot her."

Arianna stood firm, continuing to calculate in her mind. Something flared in Tristan's eyes before he lowered the gun and aimed at Dani, who was unconscious on the floor. "Or maybe I'll shoot her."

"Okay," Arianna said, lowering the gun and holstering it before showing her palms. No way was she going to take a chance with Dani and Maverick lying unconscious and no ability to even try to avoid a shot.

"Seriously?" Raquel squeaked. "You didn't care when he was going to shoot me, but of course you care about Dani. I hate you as much as I hate her right now."

"As much as I love this family drama," Tristan said with an exasperated eye roll, "we've got to go. Raquel, grab the antidote and come with me."

"I don't trust you—"

"You don't really have a choice. It's me or the people you just betrayed."

Raquel hesitated and he shrugged. "Fine, have it your way." He aimed the gun at her and Arianna screamed, "No!"

"Okay!" Raquel said, tossing the crowbar to the ground. Reaching inside, she grabbed the box with the antidote and approached Tristan. "Let's go."

Keeping his weapon trained on Arianna, he backed out of the room, ushering Raquel to go ahead of him. "I have a first aid kit in the car. Probably won't help Dominic, but it's better than nothing. I'll leave it on the north end of the lot."

"I'm *really* fucking confused. Now you want to help Dom?"

"There are things in play here that need to happen. I'm not interested in all this." He circled his hand. "I'm interested in starting a war. And that won't happen until Cromwell gets the video footage he needs of Dani. He has a vision of painting her as a villain. I have two men waiting outside, and I'll tell them you escaped but you have to go now. There's a back door emergency exit at the end of the secondary hallway. Use that instead of the front entrance."

Retreating, he gave a mischievous grin. "Oh, and one more thing. There's a false bottom in the drawer where Dani hid the antidote. Make sure you check there before you leave."

"How in the hell do you know that?"

"I make it my business to know things, Arianna. Now hurry the fuck up." Giving a nod, he rotated and fled to catch up with Raquel, who'd already disappeared.

A moan sounded and Arianna turned to find Dani wiggling on the ground as she cupped her head. "What the hell?" she groaned.

"Raquel hit you," Arianna explained, rushing over. "Long story. Mav's unconscious. Let me try to wake him." Rushing over, she crouched and turned him to splay on his back. Slapping his cheek several times, she called his name.

Suddenly, his eyes flew open and he gasped. Sitting up, he shook his head rapidly as if trying to clear it. "What the fuck happened?"

"I actually remember," Dani said, rubbing the back of her head. "Raquel hotwired a car and showed up with a crowbar. Jesus, my head is pounding."

"Dominic was hit," Arianna said, pointing to the door. "I have to get back to him. Tristan said he'd leave a first aid kit in the parking lot."

"Tristan Holder?" Maverick asked, confused.

"Yeah. Lots to catch up on. Can you two manage while I go retrieve Dom? Tristan said to exit through the back emergency exit so his men don't see us."

"Go," Maverick said, shooing her as he scooted toward Dani. "We'll help each other."

"There's a false bottom in the drawer. Check it." Rising, Arianna broke into a sprint toward the front of the lab, racing toward the man she loved while praying it wasn't too late to save him.

Once Maverick and Dani gained their bearings, they stood and searched the cabinet. Finding the false bottom, they lifted the top, and Dani breathed a sigh of relief when she saw the two vials inside.

"Well, it's not a full box, but it will have to do." Retrieving them, she walked back to the lab and located two cloths, carefully wrapping both vials before placing them in her bag. Rushing from the lab, they found Arianna dragging Dominic down the hallway toward the back exit.

Dani observed his shallow breathing and lowered to take his pulse. "Pulse is faint, but it's there and he's breathing. Maverick, can you carry him?"

"I'll help," Arianna said, her face a mask of concern. Sliding her arms under his knees, she gathered him in her arms as Maverick lifted him under his chest. They carried him through the back exit and through the woods to the truck. Dani jogged toward them, extending the first aid kit.

"Found it on the edge of the parking lot."

Maverick and Dani assessed the wound as Dominic lay in the bed of the truck, concern lacing their features.

"It was a clean shot and I think we can manage the bleeding with constant pressure," Dani said. "But we also need to keep moving. The silver lining is that he's unconscious, which means he's not feeling pain."

"I'll continue to apply pressure as you drive," Arianna said, crawling in beside him and cradling him in her lap. Pressing a clean shirt to his wound, she gently stroked his short hair as his head rested in her lap. It was a poignant gesture, so different from her sister's gruff exterior, and Dani felt the curtain of realization lift as she nodded.

Climbing in the passenger seat, she massaged her throbbing head as Maverick drove. Once they were speeding down the open road, he reached over and clutched her hand. "You okay? Besides the pounding in your skull that probably rivals mine?"

"I'm fine," she said, stunned as she recalled Arianna's soft strokes on Dominic's head. "Ari's in love with Dominic," she whispered.

Maverick's eyes narrowed. "What makes you say that? They barely tolerate each other."

"That's Arianna's love language," she said, breathing a laugh. "The verbal quips and zingers. It's always been how she communicates."

"I'll be damned," he mused. "I won't deny I've noticed the energy between them. It's fucking intense."

"I hope he's okay." Gripping the window frame, she watched the fields zip by. "Did we fail, Maverick?"

"Not yet. Let's find a place to camp, regroup and get some rest. We haven't failed yet, sweetheart."

Gripping his hand, she drew upon his strength as he drove them far away from the lab.

Chapter 30

They found a clearing in a thicket of woods, the canopy of trees a perfect shield from the outside world. They took turns sleeping around the fire Arianna built, continuing to wake each other to ensure they monitored any concussions. Dani used the meager tools in Tristan's first aid kit and stitched up Dominic with the needle and thread she'd packed from the farmhouse. They'd each packed random trinkets and supplies they thought might come in handy, and Dani was thankful she'd thought to toss them in.

She'd also packed the antibiotic ointment and made sure to slather it on Dominic's stitches when she was finished. His pulse was stronger as he slept, which was promising. Once the sun rose, they decided to stay another day as Dani and Maverick took the ibuprofen Dani had also stashed. After two days, they felt it was time to move.

Tristan had also left a SIM card in the first aid kit, which Arianna studied by the fire. "Ready to see what's on here? We have seventy-five percent battery on the phone but need to use it sparingly since we don't have the generator to charge it anymore and Dani still needs to watch the videos each morning."

Maverick inserted the SIM card. After the information loaded, he pulled up a series of images. Studying them, his eyes grew wide. "Tristan supplied us with maps of all the known black-market compounds. And he made a list of the leaders with detailed instructions of which ones we should approach first."

"And?" Arianna asked.

"This one," he said, showing them the screen. "It's in Cumberland, Maryland, near the border of Pennsylvania."

"We have enough gas to get there?" Dani asked.

Maverick nodded. "The leader is supposedly a former US senator named Arthur Reyes."

"I remember that name," Dani said. "Wasn't he mulling a run for president? He was a centrist who was popular with both political parties, right?"

Maverick and Arianna's mouths fell open as they gaped at her.

"What is it?"

"Sweetheart, Arthur Reyes rose to prominence *after* you started working at Sendaxa."

"Holy shit," she whispered, rubbing her forehead. "I remember him...I remember his popularity."

"Dani, do you remember our wedding?"

Gazing into his eyes, her lips ticked down as she shook her head. "I don't remember that. I'm so sorry—"

"That's okay," he said, inching closer and pulling her into his arms. "You remember something and that's amazing."

"Maybe my memories are going to return in a slow drip as I heal." Rubbing her head, she shot him a derisive look. "I mean, getting hit again certainly didn't help."

"Maybe it knocked things right again," Arianna interjected.

Laughing, Dani lifted a shoulder. "Maybe."

Maverick held her, rocking them back and forth as Arianna leaned over to check Dominic's wound. "We need to leave this site tomorrow. We can find a new camp along the way."

"Agreed. We'll take it day by day and approach Reyes's compound when we're stronger."

"Hopefully, we can find an abandoned school nearby and use their lab. We'll need one with a generator so I have electricity. Then, I'm going to figure out what I put in this antidote and replicate the shit out of it."

The conversation continued well into the night before they all took turns keeping watch so they could sleep.

Tristan stood in Luthor Cromwell's office, lurking in the corner as Raquel waited in the center of the expansive room. Luthor stood off to the side, slowly sipping one of the deep brown scotches he kept in the fancy crystal decanters that lined the bar. Tossing back his glass, he chugged the final drops before setting it down and approaching Raquel.

"Well, my dear, you were certainly a curveball we didn't foresee," he said in his raspy voice. Tilting his head, he studied her like a bug under a microscope. "You almost ruined my plans. I needed the footage of your sister breaking into the lab and attempting to steal the antidote. I plan to show it as proof of her treachery during her public trial. It will garner support for me as I continue to build a new government under the Sendaxa umbrella."

"I...I'm sorry," Raquel said, knuckles white as she clenched the box that held the antidote. "I had my own plans, and I finally gained the courage to enact them."

"Tristan assures me I shouldn't hunt Dani down yet. That I should use the footage to convince people she's trying to resume production of EverLife and harm others. No one knows she was trying to steal the antidote. What do you think, my dear?"

Her throat bobbed as she rapidly blinked several times. "It's always better to write your own narrative. I see the logic in that argument."

"I agree." Extending his palms, he waited, urging her along. She placed the box in his hands and he opened it, his thin lips forming a sinister grin as he gazed inside. "You say you can create a new antidote that will extend the effects of EverLife?"

Nodding, she lifted her face to his, causing a jolt of admiration to shoot down Tristan's spine. Her expression was clear and rather confident for someone who was standing in front of the most powerful—and most evil—man in the world.

"I can make an antidote that will dull the EverLife side effects but cause the body to retain the cravings. It will create a need for EverLife so great I can't see anyone who's addicted stopping."

"Constant consumption," he drawled, pleasure in his tone. "A product no one can live without. It will give Sendaxa ultimate power."

"Sendaxa is already powerful," Tristan muttered, unable to stop himself. "How much more do you need?"

"If I want your opinion, I'll ask for it, Tristan," Luthor scolded, his expression stern. Clenching his jaw, Tristan forced himself to remain quiet. The two bodyguards along the wall pierced him with their gazes, and he glowered at them, suppressing the urge to flip the bastards off.

Resettling his attention on Raquel, Luthor slipped his fingers under her chin, tilting her face to his. She was almost a foot shorter than Luthor, and something protective welled in his chest as the wicked man loomed over her. Although she'd concocted an illicit secret plan to dupe her sister, Raquel wasn't a soldier, nor did she truly understand how evil someone like Luthor could be.

She was much like his sister had been before she'd fallen under Luthor's clutches. Tristan hadn't been able to save Jessica, but he could sure as hell keep Raquel from being drawn into Luthor's inner circle. Perhaps saving her would bring him some peace to counteract his abject failure with Jessica.

"I assume you'll need shelter," Luthor continued, a sinister gleam entering his eyes as he held her chin. "Of course, you will have to *earn* your place here. I don't appreciate freeloaders."

"I told you, I will work on the antidote and anything else you require." She stepped back, pulling away from his grasp. "Surely that's payment enough. I'm a very competent scientist and worked with my sister for years in Bethesda. I have knowledge that will benefit you."

"That will pay for your food and clothing," he said, leaning his hip against the nearby desk, "but lodging is a separate matter. I have several apartments I could offer, but they will require other forms of restitution."

"She can stay with me," Tristan blurted before he even felt the words pass his lips. "It will allow me to gather intel on her sister and their team, and monitor Raquel as she works. I'm still not sure we can trust her. Her sister could've planted her here to destroy us from the inside. We can't be certain."

"I assure you, I am not a spy," Raquel said, glaring at him.

Tristan glowered back, attempting to inform her with his gaze to shut her mouth before she said something that made it impossible for him to save her from the vile man.

Her eyes widened a bit as understanding dawned, and she turned to face Luthor. "But I can see why you might be suspicious. I'm happy to stay with Tristan if it will calm your doubts."

Luthor's eyes traveled over her body, raking over her curves in the baggy clothes as if he were considering a mare for breeding. Finally, he waved a dismissive hand. "Fine. Stay with Tristan so he can keep an eye on you. I will require regular reporting about how the new antidote is progressing."

"Yes, sir," Raquel said.

"Go on, then," Luthor said, dismissing them as he stalked behind his desk. "I have a ton of video footage to sift through and manipulate to ensure Dani looks as guilty as possible from the break-in. Tristan, you'll take Raquel to the lab tomorrow morning and get her situated?"

"Yes." Stepping forward, he gripped her forearm. "Come on."

Yanking away, she shot him a hateful glare. "I can walk on my own, thank you." She strode ahead of him, out of the office and into the elevator as Tristan entered behind her. Once the doors whooshed shut and they began the descent to the lobby, Tristan hit the emergency button, halting them in between floors.

"What are you doing?" she gasped, clutching the walls.

Stepping forward, he tried to talk some sense into her obstinate little head. "You listen to me, little mouse. I just saved you from having that old man's dick shoved between your lips for the rest of your days here. He's a monster, and you'll do well to remember that."

Her mouth fell open, shock covering every inch of her expression, and he had to tame the urge to laugh. Whether she liked it or not, she was about to get a dose of the harsh reality she'd entered.

"You hate your sister, but at least her motives were pure. You won't find purity here." He pointed at the closed doors. "All you'll find is a madman intent on destroying what's left of the world. I aim to fix that, and because I'm a nice fucking guy, I'm going to save your ass too."

"I do not need saving from the likes of you, and I would appreciate it if you stopped screaming in my face!"

"Don't test me," he said, leaning closer. "I feel an urge to protect you, but my goodwill only extends so far. You're a smart woman—much wilier than I gave you credit for—so you'll understand this in time: I'm your only ally here. If you're as intelligent as I think you are, you'll accept that and work *with* me instead of against me. Are we clear?"

"Yes," she whispered as a fear swirled in her eyes.

"Good." Drawing back, he punched the elevator button, resuming their trip to the lobby. When they exited, Tristan cursed as his ex-wife sauntered toward them.

"Oh, I...uh, hello, Tristan," Grace said, eyebrows drawn together as she assessed Raquel.

"Grace," he said with a curt nod.

"Hello," she said, extending her hand. "I'm Grace, Luthor Cromwell's wife."

"Raquel," she said, shaking her hand. "I'll be working for Luthor to improve the antidote distributed in the District."

"I see." Lifting her gaze to Tristan's, she released the woman's hand as her nostrils flared. "Raquel is a pretty name. Pleasure to meet you."

A muscle in Tristan's jaw clenched as he gazed into his ex-wife's eyes. For a fraction of a moment, they reflected the pain and heartache that simmered in his own. Then, the mask returned as Grace's expression turned blank.

"I wish you well," she said, stepping into the elevator and pressing the keypad. The doors whooshed shut as Tristan encircled Raquel's wrist.

"Come on," he ordered, leading her outside.

She stayed silent as they walked the ten blocks to his apartment. The small den had a pull-out couch, and he informed her it would be her room for the foreseeable future. After rummaging for some boxer shorts and a t-shirt, he tossed them on the bed before pointing to the half bath outside.

"You can use that for now. Do you need anything else?"

"I have supplies from the farmhouse in my bag," she said, sitting on the bed and swiping her thick brown hair off her forehead. "Been using the same toothbrush for a while, but I guess it's better than nothing."

"We can get supplies this week. Inflation is rampant inside the walls since our currency is from a government that no longer exists. It's become a wild west mentality of sorts. I assume Luthor will begin to print his own currency soon, which will exacerbate his power."

Those clear green eyes studied him as she gnawed her lip. "I can tell you don't like him. You must have your own plan to take him down. I'd love to hear it. Perhaps we can work together to see if our interests align."

Leaning against the doorframe, he narrowed his eyes. "I bet you'd love to hear it," he muttered. "I'm not interested in aligning with anyone. For some reason, I've decided I want to protect you, so let's leave it at that." Grasping the doorknob, he backed out of the room. "Good night, Raquel."

"Wait," she called, lifting her hand.

Sighing, he crossed his arms. "Yes?"

"The woman I met. Grace. You two have a history."

"Yes."

Nervously licking her lips, she smiled. "It was nice of her to comment on my name. My mom loved that name."

Tristan's heart squeezed in his chest, sure as if a fist had reached inside his chest and crushed it. "We loved it too."

"We?"

"Grace and I. It was the name we picked for our daughter."

"Oh." Raquel's eyes lit with curiosity. "Is she...?"

He shook his head. "Grace lost the baby when she was five months pregnant."

A ragged breath escaped Raquel's lips. "I'm so sorry."

"Thank you. As I said, I have a compelling urge to protect you. Perhaps I'm nostalgic because of your name. Regardless, it's important to remember you're never safe in this fucked-up world. I'll do my best, but you need to be smart and alert."

Nodding, she straightened her shoulders. "I understand. Thank you, Tristan."

"You're welcome. Good night."

Striding up the stairs to his room, Tristan yanked off his clothes, crawling into bed as exhaustion set in. Harshly rubbing his eyes, he wondered how in the hell he'd ended up with a stowaway scientist. That definitely hadn't been in his plans, but now that she was here, he'd do his best to keep her safe.

Closing his eyes, he thought of Jessica. And then of Grace. And eventually, about the baby they'd lost so long ago. Sighing, he switched off the lamp, understanding he needed sleep so he could forge ahead when the sun rose.

CHAPTER 31

The team arrived at the Cumberland, Maryland, black-market compound on fumes, causing Dani to breathe a sigh of relief. She and Maverick exited the truck, leaving Arianna in the back with Dominic. He'd awoken that morning in severe pain, and Dani had urged him to rest. She hoped they could get their hands on better medical supplies if Arthur Reyes allowed them inside the compound.

Approaching the tall wooden doors, Maverick lifted his fist and pounded. A voice yelled from behind, "Who goes there?"

"My name is Maverick Ward. I was the head of security at the Sendaxa lab where EverLife was created. My wife, Danica, is with me, and we want to speak to Arthur Reyes."

Muffled voices sounded behind the door before a deep voice called, "It will be a few minutes."

He and Dani waited, glancing ever so often at Arianna and Dominic in the bed of the truck several feet away. Finally, the huge doors swung open, and a man with a rifle slung over his back stepped outside. Several men flanked him, all armed, and Maverick showed his palms.

"I have a gun on my belt, but you're welcome to confiscate it. We come in peace."

The leader gestured with his head, and one of his soldiers stepped forward to frisk Maverick and remove his gun. He also frisked Dani before returning to the leader and handing him the firearm. "They're both clear."

Placing the gun in his belt, the man regarded them under the bright morning sky.

"You're Arthur Reyes?" Maverick asked.

"Yes." His eyes trailed to Dani. "And you're the woman who destroyed the world."

Dani squared her shoulders before nodding. "I am. There is no excuse, so I won't try to make one. All I can say is that I will work until my dying breath to repair the damage. I have two vials of antidote, and if you'll help me find a warehouse or an abandoned school with any sort of science lab, I can figure out how to replicate it and begin to save people."

His eyes narrowed as his nostrils flared. "Can you bring back my sister, who died from the meaningless addiction she formed to your despicable drug?"

Dani's shoulders hunched as she shook her head. "I can't and I'm sorry. I know this doesn't mean anything, but my intentions were good. I never meant to create something that would harm so many."

"And yet you did" was his ominous reply. "Perhaps we should drag you inside and place you on trial for your transgressions."

"Hey," Maverick said, holding up his hands, "we came here in peace, Reyes, and I'm not above killing anyone who tries to harm my wife. There's a very capable soldier in that truck"—he pointed over his shoulder with his thumb—"who's ready to rush toward me, throw a rifle in my hand, and blast all of you full of bullets—"

"You're threatening me?" Reyes asked, cocking a brow. "You are aware I'm surrounded by ten armed guards, right?" He gestured toward his men.

"Fuck this," Maverick said, turning toward the truck to summon Arianna.

"Wait," Dani said, clutching his wrist and squeezing to calm him. Facing Reyes, she straightened her shoulders. "My husband has a protective streak, but he means no harm. And you're right. I should die for my crimes, and I'm willing to face the consequences of my actions. But first, I'd like to use my skills to try and help the ones who remain."

Dani stepped toward Reyes as Maverick gripped her arm to halt her. "No, Mav," she said, gently removing his hand. "I need to face this, and you need to let me."

His eyes pulsed with concern, but he finally released her. Stepping forward, she stopped when she was mere inches from Arthur Reyes. "I have amnesia and don't remember much about the past few years, although flashes of memory are slowly returning. One thing I do remember is your kindness and your involvement in a plethora of community activities benefiting so many. You were an activist before I royally fucked up and ruined everything. I'm asking you to let me help you so you can help others again. After that, I will surrender to your soldiers and you can put me on trial."

Reyes's eyes narrowed as he contemplated. "You're willing to die for your crimes?"

"Yes," she said, her tone firm. "But not before I repair the damage. That is something I can't live with...and I can't die knowing I didn't try. I hope you can understand."

Rubbing his chin with his fingers, he pondered. "I didn't expect you to be noble. Luthor Cromwell paints a terrible picture of you that has disseminated to all the black-market compounds."

"I would argue that Cromwell is the villain here. Perhaps I was a pawn, and an unwitting one at that, but I'll take responsibility." She gestured toward Maverick. "My husband, his best friend and my sister make up our small team. We could've stayed hidden and survived on our own. Instead, I'm here, asking you to let me make things right. I want you to judge me by my future actions, not the actions of my past." Reaching toward him, she covered his forearm. "And I'm very sorry about your sister," she rasped, emotion in her voice as her eyes clouded with tears. "I can't imagine the pain of losing her. When I lost my mother to cancer, I thought I might drown in grief. I'm just...well, I'm sorry, Arthur."

Releasing him, she stepped back, willing and waiting for whatever decision he wished to render. Finally, his features softened, and his lips formed the barest hint of a smile. "Thank you for your condolences. She was a wonderful woman. Vibrant and full of life."

"I'd love to hear her story. She deserves that. All the victims of this senseless crisis do."

Inhaling a deep breath, Reyes lifted his gaze to Maverick. "Either your wife is very genuine or she's a great actress."

"I assure you, she's a terrible actress. If she doesn't like something or believe in it, she has no ability to hide her disapproval." His lips twitched as he gazed reverently toward Dani.

A low chuckle escaped Reyes's lips. "I think I believe you." Facing the man on his right, he asked, "We can put the four of them in the abandoned middle school on the northside of the compound. I believe it has all the remnants of a science lab and a generator, yes?"

"Yes, sir."

Turning to Dani, he asked, "Will that work?"

"If it's the best you've got, I'll take it," she said with a nod. "As long as we have a roof over our head, access to a lab and a generator, I'll work like hell to replicate the antidote. Do you have access to any facility with production capabilities?"

"There's an abandoned factory within the walls of our compound. It's no longer functional but can be resurrected with some effort, I would imagine."

"Good. Producing mass quantities of antidote is going to be difficult. Once I figure out what's in the formula, I'm going to need to tweak it to make it more natural so we don't rely on synthetic chemicals. Plants will need to be harvested to supply us with ingredients. It's a huge undertaking, but one worth executing."

"I appreciate the foresight. We're bare bones inside the walls. The school will have cots where you can sleep and a well in the back. There's a generator that can power your lab work."

"That will work," Maverick said.

Reyes nodded before pointing toward the entrance. "Drive your truck inside, and one of my men will drive you to the school. If it's empty, he can refill it along the way. We've been sending out search parties to collect gas from abandoned vehicles and refueling stations."

"Thank you," Dani said, grateful for his acceptance. "I promise you, I'll do my best."

Arthur's eyes roved over her, clear and contemplative as he assessed. "My dear, I'm counting on it," he said before turning to step back into the compound.

Returning to the truck with Maverick, Dani climbed into the passenger seat and attempted to calm her pounding heart as they drove onto the compound.

Chapter 32

Dani observed the compound on the short drive to the school, noting the solemn atmosphere. Some houses had large red *X*s sprayed on the front and boarded-up windows. Others were still habitable, and several children appeared as they neared the school. They ran alongside the truck until it stopped, and Dani stepped out to greet the kids.

"You're the bad woman who created EverLife," one of the children said, curiosity in his deep brown eyes as he studied her.

Dani nodded. "I am. I'm here to fix what I broke. Was this your school?"

"I wasn't old enough to go here yet. This was the middle school."

She cocked a brow. "I bet you can still show me around though. We need a place for my friend Dominic to rest. He's hurt and needs to recover."

The boy's gaze drifted to the back of the truck, where Arianna and Maverick were helping Dominic, who swayed on his feet as he slid to the ground. Arianna urged him to sling his arms over their shoulders before leading him toward the entrance.

"I can show you," the kid said, waving his hand. "Come on."

The driver Reyes had assigned tipped his ballcap before climbing back in the truck and driving away.

"Guess they're keeping the truck," Dani murmured as they followed the kids inside. She admired Reyes's confidence and acceptance, and felt a small well of gratitude that he was still alive. They would need altruistic, competent leaders for the huge undertaking ahead.

"You can put him there," the boy said, leading them through a doorway marked "infirmary" and pointing to the stretcher bed in the middle of the exam room.

"Perfect," Dani said, squeezing his shoulder. "Thank you..."

"Chris." His gap-toothed grin was adorable.

"You're a great helper, Chris. I'll remember that and might need your help again."

He gave a vigorous nod as Arianna and Maverick situated Dominic in the bed.

"You married?" Chris asked, pointing to Dominic.

"I'm actually married to that one," she said, tilting her head toward Maverick.

Chris's gaze drifted toward Arianna. "Is *she* married to him?"

"*Pfft,*" Arianna said, backing away from the bed. "In his dreams. Is there another couch in this dump?"

"I can show you," one of the other kids chimed, and Arianna smiled before following the boy from the room.

"You two can sleep in the guidance counselor's office," Chris said. "It's two doors down, and the couch pulls out to a bed."

Dani leaned down and rested her hands on her knees to stare into his eyes. "Thank you, Chris. Maybe you can come back tomorrow and help us again? I think you're going to end up being a very valuable member of our team."

Biting his lip, he gave a quick nod before bolting from the room as the two remaining kids followed him.

Striding toward Dominic, Dani pressed her palm to his forehead. "He's still got a fever. Let me see what provisions they've got here. I'll clean and rebandage his wound."

"I'll go check on Arianna and scope out the guidance counselor's office," Maverick said, leaning down to kiss her cheek. "Come find me when you're done."

After he skirted from the room, Dani searched the cabinets, finding most of them empty. There were a few bandages, a bottle of hydrogen peroxide and some ibuprofen in a drawer, so she set them on the counter before shrugging off her pack. Retrieving the first aid kit, she stacked the contents on the counter and got to work.

She helped Dominic tug off his shirt before urging him to lie back so she could tend to his wound. It was ugly, but it would heal. Thank god. Losing Dominic would've wrecked her, and she needed to be in the right mindset to replicate the formula. Since she couldn't remember shit, she was going to have to study the antidote intensely, and needed to be focused.

"Arianna," Dominic whispered through chapped lips as Dani finished cleaning his wound.

"She needs some space," Dani said, opening a bandage and removing the adhesive covering.

Dominic's brown eyes darted between hers, laced with remorse and regret. "I didn't know," he rasped.

"Me neither." She pressed the bandage over his wound, lightly patting it in place. "She's not really a sharer."

Huffing a laugh, Dominic nodded against the pillow.

"She's going to fight it," Dani said, her lips forming a sad smile. "You know that, right?"

His Adam's apple bobbed as he nodded.

"You're both scared to love," she said, rising and retrieving the vial of petroleum jelly from the counter. "For different reasons, but they're all valid." After gathering some on her fingertip, she gently rubbed it over Dominic's lips to ease the chapping. "Don't let her push you away. She deserves love, Dom. She's never met a man worthy of her, nor someone who is strong enough to see past her walls and fight for her. I know you can do it. But let's get you better first, okay?"

His eyes drooped as his head barely moved in acknowledgment. Dani cupped his shoulder as he drifted to sleep. Rising, she made sure he was tucked in before she exited to find her husband.

Dani and Maverick decided to turn the guidance counselor's office into their bedroom. It offered privacy, and the pull-out couch was a bonus.

"Maybe the old counselor snuck in a nap or two when no one was looking?" Maverick teased as he arranged the bed.

"Maybe. Now that we're settled with sleeping quarters, we have a lot of tasks to complete to make this place functional so I can work."

There was no running water to the school, which Dani would need to remedy. In the meantime, Dani and Maverick washed off the grime of the day in the staid, multi-stalled bathroom next door with some of the water left in jugs by Arthur's men.

Once they were finally alone, situated in the pull-out bed, Dani slid her arms around her husband, thankful to have him by her side. Resting her cheek on his chest, she gently ran her fingers through the prickly hairs as they relaxed in the dark.

"Well, we made it to Phase II," she said, placing a sweet kiss on his pec. "We're really in it now."

"For better or worse," he said, sifting his hands through her hair as she nuzzled against him.

"The past few years were *definitely* worse," she droned, rolling her eyes. "But there were some good times before that. The times when you wore me down, even though I insisted we weren't right for each other." Resting her chin on his chest, she grinned. "That first time you told me you loved me, after we'd been dating for several months. You finally talked me into bed, and I hadn't been with anyone in a while. I figured I'd scratch an itch with you because having sex with someone as hot as you might never happen again. But you slid inside me, and threaded your fingers through mine, and told me you loved me. It was one of the most perfect moments of my life."

His eyes shimmered with wetness, unashamed, as he ran his fingers over her cheek. "You remember," he whispered, his tone reverent.

"I remember." Cupping his jaw, she traced her thumb over his lips. "I don't remember it all, but I remember enough to know this is real. I think I'll remember more each day, and hopefully, one day, I'll remember everything. The details of my work at Sendaxa and what happened there are still vague, but I remember you, Mav. How could I not?" Sliding to press a kiss on his lips, she straddled his thighs, longing to bring him inside her. "I love you."

"Dani," he breathed, searching for her...easing inside her once he was coated with her essence.

Staring deep into his eyes, she rode him, gliding over his sensitive skin, overcome with feeling.

"I've waited so long to hear you say it again. It was torture to tell you and not hear it back. I love you, sweetheart."

Pressing her palms to the mattress, she rose above him, undulating her hips to increase the pace. He whispered words of love, rising to meet her urgent thrusts as their skin heated with desire. Lowering her mouth to his, Dani surged her tongue inside, tasting the man who was her eternity.

His strong arms wrapped around her, cupping the tender flesh of her backside as his other hand slid between her legs. Breaking their kiss, he gazed at her with hooded eyes as his talented fingers found the sensitive spot under the hood of her sex. Circling with firm pressure, he continued to love her as she writhed above him.

"Mav..." she cried, closing her eyes as pleasure overwhelmed her. "*Oh god...yes...*"

"Fuck, you're perfect like this. So tight and hot when you take me deep..." he rasped, his cock throbbing inside her.

The words sent shockwaves of heat through her body, causing her cells to ignite as she increased the pace of her hips. Tossing back her head, she closed her eyes, allowing herself to fall. Succumbing to his firm strokes on her clit as he claimed her, she launched into the climax, groaning with pleasure as he moaned below her.

Her inner walls milked him as he shouted her name. Clenching her ass in his broad hands, he anchored her, pumping inside her with furious strokes before his body stiffened and he joined her in the abyss. Jets of release coated her core as she collapsed against him, craving him upon every inch of her skin. His body convulsed in tiny bursts before he hummed in approval against her neck.

"Damn, babe, that was good." Nuzzling her neck, he encircled her with his arms as she burrowed against him.

"We have a lot of sex to make up for," she teased, running her nails over his chest. He shivered beneath her before nipping her earlobe.

"That we do. We'll fit that in between bouts of you working to save the world. I mean, go big or go home, right?"

Snickering, she nodded. "Truth." Resting her chin on her hand, her thoughts drifted to her sister. "I can't believe Raquel betrayed us. Geezus, Mav. I never saw it coming."

"Do you think you can forgive her?"

Sighing, she shrugged. "I don't know. I'm pissed as hell. But no matter how angry I am, we have to save her. Once she's safe with us, we can figure out the rest."

Maverick nodded as he caressed her.

"Arianna will feel the same. She'll want atonement, but she'll want to save Raquel first. Better to be punished by your family than your enemies."

"I imagine her first goal will be helping Dominic regain his strength," Maverick said. "Now that we know he's going to make it, we can help rehabilitate him while you work in the lab. We need him strong."

"Thank god he survived. He's healthy and his prognosis is good. I think he can regain his strength over the course of a few weeks if he's willing to train with you."

"He will. The man's a stubborn SOB, and Arianna will push him. He needs that."

"They need each other," Dani said softly, aching for her sister to find the love she deserved. "Who better to tear down walls than someone who erected ones just as thick?"

"There's my optimist," he teased, chucking her nose.

"I just want her to be happy," she whispered, pressing her cheek to his chest. "They both deserve that."

Feeling her lids grow heavy, Dani relaxed into her husband's body, soothed by his soft strokes against her skin. Although the tomorrows were unknown, Dani reveled in the knowledge Maverick would be by her side for the journey. His strength was her guidepost; his love, her unwavering reminder she still was deserving, even after the pain she'd involuntarily unleashed.

Dwelling on the destruction wouldn't bring her peace, but mending and repairing it might. Resolved, she vowed to do her best to save the world she'd inadvertently destroyed, one tomorrow at a time.

Before You Go

Thank you for starting this new journey with me! As much as I LOVE writing my Etherya's Earth books, I need to keep things fresh and pepper in new stories with different elements from time to time. I hope you loved Dani and Maverick as much as I did.

Ready to see what happens between Arianna and Dominic? You'll find out in Book 2 of the Sendaxa Chronicles trilogy, *Scorched Redemption!*

Want to read another steamy dystopian box set? Check out my **Prevent the Past** trilogy! Wishing you lots of happy reading and thank you for supporting indie authors! - *Rebecca*

Scorched Redemption

The Sendaxa Chronicles, Book 2

By

REBECCA HEFNER

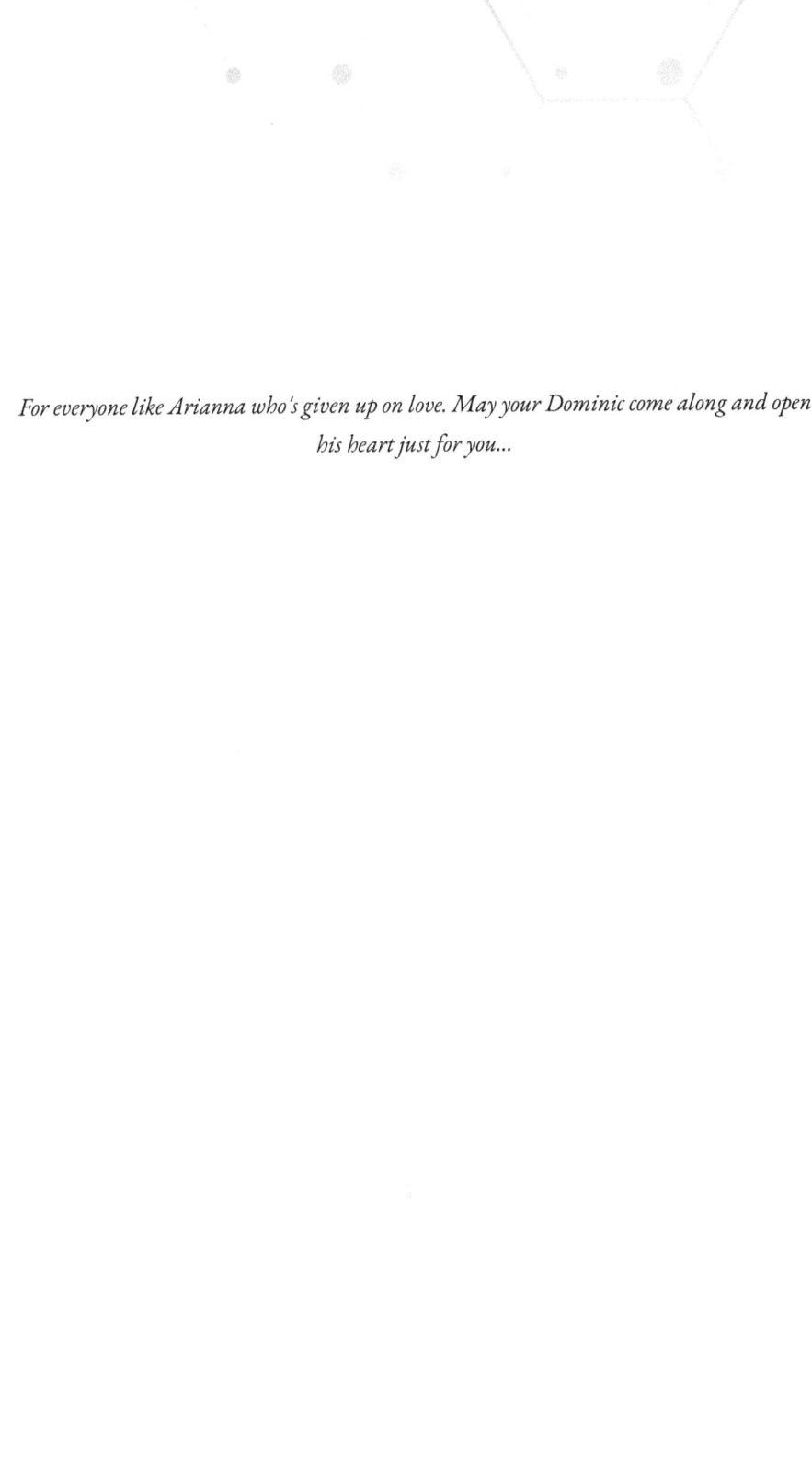

For everyone like Arianna who's given up on love. May your Dominic come along and open his heart just for you...

Chapter 1

Sometime in the not-so-distant future...

Dominic Cavalleri gasped before jerking upright and placing his hand over his heart. The organ threatened to beat out of his chest as he glared at the woman at the foot of the bed. Arianna Lawson stood tall, banging a spoon on a pan as she yelled, "Rise and shine!"

"Jesus, Ari," he said, clutching his pec. "Are you *trying* to give me a heart attack?"

"You're not very good at dying," she said, planting the fist with the spoon on her hip. "So I think your ticker's just fine."

Releasing a breath, he ran a hand over his short hair. "I was shot three weeks ago, in case you don't remember. My body's still recovering."

"Tell it to someone who cares, old man." Striding forward, she cocked a brow. "It's time to train. Since you did five miles yesterday, we're going to run seven today. And then, target practice."

"Fucking drill sergeant," Dominic muttered, lifting the covers on the medical stretcher that doubled as his bed. When his feet touched the floor, he stood—slowly, so he didn't lose his balance.

"Best drill sergeant you'll ever have," she muttered, eyeing him warily. "You okay? Don't faint on me."

"I'm good." Dominic touched the laceration at the juncture of his neck and shoulder. Thankfully, Dr. Danica Lawson-Ward, Arianna's sister, had been nursing the wound, and it was healing nicely. Although their mission to retrieve the EverLife antidote had been messy, it had been successful—and Dani was now hard at work trying to replicate it.

"I just need to clean the abrasion and wash off," Dominic said, grateful the abandoned school they were inhabiting now had running water. The compound's leader, Arthur

Reyes, had tasked some former contractors and plumbers with restoring the plumbing from a nearby well. It certainly made things easier in their dystopian world.

"I'll be by the front door in ten minutes. Don't make me wait. I've got shit to do today." Pivoting, she thrust her chin in the air and stalked from the room.

"Infuriating woman." Dominic headed to the bathroom, complete with stalls and functional sinks. After rinsing off and cleaning his wound, he applied a fresh bandage before throwing on some of the sweats Reyes's men had given him. After tying his sneakers, which had lasted surprisingly long in their dystopian world, he went in search of his training partner.

"About time," Arianna said, pushing the door open and ushering him outside.

Dominic squinted at the bright sun, wishing he still owned trivial things like sunglasses. Before the world ended, small luxuries were easily taken for granted. Now, humanity existed in a fragile balance between survival and extinction. Only time would tell which path they would take.

"I figured we'd jog to the outer wall and do some laps," Arianna said, planting her feet wide and bending over to stretch. She moved from side to side, and Dominic had to squelch the urge to look at her breasts as the neckline of her shirt bared her cleavage. Her firm ass stuck high in the air, and he licked his lips, suddenly longing to place his palms on the smooth skin...

"Earth to Dom," she said, rising. "Ready?"

Nodding, he did a few stretches before falling into step beside her. They jogged at a quick, no-nonsense pace, and he inhaled the warm air into his lungs. It was almost September, and soon the leaves would begin to turn, but for now, he basked in the heady late-summer breeze.

Every so often, he glanced at Arianna, acknowledging how lucky he was to have her as his training partner. She'd been an excellent soldier and high-ranking officer in the US Army before she'd retired to pursue her own security business. The world had fallen apart, so she hadn't been able to fulfill that dream. Protecting her sisters and saving humanity had become her new calling, and she excelled at it.

When Dominic first met Arianna, he'd made the mistake of judging her like many others did. As someone who was harsh and unyielding. And yes, Arianna Lawson definitely had those qualities.

But as he got to know her, he began to see the gruffness for what it was: a shield to guard herself from getting hurt. Arianna had always been a protector and safeguarded herself since no one had ever thought to protect her. The stern, uncompromising woman who didn't appear to need anyone.

Dominic had been drawn to Danica, who was much more open and trusting. Through the shared grief of losing her mother and Dominic's sister to cancer, they'd formed an intimate bond.

Dani helped Dominic cope with the deaths of his family members, which were both tragic and senseless. His parents had been murdered during a robbery at their Washington, DC, home. Although the perpetrators were eventually caught and sent to prison, that outcome offered little solace to Dominic.

And then, barely a year later, his sister, Pam, was diagnosed with stage-four cancer. When most of her friends were celebrating their twenty-first birthdays by tossing back their first drinks, she'd succumbed to the deadly disease, leaving him alone in a world comprised of pain and heartache.

Dominic had been left scarred—both mentally and physically—since he carried a nasty scar from his Middle East deployment almost two decades ago. Courtesy of an overzealous rebel soldier with a machete, the jagged laceration ran from the outer corner of his eyebrow, across his nose, and ended at the opposite corner of his lips.

The pain from that scar had been temporary, although he'd wear it for the rest of his life. The agony from the loss of his family was an invisible wound he carried inside, deep within the heart he'd shut down long ago.

Danica had been the one exception. Since she was married to his best friend, Dominic knew loving her was safe—that he would never act on it since she adored Maverick. It allowed Dominic to imagine he still had the ability to feel *some* sliver of emotion.

And that's where he and Arianna were *exactly* alike.

Because his love for Dani had been a shield. One to protect him from ever again experiencing the pain he felt when his parents and sister died.

Dominic had convinced himself to love someone unavailable so he wouldn't get hurt.

Arianna had just given up on love completely. They were two broken souls rotating in the same orbit.

Getting shot was the wake-up call Dominic needed. He realized it was time to stop romanticizing something that wasn't real. If his soul hadn't been broken, he might have stopped to appreciate what was right in front of him. If anyone was a match for Dominic, it was Arianna. The stoic, fierce woman who pretended not to care.

He would admit she was a good actress. He hadn't seen any indication of her true feelings. Not until he was bleeding out on the cold laboratory floor, holding his neck as she begged him not to die.

In that moment, Dominic had seen every ounce of emotion the woman kept bottled inside. Her gorgeous hazel eyes had swirled with pleading, longing and...*love*. Dominic was no expert at emotion, but he couldn't deny the intensity that passed between them in that moment.

The moment he'd realized he might actually be ready to try and love someone again. That it might be worth the risk if it was *her*.

"Stop staring at me," she droned, the words breathy as she jogged. "And if you look at my tits again, I'll break your kneecaps."

Dominic pursed his lips, silently admitting he'd stolen a glance or two at her breasts as she jogged. They were small but perfectly proportioned for her strong, tall body, and he suddenly wondered how well they would fit in his palms. Glancing down, he imagined cupping one with his hand and trailing his thumb over her nipple. Would she moan with desire or punch him in the face if he tried? Hell, she'd probably do both, but he figured suffering through the latter was worth it for the pleasure he'd experience from the former.

"What are you smirking at?" she asked, jogging to the high metal wall before stopping and bending over to catch her breath. "Let's take a breather before we begin the laps."

Dominic used the break to stretch, his body still sore from the injury. Swinging his tattooed arms around in large circles, he relished the ache in his healing muscles. He was recovering well—thanks in part to Arianna's ceaseless efforts to train with him—but stopping to stretch was a good call. At forty-one, he was no spring chicken, and knew that constant movement was essential for increasing blood flow and ensuring his muscles didn't cramp.

"I'm laughing at how you can't help yourself. You love busting my balls, Ari."

"You make it easy," she said with a shrug. "And I told you not to call me that."

"I think the habit's formed, sweetheart. Sorry—"

Arianna gripped his jaw, quick as lightning, and squeezed. It hurt like hell, but she didn't punch him in his wound, so he figured he'd take the win. If she really wanted to hurt him, that's where she'd aim, and they both knew it.

"And you definitely don't want to call me *that*," she warned, her fingers tightening against his stubble. Her glare was fierce, her almost-six-foot frame imposing even though he was half a foot taller. "I demoted men for calling me that back in the day."

Ever so slowly, Dominic slid his palm over the silken skin of her wrist. "Message received." Tugging her hand from his jaw, he held fast when she tried to pull away.

"Hey!"

"I'm not one of your subordinates, Arianna," he said, careful to use her full name so she wouldn't focus on something trivial. In truth, her nickname suited her, and he doubted it bothered her when he used it. But it was something else to hide behind. Another defense she could use to pretend she hated him.

"I know that," she said, attempting to yank her wrist from his grasp. "Dom—"

"Stick your hand in the rattlesnake's den and you're going to get bitten." He released her, a bit breathless from the feel of her skin against his palm.

Her cheeks flushed under her half-shaven head as angry eyes studied him under long, dark lashes.

"I'm not scared of you, Arianna."

A puff of air exited her lungs as her expression became confused. "I know. That's one of the things I like most about you. You're able to put up with my shit."

Dominic smiled at the concession, which he rarely experienced with her. "I didn't think you liked anything about me," he softly teased.

"That's the *only* thing," she said, her tone acerbic as she backed away. Her long fingers rubbed her wrist as she studied him, and he wondered if she mourned the loss of his skin against hers too. "Come on. Break's over. We need to get your heart rate back up."

Frustration set in as she retreated behind her shell. Aching to say something before the mask fully returned, he stepped forward. Her muscles stiffened, but she stood her ground, spine straightening as she gazed up at him. He towered over her, his broad shoulders tense in anticipation of the conversation they needed to have. Neither of them had acknowledged what happened in the squalid laboratory hallway when he was shot, and he felt it was time.

"Are we going to talk about what happened at the lab?"

A challenge entered her gaze, and admiration swelled at her pride. Arianna was confident and sure of herself, and damn, it was attractive. Not only did it set his body on fire, but he had a sneaking suspicion she let it go in the bedroom. That when she found the right partner, she would open herself up and let him take control.

And lord help him, but he wanted to be that man.

"There's nothing to talk about. You survived and Dani got the serum. The woman you love is safe, and we've moved on to Phase II of our plan."

Dominic's eyes narrowed as he battled to keep the frustration at bay. Although he loved verbally sparring with her, dismissing their feelings was beneath them both. If she wouldn't admit them, at least he could.

"You know my feelings for Dani were...something born from mutual experience," he said, shaking his head.

"Of course." Stepping back, she raised her arms in a stretch before kicking both legs to reinvigorate them. "I mean, everyone loves Dani. Makes complete sense. Let's go. I've got practice with the kids in an hour."

She turned and began jogging beside the metallic wall that surrounded the compound. Smiling at the fact he'd been thoroughly dismissed, he jolted into a sprint to catch up with her. Arianna had been a premier athlete in college and had led her team to the college softball tournament. When she'd discovered the kids in the compound had organized a makeshift wiffle ball league, she'd offered to coach them.

Chris, one of the children who'd helped acclimate them to the abandoned school, lit up at her offer. She'd been coaching them for two weeks on the grown-over baseball diamond behind the school. Dominic thought it spoke volumes about her character. She could pretend to be a heartless grump all day long, but the woman was selfless in every way.

And she deserved to be loved that way in return.

As Dominic's feet moved in tandem with hers, he stole another glance out of the corner of his eye. Her skin glistened with a sheen of sweat, and he envisioned licking it away as she moaned his name...

He'd been a blind idiot with her for far too long. Thankfully, the universe had decided it wasn't his time yet. He'd survived a near-fatal blow, and he wouldn't squander the opportunity to do things differently this time.

This time, he would break down Arianna's walls, even if she fought him the entire way.

And when he succeeded, perhaps they would finally experience the profound emotion they were both so terrified to feel.

Perhaps, together, they could learn to love without pain.

Inhaling the fragrant air, Dominic ran beside the woman who consumed his thoughts, determined to make it happen.

CHAPTER 2

Arianna Lawson placed two fingers between her lips and gave a loud whistle. "Okay, boys. That's enough for today. Head back to home plate."

Several kids ran from the outfield as she placed her hand on the catcher's shoulder. "Nice job, Chris. You're getting quicker at popping up from the catcher's position. I can tell you've been practicing."

White teeth flashed under his thick mop of brown hair. "Thanks, Arianna. I wanted to pitch, but no one told me being a catcher was so fun."

"Pitchers get all the glory, but catchers are the anchor. You're a natural leader, and you're good at anchoring the other kids."

He beamed under her praise as the children surrounded them.

"Great job today, guys," she said, clapping her hands in a few solid claps. "I might be leaving on a mission soon, and when I go, I'm leaving Chris in charge. I want you all to keep practicing, okay?"

"Yes, ma'am," they chimed.

Arianna smiled, remembering the days when grown men had addressed her that way. Times had changed, but she still enjoyed the thrill of leading a team. Even if they were a bunch of kids learning to play wiffle ball.

Splaying her hand above the ground, palm down, she waited until they'd all rested their smaller hands atop hers. "Gooooo, team!"

They raised their hands in a simultaneous cheer before gathering their tattered gloves and balls to head home.

"Well, Ari. It seems you've already got the 'mom' thing down pat," Dani said, smiling broadly as she approached.

"They're cute," she responded with a shrug. "What can I say? I was doomed the first time they asked me to play with them. Adorable little bastards."

Chuckling, Dani crossed her arms over her chest to ward off the chill. Although the morning had been warm, a cold front seemed to be moving in. Glancing toward the rapidly darkening sky, Arianna jerked her head. "Come on. Let's head back to the school before it rains."

Nodding, Dani slid her arm around Arianna's waist, the gesture representative of her caring nature. Arianna wasn't overly affectionate—to put it mildly—but they'd been through some pretty rough shit lately, and she loved her sister immensely. Placing her arm over Dani's shoulders, they walked silently as the gravity of their current situation loomed between them.

"We have to go get her, Ari," Dani said softly, concern in her green eyes as she glanced up at Arianna. "Raquel fucked up royally, but we can't leave her with Cromwell. Whether she believes it or not, she's in danger."

"I know." Anger hummed deep within as Arianna contemplated Raquel's betrayal. They'd both trusted their little sister, never understanding she posed a grave threat.

Raquel blamed Dani for denying her a proper goodbye when their mother died from cancer. In a twisted act of revenge for that supposed misdeed, she'd betrayed them all. Raquel had been responsible for the blow that caused Dani's amnesia. Now, she was living in the DC Sen City controlled by Luthor Cromwell, the notorious man who'd funded the drug that destroyed society and created their dystopian world.

Sadly, Dani had been the scientist who created the drug, although she'd been an unwitting pawn. Now that they'd retrieved the antidote from the Sendaxa lab in Maryland, Dani was intent on creating a remedy to battle the EverLife addiction that crippled so many.

Curing humanity would mean defeating Luthor Cromwell, who now commanded what remained of the US military—and also the man who was harboring Raquel in exchange for her extensive knowledge as a botanist. Her expertise could be used to create more addictive drugs and extend Luthor's domination of their broken society. Arianna loved her two sisters, and vacillated between heartbreak and fury at Raquel's betrayal. No matter how angry Raquel was, deceiving your family was a concept Arianna would never understand.

"You need to keep working on replicating the antidote, so I'll go to the DC Sen City and get Raquel," Arianna said.

"It's dangerous—"

"Yeah? Thanks for the heads up."

Breathing a laugh, Dani sighed. "I can't lose you too. I'll only feel comfortable if Maverick and Dom go with you."

"No fucking way. I don't need a babysitter. I can rescue her myself. You need Maverick here. He's formed an alliance with Reyes, and you need a trained soldier to remain behind. The people here have been good to us so far, but that could change anytime. I won't leave you unprotected."

Stopping, Dani pulled away and turned to face her. Placing her hands in her back pockets, she kicked the ground with the toe of her sneaker. "Then I guess Dom will have to go with you. Do you think he's ready?"

Arianna's lips thinned. "I don't need him. I can do it myself—"

"That's not what I asked," she said, softly but firmly. "Do you think he's healed enough to go with you?"

Arianna's lips fluttered as she crossed her arms. "Probably. He didn't croak when we ran seven miles this morning."

Dani pursed her lips, obviously trying to contain her smile as Arianna rolled her eyes.

"This isn't some grand love story, Dani. I told you, I don't want that shit. I want you to save the world so I can get away from people, not form *more* relationships. Stop trying to matchmake or whatever the fuck you're doing."

Her sister's eyes darted between hers as silence stretched between them. Finally, she stated the truth. "He knows how you feel. Why are you pretending you don't care?"

"He doesn't know shit," she said, kicking the ground. "And he loves you—"

"No," she said, showing her palm. "I'm not letting you hide behind that anymore, Ari. I have lots of notes in my journal to remind you that you deserve love and to stop pushing it away." She flashed a cheeky grin. "And Dominic's a good match for you. The whole sexy scar thing," she pointed at her face, indicating where Dominic's scar resided, "plus the way he looks at you when he thinks no one is watching... It's really cute."

"I'm banning you from writing about me in your journal. It's annoying."

Dani bit her bottom lip to contain her smile. "Sorry, but I need my notes to remember what the hell I'm doing. I'm getting more flashes of memory back every day, but I'm nowhere near one hundred percent." She patted Arianna's upper arm affectionately. "And you're one of my favorite people to write about, so you're staying in."

Releasing a frustrated breath, Arianna ran a hand over the silky dark hair that covered half of her head. "Fine, but a discussion about Dominic is off the table. It doesn't matter anyway. I have one objective: to help you save the world. I know you won't be able to fully concentrate on doing that until Raquel is safe. Even though you're pissed, you don't want her dead. So, I'll go to Washington, DC, and get her. Alone."

Dani squinted one eye as she contemplated. "You know, even if I agree, Dominic won't let you go alone. He'll insist on going with you, especially if Mav stays here with me."

"Doesn't matter. I'll leave when he's sleeping."

Emitting a resigned laugh, Dani stretched out her hands. Arianna took them and held tight.

"You know I want you to be happy, right?" Dani whispered, her eyes filling with tears as her voice tuned raspy. "I hate that you fight being happy, Arianna. Mom would want more for you."

"I'll get what I want when you replicate the antidote," she said, squeezing Dani's fingers. "I'll finally get to have a kid and live off the grid where I can get some peace and quiet."

Dani's eyebrows lifted as excitement laced her expression. "Dom's kid?"

Laughing, Arianna tugged her sister against her side as they resumed walking. "Everyone always says I'm the stubborn one, but I don't hold a candle to you."

"Truth."

They walked arm in arm until they reached the school that was their makeshift home. "Once I'm done in the lab, I'm going to make dinner in the old home economics room. We can discuss your mission to retrieve Raquel while we eat."

"Fine."

"Okay, I've got to get back to work," Dani said, waving as she backed down the hallway toward the old sixth grade science lab. "I'm getting closer, Ari."

"It's been three weeks. Give yourself some grace. I know you can do it."

Her sister nodded before turning and striding away.

Arianna entered the bathroom, which had stalls and rows of mirrors above functional sinks. After washing off the grime of the day, she trailed to the gymnasium, intent on getting in one more workout before dinner. If she was going to rescue her sister, she'd need to be fit and ready.

Especially if Dominic came with her.

Frowning, she debated the pros and cons of having him by her side. He wasn't in prime condition since being shot, but the man was recovering like some kind of cyborg. Whatever physical limitations he had wouldn't hinder him.

But having him near her might compromise her mission. After all, it was hard to continue to pretend indifference when he was around all the damn time.

And Arianna was intent on remaining indifferent.

She'd played the love game before, several times in her life. Each time, she'd been badly burned. Each man had tossed her love back in her face as if it were trash flitting along a filthy street.

If she allowed Dominic in and he ultimately rejected her, she wasn't sure she'd survive. After all, she loved the man to the point of distraction. It was utterly ridiculous and completely uncontrollable.

And he'd already rejected her countless times anyway. Every time he gazed longingly at Dani when Arianna had been there. Every time he looked past her to see someone he truly *wanted* to see.

No one had ever wanted to see her. And damn it, she was tired of caring or wanting them to try. Smart people eventually stopped doing the same shit and expecting different results. And she wasn't a genius like Dani, but she was pretty fucking smart.

Although Dani was her adopted sister, they shared a bond more solid than blood. Arianna's birth parents had died in a car accident when she was only four years old, and Cynthia Lawson had adopted her even though she was young and most likely unprepared for a child.

Arianna loved Dani from the first moment she felt her kick beneath Cynthia's swollen belly. They grew up as sisters and confidants before eventually experiencing the death of Dani's father, Bill, and the immeasurable heartache of Cynthia's death from cancer.

So much fucking loss. If Arianna took the time to dwell on it, she'd probably drown in grief.

Grief and loss...and *pain*...had no place in their dystopian world.

Picking up the dumbbells, Arianna began to furiously pump, working her biceps as she stared into the faded mirror. Gazing into her own eyes, she vowed to keep the wall between her and Dominic Cavalleri firmly in place.

Because if she let her guard down and he decided to discard her as thoughtlessly as every man had in the past—or leave her as most of the people she'd ever loved eventually did—it might break her.

Observing him love Dani reaffirmed that emotional connection wasn't in the cards for her. Allowing Dominic inside only to lose him as she'd lost everyone else wasn't an option.

She'd survived losing her adoptive mother and her sister's betrayal.

Hell, she'd survived the end of civilization as they'd known it.

But Arianna knew she wasn't strong enough to survive gaining—and then losing—the love of her fucking life.

So, she would push him away and hope the stubborn man got the message.

Arianna Lawson's heart was closed for business, and she didn't plan on opening it ever again.

Chapter 3

D r. Danica Lawson-Ward gazed into the microscope, absently murmuring to herself as she studied the liquid specimen on the slide.

"The cyclotides are working," she whispered excitedly. "Holy shit!"

"Am I going to get fired if I don't know what cyclotides are?" a deep voice asked in her ear.

Smiling, she glanced up at her husband as his arms encircled her from behind. "I think I'll let you live. And do you work for me anyway? I think you work for Reyes, whether you want to admit it or not."

Maverick's lips curved. "For a guy I was going to murder the first time I met him, he's turned out to be pretty cool."

Breathing a laugh, Dani turned and slid her arms around his neck. "You're basically his second-in-command at this point."

His features tensed as he nodded. "Although I detest the thought of more fighting and destruction, we're going to have to protect ourselves if we want to distribute your formula to the masses. And we'll eventually have to take the offensive. We need to be prepared and I like being on the inside."

"As long as you protect yourself first," she said, tightening her arms. "I just barely remembered who you are. I need to make up for lost time."

"Any new memories today?" he asked, tapping her forehead.

"Did we take a vacation to Peru?" She squinted one eye as a vague memory appeared at the edge of her consciousness.

"Yep. You complained the entire time we hiked to the top of Machu Pichu, but once we got there, it was breathtaking."

"I'm sure I did no such thing!"

Chuckling, he brushed her nose with his. "You did, but your expression when we finally made it was worth it." Stealing a kiss, he nipped her lip. "I'm happy you remember."

"I remember some of it," she said, pecking his lips before releasing him. "But not enough. It's frustrating as hell, but I'm trying not to waste energy on things I can't control."

Craning his neck, he glanced at the microscope. "How's the new antidote coming along?"

"Good." Pointing to her scribbled notes, her finger slowly ran across the page as she spoke. "The original antidote we retrieved from the lab was mostly comprised of plant and herbs. It's as if I knew I might need to reproduce it outside of a lab with elements commonly found in nature."

"My wife, the genius," he said reverently. "You knew Luthor was bad news toward the end, so that doesn't surprise me."

Dani glowed at his praise, his support a stabilizing presence against the turmoil that swam deep in her gut. Although she'd awoken with barely any memory of the past five years, she'd felt safe with him from the first moment she opened her eyes. It didn't make sense to her logical, scientific brain, but she couldn't deny the tangible energy that connected her to Maverick.

Returning to the topic, she continued. "I'm trying to rebuild the antidote with naturally occurring plant elements so we can mass produce it. I'm also attempting to create something that's also a cure, so it's challenging."

Maverick cocked his brow. "But you love a challenge."

"Damn right I do," she said with a firm nod. "I'm close, Mav, and I'm determined to create an antidote that's even more effective than the one I created in the lab."

"So, tell me about cyclotides."

Blowing out a breath, she hesitated as she tried to explain in layman's terms. "Cyclotides are organic peptides found in violets and pansies that bond with opioid receptors. In theory, if injected into the blood stream, cyclotides can bond with the receptors first so EverLife never has a chance to induce the high that leads to addiction."

His eyebrows lifted. "So, they could be preventative?"

"Yes. But I also want to include compounds that will reverse cravings for anyone already addicted. The plants I've identified that work the best so far are milk thistle, St. John's Wart, ginger and cayenne pepper."

"Cayenne pepper?"

"It's a potent provitamin. If I can get all the elements combined in the right portions, it just might work."

"Sadly, there are almost fifty subjects for you to practice on in the clinic."

The clinic was a run-down regional hospital that had been abandoned when society collapsed. It sat inside the compound's walls and had two generators that allowed it to function as a care facility—barely. Former nurses and physicians volunteered to help the addicted and sick, and Dani would eventually test her new formula on the patients there.

"I have no doubt you'll knock it out of the park," he said, reassuringly squeezing her shoulder. "What can I do to help?"

"I need a team to scout for the various plants so I can add them to the garden behind the school. Some of them already grow here naturally, but others will require scouting beyond the compound. I wish Raquel was here so she could help me. She knows more about plants than anyone."

"I know," he said, his tone sympathetic as he shook his head. "Such a damn shame. I'm no expert, but I can try and scout for you."

"I'll just need your protection as we search outside the walls. I should be able to find everything I need if we dedicate the time to looking."

"Of course." His eyes darted between hers. "But if I'm protecting you, that means I can't go with Arianna to rescue Raquel."

"Dom's going to go with her. We spoke about it this afternoon."

"And she agreed?"

"She, uh..." Clearing her throat, Dani shrugged. "I'm not actually sure, but I'm putting my foot down. Ari's tough, but there's no way she's going to DC by herself. End of story."

"There's my slugger," he said, flashing a grin. "And Dom's ready to travel?"

"I've been treating his wound, but it's healing better than I could've hoped. I don't see it hindering him."

"And are we sure Arianna won't strangle him?" he teased.

"I'm hoping they'll tangle in other ways, if you catch my drift." She waggled her eyebrows.

Maverick's expression warmed as he studied her. "My optimistic scientist. I hope it happens."

"On that note, I need to finish my notes before I cook dinner. It will probably get a bit explosive when I insist on Dom accompanying her. I need to prepare."

"You've got this," he said, kissing her forehead. "Need help?"

"Can you get a pot of water boiling? I found a box of pasta and a jar of sauce in one of the cabinets in the home economics room, so we're having spaghetti. I'll be there shortly."

Nodding, he winked before pivoting and heading out the door. Tilting her head, Dani observed his firm ass and broad shoulders, the corner of her mouth ticking up as she inwardly squealed with the zeal of a teenage girl.

"God, he's hot," she breathed before turning back to the microscope to get to work. After logging the rest of the session notes, she capitulated to her growling stomach and headed to cook dinner.

Chapter 4

An hour later, Arianna entered the home economics room, mouth watering at the decadent smell. Approaching Dani at the stove, she inhaled deeply.

"I forgot how good pasta smells. Yum."

"Since we have to divide it into five servings, I also made a salad for everyone. It won't be a huge meal, but the spinach growing in the garden out back is fresh and we need veggies."

"Why do we need five servings—?"

"Because you have an extra guest," Arthur Reyes's deep voice chimed as he breezed into the room. Arching a brow, he gestured toward Dani. "She invited me."

"We're going to discuss your trip to retrieve Raquel, and Arthur has all the cars since he's in charge of the compound," Dani said, her expression laced with a twinge of guilt at the omission as she shrugged. "It's better if we strategize together."

Arianna's gaze raked over Arthur. He'd been kind to them so far, but she was skeptical of everyone in their post-apocalyptic world. Arthur Reyes had been speculating a run for president before society fell apart, and she sometimes wondered if his motives were pure. Did he truly want to help rebuild the world, or did he want to replace Luthor Cromwell and seize ultimate power himself?

"I like that she doesn't trust me," Arthur said, annoying Arianna as he referred to her as if she wasn't in the room. "It keeps me honest."

"Honesty isn't really what I'm worried about," Arianna muttered, picking up two of the salad plates and setting them on the table Dani had set for dinner. "I'm just wary of egomaniacs who want to rule the world."

"All the more reason to take down Cromwell," Arthur said with a thoughtful nod.

Arianna just grunted as she continued placing food on the table. Dominic and Maverick strolled into the room, and Dani turned off the stove.

"Grab it while it's hot, guys," she said, waving them over.

Arianna served herself a fifth of the noodles and sauce, careful to only take her share so everyone had an equal portion. Once they were seated, Maverick smiled at Dominic.

"How are you feeling today, man?"

"Good. Arianna pushed me on our run this morning, but it was exactly what I needed." Rubbing the bandage over his wound, he smiled. "It's just an annoying gash at this point. It alternates between slightly stinging and itching ever since Dani remove the stitches."

"Thank god the bullet didn't hit a major vessel," Maverick said. "You were really lucky."

As they spoke, Arianna recalled the moment when Dominic had been sprawled before her, blood gushing from his neck as he struggled to breathe. It had been one of the most terrifying moments of her life. She'd begged every god she didn't believe in to save him—even if he was in love with Dani and would never love her back.

His words from their jog resurfaced, causing her to form a slight scowl. *"You know my feelings for Dani were born from mutual experience."* Inwardly scoffing, Arianna bristled. He could deny it, but she'd seen his feelings for Dani on full display more times than she could count. He was gentle with her. Soft. Compassionate. Everything one should be for someone they loved...

"Ari?" Dani asked.

"Huh?"

"You zoned out there for a second," she teased. "I was telling Arthur that you agreed to go to DC to retrieve Raquel."

"Uh, yeah," she said, running her palm over the nearly bald side of her head. "I've started growing this out so I won't stand out as much. Being almost six feet tall with broad shoulders is already noticeable enough, but I'd like to try and be inconspicuous as I infiltrate the city. Not an easy feat."

"And I told Maverick that you agreed Dom should come with you," Dani continued, her tone firm. "That way, Mav can stay here and help us at the compound."

Arianna's expression turned deadpan. "I agreed to no such thing. Dom needs to recover. I'm going alone."

"No fucking way," Dominic said, his tone low and immobile. "I'm coming with you."

"I don't have time to play nurse—"

"I'm well enough to help you, Ari," Dominic interrupted, annoying her with his bossy tone. "And our chances are better if we work together."

"I know I'm new to the inner circle," Arthur said, showing his palms, "but I agree. And I think you two could actually complete *two* missions while you're there."

Arianna stared at the ceiling in frustration. "Oh, great. Another man's opinion I don't need. I'm all ears."

"*Ari...*" Dani warned.

Arianna just glared at her as Arthur continued.

"I understand that rescuing Raquel is important to you. I'd like to say I wouldn't have the same deference for a traitor, but if it were my sister, I'd probably go through the depths of hell to save her, even if she betrayed me."

"We're both pissed and heartbroken," Dani said, her shoulders deflating as she shook her head. "But she's our sister and we promised our mom we'd take care of her."

With a compassionate nod, Arthur continued. "As you all know, I have a well-trained team of spies who are excellent at obtaining information from DC. All signs indicate a rebellion is brewing inside the city walls."

"Tristan Holder indicated the same to me when we spoke in the lab," Arianna confirmed.

"I'm aware. Knowing this, I'd like to ask you to approach Tristan when you're in the city. It seems he's playing both sides of the fence, considering that he let you live during the lab break in, and I want to see if we can pull him to our side."

"To what end?" Arianna asked.

Sitting back, Arthur thoughtfully rubbed his chin. "I want an ally on the inside. Once Dani has a working antidote, we're going to eventually storm the city. It will be easier to take Cromwell down if we work with someone from his inner circle, especially if a rebellion is already forming. I would bet that Tristan is involved."

Arianna chewed as she mulled. Considering Tristan's actions at the lab, it was possible they could form an alliance. "I don't trust him, but I think you're right. He's certainly not Cromwell's biggest fan."

"If you can make contact with him, I have a secret radio channel set up between our compound and several others. We'll loop him in and hopefully work with him to formulate a plan to infiltrate DC. It's time we took it back for the people."

"And who will lead them then?" Arianna asked derisively. "You?"

Arthur's eyes flared with equal parts mirth and annoyance as he smirked. "Perhaps. I've done a pretty good job running this place. The sick and addicted are treated well in the clinic by volunteers. Children who lost parents are taken in by adults who want to help. We're a highly functioning compound considering the state of the world and lack of resources."

Arianna studied Maverick and Dani as she contemplated. "You two okay with this?"

"If it's not Reyes, it will be someone else," Maverick said, resignation in his voice. "Better to go with the devil we know—"

"Hey," Arthur interrupted, cupping Maverick's shoulder, "am I the devil in this situation?"

Grinning, Maverick shrugged. "I think so. But you've given us shelter and your actions have been honorable." Looking at Arianna, he arched a brow. "I trust him, Ari."

"To be clear, I'll need a competent, trustworthy leadership team if we successfully wrest power from Cromwell," Arthur said, lifting a finger. "I want you on that team, Maverick. Maybe that will help ease your concerns, Arianna. Someone you trust will be nearby to keep me in check."

Arianna's eyes narrowed. "I thought you two were ready to settle down and have a bunch of babies once Dani healed everyone."

"I've got a few good years left in me and I think we can do both." Maverick slid his fingers over Dani's wrist and gave a gentle squeeze. "And I want to help. Rebuilding the world is going to be hard enough. Might as well finish the job we started."

Swallowing the last of her pasta, Arianna pushed the plate away and rested her chin on her hand. Her lips fluttered as she expelled a breath, causing the hair above her forehead to flit. "Fine. If Mav's involved in your regime, I'm in. But first, Dani has to finish the antidote and we have to take back the city."

"I've already got a team ready to scour the forest until we find the rest of the plants and herbs I need. I'm close to having some compounds I can test on the addicted clinic patients."

"Thank god," Arthur said. "We keep them alive with the shitty antidotes we get from black-market dealers, but they're full of dangerous chemicals. We need your pure antidote, Dani."

Arianna found his tone sincere and made a silent note to ease up on him. Saving lives was a worthy endeavor, and she wanted to do her part. "I'll approach Tristan while I'm in the city, and I have some old contacts I can try and track down to get information on a possible rebellion. Not sure if they're still in DC, but it's worth a shot. I'll need all the details on the secret radio channel so I pass on the correct intel to Tristan."

"*We'll* approach Tristan and Arianna's contacts," Dominic corrected as Arianna scowled. "And I'd like a full briefing too."

"I'll brief you both in the morning, if that works," Arthur said, rising. "Meet me at the abandoned gas station down the road from the school. After the briefing, we can pick out a car for you to drive to DC." Facing Dani, he gave a slight bow. "Dinner was lovely, thank you. Do you need me to help clean up?"

"No, I'll do it," she said, waving her hand. "Washing dishes is cathartic for me. I need some mindless activity after stressing my brain all day."

With a polite nod, he waved to everyone before departing.

Arianna threaded her hands behind her head, studying everyone as they finished dinner.

"Rescue Raquel, get Tristan on our side, and figure out if a rebellion is forming. Piece of cake."

Dominic shot her an acerbic look, understanding the mission would be extremely complex. "The city is heavily fortified, but I know it well since I used to live there. We'll need to find a place to stay that takes cash and stay off the grid."

The legs of Arianna's chair scraped across the floor as she stood. "I lived there too," she said, already frustrated that he was making decisions for her. Approaching him, she glared down as she lowered her voice. "And let's get one thing straight. *I'm* the leader of this mission. You can come with me, but I give the orders." Without waiting for a response, she strolled out of the room.

Chapter 5

D ominic pursed his lips at Arianna's departing figure. Glancing between Maverick and Dani, he grinned. "She seems thrilled I'm going with her."

Tossing back her head, Dani broke into a laugh. "Ah, Dom. Thank god you're not easily intimidated. She's my sister and I adore her, but damn, she's scary sometimes."

Chuckling, Dominic regarded the woman he'd convinced himself he loved for years. He still carried unwavering affection for Dani, but something had changed when he'd been shot. Visions of Arianna's multicolored eyes brimming with tears as she silently begged him not to die flashed in his brain, and he remembered the full force of the buzzing energy that always vibrated between them. It was much more powerful than anything he'd felt for Dani, and he cursed himself that he'd overlooked it for so long.

"Is it weird that I like how intimidating she is?"

Dani's smile widened into a full-on beam. "Nope. It's about time someone did."

Affection swelled at her obvious love for her sister as he stood. "I'm going to talk to her. She'll be fine, and I won't let anything happen to her."

"I know you won't," Dani said. "Go on so my husband can wash the dishes with me."

"Did I agree to wash the dishes?" Maverick teased, squinting one eye.

"I'll let you seduce me by the sink," she said, standing and grabbing two empty plates as she winked.

"Hot damn. Hand me a sponge, woman."

Dominic saluted them and thanked Dani for dinner before heading to find Arianna. Since he'd developed an insatiable need to know her whereabouts after his injury, he knew she liked to watch the sun set atop the old hill that crested behind the school where the withered pavement met the forest.

Exiting the double doors, he trailed over the asphalt and up the grass-covered hill, marveling at how tall and regal she appeared in the waning light of the sun. It washed over her bronzed skin, her shoulders and neck visible under her black tank top. He approached slowly, annoyance welling when her shoulders tensed.

"Can't get any damn privacy on this godforsaken compound," she muttered, staring in the distance as he neared, refusing to turn and acknowledge him.

The defiant gesture only made him more determined to infiltrate those thick walls. Stepping beside her, he slid his hands in his back pockets, gazing at the orange glow of the setting sun.

"We'll be more effective together," he finally said, judging her reaction from the corner of his eye as he stood firm. "And I'm fine with you being in charge."

She shot him a droll look. "Is that so? I wasn't aware I asked your permission."

Cocking a brow, he turned slightly toward her. "You haven't. Yet. There might be a time for that, but I don't think we're there yet."

Rotating to face him, she held up a finger. "This is about rescuing Raquel and making contact with Tristan. That's all. We'll work together as teammates and return to the compound once we've accomplished our task so we can formulate next steps. I don't know what nonsense Dani filled your head with, but I want no part of it."

Crossing his arms, he planted his feet as he waited. "Are you done?"

Scoffing, she turned away to stare at the horizon again, perhaps so he wouldn't see the emotion in those stunning eyes. "Yeah. And you're damn right I'm in charge." Grimacing, she began kneading the muscle between her neck and shoulder. "Damn it. I think I pulled something when I did weights today."

Sliding behind her—carefully, so she didn't run—he gently encircled her wrist. She bristled, her nostrils flaring as he slowly lowered her arm. Replacing her fingers with his, he began to massage her inflamed muscle.

Her throat bobbed as she continued to stare at the yellow-orange glow in the distance. The pulse on the free side of her neck throbbed in tandem with his firm movements, indicating she wasn't as unaffected by his touch as she portrayed.

Leaning closer, he could see the fine black hairs that were beginning to grow on the shaved side of her head. Placing his lips near the shell of her ear, he softly spoke. "You have a knot."

"No shit."

Breathing a laugh, he continued to work the muscle. She eventually closed her eyes and leaned her head forward, allowing him greater access. Joy reverberated in every cell of his skin as she opened herself to him, if only slightly.

"When we were in the lab—"

"I don't want to discuss that," she interrupted. "I told you—"

"When we were in the lab," he repeated, squeezing her shoulder as she grunted, "I was under the impression you didn't want me to die. Was I wrong about that?"

Sighing, she shook her head. "Of course I didn't want you to die." His fingers mourned the loss of her soft skin as she drew away and turned to face him. Gazing into his eyes, her tone was solemn. "But I'm a proud woman, Dom, and I'm not some fucking rom-com movie heroine."

His lips twitched. "No one would accuse you of that, Ari. Especially not me."

Mirth flashed across her strong features before they returned to the firm mask he was used to. "I'm not Dani. Get that through your fucking head. I don't need saving and I sure as hell don't need a man. We'll accomplish our mission and that's it. Are we clear?"

His eyes darted back and forth between hers as that palpable energy resonated between them. Deciding now wasn't the time to fight this battle, he relented. "We're clear."

"Good." With a nod, she breezed by him and began trudging down the hill.

"I just have one question," he called, hope surging in his chest when she halted.

"Yeah?"

"Who are you trying to convince? Me? Or yourself?"

Her features contorted into the scowl he'd somehow come to treasure before she lifted her hand and extended the middle finger. Unable to contain his grin, he absorbed her angry glare before she resumed the trek and disappeared into the school.

Facing the now-gray horizon, Dominic anticipated being near her as they completed their mission. Her goals were clear: rescue Raquel and acquire Tristan as an ally.

Dominic shared those goals, but he also had one more he was determined to accomplish: he was going to shatter Arianna's walls if it fucking killed him. And then, he was going to divest her of the notion she was in charge.

For, when he finally infiltrated her steely defenses, Dominic would revel in showing her how pleasurable taking orders from the *right* man could be...

Chapter 6

The next morning, Arianna sat beside Dominic in the office of the abandoned gas station. After a restless night spent thinking about the upcoming mission, she felt a twinge of guilt that she'd stormed off after their conversation. Even if she wanted to go alone, he was intent on helping her, and there was honor in that. Plus, he'd agreed she should lead the mission, which deflated her need to argue with him—about *that* at least. Pity, since arguing with Dom was one of her favorite pastimes.

Perhaps her favorite of all, if she was being honest.

Once they were finished with Arthur's briefing, she promised to make peace with her unwanted companion. The decision had been made. She could at least try to be amenable. Even if the idea made her grit her teeth in frustration.

Shaking her head, she willed herself back to the mission at hand. Arthur sat on the edge of the desk as he rotated what appeared to be a homemade transmitter in his hands.

"This was fashioned by a self-proclaimed geek here on the compound," he said as he slowly showed off the device. "If one has a shortwave radio and knows the frequency, they can receive secret messages."

Lifting the nearby radio, he sat it on the edge of the desk and raised the antenna. Arianna vaguely remembered radio units from her childhood but wasn't intricately familiar with them.

"It's confusing after living with cell phones and internet for so long," Arthur said, smiling at her perplexed expression. "But it's all we've got left. You can leave this radio with Tristan and tell him to tune to the 4930 Khz frequency. I'll communicate with him in Morse code until I verify his identity. Then I'll create a new code between us to plan the siege on the city."

Arianna tilted her head in agreement. "Good idea. No one can intercept the messages if they don't know the code."

"Bingo." Arthur handed her the radio, and she slipped it into her backpack.

"Now, let's talk cars," Arianna said, a twinge of excitement in her voice. "I'm hoping you have a red 1964 Porche 911 with my name on it."

Arthur tossed back his head and laughed. "I'm not sure whether to deride your optimism or admire your taste in cars." Rising, he gestured for them to follow him outside. "Your choices are a bit less exciting. Blue sedan. Black pickup. White SUV," he finished, pointing at each car parked beside the building.

Arianna glanced at Dominic. "I think the sedan is best. It will get good gas mileage, and we can find a place outside the wall to hide it until we need to return."

Dominic rubbed his chin as his eyes narrowed. "The pickup and the SUV will give us more cover if we get attacked by any deserters or Sen Force troops on the journey."

"Yeah, but they'll guzzle more gas and are harder to hide in a forested area."

Dominic grinned at Arthur. "She's the boss. We'll take the sedan. You've calculated the optimal route?"

"It's best if you take old Route 7. It's more rural than other roads, so it will hopefully keep you off the radar." Reaching behind his back, he pulled a folded map from his belt. "I've marked the route for you. It will take you a little less than three hours to get to DC, and you'll end up near the old Chain Bridge Forest neighborhood, where you can hopefully find a good spot to hide the car. That neighborhood was abandoned when the residents moved inside the city walls."

"And then we'll cross the Potomac River and do our best to infiltrate the wall unnoticed," Arianna said, arching a brow as she took the map. "It's going to be fun."

Arthur smiled. "I like your sense of adventure, Arianna. As we've discussed, crossing the Chain Bridge is the best choice since it's the narrowest part of the river. My informants tell me there's a vulnerable spot in the wall about a mile south that's only patrolled by two Sen Force soldiers."

"Are there cameras as well?" Arianna asked.

"Yes. One on each side of the vulnerability. You'll need to shoot them to disarm them after you disable the guards. Since we're trying to save lives here instead of end them, I left some tranquilizing guns in the travel pack I prepared for you." He tapped his neck. "Shoot them here and the guards will be out for hours."

"We appreciate the supplies," Dominic said. "I'm assuming you'll give us real guns too?"

"The travel pack is full of cash, a few gold bars and two hand guns," he said, gesturing toward the office they'd just vacated. "I also left some bullets, but my supply is limited."

"Then we'll have to be precise," Dominic said. "We plan to leave around noon so we have time to stash the car and hike to the crossing once it gets dark. Our chances of breaching the wall are better under the cover of night."

"I wish you both a successful mission," Arthur said, extending his hand to shake Arianna's and then Dominic's. After giving them both a good-natured salute, he pivoted and headed toward the main path that led to the center of the compound.

"He's thorough. I'll give him that," Arianna said, gripping the straps of her backpack as she stared up at Dom. His six-foot-six height and broad shoulders made him one of the only men she'd ever found physically imposing. And yet, there was an innate gentleness under his stoic exterior. One that made her feel safe and slightly terrified at the same time. It was that gentleness that called to her when she closed her eyes late at night and imagined his deep voice in her ear as he ran his fingers over her skin...

"Who's going to drive?" she asked, observing his jagged scar glint in the sunlight. It was somehow ominous and sexy at the same time, and she wondered why it only served to increase her attraction to him. It made no sense, but she yearned to trace her finger over the ragged laceration. To trail from the edge of his dark eyebrow, over that firm nose, and to the corner of the full lips she'd envisioned kissing the most sensitive places of her body too many times to count.

"We can take shifts," he said, shrugging. "I'm sure you'll have to stop and pee every hour."

"*Pfft*," she said, unable to control her grin at his teasing. "I've got kidneys of steel. You'll see."

Dominic smiled before glancing at the car. "We need to stock up on water and food. Not too much but enough to sustain us if something goes wrong."

"I'll raid the kitchen at the school." Kicking the ground with the toe of her boot, she cleared her throat. "I...uh..."

"Yesssss?" he asked, arching a brow.

"Well, I just..." Huffing, she rolled her eyes. "I know I'm not the easiest person..."

"You? You're a basket of butterflies, Ari."

Expelling a breath, she stared into his deep brown eyes. "I guess you're going to use my nickname whether I like it or not."

He stepped closer, forcing her to tilt her head. Determined not to shrink, she straightened her spine.

Leaning forward, he spoke in that butter-rich tone as his warm breath washed over her cheeks. "Does it really bother you?"

Her throat bobbed as she contemplated. "It's something people who know me call me. And you don't know me."

He recoiled slightly, hurt flashing across his features before he shook his head. "I know enough. I know you were trying to thank me for coming with you just now, even if you did a piss poor job at it."

Scoffing, she rolled her eyes. "That's what I get for trying to be nice."

"And I know we're going to have the best outcome if we get along. So, let's both just admit we're in this together and be nice to each other."

"I'm nice," she said, frowning.

"Oh, yeah? I really enjoyed you flipping me the bird yesterday."

She bit her lip, loving the resulting flare in his eyes. The sizzling energy between them had only intensified since his injury, even if she refused to acknowledge it.

"I'll try to be nice," she said, capitulating. "It's not really my MO."

Leaning closer, he tilted his head as he studied her. "I think Chris and the other kids would beg to differ. And Dani and Mav too. You're nice in your own way. Just not to me. I wonder why?"

"Because you're annoying," she snapped before quickly realizing it was that knee-jerk reaction she needed to control. "We both annoy the hell out of each other. But I don't want to argue with you. We need to be in sync. So I'll do better."

"You don't annoy me," he said, his tone genuine. "Not anymore. Getting shot will open a man's eyes."

"I've heard you tell Mav you want to strangle me."

"Maybe once or twice," he said, grinning. "But I think you're a good person under that harsh exterior, and it's time for us to be friends."

"Friends," she responded morosely.

"For now." His eyes lowered to her neck and collarbone before lifting back to hers. A challenge simmered deep in the brown orbs, and her knees threatened to buckle. "I'm game if you are."

Overwhelmed with the intensity between them, she took a step back. "Okay, *friend*. We'll give that a try. Maybe you can..." She trailed off, suddenly embarrassed for some reason.

Dark eyebrows lifted as he waited.

"I mean...uh, maybe you can tell me about Pam and your parents. I've always wanted to hear the story from you, and I can probably relate since my mom and my birth parents...you know..." Fumbling, she shook her head. "Shit, I'm bad at this."

His warm laughter surrounded her as he reassuringly cupped her upper arm, causing tiny bumps to spring up underneath his palm. "You're doing fine. And I'd love to tell you about them. You've never asked so I didn't want to bother you with my sad stories."

"I stopped asking people to share their stories with me a long time ago" was her solemn response. "And you always had Dani to talk to." He opened his mouth to respond, and she held up a hand. "Regardless, I'm asking now. In the whole spirit of being *friends*." She made quotation marks with her fingers.

Something akin to admiration laced his features. "I know it wasn't easy for you to ask. Someday, maybe you'll tell me why you stay locked inside that shell." He gently tapped her shoulder above her collarbone. "I think you've got some stories to tell too."

Arianna didn't share her pain with anyone. No matter how friendly they became, she couldn't fathom opening herself up to Dominic and exposing the deep-rooted ache she'd always felt just by being *her*. She was an outsider. Different. She always had been since she'd lost every blood relative at four years old.

Cynthia Lawson had brought her into their family, and Arianna had loved her to distraction, but she'd never shaken the feeling of not belonging. Instead of trying to fit in, she'd eventually accepted her place in the world and reacted accordingly. Even her hair was a fuck-you to the norm.

That lack of belonging was where her deep-rooted need to have a biological child stemmed from. Arianna longed to have at least one person on the planet who shared her blood. Who was *part* of her. Someone who wouldn't be able to hurt or leave her as so many others had.

A child she could love without fear.

To protect that child, she would create a safe space. A place only for the two of them, secluded and serene. A place where her child felt wholly loved and connected to the mother who'd born her.

Arianna craved that connection in ways that almost frightened her sometimes. But she guessed that meant she hadn't completely given up on feeling basic human emotion, so she allowed the need to exist deep in her heart.

"Oh, yeah," Dominic said, his smile deepening. "There's a lot to unleash in there. I'd love to hear it. Even strong people need a shoulder to lean on sometimes."

"Let's start with your stories and we'll get to mine eventually," she said, inwardly promising she'd never share her most personal stories with him. But she was a damn good listener, and she'd always imagined comforting him like Dani had. Did she have the capacity to do it? That remained to be seen. But at least she could try. "But don't piss me off or we'll be back to square one."

Laughter bellowed from his throat as he shook his head. "Damn, you're funny. Do people know you're this funny?"

"People don't know me at all. That was kind of my point."

His expression turned reverent as he gazed at her. "Well, I can't wait to be one of the few that do."

Her mouth turned dry as she licked the roof, her heartbeat quickening as she looked into his eyes. Struggling to breathe, she tried to form a pithy comeback, but it lodged in her throat.

"You don't have to end every conversation with a retort, Arianna," he said, smiling as his eyes slowly darted between hers. "Come on. Let's check the tires on the sedan and make sure it's ready."

With that, the man who consumed her every thought walked toward the car, seemingly oblivious that her body was on fire and ready to explode. As he crouched down beside the tire to examine the ridges, one striking thought blazed through her mind: *Girl, you're in trouble.*

Pushing it aside, she trailed over to help her *friend* prepare for their journey.

Chapter 7

The sedan was prepped and ready to go promptly at noon. Maverick hugged Arianna before Dani stepped in to crush her in a deep embrace.

"Pretty strong grip for a scientist," Arianna teased, squeezing her back. "Get that antidote done while we're gone, okay?"

Dani released her and saluted. "Ten-four. Be safe, Ari. I love you."

"Love you too," Arianna softly replied as Chris scampered toward her, a trinket in his small hand.

"My sister made this for you," he said, holding up what looked to be a charm bracelet. "I told her bracelets were dumb, but this one is pretty cool."

Arianna's heart swelled as she examined it. A tiny leather strap held various acorns and dried flowers, and it was quite pretty.

"Tell Jenny I said thanks," she said, sliding it onto her wrist. "And thank you too. Be good while I'm gone, okay, kid?"

Chris nodded, his hair flying in the light breeze before he turned and jogged away. Arianna glanced toward Dominic, noticing the admiration in his expression. Rolling her eyes, she straightened her shoulders, not wanting to come off as a damn sap. "Let's go. I'll drive first shift."

They said their last goodbyes and hopped into the sedan. Dominic's large body barely folded into the car, and he adjusted the seat to accommodate his long legs. Chris and several other kids appeared beside the car, running along as she slowly drove toward the entrance. They eventually disappeared from view as she gained speed before stopping at the large doors that comprised the entrance to the compound.

Arthur Reyes stood guard, surrounded by several armed men. He lifted his hand and circled it, and two of the men pushed each massive door open. Waving to them, Arianna put the car in drive and headed outside of the walls for the first time in several weeks.

As they pulled onto the rural roads, Arianna took in the signs of desolation and destruction. Power lines lay strewn across fields, disconnected and disassembled for survivors to use for warmth and kindling. Several houses they passed had large red *X*s on the front doors—the symbol that the residents had died when society collapsed. Most of the businesses were looted, their windows broken as dirty signs hung above empty stores.

Millions had died over the past few years. Most from EverLife addiction. Some from collateral damage from the fact that Luthor Cromwell had ordered the Sen Force troops to destroy all electricity and technology outside the Ten Cities. Only those cities—DC, Miami, New York and the other largest cities in America—had been spared. Cromwell now controlled what was left of the US Army, and his newly renamed Sen Force troops had pledged their loyalty. That was the cost of protecting their families inside the walls, where technology and societal norms still existed in some capacity.

"You look serious over there," Dominic said, lifting his eyebrows.

"I was thinking about our former counterparts. All the soldiers who pledged their allegiance to Cromwell so easily. It's going to be tough to mount an offensive if they remain loyal to him."

"Lack of a strong leader will forge weak alliances," Dominic said. "We need someone to fill the void and give them a reason to fight for good instead of evil."

"And you think Reyes is that man?"

Lifting a shoulder, he shrugged. "I think he's a big step up from Cromwell. And he wants the job, which makes him just crazy enough to possibly succeed."

Arianna laughed. "For real. I'm done with war—and with people in general, if I'm being honest. Once we save the world, I'm going off the grid."

"Yeah?" Leaning his temple on the headrest, he studied her. "Where to?"

"None of your business. That's the entire point of disappearing. No one knows your destination."

His low-toned "hmm" caused her to give him the side eye.

"Did you have a comment?" she asked, her tone dripping with sarcasm.

"Nope," he said, spreading the map Arthur had given them over his lap. "I'm just really good at finding people who don't want to be found. I did it with terrorists in Pakistan and Afghanistan for years."

"Dani and Mav will be settled down with kids by then, so finding me is irrelevant. I'll visit them when I want to see them."

He just uttered another grunt, causing her to squish her fingers on the wheel, imagining it was his throat. It's not like he would come looking for her. Sure, they were teammates because circumstances demanded it, but once they weren't forced together, she doubted he'd care to look for her. Dominic had his own life, after all.

The subject of her thoughts studied the map as she drove, and she assumed the conversation was finished until he spoke.

"You don't want to have kids? The way you are with Chris and the others... You'd be great, Ari."

"I know," she said, trying to remain nonchalant at the reverence in his voice. "I'll just be great without a partner."

A slow smile curled across those full lips. "Yeah, but wouldn't it be more fun to do it with someone else?"

She exhaled an annoyed breath. "Never met anyone I want to spend that much time with. I'm all set."

He shot her a disbelieving glance but remained silent. Reminding herself not to tangle with him since she'd promised to be nice, she pressed her lips together, determined to end the uncomfortable conversation.

"Just continue on this road for forty-five minutes and then we'll hit the fork that leads to Route 127. That eventually merges with Route 7."

Arianna clenched her jaw. "Got it."

His lips twitched as he glanced toward her. "I know you studied the map and want to tell me to fuck off. I appreciate your restraint."

Breathing a laugh, she relaxed her shoulders. It was amazing how well he could read her. And somewhat terrifying too. "I know you're trying to help." She pushed the power button on the radio and selected the CD option. "Whoever owned this car was a huge Grateful Dead fan. Get ready to binge some Jerry Garcia."

"I like the Dead," he said, stretching out his legs and resting his hands behind his head. "Bring it on."

They drove as Jerry serenaded them, the silence between them easy. Arianna wasn't really a talker and liked the fact they could chill without it being weird.

When they reached the juncture with Route 127, she pulled the car into a wooded area and parked.

"You didn't even make it an hour," he teased, the curve of his lips sexy as he reached for the handle.

"I had an extra cup of coffee for the drive," she retorted, exiting the car and stretching. "Give me a break." Observing the trees, she pointed to one. "I'm going to take care of business over there. Then I'll keep watch while you go."

Dominic nodded, doing his own stretches as she observed the white bandage on his neck. It moved as he rotated and swung his arms, and she swallowed thickly, thankful he'd accompanied her even if he wasn't fully recovered.

"If you're not going to go, I'll go—"

"Yeah, sorry," she said, shaking her head before approaching the tree. After surveying the area, she relieved herself before heading back and ushering Dominic into the woods.

He returned, his hands still fastening his belt buckle, and she felt a rush of heat over every inch of her skin. Had he ever used that belt to restrain a lover? And why was the thought so damn hot?

Although Arianna was tough as nails, she'd always fantasized about having a dominant lover. Someone who could handle her rigid demeanor and urge her to let go. To actually *feel* like the woman the world rarely allowed her to be...

The belt clicked simultaneously as her gaze rose to lock with his. Those brown eyes simmered as he hooked his thumbs in the belt, his eyes raking over her as she struggled to breathe.

"You ready?" he asked in that deep baritone that made her bones liquify.

"Uh, yeah. You want to drive the next leg?"

"Sure."

He maneuvered his large body into the car, adjusting the seat farther back as she sat beside him. Thick, tattooed arms turned the wheel as they resumed the drive, and Arianna noted the broken pavement on the two-lane road as she stared out the window.

Something glinted in the side mirror and she leaned forward, squinting at the reflection. As her heartbeat quickened, she turned to look through the back window.

"What is it?" Dominic asked, his eyes drifting toward the rearview mirror.

"I thought I saw something." The road stretched behind them, clear and desolate.

"Hard for stragglers to find gas unless they got it from a compound," he said, the words reassuring although his shoulders were tense.

Nodding, she maneuvered back into the seat and ran a hand over the fuzz now growing over the bald side of her head. "I'll keep an eye out. Just drive and keep up the pace. My grandpa drives faster than you."

"I'm assuming your grandpa is dead," he said, arching a sardonic brow. "May he rest in peace."

"And he still drives faster than you. Kick it into gear, old man."

Arianna knew Dominic was in his early forties, so they were close in age since her fortieth birthday was fast approaching. Still, it was fun to chide him—and he definitely drove at a slower pace than the one she'd set earlier.

When they reached the juncture of Route 127 and Route 7, they stopped to take another break in a wooded area. Dominic headed into the brush first, followed quickly by Arianna, who admitted she needed more bathroom breaks than she had in her twenties. But she'd never admit that Dominic was right—to his face, at least.

She'd barely gotten her pants zipped when she heard a twig snap behind her. Gasping, she pulled the gun from her belt and aimed at the origin of the sounds. Ears perked, she waited, keeping her breathing calm so it didn't obstruct her hearing.

Another twig snapped and she whirled, grip firm on the gun as she planted her feet. A man stepped out from behind the brush, gun held firm as he grinned. "Well, well. What do we have here?"

Arianna felt a presence behind her and rotated—fast as lightning—and jutted the base of her hand into a man's throat. The karate chop caused the man to gasp before he gripped his neck. Aiming the gun, she shot his kneecap.

The man screamed with pain before dropping to the ground and gripping his knee. Turning back, she aimed between the other man's eyes. "I won't aim for your knee," she said through clenched teeth. "So you can run or you can die. Your choice."

Fear flashed in his eyes as he spoke into the watch around his wrist. "They're approaching on Route 7—"

The man's eyes widened before a trickle of blood appeared between his eyes. The red liquid glimmered in the afternoon sun as it ran toward his nose before he collapsed on the ground.

"Good shot," she said, sensing Dominic beside her. "I was going to let him live...I think. The bastard didn't even let me get my pants buttoned. Asshole." She placed the gun in the holster at her waist, annoyed that her hands were slightly shaking. She was usually steady on her feet, but being attacked while finishing up taking a piss would make anyone feel vulnerable.

"Here," Dominic said, closing in and covering her hands. "Just breathe." Deft fingers encircled the button, lacing it through the hole as she expelled a calming breath. Once fastened, he rested his palm over her hip, the gesture comforting as he gauged her reaction. "Sorry I wasn't there. I'd opened the trunk to get some water—"

"It's fine," she said, her voice raspy as she backed away from his stabilizing hand at her waist, surprised how much she wanted to lean toward him and let him support her. Arianna never leaned on *anyone*, and the uncomfortable feelings that surfaced were sticky and raw.

Glancing over, she noticed Mr. No More Kneecap was unconscious. "What are we going to do with him?"

"We're going to wake him up and ask him who that was on the other end of his watch," Dominic said, pointing to the dead attacker. "They're not wearing Sen Force uniforms, but they don't have deserter marks either. They could be independent mercenaries."

Mr. No More Kneecap groaned, his eyes fluttering as he lolled on the ground. "I'm not telling you shit," he rasped.

Arianna observed him clutch the gun at his side, and she lurched but was too late. The man lifted the gun to his temple and released a clean shot.

"No!" she yelled, drawn back by Dominic's firm grip around her arm. "Damn it, I wanted to question him."

The man released his last breath, his body going limp on the ground as she sighed. "Let's take both watches as evidence. Maybe we can figure out who they were communicating with."

"They might have trackers," Dominic said, striding over to remove the far man's watch.

"He already told whoever was on the other end we were approaching on Route 7. Tracker or not, they know we're coming." Leaning down, she removed the other watch.

Returning to Dominic's side, she lifted the gadget, studying it. "Looks like a modified smart watch. Maybe it has radio technology like Reyes is using."

"Maybe. Come on. I don't want to linger here any longer."

Arianna followed him back to the car, unsettled at the fact that someone knew they were approaching DC. Wondering who the hell was on the other end of the transmission, she climbed into the car, quiet and pensive as they resumed their trek.

Chapter 8

They arrived at the abandoned Chain Bridge Forest neighborhood as the sun hung low in the afternoon sky. Dominic spotted an overgrown path and followed it until the car was shrouded by trees.

"It's as good a spot as any," Arianna said, stretching before she reached in the back seat and began securing her supplies.

"Hopefully it will be here when we get back."

After shrugging on her backpack—filled with ammunition, small rations of food, and the money Reyes had given them—she jerked her head. "Let's go."

They hiked quietly through the forest, both alert as they listened for signs of life. Aside from the random squirrels and birds, all was clear.

Dominic's hand encircled hers, drawing her to a stop as she frowned. "The crossing is that way."

"I know," he said, squeezing her fingers. "But look at that."

Arianna followed his gaze, her eyes widening at the words spray-painted on the tree: *Cromwell must die.*

"A sign of the rebellion Reyes mentioned," she said.

Leaning closer, he studied the writing. "Could be deserters, but the message is pretty clear."

"Looks like Tristan might get his war after all."

Dominic nodded before resuming the hike, and Arianna followed him, thoughtful as they meandered through the forest.

As the sky turned from cloud-spattered blue to early evening orange, the trees cleared and they approached the riverbank. Arianna's black boots pushed into the soft ground as she gazed across the gurgling water.

"Arthur said it will come up to our waist if we cross here." Clutching the straps of her pack, she sighed. "Might as well get on with it. We'll need to dry off on the other side so we don't leave a trail of mud."

"I'll lead—"

"I thought we agreed I was the leader of this mission," she interrupted.

"You are, but my mom raised me to be a gentleman." Stepping forward, he planted a foot in the water and turned back, extending his hand.

Arianna did her best to ignore the flip-flop of the organ now pounding in her chest as she slipped her hand in his.

He led her down, air hissing through her teeth as the cold water rushed against her legs through her black pants. "I thought it would be warmer."

"It's almost fall," he said, releasing her hand to wade through the water a few feet in front of her. "Must be getting some colder flow from the north."

Arianna grunted as she followed him, aware of the tiny chill bumps that lifted the hairs on her arms. The water breached her waist, and she breathed a sigh of relief they were halfway through. She scanned the tall metal wall that glowed in the last waning sunlight, wondering if they were being watched. She rested her palm on the handle of the gun at her waist, comforted by the fact she could at least put up a good fight if they were ambushed.

Dusk had settled in by the time they crested the other side. Dominic led her to a large tree before removing the towel from his pack. He dried his legs and boots before touching the bandage at his neck. Grimacing, he pulled it off and gently rubbed the tender skin.

"Does it hurt?" she asked, feeling slightly guilty that she'd been such an ass about him coming on the trip when he was still recovering.

"More like a throbbing itch," he said, shaking his head. "I want to scratch it so fucking badly."

"Here." Taking his towel, she located a dry spot and tenderly dabbed his wound. "I'm in awe of how fast you're healing. And I..." Drifting off, she was flooded of visions of him bleeding profusely on the squalid Sendaxa lab floor. "I'm really glad you're okay, Dom."

"I know you are." His velvet voice washed over her, smooth as melted butter slipping into every cranny of a warm English muffin.

Swallowing thickly, she backed away and dried her pants before shaking out the towel. Folding it, she handed it to him so he could stuff it back in his pack.

"Remain alert," he softly commanded. "I'm going first. But you're still the boss."

"Dom—"

"I'm going first," he repeated, his tone unequivocal. "Let's go."

Narrowing her eyes, she nodded and pulled her gun from her holster. They walked slowly toward the wall, the metal slabs growing taller and more menacing as they approached. When they reached the perimeter, she peered toward the top, which she estimated to be thirty feet high.

"No lookouts or cameras spotted, but that doesn't mean they aren't there."

"Agreed" was Domnic's soft reply. "Arthur said the weak spot in the wall was about a mile south."

They trailed along the wall, Arianna following close behind Dominic, unwilling to examine why she felt so comfortable letting him lead. She seldom trusted people enough to give them that much control, but he was a rare exception. Somewhere along the way, she'd come to trust him more than anyone except Dani and Maverick. Grappling with the weight of the realization, she rapidly shook her head, reminding herself to focus on the task at hand.

Arianna could feel the heat from his large frame as she stayed close behind him. Dusk turned to darkness, and he pulled out a small flashlight, illuminating the juncture where the wall met the grass. Ariana mentally calculated the distance and eventually tapped Dominic's shoulder.

"We've gone about a mile," she said, stopping to peruse the wall. "Let's start looking for the weak spot."

The sound of a gun cocking behind them caused Arianna's eyes to widen. Whirling around, she aimed into the darkness.

A man stepped forward, his strong features laced with annoyance and derision. "I've got several men within shooting distance. Lower the gun, Arianna."

Frustrated they'd been discovered, she sighed and followed Tristan Holder's command.

CHAPTER 9

D ominic placed his palm on Arianna's shoulder blade, silently reassuring her as he stared into Tristan's hazel eyes. They glinted in the darkness as the man slowly approached. He made a *tsk, tsk, tsk* sound before arching an eyebrow.

"Looks like someone's trying to break into the city."

"It was you on the other end of the transmission," Arianna said, her muscles tense under Dominic's hand.

Lifting his wrist, he rotated it in the dimness. "Smart watches still work in the city...*sometimes*. Hell of a thing. Cromwell allows some of us to use technology...for now."

"You already proved in the lab that you're not going to kill us," Dominic said. "So what's the next move?"

Tristan scrunched his features. "Killing you would be fun, but you're right. You're both more useful alive to me than dead. Speaking of, did you kill the spies who told me you were coming?"

"Yes." Arianna lifter her chin. "We didn't want to, but they attacked us. We killed one and the other took himself out."

"Pity." Craning his neck, he spoke to Dominic. "You have a bad habit of killing my men."

"Your men have a bad habit of making poor decisions."

Pursing his lips, Tristan nodded. "Can't argue with that. Well, now that we're all here, let's get the party started. I need you two to do something for me. Once you complete the task, I'll tell you where Raquel is." His gaze traveled to Arianna. "I assume that's why you're here."

"We're not doing any *task* for you," she said, bristling. "We're here to get my sister, do some reconnaissance, and give you a message from Arthur Reyes. After that, we're out."

A slightly sinister chuckle left Tristan's chest. "So combative. The Lawson sisters have that in common."

Concern laced Arianna's features. "Is Raquel okay? I swear, if you or Cromwell have hurt her—"

"She's fine," he said, showing his palm. "I've been protecting her."

Arianna crossed her arms and expelled a dismissive breath. "I bet."

"Luthor has tasked her with amplifying both EverLife and the pure antidote. He wants the former to be stronger and the latter to be weaker but still effective. I'm no scientist, but she seems to be making progress."

"To what end?" Dominic asked.

Tristan shrugged. "Addicts are easy to control. The more effective the drug, the more powerful he is. He speaks about raiding Arthur's compound to extradite Danica for public trial, but he hasn't acted on it yet."

"Why?" Arianna asked, rubbing her arm in the wake of the chilly air that swirled around the wall.

"Because he's developing a new drug. One similar to EverLife, although it doesn't extend lifespan. It increases muscle density and strength. Once it's ready, he's going to pump the Sen Force soldiers full of it and begin attacking the compounds. Arthur's compound will be first."

"Shit," Arianna breathed. "A real-life Captain America drug. Cromwell will be invincible with an army like that."

"Since we can't let that happen, I'm going to need you two to destroy the lab where that drug is being developed."

"Why can't you do it?"

"Because I can't be caught on camera working against Cromwell." Leaning forward, he flashed a sinister grin. "But *you* can."

"We don't have time for this—"

"If you want my alliance and you want me to lead you to Raquel, this is my price," Tristan interjected. "I assume Reyes wants someone on the inside to help his cause. I'm hoping he's going to start the war I so desperately want."

"It would be nice to dethrone Cromwell without war," Dominic muttered.

"That's a fantasy you should let go of now. There will be a war, and at the end of it, we'll see who rises from the ashes. I don't really care who takes over for Cromwell as long as I kill the bastard."

"And if we don't destroy the lab?" Arianna asked.

"I'll kill Raquel."

Scoffing, she turned to look at Dominic. "Maybe we should just shoot this mother-fucker. He's really pissing me off."

"We need him, and he knows it," Dominic replied, warily eyeing Tristan. "You'll get us the explosives?"

"There's a hotel in LeDroit Park at the corner of 2nd and T Street where you can stay while you're here. It's off the grid and not very safe, but I think you two can handle yourselves." He smirked, causing Arianna to grit her teeth. "Devon at the front desk is expecting you. He likes to be paid in gold. I'm assuming Reyes provided that, along with cash."

Arianna gave a curt nod.

"He'll put you up in a room for a few days so you can get the job done. I left a bag with him that has a map of the lab and all the materials you'll need. It has a lock with the code 10-09."

"Raquel's birthday," Arianna said softly. Sighing, she rubbed her forehead. "If we agree to do this, I'm going to need assurance Raquel is okay. I still have contacts here and have no doubt I can track your location in a matter of hours."

"There's no need to come looking for me, Arianna. I want information and action as much as you. And if you're looking for intel on a rebellion, I'm happy to tell you what I know."

"We assumed you'd be part of the rebellion," Dominic said.

"I want to murder Luther and that's my primary goal. Others have the goal of taking him down and trying to rebuild society. I don't know who all the players are yet. I think my proximity to Luthor keeps the rebellion leaders from approaching me." Lifting a finger, he arched a brow. "Remember, I technically work for Luthor. I have reasons I need to keep him close and keep up that deception. Whoever is leading the rebellion doesn't trust me yet."

"That makes two of us," Arianna muttered.

"Taking out Dr. Ziegler's lab is important for the future of any rebellion," he continued. "You must understand that Cromwell can't get his hands on a super-soldier drug. It would cement his future as leader for decades."

Dominic looked at Arianna, seeing the same acknowledgment in her expression that welled in his gut.

"And we're just supposed to believe this isn't a trap for us to walk into? Since you do technically work for Cromwell," she said, repeating his words.

Sighing, Tristan rolled his eyes. "So dramatic. I want the super-soldier drug destroyed and have no one inside the wall I trust to do it. You two are pretty effective at blowing shit up," he said, pointing between them. "So why not help me? It's a small price to pay for my help in return."

Inhaling a labored breath, Arianna nodded. "Fine. It will save us from having to find our own lodging, which would waste valuable time. I'm in if you are," she said to Dominic.

He nodded, and Arianna turned back to Tristan. "We'll surveil the lab and get the job done as quickly as possible. After that, how will we know where to find you?"

"I'll find you," he said, backing away. "And don't get caught. You're on Cromwell's turf now, and he'll most likely publicly execute you two if he gets his hands on you. When you're finished, I'll lead you to Raquel, although I'm not sure she'll go with you. She's feistier than I originally thought."

"She'll come with us even if I have to drag her out of this fucking city," Arianna said.

Tristan pointed toward the wall. "Wait ten minutes and then enter a hundred yards south of here. Two soldiers guard that section of the wall, but I'm sure Reyes already armed you with that information. Once you take them out, there's a rip in the metal where you can ease through. You'll have to feel around to find it. There are two cameras atop the wall that one of my cyber-tech soldiers rewired so the feed is on a loop."

"Crafty," Dominic said, impressed with his forethought.

"There shouldn't be any soldiers on the other side, but definitely stay inconspicuous. It will take you a few hours to walk to LeDroit Park, and Devon knows you're coming."

With one last nod, he breezed past them, heading toward the nearby woods.

"You're not going back inside the city?" she asked.

"I have something to attend to outside the walls," he said cryptically. "I'll be keeping an eye on you both. Be careful."

"Wait," Arianna said, removing her pack and digging out the radio. "Arthur wants to communicate with you using Morse code and on the 4930 Khz radio frequency. He wants to see if you're amenable to working together."

"I might be," Tristan said, taking the radio, "if he agrees to start the war I'm looking for. I've noted the frequency," he tapped his temple. "Thank you. Work fast and good luck." Pivoting, he advanced toward the nearby woods, disappearing between the trees under the starlit sky.

"Bossy fucking bastard," Arianna said, lifting hesitant eyes to Dominic's. "Are we really going to do this?"

"Honestly? It gives us a place to stay and a reason to stay in contact with Tristan, who claims to know Raquel's whereabouts. Plus, blowing shit up with you will be fun."

Her breathy laugh washed over his skin, and he reveled in her proximity. Long, dark eyelashes glistened in the moonlight as she stared at him, contemplating.

"Well, then I guess we need to haul ass to LeDroit Park. From what I remember, it's about seven miles from here. I wouldn't mind a bed and a roof over our heads so I can sleep."

Nodding, he loaded the tranquilizer guns and handed one to her. "We only have four darts, but I'd rather not have to reload. Let's get a clean hit the first time."

"Done," Arianna said, gripping the gun.

They stalked slowly toward the vulnerability in the wall, ears perked as they listened for danger. When they were twenty yards away, Dominic spotted two guards slowly pacing around the wall.

"You take the one on the left and I'll get the one on the right."

With a tilt of her head, she moved forward in the darkness, extending the gun and squinting one eye as she aimed.

Watching Arianna wield a weapon was a thing of beauty. Entranced by her, he reminded himself to stay focused. Her jaw clenched seconds before a puff sounded from the barrel of the gun. The soldier on the other end gasped, clutching his neck as the dart connected.

The second soldier whirled to face his counterpart, and Dominic seized the situation. Aiming at the man's exposed jugular, he released the dart, adrenaline surging through his veins when it met its mark. Both men grasped their necks before falling to the ground, unconscious.

They approached the fallen men cautiously, Arianna gently kicking one in his thigh to make sure he was down. Crouching, she removed the rifle from his shoulder. "Don't mind if I do. This will pair nicely with my Glock. Thanks, buddy."

Dominic quickly divested the other soldier of his rifle and slung it over his shoulder. Arianna approached the grooved metal wall and ran her hands over it. Her eyes grew wide when she felt a break in the consistency and stuck her hand through. "Here it is. Help me pull it back."

Dominic tugged the metal, opening a small hole for her to crawl through. After he squeezed his large frame through, they reset the metallic flap. Arianna wiped her hands on her pants as she stared at the glow of the far-off city. "It's been a while since I've seen lights that bright."

"I miss the city sometimes, but I doubt it's anything like what I remember. This place is a gilded cage for addicts," he said. Pointing toward the lights, he squinted. "Let's walk along the river until we hit K Street. Then we'll veer east."

Nodding, Arianna walked beside him in comfortable silence. Talking would've made noise, and they needed to remain alert. Eventually, they reached K Street and veered toward LeDroit Park.

Although the city twinkled in the distance, Dominic noticed the signs of their post-apocalyptic world. Many buildings had wooden boards nailed across the entrance, some with a red or black X spray-painted across them. As they walked along the paved but somewhat unkempt streets, they passed several families living in tents.

There were no cars on the roads, which created an eerie silence as the streetlights buzzed above, powered by energy from the remaining power plant to the city. Reyes had informed them that Cromwell directed most of the energy to the downtown region of the city he and the other wealthy cronies inhabited, leaving the rest of the city to function on generators or without energy at all.

Gas was now a high commodity since all trade from oil-producing nations had stopped. Each nation was now isolated with billions across the world dead. Bicycles and walking were the main modes of transport in the city, and Dominic doubted they'd even see a car until they approached downtown. Even then, they likely wouldn't see many.

Still, the city fared better than the black-market compounds, which had no access to resources they couldn't generate on their own.

Arianna frowned at the destruction as they paced. "So many homeless people," she said as they passed several more tents. "You'd think Cromwell would want to clean this up."

"It's a reminder for people inside the walls of what can happen if they don't stay compliant," Dominic said. "I doubt these people are getting any sort of clean antidote. He probably feeds them one that barely keeps them alive between EverLife injections."

"So fucking sad," she murmured, clutching the straps of her pack as they walked.

Some streets showed more destruction than others, and he observed clean, tree-lined streets in between the more run-down areas. Dominic figured these were the parts where the middle-class lived. Perhaps people who hadn't succumbed to EverLife addiction who still worked downtown and tried to live a normal life—or whatever amounted to "normal" in their desolate world.

After several hours of walking with only a few breaks, they entered the LeDroit Park section of the city.

"Damn, that was a long walk," Arianna said, rubbing her neck as they approached the corner of 2nd and T Streets. "I'm ready to crash."

Gazing up at the sign that read Mayflower Motel, Dominic raised his eyebrows. "This must be it."

The worn brick three-story building had seen better days, but if it had a bed and some running water, he'd be happy. The wooden door creaked as he pulled it open, gesturing Arianna inside before approaching the dimly lit front desk.

A man snored behind the desk, arms crossed across his chest as he leaned back in the black office chair. His feet rested on the counter before him, and Dominic cleared his throat.

The clerk's eyes flew open before he reached for the gun on the counter. Snaking his arm out, Dominic caught the man's wrist before he could grab the weapon.

"Calm down, man. Tristan sent us."

Recognition lit the clerk's eyes as he straightened his spine and gave them both a once-over. "Ah, the two rebels. He said you'd have gold for me." Leaning forward, he whispered, "If you also have a stash of EverLife, I take that as payment too."

Dominic scowled as he reached into the pack Arthur had prepared. "Just gold, man. I'm assuming you're Devon?"

"One and the same," he said, taking the gold bar. "This will get you a few days. After that, I'll need another bar."

"Fine," Arianna said with a nod. "Will that cover two rooms?"

Devon's lips curled into a mischievous smile as he glanced between them. "No pleasure on this business trip, hmmm?"

Reaching over the counter, Arianna clutched his collar as he yelped. "None of your fucking business. This is an important mission and we don't have time for small talk. Do you have two rooms?"

Sputtering, Devon shook his head as Arianna released his collar. "Only one," he rasped. "Sorry. I told Tristan we only had one vacancy. It has a double bed and a couch in the main room."

"That will do," Dominic said, his tone firm so Arianna wouldn't argue. "Give us the key and we'll let you get back to sleep. And if anyone asks about us, keep your mouth shut. Here's something for your silence." Drawing out several hundred-dollar bills, he set them on the counter. "If we finish our stay and you've remained silent, we'll give you another gold bar."

"What stay?" Devon asked cheekily, shrugging.

"Exactly," Arianna said, grabbing the key and the bag Devon set on the counter.

"That's from Tristan. It has improvised explosives inside, so be careful."

Arianna peered inside the bag before closing it. "I assume this dump doesn't have an elevator?"

"Your room is on the second floor, and no, you'll have to take the stairs." He pointed down a dim hallway. "You'll see them."

"Thanks, man," Dominic said with a salute. Arianna shot Devon one last stern glare before stalking away. Dominic followed her, his eyes focusing on her firm ass as she climbed.

He followed her to room 203, waving his hand in front of his nose when they stepped inside. "Smells musty."

"As long as it's relatively clean, who cares?" She opened the door in the small foyer and grinned. "Bingo. There are clean sheets and blankets in here. I'll sleep on the couch."

"No way," he said, reaching past her to grab a blanket. "I'll take the couch. You take the bed."

Her expression turned droll. "Dominic, you're still healing. I'm not that big of an asshole to deny you the bed. You need rest more than I do."

Without thinking, he gently encircled her wrist. Her pulse beat strongly beneath his fingers as he gazed into her eyes, mesmerized by the green and brown hues in their depths. "If you think I'd let you sleep on the couch, you know nothing about me. I'm old school, Ari, and you're taking the bed."

Her throat bobbed as she stared up at him, and the debate whether to argue with him flared across her strong features.

"You use the bathroom first and then I will. Hopefully there's hot water, but I'm not holding my breath."

"I'd argue with you," she whispered, gently tugging her wrist from his grasp, "but I'm honestly too damn tired to summon the energy."

Feeling the corner of his lips tick up, he gestured with his head. "Go on so I can get in there."

She hesitated for a few seconds before nodding and walking to the small table on the far side of the room. After setting Tristan's bag on top, she entered the bathroom that sat between the tiny main room and the bedroom. As she brushed her teeth and washed off the grime of the day, Dominic placed fresh sheets on the double bed. Their accommodations wouldn't be featured on a luxury homes tour, but the room was passable.

Arianna skirted by him, heading into the bedroom and closing the door so only a crack remained. Dominic entered the bathroom and washed his face and neck before brushing his teeth with the contents of the small travel case he'd packed. He examined his wound in the murky mirror, noting the most recent scab was peeling and the skin underneath appeared red and healthy. Pausing to express a moment of silent gratitude, he exited the bathroom to find Arianna making up the couch.

She spread a blanket atop the sheet she'd laid out under a pillow she retrieved from the closet. Straightening, she lifted a shoulder. "It's going to be uncomfortable. Are you sure?"

He nodded, inwardly acknowledging he wanted to sleep in the bed...with *her*. To wrap his body around every inch of her firm curves and rest his face in her nape as she slept. For a man who'd sworn off affection for so long, it was a strange sensation—but it was real. As real as the emotion on her stunning face had been when she'd gazed into his eyes and begged him not to die...

"Dom?"

"Yeah, I'm fine with uncomfortable. I slept on the ground in the Middle East for years." Approaching the couch, he tugged off his shirt before sitting down and removing his boots.

Arianna's eyes widened slightly as she backed away. Clearing her throat, she uttered a scratchy "Good night" before heading toward the bedroom.

"Ari?" he called from the couch.

Turning, she rested her hand on the doorframe, her body silhouetted by the faint lights that shone through the bedroom window. "Yeah?"

"Thanks for making up the couch. It's a nice gesture from a woman who tries so hard to pretend she doesn't care."

Her eyes narrowed as anger reddened her cheeks. Shooting him a glare, she stepped across the threshold and shut the door with a firm *thunk*.

Chuckling, Dominic lay back on the couch, resting his hands behind his head as he stared at the popcorn ceiling. Damn, he loved riling her. Shuffling under the blanket, he flipped to his side and clicked off the lamp on the side table.

Settling into the lumpy cushions, he closed his eyes, anticipating the moment when he riled her just enough to see her anger flare into full-on passion. Confident that day was close, he relaxed into the couch and succumbed to exhaustion.

Chapter 10

T ristan trudged through the dense woods toward the small cabin he'd built. He felt it best to have a refuge outside the walls where he could store supplies and ammunition on the small chance Luthor discovered his true intentions. After unlocking multiple locks on the front door, he stepped inside, sliding the three deadbolts he'd installed into place.

Striding over to the wooden table that doubled as his desk, he sat down to study the documents strewn across it. He pulled the folded notes from his pocket and smoothed them out next to others he'd collected. Studying them, his brow furrowed.

He'd compiled a list of all the cryptic phrases and keywords he'd heard over the radio transmissions he'd monitored over the past few months. Eagle. Tomato. Butterfly. All random words that had been transmitted more than a hundred times. They represented a secret code he didn't understand—and Tristan hated not being in the know.

If anyone was planning a rebellion, it should be him. He had close access to Luthor and wanted to murder the bastard. But Tristan's affection for his sister, Jessica, was a weakness, and whoever was organizing the rebellion must know that.

Which meant they knew too much about him. The thought prickled Tristan's spine as he rested his forehead on his steepled fingers, studying the notes but failing to come up with any answers.

There were cryptic spray-painted messages all over the city if you chose to look. Many of them called for Cromwell's ouster—or even his death—and they were quickly cleaned up by the sanitation crews Luthor employed. Tristan knew Luthor was afraid that if enough people saw them, they'd get the idea a revolution was possible.

Nothing terrified Luthor more than the thought of losing the power he'd so unscrupulously gained.

Releasing a sigh at his inability to discover who was behind the secret transmissions and spray-painted messages, Tristan stacked everything on the desk and prepared to head back inside the city. After bolting up the cabin, he returned to the vulnerable spot in the wall, noticing the two soldiers who lay unconscious on the ground with darts in their necks.

"Idiots," Tristan muttered, sliding through the tear in the metal wall before pushing the two slabs back together. He lifted his watch to his wrist as he approached the Jeep he'd left parked about half a mile away. "You can unloop the cameras now," he said into the smart watch.

A text appeared on the face that read **10-4.**

Bodie, the tech genius Tristan paid handsomely for his help and silence, was a valuable asset to Tristan's agenda. He'd tasked him to surveil for rebellion chatter on what remained of the internet and chat boards, but so far, he'd come up dry.

After all, the internet was a shell of what it used to be. The majority of residents in the city were hooked on EverLife and embroiled in a constant cycle of injecting the drug and then purchasing Luthor's watered-down antidote. Social media no longer existed. The shell government controlled the infrastructure and cell towers, so it made sense people were communicating over radio.

Tristan was just pissed he wasn't part of the communication.

Ten minutes later, he parked in the overgrown field across from his townhome in the inner part of DC. He made sure his bag was zipped before heading inside. Raquel would be there, and he didn't want her discovering the radio from Arthur Reyes.

In fact, he didn't want her to know Arianna and Dominic were in the city at all. The persistent little scientist might try to find her sister, and Tristan wanted her to remain focused on her work for Luthor. That would keep Raquel busy while the lab was destroyed.

Tristan had been glib in his conversation with them earlier, but having Arianna and Dominic destroy Dr. Ziegler's lab was imperative. They had a small window to defeat Cromwell before he became invincible, and having a shit ton of synthetically grown super soldiers wasn't an option.

Tristan was quiet as he locked the door. Raquel's soft snores emanated from the living room where she slept on his pull-out couch. She'd been a rather unassuming houseguest so far, leaving early each morning for the lab and returning around seven o'clock each evening. They rarely interacted—after all, Tristan wasn't looking to make friends. But

Raquel reminded him slightly of Jessica, and sheltering the woman in his home would prevent her from ending up like Jess had.

Sucking off a deranged demagogue just to get her hands on more EverLife.

Rubbing his chest as he trudged up the stairs, Tristan acknowledged the burn from the knowledge that Jessica was lost. Even if he killed Cromwell, she wouldn't get back the years she'd lost to addiction and pain.

And still, knowing that, Tristan wanted to try and save her. Hell, he wanted to save everyone from living in the world Luthor Cromwell had created. Sandwiching his hands between his head and the pillow, he lay in bed and stared at the darkened ceiling, hoping like hell he could start the war he wanted. Even if the rebellion wanted nothing to do with him.

In the end, Tristan was convinced that war was the only way to take Cromwell down and defeat the loyalists in the army that now revered him.

And in the chaos of war, Tristan would finally be able to murder the bastard.

Half-thrilled and half-ashamed at the pleasure that thought gave him, he closed his eyes and focused on the darkness behind his lids.

Chapter 11

Arianna awoke to a few sore muscles in her neck, courtesy of the lumpy pillow that would take some getting used to. Guilt gnawed at her that Dominic had slept on the couch, so she decided to scrounge up some breakfast for them. They had some rations in their bags, but she remembered seeing an awning with the word DELI scrawled on it at the end of the block. If she was lucky, it might just be open and serving hot breakfast.

Dominic lay sprawled on the couch, one arm over his eyes as he snored. Snickering at the deep sounds, she tiptoed out of the room and down the stairs. The sun was bright as she made her way onto the sidewalk, and she lifted her face to the sky to soak in the rays.

Small pleasures like warm breakfasts ordered on a whim hadn't existed in Arianna's world for some time. Although she was thankful for the chickens and garden at the farmhouse they'd inhabited in Virginia, eating the same thing every day wasn't exactly titillating. When she neared the deli, she inhaled the delicious aroma that emanated from the building, closing her eyes to savor the smell. A bell rang above as she pushed open the door and entered.

A middle-aged Black woman stood behind a counter ringing up orders as a tall Black man cooked at the grill behind her. Closing the cash register, she smiled and asked, "What'll it be?"

"Two bacon, egg and cheese sandwiches on a bagel if you have them."

"Coming right up," the woman said with a nod.

Arianna's mouth watered as she waited, anticipating the hot, fresh food. She hadn't had a bagel in ages.

"I'm new to the neighborhood," she said, craning her neck to watch the cook crack open the eggs on the grill. "It's nice to see you all are in business since so many stores are boarded up."

"Name's Deandra," the woman said before gesturing her head toward the cook. "And that's my husband, Ron. We never touched EverLife and just kept making food once the world collapsed. We live upstairs and stay in our own little corner of heaven." She arched a sardonic eyebrow. "As long as we don't bother anyone, we do just fine."

"Do you still get food deliveries? I notice there's not really any traffic. Not like there used to be, anyway."

Crossing her arms, she leaned on the counter behind the register. "How long have you been gone? Things have changed a lot here since Luthor Cromwell closed off the city. We still have some technology, but it's sparse. And I keep chickens, pigs and a garden in the back. Food distributors kind of fell by the wayside when EverLife took over society."

"I bet," Arianna said, admiring her resiliency. "Looks like you figured it out."

"For now." Ron wrapped the sandwiches and dropped them beside the register. Deandra placed them in a brown paper bag before tapping a few keys on the register. "That will be $27.50."

"Wow." Arianna pulled thirty bucks from her pocket and handed it over.

"Inflation is the name of the game around here," she said, stuffing the money in the register drawer before closing it. "We're open seven days a week so stop by anytime."

Leaning in, Arianna lowered her voice. "I also noticed some messages of dissention spray-painted around town. You know anything about that?"

Deandra lifted her brows. "Information costs a lot more than the sandwiches. How much you got?"

Chuckling at her candor, Arianna straightened. "Not enough for today, but I'll be back. Name's Arianna. See ya." With a salute, she exited, ready to devour the hot sandwiches.

When she entered the hotel room, she locked the deadbolt before turning and calling Dominic's name. Walking through the tiny foyer, she saw him rise from the couch, his boots haphazardly thrown on but only one actually tied.

"Dom?"

Pacing toward her, he gripped her upper arms and squeezed so tightly it reminded her of the tourniquet the nurses used to wrap when they needed to draw blood for her army physicals. Bristling, she asked, "What the hell—?"

"Goddamnit, woman," Dominic exclaimed, his fingers digging into her skin. "I'm going to fucking strangle you."

Dominic stared at Arianna's stunned expression as fury bubbled in his chest. When he'd woken up to find her gone, he'd immediately transitioned to full-blown panic mode. He'd been in the process of hastily tying his boots when she entered.

"Do you not understand the meaning of 'we're a team?' Did you even think about telling me where the hell you were going?"

"Okay, *Dad*," she scoffed, backing away from the death grip he had on her arms and holding up a bag. "I went to the end of the block to get breakfast. We both have to eat, right?"

"This isn't about me keeping tabs on you," he said, frustrated at his overreaction, but needing her to understand it was unacceptable for her to continue insisting on doing everything on her own. "We're each other's only ally in this city, Ari. You can't disappear without telling me."

"Jesus," she muttered, tossing the bag on the cheap coffee table and throwing up her hands. "I'm a big girl, Dom. I can walk to the end of the street without your help."

Clenching his fists, Dominic looked to the ceiling and prayed for patience. "Don't do it again. I mean it, Arianna. If you even think of leaving my presence, I want to know. Otherwise, I can't protect you."

"I don't need protecting," she said through clenched teeth.

"I don't give a shit what you think you need. I won't be the one who returns to Arthur's compound and tells Dani her sister is dead because I wasn't there to help her. Don't leave my sight again without telling me."

She scoffed, red splotches appearing on her cheeks as her eyes flashed with anger. "God forbid you have to disappoint your *precious* Dani." Pivoting, she stomped toward the bedroom and slammed the door.

Emitting a curse, Dominic lowered to the couch and rubbed a harsh hand over his face. He immediately realized he'd handled the situation terribly, but he'd been terrified when he'd woken up to find her gone. He'd just gone into military mode, determined to find her.

Now that he had a moment to gather his thoughts, he pondered why his reaction had been one of pure terror.

Probably because they'd reached the point where she was starting to let him in. She'd accepted his offer to be friends, and if he had it his way, soon they'd cross the line to lovers. He was man enough to admit that he wanted her, not just her body—although he certainly wanted every inch of her tanned skin pressed against his. But more importantly, he wanted her openness. Her trust.

Her...*love.*

Yes, he knew that somewhere deep inside that hard shell, Arianna loved him. He'd seen the sentiment clearly in her face in that moment in the lab when the world had stood still. Nothing had mattered but the emotion shining in the woman's eyes who he'd finally seen for the very first time.

And damn it, he wanted to see that emotion again.

Of course, he couldn't see anything if she was dead, which was why her little disappearing act had ruffled his usually controlled feathers.

Sighing, he picked up the bag and opened it, closing his eyes as he inhaled the smell of bacon and eggs. Removing one of the foil-wrapped sandwiches, he walked to the bedroom door and knocked.

She pulled it open a few seconds later, glaring at him with annoyance and frustration. Lifting the sandwich, he flashed a grin. "Peace offering?"

She snatched the sandwich from his hand before slamming the door in his face. Dominic's lips twitched at her obstinance. Returning to the couch, he opened the remaining sandwich and ate in silence.

Arianna eventually strode into the living room, planting her fists on her hips as she stared at him. "I'm sorry," she finally said, surprising Dominic as his eyes widened. "I didn't want to wake you. I didn't even think you'd be worried about me. I'm not used to having people care that I'm gone."

He released a deflated breath. "I care."

Her gaze lowered to the floor as her throat bobbed. "And I know you don't want to bring Dani bad news. She's important—"

"So are you," he interrupted, rising and coming to stand in front of her. "And I'm getting pretty tired of you twisting everything I say to make it about Dani. This is about *you*, Arianna."

"You're the one who brought her up—"

"Stop," he said, shaking his head. "Just stop. Honestly, I think it's time we stopped hiding in general and really started talking. I'm done pretending nothing happened in the lab."

Her eyes clouded with fear, and Dominic's heart cracked at the intense doubt and pain there. Just the mere mention of discussing her feelings seemed to terrify her. Man, they really were a pair of broken souls. Both afraid to acknowledge the emotion that roared within because love had been disastrously painful for both of them.

"Arianna—"

"Not yet," she said, holding up a hand. "I'm just…" She shook her head. "Not yet. But I'm sorry about leaving without telling you. I won't do it again."

The corner of Dominic's lip ticked up. "Did I just get a concession from you?"

She arched an eyebrow, the move sexy enough to send a jolt of desire through his frame. Fuck, she was absolutely gorgeous when she let those shields down and actually smiled at him.

"Yes. Don't blow it by being a dumbass, okay?"

Laughing, he exhaled a short breath. "Okay."

"Now, if you're done berating me, let me tell you about Deandra. She owns the deli and I think we can get some information from her—if we pay up."

Intrigued, Dominic gestured toward the couch. "I'm all ears. After that, we can plan our surveillance tactic for Dr. Ziegler's lab. We'll want to scope it out at night to retain cover. In the meantime, we can try and track down your old contacts and see if they have any intel on the possible rebellion."

Lowering to the couch, her face lit with excitement. "Sounds like a plan. The first thing I noticed about Deandra was the knowledge lurking in her eyes. I'm pretty sure she sees everything that happens on this block. And perhaps even farther than that…"

Chapter 12

Once Arianna caught Dominic up on her visit to the deli, they sifted over Tristan's map, studying the details of Dr. Ziegler's lab.

"It seems pretty straightforward," Dominic said, eyebrows drawn together as he traced the map with his finger. "It's a one-story warehouse and the lab is in the middle. We can enter through this back door, and if we light the explosives here"—he tapped the map—"that will give us time to exit before the lab explodes."

"Tristan labeled every spot where the guards stand at their posts," Arianna said, noting each X drawn on the map. "He also indicated each of the two guards at the back door take a bathroom break each night at midnight and one a.m. respectively. So, if we break in and blow up the lab at midnight, we'll only have to disarm one guard."

He nodded as he calculated the steps of the mission in his head.

"And we still have two tranquilizer darts left. Hopefully, we can do this without killing anyone. I think we can surveil tonight to confirm the timing and carry out the mission tomorrow if everything checks out."

"Agreed."

"In the meantime, I'm not content to sit around and wait for Tristan to lead me to Raquel. I want to approach my contacts and see if they know where he lives or anything about the rebellion."

"Okay. Are you sure they're still in DC?"

"Not at all," she said, lifting a shoulder. "But there's only one way to find out."

Two hours later, they navigated to the Columbia Heights section of the city. Arianna led Dominic through the parking lot of an abandoned Target superstore before they crossed to the next block. It was lined with brick apartment buildings and appeared quite normal in the chaos that now consumed the world.

"Pretty nice street," Dominic said thoughtfully. "It looks like someone is maintaining the cherry blossom trees."

Arianna observed the row of manicured trees in front of several of the buildings. "Guess some people try to hold on to a semblance of normalcy even if the world has turned to shit. Gotta love the optimism."

"I feel like I'm in a quasi-reality," he said, shaking his head. "It's still DC, but it's so...quiet."

The rumble of an engine echoed in the distance before growing louder. Arianna's gaze swung to Dominic before they jetted behind a large oak tree. Resting her palm on the bark, she craned her neck, observing a large tank meander down the street. Two black military-style Jeeps followed behind, causing the hairs on the back of her neck to stand up.

"A show of power from Cromwell?" Dominic asked softly.

"Probably. Never thought I'd see tanks on the streets of DC, but this is where we're at."

They waited until the vehicles disappeared before resuming their walk. Eventually, Arianna halted in front of a building with an awning that read The Stalwart, and pointed toward the top of the building. "He lives on the fourth floor. Or he used to. We'll see."

The lock on the door that led to the lobby was broken, so they slipped inside and eyed the elevator. "I'm not getting on that thing," Arianna said, grimacing at the dilapidated buttons and graffiti on the elevator doors. "Let's take the stairs."

Dominic followed her, acknowledging he was perfectly content to always allow her to lead him up any flight of stairs. Watching her ass sway was quickly becoming his favorite pastime.

When they reached the fourth floor, each breathing a bit heavier, Arianna stopped before the door labeled 412. She knocked and waited, glancing at him as something shuffled behind the door.

It swung open revealing a tall man with brown tousled hair wearing a pair of boxer shorts. Thin legs extended to bare feet, and he rubbed his chest, which was smattered with small patches of scraggly hair. Confusion clouded his sleep-filled eyes as he asked, "Arianna?"

"Hey, Matt. Long time."

"I'll say. Uh, what are you doing here?"

A woman appeared behind Matt, wrapped in a robe with a surprised expression. "Ari?"

"Hey, Susan. Guess you two are still together. Saves me from tracking you down separately."

Matt shook his head in rapid movements as if trying to snap back to reality. "I thought you were dead."

"No such luck," she said, patting him on the arm and breezing inside. "Throw on some clothes and I'll tell you where I've been. Then I'm going to need to pick both your brains."

"I'm Dominic," he said, thrusting out his hand. "I've heard absolutely nothing about you."

"Oh, where are my manners?" Arianna asked, plastering on a fake smile as she blinked rapidly. "Dominic, meet Matt. My former fiancé."

Dominic couldn't have been more floored if the building collapsed beneath their feet. Fiancé? He hadn't realized she'd ever been engaged. Especially to a scrawny guy like this who she could've chewed up and spit out in a matter of seconds. "Nice to meet you."

"Uh, yeah. You too, man. This is Susan. We'll toss on some clothes and be right back."

Arianna snooped around the living room, looking at the framed pictures on the shelf as they waited.

"Your contact is your former fiancé?" Dominic finally asked.

"Yeah, so what? He pretended to love me so I'd promote him—and it worked. Last time we spoke, he had top level security clearance, so it would be stupid to let our past interfere with any intelligence I can gather."

"You could've told me," he said, eyebrows drawing together.

"Why? It doesn't matter. Besides, he owes me."

"For what?"

"For fucking Susan while we were engaged."

Dominic allowed the uncomfortable feelings surge as Matt and Susan reentered the room. Anger Arianna hadn't told him they were approaching her ex. Annoyance at her implied indifference that Matt cheated on her. Jealousy that the man had ever touched her. His eyes raked over Matt's lanky frame. *This* guy had seduced Arianna? Dominic could barely believe it. He wasn't nearly...*enough* for her.

Matt led them to the couch, and Arianna sat down, rubbing her thighs before speaking.

"So, you're still in this dump?"

Breathing a laugh, Matt rubbed his forehead. "Still a ball buster. Yes, we managed to stay inside the city and stay clear of EverLife...for the most part," he said, eyeing Susan.

"Hey, everyone was taking it," she said with a guilty shrug. "I was curious. But thank god I only tried the pills and never injected the shit. My stomach hurt terribly after the first dose, and I was pissed at the side effects. Later, I realized how lucky I was that I couldn't tolerate it."

"And I never tried it," Matt said, leaning back and lacing his hands behind his head. "I mean, I look young enough anyway."

Arianna rolled her eyes. "I can see your ego's still intact. But more importantly, do you still have security clearance?"

"I have some," he said, shaking his foot as it crossed over his knee. "Luthor Cromwell assigned me as bodyguard to his socialite niece. He has a soft spot for her, and she's not the brightest twenty-four-year-old I've ever met. Since his family members are targets, he wants her protected."

"So, you left the army."

"More like transferred. Luthor required an oath of loyalty when he took over as commander once President Johnson overdosed on EverLife. I had no desire to pledge it, and we were going to leave the city." He reached over and clasped Susan's hand. "But I had an acquaintance who told me about the security job and helped me land it."

"This acquaintance must be close to Luthor," Arianna said.

"Tristan works for him, yes."

Dominic spared a glance at Arianna. "He's got his hands in everything, hmm?"

"You know Tristan?" Matt asked.

"Yeah. In fact, Raquel is staying with him. Do you know where he lives?"

"Raquel is in the city?" Matt sat forward, resting his forearms on his thighs. "I had no idea. I don't know where Tristan lives, but I can certainly find out."

"That would be helpful. We're here to rescue her. I don't want to divulge the details, but she made some bad decisions and we're afraid for her safety."

"Is she one of the new scientists working for Luthor?" Matt asked, rubbing his chin. "I heard Selena mention there were a few new members added to the antidote development team."

"Yes," Dominic said, assuming Selena was Luthor's niece.

"Well, that's a development." Matt arched a brow. "What else do you need?"

"We want to uncover information on the possible rebellion that's forming. It's obvious from the cryptic messages spray-painted across the city that dissention is brewing."

"Something is brewing, but I'm not on the inside. I keep to myself and focus on doing my job. It seems the best path to not getting myself killed."

Dominic's nostrils flared as annoyance surged. Ol' Matt seemed like a bona fide pussy, and he couldn't believe he'd ever laid a hand on Arianna. Had she actually been pleased by this guy?

"And do you still work for Colonel McGrath?" Arianna asked Susan. "He was high-ranking enough that you had access to classified information. We'd like to know about the top-secret lab where Dr. Ziegler is developing the soldier-enhancing drug."

"No one's supposed to know about that," Susan said, fear flashing in her eyes as they widened. "Who told you?"

"Your buddy Tristan. He's annoying as hell but knows a lot of secret shit. I wasn't sure whether to believe him, but it seems he was telling the truth."

"Sadly, he is," Susan said, slowly tracing the couch with her fingers. "Many people I work with are terrified at the thought of a super-powered drug created to enhance soldiers' strength."

"So you do still work for him?"

Her cheeks puffed as she exhaled a breath. "Yes. Colonel McGrath pledged loyalty to Luthor, and although I still work for him, it's not like it used to be before the city was walled off. The internet is controlled by Luthor's hackers, so my executive assistant duties have been diminished. I mostly ensure the colonel receives any transmissions or secure emails sent by Luthor or his generals, and water the plants." She shrugged. "I'm getting paid in cash now that the banks collapsed, but I'm not sure how long that will last. There are grumblings that Luthor is going to create his own currency."

"Even though the city has technology, it seems like it's not really accessible," Dominic said.

"It's not." Rising, Susan walked to the kitchen and returned with a smart watch. "This stopped updating months ago, and many of my friends have noticed the same with their phones and tablets. Luthor is slowly cutting off technology to those of us in the city who aren't in his inner circle. Thankfully, Matt's phone still works since it's part of his security package for Luthor's niece. Luthor only allows one cell phone company to exist within the walls, and it's too expensive for people outside of his affluent circle to afford the service."

Leaning back, Arianna crossed one booted foot over the other. "Do you think that's why a rebellion is forming?"

"People certainly hate losing access to technology," she said, "but I think the more pressing issue is that people in the city are beginning to see the truth. Luthor has been clear that maintaining power is his ultimate goal. He'll surround himself with people who have the wealth and connections to make that happen."

"And he'll have no regard for anyone else," Dominic said.

"Exactly."

Matt leaned back, stretching his arm across the back of the couch as he spoke. "Even though I want no part of the rebellion—I mean, I like living, thank you very much—I do think the people who aren't in Luthor's inner circle will try to challenge him. It's going to be tough without any weapons or technology."

"Not if they have backing from the compounds beyond the city walls," Arianna said, cocking an eyebrow.

Straightening, Matt's gaze grew serious. "Is that a possibility? I thought all the compounds were filled with addicts and crime."

"Because that's what Luthor wants you to think." Tilting her head, Arianna asked, "If you had to track down Raquel, where is the first place you'd look? Tristan says he's going to lead us to her eventually, but I'm not putting all my eggs in that basket."

Matt's expression turned contemplative. "Probably at Luthor's black tie birthday party tomorrow. Many of his officers will be in attendance, along with his acquaintances. I would imagine he'd invite the scientists to tout the development of his precious drugs."

Arianna looked at Dominic, and he saw the unmistakable glow of sisterly concern in her eyes. "If that's the case, we should try to infiltrate the party before blowing up the lab. Maybe we can find Raquel without having to do Tristan's bidding."

"We should still scope out the lab tonight just in case," Dominic said. "But I'm open to waiting on blowing it up if we can gain access to the party."

"I can get you on the list," Susan said. "That's something I can still access from Colonel McGrath's office."

"Excellent." Rising, she pointed between them. "I wasn't sure you'd come in handy when I found out my fiancé was fucking my commanding officer's assistant. But it seems it all worked out in the end, hmm?"

Standing, Matt opened his hands in a shrug. "That was ages ago, Ari. And it was for the best, wasn't it? We were never right for each other."

"It probably was since you fucked me just to get promoted. You got what you wanted and now you both can do me some favors for being huge dicks. So, yeah, I guess it was worth it." Facing Dominic, she jerked her head toward the door. "Come on. Let's allow these two to get to work. I want the location of Tristan's apartment and access to Luthor's birthday party by tomorrow morning."

She stomped toward the door and Dominic followed her, aware of the swirling emotions deep in his gut. Arianna was a master at appearing indifferent, but he understood it was just a mask. A very complicated, impenetrable mask. Inside, she was clearly hurting at the reminder of Matt and Susan's betrayal, and he desperately wanted to comfort her.

Of course, he'd learned long ago that trying to comfort Arianna when she had those walls up was like trying to get two rattlesnakes to cuddle. The chances were between zero and none.

"Arianna?" Susan called, following them to the door and wrapping her arm around Matt's waist. "For what it's worth, I'm really sorry. You didn't deserve the way we both treated you."

"You're right," Arianna said, opening the door and crossing the threshold. "And I don't need an apology. I need information and action. I'll be back tomorrow morning and expect everything to be ready. Don't make me get grumpy. Neither of you want to see that."

Dominic's lips twitched as he stifled a laugh at the fact the woman was always grumpy. But she was right. They seemed smart enough to understand it would be easier to help her than to get on the wrong side of her trigger finger.

"I need more time than that, Ari," Matt said.

With a frustrated huff, she pivoted. "That deadline is firm." Resting her hand on the butt of the gun strapped to her hip, she arched an eyebrow. "Are we clear?"

Matt's throat bobbed as he eyed the gun. "We're clear."

With a nod, Arianna descended the stairs.

"He's scared shitless of you," Dominic remarked as he followed behind her.

"Yep. I think he always was."

When they reached the lobby, Dominic encircled her wrist, drawing her to a halt. "There's no way in hell that guy did it for you, Arianna. What did you see in him?"

An almost wistful smile played with her stunning lips as she contemplated. "For a moment, I think I saw normalcy. Acceptance. And maybe a hint of love."

Dominic's features scrunched with disbelief, and she laughed. "But you're right, he was terrible in bed. I almost feel sorry for Susan." Lifting a finger, she grinned. "Almost."

Chuckling, Dominic shook his head. "Wow. You're really over it. I guess that's admirable, although I'd still be pissed."

Her shoulders deflated slightly as she kicked the ground with the toe of her boot. "It's pointless to get riled up over something you were never meant to have in the first place. I realize that now."

Dominic studied her as she stared at the ground, not meeting his gaze. "You deserve love, Arianna. I'm sorry you stopped believing that somewhere along the way. I'm even sorrier that asshole reinforced the belief." He jutted his finger toward the stairs. "He's not even close to worthy of you."

Her eyes finally met his, filled with a soft vulnerability that he'd rarely seen—jolting his heart into overdrive as energy pulsed between them.

And then it was gone, replaced with the hard steel and cool collectiveness that usually resided in her green-brown flecked orbs. "You're right. He's a fucking douche, but I'll take his help, and Susan's too."

She strode onto the sunlit street, waving him along as she set a brisk pace. "Now, come on. I need to know where to find a dress for this fancy party, and I bet Deandra can help me. I want your opinion on her and Ron."

Thrilled that she'd openly admitted she wanted his assessment, he fell into step beside her and headed back to LeDroit Park.

CHAPTER 13

D ani trudged through the forest, scanning the shrubbery as her husband trailed behind. Thankful for his protection—and the other three men Arthur had tasked to come with them—she crouched to examine a plant with dark green leaves.

"Holy shit," she breathed, touching the hairless, pointed leaf. "It's a milk thistle."

Maverick lowered beside her, eyebrows drawn together as he studied it.

"See the white marbling on the leaves? That's where it gets the 'milk' moniker from."

"Thrilling stuff," Maverick teased.

Swatting his chest, she laughed. "Do you know what this means, Mav? I've got them all! All the plants I need to replicate the serum. I mean, I think I do," she said, rubbing her forehead. "We'll only know once I test it on the mice we inject with EverLife, and if that works, on the patients in the clinic."

"What do you need me to do?"

Dani gazed at the man she'd woken up beside that morning, recalling the ardent pounding of her heart. She'd read a note in her own handwriting that informed her to watch several videos on a smart phone, and Maverick had laid still beside her as she viewed them.

As the videos progressed, a sense of *knowing* had washed over her. Like she'd watched them countless times and she was safe. Afterward, she'd rolled over and cupped her husband's jaw.

"Champagne," she whispered, running her thumb along his stubble. "We used to drink champagne together, didn't we?"

His expression shone with love as he nodded. "You're remembering things faster every day, slugger. I'm proud of you."

Blood pounded in Dani's frame as she accepted her intense attraction to a man she didn't remember but who her body very much recognized. The yearning to reach for him and wrap herself around his muscled body thrummed through every cell.

"Not yet, my naughty little geneticist," he said, kissing the tip of her nose. "We've got plants to hunt today. But tonight, all bets are off." He'd arched a sexy eyebrow before sliding out of bed, leaving her rapt with anticipation of revisiting the conversation once the day was over.

Returning to the moment, she wiped her hands on her pants and rose. "I need you and the men to extricate all the plants you see with the white marbling. We'll plant some in one of the overgrown areas behind the school. It's invasive, so we don't want to plant it in the garden."

"Got it," Maverick said with a salute.

"I'll remove the leaves when we get back to the compound and start testing combinations with the other plants immediately."

"Is it weird that I'm slightly turned on by you discussing plant combinations?"

Tossing her head back, she laughed. "Yes, it's very weird. Also, remind me to write this moment in my journal. Even if I don't always remember, it's times like these that I understand how easily I must've fallen for you. That killer smile and sense of humor must've knocked me off my feet."

"You never stood a chance," he said, leaning in to peck her lips. "Plus, I'm amazing in bed."

Mirth danced in Dani's heart as she gazed into his gunmetal gray eyes. She made a mental note to document this moment in her journal for the days her memories were scarcer. Some days were better than others, according to her notes, but her journal held a plethora of information about her husband.

"I have a lot of reminders in my journal to tell you I love you," she said softly. "That it makes you really happy when I say it back."

"Only if you mean it, sweetheart," he said, tucking a strand of hair behind her ear. "I don't want to push you."

Swallowing thickly, she whispered. "I love you. I feel it so deeply right here." She rubbed her fingers over her heart.

"Babe," he murmured, sliding an arm around her waist. "Keep telling me that and I'm going to ravish you in a pile of milk thistle."

Wrinkling her nose, she drew back. "That would be really uncomfortable, but I appreciate the effort."

Maverick winked before calling the other men over. After giving instructions, they gripped their shears and shovels and began to dig up the plants.

Dani watched them work, hope welling in her heart that she was close to a cure. The crushing weight of guilt lodged in her throat, and she joined the others, shoveling the dirt away with firm resolve. Reveling in the burn her muscles experienced from the manual labor, she silently envisioned saving the world from the destruction she'd wrought.

Chapter 14

That evening, long past sunset, Arianna and Dominic stood on the hill above the Dr. Ziegler's lab. They'd walked almost two hours to get to Glover Park, the neighborhood where the lab resided.

Dominic crouched behind the trunk of the large tree, peeking around the right side as Arianna scouted from her perch to his left.

"Two guards as we expected," she said, eyes narrowed as she gazed into the distance. "It will be midnight soon. Let's confirm they take breaks as Tristan indicated."

Dominic nodded, palm pressed to the rough bark as they waited. Sure enough, at the stroke of midnight, one of the guards disappeared inside.

"The lab isn't as big as the one we infiltrated to get Dani's antidote," Arianna said. "We should be able to breach it and light the explosives quickly."

"Unless we run into extra guards inside we didn't anticipate. If Cromwell really is working on a drug that powerful, you'd think he'd have more than two guards outside."

Arianna shot him a droll look. "Or he might just be arrogant enough to believe no one would challenge him. Power can make a man drunk with overconfidence."

"True." Standing, Dominic gripped the strap of the rifle slung behind his back. "I think we've gotten the surveillance we need. I'd be worried to enter a mission on such little prep time with anyone but you, but I know we can knock this out."

She seemed pleased at his praise, causing warmth to spread through his frame. A satisfied smile flirted with her lips as she rose. "Well then, I guess it's time to head back to our shitty hotel. I have to say, I miss cars. Maybe we can find a damn bike or something. Walking is good conditioning but not the most practical method of transportation."

"You're telling me," Dominic said, feeling exhaustion set in at the nearly four-mile walk ahead. They would get back to the motel around two a.m., and at least he could get several hours of sleep before Arianna woke him up for their morning jog.

"Speaking of conditioning," she said as they trudged through the quiet neighborhood. "How's your injury?" She tapped her neck where it met her shoulder. "Haven't heard you complain, which is really fucking cool. I'm glad you're not a pansy."

Breathing a laugh, he rubbed the slightly puffy scar. "It feels good today. Dani said the bullet hit the optimal place for me to bleed profusely but otherwise not suffer any long-term damage."

"Lucky bastard." She flashed a grin. "If they ever reinstate the lottery, you should play."

"Only if you coach me. I'm convinced our morning training sessions helped. I appreciate you taking the time to help me condition."

"What the hell else was I going to do?" she asked, shrugging as her boots stomped the grass in the field they entered along the path. "There's nothing to do on Arthur's compound except figure out how to save the world. And Dani's got that covered."

"I think we're all doing our little part." Glancing at her out of the corner of his eye, he asked, "Are we going to talk about Matt and Susan? Or is that subject closed?"

"There's really nothing to talk about. We met when I was his commanding officer, dated, became engaged. You know, all the shit normal people are supposed to want. Then I found out he was fucking Susan, and we got in a huge argument where he basically admitted he was with me to advance his career."

Dominic let that settle in, understanding how much it must've hurt to hear those words.

"He said it just like that? What a dick."

"Just like that," she said with a nod. "But I appreciated the honesty. It was nice to finally get some from him."

Pursing his lips, Dominic reminded himself to tread lightly. "Something like that would make it hard to trust a man again or to even want to be in a relationship."

"It wasn't the first time," she said flippantly. "My college boyfriend cheated on me with my roommate. There's something about me that makes men stick their dicks in other women. Not sure what it is, but I'm smart enough to stop repeating the same actions and expecting different results."

"Or you could've just dated jerks who weren't ready for a woman like you."

She scoffed. "Yeah, maybe. Anyway"—she waved a dismissive hand—"that's all there is to the story. If you're in a mood to talk, you can tell me about Pam. What was her favorite song?"

Joy rippled through him at the question. It was a thoughtful one that no one had ever asked about his sister. "'Make You Feel My Love,'" he said, his voice gravelly as emotion welled. "The Garth Brooks version. Pam loved Garth."

"That's a good one. What was her favorite food?"

They continued on for several minutes, Arianna asking questions about his sister that caused fond memories to swell—along with the painful ones.

"Her favorite movie was *Love, Actually*," he said, his boots quiet on the sidewalk in the tree-lined neighborhood they were currently crossing. "She loved that scene where the girl sang the Mariah Carey song."

"If you tell anyone I admitted this, I'll deny it, but that Mariah Carey Christmas song is dope. I'm a sucker for it."

Dominic made an *X* over his heart. "It's in the vault. Music can bring out something in a person's soul. On Pam's last day, she asked me to play 'Make You Feel My Love' for her. She said she wanted to hear Garth and imagine what it would be like to fall in love one last time. I'll never forget her expression as she lay in the bed, eyes closed and a huge smile on her face. She was so happy." He cleared his throat as his vision blurred from the tears that stung his eyes.

"Mom was the same way," Arianna said, her tone solemn. "Not with a song, but she took my hand and said the sweetest things to me. Then she closed her eyes and squeezed my wrist. She was very weak and it must've taken a lot of strength. When she opened them..." Her throat bobbed in the moonlight as she paused. "She looked at me with so much love. More than anyone in my life ever had. It was...beautiful...and peaceful."

"Those last moments are special. I can see why Raquel was upset she didn't get to say goodbye to your mom, although she had a pretty shitty way of making you pay for it."

"I'll say. I'm going to give her hell once I rescue her."

Entranced by the ease of their conversation, Dominic fought the urge to reach over and grasp her hand. They were sharing intimate details about meaningful and private moments in their lives, which he knew Arianna rarely did. It moved something deep within, and he realized he craved *more*.

More intimacy with her. More glimpses of that soft smile instead of the harsh frown. More moments where it was just the two of them, comfortable and open.

A loud snap sounded behind them and Dominic whirled around, slinging his rifle over his shoulder and assessing the darkened surroundings. Were they being followed?

Arianna did the same, feet firmly planted as she held the rifle to her shoulder, aiming in the distance.

"Do you see anything?" she whispered.

"No, but that doesn't mean no one's there. Stay alert."

They began to slowly back down the street, still facing the direction where the sound originated. A gun cocked to Dominic's left, and he snapped his head. He saw the flash of dark metal before a Sen Force soldier appeared from behind a tree.

"Run!" he shouted to Arianna, and they began a full-on sprint down the sidewalk toward the nearby woods. Bullets whizzed past their heads as they ran before darting behind a brick apartment building. Dominic spotted a large metal dumpster and called to Arianna.

"Take cover!"

They crouched behind the dumpster, breathless as Dominic assessed the situation.

"I spotted four men," he said, lifting his eyebrows for confirmation.

"Same. Do you think they followed us from the lab or they were out on patrol?"

"Not sure, but I saw the Sen Force badge on their uniforms." The Sen Force logo had replaced all other insignia on US military uniforms when Luthor Cromwell seized control of the government.

"Our best bet is to draw them in so we can line up our shots. I can lure them toward us, and you can take them out."

"I can advance while you stay here. You're healing and I'm in better condition—"

"No," he said, his voice firm as he cut her off. "You stay here and aim for their necks as I draw them in."

A muscle ticked in her jaw. "Stop trying to be a fucking hero, Dom—"

"Not up for discussion. Stay sharp." Before she could argue, he straightened and emerged from behind the dumpster.

The Sen Force soldiers immediately spotted him and advanced, and he sprayed bullets from his rifle, confident Arianna would systematically take them out. Sure enough, a bullet fired from the darkness behind the dumpster, lodging in one soldier's throat. He gasped and clutched the wound before falling to the ground.

Another man behind him lowered to check his pulse, and Arianna took the opportunity to shoot him in the lower back. He collapsed atop the other soldier, his body limp.

The remaining two soldiers wised up and hid behind the bricks on the far side of the nearby building. Rejoining Arianna behind the dumpster, Dom spoke in short, clipped words.

"Good job," he said, frustrated at his erratic breathing. "I'm going to advance on the remaining two. When I draw them out, shoot them."

"Not this time," she said, crossing behind him and craning her neck to look down the sidewalk to where the other men hid. "I'm advancing and you shoot."

"No." He circled her wrist, drawing her back. "I won't let you—"

"It's not your choice." Yanking her wrist from his grasp, she whisked onto the street and began advancing.

"Stubborn fucking woman," he muttered, fury lacing with fear that she would put herself in danger, especially when he was the one who should protect her.

It was an antiquated thought for a woman as tough and progressive as Arianna, but hell, Dominic was old school and he protected what was his.

And Arianna was *his*, goddamnit.

As soon as they finished taking down the bastards who were hunting them, he'd make sure she got the message. No more waiting. No more pretending. The present moment showed just how fleeting life could be, and he was done denying there was something between them. Dominic was ready to take action.

But first, he had to ensure they stayed alive.

The first soldier darted out from behind the brick, shooting at Arianna as she strategically advanced between the trees that lined the street. Dominic planted his feet on the sidewalk, lifted his handgun and aimed at the man's forehead. He didn't stand a chance.

His eyes widened before blood began to trickle from the bullet wound. Crumpling to the ground, he exhaled his last breath.

Arianna approached the last soldier as Dominic fought the urge to scream for her to retreat. Terror pulsed through his body at the thought of losing her, and he waited with bated breath for her to draw the last soldier out. When he appeared, Dominic shot him in the thigh. The man grimaced, dropping his weapon to grab the injured flesh, and Dominic took the opportunity to shoot him in the other thigh as well.

He and Arianna both jogged up to the man, who was now rolling around in intense pain on the sidewalk.

"Did you follow us?" Dominic asked, kicking the man in the kidney. "Answer me!"

"We patrol this neighborhood for Sen Force," the soldier said through clenched teeth. "We noticed you walking and hadn't seen you before. I swear, that's it."

"I actually believe him," Arianna said.

The soldier gagged several times before relaxing on the ground, unconscious. Lights began to illuminate the surrounding homes and apartment buildings, and Arianna jerked her head. "Let's go."

They ran out of the neighborhood, following the trail they'd taken earlier to get to the lab. As they made their way back to LeDroit Park, Dominic felt his anger grow from a dull throb to an all-consuming burn. He was pissed Arianna had put herself in danger and could tell she damn well knew it.

"I don't take commands from anyone, Dominic," she said, her tone angry as they moved at a fast pace.

"It's not about taking commands," he spat out. "Your insistence on doing everything on your own is going to get us both killed."

"I told you to stay on Arthur's compound," she gritted. "I work best alone."

Dominic remained silent, worried he was going to say something he couldn't take back. Deciding to shelve the discussion for now, he focused on controlling his seething frustration.

One thing was fucking certain: when they got back to the motel, he was going to lay everything on the table with Arianna and outline new rules. No more solo decision making. They were a team, and she needed to start respecting that.

And when he was done imparting the new rules, he was finally going to take advantage of all that energy that buzzed between them.

Dominic was ready to claim Arianna in all the ways he should have over the years they'd known each other. All the times he'd stupidly overlooked her.

As they trudged through the city, he kept repeating the same phrase in his head.

Tonight, Arianna Lawson is **mine***.*

Chapter 15

Arianna could tell Dominic was pissed she hadn't let him take control during the ambush. What he couldn't understand was the surge of abject terror she felt when he stepped onto the sidewalk to draw out the soldiers. Every heart-wrenching scene from the moments he'd been bleeding out on the lab floor had flashed through her brain. It had been the worst moment of Arianna's life—where she was sure she'd lost the love of her damn life—and she wasn't apt to repeat it.

In an effort to prevent him harm, she'd lurched from behind the dumpster to draw out the remaining two soldiers. Hell, she was more than competent and didn't take orders from anyone.

Not even Dominic, no matter how she felt about him.

Anger clouded his features as they entered the lobby of the motel, Devon straightening behind the desk as he yawned. "Hey, guys. Late night—"

"Shut it," Arianna snapped, annoyed at the attempt to chit chat. Not only was she not in the mood for polite conversation, but she was growing more furious by the minute. Dominic was upset at *her*? Annoyed at his entitled anger, she climbed the stairs, ready to shut herself into the bedroom and cool down before they got into an argument.

When they entered the foyer, she stalked to the small kitchen table and removed her weapons. They slammed on the cheap wood with ominous clanks before she returned to the entrance hallway to kick off her boots. Anxious for some solace to gather herself, she turned to walk to the bedroom. Dominic's hand snaked around her wrist, forcing her to halt.

Arianna pivoted, anxious to run from the feelings that pulsed in every cell of her body when he was near. Furious at being manhandled, she attempted to yank her arm from his grasp. "Let go of me!"

Fire flashed in his eyes and a muscle ticked in his jaw. His gaze bore into hers, dark and fierce as he pushed her toward the wall.

"What are you—?"

"Not this time," he said, the arousal-laden timbre of his voice shooting sparks of desire through her frame. "No more running, Ari." Pressing her to the wall, he stepped forward, crowding her. The roof of her mouth turned to dust, dry as sandpaper as his evergreen scent overwhelmed her.

Tilting her head back, she stared into his eyes, determined not to look away. The firm muscles of his pecs brushed her breasts under her functional black t-shirt and bra, and she had to suppress the urge to whimper. God, her nipples were hard. Closing her eyes for the briefest second, she willed away the desire.

Lifting her lids, her nostrils flared as she spoke through clenched teeth. "Let. Me. Go."

He scoffed, the arrogant sound sending fury down her spine. Bristling, she yanked her arm again to no avail.

"You're a damn good fighter, Ari, but you forget one thing," he said, his deep voice gravelly.

"And what is that?" She lifted her chin, defiant under his heated gaze. Every single muscle seemed frozen by the warmth of his strong body.

Labored breaths escaped his lips, although they were nowhere near as frenzied as the choppy pants that exited her lungs.

"I'm bigger than you," he murmured, lifting her wrist above her head and pressing it to the wall. His fingers cinched on the soft flesh there—perhaps one of the softest places on her shaking frame besides the tender skin of her inner thighs, which were now trembling as slickness gathered between them.

"Bigger doesn't mean stronger," she grunted before lifting her free hand, intending to punch every tooth out of his mouth.

He caught her balled fist in his palm as if she'd aimed for it. Sputtering, she cursed and struggled against him as he lifted that arm beside her other one. Securing her wrists tight in one hand above her head, he closed the remaining distance between them, fully aligning their bodies. The contact drove her insane with lust, and she looked away, unable to meet his eyes.

He cupped her chin and forced her to meet his gaze.

The urge to lodge her knee in his balls roared, and recognition lit his brown irises. Full lips curled into a sexy grin as his warm breath skated across her cheek. "Don't do it," he murmured. "I desperately need that part of my anatomy."

"Not around me," she said. "I'm not Dani."

Dark eyes roved over her face, contemplative and hesitant. "Using Dani as an excuse isn't going to work anymore," he finally said. "My feelings for her were a coping mechanism. I know you understand that somewhere in that infuriatingly hard head." Sliding his fingers to her temple, he gently tapped. "They weren't real—"

"Of course they were real," she said, frustrated at the incessant pounding of the treacherous organ in her chest. "Everyone loves Dani. She's gorgeous, brilliant, funny. It makes perfect sense."

Sliding his hand from her temple to her neck, he placed his palm over her pulsing vein. The pad of his thumb caressed the sensitive skin as he spoke. "Dani is easy to love, but that's a completely separate topic."

Annoyance—and a hefty dose of pain—sliced through her, and she squirmed against him, trying to wrench her wrists from his death grip above her head. "Let me go!"

"Wait," he said with a frustrated shake of his head.

"So you can tell me how much you love my sister? That's fucking weird, Dom."

Thick nostrils flared as his eyes darted between hers. "Jesus, woman, you're infuriating."

"*I'm* infuriating? You just told me you loved my sister while you're holding me in some sexual death grip against the wall!"

Huffing a laugh, he shook his head, appearing to try and rid it from the strange conversation. "I said Dani is easy to love because it's true. She isn't as stubborn and immobile as some other women I know." Arching a brow, he shot her a heated glare.

"If I wasn't stubborn, we'd all be dead. It's what makes me a good fighter."

"True." Ever so slowly, he leaned forward, his lips only a hairsbreadth from hers.

Ari gasped, mortified her knees were close to buckling. His warm breath enveloped her and she fought the urge to close her eyes and lean into his massive frame.

"You're stubborn...and fierce...and gorgeous..." His lips brushed hers as he spoke the words. "And you're not easy, Ari. You require effort and dedication, and I was lazy with you for far too long."

"I don't want your effort—"

"Liar," he whispered, resting his forehead against hers. The skin of her face tingled in every spot his skin pressed against hers. "I think you want me as much as I want you."

She shook her head, terrified of the intense feelings clamoring to breach the surface. "No, I don't."

He gazed into her as their breaths mingled. "You're not easy to love, sweetheart," he said, the words surrounding her and causing her to shiver. "But I'm tired of easy. I took that route for a long fucking time because I was broken. I didn't see what was right in front of me."

Scattered breaths exited her lips as arousal ripped through every cell in her body, burning her from the inside out. "I won't be a substitute for Dani, and I don't do romantic relationships," she said, lowering her gaze, unable to meet his eyes. "I'm not cut out for any of that shit—"

"Shut up," he interrupted, squeezing the juncture of her neck and shoulder. "Just shut up and feel, Ari."

Emotion swamped her as she felt the sting of tears. How long had she loved this man who was in love with someone else? Her own *sister*, although she understood why he'd chosen Dani. Men always chose other women above her. It was a lesson she'd learned countless times and was too exhausted to repeat.

But now he was holding her, whispering about love and a thousand other things her brain couldn't process. Mortified, her heart pounded as tears clouded her gaze.

"*Shhh*," he whispered, empathy lacing the hushed command. "I'm sorry I fucked this up so badly, but that ends today."

Pushing the emotion away, she capitulated, trying to regain some control. "If you want to fuck, just say so. It's been a while, and I can see the benefit of blowing off some steam—"

"No," he interjected, covering her lips with his thumb—the dominant action so sexy her legs almost gave out. "I'm going to *make love* to you, Arianna. You deserve that, and I'm going to give it to you."

Releasing her wrists, he snaked his arm around her waist and dragged her against his body.

Arianna held her hands high, unsure what to do. If he fucked her with emotion instead of just raw sexual energy, it would be over for her. She'd probably fall so much deeper in love with him she'd be unable to fight it. And fighting was all she knew.

"I don't make love," she rasped, "I fuck. So if you want to fuck me, do it. Otherwise, I'm not interested."

Those sexy lips curved into a sensual grin that damn near set her panties on fire. Squirming, she acknowledged she'd have to lower her arms soon since they were trembling like the rest of her traitorous body.

"Challenge accepted. Put your arms around my neck, sweetheart."

"Don't call me that."

His lips twitched. "Put your arms around my neck, Arianna."

Lulled by his soft command, she lowered her arms and clenched them around his neck.

"*Good girl.*"

Shivering at the silken words, her body vibrated when a mischievous glint entered his eyes.

"You like being praised," he murmured, pressing every inch of his body against hers. "I'll remember that. As long as you're good, I'll reward you—"

"You talk too much," she hissed, spearing her nails into his neck. He uttered a curse before she inhaled it from his lips, closing her mouth over his.

A deep groan rumbled in his chest, and Arianna felt it to her core as he lowered his hands and cupped her ass in both palms. Lifting her, he pushed her back into the wall as he surged his erection into her core. Her legs encircled his waist, clutching for dear life, trusting him to hold her since her body was out of control with rampant desire.

Squeezing him with every ounce of strength she possessed, she thrust her tongue in his mouth, aching to taste every inch of the man she'd silently loved since the day they met.

Chapter 16

D ominic devoured Arianna's lips, overcome with her taste and smell. Her tongue flitted over his, smoother than the finest silk, and her legs squeezed him so tightly he thought his hips might break. Who cared when his tongue was buried inside her hot mouth and his cock was cradled in her sweet warmth? Aching to lose their clothes, he lifted her from the wall, never breaking their kiss as he carried her to the bedroom.

Once his knees brushed the mattress, he felt her pull away as she anticipated him releasing her. "Not yet," he murmured into the wet heat of her mouth. "Keep kissing me."

She rewarded him with a lusty purr, the sound crawling down his throat and driving him mad. Clutching her for dear life, he threw himself into the kiss of the century, sliding his tongue over every crevice of hers before retreating. Placing a soft peck on her lips, he expelled a deep, satisfied breath as he waited for her to open her eyes.

Lids laced with long, black eyelashes slowly rose, the irises behind them glassy with desire and a slight bit of doubt. Dominic's insides swirled with lust and emotion as he ran a hand over the baby hairs growing over the shaved side of her head. "Goddamnit, you're beautiful."

She stared back, weary and breathless as she seemed to ponder.

"I don't have protection," he said, gazing deep into her eyes. "But I haven't been with anyone in years."

"Neither have I," she said, "but I can still get pregnant."

A surge of possessive satisfaction zipped down his spine at the thought. It was misplaced and light-years from where they were now, but Dominic couldn't deny its vehemence. The thought of her strong, gorgeous body full with his child sent a shot of renewed arousal to his dick, and he undulated against her core, pleased at her resulting gasp.

"I'll pull out, but only if you say it's okay."

Her eyes darted between his as she contemplated. Inhaling a deep breath, she nodded. "Okay."

Joy surged through him so intensely he realized he needed to set her down before he damn near collapsed. Resting one knee on the bed, he gently lowered her, her back pressing against the bedspread as she stared up at him.

Her hair was braided into a thick strand, and he drew it across the bed, fanning it from her head so she could relax. Stunning eyes with those thick-as-hell lashes stared back at him above her angular nose and swollen lips. God, how could he have wasted time on Dani when *she* had been in front of him? He really was a goddamn idiot.

"You're staring," she whispered, eyebrows drawing together.

"It's all I'm capable of at the moment," he murmured, tracing her soft skin from the corner of her eye to those luscious lips. "I've been fantasizing about this moment for a while."

The tip of her tongue darted out, and she slowly ran it across her lips, wetting the luscious flesh. "What did I do to you in these fantasies?"

Groaning, he wedged her legs open with his, craving her core against his cock. "You used those pretty lips to suck me dry, Ari."

Red splotches marred her cheeks, making her look adorable as he loomed above her. He'd rarely seen her like this—relaxed and open—and it set something free deep within.

"And you opened up to me and let me fuck you until we both screamed." Undulating against her, he reveled in her quick inhale.

"So stop stalling and let's do it."

Chuckling, he nudged her nose with his. "Yes, ma'am."

Rising, he tore at his clothes, dragging them off as she reached for hers.

"Wait," he commanded, tossing his shirt on the floor and kicking off his boots. "I want to undress you."

She stilled, those brilliant eyes glowing with desire and a slight hesitation, before sliding her hands over her head. She was spread in front of him like a gorgeous present he couldn't wait to unwrap.

Once he was naked, he strode toward her, staring deep into her eyes as he tugged off her pants before gripping the hem of her shirt. Lifting from the bed, she allowed him to pull it off and throw it aside before he traced the hem of her bra.

"No lacy lingerie here," she murmured, gauging his reaction from half-lidded eyes. "I hate fancy shit like that—"

"You're fucking perfect," he interrupted, unable to stop himself from running his palm over her breasts, covered by the black fabric. "I'm going to tell you every goddamn hour of every goddamn day until you believe me, Ari."

A joyful laugh escaped her throat, causing him to smile. "Wow. You like the functional underwear. I'm not sure what to do with that."

Stretching over her, he softly pressed his lips to hers. "I like anything you wear…"

Her lips caught his, capturing the words as he groaned. Undulating his hips, he pressed into her core, feeling the damp heat. Tremors shook his frame as he recognized the inevitable. He'd promised himself he'd go slow the first time—that he'd savor every second—but now that he was stretched above her, he admitted the lie.

"I need to fuck you," he rasped in her mouth. "I don't think I can go slow—"

"Take off my bra," she whispered, her breathing heavy as he removed the garment. His fingers shook as he slid her underwear down her long legs before tossing them away. Inhaling a deep breath, he froze, needing to bask in the vision before him for just a moment.

Slightly curved hips led to thick thighs and strong calves, the skin covered with a sheen of dark hair he craved against his palms. Dying to touch her, he rested his fingertips on her inner thighs, pressing her legs open and baring her glistening pussy.

"Not a lot of time for self-care," she murmured, opening beneath him. "I don't think I've shaved my legs—or anywhere else besides my head—in years."

"You're stunning," he whispered, running his palms over the soft skin of her legs, reveling in the slight luster of silken hair that felt so good against his skin. Continuing to caress her, he let his eyes travel over her pert breasts, the nipples tight and pointed in the exposed air. The areolas were dark—so much darker than the surrounding skin—and the contrast set him on fire.

Dominic knew Arianna didn't open herself to many men. The fact she would open herself to him shattered something deep inside his soul as he stared at her. Determined to thank her properly, he glided his hand up her thigh, shivering at her quiet moan as his fingers rested against her wet opening.

"Ari," he whispered, dragging his finger through her slickness. "You're dripping for me, aren't you?"

She gave a slight nod, her braid moving against the comforter as she gazed at him.

Placing two fingers at her core, he stared into those brilliant eyes before gently easing inside and coating them with her essence. White teeth toyed with her bottom lip as she rose to meet his fingers.

"*Good girl*," he growled, loving how she shivered at his praise. She certainly didn't need praise in other areas, but he understood that strong women sometimes liked to be dominated in bed. It provided a brief moment they could relinquish the need to be resilient and could just focus on *feeling*.

"I see you," he almost whispered, lifting the fingers now coated with her slick and touching them to her nipple. "I'm going to take care of you." Gazing into her eyes, he spread her wet arousal around the turgid nipple.

"*Oh god...*" she moaned, head thrown back as the pulse pounded in her neck. "*Dom...*"

"Don't look away," he softly commanded, lowering his fingers to press inside her again. Circling her tight vise, he gathered more wetness before lifting to coat her other nipple. "I want to look into those pretty eyes when I kiss you..." Spreading the slick over the tight bud, his cock jerked when she retrained her gaze on his. "And when I fuck you."

The curves of her breasts trembled slightly beneath the now-glistening nipples, and Dominic struggled to breathe. Sliding his hand beneath her knee, he wrapped her leg around his waist, the tip of his cock searching for her wet, pulsing core. Hissing at the contact, he lowered his head, eyes locked with hers as his mouth hovered above her nipple. Gazing into her soul, he closed his mouth around the tight bud as he began to push inside her.

Her resulting whimper sent every remaining drop of blood to his cock as he pushed deeper, lapping her nipple with his tongue as he inched inside her. Tight wetness met his steel, clenching his most sensitive place as he sucked her between his lips. Desperate for a stronghold, he reached for her, sliding his fingers into the hair beneath her braid and clutching for dear life.

"That's right, Ari," he rasped against her nipple, slowly dragging his sensitive flesh through her wet core before kissing a trail to her other breast. "You're mine now."

"I'm not anyone's—" she choked before gasping when he closed his teeth around her nipple, gently biting.

"So goddamn difficult," he grunted, increasing the pace of his hips as he licked the turgid bud to ease the sting. "It's one of my favorite things about you."

Her lips fell open with a soft cry as he increased the pace, his cock now sliding back and forth through her warmth as he struggled to hold on. Determined to please her first, he sucked her nipple deep, giving it one last, firm pull before lifting and withdrawing.

"Dom?" she asked, confusion lacing her expression beneath her flushed cheeks.

Unable to speak, he encircled her wrist and drew her toward the edge of the bed. Too impatient to gently instruct her, he pulled her to her feet before placing his hands on her hips and turning her to face the bed. "Get on your knees," he commanded.

"What the—?"

Grasping her braid, he gently tugged her head, reveling in her arousal-laden gasp. Nudging her with his hips, he pressed his lips against the shell of her ear. "Get on your fucking knees, Ari."

Arduous breaths exited her lungs as she followed his command, her submission sending a surge of joy through his veins so intense he almost whimpered. Pressing his chest to her back, he urged her to rest her head on his shoulder by tenderly tugging her braid. Once she was flush against him, he pressed his cock between the firm globes of her ass.

Resting his forehead to her temple, he spoke softly in her ear. "Open your legs."

She complied, widening her knees on the bed as he glided his fingers across her hip, reveling as the skin quivered beneath before reaching her mound. Sliding his fingers between her wet folds, he searched for her tight sensitive nub.

He began to rub her clit in concentric circles as his warm breath fanned over her ear. "If you think I'm going to get off without you coming first, you don't know me, Ari. All I want is to make you feel good." Searching for her opening with the head of his cock, he groaned when he found her slick core. Pressing against her as he stimulated her clit, he began to push inside from behind as she purred.

"That's it," he hissed in her ear, determined to make her scream before he sought his release. "Now, I need you to come for me."

"Dom..." she cried, lips glistening from the ardent swipes of her tongue as she undulated into his fingers, her body taking the sharp jabs of his cock as if she were made for him.

"So sweet and wet..." he crooned, his fingers moving furiously over her clit as he fucked her from behind.

Scoffing, she pressed her face against his neck. "I'm *not* sweet."

Chuckling, he bit her earlobe, pleased when she mewled in approval. "Your pussy is the sweetest thing I've ever felt around my cock. Now be a good girl and come around me. I want to feel you gush all over my fingers. Do you hear me?"

"I can't...*oh god*," she rasped, reaching behind to grasp his hips as they hammered against her. Uncontrollable tremors shook her frame, and he knew she was close.

Short, pointed fingernails speared into the flesh of his ass as her body bowed and she screamed his name. Overcome with joy, he pressed his cheek into her temple, kissing her as he murmured words of praise and desire. The muscles of her core spasmed, milking him as he thrust between the wet, plushy folds. Gratified he could bring her such pleasure, he held her tight, cupping her mound as her body quaked and vibrated against his.

Needing more, he gently pushed her to the bed, pressing her chest to the soft mattress before securing her hips with both hands. Lifting her to her knees, he clenched tight as he began to pummel her with his hard cock.

"Jesus, you're still coming around me..." he groaned, tossing his head back and closing his eyes against the onslaught of pleasure. The sounds of their wet flesh slapping together rang in his ears as he fought to hold off his release. Gritting his teeth, he realized the pleasure was too much to bear. Giving in to the overwhelming bliss, he fucked her as his release gathered at the base of his cock.

Screaming unintelligible words, he gripped her shoulder, holding firm as he pumped inside her, feeling the jets of release form before he pulled out and began to come.

He covered her body, wrapping his arms around her as he emptied everything against her smooth back. "So fucking good," he groaned, burying his face in her neck as jets of release drenched her ravaged body.

They quaked and shuddered, lost to desire as they clung to each other, uttering indecipherable words while pleasure threatened to drown them. Eventually, Dominic lost the ability to move, the orgasm draining every ounce of energy from his frame. Unable to support himself, he collapsed further, thankful she was strong and could support his weight.

Overwhelmed by her scent and the way she instinctively curled into him, he nuzzled her neck and slid his arm between her breasts, drawing her closer.

"Ari," he whispered, wrapping his leg around her thigh, curving her into his body as he haphazardly spooned her atop the soft mattress. "Good grief," he mumbled, trailing soft kisses over the back of her neck, thrilled when tiny bumps rose against his lips. "Is that what it's going to be like every time I fuck you?" Squeezing her, he aimed to merge every cell in his body to hers. "I'm not sure I'll survive."

Wriggling her ass into his sated body, she chuckled. "Who says this wasn't just a one-time thing?"

"*I* say," was his quick response before he nipped her earlobe, causing her to quiver in his arms. "I can't live without fucking you again. It's impossible."

A contented purr exited her lips as she relaxed against him. "You lived this long and did just fine..." Yawning, she snuggled deeper into his embrace.

"I was a fool," he murmured, kissing the shell of her ear. Reaching over, he grabbed some tissues from the dresser and wiped the skin between them, cleaning his release. Tossing them away, he snuggled against her again, acknowledging how perfectly she fit into the grooves of his body. "Never again. Do you hear me? I'll apologize for eternity if you let me keep fucking you."

A soft laugh rumbled from her throat. "We'll see. For now, I need sleep. Sun will be up soon so we can jog..."

Inhaling her scent, he burrowed deeper into her as his eyelids grew heavy. "Or we could sleep past sunrise like two normal people who just had amazing sex and forget the world is a dumpster fire."

Her resulting grunt was the perfect response, causing him to grin as he held her. Part of him wanted to push her—to make her admit what they'd done was light-years from a quick, meaningless fuck. She'd sucked every piece of his soul into her gorgeous body, and he never wanted it back. Could she open herself up enough to admit her feelings?

Hesitant to rile her when she was so warm and pliant against him, Dominic decided to table a serious discussion until after they'd made love a few more times. One day soon, he would gather the courage to tell her he was all in. That the bullet he'd taken in the lab had reset something in his brain...in his *heart*...and he was ready to take the incredible risk of trying to love again.

That *she* was worth the risk.

Gently stroking her shoulder, he nuzzled the tender skin behind her ear until her muscles grew limp. Once he was surrounded by her soft snores, he closed his eyes and gave in to the magnificent pleasure of falling asleep with Arianna curled against his body.

CHAPTER 17

A rianna awoke to the delicious smell of Dominic *everywhere*. That evergreen scent that haunted her dreams surrounded her as she rubbed her leg over his hairy thigh. Sometime during the night, they'd shifted in the bed to lay properly on the pillows. Lifting her lids, the first thing Arianna saw was the scar on his neck, the skin still slightly puffed under the healing wound.

Aching to touch him—to confirm he was okay—she touched the scar with the pad of her finger and began to gently trace it. Dominic inhaled a deep breath before turning his head on the pillow to face her.

She gazed into his eyes as she tenderly ran her finger over the laceration. "I didn't want you to draw the soldiers out last night because I was scared. I can't see you hurt again, Dom."

His lips formed a tender smile as he cupped her cheek. "I figured that was why you disobeyed my order."

Arianna rolled her eyes. "I don't care how good of a lay you are, I don't take orders from anyone."

Arching his eyebrow, he smirked. "So you're saying I'm the best you've ever had?"

"*Pfft.* Get over yourself. You're certainly the best I've had in a while though. I haven't had any interest in men in a long time."

Dominic's thumb caressed her cheek, back and forth in slow, fluid motions that made her want to curl into him and languish all day.

"But that's not going to get you out of training. We need to run at least ten miles and then grab some breakfast from Deandra. Hopefully, she'll have an update on the tailor."

They'd stopped in the deli yesterday to ask for the best place to shop for formal clothes that was inconspicuous. Deandra informed them she knew a friend who was a dry cleaner and tailor who had several tuxedos and gowns that had never been picked up. Deandra had promised to speak to him and see if he was open to lending them.

"Let's start the day off properly before we get back to saving the world," Dominic said, lowering his hand and cupping her ass. He drew her against his body, his skin warm as his cock searched for her.

"The more we do this, the more chances we take, Dom." Even as she heard the warning in her voice, she opened herself to him, allowing him inside. Biting her lip, she winced at the soreness down below.

"You okay?" he asked, halting as concern entered his deep brown eyes.

"Yeah," she whispered, pushing into him. "Just sore."

"I can stop—"

She covered his lips. "Not on your fucking life."

The smooth slide of his cock sent a warm glow throughout her body. Their cheeks rested on the pillows as they gazed into each other's eyes, the moment more intimate than she'd anticipated.

Part of her wanted to retreat behind her shell and protect all the parts she'd bared to him. But in a deep corner of her heart, she held hope that maybe, just maybe, things could be different with Dominic.

She palmed his jaw, her eyes roving over the scar that ran from the corner of one eye, over his nose, to the far side of his lips.

"It's not pretty," he muttered, fucking her in firm strokes as his fingers dug into her ass.

"I don't need pretty," she whispered, undulating into his deft movements. "I just need you to keep fucking me."

His resulting groan reverberated through every cell as he pressed her back on the mattress. Sliding over her, he loomed above as he increased the pace.

"You take me so well, Arianna," he crooned, causing her eyes to roll back in her head with pleasure. God, she could listen to that deep voice as he claimed her every hour of every damn day.

"Dom…"

"Take me deep, sweetheart," he rasped, hitting the spot inside that had been neglected for so long. Arianna's head tilted back on the pillow, and he placed wet kisses along her neck as they reached the crescendo.

With a groan, he pulled from her body, emptying on her stomach as she launched into her climax. Her muscles shook and quaked as he released above her before collapsing atop her quivering body.

Dominic's breath heated her neck as he exhaled, his face buried against her skin.

"We need to buy some condoms," she said, trailing her fingers over his back as he nearly crushed her. Another woman might have complained, but Arianna was tough and loved his weight atop her.

"I like feeling you bare around me," he said against her neck.

"Yes, but barebacking results in babies, and that's not in my plan at the moment."

Lifting his head, he studied her. "It's in your plan after Dani finishes the antidote and we defeat Cromwell."

"Sure, in a perfect world. But who knows when that will happen?"

Disappointment laced his features as he frowned. "Fine. But we're coming back to this discussion when we're both ready."

The corner of Arianna's mouth ticked up. "I told you. I've already got a plan. A turkey baster and a secluded cabin. That's all I need."

The challenge that lit his eyes was sexy as hell. "We'll see." Pecking her lips, he pushed up and slid into a sitting position. "You want to shower before we jog? We made a mess."

"Yeah." Sitting up, she ran her hand over her disheveled braid. "Give me five minutes, then you can jump in after."

"I can jump in with you," he said, his lips curling into a sexy grin.

Chuckling, she shook her head and rose. "If you do that, we'll never go running. And we both need the exercise."

Before he could argue, she slipped into the nearby bathroom and shut the door.

As she showered under the lukewarm spray—which was all they got at the shitty motel—she smiled as she ran the cloth over her sore entrance. Making love to Dominic had been even more pleasurable than she'd imagined. The way he demanded her submission, somehow knowing she craved it, had set something free inside her.

After rinsing off the suds, she stepped onto the mat and dried her skin, grinning at her reflection in the foggy mirror like a lovesick dope. No matter how much she denied it, she knew the truth: now that she'd had sex with Dominic, there was no turning back.

Covering her heart, she gazed into her eyes in the mirror.

"Careful, Arianna," she whispered.

The thrum of her ragged heartbeat was the only response to her quiet plea.

Chapter 18

After a brisk jog and another quick shower—alone, much to Dominic's chagrin—they returned to Matt and Susan's apartment. Dominic thought Arianna's head might explode when Matt opened the door and told her he hadn't yet obtained Tristan's address.

"I told you the timeline was firm, Matt," Arianna said, a muscle ticking in her jaw. "We're here to find my sister, and I know you have the resources to do it."

"Matt's shift starts in two hours, and he's going to do some digging while he's with Luthor," Susan said, appearing behind Matt and sliding a supportive hand over his shoulder. "Selena has lunch with Luthor and his wife, Grace, today. Tristan used to be married to Grace, and we think she might know where he lives."

Arianna's head whipped around. "Tristan was married to Luthor's *wife*?" Her eyes almost bugged out of her head. "That would've been good to know."

"Perhaps a possible motive for his desire to murder him," Dominic said, arching a brow.

Arianna grunted before facing Matt again. "Okay, I won't shoot you in the balls since you gave me that info. What about the birthday party?" she asked Susan.

"You're all set," she said, appearing pleased with herself. "You're on the list under the names David and Amy Ratched."

Arianna shot her a scathing glare. "Am I supposed to infer I'm 'Nurse Ratched' in this scenario?"

Dominic pursed his lips to stifle his laugh. It was pretty funny and an accurate representation of how Susan probably saw Arianna.

"Oh, that was just coincidence." She innocently batted her eyelashes.

"I bet." Arianna's tone dripped with sarcasm. "Do we need tickets or anything?"

"Nope. Just show up and give them your names. You're going to need these." She thrust out a pair of ID cards with their fake names on them.

"Well, damn," Arianna said, inspecting them before handing them to Dom. "You came through, Susan. Thank you."

Dominic stuck the two plastic cards in the side pocket of his pack, zipping it closed to keep them safe.

"I'll be home after lunch today to get ready for Luthor's birthday party," Matt said. "Selena doesn't need me until six p.m. when she's ready to head over. I can tell you if I found out anything over lunch."

"Just tell me at the party," Arianna said. "I'll find a way for us to speak privately."

"Will do."

"Okay, I've got to clean this one up and find a dress to wear." She pointed at Dominic while grimacing in distaste. "I don't think I've worn a dress in years. Gross, but necessary. Will I see you both there tonight?"

"I won't be there since Mattie's working," Susan said, hugging his arm as she nuzzled into his side. "But I hope you find Raquel, Arianna. I really do."

"Thanks. See you there, Matt." With a small salute, she turned and headed down the stairs. Dominic said his goodbyes and trailed after her, ready to try on some unclaimed tuxedos.

Two hours later, Dominic stood in front of the full-length mirror in the back of a dingy dry cleaner business that had seen better days. Deandra had come through, and she'd left Ron to man the deli while she'd accompanied them to the tailor two blocks away.

"Come on out, Arianna," Deandra called, her tone impatient. "This is the third dress you've tried on, and I'm sure it's fine."

Arianna's annoyed huff sounded from her dressing room as Dominic threaded the final button on his collar.

"I think this tux works," he said, pulling back the curtain and stepping out of the small makeshift dressing room. "What do you think?"

"Looks nice," Deandra said, approaching him. "Tommy, do you have a bowtie?"

The owner, an older man who appeared to be at least seventy, with snow-white hair and bushy eyebrows, nodded. He scuffled to the front and returned with a black bow tie. Deandra threaded it through Dominic's white collared shirt and began to tie it.

"Do you know how to do this?" she asked.

"Not really, but I'm a fast learner."

She smiled and tied the black material as she talked. "Over this way and through the loop here. See?" Tightening the bow, she beamed. "Perfect. Now, you try."

Dominic untied the material and tried to follow her instructions. Gazing in the mirror affixed to the wall, he stuck his tongue between his teeth as he worked.

"Excellent job," Deandra said, patting the bow when he was finished. "You'll do just fine tonight."

Dominic studied the woman's deep brown eyes. "You're going out of your way to help two strangers. I find myself wondering why."

Sadness crept into her expression. "We lost our son to EverLife. He was twenty-three and had his whole life ahead of him. Arianna didn't divulge much about your mission, but she told me her sister is working for Luthor. My assumption is that you're going to the fancy party tonight to find her and convince her to leave Washington, DC. Am I wrong?"

Dominic pursed his lips as he studied the wily woman. "No, but I gather you're rarely wrong, Deandra."

She emitted a good-natured scoff. "Tell that to my husband, infuriating man." Her eyes sparkled, offsetting her words. "And I also assume that once you rescue her sister, you'll regroup and return to the city to try and immobilize Cromwell."

"If I confirmed that, I'd have to kill you," he joked as the corner of his lips quirked.

Staring into Dominic's eyes, she spoke with clarity. "I hate Luthor Cromwell with a passion. I keep my ear to the ground in the hope a rebellion forms. I hear mumblings and have seen the graffiti, but nothing has come to fruition yet." Patting his chest, she lifted an eyebrow. "Maybe you and Arianna can change that."

"We'd love to know what you've heard," Dominic said. "Any information is valuable."

Deandra opened her mouth to reply at the same moment Arianna stepped out from the other dressing room. A sharp breath exited Dominic's lungs as his eyes raked over her body in the long, flowing red gown. "That's the one," he said, his mouth suddenly dry.

Arianna's eyes met his, the green flecks enhanced by the deep red color. It was simple, with a smattering of sparkles on the shoulder straps lowering to a *V* that showed off her cleavage. Noticing the flare of her hips, Dominic worked his jaw, attempting to regain his ability to speak.

"Down boy," Deandra teased, touching him under his chin and gently forcing his mouth closed. "I think your man likes it, Arianna."

"Not my man, but if it's possible, I'm happy." Stretching out her arms, she rotated in front of the mirror.

Dominic stepped toward her, his pulse pounding as he gently cupped both of her shoulders. "Holy shit. You look amazing."

"Okay, calm down," she said, but he saw the spark of pleasure in her eyes at his compliment. "You might have to help me get in and out of this thing later."

"Oh, I think he's counting on it," Deandra said, her eyes filled with mirth as she grinned.

Arianna chuckled and nodded. "Okay, we'll take it. Do we owe you anything for the clothes, Tommy?"

"No charge. Deandra's friends are always welcome to borrow my clothes," the owner said.

"Give him a gold bar," Arianna said softly to Dominic.

"Was already planning on it."

After the tuxedo and dress had been packed up, they began the short trip back to the deli.

"Deandra was going to tell me all the intel she knows about the rebellion," Dominic said as they trailed down the sidewalk.

"Was I?" she asked, shooting him a playful glare. "I don't know much, but Ron and I try our best to glean information where and when we can. Our customers talk a bit too loudly sometimes when they're in line waiting for Ron's sandwiches."

"We're grateful for anything you can tell us," Arianna said.

"We mostly hear people grumbling about Cromwell and how they detest his grip on the city," Deandra said, stopping in front of the deli. "The rich folks might like the status quo, but for the rest of us, it's not so grand." Rubbing her chin, she contemplated. "I honestly don't have much to tell. You already know the visible hints of the rebellion from the graffiti. But there is something…"

"Whatever it is, it might help," Arianna said.

Leaning forward, Deandra lowered her voice, as if she didn't want anyone else to hear, even though they were alone on the sidewalk. "Some of the conversations I've overheard speculate that the genesis of the rebellion is from *inside* Luthor's circle."

Arianna's eyebrows lifted. "Interesting. We know it's not Tristan," she said to Dominic. "Unless he was lying, which I wouldn't put past him."

"Tristan isn't in Luthor's *inner* circle," Deandra said. "He's still a paid employee, which Luthor considers beneath him."

Arianna's mouth fell open. "You know Tristan too? Is there anyone who doesn't know this guy?"

Chuckling, Deandra tilted her head. "Tristan Holder visits the deli every once in a while. He makes it his business to know what's going on in every part of the city. Sometimes, I tell him things I think he needs to hear."

"You would've made a fantastic spy, Deandra," Dominic said, admiration in his voice. "And still might depending on how things unfold."

"For you?" she asked good-naturedly. "I might consider it depending on the day." She winked. "Anyway, if I had to guess, I would imagine one of the other rich cronies might want to take Luthor down. I've heard several names tossed around, including George Luddington and James Stalworth."

"Both of whom were two of the wealthiest men in the world before it collapsed," Dominic said, recalling both men had been CEOs of huge companies and frequently appeared on the "Richest Men Alive" lists.

"And now the title of richest man has been relinquished to Luthor Cromwell. I'm not sure ol' George and James are too thrilled with that," Deandra said.

"Do you know of any specific plans?" Arianna asked.

"No. Some of their employees frequent the deli, and I overhear their conversations about how their bosses don't even bother to hide their disdain for Luthor. It might be worth investigating at your fancy party tonight."

"Absolutely. I'm sure both men will be in attendance. Rich assholes usually flock together, right?" Arianna asked.

Dominic shrugged. "Can't say I've known many rich assholes, but if they're in attendance, we'll surveil them. On another note, how functional is the Metro system in the city?"

Deandra wrinkled her nose. "Barely. Luthor had his tech team set up the trains to run automatically so they didn't need human operators. But they rarely run on time—if at all—and the stations are filled with addicts and homeless people."

"That means we should probably walk to the party," Arianna said. "It's warm today and shouldn't take more than two hours." Glancing at Deandra, she asked, "You don't happen to have any flats I can borrow, do you? My boots don't quite go with my dress, and flats are all I can manage if we walk."

"If you can wear an eight and a half, I do," she said with a nod.

"I'm a nine but close enough."

After procuring the flats from their apartment above the deli, Deandra walked them outside.

"We really appreciate your help, Deandra," Dominic said. "Thank you."

"You're welcome. Now, let me get back and help Ron. I'm already going to get a stern lecture for leaving him alone for an hour."

After saying their goodbyes, Dominic walked with Arianna to the pharmacy they'd spotted a few blocks from the motel. When they found the boxes of condoms hanging from the hooks in the narrow aisle, Arianna snatched one up and began heading to the register.

"Hey!" Dominic said, tugging her back. "You're not even going to buy the super-magnum ones? Are you trying to give me a complex?"

Arianna rolled her eyes at his teasing. "Don't flatter yourself."

Flashing her a grin, he pulled three more boxes from the hooks.

"Geez, Dom. We'll never use that many."

"Woman, I love your challenges." Leaning over, he gave a dramatic bow. "And I accept. We'll make use of every one of these suckers." Straightening, he shook one of the boxes at her.

She exhaled an exasperated breath, but Dominic caught the bare hint of a smile that tugged at her lips. "Fine. Buy them all. You can explain to Arthur where all his money went."

She strode toward the counter in that regal way that set his body on fire. After they purchased the condoms, they made their way back to the motel to get ready for the party.

"Should we break them in?" Dominic asked, waggling his eyebrows once they were in the hotel room.

Arianna chewed on her bottom lip. "I'm here for Raquel, Dom. I don't want to get distracted."

"We'll see Raquel in a few hours if all goes to plan." Closing the distance between them, he placed his fingers under her chin and tilted her head to look into her eyes. "And I can do a *lot* to your body in a few hours."

Those stunning eyes darted back and forth between his for a small eternity before she took pity on him. Her tongue darted out to bathe her lips and she finally whispered, "Prove it."

Dominic lurched for her, lifting her over his shoulder and carrying her to bed. Her high-pitched squeal was soon silenced by his lips as he endeavored to meet her challenge.

Chapter 19

L uthor Cromwell paced across the dark carpet that lined the conference room floor. His steps were measured as he circled the ornate mahogany table where Tristan sat alongside other members of Luthor's security team. Tristan wasn't always invited to these meetings since he was technically a mercenary, but Luthor was receiving reports about his small network of scientists, which included Raquel.

"How's our little botanist doing?" Luthor asked, stopping behind Tristan's chair and placing his hands over the leather headrest.

Tristan stared ahead, eyeing the men who sat across from him rather than looking up to meet Luthor's gaze. "Fine. She's usually out the door early and home by seven. She seems to take her work seriously and is an amenable houseguest."

Luthor uttered a thoughtful "Hmmm" before strolling back toward the head of the conference table. Lowering into the plushy leather seat, his eyes narrowed. "She doesn't mention her sister? Nor show any remorse about betraying her?"

"No. She's dedicated to your cause, Luthor. She hasn't mentioned Danica to me at all."

Luthor steepled his fingers and tapped them against his lips as he pondered. "Good. She's making excellent progress on a new antidote that will offer short-term relief before the addiction sets back in. It lessens the side effects, so I anticipate some of the remaining holdouts will try EverLife. It's important we get everyone in our new society on board. We can't have the majority of the population live extended lives while a small percentage experience normal lifespans."

Tristan scoffed, inwardly remarking that his comments seemed almost altruistic. As if he wanted something good for society instead of the destruction that came with each new person who succumbed to the addictive drug.

"Did you have more to add, Tristan?" Luthor asked, a warning in his tone.

"No, sir."

Leaning back, Luthor rotated slowly in the chair as he studied him. "Maybe I can finally get you on board with EverLife. It doesn't make any sense to die decades before your sister, especially since I know you love her so much."

Biting the inside of his cheek, Tristan fought not to scream. Since Jessica was vehemently addicted to EverLife, she traded sexual favors to Luthor for the drug and the watered-down antidote. Until he could find a solution, she needed to remain in Luthor's good graces to receive purer stashes that weren't filled with the toxic garbage in the antidote outside the walls.

Which meant Tristan needed to stay on Luthor's good side to protect her. What a clusterfuck.

"Not on my agenda for the moment. I'm still an old-school holdout who prefers a clean diet and exercise to stay young."

Luthor's eyebrows lifted. "For now."

Lowering his eyes to shield his hate, Tristan remained silent, hoping the bastard would move on to another topic.

"Where are we with the soldier serum, Dr. Ziegler?" Luthor asked.

The man at the far end of the table in the white lab coat cleared his throat. "I'll be ready to test on human subjects soon, sir. The tests on the mice are almost complete and very promising."

"Excellent." Resting his forearms on the table, Luthor spoke with gravity. "And the trackers?"

Tristan's ears perked as he reminded himself to remain impassive. What or *who* was Luthor going to track?

"The microchip prototype is almost complete," Dr. Ziegler said. "As you know, my counterpart, Dr. Rajmani, was an expert in microchip technology at Capital Tech. We should be able to implant the first hundred test subjects by the end of the month. After a few weeks of observation, I anticipate being able to implant them in everyone left in the city."

"And the factory near the university in Maryland has the capacity to make that many units?"

"Yes, sir," Dr. Ziegler said with a nod. "The high-capacity generators your men installed are top notch, and we have many engineers who've volunteered to work on the assembly in exchange for the antidote, whether for themselves, family members or both."

Luthor nodded as he tapped his chin. "Good. I want George Luddington and James Stalworth on the list of the first hundred people microchipped."

"They won't be happy about that, sir," Colonel McGrath said from his seat to Luthor's right. "They still employ a large number of people in the city and have influence over public sentiment. Most of our soldiers' spouses work for them in some capacity, and they're seen as benevolent employers inside the walls."

"I don't give a shit *how* they're seen," Luthor said, slapping his palm against the table. "This is *my* city and *my* government, and those two idiots are no more important than anyone else. They will be microchipped in the first wave. Are we clear?"

Dr. Ziegler's throat bobbed. "Yes."

With a firm nod, Luthor inserted his finger between his collar and his neck, loosening the fabric as the vein there pulsed with anger. "Once the trackers are ready, I want the homeless rounded up and purged from the city. All graffiti is to be cleaned, and anyone who speaks of or promotes rebellion will be exiled as well."

"Sir," Colonel McGrath said, straightening, "are you sure that punishment fits the crime? Some people still remember democracy and feel they have the right to protest—"

"Democracy died when people chose to take my drug to enhance their lives!" Luthor interrupted, rising to his feet and slicing his hand through the air. "I make their new lives possible. If they accept my leadership, they will have a prosperous life inside these walls. It's not too much to ask, is it?"

The men exchanged hooded glances as they remained silent.

"Is it?"

"No, sir," a deep voice chimed. "We are loyal to you, and this is your city. Rebels should be and will be exiled."

Tristan's nostrils flared as he listened to Zayne Danvers, Luthor's head of security.

"Thank you, Zayne," Luthor said, lowering to his seat. "Your loyalty is appreciated." Making eye contact with each of the members, he asked softly, "Do I have your loyalty too?"

"Yes, sir," they said in unison.

"Good. I'd hate to see Tracy suffer the side effects of EverLife withdrawal," he said to Colonel McGrath. "Your wife is such a lovely woman."

"Thank you, sir," the colonel replied, a muscle ticking in his jaw as he gritted the words.

Inhaling a breath, Luthor leaned back in the chair. "Dissention doesn't sow peace or prosperity. Only strong leadership and a firm hand will do in these situations. I'm glad we're all on the same page."

Glancing at the other men, Tristan wasn't so sure everyone was on board, but he'd learned to pick his battles. Now, in a room full of soldiers and security guards, wasn't the time to make waves.

His fingers tightened on the arm rests as he imagined tightening them around the evil leader's throat instead. One day soon, the day would come to overthrow the madman, and Tristan would be ready. If there was one thing he'd learned since the world collapsed, it was that patience was an asset.

One day, in the not-so-distant future, an opportunity would present itself to take down Luthor Cromwell.

And that day would be one Tristan relished for all the days that followed in their godforsaken world.

Chapter 20

S everal hours later, Dominic's fingers maneuvered the bow tie as he waited for Arianna to exit the bedroom. When she appeared, he turned to face her, noting she'd twirled her hair into some sort of fancy bun at the side of her neck.

"Didn't think the braid was elegant enough," she said, pointing to the bun. "Does it look okay?"

Dominic closed the distance between them, unable to stop himself from touching her. "It looks gorgeous. You clean up pretty well, Lawson."

Laughing, she pointed to her face. "I think I'm still flushed from our afternoon activities. The natural glow works wonders."

They'd made love twice before collapsing and taking a short nap. Feeling invigorated after the great sex and a lukewarm shower, he squeezed her shoulders. "Need me to button or zip anything?"

"No, but you could put the necklace on for me?" She held it up in her palm, and Dominic took it before she turned around. His thick fingers fumbled with the clasp of the necklace Deandra had insisted on loaning her along with the shoes, and he eventually latched it. She turned to face him and pointed at her flat dress shoes.

"These aren't really my style, but I'm not in this to win any beauty contests."

"They look fine and the dress is stunning."

"I'm worried we won't have guns," she said, eyeing their weapons on the table. "But we can't take the chance since they'll definitely frisk us before we get anywhere near Cromwell."

"We're both skilled at combat and evasion. If we need to fight or run, we'll do it." Lifting a finger, he spoke in a low, resolved tone. "We need to work together and communicate. If I give you an order, don't question it."

Her silken eyebrow arched. "And if I give you an order?"

"I'll follow it," he said without hesitation.

Her throat bobbed as she studied him. "Okay. Remember, the main goal is to approach Raquel and figure out where her head's at so we can get her out of here. If we can also discover intel on the rebellion, even better."

Dominic gave a firm nod. "If we get separated, we'll need a meeting point. Let's identify that as soon as we get there and then we'll proceed."

With the plan set, they gathered up the IDs, and Dominic slid the cardigan they'd procured from Tommy over Arianna's bare arms. The walk would take them down Rhode Island Avenue, around Logan Circle, and eventually to the downtown rooftop restaurant where Luthor's party was being held.

Once they were on their way, Arianna was quiet as they walked.

"You okay?"

"Yeah, I'm just thinking about Raquel." Tiny lines of worry appeared between her eyes. "I've got to convince her to come with us. I'm worried she won't come willingly."

"There's no use in speculating until we get there," he said.

She nodded, the gesture morose in the waning sunlight. Reaching over, he clasped her hand.

Her eyebrows lifted as she spared him a glance. "I don't hold hands, Dom."

"Okay."

She responded with an exasperated little huff but didn't pull away.

Moments later, she laced her fingers with his.

Feeling his lips curve into a satisfied grin, he held tight as they made their way down-town.

As they neared the restaurant, Arianna noticed the streets evolved from dirty to clean to pristine. The blocks that surrounded downtown were meticulously maintained, and there were no homeless encampments in sight.

"Luthor must keep this part of town spotless to maintain the illusion for his rich cronies," Arianna said.

"People can only live under illusion for so long though" was Dominic's terse response.

Inwardly acknowledging that truth, she slid her hand over Dominic's forearm as they approached a red awning that read Celine's. "There's an alley a block away," she said, gesturing with her head.

Dominic craned his neck. "That works as a meeting point. We need to identify one inside as well."

"Somewhere near the door, preferably," she agreed. Dominic opened the building glass door for her, and they were met with four security guards in black suits—three men and one woman.

"Names, please."

"Amy and David Ratched," Arianna said, smiling politely.

The man looked over his clipboard before pointing to their names. "Welcome, Mr. and Mrs. Ratched. May I see your IDs?"

Once the IDs had been looked over, one of the guards gestured toward the metal detector. "Please, ma'am."

Arianna walked through slowly, followed by Dominic, who was pulled aside by one of the men.

"Sir, I just need to do a quick check for weapons. Lily will check you, ma'am."

The female security guard did a quick but thorough check of Arianna while Dominic received a similar pat down.

"Sending up one male and one female," the guard with the clipboard said into his smartwatch. Lily led them to the elevator and pushed the *P* before backing out. "Have a good time," she said with a wave.

They whooshed to the top as Arianna took a breath to steady herself. She hadn't seen Raquel since her terrible betrayal, and several emotions whirled within. Anger for her sister's actions. Concern for her well-being. Frustration she was working for Cromwell.

"We'll get her out of here," Dominic said, reading her thoughts in the way he was increasingly becoming excellent at. "Don't lose your temper with her."

"Who, me?" she asked sardonically as the doors slid open.

Dominic smirked as they exited the elevator. A large ballroom expanded in front of them, decorated with a multitude of blue and white balloon bundles along the walls. Music pumped from a DJ booth on the far side of the room, and the wooden dance floor glowed under the multicolored disco ball.

"Can I take your sweater, ma'am?"

Arianna's eyes darted to the coat room as she shook her head. "I'll keep it, thanks." She whispered to Dominic out of the corner of her mouth, "Coat room for the indoor meet-up spot."

"Confirmed."

They scanned the room before slowly trailing along the carpeted floor that circled the smooth dance floor. Lights pulsed from the disco ball as a smattering of people danced. Arianna's eyes darted across the dim room as she searched for Raquel.

"Anything?" she asked.

"Not yet."

They approached the bar that flanked the wall to the left in an attempt to appear as normal patrons.

"Scotch neat. Macallan 14 if you have it. And a vodka soda for my wife."

Arianna shot him a droll look as the bartender scampered away to make their drinks. "He scores a few times and thinks he can order for me," she muttered.

"I know you like vodka," he said, sliding his arm around her waist. "And I also liked watching your cheeks flush when I called you my wife."

"From anger," she retorted, but her tone also held a teasing note.

"Or wishful thinking." He winked.

"I'm not really into this side of you," she said, scrunching her features and waving her hand up and down his chest. "Leave the funny quips to Maverick. You suck at them."

Leaning forward, he touched his lips to the shell of her ear. "If you want me to call you my wife again, just ask nicely."

She elbowed him in the side, half-annoyed and half-elated when he responded with a chuckle. Very few people understood her sarcastic, broody nature, and most people bristled at it. Not Dominic. He'd never been intimidated by her. Not once. Wondering if that was something to be celebrated or chagrined, she took a sip of the drink the bartender placed in front of her.

Turning, she faced the large room and squinted as she assessed. "I guess Raquel's not here yet. The room's about a third full, but we're on time. People arrive fashionably late to these things, right?"

"I guess. Want to assess the terrace before it gets too full?"

Nodding, Arianna followed him outside into the rapidly cooling city air. There were a few people scattered on the terrace, which was lined with several small couches. Dominic headed toward the edge and looked over, whistling as he observed the street below.

"So different than when I used to live here. It's technically still a city, but the hustle and bustle is gone. It's a shell of what it once was."

Setting her glass on the ledge, she rested her forearms atop the cold stone and peered down. "The world will never be the same. It's kind of sad."

"If we're lucky, maybe we can eventually fashion it into something better than it ever was."

Facing him, she leaned against the wall. "Such an optimist. How do you still have hope? Sometimes, I wonder if we're wasting our time trying to fix everything."

"You can find hope in small corners of the world if you choose to look." Extending his hand, he held up his palm. "Dance with me."

"We can barely hear the music."

"I don't need music to move with you, Arianna." He hooked his upturned fingers.

Sighing, she placed her hand in his. "This is stupid—"

He drew her into his arms, away from the ledge, as their drinks sat there, forgotten. Her arm slid around his neck as he clasped her hand, holding it at shoulder height as they began to sway.

"I've always wanted to make it up to you," he said softly as their bodies moved in a slow rhythm.

Her eyebrows drew together.

"The first time we danced at Dani and Mav's wedding. I stepped on your toes, and I'm pretty sure that's what set you down the path of detesting me."

A breathy laugh escaped her throat. "I never detested you, but you were a shitty dancer. You're much better now. How?"

Clearing his throat, he appeared slightly embarrassed. "I practiced with Raquel when we were at the farm."

"Oh, that's...weird. Why?"

His dark eyes bore into hers. "I think I had a desire to dance with you again one day and not fuck it up."

Her chest rose and fell as she gazed into his eyes, unable to look away. "With Dani, you mean."

He shook his head as a flash of annoyance crossed his face. "With *you*."

"You barely knew I existed."

"That's so far from true…" Inching closer, his nose grazed hers ever so slightly. "*You're the reason I had hope, Arianna. You always were. I knew we had a fighting chance because you were on our side.*"

Arianna's breath grew choppy as her heartbeat raged. "I just wanted to protect my sisters—"

His lips captured hers, swallowing her words as his tongue swirled over the tender skin behind her lower lip before surging inside. Arianna melted in his arms like a damn schoolgirl, overcome with his taste and smell. A high-pitched mewl leapt from her throat as she licked his wet tongue.

Suddenly, Arianna felt a tap on her upper back as someone loudly cleared their throat. Breaking the kiss, she twirled to find Raquel, arms crossed as she tapped her foot under a long light blue dress.

"Well, well. What do we have here?"

CHAPTER 21

Arianna released Dominic, tamping down the anger that surged at her sister's appearance. "What the fuck, Raquel?" she hissed. "You're working for Luthor?"

"Yes," she responded tersely. "I'm finally being appreciated for my talents and intelligence instead of being overlooked."

"Mom would be extremely disappointed in your actions and selfishness—"

"The same mother who I never got to say goodbye to because you and Dani stole her last moments from me?" Raquel extended her hands at her sides in exasperation. "Tell me again who's selfish, because that's the most selfish thing you could do to someone."

"Grow up," Arianna spat, fury in her tone. "Neither of us knew she would pass before you got to say goodbye one last time. Do you think Dani or I wanted that?"

Raquel shrugged, her shoulder-length brown hair barely touching her shoulders. "I believe you two always considered yourselves more important. Especially Dani. I'm finally out of her shadow, and I've never been happier."

Arianna studied the dark circles under her sister's green eyes and noted the hollows in her cheeks. She'd lost weight in the weeks they'd been apart, and Arianna didn't believe her bravado. "It's okay to admit you've made a mistake, Raquel. To come back with us and help Dani create a cure."

Scoffing, Raquel looked out over the now-darkened city. A muscle ticked in her jaw as she squeezed her elbows, hugging herself against the chill.

Even through all the betrayal and anger, Arianna longed to comfort her baby sister. "Raquel..." She tentatively touched her upper arm.

"Don't touch me," Raquel gritted, drawing back. "I'm not your responsibility anymore. I'm making my own life here and want to do it on my own."

"Even with the rebellion that's forming?" Dominic asked, stepping forward. "The evidence is all over the city if you choose to look. And no city can continue this level of homelessness and addiction. It won't be safe for long, Raquel."

"Then I'll die on my own terms," she said, thrusting up her chin. "I'm in the final stages of creating a diluted antidote that works wonders on addicts. It can be taken orally instead of injected and will allow people to use EverLife without withdrawal side effects."

"But they'll still be prisoners to their addiction," Arianna said, shaking her head. "That's no way to live. People need to be free of EverLife once and for all."

"Because you know what's right for everyone." Raquel rolled her eyes. "Arianna, so fucking tactical, and Dani, so fucking smart. Screw you. If people want to make the choice to take something, it's their life."

"There's no choice in addiction," Arianna said, her fist balling at her side in frustration. "You're robbing them of free will."

Straightening her shoulders, Raquel spoke without any emotion in her voice, so far from the person Arianna thought she knew. "You've lost your power to boss everyone around, Ari. If I want to work for Luthor, I will. If people want to take EverLife, they can. It's time you moved on and realized I'm done being your doormat."

Glancing toward the terrace entrance, Raquel narrowed her eyes. "You two were smart to come here instead of Dani. Luthor knows her face but not yours. Not really." Returning her gaze to Arianna's, she spoke softly. "But if I tell him my sister infiltrated the city, he's going to make you a target. Don't make me do that, Ari." Her features softened for a moment before hardening once more. "Leave and don't come back. I'm happy here."

She twirled to walk away, and Arianna caught her wrist. "Don't do this, Raquel—"

"It was done the moment you two stole her last moments from me," she said, yanking her wrist away. "Feel free to finish your dance. I guess you don't care that he's in love with Dani. I thought you had more pride than that. If you're pitiful enough to accept Dani's sloppy seconds, that's fine, but I refuse to be inferior to her anymore."

Arianna balked as if she'd been struck.

"Goodbye, Arianna. If we're lucky, this will be the last time we see each other." Raquel strode away, spine tall and majestic as a princess as Arianna gaped.

"Fucking bitch," she muttered, rubbing her forehead. "How did I never see this side of her? I'm debating running after her and punching her in her smart mouth."

"That would definitely call attention to us," Dominic said, eyes narrowed as he watched Raquel walk back inside the ballroom. "And that's the last thing we need."

Arianna sighed. "I'm going to have to forcibly remove her from this hellhole. We need to blow up Dr. Ziegler's lab so Tristan will help us. Let's do it tomorrow night so we can go on with our damn lives."

Dominic's eyes were hooded as he studied her. "Okay. Let's hang in the shadows and make contact with Matt. Maybe he discovered Tristan's address."

Her jaw was set in a firm line as she nodded.

"Don't let her get in your head," he said, sliding his palm over her lower back.

"She's not," she said, moving away from his touch. "I've always known how you feel about Dani—"

"Ari—"

"It's not a big deal," she said, cutting him off. "We need to talk to Matt and maybe Tristan if he shows up. There's nothing else to focus on but that."

Dominic's nostrils flared, and a surge of determination flashed in his dark eyes. His expression left no question that he didn't consider the conversation closed.

"We can talk about other shit when we get back to the motel. For now, I need to work this mission." She rubbed the muscles that were suddenly tense at the back of her neck. "Let's find Matt."

He tipped his head and replaced his hand at the small of her back as they headed toward the ballroom entrance. Arianna could almost feel his anger traveling through his arm into her spine. Raquel's words echoed in her head, and Arianna reminded herself that she wasn't in this for roses and love letters. She was fucking Dom to scratch an itch.

As they walked through the double doors, she hoped telling herself that would ease the ache that burned in her gut, knowing the man she loved had never wanted her first.

Annoyed at the emotion, she shut it off, determined to focus on the mission and protect her heart.

Chapter 22

Dominic stood in the darkened corner of the ballroom, aware of the change in Arianna's demeanor at Raquel's words. They'd been lodged to hurt Arianna, and Raquel knew where to hit where it hurt the most: Arianna's pride.

Dominic had rarely met someone as proud, and he cursed Raquel for pushing them back several steps. He'd made progress over the past few days, and Arianna was finally opening up to him in all the ways he craved.

Judging by the stiff set of her shoulders, they were back to square one. Just fucking great.

Imagining several inventive ways to strangle Raquel, he sipped his Scotch, reveling in the smooth taste. It had been a while since he'd had good Scotch, and since the night had gone to shit, at least he could enjoy *something*.

"There's Matt," Arianna said, her voice low as she rose to her toes. "I'm going to sidle up to him at the bar."

She was off before Dominic could respond, and he clenched his glass, frustrated she was back to making decisions without consulting him. Striding after her, he slipped into the open spot beside her as she spoke to Matt.

"What's Tristan's address?" she asked, her tone all business as Matt bristled.

"I don't know. I tried, Arianna. I made small talk with Grace at lunch and asked her where she lived before EverLife, but she's not really a talker. She mentioned living in the Kalorama neighborhood in the past, but that's all I got."

"No problem," Arianna said flippantly. "I've always wanted to shoot off your kneecaps. Maybe I'll put a bullet in each of your balls too. Seems fitting—"

"Okay, no one is shooting anyone," Dominic said, butting into the conversation. "And it looks like we can speak to Tristan ourselves." He gestured with his head toward the entrance as Tristan appeared. A slight frown marred his face above a pristine tuxedo as he scanned the room.

"Oh, goodie. Matt's balls are safe. For now," she finished, her tone ominous as she set off toward the entrance.

"Wait," Dominic said, leaving Matt behind as he cradled her elbow. "Let's draw him outside. I think the terrace is more inconspicuous."

"Fine." Her gaze lasered toward Tristan, and he must've felt the heat because he latched onto her, recognition in his eyes. She jerked her head toward the terrace, and Tristan gave a slight nod. Armed with his confirmation, she pivoted and walked toward the double doors that led outside.

The balcony was starting to crowd, so they headed toward the far corner, away from gossiping socialites and men in tuxedos smoking cigars. Eventually, Tristan made his way toward them, his voice hushed as he glowered. "What the fuck are you two doing here?"

"I came here for Raquel," Arianna said.

Tristan cocked a brow. "And how did that work out for you?"

"Terribly, as you seem to have already guessed. I need your address so I can forcibly remove her from the city. Now."

"We had a deal, Arianna. You blow up Dr. Ziegler's lab and then I'll tell you where she is." Rubbing his chin, he squinted one eye. "And yet, the lab is still functional and you're no closer to helping your sister. How annoying."

Arianna's fingers snaked around his neck, quick as lightning, causing him to gasp. Dominic saw him reach for the gun holstered at his belt and stepped between them.

"Enough!" Grabbing Arianna's wrist, he withdrew her hand from Tristan's throat. "You two are going to blow our cover."

Tristan stuck his finger between his collar and his rapidly bruising neck, attempting to loosen it. "I'm allowed to carry a gun since I'm one of Luthor's employees," he said to Arianna, nostrils flaring. "Don't make me use it."

"Asshole—" she hissed.

Dominic sliced his hand through the air, silently commanding Arianna to stop antagonizing him. "We're going to destroy Ziegler's lab tomorrow night. Where can we meet you the following morning to retrieve Raquel so we can get the hell out of the city?"

Tristan's eyes darted between them as he contemplated. "The corner of Connecticut and T Street. I'll be there at two a.m. and my house isn't too far away. Raquel will be sleeping and I doubt she'll go willingly."

"You let me worry about that," Arianna said.

"Fine." His shoulders lost some of their stiffness as he exhaled a deep breath. "I'm happy you're taking her out of here. Luthor just had a meeting with his security team, and he's going to start cleansing the city soon."

Arianna's eyebrows drew together. "Cleansing?"

"He plans to round up the homeless and relocate them outside the city walls. Everyone left will be required to be microchipped if they want EverLife or the watered-down antidote."

"He wants to track everyone?" Dominic asked, eyebrows drawing together.

"Yes. Tracking allows him to force compliance and implement a curfew. He wants all vestiges of the graffiti and rumors of a rebellion gone."

"But what if the rebellion is coming from inside his circle?" Arianna asked.

"The cronies who surround him are addicted to EverLife too. He assumes their continued compliance as long as he has the antidote. He controls the army and is the only one with access."

"His ego might be his downfall," Dominic said.

"I'm counting on it." Tristan's eyes glowed with resolve.

"We'll meet you at Connecticut and T at two a.m. sharp after we destroy the lab tomorrow night. Don't make us regret helping you," Arianna said.

"I think we're helping each other. Now, if I were you, I'd make myself scarce. Luthor will be here any minute, and there's nothing more for you to gain by staying. Rest up so you're fresh tomorrow night."

"I'm getting pretty fucking tired of you trying to give me orders," Arianna said, jabbing a finger in his face.

"Are George Luddington and James Stalworth on tonight's list?" Dominic asked, sliding his fingers over Arianna's forearm and slowly lowering it away from Tristan's face.

"I assume so. Why?"

"We're going to surveil them for a bit before leaving. We got a tip they might be unhappy with Luthor's claim to power."

"I could've told you that," Tristan said with a shrug. "The two fat bastards hate Luthor. But they're also rich and want to continue living their lavish lifestyle, complete with the EverLife injections that make them appear younger. I doubt they have the fortitude or wiliness to plan a rebellion."

"Then who?" Arianna asked. "Who has the skill and motive to coordinate something as complex as overthrowing Luthor?"

"That, my dear Arianna, is what I'm trying to find out."

Arianna glanced at Dominic. "Did he just call me *dear*?"

"That's our cue to end this conversation before I lose the ability to keep her from crushing your skull," Dominic said, tugging Arianna away. "Keep an eye on Luddington and Stalworth just in case there's something you might have missed. You can communicate with Arthur over the radio if you discover something."

Tristan nodded as they backed away. "Don't fail at the lab."

"Fuck you," Arianna murmured before Dominic led her away.

"Killing him won't do us any good," he said, leading them to the corner of the bar so they could observe their targets enter the party.

Dominic knew he needed to acknowledge the shift that had occurred in Arianna's demeanor after arguing with Raquel, but it would have to wait. Mission first. Then he would take her back to the motel and absolve her of the notion that she was anyone's second choice.

Tristan leaned on the bar, sipping whiskey as he surveyed the room. Raquel stood on the far side of the dance floor, chatting with two other scientists Luthor employed at the EverLife lab. Arianna and Dominic had slipped out several minutes ago, but Tristan had observed the chilled glances that passed between the sisters on their way out.

Absently staring at Raquel, he admitted it was time for her to go. If she stayed in the city after creating the antidote that she was nearly finished with, Luthor would have no need for her. He'd most likely force her out of the city with the homeless and addicted, so being removed by Arianna was the better choice.

Slightly *better*, he thought as his lips curved at Arianna's toughness. The woman was an immobile force. He hoped Dominic was channeling all that energy into something useful. If anyone needed to get laid, it was Arianna. The woman could afford to take down the intensity level several notches, and he had the sneaking suspicion Dominic might be the one man who was a match for her.

Luthor breezed through the doorway, his smooth face appearing slightly surreal since it should've long been wrinkled. Tristan noted the slight puff of his cheek bones. Swollen tissue was a side effect of EverLife, the drug that manipulated genes to keep everyone who ingested it looking young and virile.

Until it killed them by making them crave more, Tristan thought, frowning as he sipped his drink.

Jessica flanked Luthor's right side, and another woman whose name Tristan couldn't remember pressed against his left. Corinne? Kaylin? Hell if he knew. Luthor had a stable of women who traded sexual favors for EverLife and the antidote, and Tristan had stopped keeping count long ago.

Clenching his teeth, he watched Jessica rear her head back and laugh as Luthor whispered in her ear. Tristan would never be able to forgive himself for allowing his sister to be ensnared in Luthor's clutches. If he could save Raquel, perhaps it would ease some of his regret, if only slightly.

Everyone in the room rushed to meet Luthor, and he walked slowly across the dance floor, greeting his adoring fans. His security team was close behind, led by Zayne Danvers, who was excellent at ensuring Luthor lived. Tristan considered Zayne a thorn in his side since he was an obstacle in the way of murdering the bastard. But he couldn't argue that Zayne was extremely effective. The throng surrounded Luthor as he made his way to the bar, and Tristan's gaze returned to the ballroom doors.

Unable to control his quick inhale, he drank in the extra jolt of oxygen as Grace entered the room. She wore a fur coat, although he knew it was faux due to her intense love of animals. Not only dogs and cats, but when they'd been married, she'd had a ferret, a hamster and a parrot, along with the one-eyed cat she called Wink.

Tristan's pulse thrummed as he observed her smile, white teeth flashing at the attendant as she handed over her coat. Then she placed her hand over the jewels around her throat as if to protect them. The diamonds had been worth millions when the world had cared about things like elegant jewelry.

Unfortunately, his ex-wife still cared for those things. Which was why she'd married the richest man in the world. Tristan had never stood a chance.

Grace glided to the bar, seemingly unconcerned her husband was being groped by several adoring women at the other end. After ordering her customary glass of Riesling, she left the ballroom behind for the fresh air of the terrace.

Helpless to stop himself, Tristan followed her as if tethered to her by an unseen force. Scanning the dimness, he spotted her in the corner where he'd confronted Arianna and Dominic earlier. Her blond hair flitted in the breeze, long and flowing, and the curve of her hips in the white sheer gown reminded him of all the times he'd held her there...gripping her tight as he tried to control the raging lust that overwhelmed him when he made love to her.

Sometimes, he'd held her pale skin so hard that slight bruises would appear, and he would make sure to hold back the next time so he didn't scare her away. So his love for her didn't smother them both.

Sadly, no matter how much he'd tried, she'd slipped through his fingers anyway.

"The autumn nights are warm now," he said, noticing she didn't tense as he slid into place beside her. As if she knew he would eventually find his way to her.

Her fingers fiddled with the stem of the glass as she gazed over the twinkling lights of the city. "Climate change was too far gone before the world collapsed," she said, the slight gravel that always laced her voice still sexy to him after all these years. "I think fall nights will be warm for decades to come."

"Luthor's still got decades. Hell, maybe even a century or two if he keeps perfecting EverLife. So maybe he'll find a solution for climate change in the time he has left."

A huff escaped her lips. "Luthor doesn't care about those things. He just wants power."

Unable to stop himself, he traced a finger up her forearm, elated at her soft gasp. "Then you'll be the most powerful woman in the world."

Drawing her arm away, she turned and leaned her hip on the cool stone ledge. "Perhaps."

Those pink lips touched the rim of the glass, sipping as her eyes remained locked with his. "You're still protecting Raquel. I find myself wondering why."

He cocked a brow. "Maybe I have an altruistic streak."

Her features contorted acerbically. "More like a savior complex. She reminds you of Jessica."

Inhaling deeply, he nodded. "Maybe Raquel is my second chance to save someone from him."

Grace splayed her palm over her abdomen as the intensity between them simmered. Glancing down, she sharply removed her hand, as if she didn't realize she'd made the gesture.

"Our Raquel would've been born in late September," he said, glancing toward the stars since staring into her blue eyes had become unbearable. "She would've been ten this year."

Thin fingers gripped the rocky ledge, the knuckles turning white with force. "Yes. Ten years old in a world that's evil and lost. It's the only way I'm able to accept what happened, knowing she was saved from living in this world."

Tristan closed his eyes, the pain of the memories unbearable as they rushed in. Grace had been five months pregnant with their daughter—who they'd serendipitously decided to name Raquel—when the baby had suddenly been stillborn. He'd been out of the country for his last deployment, and when he returned, Grace had served him with divorce papers, stating the pain of continuing the marriage after all they'd lost was too excruciating.

"You gave up on us so easily," he said, shaking his head. "And you buried her without me. I've never forgiven you for that."

"I know." The words washed over him, filled with the grief she mostly kept hidden behind her elegant mask. "I've never forgiven myself. But Father also died, and you weren't here, and I saw the writing on the wall. I had to secure my future without him."

"*I* was your future," Tristan said, nostrils flaring as he clenched his jaw. "I would've taken care of you."

Leaning her elbows on the ledge, her expression grew wistful. "I was always a thing to you. A shiny object you could protect and hold in a gilded cage—"

"That's exactly how Luthor sees you, not me."

A humorless laugh escaped her throat. "You both see me that way. The difference is that Luthor is honest about it." Those gorgeous eyes latched onto his, causing his heartbeat to jolt. "I just transferred from one cage to another, but I entered the one with Luthor with eyes wide open."

Scoffing, he threw back the rest of his drink. "Well, sorry it was so shitty being married to me. Sorry I fucking loved you more than anyone on this godforsaken planet. At least you escaped the torture of being tied to me."

Her finger traced a slow, sad pattern on the ledge. "We did love each other for a time there, didn't we?"

I still love you. So goddamn much it hurts.

"Yes," he whispered, setting the glass on the stone so he didn't hurl it toward the city in anger. "For a while, it wasn't fucked up. And then, it was the three of us. Until it wasn't."

Her chin quivered as she blinked rapidly. Was she remembering the times he held her, his broad palm rubbing her belly as they tried to choose a name before he'd been deployed for that last fateful mission? The one where nothing had been the same upon his return? It was hard to tell, her face still unreadable as she stared into the blackened night.

"She would've looked just like you," he said softly. "I know it. The last thing I wanted was for her to look like an ugly wretch like me."

Breathing a laugh, she straightened, moving closer as his heart threatened to beat out of his chest. Gently cupping his jaw, she ran her thumb over the stubble. "My dear ex-husband, you are a lot of things, but ugly isn't one of them." Her cheeks flushed in the moonlight as she tenderly caressed his jaw.

He ached to reach for her...to beg her to come back to him...to ask how in the hell she could've let Luthor touch her in all the ways and places that belonged to *him*.

She dragged in a long, even breath before releasing him. "It's obvious you hate Luthor, and Jessica has no desire to be saved. I hear Arthur Reyes has one of the more functional black-market compounds, and most people know he's harboring Danica Lawson. Perhaps you should align with him. I can arrange transport for you to his compound."

"I won't leave Jessica," he said, shaking his head.

"What if I help her leave the city too?"

"The antidotes on the black-market compound are filled with shit. She needs the one here."

Grace arched a golden eyebrow. "Not if Danica is somehow working on a new antidote."

Tristan's eyes narrowed. "Where did you hear that?"

Leaning forward, she whispered, "You hear a lot when you're married to the most powerful man in the world, Tristan."

Annoyed at yet another reminder of her tether to Luthor, he grimaced. "Danica's chances of creating any sort of cure or antidote on a black-market compound are slim to none, and we both know it."

"She did it once, so her chances are better than anyone else left on the planet."

"Optimism like that will get you killed in our world, Grace. I left it behind years ago."

Backing away, she smiled. "It's not optimism, Tristan. It's *faith*, and you're terrible at it. You never had it in me, and you should have more for what lies ahead. Otherwise, what's the point of continually aligning yourself with a man you hate? Your gloom and doom mentality isn't serving you."

"It's done pretty well for me up to this point. And it's easy for a woman who wants for nothing to preach to me about faith."

Disappointment clouded her features. "I wasn't preaching, I was imploring. You're stuck so far down in the tunnel you've dug, you can't even see the light anymore."

Confusion caused him to flinch. "What the hell does that mean?"

"Mrs. Cromwell?" a voice called as a security guard dressed in a black suit approached them. "Mr. Cromwell is requesting you to be at his side as he cuts the cake."

"Of course." Facing Tristan, she smiled as her eyes roved over his face, almost as if she were memorizing his features. "Think about what I said and have some faith, Tristan. Good night."

Tristan watched her go, powerless to stop her as he'd always been. Exhausted by the cryptic conversation, he decided he'd have one more drink and then walk Raquel home so she was safe. Then, once he was alone in the confines of his bedroom, he'd try and decipher why a woman he would pledge his life to believed he had no faith.

CHAPTER 23

The walk back to the motel was quiet as Arianna stewed at Raquel's vitriol. The fact that her baby sister, who'd always been kind and loving, had devolved into the person on the terrace tonight was extremely disheartening. Perhaps the world truly was too far gone and all vestiges of goodness were slowly eroding.

And Raquel's words about Dominic? They were a good reminder for Arianna to protect her heart. No matter how much she loved him, she'd never come close to forever with any man. Experience had shown her it was impossible, and the fear that Dominic would ultimately realize that welled in her chest.

She could fuck him and even share some intimacies, but giving herself completely was off the table. She needed to focus, and being shattered by Dominic would derail her goals.

They climbed up the stairs to their room, Dominic simmering behind her, and she reminded herself to stay calm. Impassive. Unemotional. Sure, she would still have sex with him tonight—after all, sex with Dominic was incredible, and she wasn't ready to deny herself some small sliver of pleasure in their fucked-up world.

But that's as far as it would go. Meaningless sex to release some tension. Lord knew she could use it.

They entered the dim room, and Arianna walked to the small table where their guns rested. Leaning on it, she removed her shoes and rubbed her foot to soothe the sting. For someone who often wore combat boots or sneakers, flat dress shoes were an unwelcome change.

"Let's get up at sunrise to jog," she said, attempting to make normal conversation and ignore the ticking of Dominic's jaw as he tugged off his shoes, jacket and bow tie before removing his shirt and tossing it on the couch. "And if you want to fuck, that's fine, but let's make it quick because I'm beat—"

Her words were cut off as Dominic lifted her over his shoulder, knocking her breath from her lungs as he carried her to the bedroom. Shock pervaded her system as she realized how easily he maneuvered her body atop his shoulder. She was not a small woman by any means, and no man had ever had the strength—or the nerve—to manhandle her.

When they reached the bedroom, he tossed her on the bed, her back hitting the comforter as she gaped up at him. "For fuck's sake, Dom. I can walk—"

"Shut up," he demanded, straddling her and pressing his palms on both sides of her head. Arianna's heart pounded with equal parts desire and anger.

"You're the first man who's ever told me to shut up, and I swear, each time you do it, I debate letting you live."

His palm snaked around her throat, surrounding her gasp as he held her immobile. Not too hard, but firm enough that she knew who was in control. Fuck. How had she let him have control when she'd spent the entire walk home deciding to play it cool? Annoyed at how easily he played her...how much he understood her...she tried like hell to keep her muscles rigid. Tough, since every instinct in her body wanted to relax under his soft domination.

Never had she wanted to give herself to someone and let them have complete control. Never before *him*.

"You want to turn this into something it isn't," he said, his voice low with the hum of anger and frustration. "Some quick fucks to burn off energy."

"That's all it is—"

"No." His hand tightened on her neck, causing her eyes to roll back in her head with pleasure. Damn it. She fucking loved having his thick fingers around her neck. The war between her emotions and her self-preservation raged inside her rapidly heating frame as she lay beneath him.

"Look at me, Arianna."

She lifted her lids, stifling the urge to simultaneously kick him in the balls and beg him to love her back. God, her feelings for this man defied logic and upended every sense of her carefully cultivated self-control.

"Stop letting Raquel's words inside that hard head." He tapped her forehead with his free hand. "You have to let go of this notion that my feelings for you are in any way equivalent to what I felt for Dani. I refuse to keep having this same argument...or discussion...or whatever it is that makes you doubt what's happening here."

"Nothing's happening," she rasped. "We both deserve a release."

"A release?" he asked incredulously. "What you don't understand, Ari, is that I don't just need to fuck you. I need to *worship* you."

He dropped to his knees beside the bed, gripping her behind the knees and dragging her forward. When her ass hit the edge, he roughly tore the dress from her body. Cool air hit her breasts as he yanked her underwear down her legs and tossed it aside.

"Maybe if I make you scream, you'll admit what's between us." Draping her legs over his shoulders, he pressed his palms to her inner thighs. Pushing them open, his dark eyes blazed as he stared at her. "Watch me worship you, Arianna. My gorgeous, fearless warrior."

Arianna whimpered as he slowly lowered his lips to her abdomen, kissing a trail to her navel and dipping his tongue inside.

"Dom…"

"All you have to do is stay right there and enjoy this." His mouth trailed over the skin between her navel and the top of her mound, causing the skin to quiver beneath. "I'm not Matt or any of the other men you've done this with. I'm someone who gets you, Arianna. Someone who can handle you. And you're about to get fucking handled, sweetheart."

His fingers touched her slick folds before gently pulling them apart. Eyes locked with hers, he blew on her damp flesh, the sight more erotic than any Arianna had ever seen. His full lips glistened as he licked them, as if he was preparing to savor the finest dish.

"You're mine, Arianna. This pussy is *mine*. And I'm going to claim it in the way you deserve."

Her hands flew to his head, gripping since she ached to touch him. His hair was short, so there was barely anything to cling on to, but she squeezed anyway, her fingers digging into his flesh.

"Good girl. Hold on tight."

Why did her body inflame every time he called her that? Why did she crave it with him unlike any other man she'd ever known?

"Because you're mine," he said, nuzzling her slit as he read her thoughts. Closing his eyes, he inhaled a deep breath. "Fuck, I love your scent, Ari." Then all talking ceased as he buried his face in her quivering core.

His talented tongue swiped a path from her opening to her clit, causing Arianna's legs to tremble around his head as she groaned. Holding her open, he flicked the swollen bud, over and over, before drawing it between his lips. He sucked her in a deep, fluid motion, stimulating the frayed nerve endings.

"Oh god!"

His murmured "*mmm*" vibrated against her as she rocked into his mouth. Unable to control her hips, she undulated toward him, seeking the pleasure he unselfishly offered.

As his tongue continued the pleasurable ministrations, he pressed a finger to her opening, circling the damp ring before nudging inside. Arianna's head fell back on the bed, her body racked with pleasure as she welcomed his invasion.

He slid deep inside her, searching for the bundle of nerves that sat deep within. When she gasped, he released a groan and inserted another finger...then one more. He stretched her, sliding in and out as his mouth worked her clit, and Arianna moaned his name.

"No more walls," he said, lapping at her core as he fucked her in smooth strokes with his fingers. "I want all of you, Ari."

Her muscles went lax at his words, her defenses unable to remain against the blissful onslaught from his mouth and fingers. She sensed his body's change at her acquiescence. The way his shoulders sagged beneath her legs, as if silently accepting she'd finally let go.

The flicks of his tongue drove her to the point of madness as the pads of his fingers found the spot deep within that all others had failed to discover. Craving the pleasure, she let him have it all, opening her legs in wide invitation as he devoured her.

Moans laced her scattered, shallow breaths as she reached for the pinnacle. Every cell of her skin burned with pleasure, aching for release. Spearing her short nails into Dominic's head, she held on for dear life as tiny whimpers she'd never emitted for any other man leapt from her throat.

Suddenly, her back arched and her eyes glazed over before her eyelids began to flutter. Wave upon glorious wave of pleasure crashed through her frame as Dominic led her to the most magnificent orgasm she'd ever experienced.

Her body bucked and bowed, the slick honey between her legs flowing under his warm mouth, and she emitted a passionate wail, wishing the bliss would never end.

Finally, after the universe exploded and somehow reassembled itself, her muscles turned to jelly upon the bed. Lax and sated, she tried to open her eyes but couldn't find the strength.

Dominic's sigh heated the skin between her legs as they quaked around his head. All sense of control was shattered, and damn, she fucking loved it.

He slowly stood and removed the rest of his clothes before lifting her and positioning her properly on the bed. Turning off the lamp they'd left illuminated on the bedside table, he crawled in behind her. Drawing her close, he spooned her and buried his face in the soft skin behind her neck.

Arianna wiggled the globes of her ass into his hard cock, offering herself to him as she lay spent and frazzled.

"I just want to hold you," he murmured, sliding his arm between her breasts and cupping her throat with that broad hand. Fuck. His hand around her throat was quickly becoming her favorite addiction.

"I don't cuddle," she murmured, her lips twitching in anticipation of his denial of her words.

"You do with me." His hand gently squeezed her neck as tiny bumps of resulting pleasure prickled her skin.

"Holy shit, Dom. You destroyed me."

Full lips kissed her neck as he draped a thick thigh over hers. "I worshiped you in the way you need, Ari. In the way I *crave*. You're not my second choice. You're my first obsession. Now let me sleep, woman. You tired me out."

Arianna swallowed thickly, counting his slowing heartbeats as they thumped across her back. With each breath, she felt the locks and bolts that protected her heart shatter as they slowly disintegrated and disappeared.

Dominic's skillful tongue and reverent words were massively effective at destroying the carefully built walls she'd erected. Soon, there would be nothing left to deny him from consuming her and annihilating her if he ever decided she wasn't enough...if he ever decided to leave her as so many others had. Her birth parents. Her adoptive parents. Every man she'd ever thought she'd loved. Even her baby sister... They all left eventually, didn't they? Was it foolish to think this time could be different?

She waited for the metallic taste of fear to coat her tongue. When it didn't appear, she took a moment to acknowledge the emotion that welled within, realizing it felt like...relief. Somehow, for once, fear and love weren't inexorably interwoven together in the deepest corners of her heart. She just felt...*free*.

And that, she realized, was something she'd need time to grapple with. It was new and daunting, and her exhausted body needed rest to fully accept it. Allowing herself to relax, she shimmied into Dominic's warm frame as he held her in the dark.

Chapter 24

D ani assembled the syringe, gauze, vial and other components on the sterile blue sheet atop the rolling metal cart. Noticing the slight shake in her gloved hands, she took a deep breath to calm herself.

"You've got this, slugger," Maverick said, cupping her shoulder with a supportive squeeze. "And if this round doesn't work, we'll make more until we find a cure."

Dani smiled up at him, grateful for his unending encouragement. "You know, for someone who destroyed the world, I have an extremely supportive husband. I still wonder sometimes why you didn't throw in the towel when I initiated the downfall of society."

"Who else is going to accept a guy named after a cheesy eighties movie?" he teased, kissing her forehead. "I'll be right here, babe."

Scrunching her nose, she lifted the syringe and stuck it in the vial, withdrawing the milky fluid as she chided him. "And then you call me 'babe' and I debate leaving you forever."

He covered his heart as his lips formed a broad smile. "You wound me, Dr. Lawson-Ward." Backing away, he whispered "Good luck" before leaning against the wall and crossing his arms.

Inhaling a fortifying breath, Dani approached the woman lying on the infirmary bed. Shallow breaths flowed through her chapped lips as she stared at the ceiling with unseeing eyes. Dani noticed the large pupils, surrounded by reddened vessels, and the dark bags formed on the skin underneath.

"Hi, Sarah. My name is Danica and I'm here to help you," she said encouragingly, gently surrounding the woman's arm and placing it flat so the veins of her inner arm were exposed. Dragging the medical cart closer, she set the syringe on top and wet a piece of gauze with alcohol. After cleaning Sarah's skin, she wrapped a rubber tourniquet around her upper arm.

Dani tapped Sarah's arm, causing the veins to stand to attention. Identifying the most prominent one, she lifted the syringe and placed the tip of the needle on Sarah's arm.

"This will pinch a bit, but otherwise, it shouldn't hurt." Narrowing her eyes, she focused as she injected the milky serum into Sarah's arm.

Her patient's chest lifted as she inhaled a deep breath, and Dani took it as a good sign she was eliciting any reaction at all. Once the syringe was empty, she set it on the tray and removed the tourniquet. Massaging Sarah's arm, she waited, observing her reaction.

The woman's long brown eyelashes began to move as she blinked once...twice...and then more rapidly. The pulse at her neck fluttered visibly as Dani's eyes widened.

"Sarah? My name is Danica, and I just injected your arm with some medicine. You're okay." She held her forearm in a firm, comforting grasp as Sarah's eyes met hers. They were laced with confusion and fear.

"You've been addicted to EverLife and then you took an antidote that had some nasty stuff in it. Your body was under attack, but I just injected you with something that should help. How do you feel?"

Sarah's jaw worked as she tried to speak. "Where's Jenny? And Christopher?"

Smiling, Dani rubbed her thumb in gentle strokes over her skin. "Your kids are safe. They've been staying at the shelter Arthur set up for kids of addicted parents."

"Arthur Reyes? I remember him building walls around the site... Everyone was dying and we needed more antidote..."

"He's been trying to keep you all alive, but it's been tough. That's why I'm trying to help."

Leaning back on the bed, she exhaled a deep breath. "I feel...better. I'm not..."—she smacked her lips—"...craving EverLife." Turning her head on the pillow, she looked at Dani. "How?"

Glancing at Maverick, Dani felt elation surge at her words. "Go get the nurse so she can monitor Sarah's vitals," she said, her tone firm. "And then gather the team so we can pick more plants and replicate the serum. We need fifty vials immediately."

Maverick nodded and quickly left the room.

"Danica?"

"It's okay," she said, rubbing Sarah's arm. "It's possible the serum has quelled the addiction. If you continue to improve, I'll test the antidote on other patients in the clinic."

Sarah licked her parched lips. "And if it works on them too?"

Dani's mouth curved into a huge smile. "Then we're on our way to eliminating this fucking curse of a drug from the planet."

Her eyes closed in relief. "Thank God."

Dani backed away as Chris and Jenny ran into the room, followed by Maverick and one of the nurses, Rikina, who'd helped keep the clinic afloat in their squalid dystopian circumstances. Sliding her arm around Maverick's waist, Dani watched the reunion, allowing hope to surge. She wasn't sure if there were any gods left to thank, but damn it, she'd do her best to ensure everyone in the clinic—and the world—would have the ability to pray to whichever one they chose.

CHAPTER 25

After a brisk sunrise jog, Dominic and Arianna headed back to the motel to shower and plan. They spread Tristan's map of the lab over the small coffee table and discussed their prior surveillance.

"After Guard One leaves for his break, we'll shoot Guard Two with the tranquilizer dart and enter." Her finger traveled the path to the main lab on the map. "Then we'll detonate the explosives here." She tapped her finger.

"We'll need to leave through the back entrance," Dominic said, touching the map. "It's labeled exit only, but that's all we need."

Nodding, Arianna blew out a breath, ruffling the hair above her forehead. The bald side of her head was growing in, and Dominic thought it made her look exotic...and sexy.

"You're looking at me like you want to eat me," she said, and his lips curved at her teasing tone. Something had changed between them last night, and he relished the easy energy that pulsed between them.

"I think we've established that I like eating you."

She rolled her eyes as a faint smile tugged at her mouth. "So fucking cheesy. Gross."

Chuckling, he placed his palm over her thigh, unable to resist touching her. "Want to get some lunch from the deli?"

"Yes. I want to ask Deandra to watch out for Raquel if we fail."

Dominic squeezed her leg. "We won't, but I like the sentiment."

As they waited for Ron to cook the roast beef sandwiches, Arianna spoke softly to Deandra as she stood behind the counter.

"I'm not thrilled at keeping an eye out for the person creating Luthor's super drug, but I have a soft spot for you two." She patted Arianna's cheek. "I'll watch out for her. But don't die, all right? I need to know there are people like you in the world, Arianna."

"I'll do my best," Arianna said, taking the bag that Ron handed her. "And thank you." Reaching into her pack, she removed three gold bars.

"Oh, this is too much," Deandra said, pushing them away.

"You deserve more, but it's all I can give now." Arianna shoved them into her hands. "One day, I hope to return your kindness in every way I can."

Deandra's brown eyes grew teary as she hugged the bars to her chest. "Be safe. And when you return to take down Luthor, I'll be here ready to help you."

Arianna hugged her as Dominic tipped his head to both her and Ron before giving a salute. Ron saluted back, a relic of his time in the US Army when it had still existed.

After lunch, Dominic tugged Arianna close as they sat on the couch, urging her to curl into his side.

"I'm not used to this," she said, snuggling into his chest. "Don't you just want to have sex?"

He smoothed his palm over her hair, loving the texture of her braid beneath his skin. "Tell me what you want after we're done fighting."

Her fingers toyed with the prickly hairs that sprang from underneath his collar. "I want Dani to regain all her memories and live happily ever after with Mav."

"What else?"

"I want Raquel to come back to us and finally grow into the person I know she can be."

He ran his cheek over her hair. "Keep going."

"I want a daughter that has my mama's eyes. I don't remember much about her, but for some reason, I remember her eyes. They had these golden flecks in them that shone in the sunlight and crinkled around them when she smiled."

Arianna had the same eyes, filled with the same flecks between the swirls of green and brown. Dominic thought them stunning and could imagine a daughter with them.

"I want a boy, so we'll have to have two."

"*Pfft*," she exclaimed, squeezing him even as she discounted his words. "I told you, I'm using a turkey baster. It won't require the effort of dealing with someone else."

Sliding his fingers under her chin, he forced her to meet his gaze. "I'm under the impression that you enjoy our *efforts* together." He arched a confident brow.

"God, I hate that smug smile." Touching two fingers to the top of his scar, she tenderly traced them down the length of the gash. Over his nose...down to the corner of his lips, following the trail of the machete that had initially made the mark.

Dominic nipped her finger. "I think you love it. I think you love *me*."

Her breath stuttered as her eyes darted back and forth between his. "That's another reason I want a baby," she said softly, ignoring his bold statement. "I think I can love her...or him"—her lips quirked—"and not be afraid."

"You've lost a lot," he said, cupping her jaw. "We both have. It makes us fiercely protective of what remains."

"Protecting Dani and Raquel is nothing compared to how I would protect my child. Once she's here, I'll make sure she's loved and cherished in every way she deserves."

"I understand," he said, tracing his thumb over her bottom lip, "because that's exactly the way I want to protect you."

Challenge flared in her eyes, and he covered her lips before she could speak. "Instead of arguing with me about not needing anyone's protection, why don't you just let me hold you and imagine the day when you finally get what you want?"

Sighing, she buried her head into the juncture of his neck and chest. Dominic felt her body relax as he softly stroked her shoulder. In a few hours, they would be thrust into yet another mission full of danger where their very existence was on the line.

But for now, he was content to hold her and imagine himself in the future she longed to create.

CHAPTER 26

After it grew dark, they dressed in their black tactical gear, each strapping weapons to accessible parts of their muscular frames. They had the tranquilizer guns, the handguns they'd brought with them, and the semi-automatic rifles they'd taken from the two guards at the wall.

When they were strapped and ready, Dominic's gaze traveled over Arianna, his throat bobbing as his heart skipped a beat. She stood tall, with that half-mane of hair braided over her shoulder. Weapons lined her sides and the bronze skin of her arms showed off the sinewy muscle beneath.

Shifting in her black boots, her eyebrows narrowed. "What?"

Striding toward her, he grabbed her chin and kissed her. "You're fucking gorgeous. Let's go."

She looked down her body as her eyebrows ticked up. "This *is* pretty hot, if you're into kick-ass chicks."

Dominic chuckled and walked to the door, turning to peruse the room. "We'll just leave it unlocked since we're not coming back, right? I left the key on the coffee table."

"Yep. I left one gold bar for Devon on the table too. Hope he uses it for something productive instead of a vial of EverLife." She followed him across the threshold and pulled the door closed.

The trek to the lab would take two hours, and they remained mostly silent as they walked. Dominic knew she was as focused as he was on getting in, completing the mission, and then meeting up with Tristan so they could locate Raquel and get the hell out of the city.

When they finally reached the lab, they perched atop the hill that allowed visibility to the guards below. As expected, the first guard left for his break at midnight.

Arianna turned to him from her crouched position behind a large tree and gestured with her head toward the facility.

Dominic nodded and they both sprang forward, maneuvering down the hill to take out the remaining guard.

Arianna lifted the tranquilizer gun, her grip steady as she aimed, and Dominic found himself entranced as always by her skillful handling of the weapon. Her finger settled over the trigger before pulling, and a moment later, a dart landed in the guard's neck. He grasped the entrance wound and sucked in a breath before falling to the ground.

They charged forward, Dominic lowering to yank the badge from the man's chest. He swiped it over the keypad, and green light illuminated as the pad beeped. Turning the handle, he tugged open the door, and they entered.

"Stay close," Arianna commanded, turning on her flashlight and leading the way. Dominic didn't argue since he trusted her without hesitation. Although his protective streak inwardly rebelled, he knew she was the finest soldier he would ever partner with. Hell, he'd follow her into battle in any scenario, and this one was no different.

They snaked their way through the lab, the hair raising on the back of Dominic's neck as they grew closer to where the serum was stored. Something about the raid was too...*easy*, and it sent a jolt of nervous awareness down his spine.

Arianna reached the lab door, and Dominic handed her the guard's badge. She slid it over the keypad and the deadbolt clicked. Pushing the door, they headed inside the sterile lab.

Metal tables scattered the room, some covered with cages that held mice and other test animals. Arianna approached the middle of the lab and pointed at the vials that sat beside a microscope.

"Let's place the explosives here and plant more throughout the room. We can use the detonator from the hallway and then head for the back exit."

Dominic nodded as they both removed their backpacks.

Suddenly, the sound of a vial shattering caused them both to whirl toward the entrance. A man appeared, tall and dressed in black, holding a semi-automatic rifle. Dominic reached for his gun, but the man shook his head.

"I wouldn't do that, Dominic. I'm Luthor's head of security, and we're holding Raquel in his penthouse as we speak. If one bullet flies from either of your guns, I give the order to kill her." He tapped the comm device in his ear. "So, you two either come with me or she dies."

Arianna's shoulders deflated. "It's a set up."

"Of course it's a set up," the man sneered. "Do you think Luthor would let you destroy his next great drug?" His eyes remained locked on them as he called over his shoulder, "Secure them and load them onto the convoy."

Two Sen Force soldiers rushed in, and Arianna looked at Dominic with equal parts anger and terror in those stunning eyes.

"Stay strong," he said as the soldiers approached. "He won't kill us or Raquel until he has information on Arthur and Dani."

Arianna nodded quickly before the soldiers drew their arms behind their backs, securing them with zip ties. Then a black bag was shoved over Dominic's head, and a painful blow lodged at his temple before everything faded to black.

Chapter 27

Tristan stood in Luthor's penthouse home, remarking on how cold and sterile it was. One would think that a home would have some warmth, but the space was as devoid of character and ambience as his penthouse office several blocks away. Expansive windows lined the room as the city lights twinkled outside.

Raquel Lawson sat on the spacious couch in the middle of the staid living room, fire in her eyes as she glared at Tristan above the gag he'd shoved in her mouth. He hadn't wanted to scare her, but he had a plan and she played an integral part in it.

And if all went well, she'd be leaving with Arianna and Dominic, which he still firmly believed was best for her.

Zayne Danvers, the head of Luthor's security team, thrust open the double doors and entered the room with four members of his security team close behind. They wheeled Dominic and Arianna to the couch, setting them on either side of Raquel before gliding the wheelchairs to the corner. Then they assumed their places along the wall by the entrance, waiting for their next orders as Luthor addressed Zayne.

"How long did it take them to realize it was a setup?" Luthor asked.

"Not long. They didn't put up a fight when they heard we had Raquel."

"Good." Walking toward his captives, Luthor lifted Raquel's chin as she squirmed and shrieked behind the gag. "Such a sassy little thing. You've done good work in the lab, Raquel, and I appreciate it. I won't kill you, but I need you to do something for me."

She shook her head as Luthor formed a sinister sneer. Releasing her, he spoke to Zayne. "Wake them up."

Zayne gave a nod to one of the guards, who strode toward the couch with two vials in his hands. He injected one in Dominic's arm and one in Arianna's, who jolted to consciousness and yelled a muffled "What the fuck?" under her black hood.

Luthor approached and removed the hoods as Arianna struggled with the binds be-hind her back and at her ankles.

"Relax, Arianna. It's just a mild stimulant to wake you both up. I might pump you both full of EverLife soon, but it's not time for that yet," he said ominously, cocking a dark eyebrow.

"You know, I only *wanted* to kill you before this," Arianna spat. "Now, I'm *definitely* going to kill you."

Get in line, Tristan thought as he assessed the situation. For his plan to work, he'd need the two Sen Force soldiers he'd paid handsomely standing against the far wall to do their part. They weren't members of Zayne's security force, and both had small kids they needed to feed, so they were open to bribery. But first, Tristan needed to catch Luthor and Zayne unaware. A difficult task since Luthor was wily and Zayne was an exceptional guard.

"Your sister is the one I want to inject with EverLife in real time for everyone to see," Luthor said, slowly pacing as he spoke. "It's a fitting end to the villain's story. And before you point out that I'm the villain, I'll let you know that I agree."

Arianna glared at him before glancing over at Raquel and Dominic, concern in her gaze.

"The old world made me a villain with its insistence on limiting my power," Luthor continued. "If the government had just realized I was imperative to its success, everything would've been easier."

"You're a fucking plague on the world, and I won't let you near Dani!"

"That's a shame, because having you lead me to her is my master plan." Moving closer, he pointed at Raquel. "You see, I'll kill *her* if you don't. And I don't think you'll let that happen."

"What's the plan, then?" Dominic asked. "We return to Arthur's compound and you ambush him?"

"Yes," Luthor said with a nod. "You'll show up at the compound walls, and they'll open the gates, never knowing there are hundreds of Sen Force soldiers waiting in the surrounding woods."

"Fuck that. I'd rather die," Arianna said.

"But I don't think you'd let Raquel die," he said, lifting a finger. "In fact, I'm counting on it." Lifting the gun from the holster at his waist, he pressed it to Raquel's temple. "Or am I wrong?"

"Wait!" Arianna yelled, shaking her head. "Let's negotiate. There has to be a way we can help you and both of my sisters live."

Sheathing the gun, Luthor rubbed his chin. "I relish the idea of publicly injecting Dani with EverLife and allowing her to die from the side effects, but..." His eyes narrowed as he arched an eyebrow. "Capturing Arthur Reyes is the ultimate prize. His support grows alongside talk of a rebellion. His compound walls are heavily guarded, and his hackers rival mine even though they barely have access to technology. I've yet to figure out a way in besides bombing from the air, and the people in the cities are so tired of war and death."

"I see the fear in your eyes, Cromwell," Dominic said. "The people in the cities are tired of *you*. You're afraid if you bomb Reyes's compound, the rebellion that's forming will have the final push it needs."

Luthor's nose wrinkled. "Rebellion is such a dirty word, especially since I'm not a dictator. I'm a leader. One who's fair and just to those who deserve it."

"Rich assholes, you mean?" Arianna scoffed.

"People who worked hard to create something to better the world!" Luthor jabbed his finger at the darkened windows. "Everyone out there is happy. They look and feel younger, and they have everything they need. I created that!"

"You're delusional," Arianna said. "I knew that, but it's worse that I imagined."

"Enough talking," Luthor said, slicing his hand through the air. "Tristan will accompany you to Arthur's compound to ensure your compliance. I know Arthur wants to make contact with him, so he won't suspect anything when you show up with Tristan at your side."

Arianna's nostrils flared as her gaze flew to Tristan's. "Traitor," she hissed.

"I told you I have my own goals, Arianna. Sorry they don't align with yours."

"Zayne, you'll assign a guard to Raquel and hold her in my guest room as discussed," Luthor said, grabbing Raquel's wrist and tugging her to her feet. He shoved her toward Zayne and she crashed into his body, her bound feet barely holding her up as her knuckles scraped her lower back.

Suddenly, her head snapped toward Tristan, and he stared deep into her eyes, giving a faint nod. Zayne pushed her to his side as Luthor continued talking to Arianna and Dominic about his plan to approach Arthur's compound while the soldiers hid in the nearby forest.

Raquel's fingers closed around the small box cutter Tristan had slid into the back pocket of the jeans he'd forced her to don at gunpoint when he'd awoken her in his home.

Those light green eyes shot daggers at him as she'd dressed before he tied her feet and ankles and gagged her...and surreptitiously slipped the makeshift weapon into her back pocket.

Tristan knew she wouldn't be searched if she was bound, and it was the only way to get her into the penthouse while in possession of a weapon.

She blended into the background, as she often complained of doing, while Luthor droned on. Using slow, deft movements, she sawed the zip tie holding her wrists. Tristan glanced at the two Sen Force soldiers along the back wall, ensuring they were prepared to defend him if things took a turn for the worst. They stood silent, their hands crossed at their belts as Raquel broke free.

"You see, Arianna," Luthor said, approaching Raquel and waving Zayne away. Zayne moved to stand by the security guard near the door and assumed a watchful stance as Luthor cupped Raquel's shoulder. "Your younger sister doesn't hold the importance of Dr. Danica Lawson, but you know you can't leave her here to die—"

Suddenly, Raquel jabbed the box cutter forward, impaling it in Luthor's side as he wailed. His knees buckled, and he collapsed on the carpet as all hell broke loose.

Raquel rushed over to Arianna, using the box cutter to saw off her restraints before moving to Dominic. Zayne pulled his gun from his belt and aimed at Raquel.

"Should I shoot her, sir?"

Luthor held up a hand as he slowly rose to his feet, wheezing in pain. "No. I think public torture would be better. Take all three of them into custody."

Zayne stepped forward, and something clicked in Tristan's brain.

Ice circulated through his veins as the world seemed to spin in slow motion. Feeling as if he was envisioning the actions from outside his body, Tristan observed Zayne turn away from Raquel. Holding the gun with firm purpose, he lifted it high and aimed it at...Luthor.

"Actually, Luthor, I think it's time *you're* the one who's arrested."

Luthor's eyes grew wide as he sucked in a breath. "You?" he rasped. "You're the leader of the rebellion?"

Tristan remained silent, his heartbeat roaring in his ears as Zayne spoke over his shoulder. "Take Luthor into custody," he commanded his security team.

Tristan watched, stunned. He'd heard grumblings that the rebellion might be formed from people in Luthor's inner circle, but he'd never suspected Zayne.

"Think long and hard about the decision you're about to make," Luthor warned Zayne's security team. "I'm the leader of the army and the most powerful man in the world. The Sen Force soldiers stationed in every lab and warehouse in this city have orders to destroy all inventory if I die. Any of your family members addicted to EverLife will lose the precious antidote they need."

The security guards looked between each other, and Tristan's finger itched upon the trigger. It would be so easy to kill Luthor, right here, right now. But then Jessica would lose the antidote, and until Dani had created something accessible, he wouldn't chance her life.

Tristan noticed an almost imperceptible movement out of the corner of his eye and realized Raquel was pressing the box cutter into Arianna's hand. *Smart girl.* Arianna was much more dangerous with a weapon and could possibly catch Luthor unaware in the surrounding chaos.

Zayne barked more orders at his men to seize Luthor, and they remained still, the gravity of the decision looming on their faces.

Suddenly, Grace trailed through the door, her eyes heavy from sleep and her expression perplexed. "What the hell is going on in here? I heard yelling—"

Zayne seized the opportunity, snatching her against his body and planting the barrel of the gun against her temple. "No one move or I'll kill her."

Tristan aimed his gun at Zayne's head although he wasn't able to get a clean shot with Grace struggling in his arms. She squirmed and kicked, but her efforts were no match for the large man holding her hostage.

"We both know you need her alive, Luthor," Zayne said, backing out of the room. "George Luddington only supports you because of Grace. She'll come in handy as we work to sway him to the rebellion's side." Stepping across the threshold, he pulled the doors closed and something rattled on the other side.

Tristan rushed to the doors, attempting to yank them open, but they wouldn't budge. "The bastard locked them from outside. Fuck!" He slammed his palm on the door in frustration.

Arianna rushed toward Luthor, holding the box cutter high before rearing back in pain and clutching her arm. "What the—?"

One of Zayne's remaining security guards fired at Arianna, making contact with her upper arm. Raquel screamed and jolted toward her, lowering to her knees as Arianna fell to the floor. "Ari? Are you okay?"

"Shoot them!" Luthor commanded.

Raquel picked up the box cutter and rushed toward Luthor, lifting it high to strike. Sadly, she never stood a chance. Several bullets lodged in her body before she collapsed on the ground, her gray shirt rapidly turning red with blood.

Bullets flew at Tristan, and he lunged behind the large chair several feet away, taking cover as the security team surrounded Luthor before dragging him toward the door. One of the men kicked it several times and it flew open. They dragged Luthor out and away to safety.

Tristan rose and spoke to the Sen Force soldiers he'd recruited to his side. "We just need two minutes to get out of the building and into the Jeep waiting below. Go home to your families and don't tell anyone that Zayne is the leader of the rebellion."

They both nodded before exiting.

Tristan heard Arianna's soft pleading as she bent over her sister's dying body. It appeared that one bullet had only grazed Arianna's arm, but Raquel wasn't so lucky. Tentatively approaching, Tristan touched Arianna's shoulder.

"We have to go. Dominic can carry her to the Jeep."

Raquel's eyes glazed over as she stared up at Arianna. "I'm so sorry," she whispered, her skin turning pale as snow as she bled out. "I just wanted to be special for once."

"You are," Arianna said, tears streaming from her eyes as she cupped Raquel's face. "You've always been special to me and Dani. I don't know why you didn't believe it."

Raquel inhaled a long breath before her eyes slid closed. "You have to win. Tell Dani I'm sorry. And tell her bromantane is the main ingredient in Dr. Ziegler's drug."

"You tell her yourself," Arianna said, stroking her cheek. Raquel exhaled a slow, ragged breath before all signs of life left her sagging muscles. "Damn it, Raquel! You tell her yourself!" Arianna slapped her cheek, but it was no use.

"Ari," Dominic said, gently tugging her hand away. "We have to go. I'll carry her." He lifted Raquel's lifeless body and faced Tristan. "Are you coming with us?"

Tristan shook his head. "I need to find Grace. That's my first priority. After tonight, Luthor will most likely begin using the super drug on his soldiers and start attacking the compounds. Arthur's will surely be first. Tell him to contact me on the radio."

"Are you going to align with Zayne and the rebellion?" Dominic asked as he moved toward the door.

"I don't know. I need to scope out the situation and save Grace. You must know by now that she's my wife..." Swiping a hand over his face, he sighed. "My *ex*-wife. But she's not trained in any sort of combat and is completely helpless. Saving her will be my main priority. Once I accomplish that, I can focus on what happens next. Come on. We've got to get out of here."

They entered the elevator, whooshing to the lobby and the black Jeep parked outside.

"Take it while you still can," Tristan said. "Luthor will send men down here any minute. I bribed the two guards at the Francis Scott Key Bridge crossing who will let you through."

"Thank you. Your foresight is what's keeping me from beating the shit out of you for setting us up," Dominic said.

"It needed to be done" was Tristan's flippant response. "We've set something in motion now that can't be stopped. I hope you all are ready for a war. I'll be in touch...and I'm very sorry about Raquel." With a salute, he skulked off into the night.

Dominic loaded Raquel into the back seat, and Arianna climbed in to hold her. Revving the engine, Dominic drove fast as lightning toward the edge of the city, leaving DC behind.

Chapter 28

Arianna stroked her sister's hair, her head resting in her lap as they neared Arthur's compound. When they pulled up to the gate, Dominic exited the car and extended his arms, allowing the searchlights to rove over him. Once he was cleared, the heavy metal doors swung open and they drove inside.

"Please wait here," one of the guards said. "We have strict orders that Arthur has to personally approve your re-entrance to the compound."

Dominic opened the back door of the Jeep, his heart breaking at the sight of Arianna's tender ministrations on Raquel's hair.

"Ari," he softly called. "It's time for you to let her go, sweetheart. We'll ask Arthur to have the nurses at the infirmary clean and prepare her body."

Arianna's chin warbled as she nodded. "Don't let Dani see her like this, covered in blood."

"Okay."

After slowly releasing her, Arianna took the hand he offered and climbed out of the Jeep. Gazing up at him, she wiped her nose. "I was supposed to save her, Dom."

"It's not your fault, Arianna." Drawing her into a firm hug, he stroked her back as they waited for Arthur. Eventually, he appeared in one of the compound's run-down pickup trucks, his expression thoughtful as he approached.

"I assume things went badly if you two are consoling each other."

"They went really fucking badly," Arianna said, turning to face him. "Raquel is dead and Luthor knows who's leading the rebellion. He's planning on creating an army of drug-induced super soldiers, and your compound will be the first he attacks."

"Shit." Arthur rubbed his forehead. "How much time do you think we have to prepare?"

"Could be days, could be weeks," Dominic said. "But we'd be better prepared if we could track down the rebellion leader and have them fight with us."

"Agreed. Who is the leader?"

"Zayne Danvers, Luthor's head of security. He's taken Luthor's wife hostage, so Tristan is searching for them too. Perhaps you can make contact with him on the radio frequency and Arianna and I can help him search. We'll cover more ground if we combine our efforts."

"Okay." Peering into the car, Arthur frowned. "Do you all want a burial or a cremation?"

"A burial, please," Arianna said. "If you can take care of preparing her body, I'd like to plan an afternoon funeral on the hill behind the middle school. The four of us need to mourn her, even if she betrayed us."

"I'll have the body ready within a few hours." Lifting his hand high, he circled it and several men jogged over. Arthur whispered hushed directions to them before two of them hopped in the car and drove Raquel's body to the health clinic.

"You two need to decompress, so I'll have Jake drive you to the middle school." Squeezing Arianna's upper arm, he shook his head. "I'm so sorry. Another life wasted because of Luthor Cromwell's malice."

"Thank you," Arianna said quietly.

"Take today to mourn and bury Raquel, and then we can meet at sunrise to discuss next steps. I wish you had more time, but if Luthor's truly planning to attack, we need to prepare."

"I'm a soldier and have seen my share of death," Arianna said. "I'm heartbroken, but I understand the need to prevent more bloodshed."

"You two can hop in," Jake said, motioning them toward a small sedan.

When they were back at the school, Arianna listlessly headed to the makeshift room she'd claimed when they arrived at the compound. It was the former principal's office and had a large couch. Dominic followed her, determined to comfort her after the disastrous night.

She kicked off her boots and removed her pants before sitting on the couch and looking at her arm. "Fucker grazed me," she said, examining the wound.

"Be right back."

Dominic headed to the school's infirmary, noticing the first hints of dawn as they appeared outside the school windows. Retrieving some alcohol and a large bandage, he returned to Arianna.

Sitting beside her, he cleaned her wound and applied the bandage. As he worked, he noticed the flaring of her nostrils and the slight wobble of her chin as she grappled with the gravity that her sister was gone.

"Thanks," she muttered when he was finished, examining the bandage. "I should be fine with some rest." Releasing a defeated breath, she spread out on the couch and turned to face the wall. Reaching for the blanket that rested nearby, she tugged it up to her chin and closed her eyes.

Dominic removed everything but his underwear and slid in behind her. Drawing her close, he aligned his front with her back.

"You don't have to stay in here," she said, nuzzling into him as her body sent a message opposite of her words.

"You lost your sister today," he said, kissing her neck. "Of course I'm going to comfort you."

"I don't think I'm concussed even though I'm going to have one hell of a headache." She rubbed her temple. "How about you?"

"I think I'm fine too. Maverick will wake us up to debrief when he hears we're home, so I think it's fine if we get a few hours of sleep."

Nodding, she settled in as he tightened his arms around her. Her breathing was ragged as she fought off tears. He knew she rarely cried, but the day's events would spur emotion in even the most stoic soul.

"You're not alone anymore, sweetheart," he said, gently running his lips over the skin where her hair met her neck. "I thought you were finally ready to accept that."

"I've been alone for so long..." she trailed off, her voice laced with exhaustion.

Dominic held her, allowing his firm embrace to reaffirm his support.

"And don't call me 'sweetheart.'"

A laugh escaped his throat. Thankful to see a sliver of her acerbic personality shine through, Dominic closed his eyes, intent on holding her for as long as she needed.

CHAPTER 29

Arianna awoke, groggy and melancholy at her terrible failure to accomplish her goal. Sitting up, she rubbed the swollen bags under her eyes, noting that Dominic must've already risen. After tossing on some clothes, she headed to the home economics room, following the scent of bacon.

Dominic's broad shoulders stood at the stove as he flipped the bacon. Dani sat on Maverick's lap at the table, crying softly against his shoulder as he held her.

"Hey, guys," Arianna said, awkwardly scratching her arm beneath the bandage since she was uncomfortable with the display of emotion.

"Ari!" Dani cried, pushing to her feet and rushing toward her. After enveloping Arianna in a smothering hug, she drew back and studied the bandage. "Dominic said you were shot. Do I need to look at it?"

"Just grazed," Arianna said, squeezing her before releasing the hug. "I'm fine."

Dani gazed at her with red-rimmed eyes. "I can't believe she's gone."

"Me neither." Emotion clogged her throat. "I had one job and I fucking blew it."

"Hey," Maverick said, striding over and placing a supportive hand on Arianna's back. "That's the last time I want to hear that this was your fault. Raquel made her choices, and you put yourself in extreme danger to help her. We're happy you and Dom are okay."

Dominic sat the bacon on the table. "Eat while it's hot, guys."

The four of them sat, sad and solemn as they ate. Eventually, Arianna straightened her shoulders and spoke. "I want to bury her on the hill behind the school."

"The nurses are preparing her body, and Arthur is having his men make a casket," Dani said. "Burying her on the hill is perfect. She would've loved the little flowers that grow there, and hopefully her soul can find some peace there."

Arianna nodded. "After the burial, the three of us need to gather with Arthur's soldiers and form a plan." She pointed between herself, Dominic and Maverick. "Luthor is coming, and we need to brief everyone on the enhanced soldier serum, the rebellion and everything else we know."

"I wish I knew what was in the serum," Dani said, leaning her elbow on the table and resting her chin on her hand. "If I did, I could possibly concoct something to combat it."

"Raquel said there was something in it called...bromite?" Dominic asked, unsure.

"Bromantane?" Dani asked. "That's a performance-enhancing drug, so that makes sense."

"Well, let's find out." Arianna reached into her pocket and pulled out two vials. Setting them on the table, she cocked an eyebrow.

"Holy shit." Dani picked up a vial and lifted it to the light, studying it. "Where did you get this?"

"I stuffed two vials in my pocket before Zayne took us into custody in Dr. Ziegler's lab. I'm not a complete idiot," she said, playfully rolling her eyes.

"Damn, that's badass," Dominic said, reaching over and squeezing her hand. "I didn't even think to nab one of the vials."

"I'll do the thinking in this relationship, thank you very much," Arianna teased, squeezing his fingers.

Dani exchanged an excited glance with Maverick, beaming as Arianna huffed and stood. "Let it go, Dani. We like each other and he's fun to blow off steam with. That's all."

Dominic raised his hand to his mouth and whispered loudly, "She's crazy about me."

Dani chuckled as Arianna walked to the sink, refusing to get drawn into the lovey-dovey bullshit. "Want me to wash the pan?"

"I'll do it," Maverick said. "Why don't you and Dani take a walk and catch up? Dom, we can do the same."

"I'd like that," Dani said, rising. "We can remember her before we lay her to rest."

"Fine with me. After the funeral, I'll be ready to move on. Things are on a path now we can't change, and I'm ready to take on Luthor and end this shit."

"There's a cabin calling her name on a remote mountain in West Virginia somewhere," Dominic said, pointing his thumb over his shoulder at her.

"Only *her* name?" Maverick asked conspiratorially.

"I'm working on it, man. Give me some time."

Done with the annoying conversation, Arianna beckoned to Dani. "Let's head outside. I need some air."

Lacing her arm around Dani's waist, they left the men behind to reminisce about their sister and simpler times when none of the Lawson sisters needed to save the world.

Chapter 30

Hours later, they stood on the grassy hill, surrounded by the soulful songs of chirping birds in the nearby trees. Dani and Arianna were shoulder to shoulder, Maverick and Dominic positioned at their sides, solemn and supportive. The ceremony was reverent, each of them speaking kind words about Raquel as the cool breeze ruffled the fallen autumn leaves.

"I'm sorry you didn't get to say your last goodbye to Mom," Dani said, swiping away a tear as they stood by the raised pile of earth that covered her casket. "Hopefully she's with you now and you can hug her in all the ways you need."

Arianna slid an arm around her shoulders. "We failed you, and I'm sorry for that. But you can bet that I'll avenge you. Even though you pissed the hell out of me, you're my baby sister and that bastard will pay."

Embracing, they slowly swayed in tandem with the wind, their love evident as Dani rested her head on Arianna's shoulder.

When the ceremony was finished, Dani took Arianna's hand. "Remember I said I wanted to show you my progress on the antidote?"

"Yes. I need some good fucking news for once. I'm counting on you."

Grinning, Dani led the four of them to the red-brick clinic building, excitement pulsing deep in her belly. After climbing the stairs to the second floor, Arianna's eyes grew wide as she scanned the room.

Several patients were up and about, maneuvering on walkers as nurses helped them. Others sat playing chess or cards in the far corner.

Arianna slowly turned to face her sister, excitement in her eyes. "Holy shit," she breathed, her breath quickening slightly. "You created a cure."

Dani gripped her forearms, unable to control her smile. "You're goddamned right I created a cure."

Later that evening, Dani peered into the microscope, studying the serum Arianna had absconded from the lab.

"As Raquel said, it contains bromantane, and creatine too. The best way to counteract this is to create a serum from fungi that increases immune modulation."

"I've learned her language by now," Maverick said to Arianna, leaning on the counter behind them in the old middle school science lab. "In English, that means she can use mushrooms to create something we can inject into the super soldiers that will render them ineffective."

"Great job," Dani said, flashing him a grin. "Some of the *Agaricus* and turkey tail mushrooms I saw on our scouting trips around the compound should do it."

Arthur Reyes stormed into the room, causing them all to bristle.

"My lookouts just spotted a battalion of Sen Force soldiers marching toward the compound," he said, a steely determination in his eyes. "My men are ready."

"What's your current count?" Arianna asked, striding toward him.

"Ninety-seven. I wish we had more, but they're strong and committed soldiers who will fight with honor."

Maverick tugged Dani into a passionate kiss. "Stay inside the school. If the compound is infiltrated, head to the old basement gym locker rooms and lock yourself in."

"Be safe," she said, rising to her toes to peck his lips before releasing him. "I can't lose you too."

He nodded, his arms tightening into one last soulful embrace. Releasing her, he addressed Arthur. "Let's go."

"We'll arm ourselves and meet you at the front gate," Arianna said.

"Although we're outnumbered, our contingent is fierce and determined," Arthur said with a firm nod. "No one's infiltrating my compound without a fight."

Admiring his conviction, Arianna saluted him before treading toward her room to don her weapons, with Dominic fast on her heels.

Walking with purpose, she understood the gravity of the situation. Whether they were ready or not, the first battle in the war Tristan so desperately wanted was about to begin.

Chapter 31

Arianna strapped on every weapon she could fit onto her body. A knife in her boot, a gun at her waist and a rifle across her shoulder. Adding another gun on her opposite hip for good measure, she looked at Dominic. He was also loaded with weapons atop his black clothing, and she took a moment to peruse his body. Fuck, he was hot, and he was hers. If they survived, that was.

Determined to make that happen, she lifted her chin. "Ready?"

Approaching her, he lifted her chin and pressed a firm kiss to her lips. "You checking me out, Lawson?"

"Yeah." The corner of her lips ticked up. "Don't get hurt because I plan to personally remove those weapons from your body when we're done."

Desire lit his dark eyes. "I love your promises, sweetheart."

She nipped his lips, a small punishment for the endearment she swore she hated but also made butterflies flutter inside her stomach.

They marched to meet Arthur's militia, ready to fight for justice against a malicious dictator and his virulent drug.

Bootsteps pounded the ground as they approached the compound gates, and Arthur addressed the two lookouts perched at the top of the wall on either side.

"They're scattered throughout the woods, sir," one lookout said. "Armed with rifles and a few tanks."

"They underestimate us if they think I haven't trained our militia to fight in the forest in anticipation of this scenario," Arthur said, swinging the rifle around and clutching the grip. "You have the dart guns?" he asked the man in charge of the EverLife battalion.

"Locked and loaded, sir."

The EverLife battalion, comprised of fifteen men, had one job: to lodge darts full of EverLife into the Sen Force soldiers' necks. The compound's EverLife stock was diluted with all sorts of nefarious substances, which made it a perfect weapon. The darts were filled with three times the normal dose and would immobilize the Sen Force soldiers as soon as it entered the bloodstream.

Arthur ordered the gates to open, and urged everyone through them quickly so the people inside could remain protected. Arianna rushed outside, rifle held high as she scanned the surrounding trees.

A man stepped forward from the brush, the Sen Force patch on his shoulder glistening in the moonlight.

"I know him from working with Colonel McGrath," Arianna whispered to Dominic, who stood beside her in the formation.

"I'm Lieutenant Colonel Jackson," the man said, his voice cool and confident. "We've come here in peace to retake this compound for General Luthor Cromwell so he can evolve it into the next Sen City."

"We do not want your occupation, nor do we believe Cromwell has good intentions," Arthur called. "We believe his goal is ultimate destruction of our compound, and we won't allow that to happen."

"If you choose to fight, know that you are outnumbered. We have more ammunition than you can imagine and five tanks ready to fire at your compound walls." He pointed toward the thick metal grate surrounding the compound. "Although you melted down steel to fashion the wall, it won't survive a barrage by our tanks."

Arthur straightened his shoulders as his fingers tightened on his rifle. "No? We're prepared to test their readiness. To honor the rules of engagement, I'll warn you that I'm ten seconds away from commanding my men to fire."

Lieutenant Colonel Jackson sighed and shook his head. "Have it your way. If you want to die, I won't stop you—"

"Five seconds," Arthur said firmly.

Jackson backed into the brush seconds before Arthur yelled, "Attack!"

Arianna lurched forward, adrenaline in her veins as she ran toward a cluster of soldiers she spotted in a thicket of trees. Dominic was close behind her, his presence comforting in a way that had become routine. For a lone wolf like Arianna, the realization that she never wanted to fight another battle without him by her side hit hard.

And somehow, it was also the most heartening realization of her life.

Dominic swerved beside her, bullets flying from his rifle as they aimed at the Sen Force soldiers. Arianna ducked behind a thick tree, and Dominic followed close behind as he panted.

"Three down in that cluster, but there's another one at two o'clock with four men."

"Saw them," Arianna said with a nod. "I'll take the left flank."

Dominic gave a quick tilt of his head and they were off, emerging from the thicket and spraying bullets at the soldiers. A loud boom signaled behind them, followed by a flash of fire, and Arianna ducked.

"They're firing at the walls!" Dominic yelled, his breath ragged as he surveyed the nearby thicket. "That cluster is down. We need to take out the tanks."

Arianna jogged toward two fallen Sen Force soldiers and lifted the huge weapon from one man's lifeless frame. "Look what I found," she whispered, excitement in her tone.

"A rocket propelled grenade," Dominic said, eyeing the weapon. "It's the only weapon that could possibly destroy the tanks."

"Exactly," she said with a nod. "We need to approach the tank from behind since that's the most vulnerable spot. Hopefully, it will work. It's still going to be tough."

"Lead the way." Dominic's spine straightened with resolve as he prepared to follow her.

They jogged through the trees and foliage, the tank that was firing upon the wall an eerie sight in the dense woods outside the compound. The sounds of bullets and combat filled Arianna's ears as she kneeled behind a large rock and aimed the RPG.

Dominic crouched beside her, rifle aimed as he waited.

The tank exploded in a huge blaze, the ammunition inside igniting a destructive force that would leave no survivors.

"Good shot," Dominic said. "Let's move to the next tank."

They skulked through the woods, eventually locating another tank whose barrel was aimed at the compound wall. It wasn't firing so Arianna ducked behind a tree to observe it, wondering if the barrel was malfunctioning somehow.

Suddenly, the top of the hatch opened and three men climbed out, the Sen Force patch slightly visible on their uniforms in the darkened forest.

"I'm the tank commander," one man said, holding up his hands in a sign of surrender. "My gunner, driver and I have no wish to die tonight. We pledged loyalty to Luthor to feed our families. We know you have an RPG and don't want this to escalate further between us."

Arianna glanced at Dominic as the three soldiers stood silent, hands raised as they waited.

"Let's take them hostage and question them. They can give us Sen Force intel."

"Get on your knees and cross your wrists behind your back," she commanded. The soldiers complied, and Arianna placed two fingers between her lips, whistling to two of Arthur's men a few yards away. "Restrain these soldiers and tie them to a tree. When the dust settles, we'll take them inside the compound for questioning."

The men nodded and rushed toward them, securing their wrists before leading them into the forest.

"Should we move to the next tank?" she asked, arching her eyebrows.

"Absolutely," Dominic said. "It's interesting to see some of the soldiers wavering in their support of Luthor. It's a good sign."

They maneuvered through the woods, searching for the next tank when Arianna's ears perked. Surprise coursed through her when she heard someone yell, "Cease fire!"

Treading back to the compound entrance, she observed Arthur kneeling over Lieutenant Colonel Jackson as he heaved atop the ground.

"You've got a dart full of shitty EverLife in your neck, Jackson," he said, shaking his head. "It will stop your heart soon. I've called a ceasefire and need you to affirm it to your men. The ones still alive don't have to die today."

Ragged breaths formed visible puffs in the chilly air as Jackson contemplated. Turning his head atop the wet leaves, he spoke to the man Arianna assumed was his second-in-command.

"I've pledged my life to Luthor's cause and want to die with honor. This is in your hands now, son." Shallow breaths left his lungs as the drug continued to poison his blood. "May God be with you." Jackson's head lolled on the ground as his heart succumbed to the drug. His muscles convulsed in a series of spasms before he exhaled and his body fell limp.

The second-in-command lifted his gaze to Arthur's, indecision swimming in his dark eyes. Squaring his shoulders, he raised his hand high and yelled, "Charge!"

Arthur rose and sprinted toward a nearby thicket, commanding his men to regroup. Once they were gathered in the thick brush, he spoke between labored breaths.

"Spread the Sen Force soldiers out across the woods and shoot to wound, not kill. If we have enough soldiers bleeding out on the dirt, I can try and convince the new commander to surrender and offer to heal the wounded."

Arianna thought it was a solid strategy. Immobilize one by one until the enemy was fractured. Noticing that some of the men were hesitating, she stood tall and addressed Arthur. "Solid plan, sir. Dominic and I will take the east woods. You two, come with us," she commanded, pointing to the two closest soldiers.

Arthur's gaze drilled into hers as he nodded, silently thanking her for her support.

Arianna led their small group onto a nearby dirt path as others clustered together, each spreading out across different sectors of the forest.

"He needed that affirmation from you in front of the soldiers," Dominic said softly as they stepped through the brush, weapons lifted while they scanned for Sen Force soldiers. "Like I've said all along, we have a chance because of you, Arianna."

Tamping down the emotion that swelled at his unwavering belief in her, she shot him a glance. "Let's take down some soldiers first and see if we have a chance."

White teeth flashed under the stars as he grinned. "Yes, ma'am."

Confident with him by her side, Arianna trekked in the darkness, determined to make this battle count and change the course of the world for those who no longer had the ability to fight.

Chapter 32

Arianna crept through the woods, slowly wounding soldiers with shots to their thighs and arms as the night progressed. Arthur had been smart to train his men in the forest, and they were much more skilled at combat in the dense brush than Luthor's army.

Eventually, the horizon began to glow a slight eerie gray, and a whistle sounded in the distance. Glancing toward Dominic, who was crouched behind the cluster of bushes to her left, she lifted her eyebrows in a silent question.

He rose and strode toward her, positioning himself beside her as they stood in the shadow of protection of a large oak tree. "I think it's Arthur calling us back," he said, jerking his head toward the sound of the whistle.

"Agreed. Stay alert. There could still be stragglers who haven't been wounded."

They slowly made their way back to the clearing in front of the compound gates. Arthur stood tall, his gun aimed at the man Lieutenant Colonel Jackson had transferred command to before he died. Blood trickled from the man's upper arm as one of Arthur's men held him immobile.

"I can shoot you right here, son," Arthur said, the barrel of his gun aimed between the man's eyes. "Or we can talk like two commanders who want what's best for our troops."

A wail sounded in the distance, and Arianna assumed it was one of the Sen Force soldiers who'd been wounded, crying as he bled out on the forest floor.

"You're young, and I understand your desire to fight for your convictions," Arthur continued. "But your convictions are misplaced. Luthor Cromwell is not a just leader."

"And you are?" the man asked, his voice laced with pain from the wound in his arm.

Lowering his gun, Arthur stepped forward. "What is your name, soldier? I owe you the honor of addressing you properly."

The commander swallowed visibly before answering. "Major Anthony Martinez," he said, eyes darting to the sound of another wail that echoed off the far horizon.

"My sister's husband was named Anthony," Arthur said, his lips forming a sad smile. "We called him Tony. He and my sister both died from EverLife addiction."

Anthony's chest lifted with slow breaths as he contemplated. "My family called me Tony too. Those that are left still do, but there aren't many."

Compassion laced Arthur's features as he slowly extended his hand. "I'm very sorry to hear that. Although I'm technically Commander Reyes, you can call me Arthur. Can I call you Tony?"

Tony grasped his hand, giving a slow, wary shake. "Yes."

Arthur studied him as he contemplated. "Is this truly the service you signed up for, Tony? Willful alliance to a demagogue who controls the world with an addictive, poisonous drug?"

Tony's eyes lowered as his shoulders sagged. "No, sir. But the world has changed, and we must make hard choices to ensure our survival."

"So let's change it back." Arthur released his hand and took a step forward. "In fact, let's change it for the better. A world worthy of your children."

"I don't have children yet, sir, but I hope to one day."

"Then let's create something together," he said, a slight plea in his voice, alongside the firm strength. "If you're willing to discuss forming an alliance with me, Tony, I'll invite you inside to talk. In exchange, I'll send my nurses out here to tend to your wounded soldiers."

Tony's lips pursed as he contemplated.

"Aligning against Luthor Cromwell is impossible," Tony said. "He controls the entire army. The entire *world*."

The corner of Arthur's lips ticked up. "For now. But his confidence might be his downfall. I doubt he'll suspect that your battalion has formed a secret alliance with us. If we're strategic, we could turn this into an insurmountable advantage."

Tony deliberated for a small eternity as birds ushered in the day with soulful songs from the nearby trees. Another cry sounded in the distance before a gunshot reverberated in the forest with a loud bang.

Tony shuddered at the sound as Arthur shook his head. "That man didn't have to die, Tony. How many more have to die? Please..." Extending his hand, he held up his palm.

"Let me send my nurses out and come inside the walls to talk. I promise you no harm will befall you."

Tony tilted his head back and closed his eyes, and Arianna wondered if he was praying. Finally, he refocused his gaze on Arthur and lifted his hand in a salute. "Sir, I will accompany you inside if you send out your nurses."

Relief washed over Arthur's face as he saluted in return.

"Cease fire!" Tony called to what remained of his troops. "I've agreed to accompany Commander Reyes inside the compound in exchange for triage. Do not engage. Understood?"

"Yes, sir!"

"Gather the nurses and have them triage the men," Arthur commanded to the soldier who stood behind him. Stepping back, he gestured toward the front gates of the compound. "After you, Tony."

Arianna exhaled a heavy breath, releasing the tension in her weary muscles. Dominic cupped her shoulder and squeezed, silently affirming his relief as well. Lifting her gaze to his, a smile tugged at her lips as a small sliver of the optimism she so rarely felt coursed through her veins.

They were a long way from victory, but perhaps they were a few steps closer.

Sliding her arm around Dominic's waist, she pressed into his side as they walked back to the compound.

Chapter 33

An hour later, Arianna stood inside the hub of Arthur's compound as he questioned Tony. The man was talking rather freely, and she understood how many soldiers had been forced to comply with Luthor's orders due to necessity. Hopefully, Arthur would end up being the leader they needed; one who would restore society to something better. Perhaps even something whole.

"Do you know Zayne Danvers's location?" Arthur asked, leg swinging as he sat on the table, arms crossed as he questioned Tony, seated a foot away.

Tony shook his head. "We think he's being funded by George Luddington, but we're not sure. George disappeared after Luthor was injured, and Luthor has sent a search team to find him. He sent two separate teams to search Zayne and Tristan Holder. We don't think they're working together...yet."

"And Zayne is holding Luthor's wife hostage?"

"Yes. Grace was abducted the night Luthor was hurt. His desire to save her stems more from not wanting to look weak than affection, if you want my opinion. The most powerful man in the world can't have his wife murdered. Not a good look." He shrugged dismissively.

"It certainly isn't." Arthur looked toward Arianna, Dominic and Maverick. "Anything else you want to ask him?"

"I think I'm good," Arianna said. "The plan to send Tony and his troops back with Jackson's body, claiming defeat, is solid. This will cause Luthor to regroup, but he won't know Tony's secretly on our side."

Arthur nodded. "In the meantime, I'd like to send my own team to search for Zayne and Tristan. It's time for us all to unite against Luthor. Rebels, soldiers, militia—I don't care what we call it, but we're more powerful together."

"I pledge my loyalty to you, sir, and will do my best to honor our alliance," Tony said.

"You've done a good job, son. I hope this doesn't sound condescending, but I'm proud of you. Your actions today could very well pave the way for peace and are extremely meaningful."

Arthur stood and patted Tony on the shoulder as the younger soldier's shoulders straightened with pride. "We'll make sure to protect your family and all the citizens we can when we forge our attack. A clean, precise mission is best, and we'll try our damndest." He gestured to the door. "For now, my team has packed up some food for your troops. We don't have a lot to spare, but give it to your families when you return to DC. I'll communicate with you on the radio frequency we discussed."

Tony stood and extended his hand. "I was only a kid when you declared your intention to run for president, but I think I would've voted for you, sir."

Arthur shook his hand as his lips formed a sincere smile. "Maybe you'll have the chance one day. I appreciate your service, Tony."

Tony pivoted, following the team members who would lead him to the packed food.

"What a fucking day," Arthur said, scraping his hands over his face. "I'm beat."

"We need sleep too," Dominic said. "But I just want to say, you're a fantastic leader, Reyes. I'm honored to serve with you."

"Me too," Arianna said.

Grinning, Arthur tilted his head. "The great Arianna Lawson has finally accepted me. I'm humbled."

He bowed dramatically, and Arianna rolled her eyes. "Don't let it go to your head. Also, can we get a fucking bed in the principal's office? I'm tired of sleeping on a couch."

Chuckling, he hooked his fingers to call one of his men over. "There's a couch with a pull-out bed in my quarters. Move it to the principal's office at the middle school."

"On it," the man said, waving two others to follow him to Arthur's downstairs quarters.

"They'll have it there in twenty minutes and it's the best I can do."

"We'll take it."

Arthur raised his eyebrows, a knowing smile on his face.

"For sleeping," she said, exasperated. "Everyone is a goddamn matchmaker around here. I'm going to bed."

She stomped from the room, ignoring Arthur's chuckles behind her as they mingled with Dominic's and Maverick's before they followed her outside.

They briskly walked to the school under the early morning sky, and when they entered, Dani ran toward them. "Is everyone okay? What happened?"

"I'll tell you everything, slugger," Maverick said, sliding his arm around her waist. "We're exhausted, and I'm sure Arianna and Dom are ready to crash."

Three men busted through the double doors, carrying a couch and echoing hellos as they passed.

"I needed a bed," Arianna said, rubbing her tense neck. "I'm done with the couch."

"Plus, it will give you two more room," Dani said with a cheeky grin.

Arianna groaned before walking away. "Good night!" she said, flicking a dismissive hand as she disappeared down the hallway.

Dominic wished them good night as well before his footsteps sounded behind her. Knowing he would soon be wrapped around her was not only comforting, it felt *right*. She entered the principal's office, noticing the men putting sheets on the pull-out mattress.

"Grabbed a clean set of bedding from Arthur's closet," one of them said. "You should be all set. We moved the old couch against the far wall, but we can remove it if you need."

"Nope, we're good. Thanks, guys." Arianna watched them leave, the door clicking behind them before Dominic turned the deadbolt.

"What a fucking night," he said, trailing toward her and cupping her chin. "Are you okay?"

"Yes." Rising to her toes, she brushed his lips with hers before extricating herself from his grasp so they could remove their weapons. They placed them on the desk, one by one, before Arianna slipped her hand in his.

Lacing their fingers, she drew him to the center of the room atop the withered green carpet. Overcome with every emotion she felt for him, she lowered to her knees.

A visible shudder ran down his frame, causing her body to ripple with delight. Inching closer, he slid his fingers under her chin, tilting her head back. "Ari..."

"I think it's time to make some of those fantasies come true," she whispered before darting her tongue over her lips. Passion flared in his eyes, and her heart pounded at the glow of admiration across his strong features.

"You don't have to," he murmured, tracing his thumb over her wet bottom lip. "I know you're tired."

Reaching for his fly, she gazed into his eyes as she unbuttoned his pants and lowered the zipper. "I *want* to," she rasped, pushing the fabric away. "I'm filled with adrenaline and I need a fucking release. But if you want to punish me for not letting you sleep, I'm okay with that."

A long, desire-laden breath filtered through his lungs as her fingers fought to free him. "Fuck, you're perfect. You know that, right?" Palming her jaw, he ran his thumb over her cheek. "So goddamned perfect."

Arianna dragged his pants and boxer briefs down his legs until they scrunched above his boots. His shaft surged toward her, thick and turgid, the veins pulsing beneath the sensitive skin. Sliding her fingers around his length, she squeezed, thrilled at his sharp inhale.

He cupped her head, threading his fingers through the hair beneath her braid. Resting the smooth head of his cock on her lips, he softly commanded, "Open that smart mouth, Ari."

She complied, opening wide and gasping when he surged inside. He slowly began to pump between her lips, his hands holding her head firm as he stared into her eyes.

"Such a gorgeous mouth," he rasped, dragging his length back and forth over her tongue...between her lips...coating himself in her saliva as he undulated. "*My mouth*, Ari. Do you hear me?"

She nodded, feeling her eyes water as he pushed deeper, hitting the back of her throat with each solid thrust.

"Is it too much?" he asked, his deep orbs swirling with lust and emotion.

She shook her head, gripping the base of his cock and stroking it as he surged inside her mouth. God, it felt so good to have him loom above her. To know he was now a constant in her life. Gazing into his eyes, she squeezed the base of his shaft and popped him from her mouth.

"You can go harder," she said, her tone silky as she stroked his wet flesh. "I meant it when I said you could punish me." She'd never considered offering that level of submission to any man, but for Dom? Fuck, she wanted his hands everywhere—craved his marks on her skin. She wanted him to *claim* her.

Cursing, he kicked off his boots and pants, tossing them aside. Lifting her under the arms, he carried her to the bed and threw her on the mattress face-first. Laughing at the exhilaration of finally fucking someone stronger than her, she rested on her elbows as he ripped off the rest of their clothes. Hoping to entice him, she lifted her ass in the air, wriggling as he uttered a deep groan.

"Were you laughing?" he grumbled, gripping one globe of her ass in each hand and squeezing.

Nodding, she bit her lip. "You're the first man who's ever tossed me around in bed. I love that you're stronger than me—"

"No one's stronger than you" was his soft reply as he leaned forward and whispered in her ear. "You're the strongest person I've ever known, Ari."

Tears stung her eyes at the heartfelt words. "I meant physically."

Cold air washed over her ass cheek before she felt a sharp sting. Her body lurched forward as pleasure coursed through her frame.

"Mine," he gritted, his palm crashing against her burning skin yet again. His palm whacked her ass before he smoothed it, causing moisture to rush between her thighs.

"*Oh god...*" she moaned, squirming atop the comforter. "Do the other one."

His deep chuckle surrounded her as he began to smack her other cheek. Closing her eyes, Arianna gave in to the pleasure as wetness gushed down her inner thighs. To say she'd never been so aroused was an understatement.

"Look at this glistening pussy," he murmured, gripping her ass and spreading her wide. Placing two fingers against her core, he dragged them back and forth over her quivering folds. "Tell me to fuck you."

"Good lord, fuck me," she cried, clenching the covers. "I didn't think you needed an invitation at this point—"

His cock slammed inside her, filling every crevice as he aligned his chest with her back. The tiny hairs on his pecs scratched the sensitive skin of her upper back, the sensation adding to the sense of fullness from having his hard cock so deep inside her.

"I'm going to fuck you so deep you feel me in your bones," he rasped, jutting inside her with forceful strokes, the tip of his cock hitting the spot deep within that no one else ever had.

"I didn't think I could come this way..." she moaned, her fingers gripping the bed so hard she thought they might crack. "Not until you..."

"Because you were made for me, Ari," he grunted, maintaining the maddening pace as he stimulated her G-spot with every thrust.

Stars exploded behind her eyelids as she opened wider, aching for everything he could give her.

"There's my good girl." Warm breath flitted around the shell of her ear, the praise sending a jolt of elation through her frame and a fresh gush of arousal to douse his cock.

"I'm close," she whimpered, barely able to speak as the orgasm loomed on the horizon. "Fuck, Dom...it's *so good*..."

He groaned, resting more weight on her as he continued the deep, maddening strokes. Resting his forehead against her temple, he bit her earlobe, sending her headlong into a blistering climax.

Deep convulsions ripped through her core—deeper than she'd ever felt—and her spasming muscles dragged him deeper, choking his cock as he breathed her name.

"So fucking tight," he moaned, sweat dripping from his body to coat hers as she drowned in the abyss. "You're draining me...*oh god*...I can't stop it..."

He exploded seconds after pulling out, coating her lower back with pulsing jets of release. Overcome with pleasure and elation at how free she felt with him, she began to laugh, the sound joyous as her body quaked underneath his. Burying his face in her neck, he gripped her shoulders, searching for a stronghold. His strong frame trembled as he sighed her name, his body shuddering with every pulse. When he was finally spent, he collapsed against her, breathing labored huffs in her ear as she giggled beneath.

"Good grief, you're giggling," he droned, rubbing his nose against the sensitive skin behind her ear. "Since when do you giggle?"

"Since you fucked me senseless," she murmured, the words garbled since her cheek was pressed against the bed. "I usually need my clit...you know...but you got it done. I can't really talk right now, but you get the gist."

"I know." Placing a sweet peck on her nape, he sank into her, slowly relaxing as they recovered. "It's all part of my master plan to make you fall madly in love with me."

"Is that so?" she teased, aware of how the organ in her chest slammed at his words.

"Mmm hmm."

Lying there, entwined in sweaty, sated bliss, she debated telling him she'd loved him as long as she'd known him. Deciding her brain was too mushy and she wasn't quite ready, she relaxed and snuggled into him instead.

His calloused palm trailed lazily over her still-stinging butt cheek, and she smiled at the possessive yet tender strokes. "You really went for it with the spanking, Dom. Geez."

Full lips curved against her nape. "Did you like it?"

"Oh, hell yes. And I liked sucking you too. Next time, I'll let you deep throat me."

His sated shaft jerked against her back, causing her to snicker. "Guess your dick likes that idea too."

"Oh, yeah, he likes it," Dominic murmured, kissing a trail from her neck to her ear. "And I've seen you swim in the pond behind the school, so I know how long you can hold your breath. Lucky me."

Tossing back her head, she broke into harmonious laughter, unable to squelch the joy of being in his arms. His deep laughter entwined with hers, and for one moment, Arianna allowed herself to be blissfully, unapologetically happy.

A blunt finger tapped her neck, and she turned her head to stare into those deep eyes. "Yes?"

His gaze was intense as he cupped her jaw, gently stroking her cheek as he swallowed thickly. Was he...nervous?

"I want to come inside you when we do this, Ari. No more pulling out and no more condoms."

Her eyes widened as she digested the words. "I can't fight if I'm pregnant, Dom."

"Then I'll fight for you."

Swallowing the lump in her throat, she shook her head. "I can't put that burden on you. You need me. Dani needs me. The *cause* needs me."

Strong fingers stroked her cheek as he spoke in a low, soothing tone. "I desperately need you, but you also deserve to be happy. You'll be forty soon, and tomorrows are never guaranteed in this world."

"Thanks for the reminder I'm washed up," she teased, rolling her eyes.

Dominic breathed a laugh. "We're both washed up, and that means we've lived long enough to know that we have to seize happiness." He brushed a tender kiss across her lips. "Let me give you a baby, sweetheart." His expression was so genuine it almost shattered her heart. "I want to give you everything."

Flattening her lips, she struggled to keep the tears that clouded her eyes from falling. "Dominic," she whispered, slowly shaking her head on the mattress. "This is a huge decision."

"What decision? Between me or the turkey baster? I'm really hoping I have a slight edge in that competition." He squished his features, looking adorable as he waited for her answer.

Exhaling a long breath, she shifted and pulled him closer. Gliding her leg over his thigh, she contemplated him, struggling to control the heartbeat that pulsed in every cell of her body.

Cupping his jaw, she stroked her thumb over his lips. "If you give me a baby, I'm going to want forever. And no one's ever lasted forever with me. I'm not sure I'm built for that."

"Bullshit." Gliding his palm over her ass, he squeezed. "You just haven't met anyone who's built to spend forever with you. Until me."

A stupid tear fell, making her feel clumsy and vulnerable as she tried to keep her emotions in check. "I'm not ready," she said, wondering when her voice had turned to gravel. "It's too much for me, Dom."

A smile tugged at the edges of his firm lips. "God, you're so pretty when you cry," he said, swiping the tear from her cheek.

Scoffing, she rolled her eyes. "I look like a punching bag when I cry. Most men would think it's gross."

"Which men? Because this man thinks you're stunning." He squeezed her ass again as he smiled. "And this man wants to have a baby with you." His other hand grazed over her cheek as his eyes bore into hers. "This man *loves* you, Ari. If you won't say it, I'll say it. I don't want to be a shell of a person anymore. You make me want more."

Scattered breaths left her lungs as she digested his poignant words. "Dom…"

"It's okay, sweetheart," he said, drawing her close and pressing her face to his chest. "If you're not ready to say it, I'll say it for both of us until you are."

Chapter 34

Dominic held his strong, gorgeous woman as her body trembled against his chest. Suddenly, she began to cry, sobs racking her frame as she finally let emotion surge past her thick walls. Joy flooded every crevice of his body as he closed his eyes, soaking up all her past heartache and pain. Her breakdown was messy...and raw...and *glorious*, and he treasured the opportunity to finally support the woman who unselfishly supported everyone else.

"I've got you," he soothed, stroking her cooling skin as she shuddered in his arms. "Falling in love doesn't have to be a disaster."

"I swore I wasn't going to let this happen," she mumbled against his chest.

Chuckling at her stubbornness, he rubbed his chin atop her head. "Hard to believe two bastards like us fear something as basic as human emotion. But here we are."

"Speak for yourself," she said, lifting her head and swiping her arm under her nose. "I'm not a bastard. I'm practical."

"You're fucking terrified, Arianna. I'd chide you for it if I wasn't dead set on finishing this conversation and earning your trust." He slid his hand over her braid. "And seeing you open and vulnerable like this, knowing it's a side you rarely show, makes me feel like a goddamned superhero."

Wet eyes roved over his face, the hues of green and brown stunning in the small shaft of light from the lamp atop the desk. "You really do love me," she breathed.

An exasperated huff leapt from his throat. "Do you think I throw those words around often? Of course I love you, woman. How do you not know that?"

"Even though I drive you crazy half the time?"

Chuckling, he caressed her damp cheek. "*Because* you drive me crazy. You keep me on my toes and I need that. You present a challenge that I'll conquer every day if you let me."

Relaxing into the bed, she gazed up at him, licking her lips and jolting his cock as he mentally prepared for round two. *After* he'd consoled her, of course. She was opening up to him, but she was also pressed against him—sated and pliant—and he was only a man, after all.

"And you'd be happy living off the grid? I'm talking a cabin deep in the mountains where no one will bother us. Once we save the world, obviously."

Grinning, he nodded.

"It's not the most exciting life—"

Placing his fingers over her lips, he cut her off. "Every second with you is exciting, Ari. Infuriating and frustrating...but also very exciting," he finished with a wink.

Her wide smile shot a crack down the heart that she alone had repaired. The heart he'd reopened just for her.

"It won't be easy. We barely tolerate each other sometimes."

"Until we started fucking. Then you became pretty agreeable."

Narrowing her eyes, she muttered, "Idiot. Thinks his cock makes me agreeable."

Catching her off guard, he snaked over her body, drawing her arms above her head and securing them with one hand. Gently placing his other hand around her neck, he softly squeezed.

"This is the only way I want to strangle you anymore. With that luscious body beneath me as you scream my name."

Desire lit her eyes as she pushed into his hand. God, this woman would be his undoing. Her acquiescence to his dominance pushed every button embedded in his soul. He fucking loved knowing he was the only person in the world Arianna submitted to.

"And if you're not ready to say the words, I'll accept that. For now." He grazed a kiss across her lips. "But I'm going to give you a baby, Arianna. And we're going to raise it together on the side of some fucking mountain if that's what you want. Mark my words. Once we finish our mission, that's what I aim to accomplish."

The dash of vulnerability returned to her eyes, slight but noticeable as she swallowed thickly beneath his palm. "I'm afraid I won't make you happy. That I won't be...*enough* to make you stay. And it's hard for me to say that because I'm confident and it goes against my nature to doubt myself. But, with you, it's important I get it out there. I won't allow myself to enter into something that's going to fail. I've learned how painful that is and I won't do it again."

"Then we won't fail." Sliding his hand from her neck to her jaw, he stared into her eyes, showing her his resolve. "I think we can do anything as long as we do it together. And I think you do too."

"I had my doubts...but I'm coming around." Forming a sultry grin, she glided her calf over his hairy thigh. "And even though I'm a sticky mess and this has been the longest day in history, I think I have a small amount of energy left."

"Sleep is overrated," he muttered before pressing his lips to hers in a heated kiss.

Much later, when they lay sprawled on the bed after another round of epic lovemaking, Dominic held her atop his body as they panted from exertion.

"I'm too old for this," she mumbled against his chest. "You're not supposed to have the best sex of your life at forty."

"Am I the best you've ever had?" he asked, elated at the sentiment while simultaneously feeling his ego soar.

"By a damn longshot." Pressing her elbow into his chest, she rested her cheek on her fist.

"Better than the turkey baster?" Dominic teased.

"Asshole."

His deep laugh reverberated around them as he drew lazy patterns on her back. Suddenly, she slithered over him, cupping both of his cheeks as she gazed into his eyes.

"Fuck it," she whispered, shaking her head. "I'm tired of being scared too." Running her finger over his lips, she inhaled a shaky breath. "I love you, Dominic. I've loved you since you stepped on my toes at Dani's wedding."

His palm splayed across her lower back as he grinned. "I'm still going to make that up to you."

"I loved you when we started this mission together. I loved you that night we took the food to the kids by the campfire near the farmhouse."

"I think I loved you that night too," he said, running his knuckles over her jaw. "You were determined to help those kids, and I was determined to help *you*."

Her eyebrow arched. "It was annoying. I wanted to go by myself, but you're a stubborn son of a bitch."

His lips twitched before his gaze grew solemn. "I'm sorry I was too stupid to realize my feelings for you then. I'm sorry I hurt you, Arianna."

"I know." Nestling against him, she rested her cheek on his chest. "And I love you for saying that too."

"Well, it's pretty apparent we love each other. What do we do now?"

Her fingernails dug into his chest, directly over his heart, as if she were claiming it as her own. "We help Arthur and Dani save the world, have some babies and live happily ever after."

"And get married," he said, caressing her braid.

"Fine." She yawned, her voice growing sleepy as she relaxed against him. "But I don't need a ring. Just give me a gun or a weapon. Any weapon will suffice."

And that, Dominic thought as he curled his arms around her, was exactly why he loved Arianna Lawson. His brave, loyal soldier, and the woman who'd finally dragged him out of his self-imposed shell.

Holding her tight, he whispered promises in her ear as she drifted on his chest, knowing the rest of his life would be fuller just because she was in it.

Together, they would fight to free the world from oppression and addiction. When they succeeded, Dominic would finally build a life worthy of the one his sister and parents wished for him.

Because of Arianna, he would have the future he deserved.

Grateful, he vowed to love her in the way she should've always been loved: completely. Utterly. Forever.

A valiant oath for the amazing woman who would share the rest of his days by his side and deep in his heart.

Epilogue

Three weeks later

Tristan crept through the woods that surrounded the small cabin in rural Pennsylvania. Two soldiers marched behind him, both of whom had grudges against Luthor Cromwell. Tristan didn't necessarily consider them friends—after all, his social skills had been garbage since the world turned to shit and he'd become obsessed with killing Luthor. But they all shared the same cause, and that was enough for Tristan.

Glancing back, he made eye contact with both men, silently commanding them to follow. They approached the house, and Tristan tested the first stair with his toe, grimacing when it creaked.

Gesturing toward the door with his head, he indicated his intent to strike. Both men nodded, and Tristan forged ahead.

After cresting the rickety stairs, he kicked open the door, rifle clutched in his hands as he rushed inside.

"Hands up!" he called, quickly scanning the room. Two men stood by a desk at the far end of the room beside a blazing stone fireplace. Two more exited what he assumed was the kitchen, halting as their eyes grew wide.

The men by the desk faced him and drew their guns from their holsters. Tristan looked directly into Zayne Danvers's eyes, shock pervading his system at the knowledge he'd finally located him.

Golden hair flashed beside Zayne as the woman behind the desk lifted her gaze to his, annoyance in the deep blue orbs. Tristan's heart lurched with relief that she was still alive.

"Grace," he breathed, walking slowly but purposefully toward her, unfazed by the men with guns aimed at his chest. "If you hurt her, I swear to god—"

"Tristan," she said, her voice calm beneath the ringing that raged in his ears. "Put the rifle down."

Clenching his teeth, he stopped two feet from the desk, aiming the barrel at Zayne's chest. "Let. Her. Go."

Zayne looked at Grace, eyebrows lifting as he seemed to silently ask her permission.

Sighing, she rose, her face an impassive mask as she approached Tristan. Drawing closer, she stopped only inches from him and placed her index finger on the rifle. Gently pushing it down, she leaned forward.

"What the hell are you doing?" she hissed.

Tristan's throat bobbed as confusion coursed through him. "I'm rescuing you."

A breathy laugh escaped her throat before she pinched the bridge of her nose in apparent frustration.

"My men and I can take them, Grace. Let me help you—"

"Stop talking," she interrupted.

"Grace—"

"You oblivious fool," she said, fire flashing in her gorgeous eyes. "Do I look like I need to be rescued?"

Bristling, he glanced around the room.

"You could never get out of your own way, Tristan. Still, after all this time." Stepping forward, she pushed his gun aside. Crowding his space, her scent overwhelmed him as she stared into his eyes.

"You daft man. I never needed saving. Don't you see?"

Tristan's eyes widened as realization finally clicked into place.

Thrusting her chin forward, she spoke with the regality of a queen and the strength of a warrior. "Darling, *I'm* the one leading the rebellion."

Before You Go

Well, lovely readers, I had to do it. If you've read my books or followed me for a while, you know I LOVE a good twist. And man, that one was a doozy, right? Who knew Grace had it in her? I hope you're as excited to discover the conclusion to this trilogy as I was when I envisioned this story arc and began writing it!

In the next book, Fated Salvation, our tortured, morally gray hero Tristan and rebellion leader Grace are going to try and find their happy ending while helping Dani, Maverick, Arianna and Dominic save the world. I hope they succeed!

Thank you for coming on this journey with me and loving these characters as much as I do. Arianna and Dominic are some of my favorite characters I've EVER written, and I adored writing their story. Wishing you lots of happy reading and may you continue to find YOUR HEA in this crazy, intense world we all inhabit together. Reading has always been an escape for me, and it warms my heart that you spend your time and money to escape with these characters I love too. *–Rebecca*

Want to read another steamy dystopian box set? Check out my **Prevent the Past** trilogy!

Fated Salvation

The Sendaxa Chronicles, Book 3

By

REBECCA HEFNER

For everyone who supported this steamy dystopian trilogy. Thank you from the bottom of my heart. I love writing these books and am honored you spend your time and money to read them. I hope Dani, Arianna, Grace and their team save the world! Happy reading!

Part I – The Past

Chapter 1

Over ten years before the events of Scorched Redemption...

G race Albright never forgot the day she met Tristan Holder. Everything about that day—from the scent of the burning birthday candles to the sound of popping champagne corks—was embedded deep in her soul.

Her father had organized an elaborate twenty-fifth birthday party for her, and it was endearingly over-the-top, as were most things Robert Albright did for his daughter.

"What's the point in being rich if we don't spend it, dear?" her father would ask, love shining in his eyes as he patted Grace's shoulder. "And Mom would want me to take care of you. She'd be thrilled that I make you smile."

"You *spoil* me, Dad," Grace said, her smile kind since she loved him more than anyone in the world. "Mom would probably say you're making me soft."

"Soft," he said with a *pfft*. "Never. My daughter has balls of steel."

"I don't have balls at all, and don't talk like that at the party tonight. Your rich friends might faint from shock."

"Screw 'em." Robert winked. "I say what I want, and I'll spoil my daughter whenever I want. Lawrence will be here at seven, so make sure you're ready," he said, referencing their driver.

"Ten-four," Grace responded with a salute.

As she dressed for the party, Grace took a moment to reflect on turning a year older. Sometimes, she felt old. After all, most of her friends were already married to their country club husbands, and several had children.

Other times, she felt young, reminding herself she had her entire life ahead of her. Determined to seize the moment, she dressed in a gorgeous green gown that hugged her breasts and the curve of her hips like a glove. After applying a coat of makeup that accentuated her almond-shaped blue eyes, she regarded herself in the long mirror of the bedroom she still inhabited in her father's Great Falls, Virginia, mansion.

"Not bad," she murmured, running her palms over the satin of the dress. "You don't look a day over twenty-four." Snickering at the sentiment, she grabbed her clutch and headed downstairs to meet the driver.

She made uneventful small talk with her father in the limo and felt her pulse quicken as they approached the restaurant.

"Dad! The parking lot is full. How many people did you invite?"

"All your friends, and all of mine. Why waste a perfectly good party?"

"Is Luthor coming?"

"Of course," Robert said with a nod. "He's my most important client and thinks of you as a daughter, Grace."

Grace pursed her lips, biting her retort so she didn't upset him. In truth, she found Luthor to be skeevy and disingenuous, and something about him always made her feel uneasy. But his business relationship with her father was responsible for their lavish lifestyle, so she remained silent as they pulled into the parking lot.

"I also hired extra security at Luthor's request. He's paranoid now that he's the tenth richest man in the world, and thinks everyone is out to get him." Robert arched a sardonic eyebrow. "So, if you see any men with guns holstered to their belts lurking in dark corners, that's why."

"I'll try not to get shot," Grace murmured drolly as she exited the limo.

Her father smiled as he walked to her side, offering his arm. "You look beautiful, dear. Your mother would be proud."

"Thanks, Dad." Grace lifted her chin in the regal way she'd been taught from countless hours of etiquette lessons. Her mom had insisted on them, reminding Grace that acceptance into the upper echelons of society was never guaranteed. One must act refined and proper to exist in their lavish world.

Grace always thought the lessons a bit ridiculous, but she also enjoyed the spoils of her father's wealth, so she bit her tongue and did her duty. Her mother had passed away several years ago from a brain aneurism, leaving Grace as the matriarch of the family. While other women her age spent their nights dancing in dark, pulsing nightclubs, Grace spent most of her time accompanying her father to charity galas and fundraisers. Others might have found it boring, but Grace hadn't yet found her purpose in life, and going to fancy parties was familiar, so she figured she'd continue the status quo until something in her life changed.

Little did she know, it would be that evening.

She entered the party on her father's arm, noting the lavish decorations and balloons. Robert had tasked his assistant with hiring a decorator, and the room sparkled in her favorite colors—gold and green.

A band played in the far corner of the room, the music filling the room with a soft beat that was drowned out by the cheers at their entrance.

"Grace, you look stunning!" her friend Margaret said, rushing toward her and encircling her wrists. "You might just find a husband tonight."

"I'm more concerned with finding the bar," Grace replied, glancing toward the far wall. "Come on, let's get some champagne."

Margaret nodded and beckoned to her husband, Charles, who followed her like a puppy. Grace thought him incredibly boring—as were most men who ran in their circles—and she had no desire to tie herself to one of them any time soon.

After securing a glass of chilled champagne, Grace began her rounds. She understood her duty—smile, nod, and be cordial. Appearances were meaningful in her father's world, and she aspired to please him. Although she didn't necessarily crave his approval, she did crave his love. He was the only person she'd ever truly been close to, besides her dear mother, and she had an inherent desire to see him happy. Traveling in their societal circles brought him joy, so she'd continue to play her role.

Sure, it was lonely sometimes. Grace had no idea why she had trouble connecting with people. She considered herself smart and polite, and perfectly capable of interesting conversation. A casual observer would probably think she had several close friends.

But Grace was also aloof, sometimes feeling adrift in a world that seemed so big but somehow small at the same time. She often found herself wondering why people in her wealthy circles didn't want *more*. Despite all the charity galas and fundraisers, most people she knew didn't actually do anything else to change the world. Giving money was one thing, but action was another. Perhaps when she got a bit older, she could set the example by implementing positive change in the world.

For now, she pushed away the thoughts in order to mingle with the partygoers.

After two hours, Grace felt restless, yearning for a break from talking about yachts and trips to Greece. Craving fresh air, she ordered a refill on her champagne and slipped outside onto the restaurant's second-floor terrace.

The stars twinkled above as she rested her forearms on the cool stone of the terrace wall. Sighing, she closed her eyes and listened to the faint humming that leaked from the restaurant's main room. Something shuffled behind her and she whirled around, narrowing her eyes to scan the darkened corner behind her.

"Is someone there? I thought I was alone."

A man stepped forward, hazel-green eyes flashing in the moonlight as he lifted his chin. His shoulders were broad and a black holster rested at his belt. He was dressed in a black suit, his hands crossed above his belt buckle as he regarded her.

"I'm one of the security personnel your father hired tonight," he said, his deep voice possessing a gravel-laden tone that made her shiver. "I saw you slip outside and wanted to make sure you weren't alone."

Her eyes darted between his as her pulse pounded, although she wasn't sure if it was from surprise or...something else. His gaze was piercing as he regarded her, and it made her slightly uncomfortable. Heat crept up her neck as she stared back, wondering if he would break first.

The stubborn bastard stood firm, drilling her with those limitless eyes, before he smirked.

"Well, this might be the most enthralling staring contest I've ever had," he drawled, arching an eyebrow. The gesture made him appear incredibly sexy in the dim light, and Grace cleared her throat.

"It's rude to stare," she said, thrusting up her chin.

He just shrugged a dismissive shoulder.

"You can go inside," she continued. "I assure you, I'm perfectly safe. This restaurant is one of the nicest in Virginia and the only threats to my life are the dreadfully boring conversations I'm forced to have with the area's elite."

His eyes widened with surprise. "Aren't you one of the elites?"

"Yes." Her lips fluttered as she expelled a slightly exasperated breath. "Maybe the worst kind of all. I'm an elite who thinks I'm still down to earth."

A low chuckle left his throat, surrounding Grace in a blanket of warmth that caused bumps to rise along the sensitive skin of her nape. She slowly lifted her hand to rub the tiny pricks, aware that the mysterious man's eyes traveled to where her fingers caressed her skin. A sizzling energy vibrated between them, his nostrils flaring as he observed her.

Something raw and animalistic curled in her belly, and she realized it was lust. For the first time in her quarter-century on Earth, Grace felt the unassuageable tug of pure, unchecked desire.

"I don't think—"

"You're not supposed to think on your birthday," he interrupted, shifting his weight from one foot to the other. Grace's eyes roved over his tall frame, and she licked her suddenly parched lips.

"I don't have the luxury of making impulsive decisions. I think about everything."

He glanced over his shoulder to the main room where the Great Falls aristocrats laughed and mingled. Turning back, he tilted his head. "Seems to me like you have all the luxury in the world."

"The prettiest illusions are always the easiest to believe," she said, lowering her arm from her neck to wipe away the chill upon her forearm.

He took a step forward, causing Grace's spine to straighten.

"Don't bristle, little empress," he said, assessing her. "I'm just taking another look at you. If you're an illusion, I want the whole mirage."

"Empress?" she scoffed, unable to control her smile.

"Well, aren't you? All these people are here to celebrate you tonight."

Grace bit her lip as she contemplated. "I think they're all here to celebrate my father. My birthday is just the occasion."

"And is there a 'Mr. Empress?'" he asked, his tone filled with mirth and curiosity.

"No."

His eyebrows lifted slightly. "No one with a fancy boat or a portfolio full of condos waiting in the wings."

Grace's lips thinned. "Most of the eligible men I meet are about as exciting as watching eggs boil."

"Maybe you should slum with the rest of us sometimes. We're not so bad."

Breathing a laugh, she nodded. "Maybe I should."

Her breath caught when he took another step closer, the warmth from his body tangible against hers as he gazed into her eyes. He was several inches taller, and Grace tilted her head, forcing herself to meet his gaze. In other situations, she might have backed down, but for some reason, she felt a need to respond to the slight challenge in his eyes as he loomed over her.

"Damn…" he whispered, placing the backs of his fingers against her jawline. Slowly, he traced the skin there, and Grace felt her knees buckle.

"You're not what I expected, empress," he said, the tender movements of his fingers against her jaw mesmerizing. "If you know what's good for you, you'll head back inside before I show you how fun it can be to join the peasants." Leaning closer, his breath washed over her cheeks. "Or maybe that's what you secretly want."

Grace couldn't deny that she desperately wanted him to kiss her. Never had she felt the pull of consuming desire like this. Hell, she'd only had two boyfriends—one in high school and one in college—and both had been terrible in bed. She was sure neither one even knew a woman possessed the ability to orgasm.

But this man? Somehow, Grace knew that he would know *exactly* what to do with her trembling body. He would know how to find the sensitive little pearl that was now throbbing between her legs. His lips would understand how to travel over every inch of her body. And those long fingers… God, they would probably set her on fire.

"I see the dirty thoughts swirling in those pretty eyes, Grace," he whispered, sliding his fingers under her chin. Tilting her head back, he brushed his lips over hers. The touch was feather-soft, but it elicited a lusty purr from deep in her throat.

"Tell me to stop," he murmured.

Grace remained silent, her body thrumming as she contemplated whether to kiss him back or ask him to release her.

Resting his forehead against hers, he sighed. "I'm on duty, so I have to let you go." His teeth gently nipped her lip before he drew back and released her.

Grace felt the loss of his warmth in every cell of her skin.

"As much as I want to kiss you, I need this job and can't chance your dad finding us in a precarious position."

"I'm an adult and can kiss a man without my father's permission," she said, her tone regal since she was slightly offended.

His slight smirk indicated he believed otherwise, and she straightened her shoulders, embarrassed at her reaction toward him. Aiming to dismiss him, she pivoted and headed back toward the terrace doors.

"It's Tristan Holder," he called, a knowing lilt in his voice as she halted and looked back over her shoulder. "For when you come looking for me—if you're brave enough to leave Daddy's mansion."

Shooting him a glare, she planted a hand on her hip. "Screw you. I could have you fired."

His resulting smile turned his face into something so sexy Grace could feel the heat intensify deep in her core.

"See you around, empress."

Giving him her best look of disgust, she whirled around and reentered the party.

An hour later, Tristan Holder was still on her mind.

When she arrived home after midnight, he'd somehow overtaken every thought in her addled brain as she brushed her teeth and washed her face.

As the early morning light streamed through her bedroom window, Grace awoke, sweaty and groggy from a restless night full of dreams of her sexy, and undeniably rude, hazel-eyed stranger.

"Why were his lips so soft anyway?" she muttered, punching her pillow. "Guys aren't supposed to have soft lips."

But Tristan had. They were somehow soft *and* firm, and as the week wore on, she couldn't stop thinking about having them on every inch of her body.

By Friday, Grace resigned herself to the fact she would never get Tristan Holder out of her mind unless she saw him again. He'd twisted something inside her, and she needed to set it right. While her father was at work, she tiptoed into his office, not wanting the housekeeper to see her.

Shuffling through the documents, she scrolled the wheel on the mouse. In the folder labeled "Grace's 25 Birthday Party," she found a spreadsheet of all the vendors.

"Trident Security Services," she whispered, accessing the company's phone number and dialing. It rang twice before a polite woman answered.

"Uh, hi. I'm looking for one of your security personnel, Tristan Holder. He performed private security for a birthday party organized by Robert Albright last week. I think he left his...er...wallet on the terrace and I wanted to return it to him."

"Oh, that's nice of you," the receptionist chimed. "Let me give you our address and you can mail it to us."

"I was hoping I could speak to him first. Just to, um, you know, verify it's his. His license isn't inside, but there are some other identifying pieces of information."

The receptionist paused. "We can't give out our employees' information, but if you want to email me the info, I'll be happy to ask him."

Sighing, Grace rubbed her forehead. "It's fine. Sorry to bother you."

Feeling like an idiot, Grace hung up the phone.

"He left his wallet? A week ago? For god's sake, Grace. That's ridiculous." Rising from her father's desk, she stuffed her phone in her pocket and wrung her hands. "Let it go. You're two people from completely different worlds, and you'll eventually stop thinking about him. He was just...*hot*," she continued, talking to herself as she exited her father's office and trailed down the marble-floored hallway. "There are plenty of other men to obsess over. Get a grip."

Determined to move on, she plopped on the couch and turned on the latest episode of *Real Housewives*, hoping the diversion would rid the enigmatic man from her mind.

Twenty minutes later, her phone buzzed. Drawing it from her pocket, she gasped at the text message.

Unknown Number: I told you you'd come looking for me.

Furious, Grace gritted her teeth.

Grace: I don't know who this is or what you're talking about.

Sweat beaded at her temple as the text bubble appeared.

Unknown Number: Liar.

"That arrogant son of a bitch..." She quickly saved his number before her thumbs moved furiously over the keyboard as she typed.

Grace: Don't text me again or I'll call the police.

Tristan responded with an eyeroll emoji.

Tristan: Are you always this dramatic?

A surprised laugh left Grace's lips.

Grace: I'm not dramatic. And leave me alone.

He didn't respond for several minutes, causing Grace to frown at the thought that he might actually obey her order. Then another text appeared.

Tristan: If you want to see me again, all you have to do is ask.

Grace: How did you get my number? I'm pretty sure that's illegal.

Tristan: I'm in security, and we have a log of everyone who calls the firm. It wasn't hard.

Grace: I could get you fired for stalking me.

Tristan: Says the woman who needs to return my "wallet."

Grace emitted a frustrated groan.

Grace: Forget it. I never want to see you again. I had a momentary lapse in judgment. Goodbye.

Several more minutes passed before another text appeared.

Tristan: 345 Dogwood Lane, Apartment 7, Sterling, VA. If you're brave enough. I'm off on Sunday. If not, I'll lose your number. The ball's in your court, empress.

Grace pulled up the address on her phone, noting it was in the next town over. She'd planned to spend Sunday at the club playing tennis with the kids. She'd played in high school and liked to help the instructors when they held their Sunday lessons. She didn't get paid, but she didn't need the money and it allowed her to give back, if only a little.

Or...she could tell the club's pro that something had come up.

"You can't go to his house alone!" she squeaked to herself. "He could be a serial killer!"

Telling herself she'd become delusional since meeting the sexy stranger, she dismissed the idea of visiting him at all.

And promised herself she'd stick to that decision.

Which definitely made her the liar Tristan had called her when she pulled up the rideshare app on Sunday morning and hailed a car to his apartment.

Her heart pounded furiously in her chest the entire ride, and she told herself a hundred times she was crazy for visiting a stranger's home without telling her father where she'd gone. He was on a fishing trip for the weekend, so as far as he knew, she was at the club.

After the driver dropped her off, Grace rubbed her wet palms on her pristine slacks and walked down the slightly cracked concrete walkway that led to Tristan's building entrance. She located his unit number and rang the bell with shaking fingers.

"Yes?" his deep baritone chimed over the speaker.

Grace stood frozen, unable to speak as she struggled to breathe.

His sultry chuckle echoed through the speaker, both infuriating her and sending little shivers of desire over her rapidly heating skin.

"It's on the second floor, empress."

The buzzer on the front door sounded, jolting Grace as she faced the entrance. Swallowing thickly, she pushed the heavy door open and headed toward the stairs.

Wondering if she was making the worst decision of her life...

And reminding herself she didn't kiss men she didn't know...

Even if the man who awaited her inside was the sexiest man she'd ever met in her affluent but sheltered life.

CHAPTER 2

G race walked up the stairs, telling herself not to be a snob. The rickety steps desperately needed cleaning, and a dead bug greeted her as she crested the second floor, but not everyone had a live-in housekeeper. Although the building was a bit dingy, it wasn't squalid. And after all, was she really here for the décor?

"What in the hell *are* you doing here?" she muttered, rapping on the door as her heart threatened to burst from her chest.

Tristan slowly opened the door, the hinges creaking as he loomed in the doorway.

"I wasn't expecting company," he drawled, cocking a brow as Grace's eyes traveled over his bare chest and down to gray sweatpants above his bare feet.

"Well, you could've thrown on a shirt since you knew I was here," she said, annoyance in her tone.

"Where's the fun in that?" Opening the door wider, he gestured her inside. "I promise I won't bite—unless you ask."

Grace shot him a glare before breezing past him. The interior was small but clean, and she rubbed her wet palms on her jeans as she approached the plaid-covered couch. "Should I sit here?"

"Sure. Want a drink? I've got light beer, shitty wine, bottled water or whiskey."

"Water is fine. Thank you."

He disappeared through a doorway that must've led to his bedroom, because he reemerged a few moments later wearing a t-shirt. Grace frowned, silently admitting she enjoyed the view without the shirt much better.

Tristan padded over and handed her a water before sitting beside her and popping open his beer. Lifting it, he made a toast. "To slumming it."

Breathing a laugh, Grace tapped her bottle against his. "It's not so bad. And your apartment is very clean. Maybe they can hire you to remove the bugs from the stairway."

His sultry gaze lingered on her as he took a slow sip of his beer. "Yeah. We're not quite up to white-glove standards here."

Smiling, Grace forced herself to relax into the soft cushions. "Some standards are overrated."

Silence lingered as he contemplated her, and Grace was surprised at how...*easy* it was. For some reason, although her body was a frayed mass of nerves, she felt comfortable with Tristan.

"I'll be honest," he said, crossing an ankle over his knee, "I'm not sure what to do here. I don't know what your expectations were when you came here today, but I'll make polite conversation until you're ready to tell me." Tilting his head, he flashed a brilliant smile that made her stomach flutter. "So, Grace Albright, tell me about yourself."

Sighing, she ran a hand through her thick golden tresses, reveling in the desire that flashed in his eyes. "Sadly, there's not much to tell. As you know, I just turned twenty-five, but nothing much has happened to me yet. Maybe I'm here to change that."

His eyebrow lifted slightly.

"Anyway," she continued after taking a huge gulp of water. "I've probably got the same ol' boring rich girl story as every debutante in Great Falls. Wealthy father. Tragically departed mother. Trying my best to figure out life in a world I have no business complaining about but still find incredibly dull."

"I'm sorry to hear about your mom," he said softly.

"Thanks. She died of a brain aneurysm. One day she was vibrant and alive, and the next day, she was gone." Grace snapped her fingers. "It reinforced the importance of seizing each day. That's for damn sure."

Tristan nodded as his foot tapped above his knee.

"And you? Tell me about your family."

"My parents live in a retirement home in Texas. They love the community there and are thrilled to participate in the daily rounds of bridge." His lips twitched. "And I have a sister, Jessica. She's two years younger than me."

"Does she live close by?"

"She's in Florida and engaged to a douchebag who's going to ruin her life. I've given up on trying to stop the wedding. I'll just be here to pick up the pieces when she inevitably gets divorced."

"Well, that's cynical. Maybe it will work out."

Tristan scoffed. "Happy ever after only happens for people like you, empress. The rest of us just do our best while we wait for the other shoe to drop."

The sentiment made her sad, and she shook her head. "Maybe someone will prove you wrong one day. I hope they do."

"We'll see," he murmured, his expression doubtful. Shifting, his gaze grew curious. "So, what's it like to run in Luthor Cromwell's circle? He's up there with Jeff Bezos and Richard Branson. That fancy mansion he lives in must have warm bidet sprays for all his guests."

Tossing back her head, Grace broke into laughter. "He does have bidets, although I can't say if they're warm." She shrugged. "What can I say? He and my dad are close."

"They work together?"

Grace nodded. "My father is the CEO of the largest CDMO in the country—"

"CDMO?" Tristan asked.

"Contract Development and Manufacturing Organization. Companies like my father's help pharmaceutical companies like Sendaxa get drugs to market faster."

"And getting drugs to market faster makes them more money."

"Exactly. There's so much that goes into drug production, from the equipment needed for storage, to the raw chemicals, to setting up distribution channels. My dad helps Sendaxa release drugs quicker and satisfy all the FDA regulations."

"Sendaxa isn't known for adhering to FDA regulations," Tristan said. "That painkiller they released a few years ago was taken off the market."

"Yeah, that was definitely a blunder." Grace rubbed her forehead as she recalled the shitshow that ensued after the drug was recalled. "My dad lost millions in fines, and Sendaxa was fined over a billion dollars."

"All in a day's work for Luthor Cromwell, huh?"

"Sadly, yes. Sendaxa paid the fine and that was it."

"You don't seem particularly...satisfied at the outcome."

Sighing, she bit her lip as she pondered. "I mean, I'm happy Dad was able to just pay a fine and move on. He's a good man and didn't mean any harm."

"And Luthor?"

Grace's teeth fidgeted with her lower lip. "I'm not sure he's as good of a man. The experience seemed to reinforce that he can continue the bad behavior and only get a slap on the wrist."

"To living a life where a billion-dollar fine is considered a slap on the wrist," Tristan joked, lifting his beer.

Chuckling, Grace tapped her water bottle against his. "For real. Anyway, Sendaxa is Dad's most important client, which means Luthor is here to stay. Although he's not my favorite person, I understand his importance to my father's legacy."

"If he's not a good person, couldn't that be detrimental to your father's legacy?"

Shivering, Grace rubbed the bumps that rose on her arm. "Maybe. I hope that doesn't happen."

"There's that unfailing belief in happy endings again. It's in direct contrast to my ever-present pessimism."

Grace smiled, inwardly wondering if she could somehow change his mind one day. After all, being optimistic was a more positive way to life, right? What was wrong with having hope?

Tristan drank the last of his beer and shook it. "I can open another one, or I can pour us both a glass of whiskey. Your call."

Clearing her throat, she contemplated whether it was a good idea to have whiskey at ten a.m. on a Sunday with a stranger in his home.

Moving closer, he leaned toward her and whispered, "I'm not going to roofie it, Grace. Believe me, if we ever get to the point where I touch you, I want you to be perfectly aware of what's going on."

She whipped her head to face him, her nose almost grazing his. "I didn't come here to have sex with you."

A knowing glint flashed in his eyes. "Then have some whiskey with me. You're wound up and it will help you relax."

Her eyes darted between his before she nodded. "Okay."

His lips curved before he rose, striding into the kitchen and returning with two tumblers full of brown liquid.

"Sheesh," Grace said, taking the glass he extended. "What happened to two fingers?"

His eyes turned molten at the double entendre. "Why, Grace, I thought you weren't interested in having sex." The teasing lilt of his voice washed over her, drawing her further into his seductive web.

Grace didn't know much about uncontrollable desire, but this man had a magnetic stronghold over her. The energy that pulsed between them was tangible, and she leaned closer, craving it as warmth emanated from his skin.

"I'm not sure what I'm interested in," she droned, lifting the glass. "Maybe the whiskey will help me decide." Tristan clinked his glass with hers, and she took a hefty gulp.

Grace coughed and sputtered as the whiskey burned her throat. Tristan scooted closer, the side of his body pressing against hers as he patted her back.

"Jesus, woman. You're supposed to sip it." His hand caressed her back in a soothing gesture as tears stung her eyes.

"Fuck it," she whispered before tossing back another swig. "Seize the moment, right?"

Tristan grinned as he shook his head. They drank in comfortable silence until Grace felt the warm liquid coursing through her veins. After a few more gulps, she finished the glass and set it on the table. Emitting a high-pitched hiccup, she rubbed her mouth with her arm.

"That's good. I like whiskey."

"You don't say," he teased, playfully pressing his shoulder into hers. "Do I need to worry about you puking on my cheap couch?"

"Nope." Mesmerized by his strong arms as they rested on his muscular thighs, she slowly reached over and touched one of the tattoos. Emboldened by the alcohol, she gently traced the black ink that formed the shapes of a skull, a snake and an anchor.

"Did they hurt?" she asked, her voice raspy.

"Not really. I'm guessing you don't have any."

"I've always been too afraid of the pain. But with all the whiskey I just drank, maybe it wouldn't be so bad."

Gliding his fingers under her chin, he forced her to meet his gaze. "Since we've decided you didn't come here for sex, maybe you came here so I could convince you to get a tattoo. I can take you to my guy in town. He's got years of experience and will take care of you."

"I can't get a tattoo!" she exclaimed before hiccupping again. "And I'm wasted. That's a terrible time to make decisions."

Tristan arched a sexy brow. "Or maybe it's the *best* time."

Grace stared into his eyes as curiosity welled. What if she actually did something unexpected for once?

"Oh, yeah," he said, tucking a strand of hair behind her hear. "You're going to get your first tattoo today. Let me get dressed and we'll call an Uber." He tossed back the last of his whiskey and disappeared into his room before she could argue.

He emerged two minutes later, looking sexy as hell in jeans, a black t-shirt, and black sneakers. Trailing toward her, he extended his hand as he loomed above her. "Ready?"

Grace resisted the urge to shrink away. Was she actually considering this? It was completely against her nature.

"Come on, empress. Live a little."

Inhaling a deep breath, Grace clutched onto every ounce of courage she possessed and pressed her hand to his.

Chapter 3

Tristan stood beside the tattoo chair, arms crossed against his chest as he pursed his lips. He struggled not to laugh at the gorgeous creature who reclined beneath him, her face a mask of fear and anticipation as she gazed at him with those limitless blue eyes.

"Stop laughing at me!" she demanded, causing his lips to twitch. Damn, she was tougher than she appeared, and he was quickly realizing that the multiple layers of her spitfire personality ignited all sorts of feelings deep within his stoic soul.

When he'd met her on the terrace in the moonlight, his heart had stopped for one soulful moment. His eyes had traveled over her wistful expression, those plump, kissable lips, and farther down to the green dress that hugged every curve. Lust had roared in his brain, and his palms ached to caress those flared hips...

And then she'd turned, and he'd gazed into those azure eyes, and something clicked into place. One solemn, possessive word echoed in his mind as they spoke under the stars. *Mine.*

Tristan had given her his name on a whim. Something about her feisty nature caught him off guard, and he thought there might be a chance she would attempt to track him down.

Albeit, a *small* chance—but he'd been overcome with the need to see her again. To feel the strange, pulsing energy that sizzled between them. He'd never felt anything like it in his life.

When she'd shown up on his doorstep, he'd been surprised and...elated, if he was being honest. Tristan took it as an indication that she was just as curious about the sparks that had flown between them. For someone who was rather unemotional, Tristan found the indisputable connection between them intriguing.

"I'm not laughing at you, empress," he lied. "Take some deep breaths and relax. It will feel better. I thought you were drunk?"

"It's quickly wearing off," she grumbled as the tattoo artist leaned over her, the sound of the buzzing gun causing her to flinch.

"Micah will take good care of you," Tristan said, sliding his palm over hers and squeezing. "Right, man?"

"You bet." Micah gave a nod and got to work, pressing the tattoo gun to the drawing he'd made next to Grace's hip bone.

"That's a painful place to get a tattoo," Tristan said, his eyes darting over the pale skin of her hip. Jealousy flared that Micah had a front row seat to the intimate patch of skin.

"I had to choose a place my father wouldn't see," she said, squeezing her eyes shut against the pain. "He'd kill me if he knew I was doing this."

The tattoo gun buzzed and hummed as her breath grew labored. Threading her fingers through his, she squeezed so tightly Tristan thought he might lose circulation. And still, even through the threat of involuntary amputation, he held tight, wanting to comfort her. There was something about her that inspired a deep-seated need to protect, and Tristan realized he'd have a hard time letting her go when she eventually tired of hanging with the riffraff on the other side of the tracks.

Tristan was a realist, and he knew that rich women like Grace never slummed with his kind for long. Once the excitement wore off, she'd run back to her fancy country club and marry someone named Dennis who teed off at four o'clock every afternoon and then hurried home for two minutes of vanilla missionary-style sex.

But for now, Tristan clutched the hand of the regal beauty he'd met the night of her twenty-fifth birthday. She was his, if only for the moment, and he wouldn't squander his good fortune.

Hell, if he was lucky, he might just kiss those pretty lips.

He wasn't boorish enough to push her into sex. Tristan was too proud to be anyone's mistake or dirty little secret. But he wasn't above tasting that hot, regal mouth while she purred beneath him. He was perfectly fine with taking her home, giving her one last glass of whiskey, and sucking every drop from her sexy lips. Then he'd send her on her way, armed with a tattoo that would ensure she'd never forget their time together.

And maybe, just maybe, she'd come back for another taste before she married ol' Dennis.

Tristan felt his lips curve at the slightly optimistic thought. Perhaps she was already rubbing off on him; his majestic little optimist.

Tristan focused on the ink Micah injected into her skin. He thought she might pick something dainty, like a flower or a fairy, but she'd surprised him and picked a dragon. It was a simple design, with a dragon's head and a long body that ended in a curled tail.

"Why the dragon?" he asked, hoping to distract her from the pain with conversation.

"Because they're misunderstood. They have these built-in defense mechanisms like breathing fire and bony scales, but underneath, they're probably just a little lost like we all are."

The words were lonely, and he wondered how someone as wealthy and pampered as Grace could feel lost.

"I told you," she said, her lips forming a poignant smile. "Pretty illusions."

Tristan smiled back, holding her hand as Micah focused on finishing the job.

An hour later, Grace sat up and chugged the shot Micah handed her. "On the house for surviving your first tattoo. I'm impressed. Thought you were going to puke for a second there, but you proved me wrong."

"It looks so cool," she said, setting down the glass and examining her tattoo before Micah covered it with a bandage. "How long will it take to heal?"

"Use the ointment I recommended a few times a day," Micah said, shaking the tube she'd purchased to take home with her. "You want to clean with sterile, lukewarm water and fragrance-free soap at least twice a day."

"Okay," she said as he patted the bandage to make sure it was secure.

Micah helped her into a sitting position, and she swayed atop the chair. Grasping her shoulders, Tristan steadied her. "You okay?"

"Yeah." She quickly shook her head. "Just gotta get used to the discomfort."

"It will heal in two to three weeks if you follow the regimen," Micah said. "And Tristan can help you. He's gotten a few of these."

Grace pulled her American Express black card from her designer purse. "You take AmEx?"

Micah shot Tristan a droll look. "Where'd you find her, man?"

Laughing, Tristan shook his head. "Don't ask."

"Excuse me," Grace said, shaking the card. "Or would you rather I didn't pay?"

"We take cash here, princess. Nobody in this neighborhood has one of those."

Tristan pulled two hundred dollars from his pocket. "Here you go. Thanks, Micah. Keep the change."

"Always a pleasure," Micah said, standing and stuffing the cash into his back pocket. "I'll be in the back smoking a bowl. Let me know if you need anything before you leave."

"I'll pay you back," Grace said, gazing up at Tristan as she frowned. "I don't usually carry cash."

"Don't worry about it." Grasping her hand, he helped her stand, making sure she was steady on her feet before they called the rideshare back to his place.

As they sat in the back seat of the rideshare, he eyed the hip where she'd gotten the tattoo. "You feeling okay? I probably shouldn't have dared you to do this."

"Honestly?" she asked with a cheeky grin. "I feel amazing! I never do anything like this." Covering his hand atop her thigh, she squeezed. "Thank you. I feel...*free*."

As the warmth from her hand seeped into his, Tristan marveled at the joy on her stunning face. Lost in her brilliant eyes and breathtaking smile, he had the insane thought that nothing else in the world mattered other than making this woman happy.

Recreating the incandescent glow in her expression and the shine of reverent admiration in her eyes was all he cared about.

And that's when Tristan realized that even though he'd only known this woman for a matter of hours in the scheme of things, time was irrelevant when it came to matters of the heart.

Whether he was ready or not, he was falling for a rich debutante he could most likely never have.

And still, although it seemed impossible, his heart thrummed with the uncharacteristically optimistic thought that, perhaps, in some small way, Grace felt the undeniable chemistry between them too.

As they approached his building, she dug her perfectly manicured pink nails into his skin, sending pricks of pleasure-pain through his body as he gazed into her eyes.

In that moment, Tristan was overcome with the agony of ever letting her go.

So, he led her inside and promised himself he'd do everything in his power to make her want to stay.

Chapter 4

Grace followed Tristan inside his apartment, cognizant of the stinging of her freshly minted tattoo. Glancing at her watch, she noted there were hours left before her father would be home around nine p.m. She'd have to make sure she was back when he arrived—otherwise, it would lead to questions she wasn't ready to answer.

For some reason, she wanted to keep her visit with Tristan to herself, if only for the time being. Not because she was ashamed or embarrassed. Instead, it felt nice to have something that only belonged to *her*. Since her mother died, her life had been inexorably tied to her father's and his lavish world, and it was freeing to have something of her own.

Striding to the window, she glanced out toward the courtyard behind Tristan's building. She'd been truthful about not visiting him to sleep with him. That was something she wasn't ready for—yet. But the man occupied several corners of her mind, and she wanted to understand why.

The object of her musings approached, gently pressing his body to hers as he slid an arm around her waist. Grace's eyes fluttered before closing as he tenderly nuzzled her neck.

"I'm guessing we're still on the 'no sex' policy," he murmured, grazing his lips over her nape.

"I don't want to ruin this," she whispered, shaking her head. "I don't even understand it." Lifting her lids, she gazed into his eyes. "Do you?"

His palm flattened over her belly as he drew her tighter against him, the curve of her bottom fitting into the juncture of his thighs as if she were made to fit there.

"No," he rasped, his eyes sweeping her face as he studied her. "It's...intense."

She breathed a laugh. "Yeah. I'm slightly terrified, but that could just be the pain and the booze talking. But I have a couple of hours before I need to go and...I just don't want to leave yet."

"Okay." He glanced out the window. "There's a garden down the street that's pretty if you want to walk there. We could grab some food at the deli along the way. It won't be fancy, but I don't think you were expecting fancy when you searched me out."

"You've really got a chip on your shoulder about me being rich. It's annoying. I can't help what I was born into and I do a lot of charity work." She lifted her chin to emphasize her words. "And I don't look down on people who don't have the same means I do. I was just born lucky where others weren't."

"I have a chip on my shoulder because you're the most beautiful woman I've ever seen and I hate that you're going to leave eventually." Grace's heart slammed at his words. "And once you go, I'm afraid you'll never come back."

Her hand glided over his jaw, his prickly stubble so stark against her softness. "I'll come back."

"That's a lofty promise, empress."

Nodding, she ran her thumb over his bottom lip. "I know. Lock it away because I don't make promises I won't keep."

Tristan nipped her thumb and grinned. "I'll hold you to it. Come on. Let's get you some food. You must be starving."

After stopping at the deli to grab some sandwiches, they strolled to the garden. A flower-covered arch covered the entrance, and Grace found it quite pretty and serene. They walked along the gravel path until they found a bench. Once they were seated and enjoying the sandwiches, Grace surveyed the tiny park.

"Lots of butterflies here," she said in between bites. "I love butterflies."

"I definitely thought you'd go for the butterfly tattoo. You surprised me with the dragon."

"I think I was feeling bold." She flashed a grin. "Maybe I'll get a butterfly on my other hip when I get my next tattoo."

"Told you," Tristan said in that arrogant way that should've pissed her off but she found endearingly sexy. "Once you get one, you become addicted."

Grace grinned as she wiped her hands, thinking of how livid her father would be if he ever discovered the tattoo.

"I guess you're not going to tell your dad about our day together since you're hiding the tattoo."

"I don't plan to tell him...yet," she said, lifting a shoulder. "I love him very much, but he has this idea of who I'm supposed to be. I play the part and it works for us."

"Don't you get tired of pretending?"

Lifting her eyebrows, she pondered. "Yes. I think that's why I came looking for you."

Tristan nodded as he gathered their trash and walked toward the nearby receptacle to toss it in. Returning, he extended his hand. "I'm honored to be someone you don't have to pretend with."

Grace slid her hand in his, allowing him to tug her to her feet before they wandered around the garden. It was a few hundred feet in diameter, and they walked in comfortable silence as she threaded her fingers through his.

"Oh, it's an Olympia Marble butterfly!" she exclaimed, pointing to the white butterfly that perched on a nearby bush. "See the dark marbling on the white wings? They're endangered. One of the charities I volunteer for protects endangered butterflies and moths."

"It's pretty," Tristan said, squeezing her fingers. "Inspiration for your next tattoo."

Grace chuckled, wondering if she'd truly ever have the courage to get another tattoo. She'd settle into her dragon first and see how it healed. "Maybe."

Eventually, Tristan led her back to his apartment and offered her more whiskey. She declined and checked her phone.

"My dad will be back in a few hours. I should probably head back."

Tristan's gaze bored into her, filled with a yearning that shook her to her core. Closing the distance between them, he placed his broad hands on her waist and rested his forehead against hers.

"I don't want you to leave," he whispered. "And I sound like a fucking pansy for saying that, but it's the truth—"

Grace lifted to her toes, pressing her mouth to his and inhaling his words. His hands slid to her backside, cupping her and lifting her into his arms. Her legs wrapped around his waist, her arms encircling his neck as she thrust her tongue into his warm mouth.

Tristan groaned, a low hum that shot down her throat and straight to the core of raw energy buzzing deep within her rapidly heating body. He carried her into his bedroom, placing her on the bed as he devoured her mouth.

"I won't fuck you," he rasped, thrusting his fingers in her hair and twining the tresses around them as he tugged. "But I need this. I need to taste you, empress. Please let me taste you."

"Yes..." she cried, tossing her head back on the soft comforter as he nibbled her lips...and the skin that covered her collarbone...before moving lower and dragging her shirt and bra from her trembling body.

Those full, skillful lips tasted every inch of her straining frame. He tasted her tight nipples, budded into sensitive points when they hit the cool air...and then relieved when his silken tongue lapped and sucked...

And then he moved lower, dipping his tongue into her navel before he deftly unzipped her jeans and tossed them aside. He pressed tender kisses to the sensitive skin beside the bandage that covered her new tattoo. Groaning, he almost tore the scrap of lace that covered her core as he yanked it from her legs before burying his face in her dripping center.

Her sexy lover worked his tongue and fingers over the straining little bud between her legs as Grace begged for more. Spearing her fingers in his thick hair, she pulled him closer, pushing into his wanton mouth as he growled with lust.

There in a nondescript apartment with a man she barely knew but somehow trusted implicitly, Grace experienced her first earth-shattering orgasm from a lover.

After exploding beneath him, she struggled to contain the convulsions that rocked her ravaged frame. Tristan blew on her wet, ravaged core before placing soft kisses along the flesh. Slithering over her, he removed his shirt and pants and threw his thick leg over her still-trembling thighs.

"You took off your clothes," she droned, wondering how she was still able to speak.

"Left my underwear on," he said, nuzzling her neck as he held her. "Otherwise, I'll definitely fuck you, and I don't want to betray your trust. But I need to feel you against me, empress. Just a few minutes before you leave, okay?"

"Mmm kay..." she agreed, her tone sleepy as she yawned. "Just a few minutes and then I'll go..."

His satisfied hum vibrated against her skin as his limbs tightened around her. Grace reminded herself she could only sleep for a few moments and then she would leave.

Yes, just a few moments before she had to return to a reality that now paled in comparison to lying in Tristan's warm embrace on a lazy Sunday afternoon...

Chapter 5

Grace awoke to the sound of metal and wood being pulverized outside Tristan's bedroom. Rising with a gasp, she covered her breasts with her arms, shielding herself as two men stormed into the room.

"What the fuck?" Tristan yelled, moving in front of Grace to shield her.

Grace observed her father enter the room, rage lining his expression. "This is where I find you, Grace? Naked in a stranger's dingy apartment in Sterling?"

"What the hell, Dad?" she asked, peering over Tristan's shoulder as she hid behind him to cover her nakedness. "You weren't supposed to be home until nine o'clock."

"I got home a few hours early and was terrified when you weren't there." His eyes narrowed to angry slits. "I traced your location on your phone and we rushed over. I thought you were in danger!"

Grace's gaze roved over her father's two security guards as anger welled in her chest. "I'm a grown woman and can visit whomever I want—"

"Not as long as you live in my house!" He jabbed his finger as he spoke. "Do you hear me? I won't have you getting pregnant with some vagrant's child so he can steal my inheritance!"

"Your daughter searched me out, sir," Tristan said, nostrils flaring as his hands curled into fists. "And I make my own money."

"Not anymore you don't," Robert said, lifting his chin. "I'll have you blacklisted from every security job in the state if you don't stay away from my daughter. Do you hear me?"

"Dad!" Grace said, confused by the angry man in front of her. Sure, her father had always been a bit pretentious, but she'd never thought he was classist. "Tristan is right. I came here on my own free will."

"Well, we're going home now. Get dressed. And you're not to see each other again. Do you hear me? I'll be outside." He ushered the men out the door and closed it behind him.

"I've never seen him this way," Grace said, rubbing her forehead as the shock of his reaction set in. "I'm so sorry—"

"It's how the world works," Tristan said, his face impassive as he rose and gathered her clothing. Thrusting it at her, he shrugged. "I knew you'd leave eventually. At least you'll have the tattoo to remember me by."

Grace scowled as they dressed, annoyed that he would give in to her father's ridiculous behavior so easily. "This isn't over. I *will* see you again."

Tristan glanced toward the door as he contemplated. Sighing, he lifted her hand and kissed the palm. "I doubt it. Go live the life you were meant to live, Grace. I'm grateful for the day we had."

Yanking her hand away, she straightened her spine. "I just need time to figure this out. I'll be in touch."

Trying to appear composed even though she was a shaking mass of frayed nerves, she opened the door and joined her father and his security team on the other side. Robert led her down to the limo and ushered her inside before sitting across from her. As they began the drive home, he stared out the tinted window, fury evident in his expression and in the hunch of his shoulders.

"That was unacceptable behavior, Dad. I don't know what's gotten into you. Tristan was nothing but a gentleman with me."

Releasing an exasperated breath, Robert faced her and spoke in a low, solemn tone. "I've tried my best to shelter you from the evil in the world, Grace, but I fear I might have inadvertently forgotten to teach you what evil actually is. Men like *that*"—he pointed back toward Tristan's apartment building—"never go after women like you for reasons other than money or power."

Scoffing, she ran a hand through her hair. "I've never thought you were elitist, but I'm ashamed of you. It breaks my heart—"

"I'd rather you be heartbroken than broke and pregnant," Robert said, slicing his hand through the air. "And if you see him again, I'll cut off your inheritance and donate your trust fund to the local pet rescue. I mean it, Grace."

Tears welled as she struggled not to cry. "He's a good man, Dad."

"You're not to speak to him again and this subject is closed."

Overcome with emotion, Grace turned away, blindly staring out the window as she contemplated how things had gone so horribly wrong.

One thing she knew for certain was that she would see Tristan Holder again. In fact, her father's reaction had the unintended consequence of making her want to see him even more. To make things right and apologize at Robert's terrible behavior.

Little did Grace know that this night would be her first lesson in irreversible pain and heartache.

In the future, she would have many more nights where she sobbed uncontrollably and railed at the world.

But this would always be the first night her innocence was shattered.

Chapter 6

Three months later

Tristan sat on his couch studying his phone, frustrated because he knew it wasn't going to ring. His thumb trailed over the screen in a slow, sad motion, representative of the despondency that had crept into his soul when he'd blocked Grace's number.

They'd been sneaking around for several months, and the lying and deception had worn on Tristan until he couldn't take it anymore.

He'd done his best to try to win Robert to his side. Tristan had shown up at his office, and when the secretary refused to let him inside, he'd waited on the sidewalk outside the corporate building. When Robert exited, dressed in his pristine designer suit with briefcase in hand, Tristan stepped in his path, blocking him from the limo where his driver was waiting.

"Sir, if I could just have a few minutes—"

"How dare you approach me?" Robert interrupted, his cheeks growing ruddy with anger. "I have nothing to say to you."

"I'm in love with your daughter, sir, and want to earn your trust," Tristan said, encircling his forearm.

Robert yanked his arm away. "My daughter will inherit this one day." He gestured to the building. "She's all I have left since her mother died, and I won't watch her waste her life on an interloper who has no chance of giving her the life she deserves."

"You don't know me, but I'm resilient, Mr. Albright. All I want is to build something with Grace and make her happy—"

"Grace needs a man who can give her stability. Someone who came from *her* world and understands the life she's meant to have. Not someone who will build a life on her back with her money."

"I don't want her money," Tristan said, angry at the accusation. "I make my own money, sir."

"Not if I ensure you can't," Robert threatened, his nostrils flaring. "And if you don't stop seeing her, that's exactly what I'll do. Do you think I don't know she's been sneaking around with you? You have no honor, son, and your actions prove that."

"You forbade her to see me!" Tristan exclaimed. "Without even giving me a chance. And it's laughable that you would accuse me of having no honor when you're obviously having her tracked. Or are you exempt from the misdeeds of the rest of us commoners?" He crossed his arms and lifted his eyebrows.

"I had to have her followed to ensure she was safe. For all I know, you're trying to entrap her to steal her fortune."

Sighing, Tristan shook his head. "Is it so unfathomable to you that someone could love your daughter for who she is? I don't give a damn about her money. If you took any time to get to know me, you'd realize that, and you do a grave disservice to her to assume otherwise."

Robert's gaze fell to the ground as he contemplated. Returning his gaze to Tristan's, he gave a dismissive shrug. "I've been around too long and know how the world works, son. Go and find someone who fits you. Grace isn't meant for you."

"I could *make* us fit," Tristan said, a slight pleading in his voice. "In so many ways, we already do. I apologize for sneaking around, but *she's* the one visiting me. We both want this to work. Let me earn her."

A resigned expression overtook Robert's features. "You'll never be able to earn her, Tristan. The fact that you don't understand that shows me how naïve you are. It's not personal. It's just the way it is. Stay away from her before I blacklist you with every security firm from Miami to Maine." Lifting his finger, he said sternly, "I mean it. Leave. Her. Alone."

Backing away, he slid into the limo before the driver shut the door and drove away.

Leaning back on the worn cushions of his couch, Tristan expelled a defeated breath as he remembered the disastrous conversation. That night, he'd returned to his apartment with a sense of finality. Moments later, he'd blocked Grace's number. Although he wanted to make it work, he had too much pride to sneak around with a woman whose father would never accept him.

That had been two nights ago. Rubbing his hand over his heart, Tristan acknowledged it felt like two years. In the scant time he'd ceased communication with Grace, the heartache had set in. He considered himself a tough soul, but there were some connections that transcended normal feelings. His feelings for Grace exceeded anything he'd ever imagined, and he wondered how long it would take for them to abate. Would he feel them for a month? A year? Forever?

Deciding he needed to drown his sorrows, he tossed on some jeans and haphazardly combed his hair before heading downstairs, ready for a drink at the local bar on the corner. When he approached the front door of his building, he noticed Grace standing outside, her blond hair plastered to her cheeks and neck as rain drenched her.

Pulling open the door, he asked, "What the hell—?"

Her palm slapped across his cheek, the sound echoing in the vacant atrium of his building.

"You fucking blocked me?"

Tristan clenched his teeth, simultaneously admiring her gumption and wanting to wring her neck. "If you're here to win me back, knocking out several of my teeth isn't the way."

She sputtered as the rain continued to sluice over her skin and hair. "A gentleman would invite me in so I can get out of the rain."

Tristan arched a brow. "A lady wouldn't hit someone in the face."

Emitting a frustrated groan, she lifted her eyes to the darkened sky. "Lord, give me strength. I'm going to kill him before we make it down the aisle."

"What?" Tristan asked as shock ran through his veins.

Lowering her gaze to his, her eyes were filled with fire and determination. "No one makes decisions about my future but me. That includes my father. As much as I want to murder you right now, you also happen to be the one person I've ever felt free with in the entire world." Stepping closer, she jabbed her finger in his face. "You're the only man who's ever come close to making me scream—and I'm not just talking about the sex, although it's pretty fucking great."

Pride swelled as he stood silent, digesting her tirade.

"Every second I'm not with you, I feel *numb*. I feel like an imposter in a world where everyone else is human." Dropping her hand, her expression softened slightly. "But with you, I feel...*everything*." Grasping his wrist, she splayed his palm over her heart before covering his hand with hers. "And I won't give that up. So, you're going to marry me. And that's the end of this discussion."

Tristan absorbed each beat of her heart beneath his palm as he gazed into her eyes. They shone back at him filled with deep emotion and a slight fear that nearly shattered him. "You're scared I'll say no," he whispered.

"A part of me is," she said, nodding. "Because it means I'll have to fight harder until you say yes. And you *will* say yes. I think it's best if you just save us both some time and get me to a damn courthouse. *After* I dry off."

He breathed a laugh. "Your father will never let it happen—"

"It's not his choice."

"Grace," he murmured, cupping her cheek. "If I marry you, he's going to ensure I never get a security job again. My options to support us will be extremely limited."

"I have plenty of money."

"No," he said, drawing her inside and running his thumb over her lip. "I won't live on your fortune. I have to do things my way if we do this."

"A marriage involves two people, Tristan. I know we can figure this out. How about, instead of your way, we do it *our* way? Together."

Tristan mulled the sentiment. He was a lone wolf in many ways, and wasn't sure he understood the first thing about compromising in a relationship. "I'm not sure we'd be able to figure it out. And what happens then? When your father has disowned you and we're living in the real world? Have you really thought about this, Grace?"

Placing her hands on his face, she softly asked, "Do you love me?"

He released a slow breath. "Yes."

Her brilliant smile eroded every ounce of loneliness he'd felt in the past two days.

"Then marry me."

Elation at the prospect of marrying her warred with the fear they were doomed to fail.

"Tristan?"

In that moment, although it went against his better judgment, all he could focus on was her. Those stunning eyes, full of hope and love. The earnestness in her expression as she waited for him to answer.

God help him, even though he knew the odds were against them, he couldn't deny the woman he loved more than he'd ever thought possible. Sliding his fingers into the hair at the base of her neck, he tilted her face to his.

"It won't be easy, empress."

"I don't care."

Pressing his lips to hers, he sealed their fate with a poignant, solemn kiss.

"I'm going to do my best," he whispered, resting his forehead against hers. "Nothing has ever meant more to me than you. I promise to cherish you and make you happy, sweetheart. Or die trying."

"No one's dying," she said, grinning. "But we need to make it official before my father banishes me from his life forever. Once we're married, he'll have to give you a chance. I know he's going to change his mind."

Tristan's lips thinned. "I appreciate the optimism, but I doubt it."

"Well, there's only one way to find out. I think the courthouse opens at nine in the morning."

He laughed at the challenge in her voice. "Don't you want to wait and get a pretty dress or whatever women want when they get married?"

"Nope. I just want to get on with our lives."

"Okay. I'll call out of work tomorrow so we can seal the deal." He pecked her lips. "This is crazy. You know that, right?"

"Honestly? It feels like the smartest thing I've ever done," she said, shrugging. "And now, your future wife would like a towel please. I'm freezing."

Tristan took her hand, threading their fingers as he led her to his apartment. Once she was dry, he drew her into his arms, thankful she had the courage to seize their future when he'd seen no viable path to forge ahead.

And as he held her on the last night before they promised to love and cherish each other for eternity, he acknowledged it would be the easiest vow he ever made.

The next morning, Grace stood before Tristan, full of hope as they repeated their vows in front of a judge. She knew their future was uncertain and they had nearly insurmountable obstacles ahead, especially with her father's insistence they weren't meant to be.

But she'd never felt anything more in her soul than the knowledge she was meant to be with Tristan. He'd unlocked something inside her—something bold and fierce—and she'd come to crave it in the short months they'd been together.

She was certainly no expert on love, but in her mind, a connection like hers and Tristan's was extremely rare and almost impossible to find.

There, in one of the most important moments of her life, she gripped his hands and spoke her truth: Tristan was the only man who would ever inhabit her heart.

The young woman she was at that moment could never have foreseen the disastrous future ahead. Could never have imagined so much heartache and pain could follow such a happy, auspicious day.

In many ways, the last rays of innocence that had been shattered the night her father first discovered her with Tristan would soon begin to erode until only heartache and grief remained. The coming weeks and years would teach her harsh lessons about loss and disaster, and humankind's penchant for grave evil.

Eventually, she would exact retribution against those who hurt her and craft careful, meticulous plans to dismantle a malevolence that rendered the world broken and bereft.

But in that moment, as she held Tristan's hands and stared into his gorgeous hazel eyes, she was still just a woman vowing to love the man who owned her heart.

In the quiet courthouse under the soft glow of the fluorescent lights, she cemented her union and became Mrs. Tristan Holder...

Till death do they part.

Part II – The Present

Chapter 7

Three weeks after the events of Scorched Redemption

"Darling, *I'm* the one leading the rebellion."

Tristan worked his jaw beneath Grace's warm palms as she held his face. After several attempts to speak, he finally found the words, although they were less than eloquent. "Holy fucking shit."

Her pink lips curved in that sexy way that set his body on fire, and he fought the urge to grab her shoulders and shake her. *She* was the rebellion leader? Since when? And how? And why in the hell hadn't she let him help her?

"Because you were too close," Grace said, reading his thoughts as she'd often done when they were together all those years ago. Lowering her hands, she shrugged. "You're too invested in Luthor's death, and I need things to play out a certain way."

Scratching his head, Tristan regarded her. "The night Zayne kidnapped you..." He trailed off and scowled at Zayne, who was standing beside the desk in the small cabin where Tristan found them in the Pennsylvania woods. "That was a ruse?"

Arching a silken eyebrow, Grace grinned. "Pretty stealthy, right? Maybe I should've been the one that special forces recruited."

A shocked laugh escaped his lips. "Maybe so." Glancing over her porcelain skin, the swell of her breasts beneath her brown sweater, and the flare of her hips, Tristan accepted she was unharmed. "I thought you were in danger. I wanted to save you."

"Sweet but unnecessary." She batted her eyelashes, making him feel like an absolute dolt for assuming. "But we definitely need to talk. Walk outside with me? My cabin's behind this one. We have a few in this cluster, but Zayne and the men let me have my own."

"She's the boss," Zayne said, his voice filled with respect. "We're all aligned for the cause and believe in Grace's plan."

Tristan surveyed the others in the room, noting there were six additional men besides Zayne. "This is John and Caleb," he said, pointing at the soldiers who'd accompanied him. "They helped me search for you and hate Luthor as much as I do."

"You're probably hungry," she said with a nod in their direction. "Zayne, see that they get some food while Tristan and I chat outside."

"Yes, ma'am."

Gesturing for Tristan to follow her, she headed toward the cabin door and down the wooden stairs.

Tristan followed her, the act symbolic of how easily she could command him. Of how willingly he would always follow her, even when she'd left him and shattered his heart by marrying the man he loathed more than anyone on the planet.

His eyes darted to the swell of her backside in her worn jeans, so different from the fancy clothes he was used to seeing her in. He'd memorized the curves of her body long ago, although he was man enough to admit he was more entranced by her body now than when they were young. Something about the way she carried herself, and the confidence with which she swayed as she walked...

"This should do," she said, pivoting as they approached another cabin, which he assumed were her private quarters. "There are enough trees to dampen the noise if we start yelling."

Shifting his weight, he rested a hand on his hip. "I'm not planning on yelling. I just don't understand how you became the leader of the rebellion. What the hell, Grace?"

"Pity" was her soft reply as her eyes roved over his face. "I miss you yelling at me sometimes. At least when you screamed at me, I knew you cared. When you stopped yelling, I knew I'd truly lost you."

"I've always cared, even when you married that fucking bastard." Stepping forward, he pounded his chest. "Even when you ripped my goddamned heart out, Grace—"

"Okay, I take it back," she said, showing her palm. "Don't yell. I'm not ready to fight yet. I need to explain some things to you."

"You think?"

Her gaze lowered to the ground, surveying the fallen leaves as she gathered her thoughts. "There's so much and I don't know where to begin." Her blue orbs lifted to his, swimming with deep emotion. "But I guess I should tell you that I never loved Luthor."

"Your husband?" Tristan asked sarcastically.

"*You* were my husband," she said, swallowing thickly. "Luthor was a plan. A well-executed plan that I've been slowly implementing for years."

"Well, I kind of missed that when you were divorcing me in favor of marrying him," he said, angrily rubbing the back of his neck. "I thought you couldn't forgive me because I wasn't here when our daughter..." Clearing his throat, he continued. "I thought you wanted someone rich who could replace what you'd lost when your father died—"

"I know. I counted on you believing I chose him over you. It was an integral part of my plan."

Floored, Tristan's mouth fell open. "You're saying you divorced me as part of a fucking scheme? Did you fuck him for the rebellion too?"

Wrinkling her nose, she bristled. "Don't be crass. I understand you're upset—"

"He's an old man, Grace!" Tristan yelled, stepping forward and gripping her shoulders. "How could you let him touch you?"

"Who I let touch me is no longer your concern." She swatted his arms away as anger reddened her cheeks. "And we have more important things to discuss."

He scoffed. "Who touches you will *always* be my concern."

Her nostrils flared as she pinched the bridge of her nose in frustration. "I approached Luthor with the idea of marriage shortly after my father died. I had just lost the baby and was understandably distraught. You weren't here, and I had to do the best I could with the circumstances I had."

Tristan studied her, noting the secrets that lurked in her stunning eyes. "You're not telling me the whole story. I want to know *everything*, Grace."

"I'm telling you the basics," she said, her tone firm. "You can believe me or not, but Luthor and I didn't have a passionate marriage. That's why he always had women around. I wanted him to, although I'm sorry Jessica got caught up in his sick obsession. I wish I could've prevented that."

"Me too," Tristan said, sighing. "My hope is that Danica can cure the world of this fucking drug and my sister will never have to suck that bastard off again."

Stepping forward, she placed her palms on his chest. "We want the same things, Tristan. It's time to align. We need to end this once and for all."

Cognizant of the rampant throbbing of the organ beneath her palm, Tristan covered the backs of her hands. His thumbs caressed her soft skin as he gazed into her eyes. "Why didn't you tell me? I would've helped you."

"Because you get in your own way too often," she whispered, her fingers tightening on his chest in a possessive gesture that nearly caused his knees to buckle. "I couldn't have your hatred of Luthor or your doubt in me derailing my plans."

"I've never doubted you," he rasped, leaning closer so his breath mingled with hers.

"Darling, you've always believed the worst about me." Emotion shone in her eyes as she spoke. "You could never shake the belief that I shared my father's notion that you weren't right for me. Your lack of faith in my feelings for you was the one thing I knew I could count on. After all, you told me on the day I got my dragon tattoo that I'd eventually leave and never come back." Her chin wobbled. "It broke my heart that day as much as every other day you continued to believe it."

"But you *did* leave and never come back," he said, frustrated at her insistence on blaming him.

"*You* left *me*. To prove something that never needed to be proven—to me at least."

"Your father—"

"Was an old man who wanted to protect me. His views weren't personally about you. He was just a product of his environment and the forces that eventually led to his death. It was never about you, Tristan."

Needing space from her scent and her touch, Tristan backed away and studied her. "What forces that led to his death? I thought he died of a heart attack."

Grace's lips fluttered as she released a breath. Gnawing her lip, she hesitated. Finally, she straightened her shoulders and spoke with gravity. "Luthor murdered my father. I saw it and wasn't able to stop it. Shortly thereafter, I went into early labor with our baby." She covered her abdomen, a look of sharp pain covering her features. "And after I almost bled out and lost *everything*, I declared in that moment that I would bring Luthor Cromwell down."

Closing the distance between them, she straightened her spine. "And that, my dear ex-husband, is when I began plotting my revenge...and ultimately, the rebellion."

CHAPTER 8

Grace observed the shock that covered Tristan's face, still overcome with how gorgeous he was after all this time. Although he was almost forty, he'd somehow managed to become more attractive as he aged. The hair at his temples was a sexy shade of gray, and the wrinkles beside his eyes only highlighted the glints of green and honey that swirled in his hazel orbs.

Allowing herself a small moment of reprieve, she lost herself in those mesmerizing eyes as he gaped at her. Tilting her head, she remembered the small moments when they were happy...when she'd drowned in that heated gaze as he worked his body deeply into hers...

"Grace?" he called, causing her to flinch and clear her throat.

"Hmm?"

"Are you seriously going to stand there and not acknowledge that you just told me Luthor murdered your father? And you witnessed it? What the hell?"

Sadness swamped her as she covered her throat, a protective gesture against the terrible memories. "It was the worst day of my life, and you weren't here..." The words drifted off as she reminded herself now wasn't the time to get lost in memories. As much as she wanted a soulful reunion with her ex-husband, she had more pressing issues at hand.

"But we don't have time to discuss that now," she said, glancing back toward the cabin where the men she commanded waited. "How did you find me? If you tracked me down, Luthor's men can't be far behind."

"I'm not going to let you sideswipe this conversation. I need to know everything so I can help you—"

"And I'll tell you," she said, holding up a hand. "Once I figure out our next steps. We can't stay here now that I know it's vulnerable."

Sighing, Tristan placed his hands on his hips. "I'm an expert tracker, Grace. One of your men drove directly to the Scranton black-market compound to pick up supplies. Once I had his trail, you were easy to track down."

"Andy," she said, rolling her eyes. "I told him to park at least ten miles from the compound in a wooded area and carry the supplies back."

"It was sloppy, although it was pouring rain so he might've thought no one would be around to track him." Tristan's eyes narrowed. "Did Solomon Grange help you?" he asked, referencing the leader of the Scranton compound. "I've heard he's not friendly to outsiders."

"He's harboring George Luddington," Grace said. "George has promised him a position in the new government once we defeat Luthor, so Solomon has been...somewhat agreeable."

"Does George have the right to make that promise? If Arthur Reyes has his way, he'll be the leader of the new government after Luthor falls."

"George has been stockpiling weapons in a bunker near Scranton for years. Arthur will need them to take back the DC Sen City. Therefore, George can promise whatever he wants. Weapons are worth more than gold in this hellhole we find ourselves in."

Tristan arched a curious eyebrow, as if he was trying to juxtapose the savvy woman in front of him with the young woman he'd loved all those years ago.

"You won't find her here," Grace said, splaying her arms and allowing him to look his fill. "The girl you loved is dead. She died when her father was murdered by an evil narcissist and her child was ripped from her womb while you were halfway around the world. I'm the commander of the rebellion, Tristan, and I refuse to fail."

The corner of his mouth curved, jolting her heart in the way it always had. With a resigned nod, he asked, "What do you need from me? I have a direct line to Arthur Reyes through a shortwave radio channel. Do you want to contact him?"

Grace's lips formed a slow, satisfied smile. "Darling, *now* we're getting somewhere."

Chapter 9

Arianna Lawson placed two fingers in her mouth and whistled. The ninety soldiers who stood in formation before her froze, planting their feet as they awaited instruction. Pacing in front of the first line, she perused each soldier she passed.

"I'm impressed with your skills, men," she called before stopping in front of the three female soldiers on the right flank. "And women," she added with a nod.

They saluted, each showing respect before Arianna said softly, "At ease."

The female soldiers dropped their hands to their sides, and Arianna took her place in the center of the formation.

"We have ninety members in this militia. When I fought with you all the night Luthor sent his army, I was impressed with your fortitude." She lifted a finger. "But fortitude will only get you so far. Trained soldiers who fight as a team are needed to beat the Sen Force soldiers, especially if Luthor blasts them full of the super-serum."

"Yes, ma'am!" they chimed in unison.

"We've had three weeks to train, and I see improvement every day. I'm honored to serve with you all, and appreciate the time you've taken to condition your bodies and learn the skills Dominic and I have taught you."

Dominic stood behind her, feet planted far enough apart to anchor his weight as his hands crossed behind his back.

"We're working with Arthur to form a plan to take back DC once and for all. Know that your hard work will be worth it. My sister has perfected the antidote, and as soon as we wrest control of the manufacturing plants inside the DC walls, we'll begin producing and distributing the cure. This nightmare will be over, and we can go back to doing whatever the hell we did before the world fell apart."

Arching an eyebrow at one of the nearby soldiers, she grinned. "You can go back to blogging about insects on Instagram, Jones. I'm sure your fanbase misses you."

"Insects are the most interesting species on Earth, ma'am," Jones replied, deadly serious as several of the men laughed at Arianna's teasing.

"I'm sure they are, cadet. Proud of you for having the fastest ten-mile finish yesterday." Lifting her chin, she projected her voice. "Let's all aim to finish today's ten-mile run in less than seventy minutes. Our bodies won't condition themselves." She circled her finger above her head. "Get to it!"

The soldiers gave one last "Yes, ma'am!" before darting toward the far-off wall to begin the laps. Glancing to her right, Arianna leaned down and placed her hands on her knees. "You'll make sure they have water at the finish, Chris?"

The boy nodded, his face glowing with excitement at being Arianna's chosen helper for the troops.

"Good man." She patted him on the shoulder. "I'm going to have to get you something extra special for your eleventh birthday."

"Jenny and I can celebrate with our mom since Dani fixed her," he said, beaming. "We're going to have a party. Maybe you can come?"

"Tell me the time and place. And I'll bring this one too, although he's not as much fun as I am." She pointed at Dominic.

"I'm fun," Dominic said, crossing his arms as he scowled.

"Okay," Chris said before turning to jog toward the grassy knoll where the soldiers would finish their run. "Gotta make sure the water's ready. Bye, Arianna!"

Arianna watched him scamper off as Dominic sidled up beside her.

"He's obsessed with you. It's cute."

"He's got good taste," she said, grinning.

Facing her, Dominic slid his hands over her hips. "But he's not *nearly* as obsessed with you as I am." Leaning forward, he stole a kiss. "You gonna marry me today or not, Lawson?"

Squinting one eye, Arianna studied him. "Are you seriously going to ask me that every day? It's annoying. I told you, we'll get married once we defeat Luthor."

His pout was adorable, causing Arianna's heartbeat to pulse in her ears as he leaned closer. "Why wait? I want you to be my wife when we beat that bastard."

"I never knew you were so traditional," she said, unable to control her smile at his insistence on tying the knot. "Isn't it enough that you were literally inside every part of my body last night?"

Growling, he snaked his arm around her waist and pulled her against him. "I love claiming your body, but I want to claim your soul, sweetheart."

Taken by his sweet words, she tenderly cupped his cheek. "You have it." Allowing one more poignant moment before returning to reality, she brushed her lips against his and whispered, "I love you."

His resulting shiver was the perfect response to her endearment.

"Okay, enough PDA." Playfully pushing him away, she placed her palm over her forehead to shield the sun and looked off into the distance. "The troops look good. I think we have enough of a foundation to plan an attack."

"Thanks to you," Dominic said, admiration crossing his features beneath the jagged scar that ran from the corner of his eye, over his nose and to the opposite corner of his lips. Arianna found it incredibly sexy, and combined with his pride in her, it damn near made her year.

"I miss running my own squadron, so returning to the role is second nature. You're a good second-in-command. I wondered if you'd be able to let me lead, but you step up in the moments I need you, and defer during the others I don't. It's seamless."

"Because I get you, Ari, and I'm man enough to know when to follow a powerful woman into battle. With you leading us, we're poised to succeed."

Embarrassed at the tears that stung her eyes, she sighed. "Stop saying nice shit. I'm supposed to appear tough."

Chuckling, he ran his fingers over her arm. "I don't think you'll have any trouble there."

"Screw you."

"My point exactly."

She swatted his arm away before pointing toward the high steel wall that surrounded the compound. "I'm going to go help Chris prepare the water rations. You coming?"

"I told Mav I'd look over the old architectural archives of DC with him again. He's determined to find ways to infiltrate the city that aren't on modern maps. He thinks we can find several old tunnels and underground highways to gain access during the offensive. Once he memorizes them all, we'll strategize the attack with Arthur."

"Good plan. Whenever you all are ready to bring me in, I'm here. In the meantime, I'm committed to getting the soldiers ready. See you at dinner?"

"See you then."

She turned to walk away and Dominic gripped her wrist. Tugging her back, he planted a firm kiss on her lips. "Bye."

Clutching his chin, she reveled in the desire that flared in his eyes. "Don't manhandle me, Cavalleri." Drawing him toward her, she swiped her tongue over his lips. "Bye."

Groaning, he wiped his mouth as she slowly backed away, a wide grin spread across her face.

"You're going to pay for that tonight, Ari."

Lifting her hands in invitation, a challenge laced her expression. "Promise?"

Dominic just stood firm, slowly rubbing his lips as she retreated.

Flicking a dismissive wave, she turned and strode toward the wall. "God, he's so fucking sexy. Down girl. Training *then* sex. Get a grip."

Breaking into a joyful whistle, she headed to join her soldiers.

Dr. Danica Lawson-Ward stood beside the bed in the infirmary, nodding as she scribbled notes on her clipboard.

"And you're not experiencing any lingering pain at the injection site, Mr. Clarke?" she asked.

"No, ma'am," the man with kind brown eyes said, rubbing the russet skin of his arm where she'd given the injection over two weeks ago. "Everything feels fine. I believe you've cured me, Dr. Lawson-Ward. I haven't had a craving in days and I'm steady. No shaking or tremors either."

Breathing a sigh of relief, Dani smiled. "Excellent. You're our last patient, Sam, on this compound at least. Can I call you Sam? You can call me Dani."

He smiled and nodded.

"Well, Sam, I'm thrilled to say that you conclude my real-life clinical trial on this compound. Everyone is cured of EverLife addiction, and I feel comfortable producing the serum I've tested here for the masses."

"You've done a wonderful thing here, Dani," Sam said, his eyes clouding with tears. "I feel something I haven't in so long..." His voice drifted off as he cleared his throat. "Hope," he rasped. "I feel hope, ma'am."

Dani allowed the conflicting emotions to war within. Anger and doubt collided with the small sparks of longing in her gut as well. "I'm glad to hear it, Sam." She softly squeezed his arm. "I did a lot of damage, and I won't be able to live with myself until I fix what I can. Even if it will never be enough."

"It's enough," he said firmly. "You didn't have to help anyone, but you did. It's admirable. All we can hope for when we make terrible mistakes is the chance to make it right."

"From your lips to God's ears," she said, flashing a cheeky grin. "And I'm an atheist, but I still like that saying."

"Well, I'll believe for both of us." He patted her hand. "Thank you, Dani. I wish you luck on your endeavor to cure the world. I'm too old to fight in the rebellion, but I'll offer my services where I can. I want to help defeat Luthor and live in peace again."

"I'll let Arthur know of your willingness to help. There are always positions that need to be filled. Rikina will continue to monitor you during your follow-ups, but otherwise, you're free to resume a normal life. Whatever that looks like nowadays."

Sam rose and gave her one last nod, affection in his gaze, before he strode out of the room. Taking a moment to appreciate the gravity of the achievement, Dani rested her palms on the bed and closed her eyes.

"One compound down, countless more to go," she whispered. "You can do this, Dani. You *have* to do this."

Inhaling a fortified breath, she straightened her spine and trailed from the room to find her husband.

She found Maverick and Dominic in the old home economics room, studying various maps of DC. Dani approached them and cupped her husband's shoulder as she placed a kiss on his head.

"Have you identified some tunnels that will allow us entry?" she asked.

"We've found a few," Maverick said, leaning back and tapping his cheek. "But I need another kiss first, please."

Laughing, she leaned down and nipped his lips before kissing him. "How's that?"

"It'll do...for now." He winked before turning back to the maps and tracing the outline of the city in one of them. "Washington, DC, has several underground catacombs, train tunnels and old prohibition tunnels. Many of them are sealed, but we can blast through them during an attack if we need to."

Arthur Reyes walked into the room, the air of confidence and purpose surrounding his broad shoulders. Dani found him an extremely capable leader, and felt he was the perfect person to take over the new government if they defeated Luthor Cromwell.

Scratch that. *When* they defeated Luthor Cromwell.

"What have you got for me, Maverick?"

"Dom and I think these two dormant tunnels will work the best," Maverick said as Arthur sat beside him. "There's one on the northwest side and one on the southwest side. Both will probably need to be blown open at certain spots, but Dom and Arianna are excellent at creating improvised explosive devices."

Leaning back, Arthur crossed his arms over his chest. "That's good to know, but what if we didn't need to create IEDs? What if someone could supply them to us, along with all of the ammunition we need to attack Luthor?"

Maverick's eyebrows lifted. "Well...that would be great. How do you propose we accomplish that?"

"I've just been contacted by Tristan Holder," Arthur said, making eye contact with everyone as he spoke to indicate the seriousness of the moment. "He's found the rebellion leader, and we're going to chat over shortwave radio in thirty minutes. I'd like you all to join, as well as Arianna."

"Tristan found Zayne Danvers?" Dominic asked.

"He found Zayne, but he's not the leader of the rebellion," Arthur said, excitement lacing his features. "In a rather shocking twist, it turns out that Grace Cromwell is the leader."

"What?" Dani asked, lowering her stunned gaze to Maverick's.

"I'll know more when we discuss further. But it seems she has stockpiles of weapons, and she's ready to align with us."

"Wow," Dominic said, rising and rubbing the back of his neck as he digested the information. "Tristan was under the impression she was quite helpless the night she was abducted."

"Which must've been part of her plan," Dani said, eyes widening as she realized the woman's brilliance. "Good for her and very impressive."

"I'm not sure we can trust her yet," Arthur said, "but it's certainly an interesting development. We're at the point where we're going to have to take some risks, and if Grace comes through, we could be very close to ending Luthor's reign."

"I'll go find Arianna and make sure she's in the meeting with us," Dominic said. "If the rebellion truly has a stockpile of weapons they're ready to share, we should plan an attack soon. Luthor is close to perfecting his super-soldier drug, and Anthony and his men are vulnerable inside the walls."

"Agreed," Arthur said, standing and tapping the map. "Can you have a preliminary multipoint attack plan prepared by this afternoon?"

"You bet your ass I can," Maverick responded confidently.

"Excellent. And the cure is ready, Dani?"

"Everyone on the compound is cured, and the serum is also preventative from my observations. As a scientist, I'd love several more rounds of trials, but as a realist, I've seen the results and they're better than I could've hoped for. I'm prepared to distribute the cure to the masses."

"The first thing we'll do once we defeat Luthor is revamp the pharma production plants so we can produce the cure in mass quantities. Then we'll need to safely distribute it across the country and the world."

"Society will take some time to recover, but I'll walk from compound to compound if I have to," Dani said, lifting her chin. "I won't rest until everyone is free from the ravages of EverLife."

"As discussed, I'll still have to put you on trial, Dani. You'll plead your case in front of a jury of your peers, but I can't guarantee the outcome." Sympathy clouded his expression.

"I'll accept whatever outcome a jury decides. If they want to execute me, it's certainly justified—"

"Like hell it is," Maverick muttered.

Dani held up a hand. "It is, Mav. I hurt so many..." Shaking her head so she wouldn't dwell on the destruction, she continued. "But I would be honored to live out my days working for the new government to help eradicate EverLife and create more cures for deadly diseases like cancer. I hope the people will allow me the chance."

"As do I," Arthur said. "I'm proud of your efforts and honored to align with you."

Sentiment clogged her throat at the genuineness in his gaze. "Thank you, Arthur. Let's take back the world. I'm ready."

Arthur's chest rose with pride as he smiled. "See you all in an hour," he said before marching from the room.

"No way in hell are you getting executed," Maverick said, snaking an arm around her waist and resting his forehead against hers. "I won't let that happen."

"Let's hope it doesn't come to that," she said, palming his cheek. "I was really getting used to the idea of having a baby or two with you. But we're not naming them Goose."

Maverick playfully nipped her finger. "We can name them anything you want, babe. My grandma's name was Gertrude. Little Gertie would be cute, right?"

Dani grimaced. "I'm definitely going to have to let that one grow on me."

Dominic chuckled behind them. "While you all ponder baby names, I'm going to go find Arianna. I'll see you in a bit."

When they were alone, Maverick pulled her closer and pressed his lips to her ear. "My grandpa's name was Lester."

Tossing back her head, Dani laughed. "We are *not* naming our child Lester. I do want them to have *some* friends."

"They'll have my good looks, so they'll be fine," Maverick said, drawing back to point at his face. "You can't argue with genetics, babe."

Overcome with love for her gorgeous husband, she bit her lip. "I think I'll continue to be the genetics expert in this conversation, thank you very much. But you are cute."

"Oh, I'll show you cute later tonight," he said, his voice sultry. "Now that your body remembers me each morning without watching the videos, you've become very randy, my little geneticist."

"I'm remembering so much more every day, and I do recognize you when I wake up. I write about it in my journal a lot. It's this warm, musky scent that surrounds me and makes me feel safe, even when I'm scrambling to remember where the hell I am."

Empathy clouded his gunmetal-gray eyes. "One day, you'll remember everything, sweetheart. I know it." He ran a soothing hand over her chestnut locks.

Lacing her fingers through his, she tugged him toward the door. "Want to say hi to Sam Clarke before your meeting? He's my last patient on the compound, thank goodness, and he's so sweet, Mav."

"Sure, I can always squeeze in time to see my wife's brilliant work. Lead the way."

Clutching her husband's hand, Dani clung to the hope their fortune would soon change for the better.

Chapter 10

Zayne offered to accompany Grace to the clearing where Tristan's truck was parked, but she declined.

"I need you to stay here and make sure everything is packed and loaded. Then ensure the vehicles are functional and the tires are full of air. I don't feel comfortable staying here now that we've been located." She shot a pointed glare at Tristan.

"Hey, my intentions were good, and it's better I found you before Luthor."

"You've already communicated the basics to Arthur through Morse code, correct?" she asked, pointing at the telegraph machine atop the desk.

"Yes," Tristan said. "My radio and the microphone are in a backpack under the passenger seat of the truck I drove here."

"We'll be back within the hour. Make sure we're ready to move quickly," Grace said to Zayne before beckoning Tristan outside.

"Zayne is protective of you," Tristan said, slight annoyance in his voice as he led her through the woods to the faded red truck in the distance.

"It took me a while to confirm I could trust him, but he's been invaluable to my plan." She patted the frame of the truck bed as she approached. "This reminds me of the one you had when we got married."

"Shitty vehicles were all I could afford when we were married."

"We had some good times in your shitty truck," she said, running her hand over the smooth metal. "Especially in the woods where we used to hike near your apartment."

"We never had trouble making good use of a flat surface," he droned. "Until everything fell apart."

Sadness crept into the dark corners of her heart that remembered times when they were young and believed it was them against the world.

"And Zayne?" Tristan continued. "Are you and he..."

Laughing, Grace shook her head. "Not that it's any of your business, but no. I don't have time for romance, Tristan. In case you've forgotten, I'm trying to bring down my evil husband. Let me defeat him first, and then I can focus on trivial things like sex and love."

Closing the distance between them, he covered her hand atop the truck. "I still can't believe you're the rebellion leader." He slowly traced a finger down her arm, causing her to shiver in the shadows of the trees.

"Then I did a good job," she said, slowly recoiling. His proximity conjured too many memories, making her yearn for the times he'd pressed those firm lips to her ear and whispered her name... "Where's the radio?"

Tristan's eyes narrowed as he contemplated her, and Grace had a nagging suspicion he was mired in memories too. He eventually tore his gaze from hers and opened the door of the truck. Reaching beneath the seat, he drew out a backpack.

Walking toward the back of the truck, he pulled down the bed door and opened the pack. After pulling out a shortwave radio, he located the small microphone and inserted it into the transmission port. He lifted the antenna, extending it the full length, before turning the knob. A green light glowed on the radio as Tristan adjusted the dial to 4930 kHz.

Lifting the microphone, he spoke into the receiver. "This is Dragon Rider to Bird Catcher. Do you copy?"

"Interesting names," Grace said, grinning.

"It's what we came up with in a pinch," he said, with a shrug. After a few moments, he repeated the call.

"Bird Catcher here. Are you with Olympia Marble?"

Olympia Marble? Grace mouthed, pointing to her chest.

"I'm with her. Is your team there?"

"Yes, everyone is assembled and listening."

Grace took the mic from him. "Bird Catcher, this is Olympia Marble. Do you think this channel is secure enough to use our real names?"

"I believe it is," Arthur confirmed.

"Excellent. As Tristan told you, I have a supporter who has stockpiled weapons in a bunker outside the Scranton black-market compound."

"Are you willing to allow us to use them and to transport them to us?"

"Yes. My team is capable, and I assume Tristan and his men will help me."

Tristan nodded.

"How many days do you need?" Arthur asked.

Squinting, she pondered. "We have a sedan, two SUVs, and Tristan's truck now. We should be able to gather the weapons in a few days and convene with you at your compound. Once we're there and we've evaluated our stockpile, we can plan the attack."

"And we're supposed to trust this isn't a Trojan Horse plan?" a gruff woman's voice called over the radio. "That Luthor Cromwell's wife just wants to help us out of the goodness of her heart?"

"Hello, Arianna," Grace said, unable to control her smile. "It's a pleasure to finally speak to you. I don't blame you for being wary, but I assure you, my goal is the ultimate destruction of Luthor Cromwell."

"Not to be a dick, but that's exactly what a double agent would say."

Grace couldn't argue with her there. "I know trust isn't easily given in our world. All I can say is that Luthor took everything from me, and I won't rest until he's paid for every ounce of pain he caused me and everyone else. If you can't trust me, I'll forge ahead on my own, but we'll be stronger united."

Grace listened to the muffled voices on the other end as they discussed. Finally, Arthur said, "We're ready to align. We'll await you and your men. We'll need to search every vehicle, team member and weapon before you're allowed entry to our compound."

"I accept your terms. We should all arrive within the week. We'll do our best to stay off of Luthor's radar. If we're caught, I urge you to contact George Luddington at Scranton and ask for his help. He has powerful connections even though he's in exile."

"I will, although I have faith in you, Grace. I look forward to getting to know you and your team. Do you think Luthor knows you're leading the rebellion?"

"He might not know yet, but it's only a matter of time. Once he figures it out, he'll publicly execute me if we fail, so I'm counting on you, Arthur. I'm not ready to be tortured for public entertainment."

"The only person who's going to be tortured is Luthor," Tristan interjected. "I'm going to kill that fucking bastard, and he's going to choke on his own blood."

"We wish you well on your mission," Arthur said. "Tristan, please contact me with updates."

"Will do."

The static settled and Grace realized Arthur had turned off his radio. Tristan packed up the supplies before stuffing the bag inside the truck. "Should I drive the truck closer to the cabins?"

"Yes," Grace said, trailing around to the passenger side and hopping in. "We'll stuff every inch of every vehicle with as many weapons as we can before heading to Arthur's compound in Maryland."

Tristan slid behind the wheel and hot-wired the truck before putting it into gear. He drove over the high grass until they reached the cabins. Putting the truck in park, he turned to face her.

"What do you mean when you say Luthor cost you everything? Are you talking about Raquel?"

Grace's nostrils flared at the question. She could've pretended he was referring to Danica's sister, who had recently died at the hands of Luthor. But they both knew he was referring to their daughter, who'd they'd also planned to name Raquel before Grace went into premature labor at five months and lost the baby.

"Yes," she said, holding up a hand when he opened his mouth to question her further. "Not now. Let's make it to Scranton and our quarters there. They'll allow us privacy to have this conversation."

"I want some fucking answers, Grace—"

"Don't curse at me," she said, grabbing the handle and swinging open the truck door. "I'm not the same little rich girl who looked at you with stars in her eyes and hung on your every word. I was forced to become something much stronger—and much colder—when you left me behind with a baby on the way and zero support system."

"Grace—"

"Not now," she gritted, exiting the truck and slamming the door. Striding around, she waited until he got out. "When we get to Scranton, we'll have a safehouse where we'll have privacy. I want you to drop it until then."

Tristan scowled. "I will, but once we're alone, you're going to tell me everything. I won't operate in the dark."

"Fine," she said before turning to stalk to the cabin. "And don't speak to me that way in front of my men," she called over her shoulder. "I'm the commander here, and you'd damn well better remember that."

Cognizant of the emotion swirling through her body, she reminded herself to remain calm. Tristan had always stirred up more emotion in her than anyone on the planet. He'd always been the one person able to infiltrate her ice queen façade.

But she owed it to her men to show strength, and had learned long ago that emotion only led to heartache. Leaving her ex-husband behind, she marched up the stairs, ready to prepare her team for the next phase of their plan.

CHAPTER 11

L uthor Cromwell paced in front of the expansive conference room table in his penthouse office in downtown Washington, DC. His side ached from where that little bitch Raquel Lawson had stabbed him the night everything went to shit. At least her death brought him a small sense of satisfaction. *No one* stabbed Luthor Cromwell and got away with it.

"Are you all right, sir?" Dr. Ziegler asked from his seat at the table. "If your side is hurting, I can give you a painkiller."

"I'm fine," Luthor said with an absent flick of his hand. The constant stream of EverLife in his system should've led to faster healing, but Dr. Ziegler had informed him that Raquel had nicked a major vessel near his kidney. Although he'd eventually heal, the incapacitation was frustrating—especially for someone who needed to exhibit strength and confidence.

Striding to the long windows, Luthor glanced across the city. The buildings no longer seemed to sparkle in the midday sun. Instead, there was a gloomy pallor over his once-promising metropolis. Smoke rose in the distance, causing him to scowl.

"I thought I told you to arrest anyone who started a bonfire," Luthor snapped. "They're signs of the rebellion that need to be eradicated."

"My men have been advised to arrest anyone who makes sympathetic gestures toward the rebellion," Colonel McGrath said, rising and walking to stand beside Luthor. His eyes narrowed as he observed the smoke, and he lifted the walkie talkie from his belt. "Major Martinez, please send some soldiers to address the bonfire near Pennsylvania Avenue and E Street."

"Yes, sir," a voice crackled over the radio.

"Major Martinez failed in the attack on Arthur's compound, and yet, he's still in a leadership position." Luthor rubbed his chin. "How odd. Do we accept failure in our ranks, Colonel McGrath?"

"We lost Lieutenant Colonel Jackson in that battle, sir," McGrath said, a slight twinge of anger and regret in his tone. "Tony has earned the respect of his battalion, and removing him would cause strife amongst the soldiers."

"What's the point in having the strongest army in the world if we lose?" Luthor shot him a glare before heading back to the table. "Sit down, Colonel McGrath. We have lots to discuss."

Once McGrath was seated, Luthor rubbed his forehead and sighed. "I'm not sure how I've lost my grip on peace. All I've ever wanted was for humanity to live together in harmony. Long, unanimous harmony where everyone benefits from the spoils of my labor—and where I don't get arrested for the crime of being rich."

Gripping the high-backed leather chair, he slid onto the seat and rested his forearms on the table. "We must make everyone remember that I am a generous, peaceful ruler. But I am also practical, and I realize the only way we can maintain peace is to destroy the rebellion."

"Our spies have been reporting back to me consistently," Colonel McGrath said. "There's been some movement near the Scranton compound, and we'll continue to monitor that, as well as Arthur's compound in Maryland."

"I would be worried that shady bastard Solomon Grange is harboring George Luddington since he disappeared after Grace was kidnapped, but George is too much of a pretentious snob to hide on such a disparate compound. My guess is that he's hiding somewhere in the Philly Sen City. The mayor I've installed there complies with my wishes, and I've let them continue to use power and some basic technology for now."

"We haven't located your wife, sir, but it is our highest priority."

"Yes, she must be found. I can't be the most powerful leader in the world if I can't rescue my own wife."

Colonel McGrath cleared his throat. "Plus, I'm sure you want to make sure she's unharmed."

"Yes, yes," Luthor said dismissively, waving his hand. "Of course, I hope she's okay."

Luthor observed the uncomfortable looks his men gave each other and pounded his fist on the table. "Three weeks is too long! I want Zayne and Grace located immediately. Am I understood?"

"Yes, sir."

"Dr. Ziegler, are we ready to inject the first two hundred soldiers with the enhancement serum?"

"I completed the two-week observation of the first ten men I injected, sir," Dr. Ziegler said, his voice racked with nerves. "As we discussed, two are incapacitated. Their bodies went into shock and they are now in stroke-induced comas. The other eight soldiers are tolerating the drug well enough. They've all shown bouts of increased anger and irritability, but each man can now lift twice what they were able to before."

"And their healing properties?" Luthor asked.

"The strength enhancement serum combined with the EverLife in their system seems to have a positive healing effect. I cut a small gash on each of the eight men's forearms, and they all healed without a scar within seconds. A cut like that would normally take a week to heal."

"So, they could effectively sustain injuries during a battle and be able to bounce back quickly."

"In theory, yes," Dr. Ziegler said with a nod.

"We'll inject the two hundred soldiers we discussed, Colonel McGrath. They were all recruited from poor families, most of whom were ravaged when they decided to succumb to addiction rather than take the watered-down antidote I generously provided."

"Yes, sir," Colonel McGrath said. "They have all consented to receiving the super-soldier drug and have been advised of the possible side effects."

"I want to be there as they're injected. Let's plan on two o'clock today in the barracks building on Eighth Street."

"Sir, some might go into cardiac arrest or experience a stroke when injected," Dr. Ziegler said. "I'll need a full medical triage station set up in the barracks."

"Fine. Get him whatever he needs," Luthor said to Dr. Johnson, a white-haired man who he'd nominated as head of what remained of the hospital system in the city.

As Dr. Johnson nodded, Luthor addressed Colonel McGrath. "And I want the exact locations of Zayne Danvers, Grace and George Luddington ASAP. Don't make me ask again, Colonel."

"I'll have a report when we meet at fourteen hundred hours to inject the soldiers, sir."

Rising, Luthor placed his palms on the cool wood, leaning forward to emphasize his words. "I haven't done a public execution yet, but controlling the entire power structure and television streaming channels allows me to communicate directly with my constituents. I believe Zayne Danvers is an excellent choice for the first public execution. Find him so I can remind the good people of our city what happens to dissenters."

The men rose and filtered out of the room, many of them appearing slightly dejected as their shoulders hunched.

Squeezing his hand into a fist, Luthor clutched so tightly his knuckles turned white. If only power was as easy to grasp...

"You'll win them back," he murmured to himself, slowly approaching the window again. "They just need to be shown the consequences of dissension."

Placing his palm on the glass, he pressed his nose to the cool surface. "I'll remind you *all* who gave you renewed life. And once you remember, we'll all prosper together."

Silence surrounded him as he clung to the pristine glass, his loose grasp a metaphor for how quickly things could slip away if he didn't retain control.

Luthor refused to return to a world that saw him as a criminal monster. He was meant to be a leader, and the people just needed to remember his benevolence.

Failure was not an option.

Pushing away from the window, he walked to the adjoining bathroom to check his wound. Small sparks of doubt flared that Grace could somehow be involved in the rebellion, but he quickly dismissed the thoughts.

His wife was a gorgeous trophy. Someone whom he'd allowed to live because of the very lucrative business deal she'd proposed when she suggested they marry. And since her heir had died, she was the last of the Albrights, allowing Luthor to assume Robert's wealth and company.

Yes, in a cruel twist of fate, the death of Grace's daughter had secured Grace's life.

Another advantage to his marriage with Grace had been George Luddington's support. Luthor hated the fat bastard, but he'd been powerful before the world fell and had many connections. The fact that George and Grace had disappeared was certainly suspect.

"For god's sake, Luthor," he said to his reflection in the mirror as he examined the injury to his side. "What could Grace possibly gain from helping the rebellion? And even if it benefited her, she's a doormat who would never abandon her wealthy life."

Lowering his shirt over the bandage, he shook his head. "She's being held by Zayne for leverage. That's all."

Confident he understood the situation fully, he headed to inject a round of EverLife before continuing his day.

Chapter 12

The cars were ready by three o'clock, and as clouds darkened the sky, Grace realized a storm was about to roll in.

"It seems luck is on our side," she said to her team as they stood outside the main cabin. "The rain will make us much harder to track. As discussed, we'll all follow separate paths. Zayne, you and I will take the direct route, following old Highway 81. Tristan, you and your men will take the old Route 11."

Tristan nodded, his face impassive.

"Charles and Kent will drive the SUVs, taking the long northern routes so we don't draw attention. If you pass Ardor Creek, you've gone too far north. I think we all should arrive by dusk."

Grace splayed her hands to emphasize her next words. "Solomon Grange is skeptical of visitors, even though he knows we're friendly. He'll have his men search us, and we need to remember not to be antagonistic."

Tristan shot her a glare, as if he knew she was talking to him.

Flattening her lips at his angry look, she continued. "If you notice someone following you, make sure you lose the tail before you approach Scranton. Are there any questions?"

Silence followed as they shook their heads.

Steeling herself for the fact that all her planning was finally coming to fruition, Grace lowered into the vehicle beside Zayne and set off for Scranton.

Tristan approached the imposing steel walls of the Scranton black-market compound as thick clouds loomed above. The rain had let up slightly, but the ominous clouds in the distance warned more was on the way.

The perimeter compound wall was caked with mud in several places, and Tristan wondered how often it was cleaned, if ever. Narrowing his eyes, he noticed several spray-painted warnings, including *Stay Out* and *Do Not Enter*.

"It's possible we'll be separated inside, so make sure you stay alert. Keep a mental log of everything and let's make sure we compare notes. Something innocuous could end up being important."

"You got it, boss," Caleb said.

When they reached the front gates, they were met by two armed guards, rifles in hand. Stepping out of the truck, Tristan showed his palms.

"I have a gun holstered on my belt and a knife in my boot," he said. "I'm assuming you're going to frisk us. Caleb is in the passenger seat, and John is in the truck bed. They also have handguns and knives."

"Stand here," one of the guards said, pointing to an open area beside the truck. The three men complied and were frisked.

Annoyed at the loss of his armaments, Tristan reminded himself to be cordial. "When will we get our weapons back?"

"When you leave the compound," the guard said. "Grace has already arrived. She's waiting for you inside. We'll confiscate the truck and park it inside the walls until we're ready to load it with weapons."

Tristan nodded before the guards pulled open the thick steel front doors. "Walk three hundred yards down the road and you'll arrive at the old Scranton post office. It's Solomon's home base now, and they're waiting for you."

Tristan started down the damp dirt road, John and Caleb walking silently beside him as they took in the surroundings. What used to be minor Scranton roads and buildings were mostly burned out, melted to crisps and meager frames. Discarded vials and needles lined the ditches on either side of the road, and Tristan noted it had once been paved. Cracked asphalt still lined small patches along the edges, but otherwise, the road had returned to dust.

As he walked, Tristan searched for signs of life. One glaring difference between the DC Sen City and the Scranton compound was the lack of homeless people.

"I thought we'd see more people living in tents like in DC," John said.

"I heard Solomon allowed shitty, contaminated EverLife on his compound and all the addicts died," Caleb said. "He's not as altruistic as Arthur Reyes, who has a reputation for at least *trying* to only allow clean EverLife and antidote on his compound."

"And allowing shitty EverLife leads to big payoffs from dealers," John said. "Killing people has probably made Solomon rich."

"Which means he's not much higher on the sliding scale of asshole than Luthor," Tristan warned. "Stay sharp and don't trust anyone you meet here. Blind trust will get you killed."

"You trusted Grace pretty fast even though she's Luthor's wife," Caleb said. "It all seems a bit strange to me. She'd be a perfect double agent."

"She's not a double agent," Tristan said as they neared the former post office. The lettering at the top of the building had been torn away and replaced with black spray paint that read *Scranton Compound Headquarters*.

"How do you know?"

Halting, he turned to face them. "Because before she was his wife, she was mine. And I trust her implicitly, which means you both do too. Are we clear?"

They glanced at each other, each urging the other to ask the question both wanted answered.

"How in the hell did your wife end up married to Luthor Cromwell?" Caleb asked.

"Because I made a lot of mistakes I'll pay for forever." Tristan harshly rubbed his forehead. "Any other questions? Or can we get on with our fucking mission?"

They both shook their heads as Tristan struggled to contain his annoyance. Facing the headquarters, he climbed up the stairs, ready to meet the infamous Solomon Grange.

Grace observed Tristan enter the building, his two counterparts close on his heels. Solomon sat in a makeshift throne of sorts at the top of the marble stairs, and he hooked his fingers, beckoning them forward as the large doors closed behind them.

"Ah, the infamous Tristan Holder," Solomon said, gaps in his smile where several teeth had eroded. "The man who has his hands in everything, but still knows nothing."

Tristan halted at the bottom of the stairs and planted his hands on his hips. "I'm just trying my best to survive in this shithole world and take care of those I love." His eyes darted to Grace, and her heart skipped a beat at his intonation. Although he was referring to Jessica, his searing gaze left no doubt he was also referring to *her*.

Grace remained impassive, refusing to allow emotion into her expression. Love had never been the problem between her and her enigmatic ex-husband. *Believing* in their love for each other had always been the issue. Somewhere along the way, she'd lost faith in his feelings for her. Although she knew a part of him still loved the girl she'd been, he didn't know the woman behind her cultivated shell.

Tristan loved someone she would never be again. A part of her mourned that idealistic version of herself, but she'd become the person she needed to be to protect those she hadn't yet lost.

"We're all doing our part," Solomon said, gesturing toward Grace. "And your ex-wife is doing a fine job. Thanks to her efforts, our compound has remained off the radar, but I fear that luxury is now over."

"We knew this day would come eventually," Grace said, refusing to allow men to speak on her behalf any longer. "We need to mount an offensive and take back DC from Luthor once and for all. Now that Arthur's compound has been attacked, there's no reason to wait."

"The weapons George has been funneling here over the past few years are all safe in the bunker by the northern stretch of the wall. I might have confiscated a few for my own use, but most are there, along with the ammunition and other supplies."

George Luddington, who'd been lurking in the shadows behind Grace, stepped forward, balancing on a cane as he advanced. "I had a feeling you'd swipe a few," he muttered, arching an eyebrow. "But I appreciate your alliance, so I won't grumble about it."

Solomon elicited a hefty chuckle. "Good. I'll allow you to remain in your luxurious suite in the old hotel by the Lackawanna River. That's how alliances work, George. You take a little, I take a little...and everyone's happy."

Grace lifted her hand to retake control of the conversation. "Now that we're all happy, let's get on with the mission. My men and I need to get a good night's sleep so we can inspect the bunker first thing in the morning and catalog the weapons. We'll load all of the vehicles by tomorrow afternoon and leave for Arthur's compound around midnight. The darkness should provide some good cover."

"My dear," Solomon said, his voice dripping with fake affection. "You can stay longer. You've only just arrived."

"We've set things in motion that can't be undone," she said firmly. "I'll return once we've defeated Luthor, and we can discuss your future."

Solomon lifted an eyebrow, a warning in his gaze. "My future is up to me, Grace. You'll do well to remember that."

"Of course." She gave an affirming nod, acknowledging now wasn't the time to anger the man sheltering her and a shitload of weapons. "I look forward to that day. Do you have a place where we can stay the night?"

"There are several vacant rooms in George's hotel, although none as nice as the one he claimed. You're welcome to stay there. It's a ten-minute walk from here, but you'll need to drive to the bunker with the weapons."

"Thank you. Our vehicles were confiscated when we arrived—"

"I needed to check them for drugs, Grace. I can't have you smuggling in the shiny new antidote I've heard about on Arthur's compound. We have trade alliances with antidote dealers, and they wouldn't be pleased if I diluted their stash with cleaner serums."

Gritting her teeth, Grace took a second to tamp down her anger. One of her goals after defeating Luthor was to eradicate *all* of the black-market drugs with nefarious components. But she had to accomplish one thing at a time, and focusing on shady drug dealers wasn't on her agenda yet.

"Well, I'm sure you found the vehicles clean, and I'd like them back so we can load the weapons."

"My men will be outside the hotel at first light ready to drive you to the bunker. Any other questions?"

"That's it for now. Will you be accompanying us to the bunker?"

Solomon wrinkled his nose. "I wish you well, but I have no desire to dirty my hands in a war. If you win, I'll be here to enjoy the spoils. If you lose, I can claim that I never truly joined the cause."

"A man with strong conviction," she muttered. "How noble."

"Just a man who's learned to survive." His eyes narrowed. "As I know you have, Grace."

Fear darted up her spine at his tone. Did he know something? She glanced at George, and he slightly shook his head, indicating Solomon was just blustering.

"We'll head out to the hotel before it starts to rain again," she said, looking toward the high windows. "I'll report back tomorrow once we've loaded the vehicles. Thank you for your help, Solomon."

Extending her hand, she waited for George to take it. "You going to walk with us?"

"I've got no choice since the golf cart I was using ran out of gas." Gripping her hand, he sighed. "I don't move as fast as I used to before I stopped taking EverLife. Thankfully, I was able to bribe Luthor's maid to steal a stash of his clean antidote before I fled the city."

"I'm glad you're free of that garbage," she said, squeezing his fingers. "And Marcia would be too," she said, referencing George's wife, who'd passed away in her sleep a few weeks before Grace's "kidnapping." "Once we defeat Luthor, I'm happy to exercise with you to rebuild those muscles. I want you with me for a long time, George. Dad would be proud of your dedication to our cause."

"I hope so, dear. Lead the way."

She slowly led him out of the post office and down the dirt road, cognizant of Tristan, Zayne and their men following close behind.

"Once you're settled in the hotel, come to my suite," George said softly so only she could hear. "I think it's best if we talk privately."

Grace jerked her head to gaze into his eyes. "Should I be worried?"

"I overheard Solomon discussing towns along the Susquehanna River, including Dundore. I found it strange. It's a small town that's been mostly deserted since the fall of society."

"That is strange," she whispered, acknowledging the nagging worry in her gut. "I'll stop by your room around seven to discuss. Thank you, George."

When they arrived at the abandoned hotel, George gave them a quick tour of the four-story building. "The second floor is mostly vacant, except for the families that stay in rooms 201 and 202. The doors are unlocked and you can have your pick."

Grace chose room 208 since it was located in the middle of the floor near the defunct elevator bank. A stairwell ran parallel to the elevators, so she had a quick escape in the event something went wrong. The rest of the men filtered into the vacant rooms, and she noticed that Tristan claimed room 210 beside hers.

"There are some jugs of bottled water in the lobby I paid some kids to bring from the well," George said as he headed toward the stairwell to climb the last fight to his third-floor suite. "There's no power, so it's barebones, but if you search the hotel, you might find a toothbrush and some other toiletries. Use the water sparingly. Good night."

Lifting his cane, he tipped it before disappearing into the stairwell. Grace entered her room, taking note of the dust that covered every surface. Scrunching her nose, she took a fleeting moment to remember times in her life where everything had been clean and pristine.

Acknowledging those days were over, she searched through the closet, hoping to find some sheets that hadn't been infested with moths or rat droppings.

Chapter 13

Tristan heard Grace's room door close, followed shortly by the stairwell door. Pulling the stethoscope from his bag, he placed the ends in his ears and stood on the bed. Pressing the receiving end to the ceiling, he waited.

He'd overheard Grace and George speaking in hushed tones and didn't like the secrecy. Were they hiding something from him? If it was detrimental to their cause, he needed to know.

He'd learned surveillance during his time in special ops and would put the skills to good use. Did he feel guilty for spying on Grace's conversation? Absolutely not. She'd kept her role in the rebellion secret, so he considered his efforts fair play.

When she finally told him everything, there would be no need to spy.

Straining, Tristan struggled to hear the muffled words through the ceiling.

"...can't guarantee Arthur will accept the package or handle it with care..." Grace said.

Footsteps shifted above, as if she were pacing, before George answered.

"...safer with Arthur than Solomon..."

Tristan's eyes narrowed as he wondered what this "package" could be. Realizing they were going to continue to speak in code, he lowered to the bed and ran his hand through his hair.

One thing he'd learned over the years was patience. Leaning back on his hands, he crossed an ankle over his knee and waited. Minutes ticked by as he absently shook his foot, waiting for Grace's return.

Eventually, the stairwell door closing echoed in the hallway, and Grace's room door creaked shut moments later. Ready for some answers, Tristan strode to her room and firmly knocked on the door.

Grace scowled at the pounding on her hotel door. She was in the middle of brushing her teeth, thanks to the toothbrush she'd stowed in her bag. As part of her preparation, she'd armed Zayne with a toiletry bag for her before he'd "kidnapped" her. Having small luxuries like a toothbrush, nail clippers, and Q-tips were more invaluable than gold.

It was amazing what you learned to appreciate when your husband destroyed the world.

Speaking of husbands, her former one was banging down the door as if the room was on fire. After rinsing, she gripped the sink with both hands and sighed.

"You did promise him answers, Grace. Just be careful."

Striding to the door, she yanked it open and frowned. "Are you trying to wake everyone up? Our men need sleep."

"And I need answers. *Now*," he said tersely.

She arched an annoyed brow. "I'm exhausted. Can we do this in the morning—?"

He splayed his palm on the door and pushed it open another inch. "What package are you and George referring to?"

Gripping his wrist, she dragged him into the room and closed the door.

"That's confidential," she gritted, aware of the muscle ticking in her jaw.

"No more secrets." Leaning forward until their noses almost grazed, his eyes burned with anger and frustration. "I mean it, Grace."

"Fine." Walking to the bed, she sat down and removed her sneakers. Her feet were killing her, so she massaged her swollen toes as she contemplated where to start.

"Feet hurting?" he asked, his expression softening.

Nodding, she continued her ministrations. "I worked out often in DC, but nothing prepares you for hiking along dirt roads on a shitty compound. To say my circumstances have changed is an understatement." She circled her hand, indicating the sparse, faded decoration.

"Slide back to the headboard," he softly commanded.

Grace's eyebrows drew together, but she complied. Perhaps due to muscle memory from all the times in the past he'd commanded her with that deep voice.

Tristan trailed over and sat on the edge of the bed. Lifting her feet onto his lap, he began to massage them.

"*Oh, god...*" she moaned, eyes closing with pleasure as she leaned her head against the headboard. "It feels *way* better when you do that."

His warm chuckle surrounded her, making her feel like the gooey center of a hot brownie. God, she'd always loved his voice...and his laugh...and those golden-flecked irises that gazed into her soul...

"I'll keep going while you talk. Hell, maybe it will soften you up."

Squinting one eye, she grinned. "Good plan."

They sat in silence for a few moments, each easing back into the comfortability they felt when they'd been the most important people to each other on the planet.

"This is nice, empress," he said, his thumb moving gently over her arch. "I missed touching you."

Sighing, she shook her head. "I missed it too."

His gaze was hooded as it bore into hers. "What did you mean when you said you and Luthor didn't have a passionate marriage?"

She played with a nonexistent thread on her pants. "It was a stipulation of my marriage proposal to him—that he never touch me sexually. And he never did."

Questions swirled in Tristan's eyes. "That seems impossible."

"It's easy to tell a man you're not interested in sex when you've just had..."

"A miscarriage?" he asked softly.

Emotion welled in her throat. "Yes," she whispered. "Among other things."

"Tell me," he said, running his thumb over the pads of her toes in a soothing gesture. "My promise not to yell still stands."

Needing space, she drew her legs from his lap and stood. "Remember that last time we really yelled at each other? Our last terrible fight before you deployed?"

Regret marred his features as he slowly ticked his head in acknowledgment. "I relived it every day for years. It was the biggest mistake of my life."

"Fighting with me or deploying when I was four months pregnant?"

"All of the above. I never should've left." Rising, he closed the distance between them and cupped her face. "I'm so sorry, Grace. I thought I was doing the best thing for us. Your father blacklisted me, and I couldn't get a security job to save my life. It was the only path I saw to supporting our family."

"I know you thought it was best," she said, overcome by the sentiment in his eyes. "But I could've supported us—"

"No. There's no honor in that. I had to earn you and support you and our daughter."

"Darling," she warbled, overwhelmed with grief as she stroked the stubble that lined his jaw, "you had me from the second you met me on that balcony. I never needed anything else."

"It didn't make sense to me then," he murmured, running his thumb in a slow, tender stroke over her chin. "That I could be enough. I was a young fool deeply in love. Age has given me more perspective. Now, I realize that only an idiot would leave his pregnant wife and ask her to stay behind in close proximity to her father who hates him until he returns from deployment." He slowly shook his head. "I just couldn't see it then."

"I know you thought you were doing the right thing, but it broke me. I chose you, Tristan, and you chose some misplaced sense of...*obligation* to prove that you deserved me. Hell, I showed up on your doorstep three months after we started dating and demanded you elope with me."

He breathed a laugh. "You were always excellent at showing up on my doorstep and bending me to your will. You're a fantastic manipulator. I should've realized it ages ago. It makes sense you've scaled up to plan an entire rebellion."

Pride swelled at the glow of admiration on his handsome face. "I'm used to people underestimating me. It's how I survived this long."

"I need you to know that our time together was the happiest of my life, Grace." He cleared his throat as emotion laced his words. "Such a short time, but it meant everything to me."

"Before it all fell apart," she said softly, encircling his wrists and drawing his hands away from her face.

"I'm sorry I wasn't there when you lost the baby." His eyes were glassy as he flexed his fingers at his side, as if he could still feel her skin upon them. "It's unforgivable. When I returned home and you asked for a divorce, I knew it was futile to fight it. I promised to be there for you and I broke my vow. You deserved more."

"Like I said, I knew I'd truly lost you when you stopped fighting with me." She tilted her head. "I'd take arguing with you over a boring conversation with anyone else any day."

"You gave up too," he said, lowering to the bed and leaning back on straight arms. "You buried our daughter without me."

"Things moved quickly after Dad died, and I had no idea when you'd return. I had to make hard choices."

"Walk me through the choices. I need to know what happened. We never had any closure, and I can't help you defeat Luthor if I don't know everything."

"Okay, but stay there while I tell you." She pointed at the bed. "I can't think straight when you touch me. It brings back too many memories."

Crossing his outstretched legs at the ankles, he nodded, his face lined with understanding and empathy. "What did you mean when you said Luthor murdered your father?"

Grace rubbed her forehead, allowing the painful memories to surface.

"I'm going to tell you how everything unfolded, but please don't interrupt me. You can ask questions when I'm finished."

"All right."

Wanting to rid her shaking frame of its nervous energy, she began to pace as she recounted the tragic events of the past...

Grace wandered aimlessly around her father's large home, restless as she stroked her slightly distended abdomen. Ever since Tristan had deployed for his special ops mission in the Middle East, she'd been despondent. She'd begged him not to leave, but her husband was stubborn and immobile.

"Your father has blacklisted me for every security job on the East Coast, Grace," Tristan said as he furiously threw clothes into his backpack. "This special ops assignment will set me up for our future. I was lucky to get a four-month deployment and will be back before you have the baby."

"You might be back," she said, dread filling her heart. "You said they could extend the operation if circumstances change on the ground."

"I'm going to fight like hell so that doesn't happen. There are certain terrorist leaders we need to take down, and I'm going to ensure they're eradicated. Once I prove myself to the special ops commanders, I can parlay that into a job at the Pentagon. Your father has a wide reach, but it doesn't extend that far. I'm determined to support our family, and I won't depend on your father's money to raise my child."

"It's my money," she said, stomping her foot. "My mother left her family's trust to me when she died. Dad has no control over that."

"He's assured me he does, and I won't raise our child with inherited money. I'm going to build my own path and show those high society assholes that I deserve you and the family we've created."

"I don't need you to prove anything," she pleaded, grabbing his arm and halting his furious movements. Placing his palm over her belly, she pressed. "We both just need you here. Please don't go."

That had been one of many moments Grace had begged him not to deploy, but it had been no use. He'd been adamant that his way was the only way he would earn her.

Ultimately, it was the reason everything fell apart.

Before Tristan deployed, he added her to his lease and set everything up so she could maintain the apartment. But Grace quickly grew lonely and missed her father, even though their relationship was strained and she sensed Robert's disapproval of the child she'd conceived with her husband. Of course, he hadn't been on board with their elopement either, so she really shouldn't have been surprised.

Hell, couldn't a girl just fall in love and live happily ever after?

She found herself returning home often—to the place that represented happier times, when her mother was still alive and she was on good terms with her father. Although she tried her best to bury the hatchet with Robert, he'd become increasingly angry and unreasonable as he entered his sixties and grew closer to retiring and leaving the company in Grace's hands. Although she would become majority owner, she had no desire to run the day-to-day business. Still, she respected her father's legacy, and would inherit her rightful place as owner and president of the board while delegating duties to those who were better suited for Corporate America. Perhaps, then, he would forgive her for the misdeed of falling in love with someone he deemed unworthy.

To make matters worse, her father's business had become inexorably tied to Luthor Cromwell's Sendaxa Corporation. The pharmaceutical company was under all sorts of investigations and violations, and the relationship between Robert and Luthor was rapidly deteriorating.

Grace didn't understand all the details, but she knew Luthor was trying to get her father to push through approvals on certain drugs whose outcomes had been falsified. Although Grace and her dad weren't on the best terms, she believed Robert was an honest businessman and would never approve commercial production of drugs he believed would harm the public.

As Grace wandered the mansion, she heard Luthor arrive. He kindly greeted the butler and was escorted to Robert's home office. Curious, Grace crept down the hallway, noting the staff had mostly gone home since it was late. Their butler, Jerry, offered the men a drink, and Robert declined.

"Luthor's only staying a moment, and we won't need anything else, Jerry," Robert said. "You can head home. See you in the morning."

"Yes, sir." With a nod, Jerry retreated down the hallway, unaware that Grace stood in the shadows a few feet away. Minutes later, he exited the house, and she was left alone with her father and Luthor.

"I told you you're not welcome in my home, Luthor," Robert said, his tone acerbic as he sat behind his desk. Grace watched them through the slit in the cracked door as Luthor sat on the edge of her father's mahogany desk. His leg kicked back and forth in a gentle rhythm, as if he were comfortable and had no reservations that he was an unwanted guest.

"Your lack of respect is becoming dangerous, Robert," Luthor said, tracing the wood as he spoke. "With the last release of the weight loss drug to market, I'm now the richest man in the world. Some would say that makes me a very undesirable enemy."

"That weight loss drug is the last drug I'll ever push to market for you, Luthor," Robert said, leaning back in his leather chair. "I'm convinced you falsified the data about the outcome to the pancreas. In ten years, if we see a wave of pancreatic cancer, I'm going to blame you."

"People want a miracle weight loss drug," Luthor said with a shrug. "They'll do anything for it. The side effects are written on the product insert."

"Which no one reads," Robert gritted. "Regardless, you need to find a new CDMO. My company won't do your dirty work anymore."

"Pity since I'm under all these pesky investigations." Rising with the elegance of a panther, Luthor slowly paced around the desk, reminding Grace of a shark circling its prey in bloody waters.

"That's your own fault," Robert muttered.

"Perhaps. It's a shame I get punished for giving the people what they want." Halting, he gazed out the nearby window. "I have plans for a new drug. One that channels the fountain of youth and doubles a person's lifespan. I want to call it EverLife." He splayed his hand in a circle as he dramatically spoke the word. "What do you think?"

"I think developing a drug like that is expensive and requires the best minds in the world. It also would require cellular reconstruction, which, in turn, would require painkillers. Sendaxa doesn't have the best track record with safe painkillers."

"What's a little addiction when you can live two centuries?" Luthor asked, his tone sinister.

"Who in the hell wants to live two centuries? I'm barely surviving in this one."

"Ah, yes. I heard Grace's pregnancy is coming along nicely even if you hate her husband. You'll have an heir soon, Robert. Congrats."

"I told Grace I'd deny her my inheritance if she married him, but I can't bring myself to do it." He scrubbed his hand over his face. "Even though she defied me, she's my daughter and my only living relative."

"And if she were gone before she has the baby, that would leave you without an heir. In that instance, your company would automatically be absorbed by Sendaxa."

"What?" Robert asked, straightening in his chair. "No, the board would vote on what to do with Albright Industries—"

"Yes, and I, as CEO of Albright's largest pharmaceutical partner, would make a compelling case to fold your company under my wing. Don't worry, Robert. I assure you, I would take good care of it."

Something sinister trickled up Grace's spine as she listened, and she realized it was the cold rush of fear. Leaning closer, she watched through the crack as the next events unfolded.

"Well, Grace is young and has a child on the way, so I think Albright Industries is in good hands. She knows that I want George Luddington to take over as CEO if something happens to me. He's head of the board and will guide the company into the future."

"That fat bastard," Luthor said with a pfft. "He can't even guide himself away from a cheeseburger."

"We all have our vices," Robert said, glancing at his watch. "Regardless, it's time for you to go, Luthor. I don't begrudge you finding another CDMO. But our time as partners has come to an end, and my business goals don't align with yours. We've had a profitable arrangement for years, and although I no longer consider us friends, I wish you the best." Rising, he extended his hand. "I'll be polite to you in our social circles, but I think it's best for us to part ways."

Luthor slid his hands into his pockets, his lips curling into a malevolent grin. "You think you can dismiss me so easily? I'm the most powerful man in Corporate America, Robert. In time, I'll most likely become president. And you think you can just shoo me away?" He made a flicking motion with his hand. "I don't think so."

Drawing his other hand from his pocket, he appeared to clutch something in his fist. Slowly rounding the desk, he pressed his hand to Robert's shoulder and pushed him back into the chair.

"What the hell, Luthor—"

Luthor jabbed a needle into Robert's neck, pushing the stopper on the syringe forward. Cloudy liquid exited the syringe as Robert sank back in the chair, his muscles going lax.

"This is a hefty dose of that painkiller you disparaged, Robert," Luthor murmured, leaning closer as Grace covered her mouth to stifle a scream. "You see, I'm kind in my destruction. The opium inside will ensure you have a painless death. You're welcome, you bastard."

"Fuck...you!" Robert rasped, struggling to breathe as the drug coursed through his body.

Grace stood frozen, her mind screaming for her to intervene, but terror causing her to remain immobile. Petrified into a powerless statue, all she could do was watch as Luthor murdered her father.

"There, there," Luthor soothed, patting Robert's chest as he removed the empty vial and stuck it back in his pocket. "Don't worry, I've got another one in here for Grace. I'll make sure she and her unborn brat die quickly too."

Robert kicked and sputtered, fighting for his last breaths as the drug stole the life from his body.

"Once they're gone, I'll kill George Luddington and then I'll convince the board to sell Albright Industries to Sendaxa. I've always wanted an in-house CDMO. Too much red tape working with idealists like you, old friend. Now, I can approve everything to market much quicker."

"Grace... will... stop... you." Robert gasped. "She's smart."

Tossing back his head, Luthor broke into an ominous laugh. "Your daughter is a mindless twit who can't tie her own shoes without asking you first. I'll be doing her a favor by murdering her. One less vapid debutante in our elite circle, hmm?"

The words sent a jolt of anger through Grace, and she slowly regained the ability to move her fingers. Testing, she flexed them, wondering why in the hell her body was furiously shaking but she couldn't move.

"The drug is manufactured to mimic the effects of a heart attack. The Great Falls medical examiner has been paid an exorbitant sum to document that as your cause of death. Grace's death will be ruled the same."

Robert's eyes drifted closed as his head lolled on his shoulder. "Bastard... You'll burn in hell..."

"Perhaps. But I have plans, and I can't have you standing in my way, Robert. I'm sorry it's come to this, old friend." Robert exhaled his last breath as his body slumped in the chair. "Rest in peace."

No! The word shot through Grace's mind, and she willed her body to move. If she could just run to her father, perhaps she could do CPR and resuscitate him...

At that moment, a sharp pain ripped through her abdomen. Covering her belly, she screamed in pain and collapsed on the floor. Luthor's head snapped toward the door and he ran over, crouching beside her as she writhed in pain.

"Grace? I was meeting with your father. Did you overhear—?"

"Grace?" Jerry called, rushing down the hallway before kneeling beside her. "I forgot my phone and came back to get it. Are you all right?"

"Robert clutched his chest and fainted as we were meeting," Luthor said, pointing to her father's lifeless body behind the desk. "We need to get an ambulance here for both of them now!"

"Yes, sir," Jerry said, dialing 911 and lifting the phone to his ear. "I'm calling from 735 Crestwood Drive. We have a sixty-two-year-old man who's suffered a heart attack and a woman who's just over five months pregnant in distress..."

As Jerry spoke to the dispatcher, Luthor slid his hand behind Grace's neck. Having his skin against hers made her want to retch, but she knew she couldn't indicate she'd overheard his interaction with her father.

"Did you hear us speaking, dear?" Luthor asked, his dark eyes assessing her.

"No," Grace said through clenched teeth as another wave of pain shot through her trembling body. "Was just walking to the kitchen..."

"The ambulance is on its way, Grace," Jerry said, rubbing her shoulder in a soothing gesture. Closing her eyes, Grace thanked every god above that he'd forgotten his phone. Otherwise, she'd also be dead at the hands of the evil man who loomed above her.

Another wave of pain crested in her abdomen, and she realized she was having contractions.

"It's too early," she cried, tears streaming down her cheeks. "Call Tristan. Please..."

"We'll try, dear," Jerry said as sirens wailed in the distance. "The ambulance is almost here..."

Delirious from the agony of her father's death and the excruciating pain, Grace closed her eyes and allowed the darkness to overtake her...

Chapter 14

Tristan observed Grace crumple to the floor, burying her face in her hands as her body racked with sobs. Unable to comply with her request to stay away any longer, he rushed toward her and enveloped her in his arms.

"Shhh," he soothed, sitting on the floor and drawing her between his legs. She pressed her face to his neck, her tears wetting his skin as she curled into his body. "I'm here, sweetheart, and I'm so sorry."

"They couldn't reach you on your deployment. I asked the nurse to call you so many times..."

Tristan squeezed his eyes shut as shame and regret rolled through him. "I should've been there," he said, stroking her soft hair. "I can't imagine how painful losing the baby was. And you were all alone without your father. Fuck..." He tightened his arms around her. "I hate myself for leaving you."

Her tears eventually abated and she drew back, swiping her arm under her nose. Although her face was red and swollen, she was still the most gorgeous creature he'd ever seen. Cupping her cheek, he swiped the tears with his thumb. "I wish I could go back and change it."

"I know," she whispered, her throat bobbing as she swallowed thickly.

"Why didn't you tell me Luthor murdered your father?"

She pursed her lips as she contemplated. "Because by the time you came back, I'd already made my deal with Luthor...and accepted that we were over."

"Tell me why you made the deal, Grace. I'm just not getting it."

Sighing, she ran a hand through her hair. "I was the heir of Albright Industries. Luthor murdered my father in order to overtake the company. It was only a matter of time before he killed me too. So, I offered him a partnership that would give him what he wanted so I could live."

"You promised him control of Albright Industries."

"Yes. I made an offer that granted him everything he wanted but also ensured my future. I didn't want him to know that I'd seen him murder Dad. I needed to bide my time and earn his trust. I was understandably distraught after so much loss, so I needed time to mentally recover before I could plan revenge. Unfortunately, things took a bit longer than I expected. I didn't see the EverLife crisis occurring. Chalk that up to bad foresight, I guess."

"No one could've anticipated that," Tristan muttered. "And of course you needed time to mentally recover. Losing your father and the baby would devastate anyone."

"It wasn't just Dad and the baby..." she said softly.

Tristan's eyebrows drew together.

"I lost..." Her chin warbled as she struggled to maintain composure. "When I went into labor, I lost so much blood. Even though the doctors tried, they couldn't save my uterus..." She closed her eyes as two tears trailed down her cheeks. "So that's the only pregnancy I'm ever going to have."

Pain sliced through him as he digested her words. She'd lost her father, her child, and her ability to bear more children on the same day. That magnitude of loss was almost unimaginable.

"And I knew you wanted more kids... We'd discussed it several times..."

"Jesus, Grace. I wanted more kids with *you*. If you lost the ability to have them, I would've accepted that and supported you through it." Sliding his fingers under her chin, he forced her to meet his gaze. "How could you doubt that?"

"After you left me alone and pregnant when I begged you multiple times not to go?" she asked, exasperation in her voice. "Yeah, I'm not sure how I ever doubted you."

Tristan gritted his teeth as frustration for his choices—and annoyance at her ability to see any nuance in them—coursed through him. "I left for good and honorable reasons, Grace. I understand now that I made the wrong choices, but you've got to give me some credit. I did what I thought was right for our future."

"I wouldn't have *had* a future if I didn't think quickly and enter into my agreement with Luthor. He's a cold-blooded man and would've killed me, Tristan. The nurses gave him access to my room because he told them he was a family friend. I'm honestly surprised

I survived my time in the hospital. I'm very lucky he didn't slip something into my IV when I was sleeping and the staff wasn't present."

Tristan shook his head as hatred of Luthor coursed through his veins. He'd already hated the man with deep intensity for how he treated Jessica, but Grace's story only enhanced the sentiment.

"Thankfully, I befriended a wonderful nurse named Maria. I don't know what it was about her, but she was lovely and I trusted her immediately. As soon as I was cognizant enough to speak, I told her about Luthor and that he was a danger to me. I think she had something to do with making sure a staff member was always present when he visited my room."

"Thank god. Did she survive the EverLife crisis?"

"Yes," Grace said, her blue eyes darting between his as something unidentifiable swirled within them. "She lives in a small town not far from here called Dundore. She chose to stay away from the compounds and walled-off cities and live a quiet life."

Tristan's eyes narrowed. Grace and George had mentioned Dundore in their hushed conversation on the walk to the hotel.

A shuffle sounded outside the door, causing them to both gasp and whip their heads toward the sound.

"Did you hear that?" Grace whispered.

"Stay here."

Tristan jogged to the small kitchen area and searched the drawers for a knife. After locating a slightly rusted dinner knife, he ran to the front door, locking the knob from the inside before closing it behind him.

Searching the hallway, he strained to hear any noises. A door clicked at the far end of the hallway, and he took off after it, hoping to catch whoever had been spying on them. Tristan had become paranoid after years of living in a world without hope, and he didn't trust Solomon Grange not to betray them. After all, aligning with Luthor would give Solomon many benefits he might not receive with someone else in power.

Tristan barreled down the stairs and out to the grassy area behind the hotel. It had grown dark, but he could barely see the form of someone running into the nearby thicket of trees adjacent to the river. Gripping the knife, he entered the brush, hoping not to get ambushed.

"Hey!" Tristan grunted, grabbing a fistful of the runner's shirt before yanking him to a halt. "Gotcha!" Dragging the spy toward him, he glared down into angry brown eyes. "You're just a kid."

"Fuck you!" The boy kicked Tristan's shin, causing him to yelp and release his grip. The boy took off again and Tristan sped after him, gritting his teeth at the pain in his shin.

"Stop right there, you little jerk," Tristan yelled, catching hold of the boy's collar and forcing him to stop. The little tyrant reared his leg back and aimed for Tristan's balls.

"Hey!" Tristan said, his authoritative tone causing the kid to freeze. "I've got a knife, but I don't feel like stabbing a kid today. I'm not going to hurt you. Relax."

The boy panted from exertion as he stared at Tristan, his eyes filled with fear. Tristan noticed the shiner under his right eye, and he immediately released his grip. "You're okay, kid," he said, slipping the knife into his back pocket. "I don't know who gave you that shiner, but I don't hit kids. Even ones who kick the hell out of my shin."

The boy's eyes darted between Tristan's as he debated whether he could trust him.

"What's your name, and who hit you?"

"None of your business—"

"Nope," Tristan interjected, shaking his head. "We're not going to do the petulant child act. If you're old enough to spy on me, you're old enough to be a man and tell me your name and who hit you. Was it one of your parents?"

"My parents are dead," he said, sending a jolt of compassion through Tristan. "They died from EverLife addiction."

"Who took care of you after they died?"

"No one," he said, kicking the ground with the toe of his worn sneaker. "I can take care of myself."

"How old are you?"

"I'll be eleven next month."

Tristan placed his hands on his hips as he regarded the kid. "I know you were spying on me and Grace. For who? Solomon Grange?"

He shrugged.

"How much is Solomon paying you? Whatever it is, I can pay more."

The boy's eyes widened. "I get unlimited access to the commissary in the main square as long as I keep the information coming. I need food more than money."

"I can give you both. Sounds like a better deal than Solomon's giving you."

The boy frowned. "I didn't say I was spying for Solomon."

"You didn't have to...?" He drew out the end of the sentence and rolled his hand to urge the boy along.

"Nathan."

"Nice to meet you," Tristan said, extending his hand. "I assume you already know who I am since you were spying on me."

Nathan nodded and shook his hand—his grip surprisingly firm for a kid.

"Did Solomon give you that black eye?"

"Yeah, but it was my fault. I snuck some food from the commissary to a Sen Force deserter I met outside the wall on one of my scouting trips."

"That doesn't sound like something that deserves punishment."

"Solomon forbids helping deserters. He thinks they're spineless, and if the rebellion fails, he wants to be able to tell Luthor he never supported soldiers who left his army."

Tristan shifted his weight, wondering what the hell to do. He'd always had a bit of a savior complex—evidenced by the fact he'd worked for Luthor for several years in an attempt to assure Jessica was safe. Whether he wanted to or not, he felt a sense of obligation toward the scrawny kid with a shiner.

Crouching down, he beckoned Nathan forward. "Here's what's going to happen, Nathan. You're going to report back to Solomon that you spied on us and didn't hear anything." Hesitating, he asked, "*Did* you hear anything?"

"Something about Dundore...and I heard Grace crying."

Tristan swiped a hand over his face. "You're going to keep all of that to yourself. Do you hear me?"

Nathan nodded.

"We're going to catalog and load all the weapons tomorrow and then head to Arthur Reyes's compound in Maryland. I'm going to pay Solomon so you can come with us."

Recoiling, his eyebrows drew together. "Why?"

"Because I don't want you to get hit anymore, and I can use a good spy. I'll make sure you're fed just like Solomon does, and we can discuss payment once I decide how I'm going to use your...*skills*. I'll need you to act surprised when I suggest you joining us to Solomon, but I also need you to agree."

"But I don't know you," he said, trepidation in his voice. "Solomon is a jerk, but I know this compound."

"Solomon isn't a good man, Nathan—"

"And you are?"

Sighing, Tristan lifted a shoulder. "Some days are better than others," he muttered. "But today, I think I'm doing okay." Offering his hand, he waited. "What do you say? Want to align with the rebellion, Nathan?"

The kid studied Tristan's hand, gnawing on his lip as he contemplated. Finally, he placed his palm over Tristan's and they shook.

"Don't be a dick like Solomon, okay?"

Laughing, Tristan nodded. "I'll try. I'm more concerned with keeping up with my ex-wife and helping her win the rebellion."

"I'm a good spy," Nathan said, his chest puffing with pride. "I'll help you."

Tristan rose. "We need all the help we can get. Go on back to town. I'll see you tomorrow when we report back to Solomon after loading the vehicles. Make sure you're there."

Nathan nodded and pivoted before jogging away. When he reached the edge of the clearing, he turned back and waved. Something about the gesture tugged at Tristan's heartstrings, maybe because it was innocent, and he could tell the kid had lost most of his innocence long ago.

But that last heartfelt wave meant there was something salvageable there.

And for some reason, Tristan felt an urge to salvage it.

Releasing a deep breath, he plodded back to the hotel to resume his talk with Grace and inform her he'd recruited a ten-year-old spy to their ranks.

Chapter 15

Grace waited anxiously for Tristan to return. As the minutes passed, she washed her face and tugged on some old shorts and a t-shirt. Exhausted from the events of the day, she fought the urge to lie down. Craning her neck, she massaged the tense muscles there, her body reminding her she was a few years shy of forty and no longer bounced back as quickly as she once had.

Finally, the need to rest overtook her, and she slid into bed. She turned to her side, drawing the covers up to her chin as her knees curled into her chest. Within minutes, she was fast asleep.

Memories swam through her subconscious mind, parading as dreams that quickly turned to nightmares. The starkest memory was the blood the night she'd gone into labor...signifying all she'd lost.

Gasping, her eyes flew open as something tickled her cheek. Tristan loomed above her, looking rugged and handsome in the dim moonlight from the lone window.

"Sorry. I didn't mean to startle you, but I thought you'd want to hear what I found."

"Yes," she whispered, pushing herself up on her arm. "I was just going to lie down for a second. Damn it."

"Don't get up," he said, gently pushing her down as he sat beside her. Tenderness covered his features as he tucked a strand of hair behind her ear before softly stroking her hair.

"Tristan—"

"Old habits," he said, removing his hand and flashing a solemn grin. "I used to love watching you sleep."

Grace studied him as her heart pounded. "What did you find?"

Tristan told her about Nathan and that he'd ultimately invited him into the rebellion.

"You've been in the rebellion for one day and you've already tried to save someone," she teased, nudging his thigh with her knee from under the covers. "Your efforts to save people are noble, but I hate to tell you this, my dear ex-husband..." Biting her lip, she grinned. "They usually fail. You're very gallant, but terrible at executing your valiant plans."

"No shit," he muttered, swiping a hand over his face. "I ran off to the Middle East to save you and our marriage, and we both know how that turned out. I bent over backward to secure a job with a man I loathe to save Jessica, but she's still in his clutches."

"Luthor was dead set against hiring you, but I knew what you were up to. After failing to get on his payroll as a mercenary, I finally told him to hire you."

Tristan flinched. "You did?"

She nodded atop the pillow. "He thought it would bother me, being in such close proximity to you. I told him it wouldn't."

"Well, it was hell for me," he said, eyes narrowing. "Every time you walked into the room and kissed him on the cheek, I wanted to rip his throat out."

"All part of the show," she said, yawning.

"I know you're tired," he whispered, leaning closer and touching his fingers to her face. "But I don't want to leave. I'm still processing what you told me about losing the ability to have kids." He stroked her cheek as emotions warred inside her. "I want to comfort you."

"It happened a long time ago," she said, tears stinging her eyes as his image blurred. "I don't need comforting anymore."

"Bullshit."

Grace closed her eyes, refusing to let herself cry. Getting lost in painful memories was *not* on the agenda. She had a rebellion to lead and that was her primary focus.

"Let me hold you, empress," he said, the plea in his voice almost cracking her heart open. "Let me be there for you in the way I couldn't be before. In the way I should've been."

Lifting her lids, she stared into his gorgeous hazel-green eyes, knowing she'd already lost. She'd never been able to deny him when he looked at her like that. As if his soul was in his eyes, and he'd die if he didn't hold her.

"We have too much terrible history between us to try again," she said, the words feeling like a lie upon her tongue. "If you're expecting that, things are going to end very badly for you."

He breathed a laugh before running a hand through his hair. Rising, he kicked off his shoes and slowly removed his pants, his eyes on hers the entire time he slid them down his legs. He removed his shirt, and her eyes darted to his boxer briefs, which he left on.

"I'm very familiar with things ending badly, sweetheart, so you let me worry about that." Cocking an eyebrow in that sexy way that made her knees buckle, he asked, "So, are you going to let me hold you, or not?"

Grace felt her pulse in every cell of her body. It pounded in her throat, almost choking her as she contemplated. Finally, she lifted the sheets and invited him in.

His gorgeous smile would've been enough to soothe her frayed emotions.

But when he crawled in beside her and drew her against his warm, muscular frame, the familiar comfort of being in his arms pacified her long-suffering heart.

When he urged her cheek to his chest and pressed his lips to her forehead, Grace sighed against the scratchy hairs that tickled her nose.

And when he stroked her hair and whispered words of love and remorse, her enigmatic ex-husband soothed her tired soul as she drifted back into slumber.

Chapter 16

G race searched the darkness behind her closed lids, zeroing in on the pleasurable feeling between her legs. Not ready to leave the dream, her eyes remained closed as her hips undulated toward the blissful pressure. Sparks of arousal heated her skin—a feeling that had been dormant for so long, but that she remembered somehow...

A low growl sounded in her ear, followed by more pressure at her core. Warm breath rushed against her neck, followed by the brush of firm lips at her nape. Awareness dawned as she realized Tristan was cupping her between her legs. They'd often slept that way in the past—him holding her most private place in an act of physical possession.

"Tristan," she murmured. Labored pants left her lungs as her breathing accelerated.

"Hmm?" he uttered into her nape, and she realized he was still half asleep. He'd always been a deep sleeper, and he'd *always* snaked around her while they were sleeping—as if he knew he might lose her one day, so he held on extra tight.

"You're cupping my..." Exhaling an exasperated breath, she felt her cheeks flush.

She felt his muscles tighten as realization took hold. His hand froze as his chest rose and fell against her back.

"Muscle memory," he said softly, his fingers warm atop the thin fabric of her shorts.

Grace struggled to breathe as they both lay still.

His hand tightened on her core, ever so slightly, and she inhaled a sharp breath.

"Do you want me to let go?"

Silence echoed in the dark room as she contemplated.

Pressing his lips to her ear, he asked, "Or do you want me to make you feel good?"

"I told you, any romantic reconciliation between us is doomed—"

"Look who's the pessimist," Tristan said, nipping her ear. "Have the tables turned? Am I the optimist now?"

A nervous laugh escaped her throat. "You're an optimist if you think having sex won't end badly for us."

"I didn't say anything about having sex." His hand flexed atop her core again, and Grace stifled a groan. "I'm just going to make you feel good, empress."

Nerves swirled in her belly as she debated whether to run or to turn on her back and let her husband pleasure her with his talented fingers. Scratch that. Her *ex-husband*, which was why this was a very bad idea...

"Look at me, Grace."

Filled with trepidation, she turned her head on the pillow to meet his lust-filled gaze. "Let me love you, sweetheart."

Unable to speak from the lump of emotion clogging her throat, she capitulated and pushed into his hand. A broad smile curved his full lips.

"Good girl. I'm going to make you feel so good, baby..."

He slipped those long fingers under her shorts, finding her cotton panties and tracing the edge. Those burning hazel irises bore into hers as he dug under the elastic to find her bare skin.

"*Oh god...*" she cried, widening her legs to allow him better access. "It's been so long..."

Tristan's fingers swirled over her sensitive skin, sliding between her folds and rubbing the tender slit. Wetness surged to her core, coating his fingers as he groaned.

"So slick and pretty while I claim you, Grace." Leaning closer, he nudged her nose with his. "You've always been so pretty everywhere."

"My body isn't the same, Tristan. They had to cut me open when I went into labor—"

"Your body is perfect, no matter how many scars you have." He continued to stroke her as he gazed into her eyes. "One day, you'll let me see them." Pressing the tip of his finger to her wet opening, he said firmly, "One day, you'll remember that you belong to me."

With an assertive yet tender thrust, he slipped his finger inside her. Grace gasped as he inched farther inside, her muscles clenching as he assessed her.

"Relax, baby," he crooned, circling his finger in her tight warmth as she slowly released the tension from her muscles. "That's it. Let your body remember me."

Oh, how her body remembered him. Her lips fell open as she gazed at him through slitted eyes, and every cell of her skin burned. Unable to control her hips, she let go, pushing into his gentle ministrations as she allowed herself a moment of pleasure.

"I've waited so long..." he rasped, inserting another finger and stretching her as he worked his hand back and forth. "I thought I'd never touch you here again."

Grace wrapped her arms around his shoulders, holding on for dear life as he claimed her all over again. He circled his fingers, coating them with her essence before sliding them up to the tiny little bud that was rapidly swelling with desire. Dousing her clit with her slick, he made sure she was ready. Trailing his fingers back down, he slid them inside her again and pressed the heel of his hand to her pulsing clit. Closing her eyes, Grace's head fell back on the pillow as she moaned.

"God, I love watching you come," he said, moving his fingers in steady strokes inside her quaking body as he rubbed her clit with the heel of his hand. "Your cheeks flush the prettiest shade of red, and your lips swell, ready to take me."

He increased the pace and pressure of his hand at her core as his lips grazed a path from her cheek to her ear. Grace shuddered when he licked the sensitive shell before whispering dirty words. "Remember when you used to take me between those sexy lips, Grace? It's my favorite memory...and my ultimate torture...knowing it would never happen again."

"You're still a pessimist," she said, joy flooding her as she teased him.

Chuckling, he pressed his forehead to her temple. "I'm always evolving. We'll see."

Grace soaked in the warmth from his strong frame, losing herself in his sandal-wood scent. His smell had always enveloped her when they slept—and when they made love—and she attributed it to one of the many things that sparked their undeniable chemistry.

Sometimes, you just couldn't argue with nature. Their connection had always been irrefutable.

This is why she'd stayed out of Tristan's way in the decade she'd been married to Luthor, even though he worked for him, which meant they inevitably saw each other in passing. Staying away from Tristan was the only way her plan would work—and the only way she could protect those who needed it. Tristan had always been able to protect himself, and she knew if she allowed herself access to him, she'd jump right back into his arms.

This was clearly evidenced by the fact they'd been alone together for less than two days and he currently had his fingers deep inside her body. Jesus, she really had no control when it came to him.

"Stop thinking, empress," he crooned, increasing the pace of his skillful fingers. "We can save the world when I'm done making you scream. Come all over my fingers, baby. Let me feel you fall apart."

She released a deep breath, her muscles turning to jelly as she fully relaxed. Tristan's warm breath rushed against her ear, whispering unintelligible words as he brought her to the edge. Just when she thought her body might explode, her back arched and she dove into a blinding orgasm.

Wave upon wave of pleasure drowned her pulsing body as she cried his name. Her fingernails speared into his neck, causing him to emit a sexy growl as he cupped her deepest place. She shuddered and quaked, losing all control as he murmured words of praise.

As the high wore off, she lay limp, a sated grin on her face as she listened to the buzzing between her ears. Wanting one moment of unadulterated bliss, she relaxed in his arms, knowing she was safe.

Tristan placed soft kisses over her nose and cheeks as he tenderly stroked her sweat-soaked hairline. Eventually, he removed his hand from her core and brought his fingers to his lips.

Grace's eyes slid open as he licked her essence from his fingers, taking his time as he stared into her eyes. His tongue darted over his drenched skin, and she swallowed thickly, remembering the times that wet tongue had worked magic between her legs.

"Worth the wait," he murmured, his eyes shining with pleasure and that slight bit of cockiness that always drove her wild. "I could survive on just tasting you every day."

The corner of her lips curved. "I don't think that's very nutritious," she teased.

"I don't give a damn." Resting his head on his fist as his elbow dug into the mattress, he caressed the hair at her temple as he regarded her. "It's been ten years. A decade without touching you. I don't want to go another decade. Are you planning on marrying any other nefarious dictators I need to know about?"

Snickering, she shook her head as her hair fanned across the pillow. "No. But I am still technically married to Luthor. It's obviously a sham marriage that will dissolve once he figures out my betrayal. And he *will* figure it out," she finished with a shiver.

"Good. I hope to see the shine of betrayal in his eyes when I murder him. That will be a nice parting gift on his way to hell."

"So, you're not going to berate me for being married to someone else while we..." She bit her lip as her cheeks flushed.

"While I had my fingers inside you?" he asked, cocking a brow. "Now that I know you weren't intimate with him, it certainly makes things easier. But the marriage needs to be dissolved, Grace."

"It will be in due time," she said, gliding her fingers into his thick hair. "I thought you'd become more patient in your old age."

Breathing a laugh, he shook his head. "I'm almost forty, not eighty. But seeing you married to someone else, especially that bastard, will never sit well with me. You're *my* wife, Grace."

"I *was* your wife," she replied softly.

Frustration entered his expression as he exhaled a slow breath. "You'll be mine again. Mark my words."

Grace tamped down the spark of hope that welled in her chest. "We're different people now, Tristan, and I can't have any more children—"

"For god's sake, woman. One thing at a time. Let's defeat Luthor and then we can discuss all the excuses you're going to make for rejecting me again. I need to be fully focused so I can combat them."

Grace stroked his hair, wondering if he would feel the same when *all* of her secrets were revealed. "Tristan..."

A knock on the door interrupted them, making them both jump as their heads swiveled.

"Yes?" Grace called.

"Ma'am, the sun will rise soon, and Solomon's men are outside with our vehicles."

"Be right there."

Sighing, she ran her thumb over Tristan's lips, acknowledging she couldn't linger any longer.

"After we load the vehicles, I'm going to send everyone to Arthur's compound, but I need to stop in Dundore along the way."

Annoyance entered his gaze as he studied her. "Why?"

"I'll tell you everything on the way. Nathan can ride with us too if you wish."

He gave a curt nod before rolling off her, and stood and rubbed his chest. Grace's eyes roved over the taut skin of his nipples and the chest smattered with brown and gray hair. Desire coursed through her frame and she pressed her legs together, reminding herself they didn't have time for another round, even though her husband was incredibly hot.

Ex-husband. Sheesh. She was really having a hard time remembering that.

Extending his hand, he beckoned to her. "Ready to catalog some weapons? Let's pack those puppies up and get ready to attack that asshole."

Pressing her hand to his, she stood, ready to face the day.

Chapter 17

After a quick rinse from the jug of water in his room, Tristan donned his clothes and reconvened with Grace outside the hotel. The sun was barely peeking over the horizon, and it appeared today was going to be rain free. Tristan chose to take that as a good omen.

Hell, maybe he was evolving into an optimist after all.

They drove to the far side of the compound, where thick forest butted up against the high steel walls. Arriving at a tall mound of grass-covered earth, they exited the vehicles and George walked to the small wooden door.

"This leads into the bunker," he said, unlocking it with the keys he pulled from his pocket. "It's dark in there, so have your flashlights ready."

Tristan clicked on one of the solar-powered flashlights Solomon had placed in the vehicles. They headed inside the dark, musty bunker, and Tristan's eyes grew wide at the amount of weapons stockpiled on the various shelves. Rifles, handguns, and ammunition were just the beginning. Tristan noted several stockpiles of teargas, grenades and grenade launchers, night-vision goggles, and a few Javelin antitank systems.

"Holy shit," Tristan said, scanning the room. "You have Javelins? They're extremely effective in disarming tanks. This is a massive haul. How long have you been stockpiling weapons here?"

"For years," Grace replied, and Tristan noted the exhaustion in her tone. "Albright Industries had a production plant close to here before the EverLife crisis. George and I realized Luthor was growing more unhinged after the government indicted him for falsifying the EverLife clinical trial evidence. We realized he might try to stage a coup on the government and figured it was a good idea to stash some weapons here in case we had to make a run for it."

"You two have been colluding that long?" Tristan asked, pointing between them.

"Yes," Grace said with a nod. "How do you think the government knew he falsified evidence?"

"You were the whistleblower?" Tristan asked as his eyebrows lifted.

"I thought it would be the perfect opportunity to bring him down and finally enact my plan. I didn't expect the world to become addicted to his drug, making him the most powerful man on the planet. No one cared that he overthrew the government. They just wanted their precious *drug*." She spat the word as if it were poison.

"At that point, Grace was stuck in the marriage with him," George said. "There was nothing we could do, and we debated having her make a run for it."

"But I wanted to finish the job," she said, lifting her chin. "Little did I know it would take me so long. I've been planting the seeds of rebellion for a long time. It took years for me to find people I could trust and sow dissent. And now, we're finally ready." She waved her hands over the weapons, reminding Tristan of Vanna White—if Vanna were a high-end arms dealer.

"Everything is converging nicely," George said, shifting his weight as he balanced on his cane. "Arthur Reyes's willingness to shelter Danica Lawson and support her creation of a cure means we have solution to EverLife addiction. The fact that Luthor's troops didn't breach his walls means Arthur's militia is competent."

"They have Arianna Lawson, and that woman is fierce," Tristan said. "I wouldn't want to be on the other side of a war against her. Dominic and Maverick are capable soldiers too."

"Then I like our chances," Grace said. "We have some spies inside the walls, and I anticipate you have some too." She arched an eyebrow at Tristan.

Tristan thought of all the people he paid to funnel information, including Deandra and Ron, the deli owners in LeDroit Park who were experts at mining data from Sen Force soldiers who frequented their establishment.

"Yeah, I've got a few."

"And we have a sneaking suspicion that Arthur secretly converted the young Major Anthony Martinez to his side when they attacked the compound. Lieutenant Colonel Jackson died in battle, and Anthony assumed command and retreated early the next morning. They had all the firepower; all the tanks. Why would they retreat otherwise?"

"We're going to find out when we reach Arthur's compound," Grace said, stepping into the center of the room to face everyone. "Tristan and I are going to make a stop along the way. Zayne, I expect you to protect George as you all journey to Arthur's compound."

"Yes, ma'am," Zayne said with a nod.

"Thank you. Let's get to work. George has a notebook, and we're going to catalog everything in this bunker. We won't be able to fit everything into our vehicles, so take what's most valuable and document what we leave behind too. If we fail, at least we'll have a small stockpile left."

On that ominous note, the team got to work cataloging the weapons.

Around six p.m., after the weapons were categorized and the vehicles were loaded, the team drove back to the compound headquarters. Solomon sat in his makeshift throne atop the faded marble stairs as Tristan, Grace and George approached. The rest of the team stood behind them with Zayne in front.

"We're packed and ready to depart after sunset," Grace said.

"Are all four vehicles driving the same path?" Solomon asked. "Because my friend Nathan here informed me you just exited Tristan's truck. I assumed you'd ride with George to Cumberland."

Tristan glanced at Nathan, who stood beside Solomon. His eyes were downcast, and Tristan wondered if he was showing contrition since he'd spied on them again.

"George, Zayne and I need to ride in separate vehicles," she said assertively. "We can't chance being ambushed, and someone needs to lead the rebellion if I die."

"So, you'll take separate paths," Solomon said. "I find that interesting."

"I'm not sure what you're hinting at, but I'd rather you just come out and say it," Grace said. "I don't have time for guessing games."

"I just find it strange that small settlements still exist along the Susquehanna River and wonder if you'll pass them on the way," he said with a shrug. "It would be better for them if they moved into my compound. We always need skilled laborers. Cooks, nurses, seamstresses... Well, you get the drift." He circled his hand. "My spies tell me there is a woman who lives in Dundore who has a magnificent plumbing system even though she doesn't seem to possess any plumbing skills. I wonder how that's possible?

Has someone been helping her? I've decreed that no one can help citizens who live within a hundred-mile radius of the Scranton compound. Dundore sits just inside that radius."

"I have no idea." Exasperation laced her tone as she lifted her hands. "My only goal is to get to Arthur's compound so we can begin the next phase of the rebellion. The time to attack Luthor is now, so I won't be stopping for any late-night sightseeing along the Susquehanna River."

Tristan's lips curved at her grit. She'd always been someone who stood up for herself and carried herself with confidence. But this woman—the one who stood with squared shoulders and lied with conviction to a man who most certainly had a gun holstered at his waist—was fierce.

A low-toned chuckle left Solomon's lips as he rubbed his chin. "All right, my dear. As you know, I must remain skeptical of any information I receive from my spies."

"Speaking of spies," Tristan interjected. "I had the pleasure of meeting Nathan at our hotel last night." His tone held an undeniable note of sarcasm. "He's fast, but I was able to question him before he squirmed away. You'll be proud to know he didn't divulge your secrets."

Fury flashed in Solomon's eyes as he gazed at Nathan. "Is this true, boy?"

Nathan nodded as he kicked the ground with his toe.

"I can tell you're pissed he didn't tell you," Tristan continued. "I asked him not to, and I know this will displease you, so I want to offer a solution. We need a spy capable of crawling into small spaces for the rebellion. I would like Nathan to be that spy."

Solomon's eyes narrowed as he debated.

"Nathan told me he has no family left. It would be one less minor for you to take care of and one less mouth to feed."

"Fine," Solomon said, flicking his hand. "Go on, boy. And remember my benevolence. Most spies who betray me are murdered on the spot."

"Yes, sir," Nathan mumbled before joining Tristan. The boy glanced up at him with fear-filled eyes.

Wanting to soothe him, Tristan rested a hand on his shoulder as Grace retook control of the conversation. "I was hoping you'd feed my team one last meal before we depart. We left a corner of the bunker stocked with weapons as payment for your hospitality and alliance."

"The school on the next block has a cafeteria, and my cooks are already preparing the meals. I wish you luck on your journey, Grace."

"We don't need luck," she said, straightening her spine. "We need strategy, firepower, and the art of surprise. Thankfully, once we meet up with Arthur's team, we'll have all three. I won't forget your help when we win. Thank you, Solomon."

"I'm counting on it, Grace. Safe travels."

With a nod, Grace pivoted and led her men out of the post office. The team marched down the battered street, arriving at the school and locating the cafeteria.

After eating the best meal he'd had in a while, Tristan joined the others at the vehicles. They loaded inside, George and Zayne entering separate SUVs, and Tristan slid behind the wheel of the pickup truck.

Nathan hopped in the passenger side and slid beside him before Grace claimed the passenger seat. There were a multitude of weapons in the bed of the truck, covered with a tarp and rope to secure them.

"Ready?"

"Ready," Nathan and Grace said in unison.

Under the cover of night, they exited the compound walls and set off on the two-hour drive to Dundore.

Chapter 18

As they drove, Grace inwardly admitted she'd offered for Nathan to ride with them because it gave her an excuse to draw out the inevitable. Having a little boy sandwiched between them didn't lend to a heartfelt discussion during the drive.

Biting her nail, she stared anxiously out the window into the darkness. Most of the roads had deteriorated, but the highways were navigable enough. Eventually, they would exit old Interstate 80 onto Highway 11, and Tristan would have to weave the windy roads to Dundore.

"You two married?" Nathan asked, pointing between them.

"Why do you ask that?" Grace replied, grinning.

"Because you stare at each other weird. All gooey-eyed and stuff." He bugged out his eyes and made a silly face. "It's kind of gross, but whatever."

Tristan glanced over at her and smiled. "We used to be married. Maybe we will be again one day. I'm working on it."

A flash of light beamed in the passenger side window, and Grace leaned forward to focus on it. "Shit! We're being followed." Looking at Nathan, she said, "Sorry, kid."

"I've heard curse words before, lady."

"Someone's following us," she said, gripping the handle.

"I'm going to get off the highway and try to lose them," Tristan said. "You've got the handgun I gave you?"

Grace nodded and patted the holster at her belt. Zayne had trained her how to shoot over the past year, and she felt confident wielding a weapon.

"I need a gun too," Nathan said.

"Nope, but I'm sure you have a knife or some other weapon on you. You're too wily not to."

Nathan pulled the Swiss army knife from his sock and beamed. "I can stab someone's eyes out with this."

"Okay, Hannibal Lector," he said, pushing Nathan's arm down to lower the knife. "Put that back in your sock." Lifting his gaze to Grace, he instructed, "Keep an eye out and let me navigate the side roads."

Tristan weaved and navigated down dirt roads as long minutes passed. Every so often, Grace saw a flash in the side mirror, indicating the perpetrator was still on their tail.

"Screw this," Tristan said, pulling off the road into the forest. "I'm going to throw on one of the bulletproof vests and go on the offensive. You two crouch down and stay in the truck."

"Tristan—"

"They're not going to stop, Grace," he warned, exiting the truck. "Stay inside and stay down."

Grace threw her arms around Nathan and huddled in the seat. She wasn't religious, but she closed her eyes and whispered, "Please let him be okay."

Tristan grabbed a rifle from the bed of the truck. He also tossed on a pair of the night-vision goggles, acknowledging his good fortune at having a truck full of weapons.

Headlights approached on the nearby road, stopping in front of the thicket where he was now parked. Tristan had left the parking lights on. He didn't see any reason to keep running and wasting gas—if he wanted to take the offensive, he needed to lead the enemy to them.

The car stopped and two men emerged, their silhouettes lit by the headlights. Aiming for the first man's neck, he closed one eye and pulled the trigger.

The man gasped, clutching his neck before he fell to the ground.

The other man ran behind the car, taking cover before he began to spray a barrage of bullets into the forest. Cursing, Tristan ducked behind the truck and prayed that Grace and Nathan had followed his directive to stay down.

Steeling himself, Tristan gathered his courage to take the offensive. Leaving the shelter of the truck, he stealthily moved through the trees, taking shots at the car as he advanced. Every time his assailant rose and sprayed a round of bullets, Tristan ducked behind a tree to shield himself.

Eventually, he approached the tree closest to the road, understanding that was the last cover the forest could give him. Attempting to negotiate, he yelled, "I don't want to shoot you too. Come out and let's try to find a compromise."

"The time for compromise is over, Tristan," a familiar voice called. "Luthor has been trying to locate Grace for weeks and wants her back immediately."

Tristan closed his eyes and sighed. "I can tell that's you, Tom. What the hell?"

"You're the one who defected, buddy," his old friend and comrade said. "You were Luthor's top mercenary, and when you disappeared, he needed a replacement."

"Glad to hear you were there to step in," Tristan muttered.

"I always liked working for you, Tristan, although people seem to die around you a lot. I'd hate for Grace to die too. Give her to me and I'll let you go."

"No can do, *friend*," Tristan said, gritting out the word as he peeked around the tree. He could just make out the top of Tom's head behind the trunk of his car. Tristan certainly hated to kill him, but he would to protect Grace at all costs.

But first, he'd try another tactic. Aiming his rifle, he shot both driver's side tires.

"Damn it, Tristan!" Tom cried. "We're in the middle of nowhere. Are you serious?"

Tristan noticed him rise slightly, allowing him a glance at the top of his shoulder. Thinking quickly, he aimed and pulled the trigger.

Tom wailed in pain, grabbing his shoulder as he fell to the ground.

Seizing the moment, Tristan sprinted toward him, locating Tom's gun beside him on the ground thanks to the night-vision goggles. Grabbing the gun, he tossed it into the woods before planting his feet and aiming his rifle at Tom, who was writing in pain on the gravel road.

"You son of a bitch!" Tom hissed. "You shot me."

"You're lucky I didn't kill you." Aiming at the passenger side tires, he shot them both, ensuring the car was incapacitated. Then, he searched the car, finding the shortwave radio and dropping it on the ground before stomping on it to destroy it. "Hope you've got a first aid kit in there, and good luck getting back to DC with four flat tires."

"Luthor is obsessed with squashing the rebellion," Tom said, panting as he clenched his teeth. "He won't stop until he finds Zayne and rescues Grace."

Relief swished through Tristan that Luthor didn't know Grace was leading the rebellion. For now. It was only a matter of time before the truth came out, but Tristan would take every advantage possible.

"I hope you don't bleed out, man," Tristan said, shaking his head as he backed away. "You're on the wrong side of history. If you want to have a future, I'd suggest leaving DC. There's a war coming, and you don't want to be inside the wall when it erupts."

Pivoting, Tristan jogged back to the truck and yanked open the passenger side door. "You guys okay?"

"Yes," Grace said, stroking Nathan's hair as she held him. "Are you?"

Nathan nodded, and Tristan shut the door and rounded the truck. After depositing the goggles, rifle and vest back in the truck bed, he hopped in and closed the door.

"I'm going to drive quickly and continue to take back roads. Hold on tight. It's going to get bumpy."

Revving the engine, he eased back onto the road before hightailing it out of the area and toward Dundore.

Tristan did an excellent job navigating the side roads, and they managed to avoid any other vehicles—as far as Grace could tell. She directed him to drive along the river to a small cottage with a stone chimney. Since it was mid-October and still rather warm, no smoke exited the chimney, but Grace knew they used it often in the winter.

After parking the truck, they climbed out, and Grace crouched down and cupped Nathan's upper arms. "I want you to go knock on the door. A lady named Maria is going to answer. Tell her Grace and Tristan are outside and you'd like some stew. She always has a pot of stew brewing." Smiling, Grace rose and urged him inside. "Sit down at the table and enjoy it. I need to talk to Tristan before we head inside."

Nathan nodded and walked to the front door. Maria appeared, introducing herself to Nathan in the light that shone from inside. Her eyes met Grace's, and Grace held up a hand, splaying her fingers to let her know she'd be inside in five minutes. Nodding, Maria ushered Nathan inside and closed the door.

Tristan approached her, looking so handsome in the dim moonlight. His hazel eyes sparkled, the gold flecks simmering with unanswered questions. Tears welled in her eyes as she realized this might be the last moment he ever loved her. Wanting to cherish it, she cradled his face in her hands as two tears trailed down her cheeks.

"What the hell, Grace?" he whispered, palming her face and swiping away the tears with his thumbs. "What are you not telling me?"

"He was going to kill me, Tristan," she said, the words warbled from her tears. "And he was going to kill her. And I couldn't let him. She's our baby."

His chest rose and fell with labored breaths as his eyes darted between hers. "Grace..." he growled as murky awareness glowed in his eyes. "What the fuck are you saying?"

Suddenly, the front door swung open and a little girl darted out. "Grace!" she called, running toward her and jumping into her arms.

Grace enveloped her in a tight hug, burying her face in the girl's soft blond hair as emotions warred within. Joy at holding her again. Despair at the loss of Tristan's trust...and possibly his love.

After one last squeeze, she set the girl on her feet and straightened her spine. Swiping away her tears, Grace faced the man she'd loved since the moment they met.

"Tristan, I'd like you to meet—"

"Raquel," the girl said, extending her hand.

Tristan audibly inhaled as his gaze bore into Grace's. "You didn't... You couldn't have..." he said, disbelief in his voice.

"I *had* to," she pleaded, shaking her head. "I'm so sorry."

Crouching down, Tristan slowly slid his palm over Raquel's. Grace's heart shattered into a thousand pieces at the sight of his broad hand holding their daughter's.

"Hello, Raquel," he rasped, emotion lacing the words. "It's very nice to meet you."

CHAPTER 19

B lood pounded in Tristan's ears, making it hard to balance as he crouched before the girl. She stared back at him with hazel-green, golden-flecked eyes, and he knew she was *his*.

As he gazed upon her, speechless, he admitted she was a perfect amalgamation of him and Grace. She had Grace's golden hair and pert nose, and his hazel eyes and strong chin. Overcome with emotion, he struggled to process the fact his daughter, whom he thought dead over a decade ago, was *alive*.

"Sweetheart, Tristan and I need to talk out here. We're probably going to have a little argument, although we won't yell because we don't want anyone to hear us." She shot him a pointed glare, warning him not to scream at her even though he wanted to rail at the damn universe.

"Run on inside," she said, smoothing a hand over Raquel's hair. "And tell Maria we'll be in soon."

"Okay. We have stew when you all are ready." Turning, she jogged to the house and closed the door behind her.

Tristan stood and flexed his fists at his side several times, closing his eyes as he told himself to remain calm. Although he wanted to strangle his ex-wife, yelling would only attract notice, and that was something they needed to avoid.

Facing her, his nostrils flared as he stared into her eyes.

"You fucking bitch."

"Yes," she said, bracing for his anger. "I'm a bitch and deserve every ounce of your hate. You can curse me out as long as you want. I knew this day would come, and I won't deny it was a huge betrayal."

"Betrayal?" he hissed, trying like hell not to scream. "You told me our daughter died. I *mourned* her. And she's been alive all this time?"

"Thanks to me," Grace said, lifting her chin in that haughty way he sometimes found sexy. At the moment, it made him want to throttle her. "I overheard Luthor speaking to his head of security on the phone when he visited my room after I went into labor. He thought I was sleeping." Wringing her hands, she started to pace. "He had everything planned out. He was going to inject my IV with something that wouldn't be detected by the staff, and then he was going to kill Raquel in the NICU. He was just biding his time until there was a slow night shift where he wouldn't be discovered."

"Why would he need to kill a helpless baby in the NICU?"

"Um, have you *met* Luthor Cromwell?" she asked with an exasperated flail of her hands. "The man responsible for the deaths of millions of people and the collapse of society?"

Scoffing, he ran a hand through his hair. "Of course, he's a fucking tyrant, but why—"

"She was my father's heir and he wanted Albright Industries. Owning his own CDMO was the next logical step in getting his nefarious drugs to market. The government would never let him purchase one, but if the board gave their approval, he would inherit my father's company upon his heirs' deaths. Namely, mine and Raquel's."

"But George Luddington would've stopped him, right?"

Sighing, Grace shook her head. "He would've tried, but Luthor was quickly becoming the most powerful man in the world when Dad died. The other board members would've wanted his approval, and they would've voted to give him control of Albright Industries."

"So you lied to me for ten fucking years?"

"I did the only thing I could," she exclaimed. "I enlisted Maria, who was our NICU nurse, to help fake our daughter's death. I was still very weak, so George helped me too. They were able to secretly transport Raquel out of the NICU late at night in a special chamber. Maria brought her to a clinic in Scranton, and George paid handsomely for a private room under an alias.

"Before they transferred Raquel, Maria brought a body up from the morgue to replace her in the NICU." Gripping her chin, Grace recounted the terrible memories. "I wasn't able to help transport her because I was terribly incapacitated, but by some miracle, they pulled it off."

Tristan planted his hands on his hips, angrily tapping his foot as he digested the horrific story. "So, you lied to me about losing your uterus?"

"What? No. Of course not. Why would I lie about that?"

He elicited a frustrated laugh. "Excuse me if I'm having trouble discerning truth in all the lies, Grace. Jesus Christ. You looked me in the eye when I returned from deployment and told me she died." Closing the distance between them, he gripped her arms and shook her. "You told me you couldn't forgive me and wanted a divorce!"

A sob leapt from her throat as remorse clouded her features. "I didn't see any other way. I had no idea when you would be home. I couldn't get in touch with you, and you told me they could extend your deployment—"

"I told you that was unlikely."

"How was I to know? It was a black ops mission and you were unreachable." Sighing, she shook her head. "It's so easy to see my mistakes now, but I was despondent and heartbroken, and I made decisions under intense pressure to protect myself. To protect *her*." She pointed toward the cabin.

Tristan searched her eyes for any hint of malice, but all he saw was deep regret and pain.

A puff of air escaped his throat as he shook his head. "Fuck, Grace," he said, loosening his grip on her arms. "What a goddamn mess."

"I had days in that hospital to plan my revenge," she said, frowning as she recalled the past. "My father had been murdered before my eyes. My child had been born prematurely, and I'd lost my ability to ever have another one. I was a target, along with my baby daughter. The man I loved more than anyone in the world wasn't there to fight with me, and I had to take matters into my own hands."

"Don't do that," he said, dropping her arms and recoiling. "Don't say you loved me when you kept this from me. When you kept *her* from me." He angrily jabbed his finger at the cottage.

"Saying it or not saying it doesn't make it less true." She sliced her hand through the air when he opened his mouth to argue. "But I won't say it again. I understand you must hate me. But our daughter is safe, and no one but you, me, George and Maria know she's alive. And it's going to stay that way until we defeat Luthor."

Tristan studied her, unable to reconcile the shocking twist of events. Opting for a brief moment of reprieve from the argument, he said, "And Nathan."

"What?"

"Nathan knows she's alive too. Somehow, we went from childless people to having two kids to take care of in twenty-four hours."

Her lips formed a heartbreaking smile as she nodded. "And Nathan. Your latest attempt to save someone. It's very noble." Stepping forward, she lifted her face to his. "*You're* very noble, Tristan. I know you try to play both sides of the fence; to be the morally gray mercenary. But I've always known who you are deep inside. You deserved to know she was alive, and I knew I couldn't tell you if I wanted her to live." Swallowing, she whispered, "I'm so sorry."

Tristan rubbed the back of his neck, uncomfortable at the genuineness in her tone. "She called you Grace. Why didn't she call you Mom?"

"Because she doesn't know I'm her mother," she said, squeezing her eyes shut at the painful admission. "She would never have been safe if she'd known. Kids let things slip too easily."

"Unlike their dishonest mothers," he droned, arching an acerbic brow.

Her eyes snapped open. "I told you. I was committed to my plan. Marry Luthor, observe his immoral business practices, and blow the whistle so he'd go to jail. Unfortunately, that plan failed and I wasn't able to prevent him from destroying the world." She lifted her finger. "But I eventually regrouped and began to plot the rebellion, and it took me *years*, Tristan. Years where that little girl was raised to believe her parents died after she was born, and that Maria was their family friend who took her in."

Glancing toward the house, she exhaled a defeated sigh. "Years where I visited her sporadically and claimed to be a friend of her dead parents. I visited her every so often to make sure she was okay, and to ensure she knew me in some capacity. It was difficult to do so without Luthor knowing, but I pulled it off."

An owl hooted in the distant trees, and Grace rubbed her arms to ward off the chill.

"I don't even know how to process this," Tristan said, anchoring his fist on his hip.

"Solomon has been mentioning Dundore in recent conversations, which means Raquel isn't safe here. We'll take her with us to Arthur's compound, where she'll be protected while we continue the rebellion. After we defeat Luthor, we can tell her we're her parents."

"And then what?" he asked, lifting his hands.

"And then, we'll see if you can forgive me. If you can't, I'll accept that and we'll figure out a way to co-parent where you'll never have to see me."

"Or I could just take her and you'll never see her again," he said, the anger rising again. "I was a special ops soldier. If I want to disappear with her, I can make it happen."

Her gaze lowered to the grass, her shoulders hunching with defeat. "You won't need to do that. If you truly don't want me to see her, I won't fight you." Her chin wobbled. "I hope it doesn't come to that, but I'm so tired of fighting, Tristan. Once we defeat Luthor, I just want peace. So, you do whatever the hell makes you happy. I won't stand in your way."

Longing surged deep in his gut, and he took a moment to acknowledge the truth: He didn't want to fight with her either. If he were honest, what he truly wanted was to marry her all over again and try like hell to live the life they were meant to live before they'd both made disastrous decisions.

In the deepest corners of his heart, he wanted to raise their daughter together and create the life they both deserved.

And yet another part of him wanted to punish Grace. Wanted to deny her any right to see Raquel as he'd been denied all these years. That vengeful part of his soul warred with the hopeful side, and he had no fucking idea which one would ultimately win out.

"You couldn't bring yourself to tell me our daughter was alive when I was literally inside you this morning? Who the fuck lies to someone like that, Grace?"

She grimaced. "Don't be crass. I've wanted to tell you every time I saw you for years. That's why I was distant and did my best to avoid you. Laying the foundation for a rebellion against an evil dictator isn't easy. I had to stay focused, and you're the one person on the planet who destroys my focus."

Tristan scrubbed a hand over his face before hanging his head. "Fine. We'll wait to tell her we're her parents until we defeat Luthor." Stepping closer, he jabbed his finger as he spoke. "But you listen to me, Grace. I won't tolerate any more lies. If there's anything else I need to know, tell me now."

"That's it, I swear," she said, honest conviction in her eyes as they darted between his. "And I know you might not ever forgive me, but I can't have your anger changing the way you treat me in front of our team. I need to project strength, so I hope you'll keep your ire private." Her lips formed a heartbreaking smile. "When we're alone, you can take your anger out on me. But in front of our men, I can't allow it."

Cursing his traitorous heart, he acknowledged the desire to comfort her vastly outweighed his anger. Yes, he was furious at the secret she'd kept for so long. But staring at her in the moonlight, reminiscent of the night they met so long ago, all he truly wanted was to pull her into his arms and soothe her.

Even after her vicious betrayal, he longed to confirm she was okay. It was stark confirmation that he still loved her deep within and always would.

But pride was a bitch, and it was pride that held him back from embracing her. Backing away, he gave a curt nod. "Okay. The team won't know." Glancing toward the house, he grinded his teeth in frustration. "Is that place big enough for us to sleep?"

"Maria and Raquel can sleep in the bed. There's a sofa and loveseat, so you and Nathan can have those. I'll offer to sleep on the floor, but Maria and Raquel will probably let me in the bed too. It's a king, so I think we'll all fit. We should leave for Cumberland at four a.m. It will take about three hours to get there, so we'll arrive around dawn."

Exhausted, Tristan nodded and walked toward the house, wanting to be done with the conversation. He needed time to process and had so many questions about his daughter.

Was she happy? What were her favorite things? What were her dreams?

"There will be time to get to know her," Grace said softly, following behind him. "She's an amazing little girl."

Tristan squeezed his hand on the cottage doorknob, wondering if he might crush it from the weight of his fury. *Ten years.* The two words repeated over and over in his mind. He'd lost ten years with his daughter.

Filled with regret and rage, he walked inside, inhaling the fragrant aroma of simmering stew. Allowing himself to compartmentalize, he acknowledged his growling stomach and sat down at Maria's small table to have dinner.

Chapter 20

Tristan inhaled the stew, sating his voracious hunger as Raquel and Nathan sat on either side of him. He'd pretty much been rendered speechless by the news that the hushed conversations referencing Dundore had actually been about his *daughter*. Raquel had no trouble filling the silence, and she chatted away while the five of them sat at the tattered wooden table.

"Did you go to school in Scranton?" Raquel asked.

"I went before my parents died," Nathan mumbled as he finished the last spoonful of stew. "But after they put up the wall, we didn't have school anymore."

"I can study with you if you want," she said, looking at Maria. "I'm at a seventh-grade level for reading and math, right?"

"Yes, dear," Maria said, patting her hand. "Raquel spends several hours each day on her studies, and she's blazing through the textbooks Grace brought during her last visit."

"That's fantastic, sweetheart," Grace said, pride glowing in her eyes as she smiled at Raquel.

"Did you bring more books this time?"

Grace shook her head. "I had to leave my home very suddenly, so I couldn't bring any supplies. I've tried to keep you stocked up here, but you might be too fast for me to keep up with."

Raquel beamed, and something in Tristan's heart cracked wide open. Her cheeks glowed in the same way Grace's did when she was happy or excited about something. Their resemblance was uncanny.

"I can share my textbooks with you," Raquel said to Nathan. "We can study together at the Cumberland compound."

Nathan shot her a wary glance. "I'm going to spy for Tristan. I might not have time for schoolwork."

"You're a great spy, buddy," Tristan said, grinning, "but when we go to DC to fight for the rebellion, you'll have plenty of free time on Arthur's compound. You can study with Raquel. It wouldn't hurt for you to resume your schooling."

"Whatever," Nathan muttered. "It won't matter anyway if you're leaving."

"Hey," Tristan said, cupping his shoulder. "I'm leaving to fight for the cause. But when we win, I'm coming back and you're stuck with me, kid. We bartered a lot of weapons to Solomon in exchange for your surveillance skills, and I need you."

In truth, Tristan needed a ten-year-old kid with a chip on his shoulder about as much as he needed to lose a limb, but he liked Nathan and wouldn't abandon him as his parents had.

Relief shone in Nathan's eyes above that smattering of freckles.

"And how about you, Maria?" Tristan asked, pushing the empty bowl away as he leaned back in his chair. "Are you coming with us to Cumberland?"

"I recently turned sixty-eight and don't move as well as I used to," she replied, shaking her head. "I'm comfortable in this little cabin and don't want to leave. I always told Raquel that I'd grow too old one day to take care of her, and that Grace would be the one to take the reins. I'm sad that day has come, but I trust Grace to take care of my Raquel." She patted Grace's arm before encircling her wrist and squeezing.

Tristan observed the gesture as he noted Maria's slight Spanish accent. She had long dark hair with several gray streaks and deep brown eyes, and he found himself wondering what her story was. Perhaps he would hear it one day—the backstory of the kind woman who'd raised his daughter. Although he was seething at Grace's secret, he couldn't deny the woman was very nurturing and compassionate.

"Maybe you two can take care of these kids together," she continued, her almond-shaped eyes sparkling as she addressed Tristan. "Combining forces is easier than going it alone."

Tristan remained silent since he'd much rather scream at his ex-wife at the moment than discuss raising multiple children with her.

"Maria says you'll be able to give me even more books when I live with you, Grace," Raquel said, her eyebrows lifting. "That's really cool, but I'll miss the cabin. We can come and visit, right?"

"You'd better," Maria said. "I'd miss you too much if you didn't."

Raquel smiled before breaking into a yawn.

"Well, I think it's time for bed," Maria said. "Grace, you can crawl in with me and Raquel."

"Are you sure? I don't want to crowd you."

"I'll get everything ready," Raquel said with excitement. "We still have running water in the bathroom next to our room from the well and plumbing you had installed, Grace. Everyone can use it to brush their teeth."

"Thank you, sweetheart," Grace said. "Why don't you and Nathan go ahead and brush first. Do you have an extra toothbrush for him?"

"We have extras. Come on, Nathan. I'll show you."

The kids headed to the bathroom that adjoined the master bedroom, leaving the adults at the table.

"You've done such a wonderful job with her, Maria," Grace said, her eyes shining with emotion. "Are you sure you won't come with us?"

"This old lady needs to rest," she said, relaxing in her seat. "I'll miss that little girl something fierce, but it's time you save the world and raise her like you were meant to."

Lifting her gaze to Tristan's, Maria harumphed. "So, I guess you're mad as a hornet at Grace. I don't blame you, young man, but I hope you understand she made hard choices to protect Raquel."

Tristan's eyes narrowed. "I appreciate you taking care of Raquel, but you're part of the deception, so forgive me if I'm not up for a fireside chat about choices."

"Ohhh, you've got firecracker there," Maria said, rising and patting Grace's shoulder. "So growly and angry. He'll come around, dear. Maybe show a bit more of this." She placed her finger on the V of her shirt and tugged to show the curve of her breasts. "And remind him how strong and manly he is. Men love hearing that."

Tristan scowled, thoroughly unamused.

Maria's face softened as she gripped the back of her chair. "And then remind him that he's your *querido* and that you never stopped loving him. That should help as well. Good night."

She sauntered into the bedroom, leaving him alone with Grace.

"What does *querido* mean?"

Grace formed a sad smile and stood. Trailing to stand beside him, she slid her hand under his jaw. "It means 'sweetheart,'" she said softly. Leaning down, she pressed a tender kiss to his head. "Good night, Tristan."

His cheeks puffed as he released a slow breath. All these years and the woman still tied his stomach in knots. As she sashayed to the bedroom, he watched the sway of her ass, still craving her even after her treachery.

Thoroughly done with the events of the day, he marched to the couch and tore off his boots. Lying back on the soft cushions, he threw his arm over his eyes and prayed tomorrow would hold no more secrets.

Tristan awoke and stared into a pair of eyes that mirrored his own. Blinking slowly, he waited for Raquel to come into focus in the dim light.

"It's four a.m.," Raquel whispered, looking over to where Nathan was still sleeping. "Grace said to wake you up because we're already late."

Stretching his legs atop the faded couch, he nodded. "Can I get one of those extra toothbrushes you have lying around?"

She smiled, and Tristan noticed she was missing her canine on her right side.

"I want to make sure I don't lose my teeth like you did," he teased.

"I'm *supposed* to lose my teeth so my adult teeth can grow in."

He squinted one eye and contemplated. "That *sounds* like a valid excuse..."

Opening her mouth, she tugged on her other canine. "I'm going to lose this one soon. Maybe you'll see it fall out when we reach Cumberland."

"My dad used to tie a string to my loose teeth and wrap it around the door before slamming it shut. That yanked them out real fast."

Raquel's features squished. "Ew."

Laughing, he sat up and mussed his hair, trying to straighten it out since it was tousled from the scratchy couch pillow. "It's not so bad. If that one doesn't fall out soon, we can try it."

"Okay. I'll leave a toothbrush on the bathroom counter for you."

She headed back into the bedroom, passing Grace, who was leaning against the door-frame. Her arms were crossed as she gazed at him with reverence.

Striding toward her, he waited until they were so close their bodies almost grazed. Staring down into her eyes, he said, "Don't do that."

"Do what?" she asked, her voice breathless as the pulse in her neck fluttered.

"Don't look at me with those gorgeous, traitorous eyes while I'm talking to our daughter." His tone was ominous as he lightly gripped her chin. "I'm still fucking furious at you."

Her throat bobbed as she searched his eyes. "I know. But I couldn't help watching you with her. It's sweet—"

"Save it," he interjected, unwilling to soften—for the moment at least. He'd slept well on the lumpy couch, but there hadn't been nearly enough time to process everything that had happened in such a short time. "I'm not interested in your opinions on my interactions with her, Grace. So just fucking save it."

Yanking her chin from his hand, her eyes flashed with fire. "I know you're pissed at me, and you have a right to be, but you can go fuck yourself if you think I'm going to allow you to treat me like shit."

Sighing, he rubbed the back of his neck. Hell, he was barely awake and he'd never been a morning person. Anger had gotten the best of him, and he'd lashed out at her.

"I need coffee," he mumbled, shaking his head to rid it of the haze of sleep. "Does Maria have any?"

Her features softened ever so slightly. "You always were a bear in the morning. Yes, I'll make coffee while you use the restroom and get ready. We can take it with us on the drive."

"Make it strong," he said with a nod before trailing to the bathroom. Maria was helping Raquel stuff clothes into her backpack from the dresser at the foot of the bed. Stepping into the bathroom, he noticed the toothbrush Raquel had laid out for him on the counter.

Gazing into his reflection, he told himself to get his shit together and focus on the rebellion. Being mad at Grace was justified, but it wouldn't accomplish anything.

But if they didn't win the rebellion, it wouldn't matter whether Raquel was alive or not. The world would continue down its path of death and destruction, and she would have no future at all.

For the good of his daughter, he vowed to tuck away the anger and focus on saving the world. After that, he could figure out what to do with his treacherous wife—the woman who consumed his every thought.

Chapter 21

Luthor Cromwell sneered at the wounded man on his couch. Tom had shown up an hour ago, severely injured from a gunshot to his shoulder. He'd driven his car on rims for ten miles before locating an abandoned one he could hotwire—one that actually had air in the tires.

Now, he was sitting on Luthor's pristine leather couch in his penthouse office, and Luthor found himself more concerned about the leather than the man.

"Tell me again," Luthor said, crossing his arms as he paced. "Grace was in the truck with Tristan?"

"It was dark, but I'm sure I saw her, sir. Zayne was nowhere in sight."

Rubbing his chin, Luthor contemplated. "So...this can only mean one thing. My wife is a part of the rebellion. She must be working with Zayne."

"I believe they're all heading to Arthur Reyes's compound," Tom said. "They most likely took different routes so they wouldn't be ambushed together. Tristan was following a path along the Susquehanna River, and the bed of his truck was loaded with weapons."

"Interesting." Walking to the high glass windows, Luthor peered out, clenching his teeth to keep his seething anger from surfacing. Unable to control it, he strode to the cart that held his expensive liquor and grabbed a glass. Heaving it, he shattered it against the wall. Striving to regain his composure, he tugged his suit jacket before turning to face the room.

"It's futile to attack Arthur's compound again," Luthor said, addressing Colonel McGrath and Dr. Ziegler as other members of his team stood still, their eyes wide at his enraged actions. "If they want a war, they can come to us. The DC Sen City is my fortress, and I'm prepared to face them here. How are the two hundred men we injected with the super-serum doing?"

Dr. Ziegler cleared his throat, and Luthor's nostrils flared at the nervous gesture. If the man weren't so intelligent, he would've exiled him from the city long ago. He missed working with Danica Lawson, who was the most brilliant and dedicated scientist he'd ever known. Unfortunately, she wasn't on board with his methods, which was absurd. Yet another person who couldn't see the big picture.

"Seven of the men have died, sir, but the rest are doing well. Their muscle mass is increasing as the serum releases in their system. The injection will slow-release for three months and then they will need another round."

Luthor could tell by their expressions that some of his security team were appalled that seven men had died from the serum. Of course, they couldn't understand that sacrifice led to ultimate gain. One had to make hard choices to create a world that would thrive.

"Excellent. Colonel McGrath, make sure the injected soldiers are ready to protect the outer rim of the city. If they're stockpiling weapons, it's only a matter of time before Arthur and Zayne combine forces and attack us. The soldiers who received the serum will meet them outside the city, and I doubt the rebellion militia will be able to fight them effectively. If they do make it into the city, we'll have the regular battalions ready."

"Yes, sir," Colonel McGrath replied.

"And as for you," Luthor said, approaching Tom as he winced on the couch, holding his arm. "Get out of my office and come back when you can do the job without getting injured. I don't have time for subpar performance."

"I did my best, Mr. Cromwell—"

Luthor sneered and rested his hand on the holster that held his gun. "I'd suggest you follow my orders, Tom, or it's not going to work out well for you."

Tom rose swiftly and exited the room.

Turning to his men, Luthor lifted his chin and spoke with confidence. "I won't accept failure. I should've killed Anthony Martinez when he returned with his tail between his legs, but I let him live at your insistence that his death would impact morale for the troops." He gestured toward the door. "Tom barely escaped death due to his incompetence. Let this be a reminder that I am benevolent, but I also want results. Are we clear?"

"Yes, sir!" the men echoed, and Luthor flicked his hand, urging them to leave.

Once he was alone, Luthor sat at his large mahogany desk. Resting his elbows on the table, he steepled his fingers and recalled the day Grace asked him to marry her.

"I have a proposal for you," she said, her skin still so pale from her recent health trauma. "Tristan and I are over. I won't ever forgive him for not being here when I lost the baby. I

know you wish to take over Albright Industries, and as the new owner of the company, I can make that happen."

Luthor had been shocked. He'd thought her and Tristan madly in love, even if the man was gutter trash far beneath her station.

"I want to propose a marriage between us," Grace said. "I'll give you the company in exchange for your protection. We'll present a united front to the world." Lowering her gaze, she rubbed her hands over her sides in a nervous gesture. "After the trauma of losing my uterus, I'm no longer interested in...sexual relationships. Our marriage will be platonic, and you can have as many women on the side as you like. All I ask is that you're discreet."

At the time, Luthor had thought it the perfect plan. Grace was wounded and wanted protection. He would gain control of Albright Industries, allowing him to get his drugs to market faster and with much less red tape. And the little chit didn't want him to fuck her, which was a relief since he found her bland and boring.

Now, sitting at the helm of the once-great empire he created, he tapped his fingers against his lips as he contemplated.

Several years into his marriage with Grace, someone had blown the whistle on the clinical trial data he'd been falsifying to the FDA for years. It was the catalyst that had caused the US government to investigate him and what drove him to ultimately take down the government and create his own. One that wouldn't stifle his plans with red tape and investigations.

Luthor had never discovered who blew the whistle, but he figured it was someone who worked at Sendaxa. Had it actually been Grace? Had she been deceiving him the entire time they were married?

Recalling their interactions since he walled off the city and took power, he remembered how much Grace lurked in shadowed corners when he had important meetings. She was always interrupting to place a kiss on his cheek and ask what he wanted for dinner...and then she would linger and pour a drink while he carried on his business.

He'd never suspected the little bitch could deceive him.

But now, as realization washed over him, he recognized that underestimating his wife had been a grave mistake.

Grace had been gathering intel all along.

Roaring with fury, Luthor slammed his hand on the desk.

His wife had been plotting against him for years, and he'd let her into his inner circle, right under his nose.

Standing, Luthor trudged back and forth over the soft carpet. She must've seen him kill Robert all those years ago. He'd always suspected she had, but she'd never admitted it.

"Of course she didn't, you fool!" he hissed. "How could I have overlooked this? Goddamnit!"

Resting his palms on the desk, he blinked rapidly as he accepted the truth.

Grace Albright, his wife and the woman he'd never known at all, was spearheading the rebellion.

Somehow, she'd stockpiled a ton of weapons and was aligning with Arthur Reyes to bring down his empire.

"Well done, my dear," Luthor said, his tone menacing as he clenched his jaw. "All these years, you've secured access to me and tried to bring me down."

Stalking to the bar cart, he poured two fingers of scotch and lifted his glass in a salute. "To you, my duplicitous bitch of a wife," he said, then chugged the drink and relished the burn. "I can't wait to murder you like I did your father. May you drown in your own fucking blood."

Seething with rage, Luthor poured one last shot before he returned to the task of saving the world he'd created in his image.

Chapter 22

T ristan observed the Cumberland compound come into view shortly after dawn. Raquel sat on Grace's lap while Nathan was sandwiched in the middle. Once they were parked in front of the imposing compound wall, Tristan ordered them to stay in the truck while he approached the front doors.

He walked forward and the large doors swung open. Two men stepped outside, each armed with rifles.

"Please ask your companions to exit the truck, sir," one said, and Tristan waved for everyone to join him.

They were instructed to line up and lift their arms. The two men did an efficient frisk as Tristan frowned.

"Do you really need to frisk the kids?"

One of the guards pulled Nathan's Swiss army knife from his sock and held it high. "It would seem so," he said, cocking a brow.

Tristan couldn't argue with him there, so he remained silent.

Once they'd confiscated Tristan and Grace's handguns, one of the guards banged his fist on the compound door. It swung open again to reveal Arthur Reyes on the other side.

"Tristan," he said, extending his hand. "It's nice to finally meet you in person. Come inside the walls. It's not safe out here."

They all entered the compound, one of the guards driving Tristan's truck inside before locking the gate behind them.

"And you must be Grace Cromwell," Arthur said, shaking her hand. "I must say, you've surprised us all. Your team arrived last night and their armaments are impressive. Well done, ma'am." He saluted her. "I'm grateful and indebted to you."

"I'm glad we've finally reached this point," she said, smiling. "With my weapons, your militia, and Danica Lawson's antidote, we might just win this thing."

"We have no choice, so we'd better," Arthur said. "It's time for your husband's reign to end." Crouching down, he smiled at Nathan and Raquel. "And who do we have here?"

They introduced themselves and Arthur stood, his eyes narrowing on Grace. "Is she your—?"

"She's the daughter of family friends who have long passed," Grace interjected. "It's a boring story I'll be happy to tell you in private."

"Not that boring," Tristan droned, scowling. "But a private conversation is certainly best."

"We've prepared some rooms for you in the old sixth grade ward of the school that Danica, Maverick, Arianna, and Dominic are staying in. My men put some beds in there, and there's running water in the boys' bathroom."

"Ah, heaven," Grace said with a smile. "Thank you, Arthur. We'd like to freshen up and then we need to meet with you, Danica, and the others."

"I've already set a meeting for ten a.m. The children can play with Chris, Jenny and their crew while we talk. They have a wiffle ball game set for ten as well." Leaning down, he rested his hands on his knees. "Do you two like wiffle ball?"

"Never played," Nathan murmured, his eyes downcast.

"Me neither, but I can try," Raquel chimed in.

"Good." Arthur patted them both on the shoulders. "Chris and Jenny are great kids and will be happy to show you the ropes. Go ahead and follow Mike to the school in the truck. Once you arrive, he'll drive the truck to unload the weapons."

"Are you already confiscating our ride?" Grace asked, lifting an eyebrow.

"My compound, my rules," he said, showing his palms. "But I assure you, you're still the rebellion leader. I don't want a power war here, Grace. We can lead our teams together. It will only make them stronger."

"I agree."

Arthur smiled and gestured toward the truck. "Go ahead and get settled in. You'll probably run into Danica or the others at the school. We'll meet in the old home economics room at ten."

Tristan slid back behind the wheel as the others climbed inside. Mike took off in his car, and Tristan followed him to the school, ready to see Danica Lawson again.

Hope welled in his heart that she'd truly created a cure. If so, a brighter future was possibly on the way for Jessica and countless others.

They had obstacles ahead, but for the first time in so long, Tristan could feel the tide beginning to turn, ever so slightly. Gripping the wheel, he hoped his fledgling optimism wasn't misplaced. Vowing to ensure it wasn't, he prepared for the next phase of the rebellion.

Dr. Danica Lawson-Ward lifted two vials, the contents milky as she stood in front of their unified team.

"The EverLife cure has proven effective on everyone in the compound." She shook the vial in her right hand. "The workers Arthur assigned to me have helped me create three hundred vials. That's all I can produce until I get access to a factory."

Arthur nodded from his seat at the circular table. He was flanked by Arianna, Dominic, and Maverick to his left, and Grace and Tristan to his right as Danica stood before them. "The first factory we'll take over is Luthor's EverLife factory inside the DC Sen City's walls."

"He's not going to just let us in the front door, so he'll need to be dead for that to happen," Arianna said acerbically.

"That's the plan," Tristan said. "I can't wait to wipe that bastard off the planet."

"I think we're all in agreement the world will be a better place without him here," Dani said diplomatically. She shook the vial in her left hand. "This vial holds the super-soldier antidote. Thanks to the stash that Ari stole, I was able to discern what's in Luthor's serum and create something that will dull the effects."

"That's my woman," Dominic said, cupping her shoulder.

"I'm not anyone's woman," Arianna muttered, brushing his hand away. Dominic grinned, and Tristan felt his lips twitch. Those two were damn near perfect for each other. Dom knew exactly how to handle her mulish demeanor, and he honestly seemed to revel in it.

Glancing at Grace, his eyes skated over her profile as she listened to Dani. Had they ever been a perfect fit? They'd certainly been tethered together by an undeniable chemistry and had fallen deeply in love. But there was so much betrayal and heartbreak between them. Could they truly ever recover?

"I've prepared three hundred vials of this as well," Danica said, lifting a dart gun. "The militia will be armed with dart guns and our minimal supply. It's imperative they shoot Luthor's soldiers in the neck for full effect. I know gaining this type of proximity to soldiers injected with strength serum is difficult, but it's necessary. It's possible the soldiers might also go into cardiac arrest shortly after injection. Just preparing you if you see them collapse during battle."

"My wife, the badass scientist," Maverick said, glowing with pride.

"It takes a village, and I appreciate all the people you've assigned to help me with this project, Arthur. I've done my best. Now it's time for you all to kick ass."

"Let's go over the plan again," Arianna said, straightening in her chair. "Dom and I will go to DC first since we did a pretty good job sneaking in last time." She flashed a smile his way.

"I've been connecting with my tech whiz, Bodie, on a secret radio channel while I searched for Grace," Tristan said. "I can instruct him to loop the cameras at the same spot. The guards were most likely embarrassed they were ambushed, so I would guess they stayed quiet. No one wants to fail in Luthor's regime."

"That's helpful," Arianna said. "And maybe he can keep an eye out if that spot is compromised and direct us to another one."

"He can," Tristan confirmed. "I'll make sure to hop on the frequency we use before you two leave so you can communicate with him directly."

"We're going to surveil the soldiers who've been injected with the serum as they train," Dominic continued. "I want to see if we can identify any weaknesses. We're hoping Deandra can give us their training location. She's a master at overhearing Luthor's soldiers' conversations in her deli."

"Zayne, our team and I have spent years cultivating the seeds of rebellion in the city," Grace said. "If you see anyone who has an X drawn on their wrist, it means they're sympathetic to the rebellion."

"How many sympathizers do you think live in the city?" Arianna asked.

"Can't say for sure, but there's lots of dissention in the tent cities amongst the addicts. Recently, Zayne and I have noticed more graffiti and signs of unrest like bonfires popping up in the more safe and affluent places too. It's probably why Luthor sent a battalion here several weeks ago. He feels his power slipping."

"Good," Arianna said. "I hope he enjoys the last tastes of power, because we're going to douse it."

Leaning forward, Dominic rested his forearms on the table. "We'll continue to communicate with you on the secret radio channel, Arthur. We're going to head to the city tonight, and you and Maverick will lead the militia to the city in two days and arrive after sunset."

"Correct," Arthur said with a nod. "I want to train everyone on the dart guns and the new artillery before we attack. Maverick has agreed to help me, although the soldiers will miss taking orders from you, Arianna. You've whipped them into shape, and they're more loyal to you than anyone at this point."

"I look forward to helping lead when we reconvene in DC," she said with a salute. "We'll try and stay in the same hotel as long as we can bribe Devon again. We need two gold bars—one for a room and one for his silence."

Arthur pointed toward the door. "Mike is setting aside weapons and gold for you to take with you. Please be safe. We need you to win this war, Arianna. And you too, Dominic."

"Yeah, he comes in handy sometimes," Arianna teased, patting his arm as he scowled.

"Tristan, I'd love your help training the militia on the weapons too. We're fortunate to have a special ops soldier in our ranks."

"No problem," Tristan said. "I think Grace should stay here with the women and children to protect the compound while we attack—"

Grace cleared her throat and shot him a withering glare. "While we appreciate your thoughts, Tristan," she interjected, "I'm the leader of the rebellion and will join my men in battle."

Facing her, he frowned. "You're not a soldier. I don't want you to get hurt."

"That's not your decision. And I would argue I'm the stealthiest soldier of all. My planning and steadfastness led us here. I've surreptitiously stockpiled weapons for years and recruited trustworthy soldiers who can fight with us. I've sowed the seeds of uprising in the city, and I *will* be on the battlefield with you all."

Anger and fear collided in his gut as he regarded her stubborn expression. It was ridiculous for her to fight since she wasn't a skilled soldier, but neither were many of the men and women in Arthur's militia. They were just citizens of a broken world who wanted to fight for a better future. Although he was terrified for her to get hurt—or die—he couldn't deny she'd earned her chance to fight too.

"I want to do some extra training with you," he said, crossing his arms, his tone growing more serious. "If you're going to put yourself in danger, you need to be as prepared as possible."

"Fine. We'll carve out some time this afternoon and tomorrow morning."

"Fine," he said, clenching his jaw.

"*Awkwarrrrrrd,*" Arianna chimed, grimacing before she stood. "You two going to be able to stay united with all that weird tension between you? If you want some advice, you should probably just bang it out. That helped me when this one was driving me crazy." She jerked her thumb at Dominic.

Dominic stood and nipped her thumb. "Let's not dispense romantic advice, sweetheart. We've got our hands full with our own shit."

Blinking rapidly, she formed a sarcastic smile. "Call me sweetheart again in public and you're really going to have some shit to deal with."

Dominic rolled his eyes and playfully scrunched his features at her. "I told Chris we'd stop by the wiffle ball game before they're done. Come on." Encircling her wrist, he tugged her toward the door.

"I think the plan is set," Arthur said, rising, "but I'll be available for any last-minute questions."

Maverick approached Dani and plopped a kiss on her cheek. "I was totally checking you out while you were schooling us on antidotes, Dr. Lawson-Ward." He waggled his eyebrows. "I think I need some private lessons."

"Mav," she said, biting her lip. "We just welcomed Tristan and Grace onto the compound. Can you wait a few more minutes before we dive into our weird flirting ritual? I need them to think I'm a serious scientist."

Tristan rose from his chair and walked toward the two vials. Lifting the EverLife cure, he studied it with wonder. "My sister is addicted to EverLife," he said solemnly. "I can't thank you enough for creating this, Dani. Sorry I fucked up your break-in at the lab, but I had a plan and it ended with us standing right here. Thank you for giving me hope."

"You're lucky I can only remember about half of everything that happens," she teased. "I think I was probably pissed at you in the lab, but I appreciate you sheltering my sister in DC. I wish her life hadn't ended so tragically. Hopefully, I can ensure your sister's won't."

"That's very kind. I hope we can save her too."

"Let's go watch some kids crush a wiffle ball, slugger," Maverick said, extending his hand. Dani picked up the two vials and they exited the room, leaving him and Grace alone.

"I'm so happy there's a cure for Jessica," Grace said, gliding over to stand beside Tristan. "And while we're here, I wanted to suggest something to you."

Tristan lifted his eyebrows.

"I think it would be nice if you spent some time with Raquel. Dani told me there's a large pond behind the school and it has a nice walking trail around it. You two could take a walk and get to know each other a bit."

Resting his hip against the table, he smiled. "I'd like that. Did she tell you about her loose tooth?"

Grace nodded. "She's so cute when she talks about it."

Aching to touch her, he held himself back. "She looks just like you," he whispered.

"But with your eyes." Lifting her hand, she traced a finger under the curve of his eye.

Tristan grabbed her hand, holding it immobile as they stood frozen.

Her lips parted, and his gaze lowered to her wet tongue, slightly visible beneath those pretty pink lips.

"Even when I hate you, I want every piece of you," he whispered. "It's maddening."

Sadness overtook her expression. "I hope you can learn not to hate me one day," she said softly, her eyes darting between his.

"We'll see," he murmured, releasing her hand. "And I'll take Raquel for a walk along the pond after lunch." Scratching his head, he squinted. "What the hell do I talk about with a ten-year-old girl? I'm a morally gray mercenary with zero redeeming qualities."

Breathing a laugh, she bit her lip. "I think you have lots of redeeming qualities. And just be yourself. She's a talker, so she'll lead the way." She patted his arm supportively. "If you'd like to train this afternoon, I'll take you up on it. Zayne showed me how to shoot a handgun, but I'd like to practice with a rifle."

"Okay. Let's plan on three o'clock. Maverick and Arthur will be training the troops on the field, but we can find a place nearby so I can focus on thoroughly teaching you. I want you to know the ins and outs of using a rifle so you don't hurt yourself."

"The woman you profess to hate?" she asked, arching an eyebrow.

"Regardless of your deception, I don't want you dead."

"Well, that's comforting," she sighed, backing away and rubbing her forehead. "Want to go catch the end of the wiffle ball game? We can see how Raquel and Nathan are getting along with the other kids."

"Sure."

He followed her from the room, yearning to draw her back and tell her his words were a lie. That he could never truly hate her.

As they walked to the baseball field, he remained silent, allowing his anger to stifle the sentiment. There would be time for reconciliation when they defeated Luthor.

For now, Tristan's main concern was keeping his ex-wife and daughter alive.

Focused on that goal, he mentally prepared for some alone time with his little girl.

Chapter 23

That afternoon, Tristan walked beside the pond with Raquel as she chatted away. She told him of her love for butterflies and her wish to have a puppy one day. She recounted growing up in Maria's cottage and how much she loved the kind woman.

"Maria seems like a good soul," Tristan said, thankful his daughter had been safe and sheltered all these years. "What type of puppy do you want?"

"Don't care," she said, shrugging. "As long as it likes to play. Maria always said I have too much energy, so I need a puppy who can keep up with me."

Chuckling, he gazed at the top of her golden head. "You're taking the news of leaving the cabin well. I know you'll miss her."

"She told me I'd have to leave one day and live with Grace. Once she got too old to take care of me and the dictator who rules the world is gone."

"Maria told you about Luthor Cromwell?"

"Yes. She said not to be scared because Grace and her friends would beat him one day." Staring up at him, she asked, "Are you and Grace boyfriend and girlfriend?"

"Why do you ask that?"

She grinned. "Because you look at her like she's the only person in the room."

"Grace and I used to be married," he said, figuring that was common knowledge and didn't need to be kept secret.

"You're not married anymore?"

"Nope. We couldn't make it work."

Raquel's soul seemed to shine in her eyes as she gazed up at him. "Why? Grace is awesome, and she's pretty too. Maybe you should ask her to marry you again."

"I'm not sure we'd make each other happy. We didn't do a good job of it before."

"You had to be happy *sometimes* to get married," she said, as if he were daft. "Otherwise, you never would have done it in the first place."

Tristan couldn't contain his grin. "I guess we were sometimes, especially in the beginning before things got hard. We did all sorts of fun stuff together."

"Like what?"

"We went to the garden by my house that had tons of butterflies, and we always laughed at how silly the world was. When she got her tattoo—"

Raquel gasped. "Grace has a tattoo?"

Shit. Was he supposed to keep that a secret?

"Yes, but I'm not sure I'm supposed to tell you that. Don't tell her, okay?"

"What does she have a tattoo of?"

"A dragon."

"That's so cool," Raquel whispered, her eyes wide. "I want a tattoo."

"Maybe one day," he said, smoothing his hand over her hair. "Let's beat Luthor first and have you grow up just a bit more."

They continued down the dirt trail before turning around and heading back toward the school.

"Grace is going to be okay, right? I heard her say she's going with you and the others to fight."

Crouching down, he held her upper arms and stared into her hazel eyes. "I'll always protect Grace and would give my life before I let her get hurt."

Raquel's lips formed a broad smile. "You love her."

"I do. Keep that secret too. You've got two secrets now," he said, holding up two fingers. "I'm trusting you."

"I won't say anything." She made an X over her heart, the gesture cementing a new, tentative bond between them.

Straightening, he held out his hand, and she slipped hers into it so naturally it caused something to shift in Tristan's soul.

Love washed over him as he tightened his grip and led his daughter back to the school.

Grace stood at the window in her makeshift room, watching Tristan lead Raquel back from the pond. He held her small hand in his, and Grace allowed the tears to well. God, they'd all missed so much time together. Guilt gnawed at her, and she pushed it away. She'd learned long ago that guilt was a vengeful, angry companion, and it wouldn't serve her. She'd made hard choices, and her daughter was alive because of them.

Sighing, Grace changed into the sweatpants and t-shirt Dani had loaned her. Apparently, they had lots of extra clothing in the clinic from people who'd passed away. They'd all been freshly washed and were used by those remaining on the compound.

Smoothing her hand over the soft shirt, she reveled in the small pleasure of being safe and comfortable, if only for a moment. For so long, she'd been a prisoner in a marriage where she was plotting revenge. Arthur's compound offered refuge, and she'd take joy in it until they left to continue the fight.

"To *end* the fight," she vowed.

"You talking to yourself?" Tristan's voice echoed from the doorway.

Turning, she smiled and nervously rubbed her arms. "Yep. Did you have a nice walk with Raquel?"

"I did. She loves butterflies as much as you. Oh," he said, lifting a finger, "and she wants a puppy."

Grace's eyebrows lifted. "Wow. That's a lot to deal with when we're trying to save the world."

"Seriously. I told her she'd have to wait a bit." Crossing his arms, he leaned against the doorframe. Grace's eyes roved over his lanky frame, and she licked the suddenly dry roof of her mouth. Maybe it was seeing him with their daughter; maybe it was how well he filled out his black tactical pants. Whatever it was, she was suddenly flushed and craving his lips on her skin again. Anywhere would do, but the lower the better.

Tristan's eyes lit with desire, and she could tell he sensed her attraction to him. Hell, she'd never truly been able to hide it, so why start now?

"I know we were going to do rifle practice in the woods by the pond," he continued, "but Maverick is giving a tutorial on all of the weapons to the militia in a few minutes on the training field. Why don't we attend that so you can learn about the arsenal? After dinner, we can practice by the pond."

"Will there be enough light?"

"For a while." He straightened and sauntered toward her, stopping until there were only inches between them. "You scared to be in the dark with me, empress?"

Her lips curled. "The opposite. I'm afraid I might do something reckless. Secluded woods by a pond? We have a pretty awesome track record in that scenario."

Lust flared in his eyes as he emitted a soft growl. "Skinny dipping in the lake by my old apartment was definitely one of our favorite nighttime activities."

"Are we too old to skinny dip? I haven't done that since I did it with you."

A reverent look crossed his features, and she tilted her head. "What is it?"

"Raquel was asking us if we were happy when we were married—"

"I guess that cat's out of the bag," she muttered.

"It's common knowledge, so I saw no reason to hide it from her."

Grace nodded, urging him to continue.

"She asked if we were happy, and I told her we had some good moments. Skinny dipping in the lake was definitely one of my favorites."

"Mine too," she whispered, her body straining toward him as she physically held herself back.

"If you learn how to use the rifle properly, maybe we can take a dip."

Grace arched a sultry eyebrow. "A reward for my hard work? I'm going to wield that rifle like a pro once you're done with me."

"Okay, G.I. Jane, take it easy," he teased, patting her shoulder. "I just want to make sure you know how to use it well enough that you don't blow someone's head off."

"Except Luthor's," she said, lifting a finger.

"By all means, if he's in your line of vision, blow the bastard's head off."

Grace tilted her head toward the next room where he was staying. "How's the room?"

"It's fine. Nathan and Raquel claimed the room on the other side." He pointed toward the hallway. "It has two cots and he gave her his extra blanket. He's a good kid."

"I'm happy they get along and think they complement each other nicely. She can bring him out of his shell a bit, and he's street smart. She needs more of that in her life. She was sheltered with Maria, but it was the only way to keep her safe."

"I'm glad she was sheltered," he admitted, even though he hated the deception around it. "I wouldn't have wanted her near the death and destruction we've seen over the past few years."

"Me neither."

They gazed at each other for another beat before Tristan turned and headed toward his room. "See you on the training field. If you want to walk together, I'll be ready in ten minutes."

She observed his broad shoulders retreat as anticipation welled deep within. Could he possibly lower that angry shield when they trained later? Intrigued by the challenge, she sat down to slide on her shoes and anticipated skinny dipping with her husband under a star-filled sky.

"*Ex-husband*, Grace," she scolded. "Sheesh."

Accepting that he would always be her one true husband deep in her heart, Grace tied her hair into a ponytail, ready to study the hell out of some fancy, but deadly, weapons.

Chapter 24

G race enjoyed Maverick's artillery lesson under the bright afternoon sun. He was thorough and patient as he moved through each of the different types of weapons that had been stockpiled by Grace and George over the years.

Arianna and Dominic helped as well, and by the end of the two-hour hands-on session, Grace felt their militia had a much better understanding of how to wield their powerful armaments.

"We've made a list of the sharpest shooters in the militia, and those soldiers will be on the front lines with the dart guns holding the serum that will immobilize the super-soldiers who've been injected," Maverick said, holding up a piece of paper. "We'll post this list in the cafeteria on Main Street where you all gather for meals. If your name is on it, please show up at sunrise tomorrow morning for an additional training on the dart guns."

"Yes, sir!" the soldiers responded.

Arianna stepped forward. "Dominic and I are leaving for DC tonight. We're going to surveil the city, and hopefully the soldiers, and try to pass along as much information to Arthur and Maverick before you all attack. Tomorrow will be your last training day, and you'll advance on DC in two days. We'll be there to meet you, and look forward to taking back the city."

Dominic gave a solemn nod of agreement as he stood beside her, feet planted in the short grass.

"You've all trained very hard and I'm honored to fight with you." Arianna saluted, and Grace's lips curved as the militia saluted her back. It was obvious the troops deeply respected her, and Grace was proud to have her, Dominic, Maverick and Danica on their side.

A small kernel of hope bloomed in her chest, and she had the stinging suspicion they just might win.

After the weapons tutorial, Grace and Tristan joined the others for dinner at the huge cafeteria on Main Street. It was an old restaurant that had been converted into a mess hall after the compound was sealed off and had rows of tables where everyone sat to enjoy the meals that Arthur's staff prepared.

"It's very altruistic to feed everyone," Grace said to Arthur as he sat beside her in the loud dining hall. "Solomon still makes the residents of his compound purchase or barter for food."

Arthur pursed his lips as he contemplated. "Solomon has a right to run his compound the way he sees fit, but hunger leads to dissention, and dissention leads to crime and addiction in my experience. Why not feed everyone and prevent that?"

"Spoken like a generous leader. I also assume it will be a great campaign message when you assume temporary leadership of the new government we create before running for office."

Smiling, Arthur studied her. "Do you not want to lead? After all, you sowed the seeds of rebellion for years and stockpiled the weapons that will make our attack possible."

"God, no. I just want peace, and there's no peace in politics. I'll certainly support your government and help you in any way I can, but I have no desire to lead."

"Maverick, Dani and the others have said the same thing. Perhaps I'm a masochist for wanting to take over the new government, but I truly feel I can help people."

"Then you're the perfect person to be our new president." She covered his hand. "I'll certainly campaign for you."

Chuckling, he tipped his head. "I'm counting on it."

After dinner, Grace and Tristan headed back to the school to make sure Raquel and Nathan were situated in their room before they headed to the pond to train.

"I can train with you guys if you want," Nathan said, a slight yearning in his eyes. "I'll have to learn to use a rifle eventually."

"I need you rested in case I need your surveillance skills on the fly," Tristan said, noticing the boy stifling a rather large yawn as he lowered onto his cot. "Maverick and Dani are in the old guidance counselor's office down the hall if you need anything. We'll be in the rooms next door when you wake up tomorrow."

"Have fun and don't fall in the pond," Raquel said from behind the book she'd propped on her chest as she lay on her cot.

They exited and Grace gestured down the hallway. "I just need to hit the restroom and we can head out."

"Me too. Be ready in ten."

As Grace washed her hands in the old boys' bathroom, she felt the anticipation building in every cell of her body. Tonight would be the first time she and Tristan were truly alone since he'd discovered Raquel was alive.

Although he planned to train her on using a rifle, there were other issues that needed to be addressed and hard conversations that needed to be had. Staring into her eyes in the reflection, she reminded herself to be open and honest. He deserved that, and she was done with all the deception and lies.

She hoped the next chapter of her life would finally embody the happiness she craved, if she was lucky enough to survive long enough to begin a new chapter.

And she hoped more than ever that Tristan would be part of that future. As with all things in their dystopian world, only time would tell.

Chapter 25

An hour later, Tristan stood behind Grace, subtly adjusting the rifle in her hands.

"You want the butt of the rifle firmly in the pocket of your shoulder," he said, sliding it up slightly so it was better positioned. "Now, fire again."

They were in a secluded area of the forest that lined the pond, and Grace squinted one eye before firing another round. Tristan didn't want to waste ammunition, so he'd told her to go easy, but she seemed to be enjoying obliterating the hell out of the bark of the nearby trees.

"Good," he said, placing his hand on her shoulder so she'd release the trigger. "You're a natural. Are you imagining me as your target?"

She smiled up at him, her blue eyes sparkling under the rising full moon and the last remnants of dusk. "I'm imagining Luthor. I've wanted to punch him in the face so many times over the past decade. He's a misogynistic, narcissistic asshole."

"Uh, yeah. I don't think that's breaking news." Tristan slowly eased the rifle from her arms. "I think you've got the basics down. I'm going to make sure you've got a bulletproof vest and bulletproof pads on your legs under your pants when we attack. They won't protect against everything, but at least they'll help."

She formed a sad smile. "Promise me you'll take care of Raquel if I die. Luthor will certainly kill me if we make contact in the city."

"I won't let that happen."

"You can't control everything," she said, shaking her head. "And I know it's not fair for me to ask you to take care of her, but I need to know you will."

"Of course I will," he said gruffly. "She's our daughter."

Remorse swam in her eyes as she studied him. "I'm sorry. I know words are terribly inadequate, but I owe them to you."

Sighing, Tristan set the rifle on the ground and slid his hands around her waist. Drawing her close, he rested his forehead against hers. "I've been so filled with regret and rage for years," he murmured, lifting a hand to stroke her hair. "And I'm tired too—of all of it. It takes so much energy for me to pretend I hate you, when we both know that will never be the case. I might as well expend the energy somewhere else."

"That's very pragmatic," she said, nudging his nose with hers. "And very evolved. I wouldn't blame you if you hated me."

"I understand why you did it." Running his hand down her face, he cupped her chin. "Luthor is laser-focused when he wants something. If he threatened to kill her, you had to ensure he believed she was already dead."

Grace nodded, her expression laced with deep emotion.

"And attacking him from within was brilliant. It led us to this moment. But I'm still proud, Grace, and I'm not going to profess feelings to a woman who's still married to a man I detest, whether the marriage was a sham or not."

"I understand," she whispered. "I'm sorry I hurt you. It was a very regrettable side effect of my master plan."

"Once this is over, and if we both survive, we can talk about the future. When Luthor's dead and we have the ability to see past tomorrow."

Grace shivered and he pulled her closer. "I hope we make it. I'm not ready to die. There are so many things I want to do with Raquel. So many ways I want to love her and give her the life she deserves."

"Let's hope the universe gives us some clemency." Tightening his hands on the swell of her ass, he squeezed. "And to be completely clear, as much as I want to fuck you, I'm not going to fuck Luthor Cromwell's wife. When I'm inside you again, you'll only belong to *me*."

Gliding her hands up the back of his neck, she plunged her fingers in his thick hair. "I've only ever belonged to you."

Tristan growled and nipped her lips.

Slowly disengaging, she backed away and gripped the hem of her shirt. Eyes cemented to his, she tugged it from her body, tossing it on the grass before unbuttoning her pants. After kicking off her shoes, she threw her pants to rest atop her shirt.

"I assume *skinny dipping* isn't off limits with Luthor's wife—right?"

Tristan's mouth went dry as he gazed at her in her beige bra and black underwear. Her skin glowed in the murky light, beckoning to him as he flexed his fingers. His eyes roved over every inch of her skin, taking it all in before they rested on the scar that covered her lower abdomen.

"It's horrendous," she said, covering it with her hands. "I should've prepared you. The birth was traumatic, and they had to take drastic measures to save her."

A wave of compassion and shame washed over him. He should've been there for her, holding her in the worst moment of her life. Instead, he'd been off in the Middle East, convinced *his* way was the only way he could save their marriage.

Closing the distance between them, Tristan gently encircled her wrists and drew her hands away. Lowering to his knees, he placed his palms on the sides of her abdomen before tugging down the hem of her underwear to see her scar. He tenderly caressed the discolored skin with his thumbs as he reveled at her strength.

"Tristan..." she whispered, threading her fingers through his hair.

"We both made so many mistakes," he rasped, exploring the faded laceration as his fingers trailed over the coarse skin. "I'm sorry too, Grace. I'm so fucking sorry."

"I know," she warbled, tears lacing her voice. "All I ever wanted was to be with you. To be *happy* with you."

Something caught his eye in the moonlight and he shifted his hand over, lightly tracing the newer tattoo on her hip. "You got another tattoo. A butterfly." He grinned as he lifted his gaze to hers.

"That one's for Raquel," she said, her fingers massaging his scalp in pleasurable motions as her lips curved. "You're my dragon, and she's my butterfly. Those are the only two I ever got, to remind me when times were hard of what I was fighting for."

Tristan pressed his face to her scar, nuzzling the skin that had healed long ago...unsure if their hearts would ever find time to truly heal...

Grace slid her fingers under his chin, reclaiming his gaze under the rising stars. Her smile was gorgeous as she backed away, edging toward the pond as she silently beckoned to him.

She stepped into the water and sucked in a breath as she grimaced. "Holy crap, that's cold!"

Laughing, Tristan rose and began to tug off his clothes. "It's October, empress. Still warm for fall, but not ideal skinny dipping weather."

"I don't care," she said, lowering into the water. "I want to do something reckless. I've been so damn restrained for all these years."

Tristan stripped down to his boxers, loving the flare of desire in her eyes. "You left your underwear on, so you're technically cheating," he teased. Throwing caution to the wind, he removed his underwear and tossed it aside. Seizing the moment, he steeled himself for the cold and rushed into the water.

Grace floated in front of him, a gorgeous mermaid under the twinkling stars. Tristan swam toward her, capturing her in his arms. She wrapped her legs around his waist, causing him to grow instantly hard, even though the water was frigid.

"We didn't think this through," she said, mirth in her tone as she shivered in his arms. "It's fucking freezing."

Tristan tossed his head back and laughed, overcome with unabashed joy at holding her once more. "Then we'll have to keep each other warm."

She tightened her limbs around him, spearing her fingers in his hair and drawing her mouth to his.

Tristan plunged his tongue inside, swiping over every crevice of her wet mouth. Tasting...nibbling...devouring...

She purred into his mouth, setting him on fire as he swallowed the sexy sound. As their tongues slithered over one another, she glided her hand to his swollen cock. Moaning with lust and desire, she encircled his length, gently squeezing as he groaned.

"Jesus, Grace," he hissed, pushing into her hand. "That feels so good, baby."

"I missed touching you like this," she breathed into his mouth, capturing his tongue again as she sucked it deep between her swollen lips.

Tristan closed his eyes, overcome with the pleasure of his wife sucking his tongue in slow, fluid strokes as she jerked her palm over his straining shaft.

Of course, she was his *ex-wife*, but hell, how was he supposed to remember that when she was the only woman he knew he'd ever love?

"I understand why you won't fuck me," she crooned, stroking her hand up and down his cock in a pleasurable slide that would soon send him over the edge. "We're not ready for that yet. But I can make you feel good too."

Tristan undulated into her palm, reaching for the ultimate pleasure as he enveloped her mouth in deep, ravenous kisses. "*Yeah, empress...*" he gritted, biting her bottom lip before sucking it between his lips to ease the sting. "Just like that... So fucking good..."

Grace increased the pressure, squeezing him in a vise that sent shards of pleasure to every cell in his frame. Pressing his face to hers, he panted into her mouth as the base of his spine tingled.

"Going to come..." he uttered, eyes closed in sweet agony. "*Oh god...Grace...yes, baby...*"

Suddenly, his spine snapped and he lodged into a blinding orgasm. Jets of release pulsed into the water as Grace continued to stroke him, driving him mad. "No...more..." he gritted, his body jerking as he groaned her name.

Grace's hand stilled, holding his sensitive flesh as he relinquished all control. She buried her face in his neck, kissing a trail along his heated skin as he sighed.

Eventually, he softened in her hand, but she refused to let go. She held his sated length as she burrowed into his repleted body.

Tristan held her, thankful her legs were wrapped around his waist since his muscles had turned to jelly. Trailing his lips down her cheek, he pressed them to hers in a soulful kiss.

Their lips toyed and played with each other, soft and tender, as he recovered from the blissful release.

"Didn't expect that when I promised you rifle practice."

Grace broke into jubilant laughter, her throat exposed as she tossed her head back. Unable to resist, he pressed his lips to the glistening skin, dying to taste every inch of her.

After thoroughly kissing her neck, he fisted his hand in her hair and forced her to meet his gaze. "You're shivering," he said softly.

"It's really cold," she said, biting her lip. "But worth it."

Tristan tightened his arms around her. "Hold on." Praying his exhausted muscles could support them both, he carried her out of the water, placing her on her feet once they were back on the soft grass.

They dressed in comfortable silence, each shivering as the cool air hit their wet skin. Tristan reached for her hand, thrilled when she laced her fingers with his. After retrieving the forgotten rifle, he led her back to the school.

Once inside, they headed toward the shower stall in the boys' bathroom that had running water. Tristan took his time, running the soapy cloth over her body, worshiping her with his strokes as she gazed upon him.

After she returned the favor, they slipped on the clothes Danica had left in their rooms. Although they each had a room with a couch that Arthur had provided, Grace tugged him toward her room and pointed at the pull-out bed.

"There's enough room for both of us."

Tristan debated, understanding it would be difficult not to hold her as they slept. Or, perhaps, that was what she wanted.

"Please don't go," she whispered, reminding him of all those years ago when she begged him not to deploy.

His heart cracked at the intense sadness in her melodious voice. Unable to deny her, he nodded and slipped into bed beside her.

She doused the lone lamp and turned on her side, snuggling into the mattress as he lay on his back beside her. She faced away from him, and he closed his eyes, overwhelmed with the need to hold her.

Expelling a defeated breath, he rolled to his side and glided an arm around her waist. Throwing caution to the wind, he hooked his leg over her thighs and pressed his face to her nape.

She shimmied into him, her soft skin a contrast to the spiky hairs that lined his skin.

Reveling in her scent, his eyes drifted closed.

Her fingernails grazed over his arm, soothing him in long, pleasurable strokes as he faded into darkness.

For a moment, he forgot about the end of the world...and war...and death.

And he was just a man, holding his wife...the woman he loved with every ounce of his soul.

Chapter 26

G race awoke to the sight of Raquel's cute grin as the girl studied her. "Are you awake?" she whispered.

Breathing a laugh, Grace nodded. "I am now."

Raquel's gaze traveled to Tristan, who was clutching Grace as he snored against the back of her neck. Mischief entered the girl's eyes as she observed them.

Grace decided to let it rest since she was nowhere near ready to have a discussion on the birds and bees with her daughter. "Where's Nathan?"

"He's getting dressed and then we're going to head to the mess hall. We wanted to see if you're hungry."

"I am, and we have lots to prepare for before leaving for the DC Sen City tomorrow." Looking over her shoulder, she jabbed Tristan's arm. "Wake up. It's time for breakfast."

"Mmm..." Tristan murmured, sliding his hand to cup the sensitive place between her legs under the sheets. "Let me play with you first, empress..."

Clearing her throat, Grace jabbed his arm again.

"Ouch!" He lifted his head, and recognition lit his eyes as he gazed at Raquel. "Oh...good morning," he mumbled.

"Morning!" She was as chipper as he was drowsy. "Nathan and I are starving, and we wanted to see if you were hungry too."

"I'm definitely hungry, but breakfast wasn't what I had in mind."

Grace shot him a droll look at the double entendre.

"Let me get dressed, and we'll meet you at the mess hall," he said. "You and Nathan can walk together, and we'll be there in a few minutes."

"Okay. We'll save you some seats." She pivoted and breezed through the door.

Leaning on his fist, Tristan's lips curled. "Where does she get that energy from? We're both pretty fucking reserved."

Laughing, she shrugged. "Not sure. My mom was a talker and loved all the fancy parties Dad took her to. Maybe she inherited it from her."

"Maybe." His expression grew serious as he traced a finger over her cheek. "You're still my favorite thing to see when I wake up in the morning." Bumps rose along the skin of her arms as he gently traced her nose. "How are you so pretty?"

"I used to be pretty," she said, frowning. "I have wrinkles now. Luthor used to offer to inject me with tons of crap that would make them go away, but I always found a way to refuse. Thank god. His drugs are toxic."

"The wrinkles aren't so bad," he said, touching the skin beneath her eye. "I've got them too. We're old now."

Pushing to sit, she swatted his chest. "Don't put me out to pasture yet. I've still got some life in me."

"If we win, what do you want for your future?" He rolled to his back and laced his hands behind his head as he waited for her answer.

I want to marry you all over again. The words flitted through her brain as she rose and began to dress. "I want to be happy. I have no idea what that looks like, but hopefully I can figure it out."

He sat up and yawned while he rubbed his chest. Grace's eyes darted over his toned pecs and the mix of gray and dark hair that covered them, reminding herself that daydreaming had no place in her agenda.

"I'll meet you in ten minutes once I hit the restroom and get dressed," he said, rising.

He sauntered out of the room, and she all but drooled at his confident gait and broad shoulders.

"Get it together, Grace," she muttered to herself as she dug for the hairbrush in her bag.

Ten minutes later, they strolled to the mess hall and joined Raquel and Nathan. After inhaling her eggs and bacon, Grace waved to Chris, who appeared to whisk the kids away to wiffle ball practice.

Dani and Maverick strode over, and Grace asked, "Did Arianna and Dominic get into the city okay?"

"They were able to infiltrate, thanks in part to communication with Bodie," Maverick said. "Thanks for your help, Tristan."

"Hopefully, they'll get some intel for us," Dani said, sliding her arm around Maverick's waist. "I'm going to spend the day preparing the last of the vials while you all train. I'm impressed at your willingness to fight, Grace."

"My inability to bring Luthor down before he destroyed the world is my greatest failure," Grace said, pushing the plate away and rising. "I'm determined not to fail this time."

Maverick kissed Dani on the cheek before the three of them left her behind to walk to the training field. Grace spotted Zayne and her small team of men, and excused herself to approach them privately.

They formed a circle at the edge of the field, and Grace looked each of them in the eye as she addressed them. "We've worked and plotted for so long to get here," she said, her tone filled with determination. "I'm honored to fight with you and appreciative of your hard work."

"When you approached me and told me about the rebellion, I was initially suspicious that you were spying for Luthor," Zayne said, grinning. "I couldn't believe the mild-mannered woman I helped protect had concocted such a brilliant plan. He never suspected you." He tipped his head in acknowledgment. "Well done. I'm proud to be on your team."

"Thanks for taking the fall and posing as the leader," she said, patting his arm. "Luthor has probably figured out my deception by this point, but you took one for the team. I appreciate it." Glancing at the others, she spoke with reverence. "You all are brave and on the right side of history. Know that if we fail, we'll at least have failed doing what's right and just."

"Hear, hear," the men chimed.

George Luddington hobbled over, full from a hearty breakfast at the mess hall. "Just stopping by for one last huddle before you all go save the world," he said, balancing on his cane. "Arthur put me up in a cozy little house two blocks from the mess hall, but I'm ready to reenter the city. I miss the luxury of hot showers. Living on jugs of water isn't going to cut it for me."

Grace acknowledged that living outside of the conditions he was used to would be a shock, especially since he wasn't in great health. Wealthy people rarely understood the real world, but she didn't fault him for that. He'd been born into one of the richest families in Virginia, and Grace had known him her whole life.

"You've supported me for all these years," she said, squeezing his upper arm. "I could never have done this without you, George. Thank you."

"I *might* forgive you for making me pretend to like that husband of yours," he chided, his eyes sparkling. "If I ever have to go on another fishing trip with Luthor, I'll probably dive in the water and end it there."

"Hopefully, those days are over. Our deception worked perfectly. My *husband*," she emphasized the word, showing her distaste, "always believed me a vapid aristocrat without two brain cells to rub together. I guess I showed him."

Chuckling, George nodded. "You certainly did, my dear."

Grace wound down the impromptu meeting, and George meandered off the field. She and her men joined the others to prepare for tomorrow's attack.

Although the future was uncertain, they were finally taking matters into their own hands. If all went as planned, they would accomplish their goal and change the course of history.

In a matter of days, they would know for certain, and Grace was ready, whatever the outcome.

Arianna and Dominic stealthily moved through the city, making sure the deli wasn't crowded before entering. Arianna wanted to ensure Deandra had time to speak to them alone.

"What can I get you?" she called, turning to face the register and sticking a pencil behind her ear. Her eyes grew wide when she recognized them. "Well, hello. If it isn't my favorite badass couple, back from exile. How are you?"

"We're good," Arianna said. "Back to order lots of sandwiches." She slipped a gold bar across the counter.

"By *sandwiches*, I think you mean information, but Ron will make you some food anyway. What'll it be?"

"Two bagels with eggs, and he'll have ham on his too," she said, pointing at Dominic.

"She's ordering for you now?" Deandra teased before repeating the order to Ron, who confirmed it as he worked the grill.

Leaning forward, Dominic whispered conspiratorially, "I let her think she's in charge and then she lets me kiss her wherever and whenever I want—"

Arianna planted a hand on his face and pushed him behind her. "I *am* in charge, and he might get to kiss me if we can stay alive long enough to end the nightmare we're all living in."

Chuckling, Deandra hid the gold bar under the counter before wrapping their sandwiches. "Fair enough." The bell chimed as two more patrons walked in. "Meet me in the park a block north from here in ten minutes."

"She can only chat with you all a few minutes," Ron called from the grill. "Last time, she left me in a lurch."

"Oh, you hush," she said, waving her hand at him. "He's a big baby who can't work the register and cook. I swear."

"Quiet, woman!" Ron called, the words softened by the loving smile he shot her.

"I'll be there in a few," she said, shooing Arianna and Dominic from the deli.

They located the park and sat on a graffitied bench to eat their sandwiches. The words *Death for Luthor* were painted on the faded wood, along with many other messages of dissention, showing how far the rebellion had spread.

"That's a good sign," Dominic said, reading the words as he ate.

"It is. Do you think Arthur will put Luthor on trial if we capture him?"

Dominic's eyes narrowed. "I think Luthor will die in the attack. Tristan seems pretty dead set on murdering him."

"He's not the only one," Arianna muttered.

"Are you worried for Dani's trial?"

Contemplating, Arianna shook her head. "I think the jury will show her deference for creating the cure. I still have hope *some* people aren't assholes."

"Me too."

Deandra approached and sat beside Arianna, opening her hand to take the discarded wrappers. After tossing them in the receptacle beside her, she leaned back and crossed her arms over her chest. "The shit really hit the fan when you all left. Luthor sent a battalion to Arthur's compound, but you know that already. They returned with only half the men, led by a young major named Anthony Martinez." She arched an inquisitive eyebrow. "It seems you turned Major Martinez to your side."

"If you know that, Luthor surely must as well," Arianna said. "And that's not good."

"From what I've gathered overhearing the soldiers' conversations as they wait for food, Luthor sees it more as incompetence because Anthony is inexperienced. I think Luthor's arrogance blinds him from believing anyone would turn against him."

"Which is why he didn't realize Grace was leading the rebellion," Dominic said.

"You don't say," Deandra said, her mouth falling slightly open. "That wisp of a woman leading the rebellion?" Chuckling, she rubbed her palms over her legs. "How very interesting. Luthor believes Zayne is the leader."

"He's aligned with Grace, but she was the mastermind," Dominic confirmed.

"Good for her. So she really wasn't 'kidnapped' at all." She made quotation marks with her fingers. "Absolutely glorious."

"We need all the info you have on the soldiers who've been injected with the strength serum," Arianna said. "How many, where they train, any weaknesses you know of."

"Well, my dear, lucky for you, I hear *everything*." She tapped her ear. "Two hundred were injected, and seven died—"

"Jesus," Arianna breathed, shaking her head.

"I'm sure Luthor sees them as collateral damage," Deandra said. "He doesn't really view the soldiers as human. He thinks most people are beneath him."

"That tracks," Arianna said, her lips flattening in distaste. "Besides enhanced strength, does the serum have any other effects?"

"It seems to allow for rapid healing. Most likely because the soldiers are taking EverLife too. Luthor keeps them pumped full of it and gives all his soldiers the cleanest version of the antidote he'll allow so they stay young and primed for fighting."

"Do you know where they train? We'd like to scope it out," Dominic said.

"They've been training in Garfield Park, close to downtown where his headquarters are."

"Deandra, you're a goddess," Arianna said, squeezing her hand. "Thank you."

"Just remember who scratched your back when you beat that crazy old dictator." She stood and planted her hands on her hips. "Ron and I love the deli, and we need lots of renovations. Maybe Mr. Reyes can find it in his heart to help us out when he rebuilds."

Rising, Dominic extended his hand. "You can count on it, Deandra."

Deandra pointed back and forth between them. "I want an invite to the wedding. Don't leave me hanging."

Laughing, Arianna nodded. "You'll be the first to know. I'd advise you and Ron to close and lock the deli tomorrow evening, and to have some protection while you stay inside."

"Yes, ma'am," she said with a salute. "Ron will protect us. That man is fiercer than he lets on. See you all once we've entered the new world. Go get 'em."

With a final wave, she sauntered away as Arianna and Dominic prepared to spy on Luthor's troops.

Chapter 27

T he next day, a nervous but excited energy filled Arthur's compound. The morning was spent training before Arthur sent everyone home, encouraging them to spend time with the family they had left. The unspoken reality was that many of the militia members would be lost in the attack, but everyone was united in the cause and ready to sacrifice their life to regain freedom for those left behind.

Grace urged Tristan to take Raquel on another walk while she used the pen and paper Danica had given her to write her daughter a letter. She hoped it wasn't a goodbye letter, but if that were the case, she wanted her to know the truth.

My darling Raquel,

I write this letter to you in the hopes you never have to read it. If you do, please know it was written with love and a fair amount of tears.

My greatest accomplishment was ensuring your light wasn't extinguished in a world where so many others were. My greatest source of pride is being your mother. Yes, my darling, I am your birth mother, and I'm so very sorry I couldn't tell you all these years.

Maria did a wonderful job sheltering you, and was a mother to you in all the ways I craved. Getting to know you during the small visits we had over the years soothed my broken soul. I hid the fact that you were mine because the world was thrust into chaos, and I was determined to right that terrible wrong.

My separation from you, and the dissolution of my marriage from your father, are the only regrets I ever let myself suffer.

Tristan and I conceived you with an abundance of love and joy, and you shine so brightly with that joy every day. I continue to be amazed by your vivacious spirit, inquisitive mind and kind soul.

Please don't blame Tristan for not telling you he was your father. I lied to him in my effort to keep you safe, and all the blame falls on my shoulders. He will be a wonderful father to you, and I hope you both can build a future together if I'm no longer here.

I understand the huge betrayal you must feel and don't blame you if you hate me for the rest of your days. I hope they're filled with happiness in a long life where you never have to suffer. Even if you can't forgive me, I'll have the solace that my efforts weren't in vain if you seize each day with wonder and hope.

Some of my fondest memories are of the short months I was pregnant with you before your father deployed. He would rub my belly and speak to you, and he wanted you with all his heart. Please let him inside yours. You two have lots to catch up on and a beautiful relationship to build.

Live well, my beautiful girl. Carry the torch for so many others whose were extinguished. Show the world your humanity and let it be an example for everyone as they hopefully navigate new freedoms.

Love,

Your mother, Grace Holder

Wiping the tears that streamed down her face, Grace released a long breath and reread the letter. She'd used Tristan's surname because it was the one that held the most meaning in her heart. Afterward, she folded it several times and wrote Raquel's name on the outside.

Wanting to ensure the letter's safekeeping, she treaded down the hallway from her room to find Dani in the old science lab. She looked up from the vials she was preparing and smiled.

"Hey, Grace."

"Hi." Stepping forward, she held out the letter. "I was hoping you could hold onto this and give it to Raquel if I..." She cleared her throat. "Well, you know."

Dani took the letter and walked to a nearby cabinet. "I'll put it here so it's safe." She opened the top drawer and deposited it inside before returning to her seat behind the microscope. Pointing to the stool across from her, she silently asked Grace to sit.

Grace lowered onto the stool and circled a hand over her face. "You've got that inquisitive scientist look."

Dani laughed. "So, I'm a geneticist, and that means I'm really good at seeing genetic patterns in people." Her green eyes sparkled as she spoke. "It's pretty clear to me that Raquel is your and Tristan's daughter."

Grace nodded. "She is, but she doesn't know. That's what the letter is for." She pointed to the cabinet. "And Tristan only found out she was alive a few days ago. I told him she died during childbirth." Speaking the words aloud sent a wave of emotion through Grace, and she buried her hands in her face as she started to cry. "Oh, god. I've made so many terrible decisions..."

Dani rushed around the table and rubbed Grace's shoulder. "Hey, you're talking to the woman who created EverLife. I'm not sure you want to have a discussion with me about regrettable choices."

Laughter burst from Grace's throat as she lifted her gaze to Dani's. "Holy shit, you're right. You might be the only other person in the world who's made worse decisions than me."

"I could make the excuse that I don't remember half of them, but that never really works. I still feel like crap, believe me."

Grace smiled and swiped her cheeks. "It's hard because I made those choices in order to save her. Unfortunately, I thought it would happen *slightly* faster than it actually has."

Dani pulled over a nearby stool and sat down to face her. "Here's the thing," she said, swiping a hand through her shoulder-length brown hair. "It doesn't help to beat ourselves up, although I constantly want to. I just keep reminding myself that I can't change the past, but I can damn well change the future. I'm determined to cure everyone on this goddamned planet."

"That's so valiant," Grace said. "You've done amazing things here in an old run-down science lab. Imagine what you can do when you actually have a functioning lab and a factory to produce the cure."

"I imagine that every day," she replied wistfully.

Grace's cheeks puffed as she exhaled. "I'm so afraid I'm going to save the world and accomplish everything I want, only to be hated by my daughter and the man I love. I can tell Tristan wants to move on, but I violated his trust and he has every right to be angry. And Raquel..." She shook her head as she gazed at the floor. "I have no idea how she's going to handle the news that I'm her mother."

"Children are very resilient," Dani said, patting her leg. "They can also smell dishonesty and disingenuousness from a mile away. Tell her the truth—that you made hard choices because you love her. She'll understand that, Grace. I know she will."

"You make it sound so easy."

Dani grinned. "Honestly, I think it's about time something was easy. We deserve that. Let it be easy."

Grace bit her lip as she studied her. "Are you and Maverick going to have kids?"

"I hope so. As long as I'm not in prison. Let's hope the jury is lenient."

"I'll do my part to sway public opinion your way." Encircling her wrist, Grace squeezed. "Thank you, Dani. I'm not sure if you remember, but we met casually at various work events Luthor held for Sendaxa while you worked there. He held you in high regard: the brilliant scientist who would create the most important drug in history. Of course, once you figured out his nefarious tactics, his opinion of you soured. I'm not sure what you remember, but you tried to stop him. It made him livid. And that's why I know you're a good soul."

"I don't remember meeting you, but that's par for the course." She playfully rolled her eyes. "And this time, we *will* stop him. I know it."

Grace smiled, hoping they both would survive and become close friends. Dani was kind and easy to talk to, and lord knew Grace needed more friends and confidants in the world. Being married to Luthor had been a self-imposed prison, and she was ready for a new chapter of her life.

Envisioning a future without Luthor Cromwell, Grace returned to her room to prepare to depart the compound.

By the time the late-afternoon sun kissed the horizon, Arthur's militia was ready to advance on the DC Sen City. They'd packed many of the SUVs and trucks on the compound with weapons, and the remaining pickup trucks would carry multiple soldiers in their beds. All of the available gas on the compound would be dedicated to fueling the vehicles for the journey.

They would make the two-and-a-half-hour drive to DC in a caravan under the early nighttime sky for additional cover. When they reached the city, they would stop at Fort

Bennett Park and quickly arm themselves. Arianna and Dominic would meet them there so they could reconvene and join the attack.

Arthur had been communicating with Major Anthony Martinez over a secret radio channel. Since Luthor had destroyed all of the bridges into the city when he erected the wall, Anthony and his men had surreptitiously hidden row boats in the woods of Fort Bennett Park over the past few weeks. Arthur's men would use them to cross the Potomac River and rush the grassy bank outside the DC wall.

Once outside the wall, Anthony's battalion would meet them there. Although his battalion was small—thanks to the men they'd lost when they'd attacked the Cumberland compound—every ounce of help mattered. They would give Arthur's militia an additional hundred or so men, some with tanks, and that would be a huge advantage.

Arthur anticipated Luthor would send the super-soldier battalion to fight outside the wall. As they fought, Arthur's men would use the grenade launchers to try to blow the wall open. If successful, they would breach the city and enter downtown. This is where Grace played a very important role.

Her proximity to Luthor for the past decade ensured she knew the location of all of his secret bunkers. As Arthur's militia advanced, Grace would lead them to his primary bunker downtown. If he wasn't there, she could lead the militia to the next bunker, and so on, until they found him.

The primary goal was to gain Luthor's surrender and take him into custody. After that, Arthur would seize control of the city and begin the long, winding path to rebuilding the government and society.

As she sat beside Tristan in the bed of one of the pickup trucks, Grace grappled with the huge task ahead. She ran her hands over her black pants, testing the bulletproof pads underneath.

"I know they're not comfortable, but I want you safe," Tristan said.

"I get it," she responded. "They're just itchy."

"Better itchy than dead."

Since she couldn't argue there, Grace stayed silent as the wind whipped her hair on the long drive.

They eventually made it to Fort Bennett Park and parked all of the vehicles under the shelter of the perimeter woods. The men and women exited the vehicles and quickly armed themselves. The superior marksmen strapped the dart guns filled with rounds of anti-strength serum to their belts while those tasked with operating the grenade launchers strapped them behind their backs. It was a clear night with a bright moon, so there was enough visibility to see, but Arthur also ensured the marksmen armed with the dart guns were equipped with night-vision goggles for better precision.

A few men had been assigned to groups of two who would transport the Javelins across the river and launch them at any tanks operated by Luthor's super-soldiers. They could also be used to blow open the wall if the grenade launchers failed.

Once they were armed, Arthur led them in search of the row boats. As Grace stomped through the thick brush, she heard a gruff voice whisper, "Over here!"

Arthur shined his flashlight toward the sound, his teeth flashing in the dim moonlight as he beamed. "Arianna. Glad you made it to the rendezvous."

"You all are loud as hell," she said, scowling as Dominic stood beside her. Thick trees surrounded them, and Grace could see the outline of several row boats stacked along the trunks.

"What she's trying to say is that she's happy to see you too," Dominic said.

Arianna shot him a glare. "Is everybody armed?"

"Yes. The intel you sent back on the super-soldiers was invaluable," Arthur said. "Maverick and I trained the soldiers with the dart guns to aim for the head and the neck. We thought their heads would be covered with helmets, but thanks to you, we know that's not the case."

"The strength serum causes swelling in the brain, and none of the helmets fit them," Dominic said. "We saw it with our own eyes, and Deandra overheard it from many soldiers who frequented her deli."

"It's a fortuitous discovery," Arthur said. "Thank you for the surveillance. Ready to kick some ass?"

"Ready," Arianna and Dominic said in unison.

Arthur gave the command to drag the boats to the river, and the militia loaded into them and began rowing. When they were halfway across, several flood lights illuminated atop the city wall.

A loud screech echoed in the silence, causing many of the men to plug their ears. Suddenly, Luthor's voice sounded over loudspeakers that must've been attached to the wall.

"Advance any further and we will consider this an act of war," Luthor said, his tone calm and sinister at the same time. "Once we declare war, I won't hesitate to use the full weight of the Sen Force army against you, Arthur. Think about your soldiers and save them now."

Arthur waved to his men, urging them to continue.

"Very well," Luthor's voice called eerily as it rang out over the horizon. "Fire!"

Bullets began to fly from the city, and Arthur held his hands up to his mouth to yell a command. "Row until you can wade in the water and continue on foot!"

The soldiers listened, many of them jumping into the water since they could stand. They would duck every so often but continued to advance toward the riverbank.

Tristan helped Grace jump from the boat, her teeth chattering as she encountered the cool water. She marched toward the grassy bank beside several other men, noticing how Tristan made sure to walk in front of her. Her heart somersaulted at the protective gesture, and she made a mental note to kiss the hell out of him if they survived...and more. A hell of a lot more if he would let her.

But now wasn't the time to ruminate on the extent of her ex-husband's possible forgiveness. Now was the time to *fight*. Grace crawled onto the shore and followed Tristan as he jogged to a nearby bush. They ducked behind it, and Grace thanked the universe that Luthor hadn't maintained the land outside the city wall. It meant there were lots of overgrown bushes to hide behind, and Arthur's men took full advantage of that oversight.

A section of the wall swung open, and soldiers dressed in Sen Force uniforms began to filter through. Thanks to the bright lights atop the wall, Grace could discern their outlines. Their bodies were thick with bulging muscles, and they wore no helmets, so she understood these were the super-soldiers.

Arthur's troops armed with the dart guns moved in, aiming for the soldier's necks. Although they were able to take down a few, the hulking men continued to advance. With the river behind them, there was nowhere for Arthur's men to go. Faced with that inevitability, he seized the moment and yelled, "Charge!"

Arthur's troops sprang forward, firing their rifles as the sounds of war ripped through the air.

"Stay behind this bush until I come back to get you," Tristan said, rising and pointing at the ground as he spoke. "I mean it, Grace. We'll need you to locate Luthor in his bunker once we blow a hole in the wall, and you can't do that if you're dead."

"Okay," she said, her voice shaky.

He gave a curt nod and gripped his rifle in both hands as he ran to join the combat. Covering her lips with her fingers, Grace watched the battle unfold with wide eyes.

The soldiers fought under the stars, Arthur's men scurrying around bushes to take cover before emerging from the other side to attack the super-soldiers' flanks. Bullets seemed to bounce off the injected soldiers' thick muscles, giving them an air of invincibility. Grace counted about ten soldiers of Luthor's who'd fallen, but Arthur's militia had already lost over twenty-five in her estimation. At this rate, they would surely lose. Would Arthur call for a retreat or have them fight to the death?

Luthor's voice boomed "Cease fire!" over the speakers, and the super-soldiers froze, awaiting their next orders.

Arthur held up his hand, signaling for the militia to halt as he assessed.

The wall swung open again and another battalion rolled through, most of them in tanks. The tanks filed to flank Luthor's soldiers on either side. A man walked through the opening and strode forward to stand beside the leader of the super-soldier regiment.

"It seems we meet again," Major Anthony Martinez said, approaching Arthur as he stood in front of his men scattered across the riverbank. "This time, you're the one who will retreat. Luthor can hear everything we're saying," he said, tapping the receiver in his ear. "If you surrender now, he'll take you and your men into custody and let you live."

"You know I can't do that," Arthur said. "Tell your commander we came here to take back the city, and we won't stop until we succeed."

Anthony paused, appearing to listen to orders in the earpiece before backing away to rejoin the super-soldier front line.

"You've made your choice," Anthony said, lifting his chin. "We will now unleash the full power of the tanks against your militia."

Grace knew this was the moment Arthur and Anthony had discussed in secret. Instead of attacking Arthur's militia, Anthony would turn the tanks on the super-soldiers and begin to fire.

Except, in that moment, everything went terribly wrong.

The super-soldier commander snaked his arm around Anthony's neck and pulled his handgun from his holster. Grace gasped as Anthony struggled before the super-soldier commander shot him in the temple. Anthony collapsed on the ground, his body lifeless as the soldier who shot him stood stoic.

"Did you really think you could turn my own soldiers against me without me knowing, Arthur?" Luthor's sinister voice called over the loudspeaker. "The entire battalion was dead the moment you sent them back to me. I don't tolerate dissidence in my regime."

Suddenly, the tanks that flanked the super-soldiers exploded in a brilliant round of fire. Grace held her ears, barely able to tolerate the ringing in them from the excruciating sounds.

When the smoke cleared, she blinked rapidly as realization washed over.

Luthor had destroyed his own tanks and the men inside them rather than allow their disloyalty.

Major Anthony Martinez and his entire battalion were now dead.

Arthur's militia had lost an entire battalion of soldiers they'd counted on to help them win.

Fear snaked up her spine as comprehension dawned, and she whispered words only she could hear...

"Holy shit...we're all going to die."

Chapter 28

Tristan observed the carnage, barely able to wrap his mind around the crazed actions of Luthor Cromwell. The man had just killed a hundred of his own men. Yes, they'd secretly turned against him, but the action was extreme, even for Luthor.

"As you can see, I armed the interior of each tank in Major Martinez's battalion with explosives," Luthor said over the loudspeaker. "I hope this shows my determination to end anyone's life associated with the rebellion."

Tristan looked toward Arthur, whose head hung slightly as he stood still on the battlefield. Losing Anthony's battalion was a huge setback, and he could see Arthur trying to formulate a solution.

"Many of your men are already dead, Reyes," Luthor said. "End this now and surrender. I'll give you a fair public trial."

Tristan scoffed. Luthor would publicly execute Arthur if he surrendered, and everyone on the battlefield knew it.

Arthur turned to Maverick, Arianna, and Dominic, and they began a hushed discussion. Tristan jogged toward them, anxious to help if he could.

"What are you all thinking?" he asked.

Sighing, Arthur shook his head. "I don't want to lose any more men, and not having the tanks to attack the super-soldiers puts us at a disadvantage. I can surrender and you all can retreat while they capture me. You'll have to lead the militia and move quickly—"

"No fucking way!" Arianna hissed. "We're not surrendering to that asshole. Let's fight. We have the grenade launchers and the Javelins. I know we planned to use them to blow through the wall, but let's use them on the super-soldiers first."

"Those weapons aren't meant to be used on humans," Arthur said, contemplating. "I hate to senselessly kill Luthor's soldiers, and it violates the basic rules of engagement. Those weapons will rip those soldiers apart, super-serum or not."

"It's terrible," Arianna agreed, "but the future of the world is at stake. I don't think we have a choice. We can't surrender. If we lose, who else will fight? We have to seize this moment."

Crouching down, she drew circles on the ground in rapid movements. "Dom and I will lead a third of the men on the left flank. Maverick and Tristan will lead a third on the right flank. You and Zayne lead the remaining third head-on. We'll give the command to fire at will and blast those fuckers."

Arthur contemplated another moment before making the sign of the cross over his head and chest. Looking to the sky, he said softly, "Lord, forgive me. I don't see another path."

Cupping his hands over his mouth, he called, "Troops! Those to my right follow Arianna and Dominic," he said swiping his arm over that flank of the riverbank. "Those here follow me, and those to my left follow me and Zayne. Charge!"

The militia gave a rallying cry and fell into step behind their respective leaders.

Luthor commanded his men to fire at will, and the fighting resumed.

Arthur's troops advanced, each soldier stopping every few feet to plant a knee on the ground, balance the grenade launcher on their shoulder, and fire the weapon.

Although it was a slow advance due to the heavy artillery, Arthur's men succeeded in making some headway against Luthor's soldiers. Still, they were outnumbered and needed to breach the wall sooner rather than later.

"Advance to the wall and launch the grenades at it," Arthur commanded Tristan and Maverick. They led the men with the grenade launchers forward as other militia members continued the advance against Luthor's soldiers.

Tristan approached the wall, observing Luthor's men draw near out of the corner of his eye.

"Hand me the Javelin!"

He hoisted the heavy launcher on his shoulder and held it steady. Clenching his teeth, he shot the steel wall. The explosion reverberated around him, knocking him on his back as the Javelin fell to the ground. Lifting his head, he blinked to see if he'd managed to open a hole in the wall. He had, but it was small and none of Arthur's men would fit through it.

"Fuck!" he said, struggling to stand. "We must've hit a reinforced area of the wall. The hole is too small. We're going to have to launch another Javelin. Do we have any left?" They'd only had a few to begin with, and most were currently being launched at Luthor's troops.

"Maybe we can fire a grenade launcher at it," Maverick said, scanning the battlefield for a soldier who still had loaded launchers. "We've almost depleted those too."

"I can fit through it!" a voice called behind Tristan, and he whirled around to see Nathan jogging toward him.

Surprise and shock reverberated through Tristan's body as the kid spoke with excited confidence.

"I can crawl through and open the gate from the other side."

Tristan's mouth fell open as he gazed upon the kid's freckled face. "What the hell are you doing here?"

Breaking into a wide grin, Nathan puffed his chest. "I *told* you I was a good spy."

Grace felt helpless as she observed the awesome firepower being unleashed on Luthor's troops. The super-soldiers were making a valiant effort, but they were no match for the heavy artillery.

Narrowing her eyes, Grace saw a figure dart toward Tristan in the distance. Inhaling a sharp breath, she rose to her feet. "Nathan?" Afraid for the boy, she threw caution to the wind and ran to join him and Tristan at their location near the wall.

"How the hell did you get here?" Tristan asked the boy as she approached.

"I hid under a blanket in one of the truck beds with all the weapons," he said. "And when the driver parked the truck, I jumped out and hid behind a tree."

Tristan opened his mouth to say something else, but a grenade exploded in the background, causing him to cover his face with his arms. Nathan held up his arms reflexively too, and Grace fell to the ground from the reverb.

"Damn it, Grace," Tristan said, helping her up. "I told you to wait behind the bush."

"I'm going to have to get inside eventually," she said, wiping the dirt off her pants. Clutching Nathan's shoulders, she noticed his clothes were wet. "Did you swim across the river?"

Nathan nodded and pointed toward the small opening in the wall. "I can climb through it! Then I can open the wall from the inside."

"No way, kid—"

Crouching before him, she ignored Tristan. "It's really dangerous, but if you can get through that hole, there's a lever about twenty feet that way." She pointed to her left. "If you pull the lever down, it will allow that flap of the wall to swing open."

"Are you serious?" Tristan asked, arms stretched at his sides. "He's a kid, Grace—"

"I can do it," Nathan said, looking up at Tristan. "I've done much harder missions for Solomon."

Tristan lowered beside Grace. "I don't doubt your fortitude, but I don't want you to get hurt."

Nathan patted his chest. "I promise I can do it."

Grace looked at Tristan and then looked toward the battle that raged behind them. Reclaiming Tristan's gaze, she said softly, "It will allow us to open the wall. Then we can infiltrate and find Luthor. If we capture him, the fighting stops."

Tristan blew out a breath and stood. "You have to move fast. Crawl through and run to the lever. Once you push the wall open, I want you to run back that way along the inside of the wall." He motioned south with his arm. "There's a trail called Rock Creek that runs along the wall, and it has lots of overgrown trees. I want you to hide there until I come back to get you. These are orders, soldier. Can I count on you?" Tristan lifted his hand to his forehead in a salute.

Nathan straightened his shoulders and saluted back. "Yes, sir. I promise I'll hide by the trail until you come and get me."

Lowering his hand, Tristan crouched and drew the boy into an embrace as Grace's heart squeezed in her chest.

Releasing him, Tristan urged Nathan toward the opening. "Run fast. I don't want you to get shot. Now go!"

Nathan broke into a full-on sprint toward the wall. When he reached the opening, he squeezed his body through and disappeared. Grace waited for several heart-wrenching moments, hoping he would succeed. Suddenly, Arianna's voice echoed through the smoke and bullets.

"The wall is open!" she yelled. "Charge forward!"

The remaining militia members rushed the wall, fighting the super-soldiers as they struggled to enter the city.

Facing Grace, Tristan took her hand. "Ready to track down your asshole husband?"

Armed with steely determination, Grace uttered one resolute word. "Ready."

Chapter 29

Arthur's troops were able to infiltrate the city, and they scattered throughout the interior, drawing away the super-soldiers' attention so Tristan, Grace, Arianna, Dominic, Maverick and Arthur could head toward Luthor's downtown bunkers. They advanced as a team, holding rifles as Arianna and Dominic acted as lookouts. They led the way, scoping out each block ahead and ensuring it was clear before the small team moved forward. Although it was a highly precarious situation, Grace felt safe surrounded by such skilled soldiers.

They made their way down Constitution Avenue before heading north on 14th Street. When they passed the abandoned and desolate White House, Grace marveled that the once-great symbol was now an empty husk that represented days long gone.

"I always wondered why Luthor never moved into the White House," Tristan said quietly as they passed it in the shadows of the trees that lined the street.

"Because it's a symbol of a world that didn't accept his arrogance and evil," she said. "His headquarters are where he's comfortable. A sign of the new regime."

"We're approaching McPherson Square," Arianna said as they crept toward the dilapidated park. "This is his main bunker?"

"Yes," Grace said. "There's a secret doorway on the base of the statue of General McPherson. I think you all will have to blow it open."

"Dani made me some kick-ass door charges from some chemicals she found in the school lab," Maverick said, pulling them from the small pack at his waist. "We can use them to blow it open."

They moved behind a thicket of trees, assessing the Sen Force soldiers that surrounded the statue in the middle of the park.

"Ten soldiers around the base of the statue, and several scattered throughout the park," Arianna murmured.

"Confirmed," Dominic said, sliding his rifle around his shoulder and lifting it to aim. "Bet I can take out more than you, Lawson."

Arianna clutched her rifle and aimed through the leaves. "You're on."

They began to fire, each aiming for the thighs of the soldiers to hopefully wound instead of kill. Maverick and Tristan joined in, firing carefully measured shots as the officers fell to the ground one by one. They all writhed in pain as they clutched their legs, and Arthur stepped forward, retrieving a dart gun from his waist.

"I'm shooting you with sedatives, boys," he said, discharging a dart into each arm of the now-fallen soldiers as Arianna and the others confiscated their forgotten weapons. "Dani assured me it's safe. Sweet dreams of freedom," he finished acerbically.

After all the soldiers had been shot full of sedative, Maverick placed the door charges at the base of the faint outline of the bunker door. They all fell back as the charges detonated, and Maverick wrapped his hands around the stone, yanking it open.

Arthur motioned to Grace, who was still hiding in the brush, and she swiftly moved forward.

"Dom and I will lead the way," Arianna said, rifle in hand as she peered down the darkened stairs. "There's a small path of lights, similar to an airplane aisle, but that's all we've got. Stay sharp."

She stepped inside and everyone followed. Grace fell into step behind Arthur and Maverick, and Tristan walked behind.

The stone stairs were curved and led to a dark tunnel. Arthur turned on his flashlight, and they continued to advance.

They eventually reached a metal door, and Maverick pulled out another door charge. "Stand back, guys. I'm blowing this one too."

After detonation, he tugged the door open, and Arianna and Dominic rushed inside, rifles aimed. Grace entered, observing the large room, full of technology that hadn't been widely available since the world collapsed. Screens lined the walls, showing different video feeds from across the city.

A large mahogany desk sat on the far side of the room, in front of several mounted screens, and a high-backed leather chair rocked with eerily precision, indicating someone sat on the other side of the back that faced them.

Slow claps sounded from the desk, and the chair slowly swiveled. Luthor Cromwell's sinister face appeared, his eyes lit with derangement and rage.

"Well done, my friends," he said, finishing the slow clap before lowering his arms. "You infiltrated my city and are here to kill the nefarious dictator." His voice dripped with sarcasm. "I only wonder what took you so long. As the battle progressed, I decided to bunker here and wait for you. After all, running is for cowards, and I'm man enough to meet you and assume my destiny."

Arthur surveyed the bunker. "How magnanimous you are to let your men die outside the wall while you hide in a bunker and observe their efforts."

"I *saved* them!" Luthor said, standing as spittle flew from his mouth. "Every single person in this new utopia I've created. Why can't you all see that?"

"Freedom is messy and democracy is imperfect," Arthur said, showing his palms. "But they're much better than living in a regime where everyone is an addict, homeless or dead."

Luthor scrubbed a hand over his face. "You'll never understand, so I'll cease trying to reason with you. Bring in the hostages!"

Grace recognized Colonel McGrath and Dr. Ziegler as they both appeared holding two squirming hostages who were gagged and bound at their feet and wrists.

"Jessica!" Tristan called, rushing forward before Arthur slammed an arm over his chest to hold him back. "You let her go, you bastard!"

"Nathan!" Grace cried, covering her mouth as the little boy struggled in Colonel McGrath's arms.

Luthor broke into menacing laughter as he shook his head. "Ah, my doting wife. You spent so many years deceiving me, and I never suspected a thing." Perching his hip on the desk, he crossed his arms over his chest. "I've figured it all out now, of course. You were the whistleblower, all those years ago, who almost sent me to prison." He slammed his fist on the desk. "And when you failed, you plotted the rebellion until it brought you right here."

"You murdered my father!" she screamed, all the pent-up rage from years of pain and heartache causing her to lurch forward. "I vowed on that day to make you pay."

Luthor's eyes narrowed. "I always suspected you saw that. Robert was always too headstrong for his own good. Look at how he ruined your marriage to this vagrant." He gestured toward Tristan. "You did serve me well sometimes, Tristan, but your sister served me much better. I always enjoyed the times she let me go deep—"

"I'll fucking kill you!" Tristan screamed, rushing forward as Luthor held up a hand.

"They have orders to kill Jessica and the child on the spot if I'm harmed," Luthor said. "The boy sang like a bird when he was captured and defiantly told me he was '*helping the rebellion*.'" He made quotation marks with his fingers. "So, kill me if you wish, but your sister and the little brat will die too."

Tristan's expression flushed with anger as he faced Colonel McGrath and Dr. Ziegler. "Where's your humanity? This man is a mass murderer!" He jabbed his finger at Luthor.

"Many members of Colonel McGrath's family are addicted to EverLife and need my antidote," Luthor said. "And Dr. Ziegler will surely be tried and sentenced to death for the drugs he created under my regime if I lose power. They both need me to remain the sovereign leader of this city and of the world."

"My wife, Dr. Danica Lawson, created a cure for EverLife addiction," Maverick said. "Let the boy go and I'll make sure every member of your family receives it as soon as possible."

"A cure isn't possible," Dr. Ziegler said, confusion in his expression. "I've tried and can never find the right balance."

"With all due respect, you don't hold a candle to my wife. She's fucking brilliant, and she's going to rid the world of the garbage your boss created."

"Danica is the reason we're all in this situation!" Luthor exclaimed. "She alone is responsible for the destruction. I only wanted to create a world where everyone could live long lives, free from the pains of growing old."

"You wanted power, Luthor," Grace said, her nostrils flaring. "It's why you killed my father, and why you plotted to murder me and my child who was fighting for her life in the NICU. You're a fucking monster."

Luthor emitted a harsh laugh. "You always were a simpleton, just like your father. I should've killed you when I had the chance. I regret not making it a priority. There was always someone in your hospital room, and I decided you weren't worth the effort. It's one of the few miscalculations I've made in a life full of necessary decisions."

"So, where do we go from here?" Arthur asked. "We can't kill you if we want the hostages to live. How do we solve this, Luthor?"

"It's quite simple, really." Luthor walked around his desk and retrieved a handgun from the top drawer. "You all need to die. It will squash any talk of rebellion, and I can rebuild what you've broken here tonight." Lifting the gun, he aimed at Arthur. "You were a worthy opponent, but you'll be the first to die, my friend."

"Wait," a voice called, and Grace turned to see Colonel McGrath lift his gun and aim it at Luthor. Holding it steady, he locked eyes with Maverick. "How do you know the cure works?"

"My wife tested it on all of the patients in the Cumberland clinic. They've all been cured and are in good health. She has vials ready to deploy when Arthur assumes leadership of the city."

Colonel McGrath looked back and forth between Luthor and Maverick, the debate evident on his ruddy face.

"Oh, for god's sake," Luthor droned, rolling his eyes. "I don't have time for this." Aiming the gun at Colonel McGrath, he pulled the trigger and shot the man in the neck. McGrath gasped, clutching his neck as his hold on Nathan loosened. Since Nathan was bound, he couldn't run, and Dr. Ziegler stepped in front of him as he fell to the ground. Grace watched him struggle to free his binds on the cold floor, and she ached to run to him.

"Who's next?" Luthor asked, wielding the gun while a crazed expression lined his face. "Or do you want Jessica to die, Tristan?"

Tristan stood frozen, his chest heaving with deep breaths as he assessed the situation.

"I hate to make the call, but it's her or humanity," Arianna said, aiming her gun at Luthor. "I'm sorry, Tristan—"

"No!" Tristan yelled. "There has to be another way—"

A gunshot reverberated throughout the room, causing everyone to duck. Grace slowly opened her eyes to see Dr. Ziegler inhale a sharp breath as a red dot appeared between his eyes. Blood oozed from the red circle before he slumped and fell in a heap on the floor.

Turning to face the door, Grace observed a tall Black man step inside.

Luthor aimed his gun at the man, and Tristan lifted his to aim at Luthor at the same time. They both fired as the room erupted into chaos. Rushing toward the desk where Luthor had taken cover, Tristan advanced, ready to fire another round.

"You son of a bitch," Tristan snarled, slowly circling the desk. Luthor lifted his gun, and Tristan kicked it out of his hand, sending it crashing across the floor.

A sneer curved Tristan's lips as he loomed above Luthor, his gun aimed square between his eyes. "Well, well. The moment I've longed for has finally arrived. Any last words?"

Luthor reached for the knife at his belt in one last frantic attempt to save himself. Tristan's jaw ticked as every muscle in his body tensed. "Burn in hell, you fucking bastard."

And then, Tristan Holder kept the vow he'd made for so many long, wretched years.

There, in a cold bunker under a broken city, he pressed the muzzle of his gun to the evil dictator's temple and buried a bullet in Luthor Cromwell's brain.

Chapter 30

"**D**amn, Ron!" Arianna exclaimed, rushing toward the tall man and throwing her arms around him in a rare show of affection. "Deandra told us you fought in Kuwait in the nineties, but that's some sharp shooting. Thanks for the assist."

"You're welcome," he said, returning the hug before releasing her. "Deandra's got some excellent surveillance skills, but I prefer old-fashioned hand-to-hand combat. When she passed along your advice to lock ourselves inside and wait out the advance, I just couldn't do it. I needed to help if I could. For my son, Carter, who died from Luthor's horrible drug, and for all the others who also lost the ability to fight back."

"Thank you, Ron," Dominic said, extending his hand. "We're grateful."

Grace rushed over to Nathan, removing his binds and gag as Tristan did the same for Jessica. Grace pulled the boy into a smothering embrace, kissing his hair as he trembled in her arms.

"I'm sorry I got caught," he mumbled, causing her heart to shatter. "I promise I was hiding by the trail."

"You're not in trouble, buddy," Tristan said, reaching over and cupping his shoulder as he held Jessica in his arms. "You did a great job opening the wall. I'm proud of you."

Pride glowed on Nathan's face, demonstrating how important Tristan's approval was to him. Glancing at Jessica, Grace smiled. "You okay, Jessica?"

Her bloodshot eyes met Grace's, full of pain from her addiction and terrifying brush with death. "I don't know if I'll ever be okay," she whispered. "I tried to tell you all to let me die, but I was gagged. I'm not worth saving if you can save the world instead."

"Hey," Tristan said, gently shaking her. "I don't want to hear you talk like that. Of course you're worth saving. We're going to get you on Dani's cure, and you're going to be good as new. You hear me?"

Tears streamed down her face. "I'm so tired, Tristan."

"I know," he said, releasing a ragged breath. "We all are, Jess. But I'm here now, and that bastard is gone." Drawing her head to his chest, he stroked her hair as he gazed into Grace's eyes.

Grace stared back, allowing him to see her relief, and her pain...and her *love*. All the love she'd never stopped feeling for him, even after things had gone so wrong.

I'm sorry, she mouthed, caressing Nathan's hair.

He lifted her free hand to his lips and pressed a kiss to her palm as butterflies fluttered in her stomach. "No more apologies, empress. It's time to start a new era."

Jessica lifted her head to look at Grace. "I'm sorry about...*being with* Luthor, Grace. It was the only way I could get EverLife and the watered-down antidote."

"Oh, don't apologize to me," she said, grimacing. "I'm sorry you had to endure that. What he put you through was awful."

Jessica lowered her gaze to the floor, and Grace understood she had a long road ahead of her full of physical and mental healing. Hell, they all did after the nightmare they'd experienced with Luthor.

"I need a team to stay here with me as I assume temporary leadership," Arthur said, addressing the room. "Dominic, Arianna, and Zayne, would you be willing to hang back for a few days?"

"Absolutely, as long as Ron throws some bagel sandwiches in the mix," Arianna said.

"Done," Ron said with a salute.

"I'm going to send the rest of you back to the compound so we can prepare for the next phase. Maverick, please have Danica treat Jessica with the EverLife cure, and then prepare the vials we have for transport to the city. I'm going to set up clinics where we can receive the addicted patients, especially the homeless ones, and begin to cure them. I'll recruit any of Luthor's soldiers willing to pledge loyalty to a new democratic government. Any who remain loyal to him will have to be incarcerated until we can have a fair trial for them."

"Will do," Maverick said with a nod.

"I'm also going to visit the factory in Northeast DC where Luthor produced the majority of the EverLife supply. We need to begin production on Dani's cure immediately."

"I know she'll be excited to ramp up production," Maverick confirmed. "What about her trial?"

"We'll get to it," Arthur said, "but let's have her heal a couple thousand people first. I think that will go a long way toward obtaining a not guilty verdict from a sympathetic jury."

Grace could see the hope in Maverick's eyes as he nodded.

"Let's task some of the remaining militia to gather the bodies of the fallen and cremate them outside the walls," Arthur continued. "We prepared the families they left behind that we wouldn't be bringing bodies back because we have no way to properly store them. Can you take care of cataloging the names of the men and women who didn't make it? We'll have a military funeral for them and honor them in a formal ceremony in a few weeks once we have a handle on things."

"I can do that," Maverick said, extending his hand. "You sure you're ready for this, Arthur?"

He lifted his eyebrows as he shook Maverick's hand. "Whether I'm ready or not, we've got to blaze a new path. But yeah, I'm ready."

"What do you want me to do with Luthor's body?"

Arthur glanced over to Luthor's lifeless body on the cold floor. "Burn it first."

Armed with a plan, the members of the fledgling new government got to work.

Grace and Tristan returned in the caravan to Cumberland. They arrived just before dawn and as the withdrawal symptoms were setting in for Jessica.

"We're almost there, Jess," Tristan soothed, holding her trembling body in his lap as they sat in the back of one of the pickup trucks. He'd wrapped her in a blanket, and Grace admired the protective gesture. He was going to be such a good dad. She just hoped he allowed her the chance to be a mom alongside him. Although he'd declared no more apologies were needed, they had an important talk ahead of them.

When they pulled into the compound, Tristan asked the driver to take them directly to the clinic. He jumped from the truck and rushed Jessica inside, calling out for a nurse.

"I'm a nurse," a woman said, approaching them. "Is she on EverLife?"

"Yes," he nodded. "We need the cure ASAP. Is Dani here?"

"She's at the school," the nurse said.

"I can go get her," Nathan offered.

"Thanks, buddy. I appreciate it."

Grace stayed by Tristan's side as he followed the nurse, Rikina, into a triage room with a vacant bed. He lay Jessica on the crisp sheets as her teeth chattered.

"I'm going to die," she moaned.

"You're going to be okay," he soothed, rubbing her sweaty forehead. "We made it, Jess."

"Be right back with the cure," Rikina said, rushing from the room and returning a minute later with a syringe. She urged Tristan to step back, and Grace held his hand.

"Let her work, Tristan," she said, squeezing his fingers. "You've done your part."

Jessica gasped as Rikina injected the cure into her arm. Dani rushed into the room, picking up a stethoscope from the counter and plugging it in her ears.

"Status?"

"Injected with three cc's of EverLife cure-serum," Rikina stated.

Dani lifted the small light from her pocket and clicked it on. Lifting Jessica's eyelid, she examined one pupil and then the other.

"Name?"

"She's my sister, Jessica," Tristan said from the foot of the bed.

"Hey, Jessica," Dani said, observing her enlarged pupils. "You're doing great. This stuff's going to cycle through your veins, and you should start to feel better in a few minutes. My name's Danica and I'll be right here."

Grace watched their interplay, imagining how many people would soon go through the same process. "We have so many people to heal. How can we possibly do it?"

Tristan threaded his fingers through hers. "One person at a time."

"How very optimistic of my ex-husband."

His lips twitched before they fell silent, holding hands as they observed Jessica relax on the bed. Dani approached and looked at her watch. "She's going to need hours to rest and will most likely fall asleep. Rikina will monitor her. In the meantime, you must be hungry and exhausted. The mess hall just opened for breakfast."

Grace's stomach grumbled, confirming Dani's statement.

"Go on," she said, shooing them from the room. "We've got this. Go get some food and then some rest. And you probably have a lot to discuss, so I'll make sure Nathan and Raquel don't disturb you in your rooms."

Tristan glanced at Grace. "Does she know...?"

"She knows," Grace said. "She figured it out."

"Your secret is safe with me, but maybe it won't be a secret any longer?" Dani flashed a cheeky grin. "Anyway, Maverick informed me that Luthor is dead, but I'm dying to hear the whole story. Great job kicking his ass."

"It's just the first step on a long, winding path to rebuilding," Grace said.

"But at least we have something to rebuild." Dani lifted a finger. "Now, go on. If Jessica falls asleep, I'll head over and grab some breakfast. If I don't see you there, I'll assume you're *talking*." She waggled her eyebrows. "Have fun!"

Tristan spared Jessica one last look before leading Grace out of the clinic.

Chapter 31

Although she was starving, Grace wanted to remove the tactical gear and bulletproof pads. She and Tristan stopped by the school to change clothes before heading to the mess hall. They found Raquel there, chatting away with Nathan, Chris, Jenny and the other kids. When she saw them, her eyes lit with excitement and she ran across the room straight into Grace's arms.

"Hey, sweetheart," Grace said, squeezing her until her arms trembled.

"I'm so proud of you guys," Raquel said. "Maria knew you'd kick Luthor's ass one day."

"Since we just saved the world, I'll overlook the use of that word, young lady," Grace said, her tone equal parts scolding and teasing.

Raquel turned to Tristan and enveloped him in a hug. "Maverick said you all were awesome. He told us everything."

"He fought valiantly," Tristan said, pressing a kiss to Raquel's forehead. "Is he here?"

"He said he has to take care of some things, but Dani is going to come and play wiffle ball with us today. It might be our last day because Maverick said some people are going to leave the compound and move to DC now that it's safe." Tilting her head, she looked between them. "Are we going to move to DC? If we do, can we bring Maria?"

Laughing, Grace ran a hand over her hair. "These are great questions that Tristan and I need to discuss, but we're starving."

"Oh! You can come and eat. Nathan's over there. He said he snuck into one of the trucks and helped you guys! That's badass—" She glanced toward Grace. "I mean, it's really cool."

"He was an excellent soldier," Grace said, pointing at two open seats at the long table. "Save these for us."

She and Tristan loaded up their plates and sat with the kids while they ate.

A few minutes later, Grace patted her stomach and sighed. "I'm in a food coma. Time to shower."

Tristan's eyes bore into hers as he cocked a brow. "Want to conserve water, empress? I need a shower too."

Breathing a laugh, she shrugged. "I mean, why not do our part to save the environment?"

Tristan's eyes blazed with lust, and his chair scraped as he stood. "Okay, kids. Have fun at wiffle ball. Grace and I are heading to shower and nap."

As he led her back to the school, Grace noted his quick, determined pace.

"Slow down there. You're dragging me like a caveman heading back to his lair."

"I feel like a caveman right now," he gritted, leading her inside the school. "But I'll restrain myself...for now."

A jolt ran down Grace's spine, and she realized it was anticipation. After so many long, lonely years, she was finally going to make love to Tristan again. Nerves swirled in her belly as they approached their rooms.

They grabbed the towels Dani had left out before walking to the stall in the boys' bathroom that had running water. Sunlight streamed through the faded windows as they slowly removed their clothes. Tristan drew her under the spray, which was lukewarm thanks to the small generator Arthur's men had set up, and bumps rose on her skin as the water sluiced over her.

Tristan picked up the bar of soap on the small shelf and lathered his hands before soothing the bumps on her arms with the suds. Turning her to face the spray, he moved his hands along her back, running them over the swell of her backside, before crouching to wash her legs.

When her back was clean, he stood and slowly turned her to face him.

He lathered his hands again before placing them over her collarbone. Fingers spread, he gazed at her lovingly, washing her neck and the swells of her breasts as her eyes drifted closed.

"Tristan..."

"I almost forgot how pretty you are here," he murmured, cupping her breasts in his hands and gently massaging them. "How these sexy little nipples are so much pinker than the rest of your skin." He tenderly pinched each nipple before running his thumb over the taut nubs to ease the sting.

Grace gasped, every cell in her body tingling from his proximity and the ministrations of his fingers.

"You always loved when I played with you here." He squeezed her nipples again as her head fell back.

"*Oh god*...I want more..."

Tristan growled before lathering his hands again and quickly washing his body. Grace observed his rapid movements and bit her lip to stifle a laugh. Lowering her gaze, she noticed his cock springing from the nest of hair between his legs, hard and ready to claim her.

The urgency in his movements ignited something deep inside, reaffirming he still craved her as much as she yearned for him.

When they were finished, they dried off and wrapped the towels around their bodies. After reaching Grace's room, Tristan closed the door and turned the lock.

Grace sent him a questioning look.

"No one's coming in here for *hours*," he said, tossing away his towel before hooking his fingers over the top of hers as it hugged her body. "I mean it, empress. I'm going to fuck you in all the ways I couldn't over the past ten years." He yanked the towel from her body and threw it on the floor. "You ready?"

Her nipples pebbled in the cool air as she backed toward the bed. When the mattress hit the backs of her knees, she sat and leaned back. Resting one heel on the bed, and then the other, she spread her legs, inviting him to look his fill.

A slow, drawn-out breath escaped his lungs as he stared at her slick core. "Fuck yes, you're ready. Look at that sweet, sexy pussy..."

Striding forward, he dropped to his knees and pressed his palms to her inner thighs, spreading her legs wider. "This pussy wants to be touched..." Resting his cheek on her leg, he stared into her eyes as he kissed a trail from her knee to her thigh. "And it wants to be played with," he rasped, placing his fingers at her drenched core and circling them in the wet essence.

"*Yessss...*" she cried, pushing into his fingers.

"And it wants to be kissed..." he said against the skin of her thigh before his lips moved to her drenched folds. He swiped his tongue over her deepest place, growling in approval as she groaned. "And it wants to be tasted, doesn't it, baby?"

A tremor shot through her body as her clit ached for his lips...for his *tongue*...

"Yes, Tristan...*please*..."

He took pity on her, burying his face in her core and lapping at her honey. His lips nibbled and tasted her sensitive flesh, setting her on fire as her skin flushed.

"Sweeter than I even remembered," he breathed against her wet skin. "So fucking sweet..."

Grace undulated into his mouth, unabashed and unashamed as he loved her. His mouth generated torturous pleasure, reverberating through her whole body as it quivered. Tristan placed his lips over her clit, sucking the swollen bud in smooth, fluid motions as he slipped a finger inside her.

She gasped, unused to the pressure after years of abstinence.

"Take it, sweetheart," he murmured against her clit, inserting another finger and moving them back and forth. He circled the tight vise, gathering her honey as he prepared her for more. "That's it. Open up for me." His tongue flicked her clit, sending her ever closer to the edge as he worked his fingers deep inside her.

"Oh...*fuck*!" she cried, spearing her fingers in his thick hair. "I'm going to come...Tristan!"

Her back arched; her muscles straining as she squeezed her eyes closed. Bursts of gold and yellow exploded behind her eyelids as she began to come. Greedy and wanton, she pushed into Tristan's skillful mouth and fingers, emitting a joyous laugh as she drowned in bliss.

Tristan's motions slowed, his fingers stilling as he pressed kisses to her wet flesh. Grace felt his soul in each tender kiss...felt his *love* as he reveled in her pleasure.

Her body fell lax on the bed as she released a deep breath. "*Ohmygod...*" she whispered, grinning as her eyes remained closed. "So fucking good..."

Tristan hummed against her core, his palm caressing the soft skin of her thigh in long, languid strokes. Forcing her lids open, she stared at him through half-lidded eyes.

He gazed up at her, his cheek pressed against her inner thigh as he nuzzled her core. The flecks in his eyes burned with unchecked emotion, and her heart slammed.

"I want you inside me," she whispered, trailing the backs of her fingers over the stubble that lined his jaw. "I missed you so much..."

Tristan rose, placing his arms beneath her and repositioning her so she lay flat on the mattress. He crawled over her, lithe as a predator, and positioned his muscled body between her legs. Balancing on his forearms, he slid his fingers into her hair, tugging slightly in the way she'd always loved...

In the way he still remembered.

His eyes bore into hers as his cock glided through her wet folds, searching for the place it had always belonged.

"Tell me again," he rasped, his eyes searching hers as his cock probed before testing...easing slightly inside as she gasped.

"I missed you," she said, clutching his hair as her eyes stung with tears. "I'm so sorry..."

"None of that, remember?" he said, easing deeper inside as she opened herself, allowing him to claim her. "If we keep apologizing for the past, we'll never have a future." He pushed deeper, groaning as his fingers tightened in her hair. "And I want a future with you, Grace. God help me, I love you. You're the only woman I'm ever going to love, empress."

Tears streamed down her cheeks as he surged deeper, filling every crevice as she clung to him.

"*Shhh...*" Pressing his lips to her cheek, he sipped her tears, swallowing the salty essence that represented all their past pain and heartache. "Just feel me, sweetheart. Let me make you mine again."

He drew back, gazing into her eyes before heaving forward, asserting his claim in one long stroke. Grace wanted to say the words back, but her throat was clogged with heavy emotion, making speech impossible.

Tristan worked his hips, increasing the pace as he fucked her in long, pleasurable strokes. His breath grew shallow and rapid, his skin heating as he filled her over and over...

"Your body is *mine*, Grace, and I'm never letting you go again," he crooned, pressing his forehead to hers as he spoke against her lips. "Do you hear me?"

She captured his lips, unable to speak but dying to stake her claim too. She thrust her tongue inside his mouth, swirling and tangling with his as he moaned. Sweat dripped from his skin, mingling with hers as they moved in tandem. Their bodies danced in a rhythm both remembered, connected and pulsing as their breath mingled.

Tristan slid his hand under her leg, drawing it high and balancing it against his arm as he pressed his palm flat to the mattress...opening her wider...stretching her as she chortled with pleasure.

"Fuck, Grace," he rasped, his hips hammering against her as he neared the edge. "You're going to suck everything from me, aren't you?"

She purred, arching her back to allow him greater access...wanting him as deep as possible. The blunt head of his cock pressed against the spot only he knew, reigniting the tiny fires in every nerve ending of her trembling body. Gripping his shoulders, she speared her nails into his flesh, reveling in his desire-laden hiss as he slammed into her.

"Oh...*god!*" he rasped, his body lurching as he dove over the cliff. Grace joined him, sliding into the pleasurable abyss as they clung to each other. Aching to possess him, she bit his lip, holding him in her grip as her body quaked beneath him. He used to love it when she bit him during sex, and he growled with unguarded lust.

Clenching her hair, he drew her head back, baring her neck. "You fucking bit me," he rasped, raking his teeth over her skin. "Fuck, you know I love that."

Burying his face in her neck, he shuddered several times, emptying everything into her ravaged body. His muscles jerked...shaking against her own...until he released a heavy breath and collapsed against her sated frame.

Grace ran her fingernails over his scalp in the long caresses he loved. He emitted a satisfied "*Mmm...*" against her nape, causing her lips to curve. God, the deep grumble of his voice against her sweaty skin was so sexy. Wrapping her legs around him, she held tight, wanting to hold him inside her as long as possible.

Time melted away as they lay entwined. Tristan's hand searched for hers, lacing their fingers as they rested atop the bed.

His breath slowed against her nape, and he lifted his head to gaze into her eyes. Resting his head on his fist, he released her hand and touched his finger to her lips. Hazel eyes stared into blue ones filled with emotion as he slowly traced her lips.

"I'm humbled you can still love me after keeping Raquel from you," she whispered against his finger. "I probably don't deserve your forgiveness."

His lips twisted into a grin. "You probably don't. But I've just survived a decade where I was fucking miserable, and I'm smart enough to get out of my own way so I don't repeat the cycle. That's what you always told me to do, right? Get out of my own way."

Breathing a laugh, she nodded. "Yes. Sometimes, you just have to have faith and let everything else go."

"I have faith in *you*," he whispered, his tone so reverent it almost broke her heart. "And I have faith in us. I don't want to be an angry person who pushes away the person I love. That will only ensure I remain miserable." Kissing her, he drew back and smiled. "Of course, that means you have to love me too. I'm waiting, empress."

Laughter leapt from her throat at his cocky demand. "I was having trouble speaking since you were banging my brains out. And I..." Struggling to voice the words, she shook her head on the pillow. "I'm a different person from that girl you loved all those years ago. Maybe you still love her, and if that's the case, this might not work."

"We've both changed, but that doesn't mean we're doomed. Maybe we both just grew into the people we need to be to make it work this time."

Grinning, she ran her thumb over his lips. "You've *definitely* become an optimist. It's so weird."

"It's weird for me too, but it feels pretty good." The creases at the corners of his eyes deepened as he smiled.

Reality began to creep back in, and her expression grew more serious. "I can't give you any more children. It's something I want so badly, but I can't..." Her nostrils flared as wetness clouded her eyes.

"Hey," he said, cupping her cheek as his eyebrows drew together. "That's okay, Grace. I mean it. We have Raquel, and I'm pretty sure we've both fallen for Nathan too. He's a great kid."

"He is. Are you open to adopting him? I'd love to raise him and give him a family."

"I'm open." He pressed a kiss to her lips before continuing. "I have no idea how to be a dad, but I guess I'm about to get a crash course in parenting. We both are."

"You're great with them. I'd be honored to raise them with you."

"And if you want a baby after we figure it out, we can adopt one," he said, stroking her cheek. "Lord knows there are lots of kids who need parents in this world."

Grace's chin wobbled as she realized she might finally get the opportunity to live the life she'd sacrificed for so long. "I think I'd like that," she whispered.

"Okay, sweetheart. We'll discuss it once we figure everything else out. I mean, don't get me wrong. We still have a *lot* of shit to figure out."

"Well, first, you need to marry me again. I'm finally free and want to be Mrs. Grace Holder again."

"Damn, woman!" he exclaimed, feigning exasperation. "That's the second time you've demanded I marry you. I let you get away with it the first time, but this time, I'm going to give you a proper proposal. I just need a damn minute."

"I think I'd like a proper proposal. I've been married twice and never really gotten one."

"I'm not going to take the blame for you showing up in the pouring rain and demanding I marry you all those years ago." He nipped the tip of her nose. "You were so determined, sputtering and wet. You wouldn't take no for an answer."

"Because I was madly in love with you," she said, shaking her head on the pillow.

He studied her, his lips curved into a satisfied grin as he waited. "Go on, empress. Tell me now if you're going to tell me. Otherwise, we're at an impasse. I can't do this if you don't love me back. I need you to be half as obsessed with me as I am with you, or my pride is going to suffer some serious setbacks."

"Tristan..." she warbled, struggling to speak over the swell of emotion in her chest and throat. "Of course I love you. I've always loved you, even when you left and I swore I'd never forgive you." She placed her palm over his heart. "I love you in hidden corners of my soul I didn't even know existed. You showed them to me when we first met, and they'll only ever be inhabited by you."

He covered her hand against the scratchy hairs atop his chest and squeezed.

"I loved you when I made hard decisions that hurt us both, and I love the man you've become. You're complicated and enigmatic, but also deeply loyal and caring...and sexy," she finished with a grin. "I want to spend every day I have left with you, if you'll have me."

He squinted one eye. "Umm, yeah, I think I'll have you."

Tossing her head back, she laughed with joy. "Well, thank goodness. I was hoping you wouldn't reject me when you're *literally* inside me."

"Speaking of that..." Tristan slipped from her as he lifted and balanced his weight on his arms. "Let me get something to clean us up." He stood and grabbed a cloth from the dresser before pouring some water from the nearby jug into a basin. After soaking the cloth, he strode over and commanded softly, "Open those pretty legs, baby."

Grace complied, gazing upon him as he cleaned away the evidence of their loving. He returned to the basin, ringing out the cloth before cleaning himself. After spreading it over a nearby chair to dry, he walked toward her and Grace swallowed thickly, overcome by his confident gait and his sinewy muscled body.

"If you keep checking me out like that, I'm going to be back inside you in a matter of minutes," he said, sliding in beside her and drawing her to his side.

Grace curled into him, tossing her leg over his thighs as she held tight. "Well, you *did* say you were going to fuck me to make up for lost time."

Laughter rumbled in his chest underneath her ear as she snuggled against him. "I am. Just need a few minutes to recover..."

His fingers lazily stroked her hair as they drifted, their muscles slowly relaxing as exhaustion claimed them.

Grace knew he would make good on his promise to make love to her several more times before they rejoined the rest of the world. For now, she allowed herself to fall into slumber, free from the evil and heartache that had pervaded her life for so long.

Chapter 32

That evening, after lots of exertion balanced with peaceful napping, she and Tristan cleaned themselves up and headed to the mess hall for dinner. She and Tristan entered to find Dani and Maverick sitting with Raquel and Nathan.

"Well, well," Dani said, her eyes alight with mischief. "Looks like somebody had a *very* good nap."

"Uh, yeah," Grace said, feeling her face turn several shades of red as she rubbed the back of her neck. "It was really nice."

"*Pfft*," Tristan said, pulling out the seat for Grace. "I think it was more than nice."

"Okay, I'll let you off the hook since kids are present. But good for you," Dani said with a wink.

Grace faced Raquel and Nathan. "Tristan and I want to talk to you both in private after dinner. Raquel, we'll speak to you first, and then we'll bring Nathan in. We can talk by the pond."

"Okay," Raquel said as Nathan mumbled in agreement.

Grace could see the slight bit of fear that crossed his face, and she ached to soothe him. "It's nothing bad, sweetheart," she said, encircling his wrist. "I promise."

He nodded, and they proceeded to eat one of their last meals on the compound.

Afterward, Grace asked Nathan to hang back with Dani and Maverick for a few minutes before joining them by the pond.

The three of them walked toward the water, Raquel chatting in between them as they held her hands. Grace glanced over her head toward Tristan, smiling as her heart threatened to pound from her chest.

When they arrived at a soft patch of grass on the bank of the pond, they lowered to sit in a small circle.

Grace cleared her throat and nervously rubbed her hands over her thighs. "Sweetheart, there's something Tristan and I need to tell you. It's a secret we couldn't tell you for a long time, but we're ready now."

"Why couldn't you tell me?" she asked, her eyebrows lifting.

"Because the dictator we fought in the city—"

"Luthor Cromwell," Raquel interjected.

Grace nodded. "Luthor was a terrible man, as you already know. Because of his relationship to me, he threatened to hurt you."

"What relationship?"

"Luthor was partners with my father before the world collapsed. During those years, he threatened my father, and eventually me and...you." Clearing her throat, she ran her hand over the soft grass. "I couldn't let him hurt you, so I hid you from him with Maria so he wouldn't find you."

Confusion marred her features as her eyebrows drew together. "Maria told me she rescued me because my birth parents died."

"She did rescue you, sweetheart, but your parents weren't dead. That was something Maria and I told you to protect you." Tears filled her eyes as she scooted closer and placed her hand over Raquel's thigh. "It was something I never wanted to hide from you, but I didn't know any other way to keep you safe."

Her eyes searched Grace's as realization set in. "Are you my mom?"

A sob tore from Grace's throat as she nodded. "I am, and I love you very much. I know you might be mad at me for not telling you, and if you are, I understand—"

Raquel jumped into her arms, hugging her as emotion washed over Grace in overwhelming waves. Clenching her daughter tight, she allowed the tears to steam down her cheeks as she rocked her in her lap.

"I'm so sorry, sweetheart," she whispered. "I wish we hadn't lost so much time."

Drawing back, Raquel wiped away Grace's tears. "I'm not mad. You don't have to cry. Honestly, sometimes I wondered if we were related and you just didn't want to tell me. We look a lot alike."

"We do," Grace said, smoothing her hair. "And I'm so proud you're my daughter, Raquel. You're the best part of me."

Raquel slowly looked toward Tristan. "Since you were married, does that mean you're my dad?"

Grace saw the sheen of wetness in Tristan's eyes. "Yes, sweetheart."

Raquel reached for him, and he scooped her into his lap, squeezing his eyes as he held her.

"And there are some things we want to talk to you and Nathan about," Grace said, looking over the horizon. Sure enough, Nathan trudged over to them, his shoulders slightly slumped as if he were expecting bad news.

"You said to come out in ten minutes," he said, crossing his arms. "If you're not ready—"

"We're ready," Grace said, patting the ground beside her. "Sit here."

He lowered beside her, and she cupped his shoulder. "We want to talk to you to tell you something good, Nathan. Well, we hope you'll think it's good."

His eyebrows lifted as he waited.

"Tristan and I had a child ten years ago we couldn't keep." She smiled at Raquel. "Raquel is that child and we just told her."

Nathan glanced between them. "Okay. That's cool. Are you all going to live together now?"

"We are. We've decided we're going to move to the city and help Arthur rebuild. They have technology there, and we feel it will be the best place for you all to go to school."

"You want me to come with you?"

"Of course we do," she said, tilting her head. "We think you're very special, Nathan, and we'd like to adopt you if you want to be part of our family."

His eyes darted between Grace and Tristan's, searching for insincerity.

"What do you say, buddy?" Tristan asked. "Want to stay with us?"

His chin trembled as he nodded. "I was scared you were going to send me back to Solomon."

"One of these days, you're going to trust us, kid," Tristan said. "I know trust is hard to come by in this world, but you're family now."

Nathan studied them as the news set in. "Where will we live in the city?"

"There's a rowhome in Dupont Circle that I think would be perfect for us all to start over. It's owner recently passed and I inherited the property." In fact, she was now the owner of several new properties thanks to her husband's recent demise. "It's close to the capital where Arthur is going to rebuild, so it's an ideal location."

"Is there enough room for Maria?" Raquel asked. "We have to convince her to come with us."

"We're going to do our best. We've decided we're going to leave the compound once Jessica is better, and we're all going to return to the city. We'll stop in Dundore on the way. I'll need you to turn on that killer smile and convince her to come with us," Grace said.

"I can do it!" Raquel said confidently.

Tristan grinned. "I mean, who can resist that endearing determination? Maria doesn't stand a chance."

Grace leaned back on her hands and inhaled a deep breath. "It's a new beginning for all of us. I'm excited for our future."

There by the pond, under a dusky sky, the fledgling family solidified their tentative bond, hopeful for the days ahead.

Part III – The Future

CHAPTER 33

One year later

"**D**r. Danica Lawson-Ward, will you please stand for the reading of the verdict?"

Dani looked over her shoulder, wiping her sweaty palms on her pants as she looked at Maverick. Her husband stared back, an abundance of love and support shining in his eyes, and mouthed, *I love you.*

Releasing a deep breath, Dani stood to face the repercussions of her actions.

The courthouse had been rebuilt after Arthur assumed power, and he had appointed himself judge for Dani's televised trial. Technology was slowly being reintroduced across the country—and the world—and people from every corner of the globe were watching Dani's trial if they had access to Wi-Fi.

A jury of twelve of Dani's peers stood to her right, six on the bottom row of the jury box and six above them. She recognized a few as recovered addicts she'd cured with NewHope, the proper name that had been given to her EverLife cure.

NewHope was also a callback to Star Wars, an epic tale with its own rebellion who eventually defeated the dark side. The name had been chosen by voters in the first election of the reformed government. It was a provision on the ballot, along with the vote at the top of the ballot, where Arthur Reyes ran for president.

Now, almost a year into his term, he had proven himself as a man of the people. He, Dani, Maverick, Grace, Tristan and others on his team had worked tirelessly to heal the sick and destroy every last vial of EverLife on the planet. Although stashes of black-market EverLife still existed, Dani had faith that those would eventually be destroyed. Arthur had created a special ops division of the new army specifically trained to hunt down the remaining EverLife dealers and drug makers.

One day, the scourge would be eliminated for good.

"Foreperson, please read the verdict," Arthur said from his perch at the judge's bench, drawing Dani away from her musings.

"We, the jury, find the defendant, Dr. Danica Lawson-Ward, guilty of involuntary crimes against humanity."

A collective gasp buzzed through the room, and Dani reminded herself to remain calm. This is the verdict she'd expected, and it was an honest summation of her crimes. Making eye contact with the foreperson, she gave an understanding nod.

The foreperson, a middle-aged Black man with salt and pepper hair, returned a sympathetic smile and handed the verdict to the bailiff, who then handed it to Arthur.

Arthur took the verdict in his hands and read it over to confirm. Lifting his gaze to Dani's, he spoke with firm clarity.

"Dr. Lawson-Ward, you have been found guilty by a jury of your peers. Do you understand this verdict?"

"Yes, sir."

Arthur pursed his lips as he formulated his next words. "I chose to serve as judge for this trial because it gives me the opportunity to impose a sentence. One that is just and takes into consideration the substantial effort you've put into healing our society."

Dani licked her dry lips as her heart raced.

"You arrived at the Cumberland compound and dedicated yourself to creating a cure. You fought alongside your husband and the rebellion to remove Luthor Cromwell from power. In the year since, you've worked tirelessly to cure addicts in DC while also traveling the country and the world to cure others. Your sentence must reflect the effort you've already expended and your future efforts."

Arthur rose, and Dani's lips twitched at his slight flair for the dramatic since the trial was being streamed. The next election would be held in a year, and he knew this moment would get several million replays before then.

It was a savvy political move, and Dani admired it.

"People of the new America," he said, lifting his hands. "I understand the desire many of you still have to blame Dr. Lawson-Ward for the EverLife crisis. Although she played her part in the downfall of society, as the charges state, I truly believe it was involuntary. Luthor Cromwell was the evil mastermind, and the majority of the blame will always lie with him."

"Dr. Lawson-Ward," Arthur said with a nod, "I hereby sentence you to ten years of servitude to the new American government. You will donate your time, knowledge and expertise to creating a cure for cancer and other terminal illnesses. You will not receive payment for this work, but the government will fund your labs and research. I look forward to you continuing to improve society with your fastidious brilliance, and believe your contributions to humanity over the next ten years will come to outshine the damage from the EverLife crisis."

Dani's chin trembled as she nodded. "Thank you. I want nothing more than to discover a cure for cancer, and I will do my best to contribute to the improvement of society."

"Very well. The bailiff will escort you out to process the paperwork. You will be required to stay in DC for your ten-year sentence unless you obtain approval to leave from your probation officer. I can assign an ankle monitor, but I don't think we need that. Do you?"

Dani breathed a laugh. "No, sir. If you build a lab for me in DC, I'm a workaholic who won't ever leave it. Ask my husband." She pointed over her shoulder to Maverick.

A chuckle spread through the court at the moment of levity.

"I look forward to working with you, Dr. Lawson-Ward. Court is adjourned."

Covering her heart, Dani expelled a deep breath. Maverick rushed over, enveloping her in a hug before the bailiff could drag her away.

"Great job, slugger."

"I'm going to create my cancer cure," she said, staring into his eyes as her own filled with tears. "Finally, Mav."

"I never doubted you, sweetheart, and know you'll succeed." He cupped her face before the bailiff called her name.

"Ma'am, I need to take you to process the paperwork."

"Of course. You'll be here when I'm done?" she called to Maverick.

"I'll always be here, babe. See you in a bit."

Hope rushed through Dani's frame as she filed down the hallway to the processing room. She felt the sentence was just and couldn't wait to get started on her mission to save people from the intense pain she'd felt when her mother died.

The road to creating her cancer cure was winding and jagged—and nowhere near finished—but she was excited for the days ahead.

Her memory had mostly returned, although she still had dark spots and bad days that were a struggle. Thankfully, her husband was always by her side, steadfast and strong, helping her cope.

She would forever live with the guilt of the destruction her efforts had wrought. But now, with a firm resolution in place, perhaps she could balance the guilt with the pride she would feel when she cured the world of cancer, diabetes, Parkinson's and the many other terminal illnesses she would spend the next ten years trying to eradicate.

Dr. Danica Lawson-Ward was ready to save the world, and this time she wouldn't fail.

Arianna Cavalleri stood on the wooden porch of her home in the mountains of West Virginia. Staring across the expansive valleys, she spotted a hawk flying in the distance. Majestic and regal, it reminded her of Dani's face as Arthur imposed her sentence earlier that day. She was extremely proud of her sister, and grateful she would finally get to complete the work she'd yearned to fulfill for many years.

Clutching the wooden post on the porch of the home her husband had built with some local contractors, she inhaled the fresh air, thankful to be far away from the city. Arianna had helped Arthur and his team rebuild for several months, but then her circumstances had changed and she'd craved an escape from the technology the world was reembracing.

Call her old-fashioned, but the one thing she'd liked about the end of the world was not having to be tethered to technology every damn minute of every day. There was freedom in watching a brilliant sunset against the backdrop of ancient mountaintops without being interrupted by a phone ringing or a car horn blaring in the distance.

The front door creaked behind her, and Dominic's footsteps sounded. He sidled up behind her and covered her distended abdomen, caressing it in slow, smooth circles.

"How's our little terror doing in there?" he teased, resting his chin on her shoulder.

"Kicking up a damn storm," Arianna said, covering his hand and moving it over the spot where the baby was seemingly practicing the lambada. "She's going to be a squirrely little thing."

"We still don't know it's a girl since you refuse to go to the hospital for a proper checkup."

"Dani has checked on me during her monthly visits. I trust her, and after the past few years, I don't trust most of what happens in the healthcare industry. Talia is amazing," she said, referencing the midwife they'd hired to help Arianna when she gave birth in a few weeks. "She's all I need."

"I know you're tough, but I worry," he said, kissing her nape. "If something goes wrong during labor, we're an hour away from the closest hospital that's reopened."

"I'm going to be fine." Turning to face him, she slipped her arms around his neck. "I don't know how to explain it, but I just *feel* this is the right path. That I'm supposed to have her here, with you and Talia by my side, and that everything's going to be okay." She flashed a grin. "Since I'm a morbid pessimist, you should probably take the win on this one. I'm actually positive and hopeful about something."

Rich laughter leapt from his throat. "That's very true." Resting his forehead against hers, he swayed as the last rays of light surrounded them. "My grumpy wife, the love of my life and eternal doom-monger."

"Ohhh, I like 'doom-monger.' Let's make that nickname official. It has a nice ring."

Dominic just chuckled and shook his head. Drawing back, he formed an empathetic smile. "Dani looked good when we streamed the verdict today. I know you wanted to be there, but she was adamant you shouldn't travel this close to your due date. The sentence was what we expected."

"She's going to be just fine," Arianna said. "She's tough as nails and smart as hell. With a government lab and unlimited funding, she's going to accomplish so many amazing things. Mom would be proud."

Staring into her eyes as they swayed in a slow rhythm, Dominic asked softly, "So, you're happy?"

Arianna's nostrils flared as tears stung her eyes. "So fucking happy. Sometimes I wonder if it's all a dream, and I'm going to wake up in that goddamn farmhouse in a world that's still ravaged by death and destruction. This is real, right? I hope it's real..."

"It's real, sweetheart." He brushed a kiss over her lips. "And I'm happy too, in case you were wondering."

She barked a laugh. "I *do* wonder sometimes, but I think I'm afraid to ask. We're really secluded out here. That's always been my dream, but I know it's not yours."

Dominic cupped her chin and moved closer, his eyes boring into hers. "*You're* my dream, Ari. If you're happy, I've done my part."

A stupid tear slipped down her cheek, and she scoffed as she brushed it away. "Damn hormones. Stop making me cry. It's annoying."

His lips curled as he traced his thumb over the wet path on her cheek. "You love it. You love *me*. Stop pretending you're not obsessed with me, woman."

"*Pfft*. Go back inside. I was watching the sunset in peace before you interrupted me." She tried to extricate from his grasp, but he just turned her so she faced the mountains once more. Aligning his front with her back, he placed both palms on her belly and rested his temple against hers.

His hands slowly cradled their child as the half-moon peeked behind the horizon. As night gradually replaced day, Arianna observed the stars twinkle, wondering how many other beings were standing in their own seclusion, so far away, staring back from a world with its own problems, fears, injustices and hopes.

Eventually, the air turned chilly, and her husband threaded his fingers through hers, leading her inside to the dinner he'd prepared. It turned out that Dominic Cavalleri was one hell of a cook, and she added that to the long list of things she loved about him.

Once they'd eaten and the kitchen was clean, they slid into bed. Dominic positioned the pillow under her belly in the way she preferred as she lay on her side. He spooned behind her, wrapping his thigh over hers as he held her.

Within minutes, the familiar sound of his snores echoed in her ears as his warm breath hit her neck. Closing her eyes, she whispered to the child she already loved with a voracity she'd never known.

"Your dad is sleeping, and it's time for me to sleep too." She rubbed her belly, hoping her daughter would get the message. "Calm down in there, sweetheart. Just a few more weeks and then we're going to meet you. I can't wait."

Ignoring the wetness that clung to her eyelashes, she blamed the hormones again and exhaled a relieved breath when the baby stopped kicking.

Snuggling into Dominic's warm body, she closed her eyes and allowed him to protect her as she plunged into dreams.

Two months later

Grace smoothed her hands over the white satin dress, reveling in the silken fabric against her palms as she gazed into the full-length mirror.

"Absolutely beautiful," Maria said, her eyes shimmering with tears as she fidgeted with the veil hanging from Grace's hair. "Tristan might faint when he sees you."

"I'm not sure he'll faint, but I'm excited to have a formal wedding this time. The first time we eloped in a local courthouse, and it was a bit *rushed*, to say the least."

Maria chuckled as she nodded.

"And when we had our civil ceremony after we defeated Luthor, it was very"—Grace wrinkled her nose—"*practical*. Tristan promised me a grand wedding celebration once we helped Arthur rebuild and Dani began to disseminate her cure."

"You had the civil ceremony so you could officially become a family and start over," Maria said, cupping Grace's shoulders. "That was very understandable. But today is purely for celebration, and I couldn't be happier for you. And once today is over, you and Tristan can discuss adopting a baby. I know it's something you've wanted since we returned to the city."

"Yes. Once everything returns to normal after the wedding, we're going to discuss it at length." Leaning forward, she muttered, "Maria, this is definitely my last wedding. Please remind me of that when my husband is being surly and I want to strangle him."

Maria's melodious laughter filled the room. "You two don't fight often, but when you do, it's passionate and purposeful. That's a good thing, my dear. It means you both care. When you no longer fight with passion, the love is truly lost."

Grace thought of all her years locked in a lonely marriage for the sole purpose of defeating a man she loathed. "Tristan and I never lacked passion. I was drawn to him from the moment we met, and that tether between us has never truly broken."

"Then you're very lucky," Maria responded.

Grace took her hands and squeezed. "I'm so glad you chose to live with us, Maria. When we came to ask you to join us after we defeated Luthor, I could see the hesitation in your eyes. But my daughter is very persuasive." She flashed a grin. "You were doomed as soon as she began to plead with you."

"I was," Maria said. "I had reservations about living in the city, but I adore your family and it's been wonderful. Thank you for taking me into your home."

"Are you kidding? Thank you for saving me and Raquel all those years ago, and for raising her to be the amazing woman I know she'll become. I'm so grateful to you, Maria. You're family and a second mother to me." Pulling her into an embrace, she spoke against Maria's dark hair. "I love you."

Maria sniffled before drawing back and pulling a tissue from her dress pocket. "Don't make me cry. My makeup is done, and I'd like it to be presentable to Jack when I see him at the wedding."

Jack was Ron's brother, who'd moved back to DC after it was liberated. Ron and Deandra had introduced him into their circle, and he'd quickly become smitten with Maria.

"He's very handsome, and you look stunning, so he won't stand a chance."

"That's the plan, my dear," Maria said, her eyes sparkling.

After some final touches on her dress, they walked to the basement level of the rowhome Grace had converted into their permanent home. The house held four stories, which afforded more than enough room for their family and any visitors. Arianna and Dominic had accepted their wedding invite, which slightly surprised Grace since Arianna and Tristan weren't exactly best friends. But in the end, they'd come together for the common cause, and a bond had been cemented by everyone who'd fought together.

Arianna had also recently given birth, so Grace thought that might preclude her from traveling, but she had RSVP'd with an email representative of her brash personality.

Hi Grace,

We received your invitation and are thrilled you thought of us. Baby Cynthia is doing well, and I think my husband is going a bit stir-crazy. Therefore, we'll take you up on the invite and your offer to stay at your home.

We'll travel with everything necessary for the baby, but I'll warn you I can't cook. Dominic can, so if you want us to prepare some meals while we're there, I'll wrangle him into paying his dues for your hospitality.

I am, however, an expert at washing dishes. Feel free to put me to work. Lawsons carry our weight, and we'll only feel comfortable staying if you allow us to do so.

Also, tell your husband not to be a jerk or boss me around. He really pisses me off when he tries to tell me what to do.

Looking forward to it.

Arianna

The Cavalleri family had arrived a few days ago, and Grace had given them the entire third floor for their two-week stay. It allowed them some privacy and things had gone well so far. Arianna and Tristan had even spent a late night playing poker together, and Grace was thrilled at their comradery. She figured saving the world together could make even the greatest adversaries bury the hatchet under the right circumstances.

Grace approached the double doors that led to her home's expansive back yard. The soft sounds of the four-piece orchestra sounded, and she faced Maria to place one more reverent kiss on her cheek.

George Luddington stepped forward and handed his cane to Maria. "I can't properly walk Grace down the aisle with this thing. Please keep it for me until I sit."

"Will do," Maria said, winking before she strode through the doors to take her seat amongst the guests.

"You are truly magnificent, Grace," George said, taking her hands. "Robert would be proud."

"I miss him," Grace whispered, blinking away tears. "I know our fallout stemmed from his need to protect me, but I wish he could've seen the man Tristan was." She glanced toward the altar, where Tristan stood waiting. "The man he's become. He forgave me for terrible transgressions and is such a good father. I love him so much, George."

"I know, sweetheart," George said, patting her arm. "Robert became stressed and unable to see things clearly at the end. His association with Luthor wore on him, and I think you were unfortunate collateral damage. But his love for you was unwavering, and I know he's watching this from somewhere, elated you're happy."

"I hope so." Inhaling a deep breath, she faced the doors and wrang her hands at her sides. "Okay, enough dwelling on the past. I worked hard to get to this moment, and I only want to look forward."

George offered his arm. "My dear, I wholeheartedly agree."

Grace straightened her spine as the two doors swung open, thanks to the ushers on either side. The orchestra stilled before breaking into "Here Comes the Bride" as George led her down the carpeted aisle atop the soft grass.

Grace smiled at Dani and Maverick, Arianna and Dominic, Arthur, Deandra, Ron, Jessica and others as she slowly paced. Her lips twitched at the sight of Dominic, with his huge frame and imposing scar, lovingly holding his wisp of a daughter in his arms. It was a poignant sight, representative of the futures they helped shape for so many, and a surge of pride swelled in her chest.

She had helped save the world.

Her efforts in studying Luthor and planting the seeds of rebellion had created a new world where people could thrive once more.

Their team had been small but mighty, and she couldn't imagine working with more caring and capable souls.

They would be bonded together for the rest of their lives. Their shared remembrance of darker times would help them advise future leaders and make society a place where their children would thrive.

Or, at least, Grace hoped that was the case. The future was still uncertain as they continued to build their fledgling new world.

Grace finally lifted her gaze to Tristan, her heart skipping a beat when she observed his immaculate tuxedo beneath his stunning hazel eyes. Their children stood beside him, and Grace winked at Raquel, who looked so lovely in her violet dress.

"You look pretty, Mom," she whispered, offering her hand as Grace took it.

"Thank you, sweetheart. So do you."

She handed the bouquet to Maria, who promptly took it before returning to her seat beside Jack.

George released Grace's arm and shook Tristan's hand. "Let's make this one stick," he teased as Tristan breathed a laugh.

"Agreed. Thank you, George."

George lowered into his seat beside Maria, and Grace slipped her hand into Tristan's. Craning her neck, she smiled at Nathan, who stood to Tristan's right. He was endearingly handsome in his black suit and tie, and she took a moment to appreciate the sheer joy of holding hands with her family in front of the people she loved.

"Dearly beloved," Arthur said, smiling as he stood under the altar. "We are gathered here today to celebrate the union of Grace and Tristan. As many of you know, the happy couple technically married over a year ago in a small ceremony I also had the pleasure of officiating. The world was just beginning to dig out from its harrowing nightmare, and there wasn't time for a formal wedding. I see this ceremony as a celebration of the future we paved, and am delighted to officiate once more. However, since this is Grace and Tristan's third wedding, I assume it will be the last."

"Oh, it's *definitely* the last," Grace teased as the onlookers laughed.

Tristan squeezed her hand, his expression filled with mirth. "I've been assured my wife has no more secret rebellions up her sleeve, so we should be all set."

"Very well," Arthur said as the crowd's chuckles ceased. "You've both requested I keep this short so we can enjoy this beautiful day, and I aim to do just that. Grace, please repeat after me..."

True to his word, Arthur kept the ceremony under ten minutes as Grace and Tristan spoke reverent words of love and devotion to each other. They exchanged rings, and Tristan kissed his bride against a backdrop of raucous cheers.

When the ceremony was complete, they removed the chairs, and the orchestra was replaced by a playlist Raquel and Nathan had created together. It was comprised of upbeat songs the guests could dance to while enjoying the passed refreshments and complimentary drinks from the bar.

Grace enjoyed the ceremony immensely, secretly admitting she'd always wanted a lavish wedding. It had taken years, but she'd finally managed to have the wedding of her dreams. Her gaze wandered to Tristan, as he shared a cigar with Arthur, Maverick, and Dominic, and butterflies flitted in her stomach at his intense hazel gaze, filled with desire and love.

After all this time, her body still reacted to him just as intensely as the night he'd approached her on the moonlit balcony—the enigmatic man who'd stolen her heart and left no room for anyone else.

Eventually, the guests all returned home, with Dani and Maverick being the last to leave. They hugged Arianna and Dominic before Dani took Cynthia in her arms one last time to say goodbye.

"Aunt Dani's going to be back tomorrow, and we're going to walk in the park," she exclaimed, rubbing the tip of her nose against Cynthia's. "I'm going to tell you all about your Aunt Raquel and your Grandma Cynthia, who you were named after. How does that sound?"

Cynthia crooned in her arms, and Grace could see Dani's heart melt in her eyes.

"Are you and Maverick trying?" Grace asked, sidling up to Dani and playfully rubbing Cynthia's arm with her finger. "You've obviously got baby fever."

Dani nodded as she handed Cynthia back over to Arianna. "We were waiting until the verdict to make sure I didn't go to prison." She lifted an acerbic eyebrow. "Thankfully, since my servitude will entail just continuing to be a geeky scientist who creates cures and antidotes in a lab, we're good to go. I want to give Cynthia a cousin as close in age as possible."

"That's wonderful," Grace said. "We're also going to adopt as soon as things calm down from the wedding."

"Oh, Grace, I'm thrilled to hear that!" Dani threw her arms around her and squeezed. "We can have playdates together!"

Laughing, Grace stroked her back. "I can't wait. Arianna and Dominic will always have a place to stay with us, and I hope they'll visit often."

"She loves that cabin they've built in the mountains, but understands Dominic needs to rejoin society every once in a while. I've made her promise to visit no less than three times per year." Dani lifted a finger. "Everyone thinks she's the tough one, but when I put my foot down, it's the law. She's already planning possible dates to visit next year."

"The brilliant and resolute scientist," Grace said, grinning. "I love it. I'll help you hold her to it."

Once Dani and Maverick left and the house was quiet, Grace and Tristan stood in the kitchen, sharing a piece of wedding cake.

"*Ohmygod*," Grace moaned, taking the second-to-last bite. "This is so good. I was starving."

Tristan chuckled and speared the last piece with his fork before stuffing it in his mouth. "So fucking good. I loved seeing everyone, but that was a lot of entertaining for me."

Grace gently patted his cheek. "I'm very proud of my churlish husband for being cordial. Thank you."

His eyes narrowed. "I'm not sure I like your tone, Mrs. Holder." Taking the empty plate, he set it on the counter and hauled her over his shoulder. "It's time for me to take back control in this damn house."

Grace lightly pounded his back with her fists as she kicked her legs, the dress billowing around them. Tristan marched up the stairs as she squirmed, loving his strength as he wielded her atop his shoulder.

When they reached the second floor, he stopped in front of Raquel's room and set Grace on her feet so they could check on her. She snored softly surrounded by the posters of galaxies and quasars she'd hung on the wall. Their daughter had developed a love of space since enrolling in the reopened school system, and Grace had a hunch she would eventually end up in the newly revamped space program one day.

Tristan slowly pulled the door closed before stopping at Nathan's room to check on him as well.

When they entered the master bedroom, Tristan softly closed the door and turned the lock.

"Tristan!" Grace scolded. "We have guests. What if they need something—?"

Tristan snaked an arm around her waist, aligning his front with hers. "*No one* is getting your attention until tomorrow morning." He nipped her lips. "You're *mine* and it's time I reminded you of that, empress."

She slid her arms around his neck as her lips curved. "We have been consumed with the wedding and all the visitors, haven't we?"

"Yes. If it didn't make you happy, I'd kick them all out and tell them to rot in hell—"

"You would not," she exclaimed, swatting his chest.

"Don't tempt me." Cupping her chin, he ran his thumb over her lips. "But now it's just us, and I aim to keep it that way."

Desire curled deep in her belly as the flecks of his irises shimmered with hunger and emotion. "Well, okay then. I think my husband means business."

Tristan's hands gripped her waist, turning her so she faced the mirror atop their dresser. Cementing his eyes to hers in the reflection, he pressed his lips to her ear and murmured, "Sweetheart, you have no fucking idea…"

Tristan felt his wife shudder in his arms at his possessive words. Dying to touch her soft skin, he began unfastening the tiny buttons that lined the back of her dress. She gazed at him in the mirror through half-lidded eyes, her cheeks reddening in anticipation. Once he'd released the buttons, he pushed the dress to the floor, leaving her in a strapless bra and silky thong.

Grace stepped out of the dress as it pooled on the floor. Resting her hands on the dresser, she leaned forward, offering a salacious view of her backside. Tristan hissed, placing his hands on the globes and caressing as she pushed into his palms.

"Don't pretend you're not greedy for me to fuck you, baby," he rasped, hooking a finger in her thong and dragging it down her legs. He tossed it aside and removed her bra, baring her breasts to the cool air. Her nipples pebbled and Tristan grew rock hard, ready to remind her that she belonged to him. She'd always been his wife in his heart, even when she'd almost broken it, and he longed to solidify his possession of her.

It was something he would continue to do for the rest of their days. To remind her that she was always his first, and now she was his forever.

"You looked so beautiful in your dress," he said, gliding his hands up her sides to cup her breasts. "But you look like a goddess right now. Your skin blushes the prettiest shade of red when I play with these sexy nipples." He tweaked them between his thumb and forefinger before circling them as she moaned. "You like that, don't you?"

Her head fell back on his shoulder as she whispered his name. "Why are you still dressed?"

"Because I needed to look at you before I fuck you, just to remind myself this is real."

She slithered in his arms, turning to face him and flashing a sultry grin. "Darling, nothing has ever been more real."

Her fingers tore at the buttons of his shirt, all but ripping it from his frame before she pushed him toward the bed. Tristan fell on his back, huffing a laugh as his wife tugged his pants and underwear off.

They loved each other, heatedly and passionately, physically cementing the bond they'd reaffirmed earlier that day. When they both reached their peak, Grace's joyful laughter surrounded them as their bodies melded into one.

Tristan emptied everything into her—every piece of his soul and the love he'd thought unrequited for so many long, lonely years. As the last shudders abated, he threaded their fingers together beside her golden hair on the bed.

Panting and sated, they stared into each other's eyes for several poignant heartbeats.

When Tristan began to slip, he withdrew from her warmth and reached for a tissue. Gazing lovingly at his wife, he wiped away his release, marveling at the sight of the milky essence on the smooth skin of her inner thighs.

"I love seeing my mark on you," he murmured as he slid the tissue over her skin. "It's proof that you're *mine* and always will be."

Grace sighed, closing her eyes as her body relaxed upon the bed.

Tristan lifted her and pulled back the covers to place her on the cool sheets. She reached for him, her expression one of yearning as she waited.

Overcome with love for her, he slid beside her and drew her front against his. She glided her leg over his thighs, drawing him closer as they shared a pillow. Gazing into her eyes, Tristan noticed the sheen of tears.

"Hey," he whispered, tenderly caressing her cheek with his thumb. "That was supposed to make you happy, not make you cry."

A warbled laugh escaped her throat. "I'm crying *because* I'm happy. We finally made it here. I knew on the first day we spent together—the first day we fell in love and got tattoos—that we'd end up here. I just didn't realize it would take us *quite* so long."

"I, on the other hand, felt we had so many obstacles against us. I never should've doubted us."

"You shouldn't have. It broke my heart that you ever believed I loved Luthor." Cupping his jaw, a tear fell down her cheek. "How could you believe I ever loved any man but you? It's not possible, Tristan. I love you with every part of my soul."

"I was a stupid fool, and still a kid in so many ways. I wasn't sure I deserved you."

"And now?"

"Now, I realize I'm probably the only man who can put up with you. You're tempestuous and headstrong, and you'd probably drive any other man crazy."

She scoffed and playfully hit his shoulder. "You'll pay for that."

"See what I mean?" he asked, pulling her closer and resting his forehead against hers. "You drive me mad, woman, and I love you more each day. And now that I'm pretty sure you don't have any other secrets to reveal, we can build the life we always wanted. Together."

Grace pressed her lips to his, drawing him into a soulful kiss as their bodies relaxed. Eventually, she rested her head on his chest, and he stroked her smooth hair until her breathing grew slow and measured.

Closing his eyes, Tristan recalled the first time he'd held her this way, all those years ago when she had a fresh tattoo on her hip and the world had been vastly different.

Vowing to protect her and their children as they blazed their future, Tristan clutched his sleeping wife and pledged to be the man she deserved in the moonlit darkness of the city they'd saved.

Arthur Reyes had a fantastic time at Tristan and Grace's wedding. He'd been honored to officiate both their civil ceremony last year and their official wedding in the back yard of their lovely home. Officiating celebratory ceremonies was one of his favorite activities as president of the newly formed government, and he aimed to continue to find opportunities to do so.

It made him a man of the people, and if he were honest, he also understood it was good politics. As much as he'd promised himself he'd never turn into a slimy politician, being a leader meant you had to play the game at least some of the time.

He'd danced with Jessica Holder at the reception, quietly admitting his attraction to her as she swayed in his arms. Although he had no time for romance now, he wouldn't be president forever and would eventually want to settle down. Was there a future for him with Jessica? The answer was uncertain, but he looked forward to exploring it down the road.

Frowning at the thought, Arthur sat at his desk in the newly rebuilt White House, eyeing the papers in front of him. There would be an election soon, and several candidates had declared their intentions to run. Arthur was extremely popular with the people, thanks to the successful mission he led to defeat Luthor Cromwell. But popularity often waned, and people were fickle. Would a new leader be able to continue to build their fledgling government, or would it throw the world back into chaos, opening the door for another dictator like Luthor to take over?

And if that happened, wouldn't it be better if Arthur retained control, if only for one more term, to ensure the people were safe?

It wasn't about remaining in power. Arthur told himself this repeatedly. No, it was about doing what was right for the world, with the leader the people deserved. The leader who knew what they needed.

Zayne Danvers appeared at the door, and Arthur waved him in.

"Good to see you, Zayne. Sorry to call you so late on a Saturday. Please sit."

He sat in the chair on the opposite side of Arthur's desk, a curious expression on his face. "I'm always happy to help, sir. What do you need?"

"I'm still awaiting confirmation that the last stash of unauthorized super-soldier serum was destroyed in Scranton. I was appalled to learn that Solomon Grange got his hands on several doses thanks to his secret communications with Luthor."

"It was a disturbing discovery, sir," Zayne said. "Although Solomon has accepted the new government for now, we hear rumors that his management of the city is less than kind. He's armed every Scranton citizen with handguns and holds regular trainings to ensure they're capable with the weapons. He justifies this by stating he wants his people protected if someone like Luthor rises to power again, but many believe he might eventually convince his citizens to form a militia and assume power of the new government for himself."

Arthur sat back in his chair and rubbed his forehead. "I've publicly called upon Solomon to run for president many times. He refuses to and says our elections won't be legitimate until we've restored technology to every outpost in America. My people on the ground are trying, but rebuilding a country is no small feat. We'll eventually accomplish the task, but it will take several more years. I just hope he doesn't try to seize power by force. That's not going to end well for him."

"I couldn't agree more. And to confirm your question, all of the super-soldier serum in Solomon's possession has been destroyed. I was on site and am confident it's eradicated."

Arthur smiled at his assurance. He was a valuable member of his team and loyal to a fault.

"Thank you, Zayne. That gives me great relief."

"Of course. Will there be anything else? I promised Gabriella I wouldn't be home past midnight," he said, referencing the woman he'd started dating several months ago. "Unless you need me..."

Glancing at his watch, Arthur realized it was almost eleven o'clock. "No, you can go. Thank you for coming in at this late hour. I'll make sure you get a Friday off soon so you and Gabriella can take a long weekend vacation. Lord knows you've earned it."

"Sir, it's an honor to serve you. It's because of you that Gabriella and I have a future." Rising, he saluted, and Arthur saluted back before he pivoted and strode from the room, closing the door behind him.

Unrest and foreboding pulsed in Arthur's body, and he reached over to tug open the top drawer of his desk. After emptying the contents, he removed the slab of wood, revealing the false bottom that hid several vials.

Lifting one of the vials, he studied it against the ceiling lights of the Oval Office. If anyone discovered the stash, he would be removed from office immediately. After all, he was the one who'd written the decree that every last vial of Luthor's super-soldier serum must be destroyed.

To his knowledge, all vials on the planet had now been eradicated except the ones that remained in his desk.

The ones he hoped to never use against anyone, but increasingly feared he might have to use against Solomon...or someone else who tried to assume power but didn't earn it...or wasn't worthy.

Only a just and fair leader could rebuild their world. One who understood the people, who the people *chose*, and one who was capable of guiding them into their prosperous future.

Decrying the heavy thoughts, he slipped the vial back into the drawer and replaced the wooden panel before closing it tight.

Rising, he released a slow breath and trailed from the office, determined to protect the new world he'd created...

Never realizing how closely his inner thoughts mimicked those of the last leader who'd ruled over society before ultimately ending it.

Before You Go

Well, dear readers, they did it! Our amazing team of dystopian survivors saved the world. As always, I HAD to leave the door open just a little bit. Will Arthur continue to be the leader the world needs, or will he devolve into someone evil like Luthor? My hope is that he remains true, but with anything in these perilous times, one never knows!

Thank you from the bottom of my heart for reading this steamy dystopian trilogy. I absolutely loved writing it and have been heartened by your lovely messages and feedback that you enjoyed it too. The six main characters of this series were some of my favorite I've ever written, and I appreciate you joining me on the journey.

Please make sure to check out all of my books at **RebeccaHefner.com** and thank you for supporting indie authors! Until next time, happy reading! –*Rebecca*

Want to read another steamy dystopian box set? Check out my **Prevent the Past** trilogy!

ALSO BY REBECCA HEFNER

Etherya's Earth Series
Prequel: The Dawn of Peace
Book 1: The End of Hatred
Book 2: The Elusive Sun
Book 3: The Darkness Within
Book 4: The Reluctant Savior
Book 4.5: Immortal Beginnings
Book 5: The Impassioned Choice
Book 5.5: Two Souls United
Book 6: The Cryptic Prophecy
Book 6.5: Garridan's Mate
Book 7: The Diplomatic Heir
Book 7.5: Sebastian's Fate
Book 8: The Solitary Protector

Prevent the Past Trilogy
Book 1: A Paradox of Fates
Book 2: A Destiny Reborn
Book 3: A Timeline Restored